THE ALIEN ADVENTURES OF FINN CASPIAN
THE UNCOMMON COLD

Read more of Finn Caspian's

alien adventures!

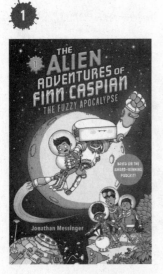

THE ALIEN ADVENTURES OF FINN CASPIAN

THE UNCOMMON COLD

Jonathan Messinger

Illustrated by Aleksei Bitskoff

HARPER

An Imprint of HarperCollinsPublishers

Library of Congress Control Number: 2020944609
ISBN 978-0-06-293221-1 — ISBN 978-0-06-293220-4 (pbk.)

Typography by Jessie Gang
21 22 23 24 25   PC/LSCH   10 9 8 7 6 5 4 3 2 1
❖
First Edition

For Griff, Emers,

and the stomp rockets they rode in on

CONTENTS

A Note About This Story

The tale you are about to read takes place approximately **36.54372 million miles away** from Earth, as the crow flies. It has been collected and woven together via various interview transcripts, recordings, and interstellar **laser screams** sent to Earth from the *Famous Marlowe 280 Interplanetary Exploratory Space Station* over the past decade.

"Laser scream" may be a new term for you, as it is still not well understood on Earth, but we don't have time to get into it here.

The astronauts who boarded the *Marlowe* were charged with **one mission: to discover a planet where humans could one day live**. Captain Isabel Caspian sends out teams of explorers. Finn and his friends are all remarkable, but Finn will always have a special place in the history books.

Because Finn was the first kid born in space.

So in many ways, Finn was born for exactly the type of situation in which we find him here in this book. But it will be up to you to decide if that makes him lucky or not.

HALL OF EXPLORERS

Abigail Obaro

Troop 301 Captain

Finn Caspian

Chief Detective

Chief Technologist

Sergeant-at-Arms

Robot

Interloper

Chapter One
Breaking News

Finn was just walking out of the library when he saw his three friends heading toward him. Abigail Obaro, his best friend, was in front. Behind her strode Elias Carreras and Vale Gil. Together the four of them made up Explorers Troop 301, and they had explored some crazy planets together. They were an amazing team.

But right now, something was different. As

his friends approached, Finn could tell they weren't on his team. It was the three of them, and the one of him.

"Uh, hey," said Finn, as the other three got closer. "What's up, guys?"

Abigail nodded and turned back to Elias and Vale.

No one said anything. No one did anything. It was silent in the hallway of the *Famous Marlowe 280 Interplanetary Exploratory Space Station*.

"So I got some new books out of the li—" said Finn.

"Cool," said Elias. He didn't seem to even notice he'd cut Finn off. "We, uh, we should get going."

"Yeah, cool," said Vale. "Super cool. See you later."

His three friends spread out to go around him. Finn held out his arms to stop them, and they all jumped back.

"Back, foul demon!" shouted Vale.

"Foul demon?" said Finn. "Vale, did you eat too much astronaut ice cream again? Actually, all three of you guys are being really weird. What's up?"

The three of them looked at each other.

"Nothing," said Abigail.

"That was the least convincing 'nothing' I've ever heard," said Finn. "You might as well have just said, 'I'm lying.' Obviously, something is going on."

Elias shrugged.

"It's not really a big deal," he said.

"I'm sure she's going to be fine," said Abigail.

Vale put his hand over his face.

"There it is," he said. "Cat's out of the bag."

"What is it?" asked Finn. "You're sure who's going to be fine? Is someone not fine right now? Is it Paige?"

Paige was Finn's little sister. And she was super talented at getting into trouble.

"No!" Abigail exclaimed, seeming relieved. "No, of course not. Paige is totally fine."

"Oh, good," said Finn.

"Well, I guess that's it then," said Elias. "See you, Finn!"

"No!" said Finn. "Who are you guys talking about if it's not Paige?"

"Eh, forget it," said Abigail.

"I can't forget it!" Finn shouted. "Like you

guys said, the cat's out of the bag!"

"Just put the cat back in the bag," said Vale.

"I can't!" said Finn. "The cat's out and is now scurrying down the hallway."

"I don't know," said Elias. "The cat seems kind of sleepy to me. She might want to go back in the bag and rest."

"The cat ate like fifteen candy bars and is bouncing off the walls," said Finn.

"I think the cat loves bags," said Abigail. "And just needs to find the right bag to settle down in—"

"Cats hate bags!" shouted Finn. "This cat thinks bags are bad. Bad bags!"

"Your mom is a snot monster!" yelled Vale.

And with that, Finn slumped against the wall, hand over his heart.

"She is?" he said.

Abigail nodded, but didn't come near him.

"So that means," said Finn, "I'm going to be a snot monster, too."

All three of Finn's friends nodded and took a step away from him.

"Sorry about that whole cat thing," said Abigail. "But, you know, not sorry enough to give you a hug over it or anything."

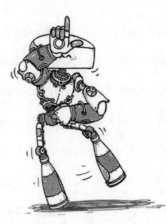

Chapter Two
Isolation Vacation

No one likes getting a cold. No matter where someone is in the universe, the symptoms are the same: runny nose, watery eyes, cough, sore throat, the redness on that little part of the face where the nostrils meet the upper lip (that's the worst).

But on a space station, a common cold can

be a disaster. Every breath you take on a space station, someone else has already taken it. You're just borrowing that bit of air until you puff it out of your lungs for someone else to inhale and use for a second. And with all that air swapping comes germ swapping.

Of course, the *Marlowe* has excellent air filtration systems, but a cold virus is the trickiest life-form in the known universe. The cold is basically a biological ninja, sneaking in and side-kicking your sinuses no matter what defenses you've put up.

So it's a policy on the *Marlowe* that if any astronaut gets sick, their whole family must be quarantined immediately. Quarantine is like being grounded. You have to stay in your room, no one can come visit you, and the only people you can talk to are the ones in your family.

It's punishment by boredom, even though

you didn't do anything wrong.

If you're a little sick, you may only have to be quarantined for a couple days. If your cough never stops, you'll be quarantined for a week or two. If you are, as Vale said, a "snot monster," you could be in your tiny compartment with just your family for as long as a month, until everyone is cleared.

"Thith will be fun," said Finn's mom, Isabel Caspian, the *Marlowe* captain. Her cold had so filled her sinuses with snot that she sounded like her head was inside a pumpkin. "Don't be tho thad, Finn. It will path by before you know it. Who wanth to play Monopoly?"

And so the Caspian family—mother Isabel, father Leon, son Finn, and daughter Paige— began playing their first of many games of Monopoly.

"It's not fair that I have to be here even though I'm not sick," said Finn.

"Yeah," said Paige. "You guys are all gross and sick and I'm fine. Also, it's not fair that you make me be the thimble in Monopoly. Who wants to be a thimble? What even is a thimble?"

But of course, by the next day, both Finn and Paige were full-fledged snot monsters.

A few times a day, every day, Captain Caspian would sit at a computer in their family's living room, going over reports on the *Marlowe*'s travels and sending advice and commands to the rest of the ship. The space station outside the Caspian compartment continued to make its way across galaxies, even though the four snot monsters couldn't see it.

Foggy, Finn's robot, got to come and go as he pleased. The entire family would have to huddle in Finn's parents' bedroom, door closed, so Foggy could open and shut the front door without letting out contaminants. Sometime in the third week, it got a little old.

"Hello, Caspian family!" Foggy yelled from the hallway. "Please exit the living room so I may come in."

"Ugh," said Paige, putting down a crayon. "Let's drop everything. Finn's sidekick wants to come in . . . *again*."

The family got up, retreated to the parents' bedroom, and shut the door—as they did every time Foggy came to visit.

"Tell Foggy he can come in, Finn," said Captain Caspian.

"All clear," mumbled Finn.

"You have to yell it, Finn," said Captain Caspian. "He's not going to hear you."

Truthfully, Finn didn't want to yell it. Foggy was always so upbeat. Sometimes when he was sick, Finn just wanted to feel miserable.

"All clear!" Finn shouted. They heard the front door open and close, and they all filed out into the living room.

"Hello, Caspian family!" said Foggy.

"You already said that," said Finn.

"I am so pleased to see you!" shouted Foggy. "Even though I am not pleased to see you looking so terrible. I wish I could help you all. I'm sad you're all feeling so bad. If there's anything I can do, please tell me."

"I still can't believe you choose to come in here with us," said Paige. "There's no way I'd volunteer to hang out with Finn every day."

Finn considered which Monopoly piece to throw at his sister.

"But he is my boon companion!" Foggy exclaimed. "My true pal. My friend-to-the-end! There is no way I would ever abandon him here to his snot monstrosity!"

"Foggy, please," said Finn. "A little less loud."

"I am sorry," said Foggy. "Robots, as you know, cannot get sick."

"Yes, you've said that," said Finn.

"So, I do not know what it feels like to be sick," said Foggy.

"I know," said Finn.

"So while you are wretched, I will just observe you, so I may learn about what being sick means," said Foggy.

He sat down on the coffee table across from Finn and stared at him as Finn pushed a tissue up his nose.

"You have a little flag dangling from your nostril, Finn," said Foggy.

"It's not a flag, Foggy, it's a—"

"I have an idea!" shouted Foggy. He sprang to his feet. "Dance party!"

Foggy pushed a button on his left arm and

music began playing out of his torso. He started twirling his hips and pointing his finger in the air. He looked like he would tip over at any second.

"Foggy, please!" shouted Finn. "I don't feel well. I don't want to talk. I don't want to move. And I definitely don't want to dance."

"Yeah, none of us want to see that, either," said Paige.

Finn coughed and spittle flew out of his mouth all over Foggy's chest.

"Ew," said Finn. "Sorry, Foggy."

"It's okay," said Foggy. "I'm sure it's harmless."

"Do you want a tissue?" asked Finn.

Foggy looked at the one dangling from Finn's nose and shook his head.

"Definitely not," he said. "Let me just run a cleaning program. One moment."

Foggy beeped and whirred. A small squeegee

emerged from his side. It wiped up Finn's spit and returned to his body.

"There," said Foggy. "Now I won't spread those germs throughout the *Marlowe*."

"Are you leaving?" asked Finn. He was in a bad mood and wanted a little space.

"No way," said Foggy. "I have lots more observations to make!"

He sat down and stared hard at Finn. For a long time.

"Um, you know what, Foggy?" said Finn. "You can go. Please. Feel free."

"Okay," said Foggy. "If that would make you feel better."

"It would," said Finn.

Foggy stood up, knocking over the

Monopoly board as he made his way toward the door.

"Oh, so sorry," he said.

The family all looked at him.

"I. . . I had all the railroads," said Finn.

"I'm sorry for the trouble," said Foggy. "But could you please?"

He pointed to the bedroom door. Every Caspian in the room sighed. They slowly walked toward the bedroom.

"It's not fair," Paige whined.

"It's definitely not fun," said her dad.

"Finn, you really shouldn't talk to Foggy that way," said Captain Caspian.

"But he was staring at me," said Finn.

"You know you're very lucky to have him," she said. "He's a good friend to you, and there are millions of kids on Earth who would die to have their own ro—"

"Um, excuse me, Caspian family," said

Foggy. "Could you please close the door? So I can leave? It's awkward to stand here and listen to you."

Captain Caspian closed the door and Finn flopped on his parents' bed. No one heard Foggy stifle a small, robotic cough as he left.

Chapter Three
Mission Pretty Possible

"Finn! You're alive!" shouted Vale as he ran down the hall. Finn had just taken his first step out of his compartment.

"Yep!" said Finn. "Four weeks, three days, seven hours, thirty-five minutes, and let's call it an even thirty seconds since I was quarantined."

"Sorry I called your mom a snot monster!" said Vale.

"What was that, Vale?" said Captain Caspian, following Finn out into the hall.

"Um," said Vale. "I said, I'm sorry I called your mom *not*-a-monster. Finn was calling you a snot monster. Right, Finn? And then I was saying, 'no, she's *not* a monster.' That may have sounded like 'snot monster,' but it was 'snot a monster.'"

"So if you were defending me, why were you apologizing?" said Captain Caspian. She smiled at Finn. She knew that she made Vale nervous, and she was enjoying this.

"I wasn't!" said Vale. Sweat rained off his forehead. "I wasn't saying, 'I'm sorry,' like, 'my mistake.' I was saying, 'I'm sorry,' like, 'No way. Nuh-uh, Finn Caspian. Excuse me? I'm sorry, you are NOT going to call your mother a snot monster in front of me! I'm sorry, but that is *not* okay.'"

Captain Caspian was laughing hard enough now that Vale realized she was just joking with him.

"Oh, I see," said Vale. "You guys get locked up together for a month and all you do is plan a joke on me?"

"Vale!!" Foggy came bounding out of the compartment. "Ah, my dear old friend, Vale! Oh, how I've missed you!"

He picked up Vale in a bear hug.

"Thanks?" said Vale. "Finally someone misses me. And it's the weird robot who saw me yesterday."

"We all missed you, Vale," said Captain Caspian. "And I'll miss you even more when you go out on your new mission!"

"What?" asked Finn. "Really?!"

"Yes," she said. "While we've all been cooped up for the last few weeks, I've been planning the next Explorers Troop 301 mission. Vale, why don't you go get Elias and Abigail and tell them to meet us in the map room. Finn, you and Foggy come with me."

Vale ran off to get them.

"Finn, I want to talk to you before the others arrive," said Captain Caspian. "I hope you'll take this mission seriously."

"I take every mission seriously, Mom," said Finn.

"I know, but this one is especially for you," she said.

Finn tilted his head. "What do you—"

"Here are the sickos!" Vale yelled as he ran in with Abigail and Elias.

"I missed you guys!" Finn hugged them both. "No germs, I promise."

"Just your usual germs, you mean," said Abigail.

Everyone got quiet. That's what it was like in the map room. Something about the place made the explorers feel like they should be subdued.

The room was round, dark, and had a domed ceiling. On the walls were maps of planets *Marlowe* explorers had ventured to in the past. In the center of the room a projector rose out of the floor. It shone a giant map of Galaxy Fishbone on the ceiling. (The *Marlowe*

had long since run out of names for all the galaxies they visited, so Paige got to name this
one.) At the center of the map was a bright red
star. About fifteen planets surrounded it. They
were all different colors.

"It's incredible," said Abigail.

"It is," said Captain Caspian.

Captain Caspian pressed a button on the
console in front of the projector, and fourteen planets shrunk away. The image of a blue
world, seven planets from the star, grew on the
ceiling.

"That's it," said Captain Caspian. "That's
where you'll be going."

"What is it?" asked Elias.

"We don't know the name, but we do know
that it seems peaceful," she said. "There's no
reason to think anything down there would
want to hurt us." She had said this to them

before. And every time she said it, she'd been wrong.

"Any*thing*?" said Elias. "I thought we tried not to call aliens 'things' because it made them seem like objects."

"You're right," said Captain Caspian. "But those aren't aliens living down there. They're robots."

"Robots?" said Foggy.

"Yes," said Captain Caspian.

"Only robots?" asked Foggy.

"Yes," said Captain Caspian. "It's really unusual. As far as we can tell, it's all robots. It's time to visit a planet of some metal beings just like you, Foggy. You've been cooped up with us sick humans long enough."

"Amazing!" yelled Foggy. "I'm positively delighted! Cough, cough!"

"Did you just cough?" said Finn.

"No," said Foggy. "Don't be silly! Off to the robot planet!"

"Hold on," said Abigail. "Normally we look for planets where humans could live. Why are we going to this one if it's all robots?"

"You're right," said Captain Caspian. "We don't think this planet is for humans, since there are no life-forms other than the robots and it's very cold out there. But we would really like to understand how such a planet came to be."

"Oh, this is gonna be awesome!" shouted Elias. "I wonder if they'll let me take any robots apart to see how they work."

"I don't think so," laughed Captain Caspian. "But I'm glad to see you're excited. We should all appreciate how wonderful robots are."

Captain Caspian looked at Finn. Finn knew she meant him.

"Perfect," said Foggy. "Tallyho, let's go, pip pip, cough cough."

"Did you just cough again?" said Finn.

But Foggy didn't answer. He was already gone. He'd flown down to the explorer pod bay and was already sitting in the tiny ship that would take the explorers down to the planet. Seat belt fastened.

Chapter Four
Robot Reception

"Huh," said Abigail. She peered out the explorer pod window. They were just entering the atmosphere of the planet below.

"What is it?" said Elias. "Please tell me nothing bad."

"Nothing bad," said Abigail. "Definitely weird. But I'm still going with nothing bad."

Finn strained to see out the window, as well.

In the distance, he could see what looked like a small village. But right below them, outside a big stone building, a group of robots stood looking up at the ship.

"What's so weird about that?" said Finn. "They're just there to welcome us. My mom sent a signal down. They know we're coming."

"Sure," said Abigail. "But . . . wait a second."

"Oh, I can't wait!" said Foggy. He'd already unbuckled and was pressed against the window.

Finn watched as the robots moved, all at once. There were maybe twenty metal creatures on the surface of the planet, all of them human-oid. They shuffled around until they formed a circle. Then, at the same time, they all raised their right arms, one finger pointing to the sky.

"Are they pointing at us?" asked Finn.

"Wait for it," said Abigail.

Then the robots danced. There was no other way to describe it. They shook it to the left.

They shook it to the right. They all moved in unison, arms waving, legs kicking, robot hips swinging like no one was watching.

Finn and Abigail laughed.

"What is it?" asked Elias, who was seated in the back of the pod. "I can't see."

"They're dancing," said Finn.

"Specifically, I think they're doing some kind of Hokey Pokey," said Abigail.

"Ah yes, the universal dance," said Foggy. He could barely contain his excitement to meet his fellow robots.

Abigail tried to land the pod a safe distance from the robots, but as their ship got closer to the ground, the robots fanned out. They seemed to want the ship to land in the middle of their circle.

"Um, generally it's not a good idea to run toward a landing spacecraft," said Abigail. "I don't want to squash any bots."

"Oh, you won't," said Foggy. "We are far too intelligent for that."

"We?" said Finn. "Aren't you one of us?"

The pod jerked as Abigail touched down. When Finn looked up, Explorers Troop 301 was surrounded.

Foggy was the first off the ship.

"Hallo, new friends!" he shouted as he landed on the flat, rocky surface of the planet. The ground was shiny and marbled, like a kitchen counter. "We come in peace!"

"The captain is supposed to make the first greeting," grumbled Abigail. "But I guess you can have this one, Foggy."

The robots didn't respond, but they did start dancing again. The circle drew tighter as the robots closed in on the ship. They snapped their fingers and shimmied toward the explorers as each astronaut disembarked.

"I'm Abigail Obaro, captain of Explorers

Troop 301," shouted Abigail.
"We come from the *Famous
Marlowe 280 Interplanetary
Exploratory Space Station*. We
mean you no harm."

The robots' dance became simpler as they
got closer. Now they were doing a very basic
Running Man, arms and legs pumping up and
down.

"Should we be worried?" whispered Elias.

The robots were now just a few yards from
the explorers.

"Why aren't they saying anything?" Finn
asked.

Now the robots were just a few feet away.

"We come in peace!" Foggy shouted again.
He was boogying as best he could in response.

The robots continued to close in on them.
Finn could feel sweat bead inside his helmet.

"This is not good," whispered Abigail.

"There's no music," said Elias. "Who dances to no music? This is creepy."

The explorers pressed into each other. The robots came closer.

"I got this," said Vale. "Leave it to me."

Vale Gil, the troop's sergeant-at-arms, had spent the most time in combat training. He stepped in front of his friends.

"Here we go," he said.

"Vale, be careful!" shouted Abigail.

Vale bent his elbows, raised both hands, and faced the closest robots. Confronted with a horde of twenty robots closing in on him, Vale did the only thing he could think to do.

He danced.

Vale began to perform the worst robot dance you've ever seen. His legs and arms pumped up and down as Vale jerked his body left, right, and forward. He slid, he shimmied.

"Uh," said Vale. "Uh. Yeah. Uh."

The robots stopped advancing. They all stood and watched Vale. Vale barely noticed. He was so impressed with his own moves.

"Come on," said Vale. "Join the party!"

Reluctantly, all the explorers began dancing their own version of the robot dance.

They were on a new planet. They were millions of light-years from Earth. And yet here they were, mechanically raising and lowering their arms, dancing to no music.

"Loosen up, Elias!" shouted Foggy. "It's all in the hips!"

One robot stepped forward.

"You," said the robot. It pointed at Foggy. "You are like us. Yet you are with them."

"Yes," said Foggy. "And we are so happy to be here."

"We are happy to have you here," said the robot. "I am called 2111222111122121222."

"Nice to meet you, 2111222111122121222," said Foggy. "My name is Foggy. These are my friends, Finn, Abigail, Elias, and Vale."

"Why are they still dancing?" asked 2111222111122121222.

The astronauts had been too nervous to stop. But now they all felt silly. They awkwardly stopped dancing, as if someone had suddenly stopped the music.

"Better," said 2111222111122121222. "That was not good dancing."

"Hey!" said Vale.

"Except you," said 2111222111122121222. It pointed at Vale. "You got the moves."

"I *knew* it!" said Vale, pumping a fist.

"Come with us, Foggy and friends. We invite you to our homes."

Chapter Five
Metal Paradise

The robot known as 2111222111122121222 walked beside Foggy, the kids trailing closely. The rest of the robots had dispersed in different directions. Finn figured they must have all gone to their robot homes.

"How many of you are there?" Finn heard Foggy ask 2111222111122121222 as they walked. "I counted twenty-three back there, including yourself."

"Yes, there are twenty-three like me," said the robot. "But there are many more not like me."

"Do you mean there are different types of robots on this planet?" asked Elias. As the chief technologist of the troop, Elias was the biggest robot fan. He'd tried to build his own robots in the past. And while he hadn't pulled it off just yet, he had a notebook full of designs.

"Of course," said 2111222111122121222. "Just like I'm sure there are many different types of whatever you are wherever you come from. Just today, I've spoken with a number of different friends, including 1112212121212, and 22221111221212121222. And do you know what 22212121111111 said to me just this morning?"

"Nope!" said Vale.

"She told me 111222121222221112212 was going to kick 121212122222121222 out of his house if 121212122222121222 didn't just admit that 111222121222221112212 was a better dancer."

2111222111122121222 laughed. Foggy joined in.

"Ha!" he said. "Ho ho ha. That is so 111222121222221112212."

"Isn't it?" said 2111222111122121222.

"You all have names like that?" asked Vale. "Just ones and twos?

"Yes," said their robot host. "It is very efficient."

"How do you remember them all, though?"
asked Vale.

"Oh, we have a trick," said
2111222111122121222. "For instance,
111222121222221112212 has one dimple on his
face, one scratch on his arm, one antenna on his
head, two eyes, two feet, two hands, one neck,
two lights on his head, one light on his foot,

two buttons on his chest, two buttons on his back, two wheels under his left foot (but you can't really see them, so that's not that helpful), two wheels under his right foot (but you can't really see—"

"Please stop," said Vale. "My human brain hurts."

"You could just call him Lou," said 2111222111122121222. "He prefers that. Most of us have nicknames we've given ourselves."

"Do you have one?" said Vale.

"Yes," said 2111222111122121222. "I call myself SuperAwesome."

"Oh," laughed Vale. "I guess if I could name myself, I'd call myself SuperAwesome, too."

"You would actually be KindofAwesome, since I am SuperAwesome," said Super-Awesome. "Now, let's go inside, shall we?"

"And that guy called himself Lou?" laughed Vale. "Why would—"

"Shhh, Vale," hissed Foggy as SuperAwesome went ahead, entering a large stone building. "Don't embarrass me."

"Vale is just joking around, Foggy," said Finn. "Robots can take a joke, can't they?"

Foggy rolled his eyes.

"Just let me do the talking," he said. "Cough cough, cough cough, spittle."

"What did you just say?" asked Finn.

"I said just let me do the talking," said Foggy.

"No, after that," said Finn. "Did you cough? Foggy, are you sick?"

"Gah," said Foggy. "That's such a human way to think. Of course I'm not sick. Robots can't catch colds, Finn. Wise up!"

Foggy hurried to catch up to Super-Awesome.

"Was that weird to any of you guys?" asked Finn.

"Very," said Elias. "Something isn't right with Foggy."

"Right?" said Finn. "He's never been that rude to me before. He's always been just happy to be my friend."

"No, I meant the coughing," said Elias.

"Oh, yeah," said Finn. "That, too."

Chapter Six
Movable Feast

"And so then 212121221122121222222111 said, 'Give me a break! At least I'm not a part of the 1111111 generation!'"

SuperAwesome slapped the table, laughing hard at her own joke.

The explorers were sitting around a large, rectangular stone table. SuperAwesome sat at the head of it. Seated beside her was Foggy, laughing just as hard as she was. Around the table were all kinds of robots. Some were as small as ants, some were as round as bowling balls, some looked like walking fish. Others were more like Foggy and SuperAwesome: they had heads, arms, and legs like humans.

All the robots had been called together for this dinner to welcome the explorers. Except there wasn't any food served. The bots were plugged into outlets wired into the table. Apparently, the electricity at this particular table was delicious, because the robots seemed to be having the time of their lives. The explorers sat together, silent, confused, and hungry.

"Do you have any food?" said Vale. "I'm hungry and I was always told not to stick my mouth on electrical outlets."

"Hahaha," laughed SuperAwesome and several of the other robots. "We have heard of this! You require 'food' to keep going. You creatures with bodies are so funny, aren't you? Here, let's see if we have some 'food' for you."

Every time SuperAwesome said the word "food," it sounded like she thought it was the funniest word in the universe. A handful of robots fell out of their chairs at the mention of the word.

"Tell me, Foggy," said SuperAwesome. "How are you able to stand it, being with these funny little fleshy creatures all the time?"

"Oh, it's not so bad," said Foggy. "You get used to their weird habits."

"Not so bad?!" shouted Finn. "Foggy, we're your family."

"Family?" asked SuperAwesome, sounding scandalized. "Do you— Ah, never mind, here is your food."

A tall, round robot with a tray balanced on one hand entered the room. He lowered the tray onto the table in front of the astronauts.

On it was a very neatly arranged pyramid of smooth, rectangular stones.

"There you are," said SuperAwesome. "Food for our flesh friends."

The explorers were aghast. Foggy shifted uncomfortably.

"I don't mean to be rude, SuperAwesome," said Abigail. "But this isn't food for humans. If we try to bite into any of these rocks, we'll break our teeth."

SuperAwesome took in this information as though she were reading the newspaper.

"Foggy, tell me, are they always like this?"

"Not all the time," said Foggy. "But you should try being in the same room with them for a month straight. It's no electricity picnic like we have here I can tell you that cough cough."

"I bet," said SuperAwesome.

"Foggy," said Finn. "Could I speak to you alone for a minute?"

Foggy sighed and made a show of slowly getting up from the table. He walked out the door and Finn joined him outside, on the smooth stone courtyard of SuperAwesome's home. The light from the planet's star glinted pink on the ground.

"What is going on with you?" asked Finn.

"Oh, I'm sorry, Finn," said Foggy. "I know I'm not being a berry good friend. But I want dose robots in dere to like me, and it seemth like they don't like you very much. Tho for jutht thith one planet, can I be a little rude to you?"

"First of all, no, that's not how friendship works," said Finn. "If you're my friend, then you have to be my friend all the time. But that's not what I meant. Why do you keep saying 'cough cough'? And you sound weird. I'm worried about you."

Foggy shuffled his feet and looked down.

"It's nothing cough cough," he said. "It's jutht a little habig I picked up, cough cough cough *CUFFWAWFF*, cough."

"It sounds like you're sick," said Finn.

"Ha, that's ridiculouth," said Foggy. "I'm a robot, I can't get sick."

"I know, but what else could it be?" said Finn. "I think we should pack up here and go back to the *Marlowe* to get you checked out. It's not like humans could ever live here anyway. The only food they have are those rocks that are hard as . . . um . . . rocks."

Foggy let out a loud electronic hiss that sounded like *SKROOOONNNNKK.*

"Did you just clear your throat?" asked Finn.

"No," said Foggy. "I'm perfectly fine. And all our travels are all about humans. Finally we find a planet with some of my fellow robots, and you want to leave right away."

"Foggy, our mission is to find a planet where humans could one day live," said Finn.

"But your mother said the mission on this planet is to better appreciate robots," said Foggy.

"I appreciate *you*, Foggy," said Finn. "But these other robots . . ."

"My mission, right now, is to go back in with my robot friends, plug in for a delicious

dinner, and have a few laughs cough cough
CUFFAWFF puke."

A little spark flew out of Foggy's mouth and
died in the air.

"Foggy," said Finn.

"It's nothing!" said
Foggy. He marched back
into SuperAwesome's
building.

"Now, where were
we?" said Foggy.

"You were telling us cough cough *CUF-
FAWFF*," said SuperAwesome.

"Oh, right," said Foggy. "COUGH
COUGH COUGH *BLECH*."

Foggy fell over, clanging on the stone floor.

"Foggy!" shouted Finn.

"Leave him alone," said SuperAwesome.
"Let one of us take care of him. COUGH
COUGH *CUFFAWFF*."

"No, he's my friend!" shouted Finn.

"2221121222, 121111212121, and 12222122222, please escort these *humans* outside," said SuperAwesome.

Before Finn could say another word, three big, round-shouldered robots had grabbed Abigail, Elias, and Vale and yanked them out of their seats. There was nothing Finn could do as they were all ushered back outside.

"FOGGY!" yelled Finn.

"Goodbye, humans!" called SuperAwesome. "Don't bother coming back!"

Chapter Seven

Call a Waambulance

"Ugh, I don't like that SuperAwesome and her 12121222s or whatever," said Abigail. "You'd think that someone who coordinates a big welcome dance like that would be a much nicer person."

"She's not a person," said Vale. "That's the problem. They're all just a bunch of robots."

"Hey, so is Foggy," said Finn. "It doesn't

matter that they're robots. We need to help Foggy, and I'm guessing we're going to need to help them, too."

"Yeah, I'm with Finn," said Elias. "Just because someone is a robot doesn't mean they don't have a heart."

"I'm going to let that one go," said Abigail. "Okay, so what's up with Foggy, and how do we help him?"

Finn told his friends about his conversation with Foggy, and the spark that had flown out of Foggy's mouth.

"I know this sounds weird," said Finn, "but I think he's sick."

"Robots don't have hearts," said Vale. "And robots don't get sick."

"But robots can get a virus," said Elias. His three friends all looked at him like he'd just declared his name was 1212222122.

Elias explained that computers and robots

can't get sick like humans do. A human usually gets sick from germs or viruses: little microscopic organisms that invade humans. They get into their noses or mouths, and sometimes into their blood.

"Gross!" said Vale. "I'm never breathing again."

"You should also start washing your hands

more," said Elias. "But that's a story for a different time."

He went on to say that germs can't hurt computers. Without a living organism, the germ or virus can't survive. But a "virus" for a computer is a completely different problem. Computers run on their own language: a code. And if there's something wrong in the code— either a bad piece of code was slipped onto the computer, or a piece of code on the computer got broken—then that computer could get a virus.

"So something broke inside of Foggy?" said Finn.

"That's my guess," said Elias.

"It must have happened when he visited you guys in quarantine," said Abigail.

"The cleaning program," said Finn. "He ran a cleaning program when I spit on him!"

"Ew," said Abigail. "You spit on him?!"

"No, I coughed and got spit on him," said Finn.

"Oh, yeah, way better," said Abigail. She took one step away from Finn.

"Dude, you don't cough into your elbow?" said Vale. "It's like I hardly know you."

"But Elias said a sick human couldn't give a virus to a computer," said Finn.

"Right," said Elias. "So who knows how this happened?"

The explorers all stood in silence, thinking about how to solve this problem.

"Well, whatever happened, it seems like Foggy is contagious," said Elias. "SuperAwesome sounded SuperGross when we left."

Finn put his hand on Elias's shoulder.

"So if the problem is with Foggy's code," said Finn, "do you think you could fix it? If we got Foggy alone?"

Elias shrugged.

"Maybe."

"Okay," said Finn. "Great. All we have to do is go in there and convince SuperAwesome to give us back Foggy, and then we can see what's wrong with him."

"Why don't you just ask SuperAwesome right now?" said Vale. He pointed at the robot stumbling out of the building.

"What have you done?" asked Super-Awesome. The robot lurched toward Finn. Finn jumped back just in time. SuperAwesome fell to the ground.

"You," said the robot. "You did this COUGH *CRAFFLOFF* puke puke *blech*."

Two sparks and a little bit of sizzled wire flew out of SuperAwesome's mouth as the robot's eyes closed. She lay still.

"Oh boy," said Abigail.

"They've done this to her!" shouted a robotic voice inside the building. "Get them!"

The three tall, round-shouldered robots came bounding out of the building.

"Fun times," said Vale.

"Hope you're feeling one hundred percent, Finn," said Abigail. "Because I think we need to run at about one hundred miles per hour."

Chapter Eight
Nowhere to Run to, Baby

The four explorers ran as fast as they could toward their explorer pod. They were lucky that the robots chasing them weren't particularly speedy.

"If we climb in there," shouted Abigail, pointing at the pod, "those robots will just pry the ship open. They could really damage it."

"Okay," said Finn. "Then let's run past it and make our way to the next building. We can try to lose them over there."

The explorers all ran straight past their ship to the village of small buildings just beyond it. Finn had spied it from the explorer pod but hadn't thought of it again until now. They ran through the narrow alleys of the town—robots apparently didn't need cars, so there were no streets—and tried their best to go unnoticed.

The alleys were teeming with robots of every different shape and size. Finn accidentally stepped on a few tiny ones, but they seemed designed to recover quickly.

"Sorry!" Finn would shout, but the tiny robots would just pop back up into their proper form and wave their hands. It was like Finn stomping on them was nothing more than a bit of rain.

The guards spotted them, and the explorers dove deeper into the maze of alleys in this village. Vale noticed a bucket full of black goop and knocked it over as they ran past.

The guards slowed down and walked carefully through the goop, like it was glue that was going to dry and trap them in place.

"Okay," said Finn as they dodged around another corner. "I think we've lost them."

"What are you?" asked a round robot flying just over the explorers' heads.

"We're robots!" shouted Elias, stepping forward. "Newest models. Never seen anything like it. Can't keep us on the shelves!"

"Robots?" said the flying bot. It stuck out a small stone wand and poked Vale in the shoulder. "You're awfully squishy."

Vale grabbed the wand out of the robot's hand and poked it back.

"And you're a little too pokey!" shouted Vale.

The bot spun away from the explorers and caught sight of the three tall robots making their way through the crowded alleys.

"Over here!" shouted the
flying bot. "Guards, guards!
They're over here!"

"Snitch," said Vale.

"Squishy," said the flying bot.

The explorers turned down an alley. It was
a dead end. Nothing but smooth, shiny stone
walls. Behind them, the guards blocked the
only way out.

"What have you done to Queen
2111222111122121222?" asked the first guard
to step into the alley.

"She's your queen?" asked Abigail. "So the
robot who was frazzing out back there was . . .
your . . . queen?"

"Answer us!" shouted the second guard bot as
they stalked closer to the kids. Finn, Elias, Abigail, and Vale pressed their backs against the wall.

"Yeah!" said the third guard. "Cough cough puke *blech blurp.*"

The guard fell over, a drip of oil spilling from his mouth. The other two guards made equally gross sounds and keeled over, forming a guard pile in the middle of the alleyway.

"Um, what do we do now?" asked Vale.

A door opened beside the explorers.

"Come on, in here." It was the flying bot. "This is my house. Bring them inside."

"Why should we trust you?" asked Vale.

"Because those are three of the queen's guards," said the robot. "And the second any-one sees them lying on the ground, you can bet another hundred will be on their way."

"Yeah, but you could be a spy for the queen," said Vale.

"*You* could be a spy for the queen!" shouted the robot.

"Oh wow," said Vale. "I never thought of that. You're kind of blowing my mind."

"We are not spies!" shouted Elias. "And here's hoping you aren't, either. Thank you for your help. I accept on behalf of my friends."

"Don't thank me yet," said the robot. "You guys have to carry those suckers in here."

Finn watched as Abigail, Elias, and Vale each grabbed a guard by the feet.

"Oh, come on," said Abigail. "You're not sick anymore. Grab a robot head and help."

Chapter Nine
The Plot Sickens

"My name is Luxor," said the robot, after the explorers had dragged the three guards inside. "I'm not going to bother to tell you my number name because I was stripped of it long ago."

Luxor told the explorers he had once worked for the queen, but after a disagreement with her over the proper way to dance the cha-cha, Luxor was thrown out of the imperial court.

"That's why you snitched on us," said Vale. "So you could get back in SuperAwesome's good graces."

"Yes, that's true," said Luxor. "But please. That's Queen SuperAwesome to you."

"*Queen* SuperAwesome!" exclaimed Vale. "That has to be the best name ever. I still can't believe that guy called himself Lou."

"You guys met Lou?" asked Luxor. "How is that old bag of bolts, anyway?"

The explorers shrugged. They didn't know if Lou had caught the virus or not.

"Never mind," said Luxor. "The point is that when Queen SuperAwesome threw me out, I lost touch with all my friends. They turned their backs on me. I never thought that would happen. And the last thing I need is word getting around that I had a pile of the queen's guards outside my door."

"Thank you for your help," said Abigail. "I

am Abigail Obaro. I'm the captain of Explorers Troop 301. We're visiting from the *Marlowe 280 Interplanetary Exploratory Space Station*."

"Fancy," said Luxor.

"Thanks?" said Abigail. "We had a robot friend with us. He became fast friends with Super—the queen. But he got sick."

"Ha!" said Luxor. "Robots can't get sick."

"Sure can," said Vale. "Elias, tell him everything."

"They can get viruses or glitches in their software," Elias explained. He told Luxor what they had seen happen to Foggy and then to the queen, too.

"And now, apparently, these guards," said Finn. "Elias, do you think you can see what's wrong with them? Maybe if we can figure out what's happening, we can fix Foggy and the queen."

"Wait, you brought a bunch of virus-infected

guards into my home?" said Luxor.

"You told us to!" said Vale.

"Don't worry," said Elias. "My theory is that the virus spread when all those robots plugged in at dinner. Luxor, so long as you don't connect to the guards, you should be fine."

"Okay," said Luxor. "But just in case . . ."

Luxor placed blankets over the guards.

"That's . . . not . . . ," said Elias. "Why do you even have blankets? You know what, never mind. I need to take one blanket off so I can check out this guard."

Elias knelt down and found a panel on the back of the robot. He pried it open, exposing the robot's circuitry.

Elias tapped some numbers on a keypad in the robot's back. A long string of numbers raced past on a small screen.

"I can't look," said Luxor. "I think I'm going to be sick!"

"Is it that bad?" said Finn.

"Well, it's not going to be easy," said Elias.

"Okay," said Finn. "Elias, you work on that. I'm going back to the queen's house."

"Are you crazy?" said Vale. "Don't you remember that we were chased out of there and basically blamed for taking down the queen of the entire planet?"

"Yep," said Finn. "But that's where Foggy is."

"So that's where we'll go," said Abigail.

Finn shook his head.

"Oh, come on!" said Abigail. "We're not going to let you go on your own. Foggy is our friend, too."

Finn smiled.

"Vale, you stay here with Elias and protect him if any of these guards wake up and give him trouble," said Finn. "Luxor, you come with Abigail and me."

"Me?!" shouted the robot. "Why?!"

"Because," said Finn. "You're our ticket inside."

Chapter Ten
Fireworks

"Oh, this is so exciting!" exclaimed Luxor as they left his house.

"Why are you so excited?" asked Abigail.

"Because!" Luxor answered. "In every great story about a knight or a warrior, they are sent on an impossible mission by a king or queen. And the hero must prove his or her worth by completing several trials. Luckily, in this story, there are three warriors. You two and me."

"We're not warriors," said Finn.

"You are now," said Luxor.

"And we weren't sent on a mission by the queen," said Abigail. "We're working against the queen."

Luxor lowered his voice to reflect the drama of the situation and said: "These are your trials."

Abigail rolled her eyes at Finn and laughed. If they were going to go on this impossible mission, they might as well have a robot narrator with them. They walked out into the alleys of the village, Luxor hovering just above their heads.

They tried to keep their eyes down and be as unnoticeable as possible.

"Okay, Luxor," said Finn. "Now, if we run into anyone who recognizes us, you need to tell them you've caught us. That way you get to be the hero for the queen, and we get into her castle without any trouble."

Luxor smiled and nodded. He seemed pleased with the plan.

"Walk a little stiffer, Finn," whispered Abigail. "Like your arms are made of metal."

Finn did his best to walk robotically. They'd already made it halfway through the village, and no one had raised a metallic eyebrow at them.

"It's working," he whispered. "No one suspects a thing."

"CLEAR THE WAY! CLEAR THE

WAY!" shouted Luxor above their heads. "VILLAINS COMING THROUGH. THAT'S RIGHT—I, LUXOR, HAVE CAPTURED THE VILLAINS WHO ELUDED THE QUEEN'S GUARDS NOT SO LONG AGO! PLEASE MAKE WAY SO THAT I, LUXOR, MAY RETURN THEM TO THE QUEEN'S CUSTODY!"

Finn gasped. Abigail poked Luxor in the belly.

"Luxor! That's not helping!" she shouted.

"TELL YOUR FRIENDS, TELL YOUR ENEMIES THAT IT WAS I, LUXOR!" The robot was shouting to everyone in the village. "THE QUEEN HAS NO BETTER FRIEND THAN LUXOR. THAT'S L-U-X-O—"

"We better run now," Abigail told Finn.

But just then, a robot shaped like an upside-down pear floated in front of them, blocking their path.

Luxor stopped talking and he stopped flying. If a robot could go pale, Luxor would have been white as a sheet.

Finn recognized the strange-looking bot immediately. It had been at their dinner with Queen SuperAwesome when they'd landed. "I know them!" shouted the robot. "You're right, Luxor, you fool! You have captured the scally-wags."

"Scallywags?" asked Abigail. "What are you, a pirate?"

"How dare you!" shouted the pearbot. "I am 212222122221111, chief chef of our world. I made you the little stone bricks you so rudely declined to eat!"

"I love a tasty stone brick!" said Luxor.

"Oh, be quiet, Luxor," said the chef. "I can take them in from here, cough cough."

"Hey, these are my prisoners," said Luxor. "And besides, this has to be our first trial."

"These fleshy creatures cannot go to the queen," said 212222122221111. "They must be brought to the dungeons!"

"Dungeons!" shouted Finn. "Why do robots have dungeons?"

"Yeah," said Luxor. "Why do we have dungeons?"

"Enough!" shouted the chief chef. "The

dungeons are the caves and tunnels that run below this village. They have always been there. We have been slowly filling them with black tar to reinforce our streets and buildings. But now we can fill them with you!"

212222122221111 reached down and grabbed Finn by the shoulder.

"Let's go!" the robot shouted. "I will *CUF-FAWFOFAFFFAFOFF.*"

"You'll what now?" asked Luxor.

But the chief chef couldn't answer. He took a step back and opened his mouth. Out poured a waterfall of sparks.

"Oh, he's got a bad case," said Abigail.

The chef coughed again, and a small, whistling tube, almost like a tiny firework, shot out of his ear.

"Uh," said Finn.

"Puke puke *pukity* puke," said the chef, and a long, thin rocket shot out of his nose, up into the sky, and exploded in a spray of sparkly golden lights.

"The virus makes fireworks?" asked Luxor.

"It must do different things to different robots," said Finn.

"*BLURPY!*" shouted the chef, and four streaking fireworks flew out of his ears, up above the village, and sent blue and green sparkles raining down on the rooftops.

"Oooohhh," said the robot villagers.

"They like it," said Luxor.

"No, this is bad," said Finn. "We need to

stop this now or someone else is going to come grab us."

Finn looked around. He spotted another vat of the goop they'd used on the guards. He ran over to the side of a building and grabbed a hose, yanking it off its faucet.

"Hey, that's vandalism!" shouted Luxor. "You heard the chief chef! They need that to fill the dungeons!"

"No, *that's* vandalism," said Finn. The chef was now hiccupping like mad and the fireworks were growing increasingly larger. If one rocket shot off in the wrong direction, someone could get hurt.

Finn put one end of the hose in the bucket and pointed the nozzle at the chef. There was a small lever on the side and he cranked it as hard as he could.

"Here we go!" shouted Finn.

Ploop.

A tiny squirt of goop came out the end of the hose, doing nothing more than dirtying the chef's toes.

The chef hiccupped and shot a rocket straight at Luxor. It bounced off the flying bot's round belly and crashed onto the ground nearby.

"I'm okay!" shouted Luxor. "But hurry up already! Really crank it!"

Finn pumped the lever on the hose as fast as he could. He then flipped it one last time, and a rush of goop flew out of the nozzle. It was like a firehose of disgusting black glue. But it did the trick. The goop put out the fireworks in the chef's belly, and the robot collapsed onto the ground.

"Our first trial is complete!" shouted Luxor. "The chef is defeated, and we may now proceed to the queen."

Chapter Eleven
Swarm and Cozy

Finn, Abigail, and Luxor raced out of the village. It's hard to stay hidden once you trigger a fireworks show in the middle of a town.

The two explorers ran as fast as they possibly could, until they were in the clearing separating the village from the queen's palace. The only thing between them and Queen SuperAwesome now was their explorer pod, which looked positively peaceful parked on the smooth stone.

"I really don't like battling these robots," said Finn.

"Why?" asked Abigail. "They don't seem to feel too bad about battling you."

"Yeah, but Foggy," said Finn. "I love Foggy. And he's a robot. And for some reason, all these robots have this idea that they're better than we are."

"Can you shoot fireworks out of your nose?" said Abigail.

"Ha-ha," laughed Finn. "Maybe if I drink enough soda. Anyway, Foggy just seems like such a different robot down here. We have to get to him so Elias can make him better, and then we'll take him home and figure it all out."

"But Finn, what if Foggy doesn't want to figure it out?" asked Abigail. "What if he wants to stay with his robot friends?"

"Then I will be really sad, and I'll eat like eight ice creams when we get home," said Finn as they passed the explorer pod. "But it doesn't matter. Because Foggy will want to come with us. I just know it, and— Oh, hey, that looks bad."

Finn's feelings had to wait. The robots were coming! How many of them were there? Thousands? Millions? Teeny-tiny robots, the kind that bounced back when Finn stepped on them. They were swarming out of the palace and coming straight for Finn and Abigail.

"Oh, ew," said Luxor. "These little disgusting things."

Luxor flew up about ten feet above their heads.

"Good luck!" he said. "I'll just be up here."

"I thought you were a warrior!" shouted Finn.

"This is just the second trial," said Luxor. He flew farther away from the tiny robots. "I'll take care of number three. Promise."

Finn and Abigail had nowhere to go. They ran back to the explorer pod and climbed up on top of it. They needed to get up high.

The tiny robots were like a swarm of insects. The shiny stone ground turned black with them as they rushed toward the explorers.

"I don't see any weird goop around," said Abigail.

"Yeah, what are we going to do?" said Finn.

"Wait, shhh, listen," said Abigail.

The microbots were so small, their voices were barely louder than a whisper. But together, they grew louder. Tiny *blurb*s and coughs that added up to one big virus.

"They're sick, too," said Abigail.

"Ugh," said Finn. "What do we do now? We know stepping on them won't help. They'll just bounce right back."

"I have an idea," said Abigail. "It's weird, though. So you stay here, and if it doesn't work, make sure you still get to Foggy."

"What?" asked Finn. But Abigail was already gone.

She jumped down onto the ground just as the microbots reached the pod. The tiny robots paused for a moment, like a tidal wave right before it crashes. Abigail lay down on the ground and the swarm surged over her.

"Abigail!" shouted Finn. "No!"

Abigail was covered with so many little

robots, Finn couldn't even see her anymore.

"Abigail, can you hear me?!"

There was no answer. The microbots started to make their way up the pod's walls, too. They were going to overtake Finn at any moment. There wasn't much he could do. He could try to get into the pod and away from the swarm. Or he could do something crazy.

He knew if it were him down there, Abigail would do something crazy. So would Foggy.

He jumped down to where he thought Abigail was, and he could hear their little voices. They were spreading all over him. In between coughs, they were saying things like, "Ha-ha! Take that! And that! Who's stomping who now?"

But Finn also heard something else.

"Hahahaha."

It was Abigail's unmistakable laugh.

"That tickles."

Finn reached down and began sweeping microbots away, trying to find Abigail. He didn't want to hurt the bots, but he also needed to save his friend.

Finally, his fingers struck the glass of her space helmet. He cleared the robots away so he could see her face.

"It's okay, Finn," said Abigail. "I'm fine."

"But what are you doing?"

"I'm getting tickled," she said. "If I were a tiny robot, I think I'd get tired of being stepped on all the time. So what's the one thing that would make me feel better?"

Finn heard another tiny, whispered chorus of microbots. "Stomp stomp. Take that!"

"You'd want to stomp back," said Finn.

"Exactly," said Abigail. "They just want their tiny revenge."

Finn laughed. He lay down next to her.

"Have at it, tiny robots!" shouted Abigail. "You have defeated us!"

Finn couldn't stop laughing.

"You're a genius!" he shouted between chuckles. And the two of them lay side by side as the microbot swarm passed over them, stomp-ing away, tickling them the whole time.

"Okay, they're gone now!" said Luxor. "You can get up. Weirdos."

Chapter Twelve
Trash Day

As Finn, Abigail, and Luxor made their way toward Queen SuperAwesome's palace, Finn heard a piercing scream. It came from the village behind them.

"AaaaaAAAAAAAAHHHHHHHHH!"

"Up there!" shouted Luxor.

Some sort of hovering disc was flying

toward them. It had to be a robot. Finn and Abigail knew what real spaceships looked like. They lived on one, for crying out loud. And this disc did not look like a real spaceship. It was more like a cartoon flying saucer—round like a plate, with a small bubble in the middle.

As the disc got closer, the screaming grew louder. The robot wasn't screaming, of course. It was Vale. He was hanging from it upside down. And dangling from Vale's arms, also screaming mightily, was Elias.

"HELP MEEEEE!" shouted Vale as the flying robot neared Finn and Abigail. Elias was still going with the classic "AAAAAHHHH-HHHH!"

"What happened?!" shouted Finn as Vale and Elias came within a few feet of their friends. But they were much too high for Finn to grab.

The flying saucer hovered nearby, spinning around and around.

Elias and Vale spun like they were inside a washing machine.

"We were just coming to get you," said Vale.

"We fixed the guards," said Elias. "AAAH-HHHH."

"AAHHHH," agreed Vale. "And then we stopped to clean up that robot you covered in goop."

"YEEEAAaaaAHHHHH!" shouted Elias. "And then this thing came along and sort of vacuumed up Vale. Got him by the feet."

"But I don't fit!" shouted Vale. "So I'm *whoa*, stuck, *whoa*, halfway out."

"And I grabbed him!" said Elias. "But I can't pull him out."

"Okay," said Finn. "Luxor, is this the third trial?"

"Oh, sorry," said Luxor. He turned toward the explorers.

"Combatants!" he shouted. "Welcome to your third trial!"

"Cool," said Finn. "But we need to get Vale out of there before he's swallowed. Like, now. What do we do?!"

Luxor zoomed over to the flying saucer. He

reached up and pressed a button on the top of the bubble.

"*Boop*. Powered down," said the flying saucer.

It lowered down toward the ground, paused about ten feet in the air, and released Vale. Luckily, Elias was there to break Vale's fall.

"Thanks, Luxor," said Abigail. "To defeat a robot, you need a robot."

"That wasn't even a robot, you chuckle-heads," said Luxor. "That was a trash automaton. Basically, a flying vacuum. I'm insulted you thought that brainless appliance was a robot."

"Great," said Finn.

"The gang's all here. To the queen!"

"Wait a second," said Abigail. "We need a plan."

"The plan is to get Foggy out of there and get home," said Finn.

Elias put his hand on Finn's shoulder.

"But what if Foggy—"

"I know, Abigail already asked me that," said Finn. "If Foggy would rather be friends with these robots . . . then I have to let him stay. I'd have to be the kind of friend who cared more about his friend's happiness than his own."

"No," said Elias. "I was going to say, what if we can't fix Foggy? What if the virus is too strong?"

"Not an option," said Finn. "I have the best scientist in five galaxies here to fix Foggy."

"Oh, awesome!" said Elias. "Who?"

"You, buddy," said Finn. Elias was shocked.

"Finn, I'm seven," said Elias.

"That's a lucky number!" shouted Vale. "And this is boring. To Queen SuperStinky's palace!"

Vale and Finn dashed toward the palace in the distance.

"Come on, Elias," said Abigail. "No pressure."

She ran after Finn and Vale. Elias shook his head and sprinted to catch up.

"That trial was no fun," said Luxor. "What a rip-off!"

Chapter Thirteen
Long Live the Queen?

The explorers all rushed through the door to the dining hall where they'd left Foggy. There, Queen SuperAwesome sat at the head of the table. Her eyes were still closed. Her chin rested on her chest.

She was clearly still sick and unable to function.

A few of the other robots who had been at

the dinner were also still sitting at the table. If robots could look worried, these seemed desperate. One was nervously pressing three buttons on the side of its head. Another twiddled its antennae.

Finn rushed to the queen's side but tripped on something. Foggy was still beside her. He was just lying on the floor.

"No one even picked Foggy up?!" shouted Finn. "Come here, buddy."

Finn and Abigail picked up Foggy and laid him on the table.

"Elias, how did you make the robot guards feel better back at the village?"

"It was easy," said Elias. "I just had to do a simple reboot. Their numbers, the 1s and 2s, were printed on the inside of their panels. I just typed those in and the guards reset. They're good as new. I'm sure they'll be here any minute."

"Great," said Abigail. "Try that with Super-Awesome."

Elias bent the robot queen forward so her head was on the table. He peeled off her back panel to reveal the same type of keypad that was in the guards.

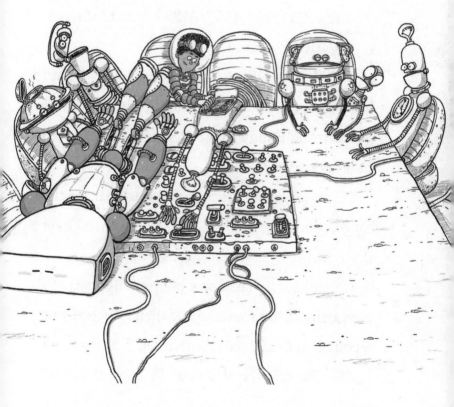

"There's no number here!" said Elias.

"Just try any combination," said Vale.

"There are probably billions of those," said Elias.

"Then try the one that's most superawesome," said Vale.

"Try 2111222111122121222," said Finn.

"Really?" asked Elias.

"Yeah," said Finn, and he blushed. "That's her name. I wanted to remember it. If she was going to be Foggy's new best friend, I wanted to be her friend, too."

"That is so sweet you would do that for the robot queen," said Elias. "Not a sentence I ever thought I'd say, but . . . here goes."

The queen beeped and booped, lights flickered behind her metal eyelids, and, after a few seconds, her head lifted.

"Get out!" she shouted. "Get out! All of you! Now!"

"Hold on," said Finn. "We just saved you."

"Yes," said Queen SuperAwesome. "After you brought that sick robot to our home. The second he plugged into the table I knew something was wrong. He gave me a virus so strong it shut down my entire system."

"Fair," said Vale.

"Just let me help my friend Foggy," said Finn. "And then we'll go."

"You are no friend of robots!" shouted the queen. "You probably gave him that virus!"

Finn's shoulders sunk.

"You're right, I did," he said. "But I didn't mean to. He got sick because he was trying to be a good friend to me. He was keeping me company when I was sick. And now I just want to make him better."

The queen seemed unconvinced.

"Hey, this may be a bad time," said Luxor. "But I just wanted to say hello, Your Majesty!

I'm the one who captured the flesh creatures and brought them back to you. You know, in case you were wanting to reinstate me as a friend of the Queen's Court."

"Oh, please," said Abigail. "We're the ones who brought you here. You wouldn't have lasted through one trial."

"Everybody out!" screamed SuperAwesome. "Guards! Take them to their ship! I don't want to see these humans ever again!"

Three new guards ran into the room and grabbed Elias, Vale, and Abigail. But Finn was down on his knees, trying to help Foggy.

"Let us go!" shouted Vale. "We're not leaving without all of us, including Finn and Foggy."

"No," said Finn. He'd taken off Foggy's back panel. "You should go."

A faint humming sound came from Foggy's back.

"You're kinda stealing my thunder here," said Vale.

The noise from Foggy grew louder.

"Finn," said Abigail. "What's wrong?"

"It's Foggy," said Finn. "I think he might explode."

Chapter Fourteen
Friends Don't Let Friends Blow Up

"Nonsense," said Queen SuperAwesome. "You don't know anything about robots!"

"Actually, Your Majesty, he does," said the chief chef, walking through the door. "He stopped me from exploding earlier. And his friend, the quiet one, saved the guards outside."

"Yeah," said Vale. "And I nearly got swallowed by one. So, you know, I learned a lot."

"Everyone be quiet!" yelled Finn. His face was red. Sweat pooled inside his helmet. "Foggy's in trouble. Elias, come here."

Elias peered over Finn's shoulder at Foggy's control panel. There, beneath a small keypad and a screen, was a glowing green light. Finn pushed back a few wires. The green light grew brighter. Some of the wires around it had melted.

"It's the battery, right?" said Finn. "It's overheating?"

"Yeah," said Elias. "He must have been really sick. Or sick for longer than any of us realized."

"But how could this happen?" said Finn. "Robots aren't affected by germs. They can't run fevers."

"Must be his processor," said Elias. "It's working overtime to try to clear out the virus."

"Because Foggy was working overtime to

help us when we were sick," said Finn. "If he hadn't cared so much, he never would have spent so much time with us. And I never would have gotten him sick."

Elias peered at the battery.

"Finn, if that battery overheats and cracks . . ."

The humming grew louder. The battery started to shake.

"Then Foggy could explode," said Finn.

The weight of it hit him like a tray full of smooth stone bricks. He couldn't let this happen to his best friend, but how was he going to stop it?

The battery vibrated. It looked like it was going to jump out of Foggy.

"Okay," said Finn. "So how did you cure the others? You typed their names into their keypads and reset them, right?"

"Yeah," said Elias. "But Foggy doesn't have a coded name like that. He's not 111212212122 or anything."

"He's just Foggy," said Abigail. "Our friend."

"Okay, so let's think of what it could be," said Finn. "What's the code to reset him?"

Finn felt like a surgeon. There was his friend, laid out on a table in front of him. The pressure from everyone hovering over him, watching and waiting, was impossible.

"You could try 36449," said Elias. "On a keypad with letters, that spells Foggy."

Finn typed it into the small keypad. Nothing.

A wisp of smoke curled up from the battery.

"You guys need to get out of here," said

Finn. "He could blow at any second."

"Never," said Abigail. She put her hand on Finn's shoulder.

"I am leaving, and I suggest all the other robots leave, as well," said the queen. "These flesh creatures don't know what they are doing. They know nothing about our kind."

SuperAwesome stood and ran out the door. The chef stayed. So did Luxor.

"Hey, I had an idea," said Luxor. "The last trial was kind of a dud. Maybe this is the final trial."

"Who cares about your trials right now?" said Vale.

"You could try 6275693," said Abigail. "That would spell *Marlowe*."

"Worth a shot," said Finn. He typed it in, but it didn't work. The battery darkened and turned a bright red. Now smoke was coming from the metal bracket holding the battery.

Finn grabbed it to try to hold it steady.

"Ow!" said Finn. The heat had burned his fingers through his spacesuit.

"I'm sorry, Finn, but we have to go," said Elias. "Now! The fluid inside that battery is combustible. It can burst into flames. If the battery cracks and the fluid leaks out and touches that metal, it'll explode. And this whole building will blow."

"I feel like I should be able to figure out this code," said Finn.

"It could be anything," said Elias. "It could be whatever the engineers on the *Marlowe* put in when Foggy was made."

"How am I supposed to guess that?!" said Finn.

"You can't!" said Abigail. "That's why we have to go."

"We have thirty seconds, max, before he

explodes!" shouted Elias. He stood up. "Guys, we have to leave."

His friends pulled on Finn's shoulders. They dragged him out the door and into the pink sunshine of the robot planet.

Behind them, the entire room glowed a bright red.

"I'm sorry, Finn," said Abigail. "I know he loved you."

"I love you guys, too," said Finn. "Remember that, you know, just in case."

"Oh no," said Vale. "He's about to do something stupid, isn't he?"

"You would know!" yelled Finn. He dove back into the palace.

Chapter Fifteen
Aftershocks

Elias, Vale, and Abigail ran for the explorer pod. The building was going to blow any second, and they had to get behind the pod before it did.

They dove behind their ship. But nothing happened. Just silence.

"Guys!" shouted Vale. "I think the explosion hurt my ears. I can't hear anything!"

Abigail shook her head.

"That's because there's nothing to hear," she said. She stood up and peered around the pod. There was Finn, dragging a very heavy Foggy out of the queen's palace.

"They're okay!" she shouted, and ran toward Finn.

Foggy woke up just as Abigail reached them.

"What are we doing outside?" said Foggy. "And why do I feel a breeze inside me?"

"Oh, sorry," said Finn. He reached back and shut Foggy's panel.

"Finnegan Emerson Caspian, I am very glad you're alive but now I have to kill you," said Abigail. "That was the dumbest, bravest, but mostly dumbest thing I've ever seen someone do."

"Can you take his legs?" said Finn. "I think we're going to have to carry him to the explorer pod. He's a little weak."

As the troop made their way back to the ship, Abigail berated Foggy for being a bad friend to Finn.

"And we found you just lying on the floor!"

said Abigail. "Could any of your new robot friends be bothered to help you up? Nope! They just left you there like trash."

"Hey," said Vale. "Lay off of trash. I have a newfound respect for it."

"I know," said Foggy. "I know. It was ridiculous of me. I was so excited about these new friends, I stopped paying attention to my good friends, and then I almost met my end. Is that a poem I just wrote? My head hurts."

Abigail buckled Foggy into his seat and took the pilot's seat. She pressed the throttle and launched the pod up toward the *Marlowe*.

Finn sat next to Foggy.

"You must be very angry with me," said Foggy. "I don't blame you."

"Nah," said Finn. "I wasn't always great to you. My mom was right. I should have appreciated you more."

Foggy smiled at Finn.

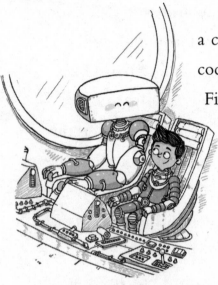

"You know, we tried a couple different pass-codes to reset you," said Finn. "Your name and then your home."

All the explorers looked at Finn. They wanted to know how he'd saved Foggy.

"So I thought about how, if I were a robot and I had a reset code, I'd probably want to come up with it myself. And I'd make it something that I would never forget. Something that I really loved."

"3466," said Foggy.

"Yep," smiled Finn.

Vale looked down at the small communicator on his wrist.

"Let's see, 3-4-6-6," he said. "That spells 'dino.' That's weird. You love dinos?"

"Finn," said Elias. "It spells 'Finn.'"

Finn gave Foggy a hug.

"You know, Foggy," said Finn. "You're going to have to change your code now."

"Why?" asked Foggy.

"I think you should change your name," said Finn. "I'm thinking something like 12121222221112212211."

The pod zoomed toward the small purple light in the distance. The *Marlowe* was waiting for them, and Finn couldn't wait to get home and stay there for a while.

THE *FAMOUS MARLOWE 280 INTERPLANETARY EXPLORATORY SPACE STATION*
HALL OF ALIENS

EXPLORERS TROOP 301 HAS VISITED MANY PLANETS ACROSS THE UNIVERSE. THEY HAVE MET, OUTWITTED, AND OUTRUN DOZENS OF ALIEN LIFE-FORMS. THESE ALIENS HAVE COME IN VARIOUS SHAPES, SIZES, AND BODY ODORS.

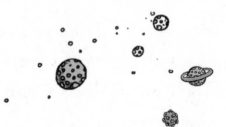

DOUG

Doug is a small alien with a big, glowing brain. He seems like he's your best friend at first, but that's just because of  the whole mind control thing. Doug is not to be toyed with. Doug is not to be trusted. Doug is, however, the Dougiest.

DEATH BUNNY

Sometimes a name just doesn't fit an alien. Sure, this alien looks like a bunny. And yes, he almost stole Troop 301's explorer  pod. And, of course, he did blow up an entire planet singlehandedly. But *death* bunny? That seems a little too extreme for a friendly and furry alien like this one!

ROCK GIANTS

They're big. They're dumb. They're crawling out of the ground and they're coming for you.

SUPERAWESOME

Robots may not have hearts. They may be just a bunch of metal, wires, and code. And they may not be friendly if you land on their planet.

But something Troop 301 has learned along the way: Give them a beat, and they'll dance to it. (Also, they will try to throw you and your friends in their weird robot dungeons.)

SAPHRITE

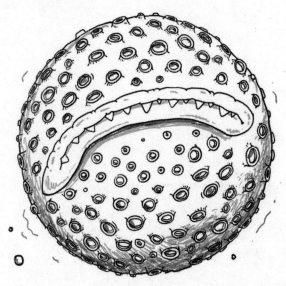

You know how your grandma is always telling you to eat more? And that a growing body needs a healthy appetite? And you practically have to dodge plates of food when you go to her house? That's what Saphrite's grandma was like. Except instead of food, Saphrite's grandma fed her planets. But, you know, same thing!

THE ALIEN ADVENTURES OF FINN CASPIAN

JOURNEY TO THE CENTER OF THAT THING

"Yeesh, I said *psssstt*," grimaced the beetle. "Don't you know what *psssstt* means?"

No one answered. They were too shocked by this enormous, talking beetle.

"It means keep things quiet, ya know?" said the beetle. "On the qt. The down low. Small ball. Mini talkie."

No one said anything, but Foggy and Vale flew down to the ground to investigate.

"See?" said the bug. "Even that. Too loud. You need to take it down a notch. Inside voices. Whisper misters. Soft vocals. The down low."

"You said that one already," whispered Abigail. "But why do we have to stay so quiet?"

The beetle seemed to laugh at this.

"Duh," it whispered. "So you don't wake up the boss. The big cheese. The head honcho. The top dog."

"And who is that?" whispered Finn.

"Who is the big kahuna?" asked the beetle. "The heavyweight? The muckety-muck and the luckety-luck?"

"Yes," sighed Finn. "Who is that?"

The beetle took another step out of the grass. Its body was even bigger than they expected. On another day, on another planet, Finn could probably ride it like a pony.

"You're telling me you don't know where you are?" asked the beetle. Everyone shook their heads. "You wanna know who the top banana is? You're standing on her."

The explorers all looked at each other, then down at the ground. The turf was rough and brown, but it wasn't that strange. They'd been on much weirder planets.

Vale picked up his foot and looked at the bottom of his shoe as if he were checking for dog poop.

"Is she like you?" asked Elias. "Is she a . . . um."

Elias caught himself. The beetle probably didn't think of itself as a bug.

"A bug?" asked the beetle. "No. Saphrite is not a bug. Saphrite is the planet eater, the colossus, the giant that all giants fear."

"I'm sorry," said Foggy. "Who is this Saphrite?"

"Yeah," said Finn. "And where is she, exactly?"

"Oh, I see," said the beetle. "You really don't know. Bubs, you're not standing on a planet. You're standing on Saphrite. She *is* this planet."

Blast off into more adventures inspired by the award-winning kids' podcast!

PART ONE

EXPOSÉ

Twenty-five years ago…

The heat rippling over the surface of Charity Marlow's blacktop driveway was one hundred twelve degrees. It was nearly one hundred nine in the shade from the scrub brush that passed for trees in her front yard.

She sat on a white iron bench in her backyard, picking at the paint flaking off the arm scrolls. A glass of sweet tea stood on the empty plant stand to her right, thinner on top, where the ice cubes melted, thicker on bottom, where the sugar settled.

Inside, the baby was crying.

She'd been going for close to three hours this time, and Charity's arms ached from holding her. Her head throbbed and her feet were sore from standing. From pacing and rocking in place. Her throat was raw from crooning, her nerves shot from exhaustion, and her patience long worn thin.

She'd decided to go inside again when the last ice cube had melted into her tea, and not a minute later.

Not a minute earlier either, even though the top of her head felt close to combusting from the heat of the sun.

She stared at the cracked earth beneath her feet, at the hands in her lap, watching her own fingers shake from exhaustion. Then she stared at her tea as the ice cubes shrank before her eyes, and still the baby screamed.

Then, the last ice cube melted.

Despair swallowed Charity like the whale swallowed Jonah, but she held no hope of being spit back out. Her arms felt like they were made of iron as she lifted her tea.

She closed her eyes while the top of her skull burned in the blazing sunlight. "Lord," she whispered, condensation dripping over her fingers from the outside of her cold glass, "won't you take this angry child and give me a quieter, happier one in her place?"

As soon as she'd said the words, she regretted them. Words spoken in pain and exhaustion are rarely meant, and Charity Marlow's were no exception.

But there was no taking them back.

The moment the last word fell from her lips, the baby stopped crying.

Setting her glass down, she listened harder but heard only silence.

She stood and rounded the bench, headed for the kitchen door. By the time she got to the house, she was running. The screen door slammed behind her and her sandals slapped the floor, competing with the thunder of her own heartbeat in her ears as she raced down the hall.

She stopped in the nursery threshold, one hand clenched around the glossy white door frame, breathing too fast. Too hard. Her chest felt like it was constricting around her heart, as if her ribs were laced up too tight.

"I didn't mean it. *Please*, I didn't mean it."

The baby was dead. Charity was sure of it. She'd committed the worst sin a mother could commit, and now she was being punished.

But there was no answer from above, so she had to take that next step forward. And the one after that.

By her third step into the nursery, she could see a chubby little fist propped against the pastel crib bumper. Anguish swelled

up from her heart and caught in her throat, a lump she couldn't breathe through, yet couldn't swallow.

One more step, and she could see the whole crib and the baby lying in it, eyes peacefully closed.

Charity sobbed and sagged against the crib rail, one hand on her daughter's round little stomach.

The child's eyes fluttered open, and Charity's shocked gasp was like a crack of thunder in the silent house. Her eyes filled with tears of joy and relief and she reached to pick up the child, already scolding herself for being such a superstitious fool.

Then the child smiled at her and Charity froze, her fingers inches from her daughter's pale pink jumper. Chills raced up her spine and goose bumps erupted all over her body.

The child laughed—surely no purer sound of joy was ever heard—and she stepped back from the crib, fear crawling beneath her skin.

The baby laughed again, and she took another step back, then another, and another, until her back hit the pale yellow wall. In that moment, as confusion, guilt and fear met within her, calling into question everything she'd thought she understood about the world and her place in it, Charity Marlow knew only one thing for sure.

That was *not* her baby.

Fourteen years ago...

The whistling tones of a calliope organ rang out from a speaker mounted over the carnival gate, the playful notes tripping up and down the musical register with a spirited energy. The kids from Franklin Elementary buzzed with anticipation, whispering excitedly to one another as they fidgeted in two semistraight lines. The music seemed to feed their enthusiasm and fray their patience.

As she approached the gate, ten-year-old Delilah Marlow clutched her brown-bag lunch and stared at the graceful form

in front of her. The woman handing out tickets wore a red sequined leotard with a black feathered hat, black stockings, and shiny black slippers. Her lips were painted bright red. Her blue eyes practically glowed beneath dramatic sparkly lashes and thin dark eyebrows that ended in a jewel-studded curlicue at each of her temples.

She was the most glamorous thing Delilah had ever seen.

"Here you go, sweetheart." The costumed woman handed her a shiny slip of red paper. Delilah's gaze lingered on the sequins and feathers as the woman handed tickets to each of the other five fifth graders in the group, and to Mrs. Essig, their young homeroom teacher. "You all enjoy your visit, and remember to look but not touch. Especially you!" She patted the brown spikes sticking up all over Matt Fuqua's head. "With that hair, you might just be mistaken for a werewolf pup!"

The other three boys laughed and elbowed Matt, but fell into a sudden awed silence as another woman in red sequins passed by—walking on her black-gloved hands. Her tiny waist was bent backward at a severe angle, so that both of her bare feet dangled over her head, her toes nearly touching the top of her skull.

Delilah couldn't stop staring.

Shelley Wells linked her arm with Delilah's as they stepped through the gate and into the carnival. "How does she *do* that?"

"She's a circus freak." Matt marched past the girls as if he owned the whole midway. "My dad says some of them are just as weird as the monsters they got in cages."

Mrs. Essig hurried to catch up with him, shooting an apologetic glance at the red-sequined woman. "They're *human*," she whispered fiercely as she grabbed the back of Matt's shirt to keep him from wandering down an offshoot of the main path on his own. "That's all that matters."

Matt pulled free of his teacher's grip. "Are we *sure* they're human? My dad says sometimes you can't tell just from lookin'. Remember the reaping?"

Mrs. Essig nodded stiffly, but Delilah knew their teacher didn't *actually* remember the reaping, and neither did Matt Fuqua. Only old people *actually* remembered the reaping, and most of them didn't like to talk about it, because they'd all known someone who'd died. Or killed. Or been taken.

Remember the reaping? wasn't just a question. It was something parents said in hushed voices. Something priests advised while they made the sign of the cross. Something politicians shouted from behind podiums. *Remember the reaping* was a warning not to let history repeat itself. A reminder for humanity not to let its guard down.

Remember the reaping was an American way of life.

The teacher rubbed her forehead and pinched the bridge of her nose. Delilah recognized both gestures. Mrs. Essig was getting another headache.

Matt shrugged, oblivious to his teacher's discomfort. "My dad says you have to be careful who you trust, because the reaping could happen again."

According to Delilah's father, Matt Fuqua was just smart enough to be dangerous. Others who'd warranted the same description included congressmen from the wrong side of the aisle and that eight-year-old from Memphis who'd figured out how to put his mother's car into Neutral before he realized he couldn't reach the brake.

Just smart enough to be dangerous, it turned out, wasn't really very smart at all.

For the next hour, Delilah and her classmates wandered along the crowded sawdust-strewn midway, clutching their lunches and staring in awe at every vibrant spectacle they passed. They didn't have access to the entire menagerie. The owner had generously offered a complimentary midway "preview" for all of the local schools, with the hope that curious parents would later attend the whole carnival at full price. But what they did see was enough to impress even the most jaded fifth grader.

Along with the tantalizing scent of the food carts and the game booths boasting all the bells and whistles, costumed circus performers gave abbreviated demonstrations to cheering children and stunned teachers. A man in a red velvet jacket and dramatic black eyeliner swallowed a series of swords on a small dais, while Delilah rubbed her throat in empathy. Five acrobats in red-and-black sequined leotards formed an inverted pyramid, their bodies bent and twisted into complicated shapes. And set back from the midway, behind velvet ropes to hold the audience at a distance, a man and woman in matching top hats and shiny red-and-black costumes juggled lit torches and breathed fire into the air.

Everywhere the children turned, a new spectacle awaited, each more extravagant than the last. But the real draw was a series of stunning hand-carved and brightly painted circus wagons that had been hauled out to line the midway. Each wheeled cage displayed a different cryptid the children had only ever seen on television, the internet, or in books. Handlers in black slacks and bright red shirts stood by, ready to answer questions or prod creatures into displaying their bizarre and sometimes unsettling features.

The first wheeled cage held a brownie, a small gnomelike creature with a long nose and pointed ears, which Matt labeled "boring" and Shelley pronounced "cute." Another held a cockatrice—a miniature dragon with dark, unsettling eyes that stared up at them from its rooster-like head. The creature had scales that glittered with each elegant movement of its long whip of a tail. Its sharp talons clicked against the metal floor of the cage, and Delilah stumbled backward when it opened its curved beak and let out a terrible crow.

The exhibit most popular with the boys, other than the woman who could twist her body until she was standing on her own skull, was a dog with three heads, each growling and snapping at the other two. As they watched, a woman in a sparkly

red bustier and black skirt tossed a bloody hunk of meat into the cage with an artistic flourish. The boys in the audience cheered as each third of the dog fought viciously over the single dinner all three mouths had to share.

All Delilah could think was that the dog must have been awfully hungry to keep stealing food from itself.

While the rest of the group remained spellbound by the savage snapping dog, Delilah wandered toward the next wagon, where a cluster of kids from another school had gathered. She had to push her way to the front of the whispering, pointing crowd, and her first glimpse of the creature in the cage stole her breath. It was like nothing she had ever seen. Or rather, it was like *several* things Delilah had seen, but never in such a seemingly random compilation of mismatched parts.

The cryptid was the size and general shape of a lion, its body covered in smooth golden fur ending with a long, slim, tufted tail. Each of her four paws was wider than Delilah's whole hand, but even more incredible was the huge pair of eagle-like wings growing from the creature's back, its feathers fading from dark golden brown at the base to nearly white at the tips. Yet what really caused the commotion was the fact that the creature's front feline paws grew up into deeply tanned human arms and shoulders, which supported an equally human neck and a human head with long, dark hair.

From the biceps up, the creature in the cage looked like a normal woman.

Mesmerized, Delilah glanced at the plaque wired to the front of the wagon. Sphinx, it read. The cryptid was a forty-three-year-old sphinx named Hecuba, who'd been taken from her mother's nest on a Greek mountainside just weeks after she was born.

Delilah tried to imagine the creature in her natural habitat. Flying across the Greek countryside on huge powerful wings. Swooping to catch a goat or lamb in her razor-sharp claws, then

taking the prize up to a massive nest on the side of a mountain. That would have been incredible to see.

Could Hecuba remember any of that life? Delilah couldn't remember anything from when she was only a few weeks old.

The sphinx turned in her tight quarters, ready to pace several steps to the other end of her cage, but when her gaze met Delilah's, Hecuba froze. Her eyes were gold and round like a cat's, and the left one peeked at the child through a curtain of dark hair. But no cat had ever looked at Delilah like Hecuba was looking at her. No bird had either.

The sphinx glared at her the way her mother did in church, when Delilah kept clicking the ballpoint pen but couldn't be scolded during the prayer.

The sphinx was looking at Delilah as if she wanted to say something.

Hecuba blinked, then continued pacing, but every time she turned toward the fascinated child, their gazes locked and Delilah's curiosity was piqued again.

"Can we ask her questions?" she asked the sphinx's handler, a large man in jeans whose thick arms were crossed over a simple red employee T-shirt. There were no top hats or sequins for handlers assigned to the most dangerous cryptids—nothing that could distract from the safety regulations.

"Questions?" The handler frowned down at her, as if he found her request very odd. "You can ask anything you want, but don't expect an answer. She don't talk. Even if she could, it'd probably be nonsense. Having a human head don't mean she has a human brain."

Delilah decided to give it a try anyway, because what other kind of brain could be inside a human head? She stepped closer to the cage, but stopped when the handler stuck one arm out to keep her at a safe distance. "Hecuba?" she said, and the sphinx stilled when she heard her name. "Do you remember Greece?"

The sphinx blinked, then narrowed her eyes at the child. A

human tongue peeked from between her dry lips to wet them, and Delilah's pulse quickened. Hecuba was going to answer. She, Delilah Marlow, was going to be the first person in history to carry on a conversation with a sphinx!

"Ha!" Someone shoved Delilah's shoulder, and she stumbled to the left. When she turned, she found Matt Fuqua leering at her. "Did you really think it was going to answer you?" Matt and his friends laughed at Delilah while her cheeks burned.

Mrs. Essig quietly rounded up her group and announced that it was time to eat their bagged lunches.

As they headed down the midway toward the petting zoo, which boasted a picnic area and hand-washing station, the parade of performers and exhibits continued. Matt stepped into the path of an acrobat doing backflips down the sawdust-strewn path, and if Mrs. Essig hadn't pulled him out of the way, he would have wound up tangled in a knot of bendy limbs and sequins.

Shelley whispered into Delilah's ear that Mrs. Essig should have let him go. Death by circus acrobat would have been the most interesting thing ever to happen to him.

The petting zoo was a fenced-off area at the end of the midway. Inside, a series of small open-air pens had been arranged across from a collection of long folding picnic tables. Mrs. Essig claimed the end of one table for her six field-trip charges and shooed them toward a hand-washing station at one end of the exhibit.

Delilah dropped her lunch bag on the chair she'd claimed, then followed Shelley toward the boxy plastic sink and soap dispensers. While the boys splashed each other and used more paper towels than they actually required, Delilah and Shelley wandered slowly past the enclosures, oohing and aahing over the young beasts on display.

Instead of the usual collection of lambs, piglets, and newborn bunnies, the menagerie's petting zoo held werewolf puppies, a centaur foal who pranced around her pen with hair the color of

wheat flying out behind her, and the most adorable little bundle of white fur identified by the sign hanging from its pen as an infant yeti.

There was also a young giant—a three-foot-tall toddler wearing a folded tablecloth as a diaper. The giant's forehead protruded grotesquely and his legs were knobby and twisted. After a second of staring at him, Delilah decided that the huge toddler was much more scared of the taunting children than they were of him.

Shelley's favorites were the werewolf pups. The plaque hanging from their pen said that they were five years old and had been born right there in the menagerie. They had a baby sister, according to petting zoo's "nanny"—a woman in black overalls and a stained red apron. But the infant was still too young to be separated from her mother, so Shelley and Delilah would have to come back with their parents to see the full display at night, if they wanted a glimpse at the only baby werewolf in the menagerie.

At the last pen before the hand-washing station, Matt and his friends had gathered, wet fingers still dripping, and were shouting to be heard over one another as they stared into the pen. "What's going on?" Shelley said, elbowing her way through the small throng of boys with Delilah at her side.

"There's no sign, so we're taking bets about what's in the pen," Matt explained. "I've got a homemade fudge brownie up for grabs, from my lunch, and Elías is throwing in a candy bar."

Delilah peered into the pen and discovered the source of the mystery. Three forms sat at the back in a semicircle, facing away from the crowd. The one on the left was the smallest and the one on the right was the largest, but all three wore what seemed to be threadbare nightgowns. Without their faces visible, their species was a total mystery.

"I say they're cyclopses," Matt declared.

Delilah shook her head. "Cyclopses are giants."

"Actually, there's a pygmy species native to a small island near Greece." Neal Grundidge pulled a used tissue from his pocket and swiped at his runny nose. "They're people-sized."

"They could be satyrs," Elías said. "We can't see their feet from here."

"Hey!" Matt shouted, gripping the pen with both hands. "Hey, turn around! We paid for freaks, so show us some freaks!"

"This field trip is free," Shelley reminded him, but Matt only wedged one sneakered foot into the pen and climbed up a foot.

"Get down!" Delilah whispered fiercely, as the nanny started toward them with clenched fists and narrowed eyes. "You're going to get us all in trouble."

"We're not leaving until you turn around, freaks!" Matt shouted, propelling himself another foot up the six-foot fence.

The creatures on the right and left of the semicircle hunched even closer to the center, but the one in the middle slowly began to turn.

Delilah held her breath, and Matt dropped onto the ground but clutched the fence with both hands. All six of the classmates watched, spellbound, as the form in the middle stood on human legs and feet and turned to face them. Long dark hair hung over her face, obscuring the source of her monstrosity, and silence fell over the fifth graders as they waited, frozen.

Finally the girl in the dress lifted one human-looking hand and pushed her hair back to reveal...

A perfectly normal-looking little girl.

"Awww!" Neal frowned. "She looks like my little sister."

"What is she?" Elías asked, as the nanny approached.

"She's not a she, she's an *it*," Matt insisted, backing solemnly away from the pen. "That's the most dangerous kind of freak. The kind that looks like us. She must be a surrogate."

"Are those her sisters?" Neal asked. "Surrogates don't have brothers and sisters."

"She's an oracle," the nanny said. "All three of them are. Right

now they mostly find lost things and guess your middle name, but someday, they'll be able to see the future."

"You think they'll see another reaping?" Shelley whispered.

Delilah hardly heard her best friend's question. When her classmates had bored of the normal-looking freak and moved on to eat their lunch, Delilah stood alone in front of the pen, staring at the child oracle, who stared right back at her through haunting golden-brown eyes. The girl was a couple of years younger than Delilah, and a lot skinnier. Her nightgown was stained. Her hair was tangled and dirty, her bare feet caked in mud. There was no food in the oracles' pen, nor any furniture at all.

When Delilah finally turned away from the girl on the other side of the fence, bothered by something she couldn't quite put into words, she could feel the oracle watching as she walked all the way back to her table and sat with her friends. That unseen gaze followed her as she pulled a sandwich from her brown bag and stared at it, suffering a sudden loss of appetite.

Finally, as she opened her carton of milk, Delilah's grim tangle of thoughts cleared enough for one to shine through. If that girl was a monster, anyone could be a monster. That's why the world was so terrified of another reaping. Because just like last time, humanity would never see it coming.

But if monsters could look like humans, and humans could look like monsters, how could anyone ever *really* be sure that the right people stood on the outside of all those cages?

"Three hundred one thousand babies were born in hospitals across the United States in March of 1980. Not one of them made it home from the hospital."

—Opening lines of a 1996 documentary entitled
The Reaping—America's Greatest Tragedy

ROMMILY

A bead of sweat rolled down Rommily's brow and soaked into the thin blanket beneath her head. In midsummer, the inside of the cargo trailer was always sweltering, and being accustomed to the dark and the heat and the relentless jostling from the road wasn't the same as being comfortable. But then, comfort wasn't a concept she remembered very well anyway. She'd been sold to the menagerie as a skinny six-year-old with wide honey-brown eyes, clinging to her older sister's hand while she whispered reassurances into her younger sister's ear.

At twenty, Rommily was still thin and her eyes were still wide and honey brown, but the rest of her was all grown-up.

For the past decade of their fourteen years in captivity the oracles had shared a single cage on wheels, just wide enough to let them sleep side by side and just tall enough to stand up in. Rommily's entire world consisted of 192 cubic feet of space, which she shared with her sisters. What little time they didn't spend staring out at the world through steel mesh was spent performing, in chains.

Rommily could recall little of her life before the menagerie, and what memories she still possessed had taken on the hazy quality of a half-remembered dream.

The overloaded semi rolled to a stop with a familiar groan and the harsh squeal of brakes, and her body rocked with the motion. Near the front of the trailer, the pup whined in her

cage, and at the rear one of the cats snorted, startled from sleep by the sudden loss of forward momentum.

The cats, she knew, always dreamed of trees, of wind and earth and prey. The pup dreamed about her mother. Rommily remembered their dreams clearly, though she hadn't been able to peek into them in months.

She sat up on the threadbare quilt that served as her pallet in the summer and her blanket in the cold. She glanced at the sister on her left, then at the sister on her right, both still asleep in spite of the narrow empty space she had left between them. She could hardly see them in the muddy darkness, but she knew their shapes by heart.

On the left was Lala, with her perpetual baby face and thin frame, dirty toes peeking from beneath her long layered skirt, even with her legs curled up to her chest. Lala was the youngest of the three, and the smartest, according to most.

On the right was Mirela, whose bountiful figure endured, though she was fed no more than the rest of the livestock. Mirela had a spine of steel, a fact evident in her proud posture. Mirie would not bend. Not for food, not for sleep, and not for comfort. Deep down, her sisters understood that if she were ever pushed too hard, she would snap, and the recoil might kill them all.

There wasn't enough room to move around in the steel crate, so Rommily sat with her knees tucked up to her chest and stared into the cage across the narrow aisle that ran down the center of the cargo trailer. A set of eyes flashed in the dark, reflecting what little light filtered through the vents in the top of the wide-load trailer.

The minotaur was awake. If he ever slept, Rommily couldn't tell. Every time she woke up on the road, the bull was watching her. Not just looking at her. *Watching* her. She wasn't sure of much anymore, but she was sure of that.

The rumble of the engine died, and in its absence voices echoed from outside, shouting orders and barking replies. Rom-

mily couldn't tell what time it was from the muddy light overhead, but the time of day never mattered anyway. Regardless of the hour or the weather, the roustabouts would start setting everything up the moment they arrived at the site, the latest in an endless blur of rural county fairgrounds. Lost time was lost money, and if there was anything old man Metzger wasn't willing to lose, it was money.

Something scraped the outside of the cargo trailer, and Lala rolled over in her sleep. Metal creaked from the left and right as the other livestock began to stir in their cages. The acrid scent of fresh urine wafted from the front of the trailer and Rommily's nose crinkled. Someone's bladder control had failed. Probably the pup's. But that was no surprise, considering how long they'd been locked in the dark.

A sudden violent squeal of metal ripped through the voices echoing from outside, and Rommily's eyelids snapped shut as mental images rolled over her. Visions still came like that sometimes, triggered from deep within her by a sight, scent, or sound.

"Take the key and lock her up," she mumbled.

The bull's eyes narrowed as his attention to Rommily intensified, but she didn't notice. She could no longer see anything but what played in her head, and even if she actually understood what she saw this time, no one else ever would. They hadn't been able to make much sense of anything she'd said since the rainy night they'd found her wandering between the cages on some Midwestern fairgrounds, drenched to the bone and dripping with enough blood to drive the cats into a frenzy.

Rommily knew that she understood more of the world than it understood of her since that night, but that frustrated her much less than the brutal realignment of her divination. Her third eye saw mostly the end of life now, and each vision chipped away a little more of her sanity. Mirela worried that she was too far gone already. Rommily worried that Mirela was right.

"Jack fell down and broke his crown," she whispered, and the words ran together like watercolors on canvas.

On her right, Mirela sat up, took one look at Rommily, then shoved her other sister's shoulder. Lala groaned and opened her eyes, ready to grump, but when her gaze fell on Rommily, the words died on her tongue.

Before either of them could try for the thousandth time to interpret their sister's words, the mighty groan of steel obliterated any attempt at communication. A second later, their cage began to tremble as the floor of the trailer shuddered beneath it.

The trailer wall behind the bull's cage separated from the ceiling with a great creak. Harsh daylight poured in through the ever-widening seams at the top of the wall and down both sides, blinding the occupants inside as the wall, hinged at the bottom, folded down like a ramp the full length of the trailer.

The effect was like opening one long side of a box to reveal its contents. Anyone unaccustomed to the sight would have been astonished by the number of wheeled cages lined up inside, neat as a child's blocks put away for storage.

But Rommily and her sisters, and the pup, and the cats, and all the others—they only stared out at the circus unfolding before them with tired, glazed eyes.

The bull didn't turn to look, not even when several big roustabouts in dusty jeans and matching red shirts climbed the ramp at his back. Their heavy boots clomped against the metal floor, and they began opening locks and pulling heavy iron chains from the axles beneath the bull's cage.

The minotaur was bigger than all three of the oracles combined, and it took eight men—all of them big and strong, and accustomed to the work—to control the roll of his cage down the ramp. If left to gravity, his cart would crash heavily into whatever blocked its path, and if there was anything old man Metzger liked less than wasted time or lost money, it was broken equipment.

While several of the roustabouts stayed behind to sedate the bull, then let him out of his pen and fit him with a work harness, the others climbed the ramp again to fetch the horse cages. The centaurs couldn't bear a load like the minotaur, but all beasts of burden would be put to heavy labor of one sort or another.

To keep them healthy enough to work, they were given extra food.

To keep them relatively safe to work with, they were given regular sedatives, which kept their minds dull.

Rommily watched as the minotaur was harnessed, leather straps fitting over his largely bovine head and massive, heavy horns before lying across enormous cords of human neck muscle. He blinked at her through a medicated daze. His attention didn't falter even when the lot superintendent started shouting orders and waving his arms, directing carts of brightly colored costumes and decorative wagon casings—huge hand-carved frames, which would be mounted on the sides of the cages when they went on display.

Mirela and Lala sat on their knees on either side of their sister, and together they watched the pre-carnival dance, a laborious routine they knew well. Everyone had a job. Every job was important. The last time someone forgot to double-check a lock, three people had died. Four, if you count the creature that got loose.

But no one ever counted him.

The beasts of burden were put to work unloading the other cages. The oracles watched, mute, as pairs of large men hauled huge posts toward the fairgrounds. Women drove tractors pulling carts full of supplies, hay, and feed.

Rommily's fingers folded around the steel mesh in front of her when the roustabouts came for her cage. The animal exhibits had been unloaded and all that remained were the specialized-service acts. The succubi. The sirens. The oracles. Soon they would be cleaned up, decked out in bright colors, and acclaimed

on the midway as dancers, singers, and fortune-tellers. But that was all for show. For profit. For later.

For now…

The rattle of chains and the metallic screech of wheeled cages. Sweat-stained clothes and growling bellies, and the aged stench of travel.

The oracle sisters rocked with the jostle of the cage as they were rolled off the trailer. They squinted against the harsh sunlight. Rommily breathed deeply in the open air, but even outside the stale livestock trailer, the menagerie still smelled like captivity. Like straw and animals and sweat and manure. Like rust, oil, and exhaust.

The bull passed the oracles' cage pulling two of the wolves' pens, linked end to end. His gaze caught on Rommily again, and he veered so sharply that the man pulling his harness turned and beat him over the head with a thick baton. Rommily could only watch, and when the small procession had gone, her focus fell on a sign revealed by its passing.

Welcome to the Franklin County Fairgrounds.

Rommily shook her head, and her grip on the steel mesh tightened. When she opened her mouth, the commotion of the menagerie swallowed her voice before even her sisters could hear it. But the words echoed in her own head long after they fell from her tongue.

"…we all fall down…"

DELILAH

On the morning of my twenty-fifth birthday, I woke up to find that Brandon had left four glossy red tickets on my night-stand. They were made from nice card stock—definitely keep-sake quality—covered in glittering, scrolling black script. My hand shook as I picked them up. I knew what they were before I even read the print.

Admission For One
To Metzger's Menagerie
The Largest Traveling Zoo
In The Northern Hemisphere

I left the tickets in the glove box during my shift at the bank, where I spent most of the day trying to tune out the excited chatter of my fellow tellers. About half of my coworkers also had tickets. The other half couldn't afford to go.

Nothing pays very well in small-town Oklahoma, and usually that's okay, because there isn't much to do in the land of red earth anyway, until you get up to the capital or out toward Tulsa. Hell, you can't even get full-strength beer with your din-ner unless you pay for an import.

But the menagerie hadn't been within driving distance of Franklin County in nearly fifteen years, and it might never

come back. Everyone who could borrow money or call in a debt would be there to see the spectacle.

Including me.

Brandon had spent a fortune on the tickets, and it didn't really matter that I would rather drive to the city and spend my birthday at the ballet, or a concert, or even a baseball game. As my mother had told me all my life, the true gift was in the intent, and my boyfriend had meant well.

He always meant well.

That evening, Brandon took my hand as we wandered down the fairground midway behind my best friend, Shelley Wells, and her boyfriend, Rick. Barkers cried out from both sides of the path, challenging us to pin the tail on the centaur, or knock down pop-up silhouettes of satyrs with a rubber-tipped archery set, or shoot the shell bras off mermaid figurines with water guns. Calliope music played at a volume only small children and the near-deaf could actually enjoy.

The noise scattered my thoughts and scraped my nerves raw. We hadn't even gotten to the menagerie section of the carnival yet and I was ready to go home.

"Hey, Lilah, did you see they have a minotaur?" Shelley pointed to a twenties-style poster tacked up next to a spinning ride advertised as "guaranteed to make you hurl."

"They didn't have him when we were kids."

I nodded, and she turned to walk backward, facing me while she shouted above the jostling, buzzing crowd. "You see a minotaur in school?"

"No. They're pretty rare." We'd seen very few live cryptids in class, and minotaurs were among the least likely to ever be studied by undergrads. They bred slowly in captivity and gave birth to only one offspring at a time. Most experts believed they'd be extinct within a century—a tragedy few in the U.S. would recognize.

"You shouldn't have quit." Shelley turned to face forward

again, taking Rick's arm, then called to me over her shoulder. "You would've been a great crypto-vet."

"I didn't quit. I just didn't go to grad school." For a while, though, that had been the plan. I'd finished my crypto-biology degree and had already been accepted into two crypto-veterinary programs before I'd realized that the only jobs legally available in the U.S. for crypto-vets would have required me to lock up my patients. Even the ones with human faces.

Those jobs were at places like Metzger's Menagerie.

Or worse: research labs, in which scientists tested everything from cosmetics to biological weapons on creatures protected by neither human law nor ASPCA regulations.

Disillusioned by those prospects, I'd moved back home to Franklin, where the median income was less than two-thirds that of the national average and my best guess on the median vocabulary looked even less promising.

A jewel glittering among small-town clods of red clay, Brandon was a newly minted pharmacist with a future in the family business. He read books and spoke in complete sentences. We'd been together since the month I'd come home from college, and—poor gift-giving skills aside—he was a very nice guy. And he truly loved me.

The only part of me that had been relieved to find such a morally ambiguous birthday present on my nightstand was the part that had half expected an engagement ring.

I wanted to be more than a small-town bank teller married to a small-town pharmacist. But I had no idea what "more" might look like, and the certainty that I'd know it when I saw it had faded with each day spent in Franklin. All I ever saw was Brandon, and all he seemed to want to see was me.

And a traveling zoo full of bizarre beasts.

The actual menagerie was behind a second gate at the end of the sawdust-strewn midway, a design no doubt intended to pull people past countless opportunities to spend money on their way

to the main attraction—the only part of the carnival not offered on a yearly basis by the county fair.

Brandon and I caught up with Shelley and Rick at the menagerie gate, where another line had formed. I recognized several of the people in the crowd as account holders from the bank, but without my name tag—Hello, My Name is Delilah. Can I Interest You in a No-Fee Savings Plan?—they didn't seem to recognize me. The family in front of us had three small children, each clamoring to touch the shifter kittens and phoenix chicks in the petting zoo. At the gate, the parents were reminded that certain areas of the exhibit, namely the succubus tent, would be off-limits to anyone under eighteen.

Rick snickered like an overgrown twelve-year-old and Shelley elbowed him. I thanked the universe for my mature, stable, predictable boyfriend, then realized that I'd just found three different ways to call Brandon boring.

When we got to the front of the line, an elderly man in a red sequined vest and a black top hat took one look at Shelley, then bowed low and pulled a bouquet of real daisies from his sleeve. He presented them to her with a flourish from one knee, heedless of his cracking joints.

Delighted, Shelley returned his bow with a curtsy, spreading the hem of an imaginary skirt, and even I couldn't resist a smile. Then she and Rick helped the poor old man to his feet.

The ticket taker resettled his hat on his head. "First time at the menagerie?"

"Kind of." Shelley stuck her nose into the daisies and sniffed. "Delilah and I saw some of it when we were kids. They didn't bring out any of the exotic stuff, though."

"Well, then, you're in for a treat!" He glanced at our plastic full-pass bracelets, then waved us inside with a grand, white-gloved gesture. "Trust me, ladies and gentlemen. You've never seen anything like *this* before."

However, that could only be partly true, no matter what they had on display behind velvet curtains and in gilded cages. Gone

were the days when centaurs roamed the plains in herds, with flocks of thunderbirds beating powerful wings overhead, but we'd grown up seeing cryptids of all sizes, shapes, and colors on television and in movie theaters. They were the villains in our horror movies, most of which drew on the reaping for inspiration. They were the hidden terrorist threats in our thrillers, the bumbling bad guys in our comedies, and the subject of scientific study in nearly every documentary I'd ever seen.

That's where traveling creature features had the market cornered. Anyone could see a werewolf on television, but the average citizen could only see one live at the menagerie. If he or she could afford the cost of admission. And Metzger's had the most diverse collection of any cryptid zoo in the country.

Metzger's was stunning. I couldn't deny that, even as I stopped to scrape a thin coating of manure and sawdust from the sole of my left boot onto the grass.

Compared to the Tilt-A-Whirl and corn-dog portion of the carnival, the menagerie was practically circus finery. The lights were brighter and the colors more vibrant. Even the boisterous organ music felt more sophisticated and dimensional. Costumed performers wandered the midway with flaming batons, balloon bouquets, and souvenir top hats, giving the menagerie the same glamorous, exotic appeal I remembered from my visit as a child. The red sequined costumes had been updated, as, presumably, had the employees wearing them, and the scents of fried dough and roasted meat still made my mouth water.

But the guilt twisting my insides into knots couldn't be calmed by junk food, and the glass of wine I'd had in place of my pre-carnival dinner hadn't helped in the least. The small line of People First protesters shouting, "Remember the reaping!" outside the front gate had only made the whole thing worse.

The People First activists wanted the menagerie to leave Franklin County. We had that much in common. However, they didn't object to the inhumane treatment of cryptids in

captivity—they were scared that the cryptids would escape and embark upon another devastating human slaughter.

What they didn't seem to realize was that if the menagerie's oddities escaped, *we would see them coming.*

We hadn't seen the reaping coming. The cryptid surrogates had pulled off the greatest con in all of history—so meticulously executed that we didn't realize the scale of the infiltration until it was far too late. Six years after the first wave, we'd *still* had no idea that our losses numbered more than three hundred thousand.

Fearing locked-up cryptids that didn't look human would do us no more good than suspecting our own neighbors and relatives of being monsters, as we'd done for decades after the reaping. But scared people can't be reasoned with. Scared politicians can't be talked down from their podiums. Scared nations pass reactionary laws without bothering to consider how much powder those legal snowballs will gather as they roll down Capitol Hill. Eventually, yesterday's outrage becomes today's normalcy.

Reactionary legislation had spawned outfits like Metzger's, where anything and everything not deemed to be human could be locked up and put on display with no limits, no boundaries, and no regulations except those meant to protect employees and spectators. Which made people like me—the admittedly quiet minority—profoundly uncomfortable.

My tension headache told me I shouldn't have accepted the tickets. My queasy stomach said I shouldn't be celebrating my birthday at the menagerie where, as a child, I'd been shocked to see three malnourished little girls locked in an animal pen wearing no more than a few filthy scraps of material. Because when *I* remembered the reaping—inarguably the most profound tragedy to ever strike the U.S.—I also remembered the millions of innocent cryptids who'd been rounded up and thrown in prisons or shot on sight for resisting arrest.

By the time I was born, several years after the reaping was

discovered, the government had begun denying citizenship and legal rights to any living being only partially human, as well as to any hybrid of two or more different biological families.

What that meant was that ligers and mules were protected by the ASPCA because they were both hybrids of two animals that share the same biological genus and family. But because the griffin is a hybrid of two different classes—Mammalia and Aves—and three different orders—Carnivora, Artiodactyla, and Squamata—it isn't recognized as a natural animal but as a cryptid "beast." Anything considered "unnatural" under such legislation was denied protection under U.S. law.

That secondary national tragedy, a clean sweep of everyone not wholly human or "naturally" fauna, had been brushed under the rug, and even mentioning it made my friends and coworkers look at me as if I'd just set fire to the U.S. flag. So I'd stopped talking about it. But I hadn't stopped feeling it.

Yet deep down, I was dying to see the strange and amazing creatures I'd studied in school, for all the same reasons that had led me to major in crypto-biology in the first place. I wanted to see the beautiful selkie emerging from her seal-skin. The troll, so tall and thick he couldn't stand up in most human-scale build-ings. The man who could turn into a cheetah at will. The part of me that objected to the confinement and abuse of such be-ings was the very same part that *needed* to see them for myself.

To understand.

Metzger's had no right to exploit the creatures in its custody, but that wouldn't end whether I looked at them or not. And who better than I to truly appreciate, rather than taunt or mock?

At least, that's how I rationalized my warring desires to both condemn and experience the spectacle.

At the center of the menagerie, towering over everything else, was the big top, an enormous red-and-white-striped circus tent with three sharp peaks that cast an ominous shadow over the fairgrounds. The entrance flaps remained tightly closed until a

paying guest was admitted, making it impossible to catch even a passing glimpse of the mysteries within. Around the perimeter of the menagerie stood a series of smaller tents and attractions, and branching from those were a series of themed subsections. Everything from the posters and cages to the costumes and music was designed with a vintage feel so that it seemed as though we'd stepped back in time.

Up first was the bestiary, where cryptid animals lounged or paced in sideshow cage wagons modeled after circus train cars from the early 1900s. They had bright, intricately carved frames and huge wooden wheels, and the beasts within were visible from both sides, through thick iron bars reinforced with sheets of modern steel mesh.

The mesh was a recent requirement, after a twelve-year-old had lost her right hand to an irritable troll in a carnival out West somewhere, a few years back.

Shelley oohed and aahed over the chimera, a beast with the body and claws of a lion, two heads—one lion, one goat—and a snake for a tail. "Delilah, look how thick and smooth his fur is!" she cried, her nose inches from the side of the cage. I gently tugged her back by one arm. Anything with claws *and* venom should be appreciated from at least two feet away. "So glossy!"

But when the creature turned to pace four steps in the other direction—the full length of its cramped quarters—I noticed that the fur on the goat head's side was matted and dirty. Obviously that half didn't self-groom.

"Here, kitty, kitty!" Shelley called, and the snake growing in place of the beast's tail hissed at her.

"He's not a kitty, Shell," Brandon said. "He's a ferocious beast capable of tearing you apart with three different jaws at once."

"He's not a he." I pointed at a sign attached with twists of wire to the bars on one end of the cage car. "*Her* name is Cleo. She's eighty-six years old, as of last spring," I said, still reading from the plaque. "Born in the wild well before both the reaping and the repeal of the Sanctuary Act, and still in her prime

today." I stepped back for a better look. "Poor thing. By the time she dies, she'll have spent three-quarters of her life in a cage."

Rick rolled his eyes. "They're animals, Delilah. They don't even know where they are."

"We're *all* animals. From the taxonomy kingdom Animalia. And you don't know what she knows or feels. Have some respect. She's your elder."

Rick laughed as if I'd made a joke. He tried to put one arm around me and when I pulled away from him, I tripped over a rock and had to grab one of the cage's bars to keep from falling. The heavy cage rocked just a little, and the chimera twisted toward me faster than I would have thought something with three heads could move. The snake hissed and the lion head roared.

I froze, intuitively trying not to trigger any further predatory instinct, but Shelley screeched and jumped back.

Rick laughed at her. Brandon pulled me away from the cage and didn't let go even after I'd regained my balance, my heart still racing.

"Don't touch the exhibits," a deep voice growled, and we turned to find a large man in a bright red baseball cap standing near the end of the chimera cage. His red polo shirt bore the Metzger's logo and the name embroidered over his heart read Gallagher. His hair was thick and curly beneath his cap and his eyes were dark gray. "Unless you want to lose a lot of blood."

"I tripped." In the glare from the setting sun, I noticed several old scars on his face and his forearms, and I wondered how many of those had come from beasts he was in charge of. And how many of them he deserved.

"Cleo's in an iron cage, surrounded by steel mesh," Rick said. "What's she going to do, roar until our ears bleed?"

The man tugged the bill of his red cap down, shading more of his strong features. "Only a fool believes his eyes over all other senses."

Shelley laughed out loud while Rick fumed, and when I

turned back for another glimpse of the large man in the red hat, he was gone.

Shelley and I dragged the guys toward the next cage: *Panthera leo aeetus.* Commonly known as a griffin.

Rick and Brandon were fascinated by the griffins, both perched on dead tree branches bolted to the ends of their massive aviary on wheels. They had the hindquarters of a lion and the majestic head, wings, and front claws of an eagle.

An eagle on the physical scale of a lion.

I'd seen them on television and studied them in school, but I'd had no appreciation for their size until I stood in front of them. They must have weighed at least five hundred pounds each.

Brandon shouted at one, unrebuked by another large, gruff handler, and was rewarded when the griffin suddenly threw his enormous wings out and flapped, as if he'd dive at us. We all gasped and backpedaled. The griffin pulled his dive up short at the last second, and I noticed that a patch on his right wing, along the top ridge, was bare of feathers at exactly the spot his wing would have hit the bars, if he hadn't stopped.

The griffin made a horrible avian screech and I covered both my ears, but when he settled on a branch closer to us, still riled up from being teased, I realized that his sharp eagle's beak and incredible wingspan were far less intimidating than his feet, a lethal cross between a lion's claws and a bird's talons.

They were huge. And sharp. I noticed a dried chunk of raw meat wedged between his first and second digits.

My heart ached for him. The griffin was obviously meant to soar the skies and stalk the plains in wide-open freedom. None of which he would get in the menagerie. Yes, griffins could be dangerous, but so could bears and sharks and alligators, yet we didn't round them all up and throw them into cages.

After the griffins came the phoenix. Shelley was disappointed when it refused to burst into flames, then rise from its own ashes for her personal amusement, even though the signs wired to its

cage said the poor thing wasn't due for a "rebirth" for nearly another month. I thought it was beautiful, even without the flames. The phoenix had a long graceful swan-like neck with plumage in vibrant graduating shades of red, yellow, and orange. Its broad sweeping tail would have made any peacock jealous.

After the bestiary, we skipped the "Natural Oddities" section, which promised us trolls, ogres, goblins, and other assorted humanoid creatures of legend. Brandon led the way toward the "Human Hybrids" section, where the sign at the entrance promised us "bizarre and fascinating combinations of man and beast."

"Come forward, come forward!" the uniformed man at the tent entrance called, waving us closer with both white-gloved hands. "Metzger's guarantees you've never seen a spectacle like this, no matter what other shows you've attended. No one else on earth has such an extensive collection of grotesque mergers of human and animal flesh as you'll find in this very tent. Wolf and man, horse and man, fish and man, bird and *woman*…" He winked at Rick. "We've got it all! And don't forget to take a peek at our world-famous minotaur! You won't find another like him anywhere else in the continental U.S.!"

"It sounds really freaky," Shelley said.

"That it is, that it is." The talker bowed deeply, top hat in hand. "But you've got these lucky gentlemen to keep you and your friend safe." He gave the guys another faux-confidential wink, and I almost laughed out loud. Brandon got nervous when he heard coyotes howl at night.

The man in the top hat glanced at our bracelets, then held back a canvas flap with a practiced flourish.

"Seriously, what's it like in there?" Shelley asked before Rick could push his way inside.

The carny shrugged with an evasive smile. "Some people love it. Gives others the willies. But what I *can* tell you is that you can't truly know who you are in here—" he laid one gloved

hand over his red sequined vest "—until you've been through *there*." He pushed the tent flap open wider.

Brandon, Shelley, and Rick stared into the darkness.

I stepped inside.

"Shock and grief echo across the United States this morning with the news that more than one million children died overnight, most reportedly killed in their sleep. Government officials and residents alike watch, stunned, as the reports continue to pour in, raising the death toll by several thousand per hour..."

—As reported by anchor Brian Richards on
U.S. Morning News, August 24, 1986

DELILAH

My ears roared with my own pulse as my friends followed me through the low entrance into the soaring tent, where a circle of faux-vintage wagon cages surrounded a bright red circus ring. The ring was empty except for a tall stool in the center, dramatically illuminated by a stark spotlight. Unoccupied bleachers lined the shadowy perimeter of the space, set up for a show to come later that night.

The farm scent was much less noticeable in the hybrid tent, where all the exhibits were at least part human, but there was yet more hay beneath our feet and the prevailing ambient noise was still the whisper of paws against hard surfaces and the occasional clomp of hooves.

Like the wagons in the bestiary, those in the hybrid tent had solid steel—or iron?—end panels, complete with massive, heavy-looking couplings with which they could be connected to the other cars. In theory. However, the rust on the hitches made me doubt that they were ever hooked to anything for very long.

Though we couldn't see inside the cars with their end panels facing us, we could see into the wagons across the ring, where vaguely humanoid beings paced, slouched, or sat in the corners of their cages, wearily trying to ignore their audience.

A woman in a red sequined leotard and red-trimmed black top hat stepped forward when we got to the entrance of the ring, defined by padded crimson ropes strung between two

shiny metal posts. "Welcome to the human hybrids tent, where every genetic atrocity you can imagine is on display to satisfy your curiosity!" Her name tag read Wendy, and she was cradling something in the crook of her left arm.

"Oh!" Shelley rushed toward the woman and the small bundle she held. "He doesn't look so atrocious!"

Wendy gave her a slick, indulgent smile. "No, this little guy is damn near adorable." She leaned into the light and I saw that she held an infant satyr, whose furry brown goat legs ended in tiny hooves. His chubby little belly and everything north of it was human, except the tiny horns growing from the sides of his skull.

I'd never seen anything cuter in my life.

"His mother just fed him, and I was about to take him back to the petting zoo." Wendy twisted toward the circle of cages with hardly a glance at her young charge. "His mother's the one at the back of—"

"Oh, can I hold him first?" Shelley asked, already reaching for the infant.

"I...um..." Wendy sputtered, obviously unsure how to answer. "I guess. Just for a second." She laid the child in my best friend's arms, while Rick and Brandon watched, dumbfounded.

"His fur tickles." Shelley ran one finger down his fuzzy shin and over his hoof, but the child's eyes never fluttered. He didn't even seem to feel the touch.

"Why isn't he moving?" I asked Wendy.

She shrugged. "He has a full belly. He's passed out cold."

That much was true, but it had nothing to do with the state of his stomach. I gently pulled back the baby's left eyelid, then his right. "He's not full, he's sedated." I frowned up at Wendy. "Why would you sedate an infant?" I demanded. Brandon put one hand on my shoulder to calm me, embarrassed by what he no doubt saw as an irrational tantrum on my part, but I shrugged him off. "He's not a threat. He's a baby."

Wendy's patronizing smile faltered. "If the reaping taught us anything, it's that a threat can come in any size." She took the baby back, and with it, her bright, cheery expression, which now looked as false as her ridiculously long, ridiculously red fingernails. "Now, if you'd like to see the kind of monster this little guy will grow into—" she swept her empty arm toward the wagon car on our left "—start here and follow the circle counterclockwise."

My gaze followed the path formed between the outer loop of wagons and the inner, twelve-inch-high circus ring. Several other customers were clustered at various points on the path.

"When you get to the far side of the circle, go through the gate to the adjoining tent for a look at our special exhibits."

Rick's eyes brightened. "Is that where you keep the mermaids?"

She nodded and gave him an almost intimate smile, as if she were letting us in on a special secret. "Along with a couple of our other rare specimens. Including the Brazilian *encantados*— dolphin shape-shifters—and our world-famous minotaur."

Brandon shoved Rick's shoulder. "I *told* you there were mermaids!"

Wendy's smile grew, and she was now ignoring me completely. "Just make sure you stay on the path and out of the center ring."

"Why? What happens there?" Shelley asked.

"At the eight-o'clock show, one of the werewolves will do a live shift. I've seen it a million times, and it's *still* incredible. You *can't* miss it!" She laughed at Shelley's worried expression. "They're chained the whole time, even inside the safety cages, and they're surrounded by armed handlers, too." She gave each of us a full-color glossy pamphlet. "And the ten-o'clock show is *stunning!*" She gestured toward the ring with a familiar, wide-armed wave. "The draco sets two rings on fire and the cat shifters jump through them." Her arm rose gracefully to take in

the soaring ceiling of the tent. "They put a bird net around the whole thing, and the harpies make several breathtaking dives. I guarantee you've never seen anything like it. It's the highlight of the evening."

I stared at the pamphlet. I *wanted* to see the draco breathe fire and the harpies swoop and dive, but wanting something didn't give one the right to have it. While I could rationalize my willingness to walk through passive exhibits I found fascinating yet morally repulsive, I could *not* justify sitting through a show in which sentient creatures were forced to perform against their will.

Though the prices Metzger's was able to charge made it clear that I took the minority viewpoint on that.

"Do the shows cost extra?" Rick asked.

"Um…let me see your bracelet." Wendy glanced at the wrist he held out. "Nope, you guys have the deluxe admission. You can go anywhere and see anything, except for the staff-only and staging areas."

"Awesome," Shelley said.

Wendy smiled and wished us a great evening, though her smile staled when it landed on me, then gestured for us to enter the ring. As we approached the first huge circus wagon, I glanced back to find her talking to Gallagher, the handler in the red cap, who'd snapped at me for touching the chimera cage.

They were both watching me.

I made myself turn back to my friends just as Shelley gasped. "He's so big!"

For a second, I thought she was talking about the huge handler, and I almost nodded in agreement. Then I realized she was staring into the first cage, a silver-trimmed green masterpiece with fleurs-de-lis and stylized howling wolf heads carved into the corners. I hurried to catch up with my friends and as soon as I stepped in front of the first cage, labeled Claudio—Werewolf, I lost my breath.

48

Claudio was *beautiful.*

His eyes were golden, like multifaceted bits of amber, and while they were clearly wolf eyes, they contained an obvious understanding—a self-awareness that ordinary wolves' eyes didn't have. His fur was thick and silver and glossy, and when he paced into the half of his cage that was lit from the overhead lights, I saw that his silver coat was actually made up of many different shades of black, white, and gray. His fur shifted with each movement, the color rippling and buckling as each individual hair reflected the light at a slightly different angle.

I stared, transfixed.

Claudio growled at us softly, padding back and forth in a cage that was much too confined, because Shelley was right. He was huge.

"I didn't realize how big they'd be," Brandon said.

"Ordinary wolves don't get that large," I whispered, uncomfortably aware that the shifter could both hear and understand me, assuming he spoke English. "One hundred seventy-five pounds, max, for males. Most are closer to one-fifty." By contrast, Claudio was two hundred pounds, by my guess—a wolf the size of a grown man—and in spite of an obviously confined lifestyle, he looked lean and powerful.

"The reality isn't like the old monster movies," I said, still speaking softly because somehow that felt more respectful of Claudio. "They don't have superpowers. They're strong and fast because they're wolves, but they're not superstrong, or superfast."

"Yeah, but even a regular wolf can rip a man's throat out," Brandon said, and I couldn't argue.

I stepped closer to the cage, fascinated, and Claudio snarled at me, lips curled back to reveal a muzzle full of lethally sharp teeth. The lump in my throat threatened to cut off my airway. "I'm so sorry," I whispered, and the growling stopped. Claudio blinked and tilted his head in an oddly human display of sur-

prise, and that stream of guilt trickling through me swelled into a veritable river, until my veins surged with it.

Claudio didn't belong in a cage, and just by coming to observe him in captivity, I'd become part of the problem.

Anger on his behalf uncoiled like a living thing deep inside me and I gasped at the hot, unsettling sensation in my belly.

"Lilah!" Shelley called as she moved on to the next cart, a green-trimmed silver inverse of the werewolf's, with full moons carved into the scrolling frame. "There's a girl wolf!"

Claudio's snarling resumed, more intensely than before, a reminder that he not only heard everything we said, but understood us, as well.

The plaque on the next circus wagon read Geneviève— Werewolf, but at first glance, the cage appeared empty.

"I don't..." Something flashed in one dark corner of the cage, two pinpoints of yellow light, there, then gone. Then there again.

Geneviève was blinking.

Curiosity got the better of me and I squinted, trying to get a better look at her, but I could barely make out a small, hunched form in the shadows.

"I can't see her," Rick complained. "What good are two-hundred-dollar menagerie tickets if the exhibits are just going to hide?"

"I think she's scared," I said. Brandon took my hand, and Shelley nodded mutely.

"*She's* scared? She's the monster. We're supposed to be scared of *her*." Rick scowled, already walking backward toward the next car, which, according to the sign, held one of only four adlets currently living in captivity.

Adlets were the wolf version of a satyr, stuck in an in-between state with both canine and human features. They were also cannibalistic, highly aggressive, and one of the most effective arguments in favor of keeping cryptids locked up.

"Hold on a minute, now, you don't want to miss this," a voice called from the darkness behind the werewolf cages. Hay crunched beneath heavy footsteps, and a moment later something clanked against the bars on the rear of Geneviève's cage.

The light reflecting from her yellow eyes blinked out.

Claudio's snarling deepened and from our right, the adlet responded with a fierce, eerie howl of its own. On the other side of the ring, hooves and paws scraped the floors of other cages as the captives paced nervously.

Unease gathered in the pit of my stomach and crawled along my arms. My hair stood on end. The hybrids' anxiety was both obvious and contagious.

"Just a sec." A handler stepped into the light falling over and through half of Geneviève's cage. He was a stout, balding man in a Metzger's T-shirt but no vest, hat, or sequins whatsoever. His shirt was stained with sweat, his boots caked with dirt, and a lit cigarette dangled from his mouth. This was a behind-the-scenes man if I'd ever seen one. He held what looked like a thick stick. "This ought to get her up for you."

Geneviève whined, and the sound reminded me of a puppy we'd had when I was in middle school, before she'd chewed up the legs of my dad's favorite chair and he'd made us give her away.

Claudio growled, accompanied by a snarl from the adlet, and when assorted hisses, growls, and the clang of metal rang out from across the ring of circus wagons, I realized that the entire hybrid section of the menagerie knew exactly what was about to happen.

"Last warning, Genni," the handler said, and though her whining intensified, her eyes did not open. Too late, I realized that the handler's stick was actually an electrified cattle prod.

"No!" I shouted, and dimly I was aware that I'd squeezed Brandon's hand hard enough to make him flinch. My other hand had crushed the glossy pamphlet.

"It's okay," the handler said. "She makes us do this all the time." He shoved the cattle prod through a small hole in the steel mesh at the back of her cage.

Geneviève yelped in pain, and Claudio's growling crescendoed until it was almost all I could hear. The handler jabbed the traumatized werewolf one more time, and she scuttled out of her corner and into the light.

Rage filled me like a bonfire lit deep inside my soul. Geneviève was a little girl, no more than thirteen years old. She trembled on the floor of her cage, knees drawn up to her chest, heels tucked close to her body in an attempt to cover herself. She wrapped her arms around her legs and buried her face in the hollow between her knees, letting her long, tangled blond hair fall down her nearly bare back.

"Oh..." Shelley breathed, clearly horrified, and this time Brandon's hand clenched mine. None of us seemed to know what to say. Even Rick looked uncomfortable.

"Stand up, honey, and let them get a look at you," the handler said, as Claudio continued to growl and pace in his cage. The male werewolf couldn't see Geneviève, but he obviously cared about her, and he clearly knew what was happening. "I'm not going to tell you again," the handler taunted, his cigarette bobbing with every word, and the girl-wolf began to tremble.

The cattle prod scraped the iron bars on its way into the cage, and Geneviève stood faster than I would have thought possible. She scrambled toward the front of her cage to escape the weapon, her eyes still squeezed closed, as if her refusal to see us somehow meant that we wouldn't see her.

In that moment, I wished more than anything in the world that I'd made my friends sit through a boring birthday dinner with me instead of using Brandon's tickets, so that at least we could have spared Geneviève this one moment of humiliation in the string of such instances that no doubt comprised her entire existence.

Genni's hair brushed the base of her spine and did much more to cover her than the white bikini bottom and tube-style swimsuit top she'd been made to wear. Her arms and legs were thin and her rib cage was plainly visible through her skin. The outsides of her thighs were peppered with pairs of red welts that could only be burns from the cattle prod.

Little Geneviève obviously resisted her handler quite often. I wasn't sure whether to be relieved by that fact or horrified by it, so I settled for a deep sense of awe that a child so young had survived—so far—an existence I couldn't even imagine.

On display. Nearly naked. Ordered to perform, and tortured for refusal.

I hated myself for being there to see it.

I started to head to the next cage and relieve Geneviève of the audience that gave her handler the chance to abuse her. But then she opened her eyes, and I was too mesmerized to move.

She had Claudio's eyes. Exactly. Beautiful golden wolf eyes in a little girl's face.

"Open your mouth, Genni, and let them have a look at your teeth." The handler circled the end of her cage, still carrying the cattle prod, and Geneviève scuttled away from him. The name embroidered on his shirt was Jack. The tip of his cigarette glowed red in the shadows.

"Genni…" he warned, and when Claudio started howling, Jack banged on the end of the male wolf's cage with the fist holding the cigarette. "Pipe down, Papa!"

Understanding crashed over me with a devastating weight and stunning intensity. The father was caged feet from his half-naked daughter, unable to protect her, yet forced to hear every offense heaped on her.

"Genni!" Jack shouted, and she turned on him, hissing, hair flying, her lips curled back to reveal long, sharp canines among the teeth in her otherwise human mouth.

"Ain't that somthin'?" Jack took a long drag on his cigarette.

"Have to file 'em down once a month, or she's likely to bite a finger off when we groom her."

"You *groom* her?" Brandon sounded sick. Shelley looked pale, and Rick was staring at his feet.

"Have to. That one won't do nothin' on her own. Has to be prodded into brushin' her own teeth in the mornin'." He brandished the forked end of the cattle prod at her and she hissed again, then retreated to the back of her cage. "No, no, don't sit down, Genni. Give the good people their money's worth." Jack turned back to us. "Wanna hear her howl? She's got a helluva voice, that one. Not much for speaking, but she howls like her mama did."

"Did?" I didn't want to ask, but I wanted to know. "She died?"

Jack shrugged, and the tip of his cigarette left squiggles of light dancing in front of my eyes. "Who knows? Sold her off last year." He turned back to Geneviève, who stood in the darkest corner of her cage. "Give us a howl, darlin'."

But Genni had had enough. She sank to the floor against the rear wall of her cage and vanished into the shadows again, closing her eyes so the twin points of yellow light disappeared.

Jack moved toward her with the prod again, and the fire burning in my belly burst into a full-body blaze.

"Leave her alone," I said, and when the entire hybrid tent went silent around me, I realized that my voice sounded...different. Not lower in pitch, but larger somehow. More robust.

Brandon, Rick, and Shelley turned to look at me, their eyes wide. Distantly I realized that my scalp had started to tingle and that the heat blazing deep inside me now threatened to burn me alive.

It was a boundless and terrible heat. And it was not entirely unfamiliar.

Creatures in cages all around the tent turned to stare. Sounds I hadn't even realized I was hearing suddenly ceased—the snort of

something equine; steady small splashes from the special section across the ring; and the constant rustle of feet and hooves on hay.

Jack was too intent on causing pain to notice the sudden silence. "It's no trouble." With his back to us, he moved toward the center of the cage to lengthen his reach. "It's just—" he twisted something at the base of the prod "—a little jolt." He shoved the cattle prod between the bars and through the mesh, and Geneviève howled when the tip touched her right calf.

"Get the hell away from her!" I shouted, and my hair rose on my scalp, as if the power sparking through me had charged it at the roots. It floated around my head, not in thin tendrils, but in heavy ropes of hair, twisting around my face in my peripheral vision.

My pamphlet fell to the ground. Brandon dropped my hand. Shelley made a strange noise as she and Rick backed away from me.

Jack pulled the prod from Geneviève's cage and turned, his mouth already open to yell at me. The first syllable died on his tongue. The cattle prod thunked to the ground. My hands found the sides of his head, and dimly I was aware that my fingers looked too dark, the nails long and vaguely pointed.

I gripped his skull and felt several tiny pops as my nails pierced the skin at his temples. Jack's eyes rolled up into his head and his arms began to twitch. His teeth clattered together and sweat poured from his forehead. Blood dripped from his temples.

I saw it all, but none of it sank in. I registered nothing in that moment except the sparks still firing inside me, firing *through* me, out the tips of my fingers and into Jack's head, where every synapse fried within him eased a bit of the demand for justice seething inside me.

How do you *like it?* I demanded, but my mouth never opened. My tongue never moved.

Shelley screamed. The sound of her terror cut through my rage and I pulled my hands from Jack's head in one swift move-

ment. I stumbled backward, horrified by what I'd done, sucking in great gasping breaths that did nothing to soothe the fire burning deep in my chest.

What had I done?

The handler wobbled on his feet. Blood leaked from four pinpoint holes on either side of his balding scalp. Eyes unfocused, he thumped to his knees on the ground, then felt around in the hay without ever looking down. His thick fist closed around the cattle prod he'd dropped and he twisted a knob on the end as far as it would go. Then he raised the prod as high as he could in both fists and rammed it down on his own thigh. The forked tip plunged through denim and into flesh.

The handler began to convulse. For a moment, no one else moved. The entire hybrid trailer watched Jack electrocute himself. Then hooves and paws began to pound against their cage floors. Wolves howled, something avian screeched, and several human mouths cheered.

"What did you *do*?" Shelley wailed.

My heart pounding, I turned to see my friends staring at me in horror, backing slowly toward the adlet cage to get away from me.

Rick tripped over the low circus ring and went down on one hip.

"I..." I looked at my hands and blinked to clear my vision, but my vision wasn't the problem. The problem was my hands. They were too long and bony, my fingers ending in narrow black points. I had needle-claws, where I'd had normal fingernails before.

Blood dripped from the tip of one. I shook my head in denial of what I was seeing—of what I'd done—but instead of settling over my shoulders, my hair was twisting around my head, if the standing-on-end feeling in my scalp could be trusted.

I backed away from the handler still electrocuting himself and from Geneviève's cage, where she stared at me through yellow

wolf-girl eyes. Panic dumped adrenaline into my bloodstream and I suddenly itched to run. To escape.

"What the *hell*?"

I turned to find Rick staring at me, one dusty brown cowboy boot on either side of the bright red circus ring.

Another handler stepped out of the shadows and kicked the livestock prod from Jack's hands. He stopped convulsing, but his eyes regained no focus. His mouth hung open.

"What *are* you?" Wendy, the woman in the sequined leotard, demanded, and I could only blink at her, because I had no answer. Yet even in my mounting terror, I knew that if I'd had an answer, I shouldn't give it to her.

You are normal. You are human. You are ours. The memory of my mother's bedtime mantra played through my head as it always had in moments of fear and doubt since I was a small child. It had never in my life felt more relevant. Or more like a total lie.

The handler in the red cap pushed Wendy aside and stomped toward me, reaching out for me. Then, suddenly, his gaze darted over my shoulder. "Wait!" he shouted, and I turned to run.

The last thing I saw before my skull exploded in pain and the world went dark was the face of the hybrid tent ticket taker in the top hat as he swung a felt-covered mallet at my head.

ATHERTON

The call came over the radio at 7:04 p.m., while Wayne Atherton was eating a cheeseburger in the driver's seat of his patrol car.

"All units, respond with your location. We got a problem up at the fairgrounds."

Wayne dropped his burger into the grease-stained bag and answered with food still in his mouth. "This is officer oh-four. I'm just off Highway 71, a mile past Exit 52." Known locally as the Sonic exit. Wayne finished his bite while four other deputies responded with their locations, then Dispatch came back over the radio with a squawk of static.

"No details yet, but there's an ambulance on the way to the menagerie and they're requesting all the backup we can send. Oh-four, you're closest, but I'm sending everyone else your way. Be careful. And don't forget your iron kit."

The iron kit. *Shit.*

Wayne slammed the gearshift into Drive and pulled onto the highway without checking for oncoming traffic. He only remembered to turn on his siren when the car he nearly ran off the road blasted its horn.

"Dispatch, how're those details coming?" he demanded as he sped down the dusty two-lane highway toward the Franklin County fairgrounds. "I need to know what I'm walking into."

A month before, a cop down near Dallas had lost an arm to an ogre drunk on Kool-Aid and impatient for his dinner.

"Oh-four, you're headed for the hybrid tent, set up near where they put the Tilt-A-Whirl at the county fair. Not sure how it happened, but it sounds like one of the hybrids got loose and injured a menagerie employee."

"A hybrid?" Wayne stomped on the gas pedal and began scanning the side of the road for the familiar faded wooden sign marking the entrance to the fairgrounds. What he knew about cryptids would easily fit between the cardboard pages of a toddler's picture book, and the only hybrids he could even name were mermaids and werewolves. "No civilian casualties, Dispatch?"

"Well, I doubt the carny's a cop, Wayne," Grace said in that exasperated tone she usually saved for after hours.

"You know what I mean. No customers hurt? No locals?"

"Hang on, oh-four." Dispatch went silent for a minute, and just as Wayne was turning onto the wide gravel path leading to the fairgrounds, Grace came back on the line. "We're only hearing about the one injury so far, and Metzger's says no one else is in immediate danger. Secondary report says the perpetrator is restrained."

Perpetrator? "If this is a hybrid attack, there's no perp, Grace. You wouldn't characterize a tiger that escaped from the zoo as a perpetrator, would you?"

"I don't make the reports, I just dispatch them. But I'm coming up with all kinds of new ways to characterize *you*."

Wayne laughed, picturing Grace chewing on the cap of her pen. "What kind of injury are we talking about, Dispatch?"

"We're not clear on that yet, oh-four, but the folks at the carnival seem to want us to take the cryptid into custody."

"This is the Sheriff's Department, not the pound!" Franklin County wasn't equipped to hold most cryptids, much less keep them for any extended period of time. Hell, some of them wouldn't even fit in a standard jail cell!

"You're preaching to the choir, oh-four. Just haul ass and watch your back."

He hated it when Grace talked like she was his boss instead of his girlfriend. Especially over the radio, where anyone could hear. But as usual, she was right. "I'll check in as soon as I know what's going on."

Wayne turned off the siren but left his lights flashing as he rolled through the menagerie's open gate, where carnies in elaborate red-and-black costumes waved him on. He drove straight down the midway with his foot on the brake, honking to warn everyone who hadn't noticed his blue-and-red strobe. Where the midway forked, another pair of menagerie employees waved him to the right, through another gate, and a minute later, Wayne could see the commotion. A large group was being held back from the entrance to a big circus-style striped tent by a crimson velvet rope and a staff of large red-clad men.

He got out of his car, lights still flashing. The crowd made way for him, and when he got to the front, he headed straight for a woman in a leotard and top hat and a man in a black Metzger's cap. "Deputy Wayne Atherton, Franklin County Sheriff's Department. Who can fill me in?"

The employee in the black cap stuck his hand out for Wayne to shake. "I'm Chris Ruyle, the lot supervisor."

Wayne had no idea what a lot supervisor was, but he walked and talked like the boss. "What happened, Mr. Ruyle?"

"We were hoping you could tell us." Ruyle lifted the closed tent flap and gestured for Wayne to go in ahead of him. Inside, a woman lay on her side on the ground, a familiar head of dark wavy hair spread all around her. Her hands were bound at her back. With iron cuffs.

Wayne dropped to his knees at her side. "That's Delilah Marlow." She'd been a couple of years behind him in high school, and all he really knew about her was that she'd been ready to shake the red dirt from her shoes on her way out of town since

before she could even walk. No one had expected that girl to come home after college, much less stay. "Dispatch said the victim was an employee. What the hell happened?" A large purple bump was already starting to rise on one side of her skull. "What did this?"

"I did."

Wayne looked up at the man who'd spoken. Then he looked up some more. The man held a black top hat and wore a red vest with *Lerner* embroidered on it in scrolling black print.

Wayne stood, anger bubbling up from his guts. *Damn out-of-towners beating up on local girls.* Franklin County wouldn't stand for such things. "I thought this was a cryptid attack."

"It was," Lerner said. "But the creature wasn't ours. She was yours."

"Mine?" Wayne followed Lerner's gaze to Delilah Marlow's unconscious form. There was hay caught in her hair and blood beneath her fingernails—defensive wounds if he'd ever seen them. "You got five seconds to start making sense before I arrest you for assault and battery."

Lerner stared at him unflinchingly, and Ruyle cleared his throat to catch Wayne's attention. "Officer Atherton, the victim is over there." Ruyle pointed toward a small crowd of flamboyantly dressed carnival employees gathered around a man seated on the ground with his mouth gaping open, staring at the hay beneath him. A trickle of blood seeped from each of his temples. A line of drool hung from his open lips. "This *girl* is the creature, and I can assure you she doesn't belong to Metzger's. So what I need to know from you is just what exactly this Delilah Marlow is, and what the hell she did to my handler."

Martin,

I'm sure you've seen the news by now, and I'm very sorry to have to tell you that your sister Patricia and her family are among the thousands of victims of this morning's national tragedy. I wanted to call, but your phone number wasn't in Patty's address book, and she was in no shape to find it for us. She and Robert are both in total shock. They lost four of their children overnight, and the police aren't sure exactly what happened. All we do know is that Emily, the six-year-old, was the only one who survived…

—From a hand-written letter by Hannah Goodwin to her brother-in-law and his family, August 24, 1986

DELILAH

A soft buzzing woke me up. Not like a bee or a fly, but like…
electricity. I was lying on something hard, rough, and cold, but
the cold was all wrong. I could feel it not just against my face
and arms, but against parts of me that should have been insulated by my clothes.

My eyes flew open as I shoved myself up with both hands, but
the glaring assault of fluorescent light—the source of the buzzing—was like a spike driven through my skull. My arms gave
out and my eyes fell shut. My cheek slammed into the floor,
and I sucked in a shocked breath.

The floor. I was lying on the cold, hard floor. Naked.

My pulse racing, I lifted my head carefully and had to breathe
through a wave of vertigo. My head throbbed fiercely. Light
painted the insides of my eyelids red. I sat up on my knees, shivering, and folded my arms over my chest to cover myself. Then
I opened my eyes again.

The glare was no longer crippling, but my headache was. I
blinked and my eyes started to adjust to the light, but the world
was a blur. Another blink, and several dark stripes came into
focus.

No, not stripes. Bars. Thick iron bars.

Panicked, I scrambled away from them on my hands and
knees until I came to a gray brick wall. I leaned my bare back

against it, my knees pulled up to my chest, and finally made myself look at my surroundings.

I was in a corner cell with two walls of iron bars and a rough concrete floor.

No.

My heart pounded hard enough to jar my whole body with each beat. The adjoining cell had a hazard-orange floor with No Occupancy painted on it in black block letters.

No, no, no, no…

Across a wide aisle from my cell were other, normal cells.

Jail.

I was in *jail*. Because I'd turned into some kind of monster and stuck my fingers through that carny's *skull*.

But that wasn't possible. I wasn't a monster, and I had never hurt anyone in my life.

Yet I could remember exactly how that man's flesh had felt beneath my fingers. I could still feel the resistance his skull had offered, then that satisfying *pop* when my fingers had breached it.

Nonononono. I buried my face in my arms and squeezed my eyes shut, but the images were still there.

A dangling cigarette.

A cattle prod lying in the hay.

Blood dripping down the sweaty man's face.

What the *hell* had I done? *How* had I done it?

Tears rolled down my cheeks and I swiped at them with both hands. This couldn't be happening. I wasn't a cryptid. My parents were human. I didn't have so much as a birthmark to be examined, much less feathers, or horns, or scales.

Yet in that tent, I'd had… What *had* I had, exactly? Weird hair? Pointy fingers? That didn't fit the description of any cryptid I'd ever studied.

I examined my hands. They were trembling uncontrollably, but looked normal, other than the blood dried beneath my fingernails.

I pulled handfuls of long, dark hair over my shoulder. My hair looked normal. Whatever I'd become had left no trace of itself. How was that even possible? The vast majority of cryptid species can't blend in with the human population—not even shape-shifters. I'd officially learned that on day one as a crypto-biology major, but like everyone else, I'd actually known it my whole life.

So how could whatever kind of creature I was blend in well enough to hide itself not just from the rest of the world, but from me? How could I not know what I was?

What else did I not know about myself? If I couldn't put faith in my own humanity, how much of the rest of my life was a lie?

I didn't mean to do it.

Terrified, I mentally relived that surreal memory over and over, trying to understand what had happened. The only thing I was sure of every single time was that I hadn't *intended* to turn into a monster and shove my fingers through a man's skull. I'd seen it happen. I'd felt it happen. But I hadn't *made* it happen. Not on purpose anyway.

And that meant I could no longer trust my own body.

I didn't realize I was pounding my head into the brick wall at my back until the repetitive thuds finally broke through the vicious cycle of my memories.

The fierce throb in my head felt like my brain was trying to burst through my skull. My hands wouldn't stop shaking. The concrete floor had sanded raw spots into my knees and my palms, as well as on more tender patches of bare flesh.

This couldn't be happening.

On my right, a door squealed open on rusty hinges. Startled, I turned to find a sheriff's deputy heading down the center aisle toward me. He carried a tall stool under one arm and a bundle of familiar material beneath the other.

The sight of my clothes in his hand triggered fresh tears as I scooted along the wall at my back. When I hit the far corner, I

stopped, cradled by solid brick on two sides. I tucked my legs up to my chest again and crossed my ankles to cover my most private parts. I was as shielded and defended as I could get, yet I'd never felt more exposed or vulnerable.

"Hi." The deputy set his stool down in the aisle, out of reach from my cell.

I rested my chin on my left knee and let my hair fall forward like a curtain, hoping all he could see were my shins, hair, and eyes.

"Do you remember me?"

He did look a little familiar, but no name came to mind.

"I'm Deputy Wayne Atherton. You were a couple of years behind me in school."

Wayne. Yes. We'd had a history class together my sophomore year.

"Where am I? Are you in charge?"

"This is the Franklin County Sheriff's Department. You've been taken into custody as a cryptid living under false pretenses. And as far as you're concerned, yes, I'm in charge."

"Did—" My voice cracked, so I cleared my throat and started over, my face flaming. "Did you take my clothes off?"

"No, that was a couple of guys from the SWAT team the sheriff called in to assist with your transport. Dr. Almaguer said he would only examine you while you were still unconscious. To check for species-identifying features."

Dr. Almaguer. My teeth began to chatter and I set my chin on my knees to make it stop. They'd called in a small-animal veterinarian to examine me—the very man who'd once put my dad's farm dog to sleep.

The deputy propped one foot on the lowest stool rung and set my clothes on his lap. "He didn't find anything, Delilah."

Because there was nothing to find. How else could I not have known?

"Are you going to give my clothes back?"

"That's up to you," he said.

I closed my eyes. He was going to interrogate me in the nude. Because he could.

"What are you?"

"I don't know."

"Make this easy on yourself, Delilah. Just tell us what you are, and you can have your clothes back." The deputy shifted on his stool and my underwear slid from the pile of clothes and landed on the floor. He didn't notice, but my focus snagged on that bit of fabric. I would have told him anything I knew for a single scrap of my own clothing. But there was nothing to say.

"I told you, I don't know what I am. *Please* give me my clothes." My cheeks were burning, but my teeth still chattered. "I'm freezing."

"Yeah, the sheriff runs warm, so he keeps the air turned down low. Especially in the summer." Atherton shifted on the stool again, and his tone softened. "Delilah, I can't help you until you help me. I got orders. So why don't you tell me what you are, and I'll not only give you your clothes back, I'll get you some water. Or something to eat. Are you hungry? Your friends said you didn't eat much dinner."

"Are they here?" Shelley's scream still echoed in my aching head. Brandon's look of horror was imprinted on my retinas. "Can I see them?"

Deputy Atherton started to shake his head, and I buried my face in the crook between my knees, sniffing back fresh tears. "Please," I said into my lap. "I didn't mean to hurt anyone and I have no idea what happened. *Please* just give me my clothes and let me see my friends."

Atherton sighed. "Ms. Wells had to be sedated. Her boyfriend took her home."

My throat felt thick, my tongue clumsy. "Is she okay?"

"She's terrified. She's not the only one. The news is out, and people don't feel safe, knowing you were born and raised here.

Knowing you went to school with their children and spent the night at their houses—and they didn't have a clue. People are starting to remember the reaping, Delilah."

Oh, *fuck*.

Terror pooled in my stomach like acid, eating at me from the inside. "They don't think I'm a surrogate, do they?" I peered at him over my knees. My hands started shaking again. "Because I *swear* I'm not."

"How can you know that, if you don't know what you are? You look human, and you lived among us for years. Just like the surrogates. What are we supposed to think?"

Panic slowed my brain, yet sped up my words. "This is totally different. I wasn't hiding or lying in wait, planning something. I didn't know I wasn't human. I *still* can't believe what happened. You have to tell them that. Tell the sheriff I'm not one of them."

"How do I know that's true?"

Terror scattered my thoughts into a maelstrom of disjointed theories. *Think, Delilah!* "There were hundreds of thousands of surrogates, but there's only one of me."

The deputy shrugged. "So far. For all we know, you could be the first in a whole new wave."

"No, that's not what I am!" My arms tightened around my shins, drawing my knees tighter against my chest. "I don't have any siblings."

"Having grown, healthy siblings would work in your favor. Being an only child does not."

"Okay… But I'm an adult!" Surely they'd figured *that* much out when they'd taken my clothes off. "The surrogates were six-year-olds."

"Yes, but even cryptids age. The surrogates are now thirty-five years old. Wherever they are."

But no one knew where they were, and that was the problem. As soon as they'd been discovered, Uncle Sam had rounded them up like rabid dogs, and no one knew whether they'd been

shot, or studied, or cryogenically frozen for later. And that was fine, because the surrogates truly *were* dangerous. They were the fucking devil's spawn.

If the government thought I was one of them, I would disappear, too.

"I'm not a surrogate." I pushed hair from my face with one hand and sat up as straight as I dared without clothes on. "I didn't steal any babies. I've never hurt a soul in my life before tonight, and *I don't know how that happened.* Think about it. If I'd known what I was, why would I go to the menagerie? Please, Deputy. You have to believe me. I'm not conspiring against humanity."

Atherton exhaled slowly. Then he stood, still watching me, and shook out my blouse. "I believe you." He stuck my shirt between two of the bars and dropped it on the floor. "But I'm not the one you have to convince." Next came my jeans, bra, and underwear, each dropped just inside my cell. "Get dressed."

I glanced at my clothes, then back up at him. "Are you going to watch?"

He blinked, obviously startled by the thought. "Of course not." When he walked down the aisle away from my cell, I realized that Atherton wasn't the enemy. He was just doing his job.

Unfortunately, his job was to extract information I didn't have, in order to help the sheriff—

Help the sheriff what?

End life as I knew it?

I lunged for my clothes, then dragged the whole pile back into my corner, where I shimmied into my underwear as fast as I could. I turned my back on the bars to put my bra on, in case he turned around, and had just stepped into my jeans when the brutal reality of my new situation hit me over the head like that carny's mallet, swinging straight for my soul.

I'll never go home again.

My legs buckled beneath me and my knees slammed into the concrete. My jaw snapped shut with the impact, but I hardly

felt it. I was a cryptid living under false pretenses, and no one would care that I hadn't known. Most probably wouldn't even believe that.

I pushed my arms through the sleeves of my shirt, but had trouble buttoning it. My hands wouldn't stop trembling.

Gone. Everything I'd ever had was probably already gone. My job. My apartment. My car. My clothes. Cryptids weren't allowed to own property or enter into contracts. Including leases.

"Deputy Atherton, I think I need to talk to an attorney." My voice had almost no tone and very little volume. I seemed to be hearing myself from one end of a long tunnel.

He turned and headed down the aisle toward me again. "They're not gonna give you a lawyer, Delilah. Cryptids aren't citizens. You have no rights in the U.S. of A., in Franklin County, or in the incorporated township of Franklin. You are now the property of the state of Oklahoma."

Property. No rights.

"Unless they decide you *are* a surrogate," Atherton continued. "If that happens, the feds will come for you."

And I would never be seen again.

I clutched my half-buttoned shirt to my chest and scooted back into the corner, pressing my spine into the seam where both brick walls met. The world seemed to be shrinking around me, as if someone were sucking all the air out of a vacuum-sealed bag. I couldn't breathe. I couldn't think.

"Is your mother still over on Sycamore?" Deputy Atherton asked, and a fresh bolt of fear opened my lungs. "They're sending someone to pick her up."

"Leave her alone." My gaze snapped up to meet his, and his brows rose. "She has nothing to do with this. She's human."

"You thought you were human, too, and you were wrong about that. Is there anything we should know before they knock on her door?"

I held his gaze in silence.

"They're already on their way, Delilah. If you know something that will keep her from getting hurt, you need to tell me."

"She sleeps with my dad's shotgun under her bed." I crossed my arms over my knees and stared at the ground. "Better call first and let her know you're coming. That, or send an ambulance in advance."

Atherton's brows rose. He unclipped a radio from his belt and relayed my mother's itchy trigger finger to someone in Dispatch.

My bare toes curled on the concrete, and I wished for a pair of shoes. My racing thoughts had stilled into a single bold question mark, and the mental silence was almost as confining as the bars caging me.

"So, what happens now?"

He pulled a thick, rusty pair of medieval-looking iron cuffs from a pouch at his back. "Come on, Delilah. Get up. It's time to meet the sheriff."

DELILAH

"Turn around and stick both hands between the bars."

The theory seemed to be that my hands were my weapons, and that with them restrained in iron behind my back I would be much less of a threat.

I complied, and the cuffs closed over my wrists one at a time. They were heavy, and the weight felt both surreal and brutally degrading. But surely if I were going to have any adverse reaction to iron—which would narrow my species down to one out of *hundreds* of kinds of *fae*—the bars on my cell would have triggered it already.

Iron was the only way that we knew of to identify the *fae*. Most of them had one feature or another that clothes wouldn't cover—feathers, a hollow back, vines growing in place of hair—but glamour was a better disguise than any clothing, contact lenses, or wigs could ever hope to be.

Once I was cuffed, the deputy let me out of my cell and guided me down the aisle. He didn't touch me. In fact, he seemed to be walking a couple of feet behind me until he had to come forward and open the door at the end of the aisle.

The moment I stepped into the open front room of the sheriff's station, all phone calls and typing ceased. The ambient nervous chatter died, and everyone turned to watch me be escorted across the room. None of the stares were friendly. Even

the people in handcuffs looked at me as if I were a slimy clump dug from their shower drains.

My face flamed. I wanted to hide, but the best I could do was let my hair swing forward to shield part of my face.

Several feet into my barefoot walk of shame, I saw Brandon sitting in a cracked plastic waiting room chair. I tripped over my own nerves and Deputy Atherton started to catch me, then changed his mind. I saw the moment it happened. He was reaching for me, probably out of instinct, then suddenly recoiled. He *flinched*—as if I were a snake about to strike, when really I was falling face-first toward the dingy yellow floor tile, unable to catch myself with my hands cuffed at my back.

Brandon stared at his shoes as I staggered, then awkwardly regained my balance on my own. I recognized tension in the cords standing out from his neck, as if he wanted to look, but was fighting the urge.

"Brandon," I called once I was steady, and my voice cracked on the first syllable. His jaw clenched, but he didn't look up. My flush deepened. "Brandon." Raw desperation echoed in my voice and a couple of strangers sneered at the tender bits of my heart and soul I'd exposed.

My boyfriend of four years was the only person in the room not watching me.

"Brandon, *please.*" My cheeks were scalding and my throat ached. But I *couldn't* believe he would abandon me without a word. He knew better than anyone else in the world aside from my mother that I would never hurt someone on purpose.

Deputy Atherton took me by the arm, evidently having gathered the courage to touch me in the face of my humiliation. "Come on, Delilah."

"No." I jerked free of his grip, and people all over the room flinched. "Say it, Brandon," I demanded, and at first he didn't move. Then my roommate and lover—one of my very best friends—stood and marched toward the exit, as if he wanted to

run, but pride wouldn't let him. "Brandon! Say it, you fucking coward!"

He froze halfway to the door, and my heart stilled along with him. Then slowly, Brandon turned. His eyes were red. His jaw was clenched. He looked at me as if he didn't even know who I was.

"How could you do this to me?"

"I didn't—"

"The whole thing was a *lie*," he shouted, and I flinched. "*You* were a lie! I trusted you. I told you everything. I ate with you and slept next to you, and the whole time you were some kind of monster, just using me as part of your human camouflage. There *is* no Delilah Marlow."

"No, that's not true. It was all real! I didn't know!" I took a step toward him, but Atherton grabbed my arm again, and several other deputies placed hands on the butts of their guns. "You have to believe I didn't know."

"I don't know what to believe." Tears shone in Brandon's eyes, but anger glowed in his cheeks. "I was in love with a woman who never even existed. I can't believe I ever let you—" His sentence ended in an inarticulate sound of disgust, and something deep inside me cracked apart. Some delicate part of me collapsed like a demolished building, leaving only broken shapes and sharp edges.

"Don't blame yourself, son," a middle-aged man called out from the waiting area. "We were all fooled in the eighties. I lost my aunt, uncle, and six cousins to those chameleon bastards, may they rot in hell."

Cheers erupted all around me, and suddenly my ribs felt too tight.

"But I—I'm not one of them! I'm not—"

"Baby killer!" a woman shouted from the waiting area.

"Remember the reaping!" a man in regular steel cuffs shouted, though the cop who shoved him back into his chair didn't seem to dispute the sentiment.

A cop in his thirties stood from behind his desk and strode toward me, and I thought he was going to take over for Deputy Atherton and get me out of there—until he spit in my face.

I blinked, stunned, as spittle dripped down my cheek.

"Damn it, Bruce!" Atherton hauled me toward another door.

Across the room, Brandon shoved the press-bar on the front exit and when he stepped into the parking lot, he took my last shred of hope with him. If my own boyfriend wouldn't stand by me, who would?

The front door closed behind Brandon, and I sniffed back tears that stung like utter rejection and humiliation. My hair fell into my face as Wayne led me into another hallway, several strands clinging to the spit on my cheek.

Finally, Atherton closed the door behind us, shielding me from the rest of the world. Or maybe shielding it from me.

In an interrogation room, I followed his instructions without truly hearing them. In my mind, the front door of the sheriff's station closed over and over, and all I could see was the back of Brandon's head.

"Delilah," Atherton said, and I realized he'd already said my name at least twice.

"What?" I blinked to clear my head and looked down to find myself sitting in a cold plastic chair with my arms looped around the back. A tug against my cuffs rattled chains I had no memory of, which evidently ran between my handcuffs and a metal loop set into the ground. I couldn't stand or even twist much in my chair without pulling my arms out of their sockets.

Before I could ask if all of the metal was really necessary, a second deputy knelt to slap a set of iron shackles around my ankles and connect them to that same hook in the ground, behind my chair. When he stood, I tried to lean forward, but the pain in my shoulders stopped me. I tried to cross my ankles, but the shackles were in the way. I couldn't move more than an inch in any direction, and that sudden severe confinement made my throat

close. The room had plenty of open space but I couldn't use any of it. Plenty of air, but I couldn't seem to breathe any of it.

"Struggling will only make it worse," Atherton said, and while there was no malice in his voice, there was no willingness to help either. "Just try not to think about it."

But I couldn't seem to manage that until the door opened, and Sheriff Pennington stepped in from the hall. He commented on my restraints with an incomprehensible grunt, then sat in the chair across a small folding table from mine.

Pennington folded his fleshy arms on the table and studied my face. "Delilah Marlow?"

I nodded, desperately trying not to squirm. "Am I under arrest?"

He snorted, then swiped at his nose with the back of one hand. "No, and I wouldn't arrest a dog for bitin' either. I'd just put the bitch down in the interest of public safety. You won't be charged, and you won't be Mirandized, because you no longer have any rights, you devious piece of shit. As long as you're under my jurisdiction, I can do whatever I want with you, and I can't imagine your lot would improve if the feds take over."

His blatant threat bounced around the inside of my skull, and anger overtook my fear for the first time since I'd woken up in a jail cell. "This isn't right, Sheriff."

"I deal in law, not morality." Pennington paused for a moment, evidently to let that little cow chip of irony sink in. "What are you exactly, Delilah Marlow?"

"I don't know," I repeated. He lifted one skeptical eyebrow, and I shrugged as best I could with my hands tightly bound behind me. "Look, if I knew, I'd tell you just to prove I'm not a surrogate."

"Unless you *are* a surrogate."

"If I were a surrogate, I'd lie. Either way, you'd have an answer. But I *don't know* what I am. I didn't know I wasn't human until tonight."

"We don't know what the surrogates were either, do we?"

Pennington pulled a palm-sized notebook from his front pocket. "So that doesn't really rule anything out for you."

I tried to find a more comfortable position, but the chains kept relief just out of reach. "Well, we know what they weren't, and none of those little monsters looked anything like I did tonight."

"About that..." the sheriff continued, flipping open his notebook to reveal a single page of pencil scrawling. "Let's put our heads together and come up with some possibilities that might keep you out of federal custody, shall we?"

And finally something in his voice clued me in. Sheriff Pennington didn't want me to be a surrogate either, because that would put me beyond his authority. The Justice Department had claimed jurisdiction over all of those cases before I was even born.

"Here're the facts, as they were relayed to me. One, your voice changed in depth and—" Pennington glanced at the notebook on the table in front of him "—quality. Says here it was deeper than it shoulda been, and it felt—" another glance at his notes "—*large*. Whatever that means. Two, your eyes changed color. Not just the irises, but the entirety of your eyeballs." He made a vague gesture encompassing most of my face, and I shuddered at the thought. "They became white, shot through with dark veins. Does that sound about right?"

I could only give him a painfully wrenching shrug, trying to hide the tide of horror washing over me. "I couldn't see my own eyes." And I'd never heard of a cryptid species which fit that description.

"It also says here that the veins in your face became black, like dark spiderwebs beneath your skin. Do you know anything about that?"

"No." But I could imagine how terrifying it would have been to see. No wonder Shelley was scared. No wonder Brandon could hardly look at me. I'd spent four years studying cryptid species, yet couldn't even identify my own. If *I* couldn't understand what I'd become, how could they?

Pennington glanced at his notebook again.

"What about your hair? Witnesses say your hair took on a life of its own."

"Sheriff, I'm assuming that if you spoke to my friends, you know that I was a crypto-biology major, with an emphasis in human hybrid species. I should know what I am. But I truly have no clue. Before tonight, I didn't even know the question needed to be asked. All I know for sure at this point is that I'm no longer a bank teller." I was no longer a driver, or a tenant, or a girlfriend, or a best friend.

I was nothing other than the property of the state of Oklahoma.

My eyes fell shut and I sucked in a deep breath.

The reality—the true *enormity*—of my loss suddenly hit me in a way that the mere intellectual understanding of it hadn't been able to. When the interrogation was over, they weren't going to send me home. I *had* no home. I was never going to count another cash drawer or make another pot of coffee ever again, no matter what I did or said. Everything that I had ever been or done or loved was gone. Delilah Marlow no longer existed.

No, Brandon was right. Delilah Marlow had *never* existed. My entire life was a delusion. A fantasy. A lie I hadn't even known I was telling.

The reality was pure hell.

Pennington closed his notebook and crossed his arms on the table again, watching calmly as I fought total, devastating terror. "Before you start feeling too sorry for yourself, keep in mind that a man almost died because of you, and up at County General, they're not sure he'll ever regain normal brain function."

A bright spark of anger surged up through my fear, and I seized it. "He electrified a little girl!"

Pennington turned to Atherton, who was stationed next to the door. "She's talking about one of the beasts?"

The deputy nodded and pulled his own notebook from the pocket of his khaki uniform pants. "A pubescent *canis lupus ly-*

canus. Female." He looked up and pocketed the notebook. "A thirteen-year-old wolf bitch. The rep from Metzger's says they have trouble with her all the time, and the customary motivational method is a low-voltage poke with a standard cattle prod."

"She was covered with electrical burns!" For a second, I forgot I was chained to the floor, and when I tried to stand, I nearly dislocated my shoulder. Both Pennington and Atherton reached for their guns.

I froze. "Relax." My pulse raced so fast the room started to look warped. "I can't even open a jar of pickles, much less break through solid steel and iron."

Atherton glared at me. "Delilah, she's not a child, she's a wolf." The deputy slid his gun back into its holster, but the fact that he didn't snap it closed made me nervous. "An animal."

"Then why was she wearing underwear?" I demanded, and the sheriff and his deputy looked at me as if I'd lapsed into Latin. "Okay, just think about it. When we put wolves on display in a zoo—a *regular* zoo—we don't put underwear on them because they aren't self-aware enough to feel modesty or adapt to social conventions and restrictions. But Geneviève was wearing underwear, which means the menagerie understands that she's *thoroughly* self-aware. And if she's self-aware, why is it okay to put a *child* on display in skimpy undergarments, then shock her with a cattle prod when she doesn't want to be seen in nothing but her underwear? You can't have it both ways."

I sank back into my chair, only aware that I'd been straining against my restraints when my joints started screaming at me in protest.

Atherton and the sheriff stared at me for a moment, obviously unsure what to say. Then Pennington dragged his chair closer to the table and scowled at me with confidence born of ignorance. "According to the law, your werewolf bitch isn't a person. She's a monster, and monsters are offered no protection under the law because them and their kind slaughtered more

than a million innocent children during the reaping alone. Who knows how many others they've killed one at a time? If were-wolves are self-aware, why didn't the pack that tore that family apart up in the Ozarks last month use that self-awareness to decide not to kill innocent people?"

"First of all, that was a pair of adlets, not a pack of werewolves, and second, self-awareness isn't the same as a moral compass," I argued. "I don't believe every cryptid should be allowed to roam free, just like I don't believe every *human* should be allowed to roam free. We have psychos, too. People kill their coworkers. Kids kill their classmates. Parents kill their own children. Those people are every bit as monstrous as the worst cryptid predator you can point to, yet they're human, just like we are."

Atherton and Pennington stared at me, and unease churned in my stomach. "There is no *we*," the deputy said, and though I'd known that for several hours by then, hearing him verbally exclude me from the rest of humanity added another layer of pain to that brutal certainty. "Delilah, you're not human."

"Yeah, well, I guess you're going to have to take a blood sample to figure out what I am, because I don't know."

"Actually, we took one while you were knocked out." The deputy glanced at my arm, which was when I noticed the small bandage in the crook of my left elbow. "They had to send it up to Tulsa. Your sample's the lab's number one priority, but it'll still take several days."

I collapsed against the back of my chair, and my aching shoulders sagged with relief. "Then I guess we're in for a bit of a wait."

The interrogation room door creaked open and we all turned as another deputy stepped into the doorway. "Mrs. Marlow's here."

Sheriff Pennington stood and gave me a grim scowl. "I'm not very good at waiting, so you better hope your mama can shed some light on the subject. Otherwise, things are gonna get real bad for you, real damn fast."

State agencies report that more than 12,000 parents have been arrested in connection with the August 24 murders of more than 1.1 million children, and an unnamed source in the FBI tells the *Boston Gazette* that that figure is still rising...

—From the front page of the *Boston Gazette*, August 28, 1986

CHARITY

When Charity Marlow's phone rang at 12:04 a.m., she knew without even glancing at the caller ID that something was wrong. No one ever called in the middle of the night to say everything was fine.

Ten minutes after she hung up the phone, Charity had dressed, brushed her hair, and brewed a pot of coffee. The deputy who knocked on her door declined a travel cup, so she made him wait while she fixed one for herself because "questioning" sounded like the kind of ordeal that would require coherence on her part.

Coherence was the very least of what Charity Marlow owed her daughter, but it was all she had left to give.

On the way to the sheriff's station, she sat in the passenger's seat of the patrol car and sipped quietly from her cup, and not once during the drive across town did she ask why Delilah was in custody. Charity had been both waiting for and dreading that night's phone call for nearly twenty-five years.

At the station, in a small room equipped with bright lights and cheap chairs, she sat across a small scarred table from Matthew Pennington, who'd held the title of sheriff for the past twelve years in spite of her consistent vote for whoever ran against him. Two armed deputies were stationed at the door, one on each side, and Charity saw no reason to pretend she didn't understand their presence.

"I suppose you want a blood test," she said before the sheriff could even open his mouth.

He nodded, but she read irritation in the stiff line of his jaw. Pennington liked to run the show. "We've got a phlebotomist from County General waiting for that very thing. Of course, you'd be saving us all a lot of time if you could just tell us what you and your daughter are."

Charity set her travel cup on the table. "Sheriff, if I weren't human, I wouldn't exactly feel inspired to bare my soul to you and your gun-toting hee-haws." She tossed a glance at the deputies beside the door, both of whom scowled at her. "But I *am* human, and your lab should be able to confirm that with little more than a microscope. And since you clearly know otherwise about Delilah… Well, I'd be just as interested as you are in what the lab has to say about her blood sample."

Pennington leaned back and crossed thick arms over the brown button-up shirt stretched tight across his soft chest. "You're telling me you don't know what species your own daughter is?"

Charity nodded. "In fact, considering that you have her in custody, I'd guess you know more about her genetic origin than I do."

"Well, you'd be wrong there." Frustration deepened the sheriff's voice even beyond the chain-smoker range. "I have her medical records. The blood test they ran at birth says she's human."

Charity nodded again, but made no comment.

"According to her record, she hasn't had blood drawn since the day she was born."

"I believe that's accurate."

"She's never been sick?" Pennington leaned forward, arms folded over the table, and Charity winced at the acrid bite of cigarette smoke clinging to his uniform. "Not once in twenty-five years?"

"Every child gets sick at some point, Sheriff. But Delilah never had anything I couldn't treat myself."

"Because you're an RN."

Charity sat a little straighter in her hard plastic chair. "Actually, I'm a nurse practitioner."

"That's right," the sheriff said, but she saw right through his sudden recollection of her employment history. "You finished your MSN when Delilah was three. Was that so that you could legally treat her yourself?"

"In fact, it was. And as her primary medical caregiver, I found no reason to run further blood tests on a perfectly healthy child." Charity looked right into the sheriff's eyes. "But I would be willing to tell you what I *do* know, if you'll go first."

The sheriff's flustered flush was so bright that one of the deputies stepped forward to see if he was okay. Pennington waved the unspoken question off and glared at the woman seated across the table.

"What we know, Mrs. Marlow, is that your daughter got worked up during a tour of the menagerie this evening and turned into the kind of creature that should have been lookin' outta one of those cages, instead of looking into 'em. She grabbed a carny by the head and sank her fingers into his skull, and when she finally released him, he turned his livestock prod up as far as it would go and rammed it into his own leg."

Charity's bold spirit—a thing of wide repute in Franklin County—faded like a blossom gone dry in the sun. She closed her eyes to hide her thoughts from the sheriff, and the face that flashed behind her eyelids belonged to a woman she hadn't seen in twenty-five years, but would never in her life forget.

"Lilah actually hurt someone?" More than two decades of secrets, lies, and guilt swelled within her as she examined every fear and doubt she'd ever had about the daughter she loved more than anything else in the world. More, even, than the husband whose heart had given out at the age of fifty-seven, beneath the burden of their secret. "I didn't think she was even capable of violence."

"Why don't you tell us what you know?"

Charity crossed her arms over her favorite blue summer sweater and when she leaned back in her chair, a gray-streaked strand of straight brown hair fell over her ear.

"Keeping your secret can't help her anymore, Mrs. Marlow," Wayne Atherton said. "We can't help her either, if we don't know what she is."

Unlike Pennington, Atherton truly seemed to want to help, so Charity cleared her throat and took a long sip of her coffee. "Almost twenty-five years ago, my six-week-old daughter disappeared from her crib."

"You're telling us that Delilah was kidnapped?" Pennington prompted after a moment of silence, but Charity only shook her head.

"I'm telling you that my daughter *Elizabeth* was kidnapped. Her middle name was Delilah, so that's what I called the changeling left in her place."

For one long moment, neither the sheriff nor his deputy spoke. Charity couldn't even be sure they were breathing.

"Changeling." Pennington seemed to be tasting the word, as if he might want to spit it back out. "So, you're saying the *fae* took your baby and left a surrogate in its place? There hasn't been a confirmed surrogate exchange since the reaping." The sheriff laid both thick hands flat on the table between them. "Mrs. Marlow, are you telling us that your daughter is part of a second wave of attack?"

Atherton slipped quietly out of the room.

"No." Charity set her coffee down and looked straight into the sheriff's eyes, so that he couldn't possibly mistake any part of her bearing or intent. "This is different. I don't know what those little monsters were, but Delilah isn't one of them."

The sheriff crossed his arms above his belly. "How can you be sure? Does she look like Elizabeth?"

"I haven't seen Elizabeth in twenty-five years, Sheriff, but as infants, they were identical."

Pennington's scraggly gray brows rose. "Sounds like a surrogate to me."

"You're wrong." Charity lifted her cup in one unsteady hand and took a sip of the cooling coffee. Then she set the cup down and took a long, deep breath. "Delilah *was* sent to deliver pain, but not by instilling terror on a national scale like the surrogates. She was left in Elizabeth's place to punish *me*. And I got exactly what I asked for."

"What—"

Charity held up one hand and spoke over the sheriff. "Elizabeth was a beautiful child, but she had an ugly temper. She cried for days and nights on end. I couldn't eat or sleep. I couldn't think straight. One day, when she was six weeks old, I prayed that the Lord would take my brand-new baby girl—the center of my existence—and send me a quieter, happier child in her place."

She pulled a tissue from the purse in her lap and dabbed at first one eye, then the other. "Now, it may be that a lot of women in my position do the same thing, and nothing comes of it. But I…" She leaned forward, and fresh tears fell from her eyes. "Well, Sheriff, I said my prayer out loud. And it wasn't the Lord who heard me."

"Who heard you?" the remaining deputy whispered.

Charity twisted in her chair to give him a censuring glance. "Believe it or not, Deputy, no one claimed credit for replacing my daughter with a more pleasant doppelgänger." She turned back to the sheriff. "So I did some research and learned that I could get in touch with whoever took my daughter if I were to nurse the child for a week, then smear a bit of her blood on a mirror and state my own child's name." More inclined toward logic than superstition, Charity had thought the whole thing sounded gruesome and crazy, but the truth was that since the reaping, anything seemed possible. The sheriff eyed her doubt-

fully, but she continued. "It worked! A woman appeared to me in my bathroom mirror, holding Elizabeth from some room I've never seen before."

"What did she say?" the deputy asked, and the sheriff scowled, but let the question stand.

"She said that in a year, if I had taken proper care of the changeling and still wanted my daughter back, Elizabeth would be returned to me."

"This woman in the mirror?" The sheriff's skepticism was fading beneath undeniable curiosity. "Did you get her name? Her species?"

"She wouldn't tell me any of that. But she looked and sounded as human as Delilah did."

"So what did you do?" Pennington said, and from across the table, Charity could see that though he held a pen, the notebook page in front of him was completely blank.

"We cared for Lilah as if she were our own. She was a delightful child. Happy and affectionate. We came to love her—I felt *guilty* for how much I loved her, when my own daughter was missing." Charity folded her hands on the table and took a deep breath. "Then the one-year mark came and went, and Elizabeth never reappeared."

"Did you try the blood-on-the-mirror trick again?" the sheriff asked.

Charity nodded. "Several times, but my summons went unanswered."

"And you never got her back?" the deputy guessed, clearly transfixed by the story.

Pennington waved one hand to silence the deputy, and when he turned back to Charity, she met his gaze with tear-filled eyes. "No, I never got Elizabeth back," she said. Then she took a deep breath and gave voice to a fear that had lived in her soul for twenty-five years, but had never before been spoken aloud.

"Sheriff, I think my Elizabeth was never returned because I loved Delilah more."

DELILAH

The weight of my mother's confession steadily pressed the air from my lungs until psychological suffocation felt like a very real threat. I tried to lean forward, staring intently through the one-way glass into the room where she sat, but again chains and cuffs held me painfully short of where I wanted to be.

However, the real trauma went much, much deeper. Brandon had been wrong—there really *was* a Delilah Marlow. But I wasn't her.

I closed my eyes and took a deep breath, trying to take it all in. Trying to understand.

I wasn't my mother's daughter.

That devastating revelation triggered a landslide of loss, leaving me crushed by the debris of my own life. I had no real name or family. No birthplace or birth date. No true identity. Added to the confiscation of everything I'd ever owned, that left me with nothing but a body I could no longer trust. Though according to Pennington, *that* was now owned by the state of Oklahoma.

This can't be real.

What was I, if I had no name, no friends, no family, no job, no home, no belongings, and no authority over my own body? What *could* I be?

Maybe I was just the good little girl my mother'd begged for. Or maybe I was the monster Sheriff Pennington believed me to

be. Maybe I was the first enemy soldier in a secret war against humanity. But could that even be true, if I didn't know about it?

A strange creak cut through my thoughts, and Deputy Atherton turned away from the window to look at me. "Delilah? Are you okay?"

When I opened my mouth to tell him just how far from okay I was, the creaking stopped. I'd been clenching my jaw so tightly we could both hear the stress.

"You really didn't know about any of that?" he said, pointing beyond the glass at my mother.

I shook my head. Even after hearing it, I wasn't sure I truly understood. All I knew for sure was that I was a changeling of unknown origin sent to torture my mother. And that somehow a punishment meant to last a year had lasted a lifetime. For what? For loving me too much?

That wasn't fair to her. She was a *good* mother. Yet if whoever'd taken Elizabeth Delilah Marlow—the *real* Lilah—had brought her back, where would that have left me? Would I have been raised by the woman in the mirror? Was she my mother?

No.

Charity Marlow had been living with her secret for twenty-five years, maintaining her silence to protect me, mourning her real daughter—a baby who'd looked just like me—in private, because the world could not know of her loss. That *made* her my mother, even if we shared no blood.

Had my dad known?

Yes.

Suddenly my father's periodic melancholy made sense. What had he seen when he'd looked at me? Could he see the difference between me and his Elizabeth? Had he loved me as much as my mother did?

Had he blamed her for the loss of their true child? Had he blamed *me*?

"If you tell the sheriff I let you watch, he'll have my badge."

Deputy Atherton's statement sliced through my thoughts so suddenly that it took me a second to understand what he'd said.

I sniffed, unable to wipe either my eyes or my dripping nose. "I won't tell him." As the only person to show me even the slightest bit of compassion, Atherton was the closest thing I had to an ally. "Thank you for letting me see my mom. What's going to happen to her?" I whispered, still staring through the glass.

He shrugged. "If she's human, she should be fine."

"She harbored a cryptid for twenty-five years. That's a felony, Deputy."

"She was protecting her kid. The sheriff would never..." Atherton didn't bother to finish. We both knew the sheriff would.

"Mrs. Marlow," Pennington continued from the next room. "As an officer of the law, I have to ask, why didn't you turn the changeling over to the proper authorities when it became clear that your daughter was never going to be returned?"

The changeling. He wasn't even using my name anymore. I'd become a thing.

"She didn't know she wasn't human," my mother said. "*I* didn't know for sure. If I'd given her to the police, they would have put her in the state refuge, where she'd have been less than a snack for the first troll or ogre to find her. She was a baby, Sheriff."

"Yes, and I'm sure she was adorable." Pennington leaned back in his chair again, and though I couldn't see his face, I could picture his patronizing expression perfectly. "A few years ago I saw a baby tiger in the zoo, over at Tulsa. It was behind a thick wall of glass playin' with its handler, chasin' a bit of string with a stuffed mouse tied at the end. That baby tiger was the cutest damn thing I ever saw in my life." He paused dramatically. "A year and a half later it ripped that same handler's arm off and bit through her jugular."

My mother didn't even flinch. "You're suggesting Lilah is like this tiger?"

"I'm tellin' you she's worse. The tiger acted on instinct. Your Lilah made a deliberate decision to—" Pennington crossed his arms over his chest. "Well, we're not sure what she did to that poor man. What we *are* sure of is that if you'd done your civic duty when she was a baby, we wouldn't be sittin' here now. I suspect the state's attorney will have a few things to say to you about that, but I could put in a word on your behalf, if you were to help us out. We really need to know what she is. You must have seen *something* when she was growing up that could help us. There musta been signs that she was different from the other girls."

"There weren't, Sheriff," my mother insisted. "That's why it was so easy for me to believe she was human, no matter where she came from. Lilah was normal. She was smart, and kind, and always the first to go to bat for the underdog. I was always *so* proud of her."

My mother's face blurred beneath tears I couldn't hold back.

"So, you never saw anything strange about her hair? Or her eyes? Or her hands?" Pennington asked, and my mother shook her head. "Not even when she got riled up about something?"

"No. There was never anything like that." My mom leaned forward, her arms folded on top of the table, and I recognized the fierce look in her eyes. "Look, Sheriff, I have no idea what Lilah did to that man, but I have no doubt that he damn well deserved it."

Deputy Atherton twisted a knob at the bottom of the glass, and my mother's voice went silent. He pressed a button on the same panel, and the glass frosted over until it became reflective again. My viewing was over.

"She loves you."

"Yeah, and I'm afraid that's going to get her in serious trouble." I rotated my shoulders in the futile search for a more com-

fortable position as he slid into the chair across the table from me. "What's next for her?"

The deputy exhaled and pushed a strand of brown hair from his forehead. "Pennington's approved a rush order on her blood test, so we should hear back within twenty-four hours, assuming she's human."

Because identifying one of thousands of cryptid species by blood was complicated, but confirming humanity was pretty quick.

"She'll have to stay here until we're sure, though."

"Can't you just let her go home? She's no threat, Deputy."

Atherton shook his head. "Standard procedure, for public safety. Anyone suspected of having cryptid blood has to stay in custody until the results are in. I'll take her some coffee and a stale cinnamon roll, but that's the best I can do."

"What about me?" I shifted in my seat, trying to ease the pressure on my shoulders. "Am I going to sit in a cell until they figure out what I am?"

"Looks like it, and you should probably consider that a stroke of luck. Pennington's had a couple of the guys out front looking at options for where to send you since before you woke up, and the very best of them is going to make this place look like a luxury hotel."

A fresh jolt of fear tightened my chest. "Please tell me Pennington's not the final authority."

Atherton shrugged. "The law's a little fuzzy on that. If that carny was in the morgue instead of the psych ward, Pennington would have to call in the state police. That's standard for all capital offenses. But since he doesn't have to make that call, he's probably not gonna. If you turn out to be a surrogate, you fall under federal jurisdiction, but that's another call he's not going to make unless he has to."

"So my fate is in the hands of the sheriff of a county with fewer than fifteen thousand people in it." My mouth was dry,

and my hands had gone numb, but because I wasn't human, they could keep me as long as they wanted without so much as a sip of water or a trip to the bathroom.

"Yes, but I think you're better off here than you would be in state custody." The deputy folded his hands on the table while I watched him through a strand of hair that had fallen over my eye. "The state reservation is over capacity. They're sendin' the overflow straight to an R & D holding facility, and that place..."

Atherton stared down at his hands, and the fact that he was clearly stalling made my heart beat too hard.

Cryptid research and development was big business, with both the government and the private sector, but regulation was virtually nonexistent. Animal activists raised hell if a pharmaceutical company wanted to test new shampoo on a sewer rat, but R & D could inject environmental toxins beneath a selkie's removable seal skin all day long and no one blinked an eye.

"They don't tag 'em or count 'em, Delilah. I made a couple of calls, and a guy in records told me that since the lab opened fourteen years ago, they've sent in more than five times the max capacity—all kinds of cryptids—and there's no record of any of them ever officially leaving the facility. But they fire up the industrial incinerator about once a week."

My pulse jumped, and I struggled to keep breathing slowly. Evenly. "What's the alternative? Hotel California?"

The deputy nodded. "Otherwise known as the Oklahoma Cryptid Confinement Center."

"Same thing." Because there, every sentence that wasn't a life sentence was a death sentence.

"The only other option I can think of would be a private collection. I know this guy out in—"

"No." Chills shot up my spine. Werewolves on leashes, declawed and walking around like pets. Selkies and naiads swimming in giant koi ponds. Fauns serving drinks at private events

in nothing but gold chains and collars. I shook my head vehemently. "I'm nobody's pet."

"That's not up to you." Atherton leaned back in his chair, his forehead crinkled in irritation. "I'm going out of my way to help you, and your appreciation looks a lot like ingratitude."

Indignation sharpened my vision until I finally saw the deputy clearly. "You want me to be *thankful* that you're willing to sell me as a living party favor instead of sentencing me to a cryptid prison?"

The deputy's eyes narrowed. "You need to take a good, objective look at what you're facing here, Delilah. OCCC is an open-population cryptid prison. There are no guards. No cells. No rules. Helicopters make periodic supply drops on the grounds. You'd fight for every scrap of food and clothing until the day some troll or adlet eats you for breakfast. Is your pride really worth dying for?"

Fuck! I closed my eyes and clenched my fists over and over, wishing that the rest of me would go as numb as my fingers.

"And at least in a collection you'd be alive and in good health. No collector is going to let any serious damage come to property he spent good money on."

Property. Damage. Money. I would be an exotic pet. An insured asset in some rich prick's ledger. Because even animal lovers keep dogs on leashes.

The deputy shrugged. "I could say something to the sheriff about a private collector," he offered. "He'd have to think it was his own idea, but that shouldn't be hard. He still thinks it was his idea to install a vent fan in the men's room, and—"

"That *was* my idea." Pennington pushed the door open and marched into the interrogation room. Atherton's jaw tightened and his gaze dropped to the table between us for a second before he stood to relinquish the chair. "But I like where your head's at, Deputy." Pennington settled across the table from me, and the chair groaned beneath his weight. "I've found a fella out near the

panhandle who's lookin' to replenish his collection. He doesn't care what flavor of freak you are, so long as we pass along the results of your blood test as soon as we have 'em."

My chest felt so tight I could hardly breathe. "What kind of collection?"

"Well, I guess calling it a collection is kinda puttin' on airs. Fella actually calls it a reserve."

Wayne frowned. "Sheriff, are you talking about Russell Clegg's operation? He's running a game park over there, bringing hunters from all over to—"

Pennington twisted to look up at his deputy, and the chair creaked again. "Atherton, shut your mouth. You know no such thing."

I swallowed convulsively, struggling to hold down what little dinner I'd had as horror washed over me in waves. "You can't just let them chase me through the woods and shoot me down like a deer!" I wouldn't stand a chance, with hunters wearing infrared goggles and hound dogs following my scent.

"Handin' you over to Clegg will save the great state of Oklahoma thousands of dollars a year in upkeep, and in the process, I'll be making the streets of Franklin County a safer place to live. Folks want you gone, Delilah. Voting folks."

"I thought you couldn't send me anywhere until my blood test comes back."

The sheriff shrugged. "After talking to your mother, I agree that whatever you are, you're probably not a surrogate. If the test says otherwise, the feds can seize you from Clegg just as easily as they could seize you from me, and as long as my check has cleared, I could not give a—"

The door to the interrogation room flew open, startling us all.

"What?" Pennington roared at the deputy who stood in the threshold.

"There's a man out 'ere wants to talk to ya, Sheriff. It's about Lilah Marlow."

"What about her?"

The deputy shrugged. "He said he'd only talk to you. We put him in the next room, now that they got Mrs. Marlow moved to a cell."

The sheriff nodded. "I'll be there when I'm done in here." His deputy disappeared into the hall, and I glanced at Atherton with my brows raised, silently asking what he knew.

He only shrugged.

As the sheriff turned back to me with more questions, I stared at my own reflection in the one-way mirror, wondering who was looking back at me from the other side, and why.

I'd already been threatened with prison, a collection, and a hunting reserve. How much worse could this stranger's plan for me possibly be?

"Ladies and gentlemen, our lead story continues to grow stranger and more disturbing. So far, in every single one of the reported cases of this mass prolicide—the killing of one's own children—it appears that one child in each family has survived, completely unharmed. Even more bizarre—all of the surviving children are six years old, each born in the same month—March of 1980."

—Continuing coverage on the *Nightly News*, August 30, 1986

RUDOLPH

"Just twist that button next to the window, and you'll be able to hear what they're saying." The sheriff's deputy still had one hand on the doorknob, clearly eager to leave the observation room. Rudolph Metzger was neither surprised nor offended. Often locals were almost as unnerved by menagerie workers and their close proximity to the beasts as they were by the beasts themselves. "They can't see or hear you. The sheriff will be with you shortly," the deputy added on his way out.

Rudolph exhaled slowly when the door closed behind the officer, leaving him alone in the dim interrogation/observation room with Gallagher.

One hundred and twelve years.

That's how long the menagerie had been in Rudolph's family. The Metzgers had been bringing quality live entertainment to small towns all over the U.S. since before cell phones and personal computers. Since before the internet brought footage of dangerous and exotic creatures into private homes with one simple click of a mouse.

Since long before the reaping and the repeal of the Sanctuary Act.

Back then, business was simple and the creature carnival was smaller. Beasts only. The chimera. The phoenix. The basilisk. Nothing with human parts could be caged or put on display, but business was good because outside of zoos and traveling menag-

eries, private citizens couldn't get an up close look at a griffin without getting their eyes pecked out or their limbs ripped off.

But the technological boom had not been good to traveling circuses.

Rudolph shrugged off bittersweet nostalgia and waved a hand at the button on the wall, his gaze focused on the occupants of the room beyond the one-way glass. Gallagher stepped forward to twist the knob, and voices filled the room.

For a while, Rudolph only watched, uncomfortably aware of the fact that if the woman hadn't been chained to both her chair and the floor, he would've had no idea she wasn't, in fact, a woman at all. She was a monster. A female monster, certainly, but *not* a woman.

Only humans can be men and women.

But she *looked* like a woman, and that was a problem.

Most monsters could not hide for long among humanity—monstrosity shone through, even among the most normal-looking of creatures. Werewolves, for instance, had wolf eyes and canines even in human form. *Ifrits* gave off an unnatural body heat and had hair the color of flames. Sirens' eyes often came in colors foreign to humanity. Each species had its tell.

But this one...

After five minutes of studying her, scrutinizing every visible part, Rudolph could see no sign of aberration. Of course, the same was true of oracles, until their eyes clouded over in the grip of second sight.

"You're sure?" he said, still staring at the female chained to the chair. Strands of her ordinary dark hair hung over her ordinary blue eyes. She was ordinary, in the human sense, but somewhat attractive.

Yet another problem.

Gallagher nodded without pulling his gaze from the subject behind the window. He was a man of few words, but he was also a man of strong instinct and no bullshit, both qualities the

old man considered himself to have in spades. If Gallagher said this beast was more than she seemed, then she was more than she seemed.

She was also the kind of exhibit that could make or break a menagerie. Rudolph could not afford the risk she represented, nor could he afford to pass up the crowds she could draw. The profit she could bring.

When the Sanctuary Act was overturned, mere months after the reaping, traveling menageries began to evolve into modern creature features, complete with humanoid and hybrid exhibits as well as specialty shows. Demand was high and regulations were few. Insurance was optional and inspections were rare in most venues. Costs were low and profit margins were wide.

At first, Metzger's had flourished.

Yet by the time Rudolph's father passed the reins on to his middle-aged sons in the late 1990s, everything had begun to change. Rubes had become skeptics accustomed to movie magic and special effects. Audiences were harder to impress and less willing to pay for the privilege. Safety regulations, inspections, and insurance for traveling menageries had become astronomic expenses in an age when customers could sue a restaurant over too-hot coffee.

Rudolph's three brothers—and their prissy, gold-digging wives—wanted no part of the circus lifestyle, and after he bought them out to keep them from running Metzger's into the ground with their own disinterest, the menagerie's liquid assets were nearly drained.

Fortunately, Rudolph had a head for figures and an eye for beasts. He could tell at a glance which werewolf pup was the hardiest of the litter and which centaurs could subsist on oats and water without compromising their stamina. Rudolph knew just how to coax the livestock into breeding, and exactly when to sell which offspring to supplement income during the rough winter months when traveling was restricted by the weather.

Thanks to Rudolph's talent and attention, Metzger's had survived when many other menageries folded. But survival wasn't enough. He wanted Metzger's to flourish!

Gallagher's discovery could help make that happen.

"We can't show her like that." Rudolph waved one hand at the glass, and Gallagher nodded. "If people think she's a surrogate, no one will come see her. And if it looks like we've put a human woman in a cage, the rubes will feel sorry for her and we'll be the bad guys. You'll have to bring out her beast. Show them she's a monster—but not a surrogate."

Gallagher scowled. "*I* will have to...?"

Rudolph sank onto the edge of the table to relieve the pressure on his bad hip. "She was your idea. She's your responsibility. I want to see the eyes, and the veins, and the claws. The audience *needs* to see those things. You will train her."

"We don't know what she is." Gallagher's focus returned to the room behind the glass. "Hell, it sounds like *she* doesn't know what she is."

"If we've never seen anything like her, the audience won't have either. Play up the mystery until you figure it out." Rudolph glanced up at the large handler's harsh profile. "She's dangerous, Gallagher. Don't underestimate her."

"She stuck her fingers through Jack's skull. There's no underestimating that."

"No." Rudolph's tone demanded his employee's full attention, and Gallagher turned again. "No matter what she can do when her beast shows itself, she's more of a threat in her human guise. Look." He pointed through the glass, where the female's jaw was clenched in anger while tears still stood in her eyes. "She's not just scared, she's *indignant*. She thinks she deserves better than she's getting."

For several minutes, they watched through the glass while the female made demands and begged for exceptions.

"She wasn't in hiding here in bumfuck, Oklahoma," Rudolph

said. "She wasn't trying to pass for human. She thought she *was* human. The world thought she was human. When audiences look at her, they will see themselves, locked up and helpless. When the other exhibits look at her, they will see possibility. Opportunity. She grew up with freedom and human privilege. She's smart, she's loud, and she has a severely inflated sense of self-worth. Her delusions make her dangerous."

Gallagher nodded slowly, and they both stared through the window again while the female shouted at the sheriff, as if fear fueled her spirit, rather than cowing it.

Rudolph shook his head to disguise the chill traveling up his spine. This female could incite riots. She could save the carnival—or be the end of everything he'd been working toward his entire life.

"You must break her, Gallagher. She is the spark, and if that spark kindles, it will burn my menagerie to the ground."

DELILAH

With no clock or watch, I couldn't be sure how long I sat alone in the interrogation room chained to the floor, but it felt like forever. At some point during my isolation and immobilization, the threats I was facing—prison, private collectors, exotic game parks—began to coalesce into a steady baseline of anxiety. My new normality, it seemed, would be fear, and once that became clear, my other, lesser complaints began to stand out.

My shoulders were a constant source of pain—dull when I sat still, sharp and paralyzing when I tried to move. My hands had gone numb again, and no amount of finger wiggling would bring back pins and needles.

My bladder, though, was the real problem, and the inability to take myself to the restroom was one fresh hell of an indignity.

When the door finally opened again, I started to insist on a bathroom break, but one look at the sheer joy on Sheriff Pennington's face stole the words right off my tongue. The hair on the back of my neck stood up; his pleasure couldn't mean anything good for me.

Pennington strode into the center of the room and waved one pudgy arm at me. "There she is. Make it quick."

Two men eyed me from the hallway. An adrenaline-charged bolt of fear shot through me with one glance at them, and I forgot about my pain and discomfort. I recognized the large man

in the red baseball cap even before I saw that *Gallagher* was embroidered on his Metzger's Menagerie polo.

The smaller, older man wore a slick-looking button-down shirt in that same shade of red, tucked into a pair of pleated black pants. He pushed past the deputy into the interrogation room, where he stared down at me from across the table.

My skin crawled under his methodical assessment. His gaze was cold and quick, efficiently inventorying my features without pausing to notice intelligence in my eyes, or tension in my frame, or fear in the rapid rising and falling of my chest with each breath.

My focus snagged on the crow's feet branching from the corners of his eyes and the wrinkles framing his mouth like nested parentheses. The script on the left side of his shirt read Rudolph Metzger.

"Any health issues?" Metzger glanced over his shoulder at Pennington, then turned again to study the chains binding me to my chair. "Allergies? Seizures? Anything communicable?"

"What the hell?" I demanded as Deputy Atherton stepped into the room, but he could only shrug. Pennington may have thought of me as a thing, but at least he'd talked to me like a person. Rudolph Metzger might as well have been examining the teeth of a racehorse.

Gallagher only watched from the doorway, his expression as featureless as the wall behind him.

"Regular bowels and menstrual cycles?" the old man continued, addressing me for the first time.

My cheeks burned. "Are you fucking serious?"

When I refused to answer, he turned back to the bewildered sheriff. "Normally we'd wait for the lab results on a cryptid of unknown origin, but since half a dozen of my own people witnessed the incident, we'll take her. You get half up front, and the other half when we have her blood work in hand. We can't register an exhibit without it."

"No." My pulse raced so fast the room started to look unsteady. "Hell, no. I am not joining the circus."

"It's not a circus, it's a carnival," Pennington said, while I tried to breathe through my fear and fury.

"Actually, it's both," Metzger corrected, without acknowledging that I'd spoken. "The menagerie itself is technically a circus—a single traveling unit, whose employees live, eat, and work together. But we engage carnival-style independent contractors who bring their own food carts, game booths, and rides at each stop." His contemptuous gaze settled on me. "This transaction doesn't require your approval. You're not joining my menagerie. You're being sold into it."

"Well, I can guaran-damn-tee you that requires *my* approval," Sheriff Pennington growled.

"Of course." Metzger glanced at his employee. "Gallagher, write the man a check."

Gallagher pulled a long checkbook from behind his back.

"Hang on now. We're gonna need more than half up front," Pennington insisted. "If you don't even know what she is, she must be rare, and rare is expensive."

Metzger gestured for the sheriff to precede him into the hall, and he took the checkbook from Gallagher on the way. "Let's talk money. But keep in mind that I'm the one assuming all the expense and risk…" Their voices faded when the door closed, and through the window set into it, I saw both men gesturing as they negotiated.

Gallagher watched me from his station near the door. His focus only strayed from my face when he studied the chair and the chains holding me in place, and after a second, I realized he was checking for weaknesses in my bindings.

"Deputy." My heartbeat hammered in my ears. "Please don't let him do this."

Atherton sank onto the chair across from me and leaned over the table. "There's nothing I can do, Delilah."

"Talk the sheriff out of it. Tell him you heard Russell Clegg pays big."

"You'd rather be hunted than sit in a cage?"

I'd rather do neither, but the drive to the panhandle would give me several hours to think. Maybe I could break free at a rest stop. The chances of that were slim, but with Metzger, my chances of escape dropped to zero; the county fairground was only a few miles away.

"Delilah." Atherton cleared his throat and glanced at the table between us. "I think you should keep your head down and roll with the punches on this. These guys look like they're prepared to do this the hard way."

"You should listen to him." Gallagher's voice was like the rumble of distant thunder.

Before I could respond, the door opened again and Metzger walked into the interrogation room as if he now owned not just me, but the entire Franklin County Sheriff's Department.

Pennington followed him, holding two checks. He handed one to a deputy whose name I couldn't remember. "Write up an invoice and send that in with it to the state treasurer, up at the capital." The deputy left, and Pennington folded the other check and stuffed it into his own back pocket. "Deputy, give 'em the keys."

"No. Please!" I thrashed against my bindings, though I knew that would do no good. I couldn't help it.

Atherton stood and gave me an apologetic look as he fumbled with his keys.

Pennington rolled his eyes, then snatched the key ring and tossed it to Gallagher, who caught it one-handed. "It's the big one with the black rubber grip."

"No." Despite the pain, I struggled frantically while Gallagher thumbed through the keys. "You can't just *sell* me!" I shouted, and a deputy with baby cheeks and big brown eyes jumped,

startled by my outburst. "You can't sell *people*! How could you all just go along with this?"

"You wanna sedate her?" Pennington asked, as Gallagher found the right key and pried it from the ring.

Metzger gave him a contemptuous huff. "It's never safe to introduce chemicals into the system of a cryptid before you know its species. Reactions vary widely. This one was raised human?"

Pennington nodded.

The menagerie owner sat on the edge of the table in front of me. "Do you have family?" he demanded, and I realized he had yet to address me by name.

When I only glared up at him, the grinding of my teeth drowned out by the panicked rush of my own pulse, Pennington answered for me. "We got her mother in a cell. Not her real mother. Charity's human, best we can tell."

"I don't know how you *can* tell, considering how normal this specimen looks. I'd keep an eye on the mother," Metzger said, and when Pennington nodded, the menagerie owner turned back to me, his voice carrying a soft, measured menace. "You're going to come peacefully, because if you don't, I'll see that your mother is charged with harboring a cryptid and public endangerment."

I studied his dark brown eyes, looking for the bluff, but I found none. He would have my mom arrested with no more regret than when he shook the dust of Franklin County off his boots and led his rolling prison into the next town.

"Fine." I couldn't drag my mother down with me, so I made myself sit still, battling competing urges to both fight and flee.

When the tension in my frame eased, Metzger stood and turned to the sheriff. "That would never have worked on a surrogate. The feds have no claim on her." He nodded to Gallagher, whom I could feel looming over me from behind, then the old man and the sheriff wandered into the hallway, talking about the proper restraint technique of a "human-lookin'" cryptid.

I jumped when Gallagher's hand settled onto my shoulder. "Relax." His voice was low and carefully controlled, but the word was spoken so close to my ear that I could feel the breath it rode on. His hand slid down my arm, like a handler strokes a horse's flank, to soothe her.

"Don't touch me!" I snapped through clenched teeth, and the light pressure of his fingers disappeared.

"I'm going to unthread the chains, then I'm going to help you up and lead you to the truck." He spoke softly as he worked, filling me in on each step before he carried it out, and when I looked up, I found Wayne watching, his expression trapped somewhere between anger and fascination. "I'll have to hold your arm as we walk," Gallagher continued. His hand brushed my bare foot, and the shackles fell away. "That's standard safety procedure."

"Do I look that dangerous?" I asked as he knelt behind me.

"Appearance isn't relevant to threat potential."

Metal clanged on the concrete, and suddenly my arms felt weightless, free of the burden of several pounds of iron chain.

The old man turned at the sound, and Gallagher tugged me up by one arm while he pulled my chair back with his free hand. My legs ached, and I wanted to stretch them. My fingers started tingling, as feeling returned, and I rolled my sore shoulders to help the process along.

When I turned to look up at Gallagher, I had to look way up. He was six foot six, if he was an inch. Maybe even taller. He returned my gaze with no visible thought or emotion, the face of a soldier. Or a stone statue. I got the feeling just from looking at him that unlike Deputy Atherton, Gallagher was burdened with neither empathy nor compassion.

Atherton, however, was suddenly nowhere to be found.

"Is she a biter?" Metzger asked the sheriff. "We brought a muzzle."

Pennington shrugged. "I'd keep it handy. That one's got a mouth like a snake."

Metzger's eyebrows shot up. "She has venomous fangs?" He pulled a small notebook from his jacket pocket. "That should narrow things down."

Pennington shook his head, looking confused. "No, she's a smart-ass."

The old man stuffed the notebook back into his pocket and stalked past him, gesturing for Gallagher and me to follow. "You should use more care when describing cryptids, Sheriff," he shot back over his shoulder, as Gallagher tugged me along. "In my line of work, similes are often indistinguishable from description."

Pennington mumbled something rude, then pushed past us into the front of the sheriff's station.

When Gallagher pulled me into the room, I had to fight for a deep breath. My gaze lost focus as it skipped from face to face in an open reception area that should have been nearly empty at 2:00 a.m. Some of the staff had stayed to help identify my species or find some place to send me. Others had stayed because there'd never been a cryptid outed in Franklin County, and I was big news.

Still others, based on the staggering hatred shining in their eyes, had evidently come just to spit on me.

"Lilah!" My mother's voice cracked beneath the weight of my name. I turned toward the sound and saw her standing, unrestrained, next to Deputy Wayne Atherton.

"Mom!" I shouted.

But Gallagher kept pulling me forward, still barefoot, after Metzger, denying me the goodbye Atherton had obviously risked his job to give me.

"Where are you taking her?" my mom demanded from across the room. I wanted to turn again, but if they thought I was re-

sisting, Metzger might demand my mother's arrest on the spot and Gallagher might produce his muzzle.

Other questions followed my mother's, and when a woman's commanding tone and professional cadence rose above the others, I looked up to see that Channel 5 had sent a small crew from Oklahoma City.

A new foreboding settled through me like sand sinking through water, and suddenly my legs felt too heavy to move. Someone had alerted the media. More reporters would follow.

"Folks," Pennington began, and I groaned when I saw him standing with his hands on his hips, feet spread wide, ready to address the public as their leader in arms. Naturally, I'd been apprehended in the middle of an election year.

As soon as the crowd turned toward the sheriff, Rudolph Metzger stopped in the middle of the station and Gallagher pulled me to a halt several feet behind him. "Ladies and gentlemen, I understand your curiosity, but I don't yet have the answers to most of your questions." The menagerie owner's voice carried with even more presence and authority than the Channel 5 reporter's, and the crowd abandoned Pennington in favor of the man who'd probably been talking for the menagerie since before he could grow a decent beard.

"What I *can* confirm for you is that Delilah Marlow has been exposed as a cryptid hidden among the good people of Franklin County, and I have agreed, on behalf of Metzger's Menagerie, to take possession of her in the interest of public safety, effective immediately."

"What is she?" The reporter thrust a microphone at him, and I realized that her cameraman had framed the shot so that Gallagher and I were both visible over Metzger's shoulder.

"How was she exposed?"

"Was anyone killed?"

"What will you do with her?"

"Is she the only one?"

Metzger smiled for the crowd—I saw it in profile—and graciously waved off the questions. "That's all I'm prepared to say tonight, but I'm excited to announce that thanks to our new acquisition—" he aimed an elegant gesture my way, and I dropped my head when I saw countless phone cameras aimed at me "—Metzger's has agreed to extend our engagement in Franklin County to indulge the hometown crowd. Come see us tomorrow night, when we will unveil our latest exhibition. We'll answer what questions we can for you then."

Horror pitched me into a stunned fog. I didn't hear the questions lobbed at us as we continued through the lobby toward the door. All I could think about were words like *acquisition*, and *exhibit*, and *hometown crowd*, and what they meant strung together in the same sentence with my name.

"Lilah!" My mom lurched forward and reached for my arm, with Deputy Atherton just a step behind her.

Gallagher slid between us without missing a step as he hauled me across the floor.

"Lilah!" She followed as closely as he'd let her. "I'll fight this. I'll get a lawyer. I'll get you out of there, honey."

But since the reaping, no court had ever deigned to hear a case brought forth by a cryptid. Some courts were even refusing to hear witness testimony from cryptids. And if she dragged him into her fight, Pennington would arrest her just to keep her out of his hair.

"Mom, don't," I said as she jogged to keep up. "I'm fine. Really. So just...don't. Okay? Promise me."

"Lilah—"

"Promise me!" I begged, as Gallagher tugged me through the front door and toward the dark parking lot, where a windowless Metzger's van was double-parked on the first row, beneath a light pole. I dragged my feet until a rock cut into my bare sole. "You have to trust me, Mom. It's better this way." *For*

you. But if I said that aloud, she wouldn't stop fighting until we were both behind bars.

Gallagher pulled me to a stop behind the van, where another handler in a red Metzger's shirt opened the rear doors, then helped lift me into the cargo area. I twisted in his grip to see Deputy Atherton dragging my mother back into the sheriff's station. Her tear-streaked face was the last thing I saw before the van door slammed shut on life as I'd known it.

PART TWO

CONFINÉ

ROMMILY

The oracle sat up in the dark, suddenly wide-awake. She wasn't sure whether the images still burned into her brain were from a dream or a vision, but there was little difference between the two anymore.

Rommily clutched the side of her cage to pull herself onto her knees in the narrow space between her sleeping sisters. Her gaze skimmed dead grass and muddy hoofprints dimly lit by lamp poles on the edge of the parking lot, but she saw none of that. The oracle's eyes were filled with another place and another time. Though she could no longer trace the threads connecting the present and the future, she understood that they were drawing closer together with every beat of her heart.

Something thunked in the dark, and Rommily's focus—a fragile thing, at best—was yanked back into the present. A door squealed open, tracing a skewed rectangle of light on the ground in front of the nearest staff trailer, and a dark silhouette emerged. The backlit outline joined another shadowy shape, then voices spoke, accompanied by the heavy footsteps of two men with rough hands and cold hearts.

"Thumb on the scale," the oracle mumbled as the handlers stomped past her cage. One was still pulling his shirt on while the other scrubbed sleep from his face with both thick hands, cursing the phone call that had awakened him.

"Balance restored." Rommily's voice carried more volume

than before, and Mirela stirred on her left, one foot peeking from beneath her brightly colored skirt.

In the distance, two points of light snaked toward the menagerie on a narrow gravel road. Rommily's grip tightened around the steel grid caging her as the hum of the engine grew louder. A current of anticipation fired through her, crackling in her ears like static. Humming in her throat like a melody.

"The blind lady."

A van pulled into the parking lot and reversed into position with the crunch of gravel. The old man got out of the passenger's seat, and Rommily retreated from the edge of her cage as he rounded the vehicle, limping on his bad hip. The old man missed nothing.

The driver stepped out and slammed his door, and the oracle scooted farther into the shadows. She watched, unseen, as the drowsy handlers opened the rear doors of the vehicle. The large man with gray eyes and a red hat jumped out of the back of the van and lifted a young woman in chains from the darkness that hid her.

The oracle's gaze narrowed on the dimly lit figure. The woman's dark hair hung limp and her eyes were dull with exhaustion, but Rommily had seen her true face. She knew the terror it could inspire.

"She won't serve her dish cold," the oracle mumbled, almost giddy with joy as chill bumps rose all over her skin. "And two graves won't be near enough..."

DELILAH

The van rolled to a halt, then shifted into Reverse, sliding me across the bench seat. Gallagher grabbed my arm to stop me from falling. He hadn't moved an inch or said a word since we'd left the sheriff's station, and his stony silence left me with nothing to think about but the inevitable indignity of being displayed in a decorative cage for an audience of my own friends and neighbors.

The van stopped again. Footsteps stomped through gravel, then the doors flew open, and a jolt of adrenaline set my chest on fire. "Please, no," I mumbled, staring out into the yellow glare of several light poles. I wasn't ready. This *couldn't* be real. How could my fate possibly be up to two men and a checkbook, with no attorney, no trial, and no defense?

How could I have fewer rights under the law than a stray dog had?

Stray dogs were never responsible for the mass slaughter of American children. Everyone knew that.

I hadn't killed any kids either. I hadn't brainwashed any parents or stolen any babies. But that hadn't stopped Sheriff Pennington from selling me to the first man to walk in with a checkbook. Cryptids would forever pay the price for the horror of the reaping.

Metzger stared into the cargo area with his arms crossed over his red satin shirt. His showman's bearing and voice had been abandoned, along with his jacket and his red suspenders. All that

remained of Rudolph Metzger, the menagerie front man, were the polished black boots he still wore and the top hat, now held in his left hand. Behind him stood two more large handlers, who looked gruff and irritated to be on the job in the middle of the night. Like Gallagher, they wore nothing sequined or shiny. These men were the power and sweat behind the glitz and the glamour.

I was officially behind the scenes of the menagerie.

Gallagher jumped down from the van, then lifted me out by both arms and set me down on gravel. Rocks cut into my bare feet. My shoulders ached and my wrists were raw from the heavy cuffs fastened at my back, but no one offered to take them off. No one gave me any shoes, asked my name, or addressed me directly at all.

"What is she?" the handler on the left asked. According to his shirt, his name was Wallace.

"She is a mystery." Metzger thumped his top hat to knock dust from it. "She's new and exotic. Very rare. That's the angle anyway, until her blood test comes back. Play it up."

The owner pulled Gallagher aside, leaving the other handlers to glare at me, bulging arms crossed over broad chests. They were a human wall, and I would not be able to breach it.

"My daughter's getting remarried on Friday, and my wife and I are watching her kids during the honeymoon." Metzger had to look way up to talk to Gallagher. "I'll catch up with the menagerie two weeks from today. You have that long to break her in and train her."

Break me in? Train me?

I sucked in breath after rapid breath, but couldn't seem to get enough air. The night was uncomfortably dry and warm, but my veins had become arctic channels, pumping tiny icebergs through me to pierce and sink all hope.

"That won't be long enough, sir." Gallagher's voice was so low and deep that I could hardly hear him. "She's spent a lifetime—"

"Make it happen," Metzger demanded.

I hunched around the cold knot in my belly, struggling to absorb everything I was hearing through filters of shock and exhaustion. Nothing felt real. Nothing but the iron cuffs.

"Delegate some of your other responsibilities and make this your primary concern," the old man said. "I want her turning a profit when I get back, or I'm selling her to Vandekamp to recoup part of my loss, and you'll make up the rest from your own paycheck. For the next six months. Understood?"

Gallagher nodded, and panic tightened my chest until I could hardly breathe. Who the hell was Vandekamp?

"Get her processed, then put her on the row. Tomorrow, start breaking her." Metzger marched off toward a long line of campers and 18-wheelers, many painted with menagerie images in the same retro style as the posters hanging all over town.

His instructions echoed in my head.

Break me? Like a stick for kindling or like a pony for riding? Break me like a date, or like a heart, or like a promise?

In the end, it wouldn't matter. I had no intention of being broken.

Metzger's footsteps faded, and I turned back to Gallagher, fighting to convert my fear into fuel for the sparks of rage flickering deep in my soul.

My entire existence was in his hands, which meant he was the biggest obstacle to my escape.

I studied him as he gave Wallace and the other handler a series of instructions involving words like *crate*, and *blanket*, and *padlock*. Gallagher was big. He was tall, and broad, and solid enough to make the others—large men in their own right—look almost delicate. I would not escape by overpowering my handler physically.

But there were other ways to overpower. My mother had shown me that in every battle from the PTA presidency to the great flower-bed debate of 2008, in which she and her army of

petunias had sent my father's ground cover packing. Pride. Love. Jealousy. Hatred. Insecurity. Any weakness can be exploited, and everyone has a weakness.

When we were in the eighth grade, I'd used a bully's insecurity to humiliate her, after she'd accused Shelley of cheating off her on a test, when the opposite was actually true. In college, I'd helped a friend get revenge on a cheating boyfriend by exploiting his rampant lust. And once at the bank, I'd used my boss's trust in me to get him fired after he cheated on his wife in the vault.

Gallagher might be bigger than the other predators I'd encountered, but as my father always said, the bigger they are, the harder they fall. Finding Gallagher's weakness would be the key to setting myself free.

Gallagher pounded on the trailer door with his thick right fist, his left still wrapped around my arm in a grip that didn't actually hurt, but probably couldn't be broken. My legs ached and my ankles were chafed from walking in iron shackles, and what I'd learned from slowly, awkwardly climbing the steep porch steps in them was that even if I could have pulled free from my captor, I wouldn't get very far if I tried to run.

The porch light came on over our heads, illuminating the aluminum steps beneath us, the dented metal door, and the mud-splattered white vertical siding of the menagerie's mobile office—a modular trailer, which could be lifted onto a flatbed truck and hauled from city to city, intact.

Gallagher had called it "the silver wagon," but neither descriptor fit.

The door was opened by a tall thin man wearing a red satin Metzger's jacket in spite of the stifling heat of the midsummer night. The name embroidered over his heart was Ruyle, and beneath that his title read Lot Supervisor.

I hated him with every cell in my body, even before Ruyle

took one look at me, then snorted. "I can't believe the old man bought another free-range freak."

Free-range? Because I hadn't grown up in captivity?

The supervisor stepped back, and Gallagher tugged me into the cramped one-room office. Inside there was barely enough room to breathe, thanks to two cluttered desks, four lockable filing cabinets, a mini-fridge, and a whiteboard schedule covered with employee names, time slots, and various menagerie act assignments.

The board slid out of focus as I stared at it. I would be listed there soon—not by my name but by my species, or by some number assigned to me on a list of inventory.

"You'd think the old man would have learned a lesson after that free-range dark elf we picked up near Atlanta last year," Ruyle continued. "That was a real clusterfuck."

Gallagher only grunted.

Ruyle kicked the door closed and turned to study me. My skin crawled beneath his appraisal.

"What is she?"

Gallagher shrugged. "She doesn't eat live flesh, read minds, tell the future, shift into an animal, or have an allergy to iron."

Ruyle made a spinning motion with his index finger, and Gallagher turned me by both shoulders, so the supervisor could finish his assessment. "No horns, hooves, claws, or fangs. Do a thorough check for feathers, scales, and fur when we're done here."

"I don't have any of that." I tried to turn and appeal to Ruyle directly, but Gallagher stopped me with one heavy hand on my shoulder. "I was examined at the sheriff's station, and they didn't find anything."

"Oh, I think we're going to want to see for ourselves." Ruyle's hand settled on my lower back, then slid low over the curve of my hip. I tried to step away from his touch, but Gallagher's grip on my shoulder tightened, holding me in place.

Rage blazed beneath my skin like a fever. "Don't touch me."

Ruyle stepped into sight again, his disappointed gaze lingering on my mouth. "Not a succubus, then. Damn shame. They would have lined up for miles to be sucked dry by her."

The mental image made me gag. The supervisor laughed while I swallowed convulsively to keep from vomiting. I *loathed* him. "What, does that offend your delicate sensibilities?"

I stared straight into his eyes, standing as tall as I could. "If I'd eaten anything tonight, you'd be wearing it. Consider that my official opinion of your business model."

Gallagher's grunt actually sounded amused.

Ruyle seized my chin in a brutal grip and I gasped, shocked by the casual cruelty. I tried to pull free, and his hold tightened until my teeth cut into my cheek and I tasted blood.

"Free advice, freak. Just because you *can* talk doesn't mean you *should*." The supervisor looked up at Gallagher without letting go of me. "If the sign out front read Ruyle's Menagerie, cutting their tongues out would be an official part of the welcome package."

Gallagher said nothing, so Ruyle turned back to me. "If I have to go find a muzzle for you, you'll wear it for a week straight, even if we have to feed you through a straw."

When he let go of my chin, I glared up at him, blinking back angry tears. "Aren't you afraid I'll scramble your brain and leave you drooling in a puddle of your own urine?"

"With your hands cuffed behind your back?" Ruyle's mouth laughed, but his eyes didn't.

"I won't always be cuffed, though, will I?" None of the "exhibits" I'd seen had been restrained within their cages.

The supervisor's eyes narrowed into angry slits beneath his deeply furrowed brow. "Three." His gaze slid up to Gallagher again. "My money's on three days before the old man sells her to R & D. Or I feed her to the adlet. We've got a pool going." Ruyle pointed to his desk, where an old pickle jar held a handful

of wrinkled five-dollar bills. "You want in? The dark elf made it a week and a half." His contemptuous gaze narrowed on me. "But I'm betting she won't make it half that."

"Get on with it," Gallagher growled, while I stared at the jar of cash bet against my survival.

Ruyle rounded his desk and dropped into the chair behind it, looking up at me with both arms folded on the cluttered plywood desk. "You're what? Twenty? Twenty-two?"

"Twenty-five, today." Gallagher sank onto the edge of a two-drawer filing cabinet, without letting go of my arm. He'd either seen my driver's license, spoken to my friends, or read a report at the sheriff's station.

Ruyle's brows rose. "Hell of a birthday, huh?" He leaned over his desk and his gaze narrowed on me. "Look, twenty-five years is a long time to spend living a lie, and I'm sure you got real comfortable with a bunch of liberties and amenities you never really had any right to. Most in your situation don't make it in the menagerie because they can't let go of the past. But if you want to prove me wrong and cost me a small fortune in fives—" he gestured to the jar of cash "—that's exactly what you'll need to do. Forget about your friends, and your family, and your car, and your job, and any other defunct delusions. They were never really yours in the first place. If you can accept your place, you could be pretty comfortable here." His hard-eyed gaze took on a lascivious gleam. "I'll see to that myself. But if you make my job hard, I will make your life a living hell."

"She's *my* charge." Gallagher's hand tightened around my arm, tugging me closer. I fought the urge to pull away from him.

Ruyle nodded. "True, you're Gallagher's problem until you're broken in and turning a profit. But I'm his boss, which means that ultimately, just like all the other beasts, you're my problem. Understood?"

"Yeah." I shrugged, trying not to let the pain in my shoulders show. "You're the boss, so you have a lot of problems."

Ruyle's jaw clenched. He glared at Gallagher. "Three days. And that's a generous estimation." Then he picked up a form from a pile of papers scattered across his desk and turned back to me. "As the lot supervisor, I'm in charge when old man Metzger's gone, which is most of the time. Even when he's here, he leaves the real work to me and our boss of livestock." He threw a careless gesture at Gallagher, without looking away from me. "Obviously, you're the livestock. I'm sure a lot of this comes as a shock, after the way you were raised, so if you have any questions…" He shrugged. "You'll figure it out."

Ruyle scribbled something on the form in front of him. "Put her in crate forty-two. With any luck, it still smells like cat piss from that leopard shifter we leased from All American." He spun the form around and slid it across the desk toward my new handler. "Give this to Nellis and tell him we'll use one of the spare wagon casings for now. I'm not going to have Alyrose fix up something special until we know your new pet's a keeper."

"Crate?" I turned to Gallagher, wincing when the cuffs cut into my ankles. "You're going to put me in a box?" Would they at least punch holes in the top, so I could breathe?

"It's just a cage on wheels," Gallagher said. "A circus wagon with the decorative casings removed for transport."

Ruyle leaned back in his chair and laced his fingers behind his head. "I think you're onto something, though. I'm sure we could find a shipping crate to stuff you in. Yesterday's high was one hundred twelve degrees." The manager shrugged. "It'd be a real shame for you to broil in your own sweat because you couldn't keep your mouth shut."

Survival instinct stilled my tongue, but terror ate away at me from the inside. He was right. I couldn't survive the menagerie. I couldn't live in a cage. I couldn't be someone else's property.

Panic crept in from the edges of my mind, where lurked all the horrifying possibilities I hadn't yet let myself consider. They could do whatever they wanted with me. *To* me. I closed my

eyes and breathed deeply, trying to tune Ruyle out, but the best I could do was mentally distance myself from the miserable existence his forms and decrees were outlining for me.

In addition to a crate number, he assigned me to uniform group C and hygiene plan A, with the caveat that if I became a security risk in the bathroom, I would lose the privilege.

Having never considered hygiene a privilege, I wasn't entirely sure what a downgrade from plan A would mean.

The supervisor also assigned me to the omnivore meal plan and gave me a wagon number, which would indicate my position in the "take down" and determine which of the menagerie's custom-built, wide-load 18-wheelers I would be "shelved" in for transport.

I couldn't fully process all the new information, and I didn't even try. But by the time Gallagher escorted me from the silver wagon, accompanied by the clank of my heavy iron bindings, the takeaway was clear.

Everything I'd ever owned had been taken. Everyone I'd ever known was gone.

I'd become the property of Metzger's Traveling Menagerie.

"According to the most current numbers, more than three hundred thousand human families lost a total of almost one million children in last week's massacre, and all of them appear to have been killed by their own parents. But what's really strange, Bill, is that the authorities are saying not *one* of those parents remembers a thing that happened in the early hours of August 24. Could *all* of those parents have been acting in some kind of subconscious state?"

—From an NPR interview with William Green, the world's foremost authority on hypnotism, September 3, 1986

DELILAH

The county fairgrounds ladies' room. Six stalls—four toilets and two showers—and a sink-lined walkway. Grimy concrete floor. White cinderblock walls, dripping with slimy condensation.

As an eight-year-old, I'd vomited in the third stall from the left after a bad chili dog at the fair. At thirteen, I'd borrowed Shelley's makeup and applied it in front of the very last sink, a willful violation of my dad's "not until high school" rule. And a week after my eighteenth birthday, I'd stood outside the fourth stall while Shelley took the pregnancy test she hadn't had the nerve to take at home alone.

But I'd never been marched down the abandoned midway in the middle of the night by a man the size of a small building, passing darkened game booths and locked-tight food stalls on our way into that bathroom. I'd never looked into the mirror and seen finger-shaped bruises rounding my chin or dark circles forming beneath each of my eyes.

I'd never been ordered to strip in front of the curtain-less shower while three men watched, their expressions ranging from Gallagher's objective professionalism to Mustache Man's leering grin of anticipation.

"I'm going to uncuff you, and you're going to take off your clothes and turn a slow circle so we can visually check you for species-identifying marks or features," Gallagher said. "Then

you'll step into the shower and thoroughly wash your hair and your body."

"No," I said, and irritation narrowed his gray eyes. "Please don't make me do this. I don't have any marks, I swear."

He scowled and turned me by my shoulders for access to the cuffs at my back, but I spun around again before he could dig his keys from his pocket.

"I get it, okay? I don't have any rights. I'm just a piece of meat you're going to lock up in a metal box." Each word killed a little more of my soul, but desperation kept me talking. "I can't stop you from doing whatever you want with me."

"Damn right," the man with the mustache said, but I only exhaled and kept my gaze on the boss of livestock.

"You can make me strip. But I'm asking you not to. As a kindness. I have nothing left but my dignity. Please let me keep it."

Gallagher blinked, and for just an instant, he looked…surprised. Then the professional blinders slid back into place, locking me out of his thoughts. "There are rules. If you refuse to follow them, we'll have to cut your clothes off and bathe you ourselves, and there is *much* less dignity in that."

I nodded, my jaw clenched to keep my chin from trembling, and as I turned to give him access to the handcuffs, he exhaled.

"I think we can forgo the flea and lice treatment."

"Ruyle says no exceptions on that." Mustache Man picked up a commercial-sized bottle from the box at his feet. "We can't afford an infestation." The name on his shirt identified him as Clyde.

"This morning she was a bank teller with manicured nails." Gallagher slid his key into the cuffs with the scrape of metal. "She's probably cleaner than you are."

Clyde scowled, but didn't push the issue.

Gallagher released my left hand, then my right, then turned me by my shoulders to face him again. He knelt to unlock my ankles, and Clyde leered at me over the top of his boss's red cap.

I crossed my arms over my chest, shielding myself from the pending visual violation. "Okay, how 'bout a compromise?" I said to the top of Gallagher's head as he freed my left ankle. "I'll strip and shower without a fuss, saving everyone a lot of time and effort—but not in front of them."

Gallagher shook his head without looking up at me as he unlocked my ankle. "Until we know what you're capable of, federal regulations dictate a three-to-one ratio of handlers to unrestrained cryptids."

I shrugged. "So make them turn around. How many of you really need to see that my back isn't hollow and my ass isn't covered in scales?"

Gallagher stood, towering over me with my shackles in hand, and I watched anxiously while he weighed the risks and benefits of my proposal. "If you try *anything*, I will never be able to trust you again. Do you understand what I'm telling you?"

A stubborn thread of anger steeled my spine as I stared up at him. "Let you see me naked, or you'll make my life hell?"

"This isn't about seeing you naked."

"Right." I rubbed my sore wrist, left raw from the sheriff's department's restraints.

Gallagher turned me by both shoulders, and I held his hard, gray gaze. "At the back of the menagerie, in a tent trimmed with a red ribbon, sit four of the most beautiful women ever seen on this earth. Succubi crave physical contact and take off any clothing we don't practically glue to their skin. So understand, Princess Vanity, that yours is not the most coveted flesh in this carnival."

I blinked, surprised by the longest speech I'd heard from him.

"It's almost dawn," Gallagher growled. "Get moving." He glanced at each of the other handlers. "You two turn around."

Only slightly mollified, I reached into the shower stall and twisted the knob. Water exploded from the showerhead and I held one hand beneath the flow, waiting—hoping—for it to

warm while Gallagher fielded protests from Clyde and the other handler, whose name was Freddie. When the water was as warm as it was going to get, I turned to find the boss of livestock watching me expectantly while the other men stood between us, facing him, but turned away from me.

Their stiff bearing and crossed arms spoke volumes, but so did their obedience. They weren't willing to cross Gallagher.

I turned away from him, and my hands shook as I pulled my sheer blouse and cami over my head together in one quick movement. Despite the warm night, I had to clench my jaw to keep my teeth from chattering. I could practically feel his gaze on my back.

My fingers fumbled with my bra hook, and by the time I pushed my underwear to the floor and stepped out of it, I was trembling all over. Reducing the spectators from three to one hadn't helped as much as I'd hoped. I was still naked and vulnerable in front of a stranger.

"Extend your arms," Gallagher said, and I jumped, so on edge that any stimulus from the world around me—the splatter of lukewarm water from the shower, the tick of Clyde's old-fashioned wristwatch, the scent of bleach emanating from the toilet stalls—was a shock to my system.

I held my arms out, silently commanding them not to shake. For a moment, there was only silence behind me. Then, "Turn around."

Exhaling slowly, I turned and looked Gallagher in the eye, silently challenging him to look away first.

His gaze held mine for several seconds. Then he made a visual inventory of the rest of me, evidently ticking off the parts I did and didn't have on some mental list.

When he was done, Gallagher gave me a quick nod. "Shower," he said, then he glanced at each of his subordinates and gave a brief report. "Nothing of interest."

I stepped into the shower, my face flaming as the other men

snickered. Something landed on the shower floor at my feet and I looked down to find a clear plastic shower kit containing a tiny bottle of shampoo and a small bar of soap.

The razor was notably missing, and I had no intention of lingering long enough to use the little tube of depilatory cream.

I washed as quickly as I could, and when I turned off the water, Gallagher nodded to Clyde, who tossed a threadbare white towel over his shoulder. I had to scurry across the concrete, nude and dripping wet, to catch it before it hit the filthy floor.

The radio clipped to Gallagher's waistband buzzed as I wrapped the towel around myself. When I reached for my clothes, he paused with the radio in hand and shook his head. "No personal clothing." He nodded to Clyde again, who knelt to pull a wad of gray fabric from the same box that had produced the ratty towel. Clyde tossed the garment over his shoulder, and I caught it with one hand, holding my towel closed with the other.

"What?" Gallagher said into his radio as I shook the material out and held it up.

"The crate's ready," a voice said through the static.

"Be right there." He clipped the radio to his belt again and eyed me expectantly. "Let's go."

I held the dress up for him to see. "This is it?" Uniform C had turned out to be a very thin, very short gray peasant dress, sleeveless and gathered at the waist. It was better than the werewolf girl's tube top and bikini bottom, but not by much.

He frowned at Clyde. "Give her the rest of it."

Clyde dipped back into his box for a much smaller wad of material, and a second later I caught a pair of white cotton underwear, tangled around a cotton bra with no wires. They were clean, and approximately the right size, but worn thin.

"These are used."

"Uniforms are community property," Clyde said without turning. "You get whatever's clean, and if you're lucky, it'll fit."

Clenching my jaw so hard my whole face ached, I stepped into the underwear without taking off the towel, then turned away from them to put the bra on and pull the thin dress over my head. When I was clothed, Gallagher nodded to his men.

They turned as I was wringing water from my hair with the towel.

"Much better." Clyde eyed the dress and my dripping hair, but I didn't understand what he meant until I glanced in the mirror behind him.

I looked like a peasant from the Renaissance Fair. Or a servant from a fairy tale—a child's story, not an actual tale of the *fae*. I certainly didn't look like I hailed from a world of cell phones, high-speed internet, and mass-produced blue jeans. And that, of course, was the point.

The uniforms, like the cages, were a visual demarcation between humanity and everything else. A symbol of the gulf imposed between us, which they probably considered especially important in my case, because I had no features to identify me as other than human.

Less than human, according to the satisfied glint in Clyde's eyes.

"Use the toilet. You won't get another chance for a while." Gallagher's focus shifted to Clyde as he backed toward the door. "Watch her while I check her wagon."

When he was gone, I stepped into one of the stalls, but Clyde's hand stopped the door when I tried to close it. He and Freddie watched, tranquilizer rifles held ready, as I urinated.

Maybe I should have been relieved that they didn't make me squat in a box of litter.

NALAH

The centaurs were snoring again. Every few minutes, one of them snorted like a horse in a stable, and the sound was like a knife ripping through the fragile fabric of the young *ifrit*'s slumber.

Nalah pushed a heavy braid over her shoulder. Light from the waxing moon shone on crimson strands threaded with so many shades of gold and orange that her hair seemed to shift and jump like live flames. No human ever had hair of such colors, nor copper eyes ringed in bronze that flashed like sparks from a bonfire.

By most accounts Nalah was one of the most beautiful *ifrits* ever born into the *djinn* peasant class, and she could never, even for a second, be mistaken for human.

On her left, Adira groaned and rolled over on her own blanket. "I can't sleep," she moaned, blinking wide blue eyes at Nalah in the dark. "The beasts reek, and it's too hot to move."

"Apologies, Princess," Nalah murmured in the soothing tone she'd mastered as a child. There was nothing she could do about the beasts, and even less she could do about the heat, but she *was* sorry for it. She understood that being caged with her was both a blessing and a curse for Adira.

Nalah was a loyal companion and an even better attendant— she was well-trained in both arts—but the heat an *ifrit* radiated by nature contributed nothing to the princess's physical comfort

in the summer. Not that there was much comfort to be found in the menagerie, where royalty and mongrels were treated with equal contempt. "Let me fix your bed, then I will brush your hair. That always helps you sleep."

Adira crawled off her blanket and tucked her knees to her chest in the farthest corner of their small cage. There wasn't much room in which to move, but Nalah made do, as she had for the entire year they'd been captives of Rudolph Metzger and his prison on wheels. In seconds, she'd refolded Adira's blanket into as thick a pad as she could manage. When the princess curled up on the makeshift pallet, moonlight shining on her pale skin and gossamer hair, Nalah folded her own blanket into a pillow and slid it beneath the princess's head.

Nalah scooted to the far side of their cage, so that any breeze that rolled through would hit Adira first, unimpeded. Then she began to run her fingers through the princess's long silvery hair, gently untangling it by hand, since they had no comb or brush, nor any other luxury, save each other's company. As she worked, Nalah hummed a traditional lullaby, one of a dozen she'd mastered by age eight, though the language and the legend it told were not her own.

"I miss the water. Do you remember the pools and fountains at home?" Adira whispered, and the wistful crack in her voice broke her companion's heart.

"I remember them fondly," Nalah said, though Adira's home was not her home. Adira's fountains were not her fountains. Adira's people were not her people.

"The water was so clean. So clear. So cold." She shifted on the makeshift pillow and moonlight glittered in her hair like sunshine on a shallow stream. "I'd give my kingdom for a fucking *glass* of water, much less a fountain."

Her kingdom.

Adira actually had a kingdom. She would have had two, if not for the menagerie. If not for imprisonment, and poverty,

and long absence from the world of shimmering lakes and fountains she was born into.

Nalah let memories take her as her fingers combed through the princess's hair out of ingrained habit, yet what she remembered was not the glittering fountains and cool pools of Adira's childhood, but the roaring flames and cozy hearth fires of her own. Roasted meat, straight off the spit. Grilled fruit and charred marshmallows on sticks. Hot, thick vegetable stews and warm teas sweetened with honey. The remembered taste of sizzling hog fat and seared tomatoes took her back to the feasts of her youth, and memories might have become sweet, warm dreams if not for the unexpected light bobbing in the night a hundred feet away.

The *ifrit's* fingers paused. Her copper eyes narrowed, trying to focus on a face in the dark, but it was the outline of his form and a familiar gait that finally brought recognition. Those, and the silhouette of the cap on his head.

"Gallagher!" Nalah gasped. Her hand flew immediately to her mouth, as if she could stuff the word back inside, but it was far too late for that.

"Ow!" Adira clutched her head, and Nalah was humiliated to realize her clumsy fingers had pulled out several strands of her companion's hair.

"Apologies, Princess," she breathed, but Gallagher had heard, and he was headed their way.

"You two should be asleep," the handler growled, tugging the bill of his cap lower on his forehead. Something clicked near his hand, and the flashlight was extinguished, momentarily blinding the girls with the sudden darkness.

Adira rose, propped on one thin arm. "You try sleeping in a cage surrounded by livestock."

"I've slept under much worse conditions," he said, and Nalah flushed at the scorn in his tone. She dreaded his disapproval, even when it was not aimed at her.

"How close are we?" Adira demanded when his censure floated right over her head.

"Close." He spoke so softly Nalah had to strain to hear him. "We've hit a delay, but we're still close."

The princess huffed impatiently. "What kind of delay?"

"The kind that's none of your business."

"You're being paid. Everything you do is my business."

The handler stepped closer to the cage and his voice became a fierce rumble. "I haven't been paid yet, *Princess.*"

Adira made an angry sound deep in her throat. When she began to braid her own hair, pointedly ignoring him, Gallagher's gaze fell on Nalah. "Try to get some sleep," he said softly.

The *ifrit*'s heart pounded so hard her dress trembled over her chest with each beat. "My needs are few and insignificant," she assured him, and the dismayed look he gave her burned all the way to her soul.

When the thud of his footsteps faded into the night, Adira laughed. "Your needs are not so insignificant after all," she teased. "Nor are they difficult to fulfill. If you offer yourself, he will have you."

"I couldn't." Nalah's cheeks flushed and the heat emanating from her swelled with humiliation.

"*I* could. Shall I offer you to him?"

"Only if that brings you comfort, Princess."

At her companion's expected reply, Adira gave a satisfied cluck of her tongue, and Nalah's flaming face began to cool. Her fingers found the princess's hair again, and she repaired the braid Adira had botched.

Moments later, the princess sat bolt upright, sniffing the air like a hound on the scent of prey. "Water." Her voice shook with anticipation. "Clean water. I need it, Nalah."

"Of course. Where...?"

"There." Adira pointed into the dark, and a second later the shadows shifted with movement. When the form came closer,

Nalah recognized both the handler—the others called him Wallace—and what he held: a bottle of water. Fresh and unopened.

She rose to her knees and cleared her throat to catch his attention. When he looked her way, Nalah released the shoulder strap holding her thin dress on and let the material fall over her calves on the floor of her cage, highlighted by a pool of moonlight.

The handler came closer, licking his lips as his gaze wandered over her firm bronze flesh. "What does Her Highness require tonight?" His words were sharp with sarcasm, but his willingness to oblige was as obvious as the bulge beneath his zipper.

"Water," the princess said, seated at the back of the cage with her legs neatly folded beneath her. "You may take her, in exchange for the bottle in your hand. Full and unopened," the princess added at the last second. They'd been burned by vague phrasing before.

"Done." The handler fumbled to open the door, then pulled Nalah from the cage as he tossed the water bottle inside. He locked the cage with one hand, the other bruising her arm.

Adira had drained the bottle of water with a satisfied belch before the first ugly grunt echoed from the shadows behind her cage.

DELILAH

Gallagher cuffed my hands in front of me with regular steel cuffs and led me out of the bathroom onto the deserted midway, where he took the tranquilizer rifle from Clyde. "You two turn in her clothes, then hit the sack. I got it from here."

"You sure?" Freddie eyed me while I curled my bare toes on the rough sidewalk.

Gallagher gave him a terse nod.

Freddie took off after Clyde, with the box containing my stuff tucked under his arm.

Gallagher took my arm and marched me toward the rear exit of the fairgrounds.

I looked up at him, but the bill of his hat shielded most of his face from the couple of lampposts we passed beneath. "Aren't you afraid I'll try to liquefy your gray matter?"

"You don't know how. That's as much a problem for me as it is for you."

"Are you sure?" The paved path ended at the open gate. The grass was scratchy but surprisingly cool against the soles of my feet. "I could just be biding my time, waiting for you to get careless."

The huge ring of keys attached to his belt jangled and clanked with every step. "I'm never careless. And if you knew how to turn back into…whatever you are, you would have tried to kill us and escape while you were uncuffed."

"I'm not a killer." No sense denying that I was a flight risk, especially when I spotted a double line of circus cage wagons up ahead. They were great hulking shadows cast into the larger darkness by a line of tall lampposts.

Gallagher made a skeptical sound deep in his throat. "Of course you're a killer. You just lack experience in the field."

"You don't know anything about me."

One dark brow rose in the shadows beneath the bill of his cap. "You're an only child. Labeled 'gifted' in elementary school. High school salutatorian. Undergraduate degree in crypto-biology from Colorado State—on scholarship—then you came back home to handle deposits and withdrawals at the local credit union."

I stopped walking to stare up at him. "How do you know all that? *Why* do you know all that?"

"My job is to break you. The more I know about you, the easier that will be."

My gaze fell and I stared at my bare feet, mentally wading through shock to process not just what he'd said, but the utter lack of emotion with which he'd said it. His job was to break me, and he would do that with no more regret than when he got dressed and brushed his teeth in the morning. Breaking me was just something else on his to-do list.

Yet he was the only one at Metzger's who'd spoken to me like a person.

"Why did you make those other handlers turn around?" I would already be one step closer to broken if he had let Freddie and Clyde watch me shower. Was that kindness just a setup for my inevitable psychological fracture? Show me mercy now, so that later his cruelty would seem all the more cruel?

Gallagher shrugged his massive shoulders. "I don't have to start breaking you until tomorrow."

"And that won't bother you because you think I'm a killer?"

For a second, I thought he'd actually answer. Then Gallagher tugged me forward again.

"I— Ow!" A jagged rock bit into my heel and sent sharp pain up my leg. I hopped on my left foot, reaching to clutch the bruised sole of my right before I remembered my hands were cuffed again.

Gallagher hauled me upright before I could fall over.

"Can I at least get a pair of shoes?"

"I can't issue anything that would help you escape." He took my arm again. I couldn't pull free, so I dragged my feet in silent protest, as well as out of caution. The dark grass suddenly felt like a minefield waiting to cripple me with every step.

For several minutes, I followed him in silence, watching the ground for rocks I probably wouldn't be able to see in the dark anyway. Then an odd equine snort startled me and I looked up to find the double line of circus wagons just a few yards away.

"Home sweet home," Gallagher said, and that fact—the visceral reality of it—hit me like sledgehammer straight to my soul.

My feet stopped moving and my mouth fell open. I inhaled as deeply as I could, but the air tasted foul. Like tyranny and manure.

"This can't be happening." The world teetered around me, and the very ground seemed determined to toss me like an angry bull. I dropped into a squat, knees and back bent, gasping, but no matter how much air I sucked in and spat out, I couldn't get a satisfying breath.

"Delilah. Stand up."

"This isn't real," I gasped, my elbows propped on my knees, hands hanging limp, cuffs and all. "This *can't* be real."

"It is, and making me drag you to your crate won't change that. Stand up."

But I could hardly hear him over the roar of oblivion devouring everything I'd ever had or been, leaving only an empty shell of me tethered to my brutal new reality by cuffs and chains.

"I'm having a nightmare," I murmured. But that wasn't quite right.

I was *living* a nightmare.

Gallagher squatted next to me and tilted my face up until I saw his gray eyes, finally illuminated in the beam from a light pole. "A cage locks other people out as much as it locks you in, and sometimes that's for the best."

"You're locking me up to protect me? You really expect me to believe that?"

"I'm locking you up to protect everyone. Where you live is not up to you anymore, but *how* you live is still your choice. I can make things a little easier for you, if you'll make my job easier for me."

Fresh anger flared in the pit of my stomach. I tried to shove him back, but that was like trying to push over a tree with my bare hands. "You're no better than your boss, offering to make me comfortable—for a price."

Gallagher's gaze hardened until his eyes looked like onyx pebbles. "I'm far worse than Ruyle." He grabbed my arm and pulled me upright. His hand tightened around my arm, and when I flinched, he let me go. "But I wasn't propositioning you. Do *not* insult me with that assumption again."

"So then, what were you offering?"

"You help me get you ready for exhibition, and I'll do what I can to make your adjustment less traumatic."

Indignation burned in my veins. I didn't *want* to be exhibition-ready, and there was no way to make any of this less traumatic. They could lock me up, but they couldn't force me to cooperate. Let them sell me—hell, let them kill me. If I'd realized anything since being sold into the menagerie, it was that I had nothing left to lose.

I turned my back on Gallagher without a word and marched toward the circus carts on my own. He caught up in three huge strides, and a few yards later, he pulled me to a stop in front of

an empty steel cage on wheels. It was the last cart on the first of two parallel rows of circus wagons and the only one without a stunning, brightly colored decorative frame—a naked version of all the other cages.

One steel mesh panel had been slid open along its track. The base of the wagon was a custom steel trailer two feet off the ground, and before I could even process the fact that there were no steps, Gallagher lifted me by the waist and set me inside the cage on my knees. The door slid shut behind me with a horrifying clang and I spun around to find him threading a padlock through two metal loops to hold the sliding panel closed.

"Wait!" Panic echoed in my voice. "Please don't do this." My eyes watered, and my throat felt so tight I had to force the words out, because this was my very last chance. "I'm not dangerous."

Why the *fuck* had I let Brandon drag me to the carnival? It was just as depraved a spectacle as I'd imagined, but I'd never expected to become trapped inside it. If I'd insisted on a birthday dinner instead, I'd be curled up next to him in bed, blissfully ignorant of the horror I'd narrowly escaped.

"I don't belong here!"

Gallagher clicked the padlock closed. "You're no different from the rest."

I couldn't argue with that. No one belonged in the menagerie.

"What about these?" I held my hands up and rattled the cuffs.

He flipped a steel peg free from its loop on the outside of my cage, and a small panel in the mesh folded down, low enough that I had to sit to slide my hands through. He pulled a key from his pocket and removed the cuffs. Once I'd retracted my hands, he closed and locked the panel.

And just like that, my world was reduced to a four-by-six cage hardly tall enough for me to stand up in.

I sat with my legs folded beneath me, and the clang of my cage being closed echoing in my head. Gallagher watched me through the steel mesh. I couldn't read his expression—it was shrouded

in shadows—but I heard the jangle of metal as he clipped his key ring to a loop at his waist. "Try to get some sleep. Tomorrow won't be easy."

As if my evening had been a stroll through a moonlit park.

It took every bit of restraint I had to keep from pleading with him again to let me go. That wouldn't work anyway, and I was done with begging.

"Fuck off," I said through clenched teeth.

Gallagher tugged his cap lower on his forehead, then retreated into the dark.

I stared in the direction of his fading steps until I could no longer hear them, then I crawled into one corner of my cage and leaned against the solid aluminum end wall, my knees tucked up to my chest. The diamond-patterned aluminum floor was hard beneath me, and the fresh, shallow claw marks were the only sign of recent occupation by the leopard shifter Ruyle had mentioned.

When my eyes had adjusted to the dim light and shadows, I realized there was a blanket at the opposite end of my cage, half-unfolded from being tossed inside. There was no pillow and no sleeping mat, and I'd been offered neither food nor water. Inmates on death row were treated better.

Of course, inmates on death row had constitutionally guaranteed rights.

I considered the blanket for a few seconds, then I closed my eyes and rested my chin on my knees. It was too hot out to sleep anyway.

"What are you?" The strange voice rumbled softly from the darkness to my left, and my eyes flew open. Two points of light shone from the shadowy depths of the green-and-silver wagon across the aisle from mine.

I stared back at the bright eyes without lifting my chin from my knees.

Metal creaked and the green cage rocked as the weight within

it shifted. A man wearing only a thin pair of gray shorts crawled out of the shadowy side of his cage into the area lit by a nearby light pole. Long lines of tight, lean muscle stood out beneath his skin, and each movement he made was smooth and graceful.

"What are you?" he repeated, the words low-pitched and gravelly.

"I'm a person."

"But not a human, or you wouldn't be here. So what are you, really?" A strand of silver hair fell over his gaunt face, hiding one shining eye.

"I don't know. My name is Delilah."

"Pas plus," he said. "Not anymore. They call me Claudio."

"They call you...?" I frowned, considering his odd phrasing. "Is that not what your mother named you?"

"My mother gave me life, and milk, and silver fur and golden eyes, but no true name, other than Little Gray Pup." Those bright eyes blinked again, studying me even as I studied them. "Claudio is the name on my pedigree. It's all I've ever been called."

Little Gray Pup. Claudio.

All at once, I recognized the wolf heads and fleurs-de-lis carved into his wagon frame. "You're the werewolf," I whispered, curling my fingers through the wire mesh. "The girl is your daughter?"

He nodded. "Geneviève."

On the tail of the name, a soft whine came from the dark cage to his right, and I found two more eyes shining at me. No cage stood across from the pup's. Mine was the last in my row.

"Go back to sleep, Genni," her father whispered, but affection softened his voice. The lights winked out when his daughter closed her eyes and I realized that because of the solid end panels, I could see into her cage from across the aisle, though he could not. But I couldn't tell from those two lights in the dark whether she was in human or canine form.

"Merci." Claudio's words were so soft I almost mistook them for the rustle of cloth from the cage to my right. "For what you did for her. Thank you," he repeated. "I am so very sorry for what it cost you."

I didn't know what to say. His daughter was the reason my life had been ripped from me, but I didn't feel worthy of his gratitude. I'd made no conscious decision to act on Geneviève's behalf. I'd had no idea what I could do, or what I would be sacrificing. I hadn't acted, I'd merely *reacted*.

I was no martyr.

For a long time, I stared at the end panel of my own cage, too overwhelmed to truly focus on anything. I was listening to the snorts and shuffles of the unseen assortment of my fellow exhibits, assuming Claudio had fallen asleep, when his gravelly voice floated toward me again from across the aisle.

"The mystery of your species is a blessing, Delilah." My name sounded foreign and beautiful, graced with his French accent and the lupine depth of his voice. "Do not rush to solve it."

"Why not?" I whispered, as his eyes flashed at me in the dark.

"It costs them less to breed new exhibits than to buy them, but they will not try to breed what they cannot identify."

Horror rolled over me in overlapping waves, and my crate seemed to rock like a boat at sea. Psychosomatic vertigo.

"Is that how you…how you got Geneviève?"

"And the four before her, each sold when they got too big for the petting zoo. She's the only one they've let me keep."

But he'd lost her mother. Grief was thick in his voice, and his pain made me ache deep, deep inside, both for his bleak past and for my own grim future.

Claudio retreated farther into his cage, and the rustle of rough fabric and the creak of metal told me he was curling up on his blanket to reclaim slumber.

DELILAH

I was still wide-awake, the werewolf's horrific warning echoing in my mind, when the sun rose to shine on my new hell. The only improvement morning brought was daylight, and after twenty minutes of starkly illuminated clarity, I decided I preferred the dark.

Daylight made it impossible to miss the filth caked into the seam where the floor of my cage joined the end panels, or the ribs showing through Geneviève's skin, even in wolf form. Or how the cheetah—werecheetah?—in the cage on Claudio's other side was missing several patches of fur, which was how I discovered that in cat form, her skin was patterned just like her fur.

The sun still hung low and heavy on the eastern horizon when the rest of the carnival came to life. The tantalizing scents of bacon and coffee reminded me that I hadn't eaten since dinner the night before.

"Flags up!" a woman's voice shouted.

When I pressed my face against the wire mesh side of my cage, daylight showed me what the night had hidden. A young woman in an apron stood in front of an arrangement of plastic tables and folding metal chairs, setting out salt and pepper shakers.

Behind her, a large man in an apron manned an open-sided food truck, scrambling eggs and flipping bacon.

At the woman's cry, a steady procession of Metzger's employees began meandering past the rows of caged chattel toward

the scent of breakfast. They formed a line—half of them large men in red polo shirts—and filled trays with heaping portions of steaming food. Coffee was poured, knives and forks clanked, and boisterous conversation rose above it all.

"Don't start drooling yet," a raspy female voice said, and I turned to find one of the cheetah shifters—now in human form—watching me from the black-and-silver cage wagon to the right of Claudio's. She was small and delicately built with smooth dark skin and a tiny waist, and she had the most beautiful orange-gold eyes I'd ever seen. According to the plaque wired to her crate, her name was Zyanya. "We don't get bacon and eggs from the pie car. Not for free anyway."

Pie car?

I decided not to ask what "not for free" meant.

"I wasn't expecting them to share." I turned back to watch the buffet line. "But I *had* kind of assumed the staff would live on corn dogs and fried Twinkies. That's what I'd eat if *I* lived in the carnival. Under other circumstances," I added with a glance at the cage floor beneath me.

"What's a Twinkie?"

That time when I turned back to the row of carts across from mine, I found Geneviève watching me with her knees tucked up to her chest, tangled golden hair hiding most of her small body like a curtain.

"Um. It's a little yellow cake filled with cream. When they're deep-fried, the outside gets crunchy, and the middle is all gooey and sweet. I'd pick a fried Twinkie over scrambled eggs any day." But I realized from the puzzled look in her golden wolf eyes that a child raised in a cage had probably never tasted either.

"Junk food comes from the grease carts, which are part of the carnival, not part of the menagerie," another woman's voice called, but her wagon was too far down the line for me to see. "They don't open until the gates open."

"Who's speaking?" I asked, my face pressed to the wire mesh.

"That's Lenore," Zyanya said, running one hand through her short-cropped dark curls. "One of the sirens. Before she was exposed, she used to sing at some county fair in Alabama."

"Mississippi," Lenore corrected. "Then one day I got sloppy, and they pulled me offstage and locked me up."

"You grew up human?" I *really* wished I could see her.

"I grew up *passing* for human," she said. "All it took was a good pair of contact lenses and a little self-control. But nothing good lasts forever, right?" The bitterness in her voice was an eerie echo of my own.

She'd grown up hiding in plain sight, and I'd never known I needed to. Lenore and I were two sides of the same doomed coin.

The staff members ate quickly, and as each stood to return his empty tray, another stepped forward to claim the open seat. Neither Chris Ruyle nor Rudolph Metzger appeared. Neither did Gallagher. Obviously the management took its meals apart from the common rabble.

As crew members passed the line of cage carts on their way back from breakfast, most stopped to stare at me. I could only stare back at them, bitterly aware that twenty-four hours earlier, my life might have made most carnies jealous, but now they looked at me like people look at dogs in the pound. As if I *might* bite, but I'd *definitely* give them fleas.

From bits of overheard conversation, I discovered they were placing bets not just on how long I would last in the carnival after my "free-range raising," but on what my species would turn out to be.

After breakfast, I watched the aproned man and woman clean up the pie car, while a steady procession of performers wandered past my cage on their way onto the fairgrounds to rehearse. Without their costumes, makeup, and equipment, I couldn't match most of them with their acts, but I passed at least half an hour trying to.

Around midmorning, I recognized the heavy clank of horse trailers being opened from farther down the rows of carts, followed by the clomp of hooves first on metal ramps, then on earth. Those were sounds I knew well, having grown up on a farm, and I could tell from the absence of equine snorts and whinnies that the handlers weren't unloading actual horses.

Minutes later, several handlers lead a line of six centaurs by my crate, and I couldn't help but stare.

They were beautiful.

Regal and proud, despite the chains and the drugged glaze of their eyes, the centaurs marched on four strong horse legs with their human shoulders squared and heads held high. The first two were Belgians, thick and powerful, their builds capable of heavy labor—a fact the staff would no doubt exploit. They shared the same dark brown coat, smooth, tan human skin, and stark blond hair, and after a closer glance at their nearly identical square chins and straight noses, I concluded that the first two centaurs were brothers. Or maybe cousins.

After the Belgians came a beautiful white Arabian, who looked almost delicate following the draft horses. She had dark eyes, fine, sculpted features, and long white hair that fell down her back to the juncture of her human and equine halves. Unlike the bare-chested men of her species, she wore an elastic sports bra of the same drab gray as my dress.

I couldn't identify the breeds of the fourth and fifth centaurs, one male, the other female, but the sixth was unlike anything I'd ever seen. He was a hybrid of man and what appeared to be white-tailed deer, based on the distinctive reddish-brown summer coat and white underside of his tail. His human half—well, one-third—was elegantly muscled with a dramatically thick neck, obviously necessary to support the massive six-pointed antlers growing from his otherwise human head.

I couldn't imagine where they kept him. His rack wouldn't fit into a standard horse trailer.

Each pair of centaurs was led by a single handler, and though the men holding the ropes were roughly half the size of the captives they escorted, the centaurs showed no inclination to resist. That was surely due, at least in part, to whatever drug had slowed their steps and glazed their eyes.

I watched the deer-man until he passed out of sight. I'd never studied anything like him in school.

"What is that last one called?" I asked, turning to Claudio, and I was almost ashamed of the interest ringing in my own voice. It was that very curiosity that supported the market for exploitative shows like the menagerie in the first place.

Claudio started to answer, but Zyanya beat him to the punch, blinking orangish cat eyes at me from her cage. "He's a cervuscentaur. The ringmaster says it every night in his spiel. The proper name for the others is actually hippocentaur."

I'd known that much. *Hippo* was the Greek word for *horse*.

On the heels of the centaurs came a line of four satyrs, which—unlike centaurs—walked upright on only one set of furry, hoofed legs. Led by a single handler, they were linked by a chain running through cuffs around their goat legs. My heart ached for them, bound together like slaves, clad only in flimsy loincloths, and my sympathy was compounded when I noticed that their ankles had been rubbed free of fur by the padded leg irons.

The satyrs were much smaller than the centaurs and couldn't carry a pack-load, but I had no doubt they would be used as beasts of burden.

As the satyrs passed, I heard the squeal of unoiled wheels, followed by the light clang of metal, which I recognized from the fold-down panel Gallagher had opened in order to remove my cuffs the night before.

When Claudio perked up in his cage, staring eagerly down the aisle, I realized that our breakfast was being served—absent the scents of coffee and bacon.

While I sat cross-legged in my wheeled pen, a new sound arose so subtly it took me a moment to realize I'd been hearing it for at least thirty seconds.

There was a thudding. A repetitive, earthy thunk, like a hammer striking the ground over and over. The sound came closer and closer, and when Gallagher stepped into sight holding a thick rope, I blinked, surprised.

He adjusted his red cap without even a glance in my direction.

A second later, the minotaur appeared, led by Gallagher's rope, tied around a copper ring piercing his bovine nose. I fell back onto my heels in astonishment. He was huge.

Eryx. I remembered his name from the posters nailed up all over town, and the minotaur was easily reminiscent of the mountain he was named for.

He was at least seven feet tall, and easily half again as wide as Gallagher, from shoulder to shoulder. Eryx stood on two powerful legs, neither fully bovine nor human, but some combination that merged huge hooves and shaggy brown hair with a mostly upright skeletal structure and the heavy musculature necessary to support such a massive creature.

His chest and arms were human, enormously muscled, and deeply tanned from years spent laboring under the sun, clothed in nothing but a much larger version of the satyrs' loincloth. The shaggy brown hair began again on his colossal human shoulders and thickened all the way over a massively muscled neck before growing thinner and shorter over his bovine head. Above and behind a drooping set of cow ears grew a pair of curved, whitish horns so thick at their base that I could hardly have wrapped both hands around them.

I stared with my mouth hanging open, only dimly aware that the thudding was the sound of the minotaur's hooves hitting the ground. I must have made some noise, because Eryx stopped, his long tail stirring dust on the ground. His heavily

lashed, brown-eyed gaze met mine, and I recognized surprise in the widening of his oddly expressive eyes.

His eyes were human.

When the slack in the lead rope tugged on his nose ring, the minotaur snorted and tossed his head.

Gallagher stopped and looked back. "Eryx," he called to the minotaur. But he was looking at me.

The bull-man snorted, then he turned to follow his handler, leaving me to stare after them both.

"He's something, isn't he?"

I jumped, startled by the disembodied voice. Chris Ruyle, the lot supervisor, stepped into sight from the end of my cage. He leaned with one shoulder against the steel frame and I scooted back to put as much space between us as possible.

"One of only three mature male minotaurs in the country. The old man paid a quarter mil for him three years ago, and he costs a fucking fortune to feed. Draws a real crowd, though." Ruyle pulled a stick of gum from his pocket and unwrapped it, then dropped the sliver of paper on the ground. "He's not as tall as a giant, but he weighs more than one. Something about bone density and muscle mass. Guess how much he eats. Go on, guess," he insisted, but I only stared back at him. "That big bastard eats fifteen pounds of high-protein feed a day, just to maintain his size. Fortunately, he pulls his own weight, and then some. No machine built can raise a tent better or faster than a minotaur. Pound for pound, they're stronger than an elephant and easier to control than a giant."

"Fascinating," I said, and though I was actually fascinated, I let nothing but boredom leak into my voice.

"If you think about it, he's the perfect menagerie freak. He works hard, brings in customers, and never talks back. Or at all, for that matter."

"He can't speak?" The question flew out before I could swallow it, in spite of my determination to show no interest.

"Nothing but snorts and *mooooo*s. Which is just as well, considering there's nothing really going on up here." He tapped his own skull, and I refrained from pointing out the irony in the gesture. "His brain is more cow than man. Eryx may be as big as a giant, but he's as simpleminded as a child."

"Children are universally young, not universally stupid," I mumbled.

"Enough about the bull." The supervisor's grin chilled me from the inside out. "Today's your big day."

"Emancipation?" I swiped one arm across my brow. "Whew! That was fast."

"Exhibition. Tonight you get to show the hometown crowd the real you."

My arms tightened around my knees. "I won't perform."

Ruyle stepped so close to the cage that the wire mesh brushed the tip of his nose. His gaze hardened. "You *will* perform, because if you're no use to the menagerie, the old man won't care much if the quality of your care…declines." His gaze held mine long enough to punctuate the less-than-subtle threat, then he glanced over my shoulder when something rattled on the other side of my cage. "Breakfast!" He made a face at whatever was being served behind me. "I'm more of a waffles-and-sausage man, myself, but you know what they say about beggars, right?"

Ruyle wandered away, whistling, and I turned to see Clyde, the mustached handler I'd met the night before, pushing a large stainless steel cart in the aisle between the two rows of cage wagons. He stopped in front of Zyanya and scooped a bloody serving of raw meat onto a plastic tray, then slid it through the fold-down panel in the side of the cheetah-shifter's cage.

Zyanya snatched the tray and set it on the floor of her pen. She growled softly as she ripped into a sloppy cut of raw meat with human hands and teeth that must have been at least part-feline. While I watched her in equal parts disgust and fascination,

Clyde served two more carts in line with my own, then gave small, bloody portions of meat to both Geneviève and her father.

Finally, the handler parked his cart in front of my cage and pulled a clipboard from a slot next to the trays. He ran one finger down a list I couldn't see, then nodded to himself, replaced the clipboard, and pulled one of the last three trays from the stack. "They don't know what you are yet, so you get a little bit of everything."

Clyde pulled a slice of white bread from an open bag and dropped it onto the largest compartment. He dipped a small plastic bowl into a stainless steel tub of water on top of his cart, then set it in the tray compartment designed for a cup. Then he scooped two small chunks of cooked meat from the center tub onto my tray and opened the panel in the side of my cage.

Clyde shoved the tray at me. Water sloshed over the edge of the bowl and soaked into my bread.

I grabbed the tray before it could fall, and my stomach growled in spite of the unappetizing nature of the meal. "What is this?" I poked at a dark blob of meat with one finger, because I hadn't been given any utensils.

Clyde glanced at my tray. "Looks like...turkey kidney. And maybe a chunk of liver."

I gagged and set the tray on the floor of my pen. I'd never been able to stomach organ meat.

"Oh, you're too good for innards?" Clyde slammed the lid on the center serving compartment. "That shit's full of vitamins and packed with calories. You really gonna waste perfectly good meat little Genni over there would be grateful for?"

I glanced past Clyde to see that the werewolf pup—still in human form—had finished her meal and was licking her semi-clawed fingers clean.

"Give it to her." I turned back to the handler. "No reason for it to go to waste."

Clyde looked at me as if I'd lapsed into Greek. "You want to give away your breakfast?"

"Just the meat. She needs it worse than I do anyway." I pushed my meal toward the closed panel, and he shrugged, then opened it. When I slid the tray halfway out, he scooped up the liver and kidney with one hand, then shoved the tray back at me and slammed the panel shut.

The handler crossed the aisle to the pup's crate, and my heart ached when the wolf-girl sat up, her golden-eyed gaze eagerly glued to the meat in his hand.

"Your new neighbor has a gift for you, Genni." Clyde held up the turkey organs, and Geneviève's mouth fell open, her attention still tracking the meat.

The handler's fist closed and he squeezed until dark red bits of turkey oozed between his fingers. When his hand opened, the meat fell to the ground in front of Genni's cage. "Don't forget to thank her," he stage-whispered to the young werewolf. Then he wiped his messy fist on a towel hanging from the cart and pushed the whole thing back down the aisle without even a glance back at me.

Genni's howl followed him.

Her hunger echoed deep within my soul.

ERYX

The minotaur stood in the shade of the brightly striped big top tent, chewing tasteless feed pellets and watching flies crawl on a pile of dung dropped by one of the centaurs when his handler refused to give him a bathroom break. The carnival staff tended to forget that hybrids were as much human as they were beast, but that wasn't the biggest blind spot in humanity's collective psyche.

Eryx had long ago realized that the only true difference between the hybrids and most of their handlers was that the handlers hid their beasts on the inside. A wolf will growl to warn that it's angry and a bull will paw the ground before charging. Rattlesnakes rattle, cats moan and hiss, and hyenas grunt and cackle. But a man will smile right in your face as he drives a knife into your heart.

Such was the nature of humanity, as Eryx understood it.

When the minotaur reached for his feed pail, his chain clanked and he glanced in annoyance at the big iron leash fastened to the cuff above his right hoof.

As he chewed, the groan of metal and the clomp of hooves drew his gaze to the somber procession passing the big top. It took all four satyrs to pull Finola and Lenore in their wheeled cage, though both sirens were more bone than flesh, lately. But the sirens didn't interest him. Neither did the succubi who followed, Zarah and Trista—twisted sisters, from twin birthing

cries to shared cages, customers, and comforts. Nor did the two succubi in the cage behind them, whose names he'd never cared to remember. A pair of centaurs hauled each of their cages, but it was the fourth cart in line—the one pulled by the buck and the Arabian—that captured Eryx's attention.

Rommily.

Her name echoed in his heart and his chest ached when he saw her.

She sat between her sisters, Mirela and Lala, all three on their knees, one colorful skirt flowing into the next on the floor of their cage. Rommily's hair was long and dark, loose curls pulled into looser waves by their own weight, and he knew exactly what those waves would smell like, if he'd been close enough to catch the hot breeze blowing through her crate.

The interactive exhibits were bathed nearly every day. They were groomed, and perfumed, and styled, because they would have personal contact with the customers, the very thought of which made Eryx's fist clench around a handful of feed pellets, grinding them into powder.

He let the pulverized protein slide through his grip into the massive feed pail, then he set the bucket on the ground and bent to drink from the trough filled just for his use, because a minotaur could not easily utilize a cup, bowl, or fountain.

Eryx had never minded the trough, but the other limitations of his bovine features bothered him more with every passing day. Sometimes the inability to speak seemed much crueler a constraint than the chains, harness, and cage that restricted his every movement.

Though the bull's muzzle was not suited to human speech, his eyes and ears functioned perfectly.

When he stood, wiping water from his snout with the back of one thick hand, Rommily and her sisters were gone, headed to the tent where Mirela and Lala would read palms and tell fortunes once the carnival opened. Rommily was no use in-

side the tent since the night they'd found her wandering in the rain, so she stood outside with the talker, one ankle chained to a tent stake, a living advertisement for what customers would find inside.

Even separated from them by a wall of canvas, she was never far from her sisters, a blessing Eryx knew she cherished, even if she could no longer clearly express such thoughts. He could see it in the way she clung to Mirela's hand when they chained her. In the way she whispered frantic, likely impenetrable secrets to Lala as their handler unlocked the cage. Rommily no longer had lucidity, but she still had her sisters.

Eryx had never met another minotaur. He'd never even seen another of his species in person, except for his mother. Though sometimes he could remember her smell and her warmth and the feel of her coarse hair when he awoke from dreams of her, he had no clear mental image of what she looked like. He didn't even know her name.

The minotaur's earliest true memory was of a box, big and rough, with splinters that dug into his fingers and the sharp points of errant nails that slashed at his face when the floor pitched and tossed him into the sides of his confinement.

He'd spent three days in that crate with only a blanket, a few bottles of water he didn't know how to drink from, and a contraption that dispensed feed pellets when he pressed on a big blue button. Sometimes he heard human voices, but more often he heard bleats, and neighs, and whinnies, and even the occasional hiss. Eryx lost control of his bladder on the second day and he was mortified by the accident, but there was no one around to see him hang his head and ram his infant horns against the sides of the box when he could find no other way to express his distress.

When the floor had finally stopped tilting, he'd heard voices and felt the rumble of a truck beneath his box. Then the world had stilled around him, and there'd been a great squeal of nails

being pried loose as one side of the crate was forced open. Daylight had blinded him as a chorus of aahs rang out from around the box. An instant later, small, eager arms had enfolded him. Eryx blinked as the child who'd embraced him dragged him onto a sunlit lawn bedecked with streamers and balloons, scattered with people in lavish clothes eating cake from little glass plates.

Rodney had turned six the day he received Eryx as a birthday present, but already the three-year-old minotaur outweighed him by fifty pounds.

Twenty-five years, eight hundred pounds, and three owners later, Eryx had yet to meet another of his own species or spend more than five minutes at a time unrestrained, but on his good days, he could almost remember little Rodney's last name. On the great days, he remembered the stories Rodney had read to him, and the colorful pictures in his big storybook, and the feel of delicate paper and brittle crayons between fingers that had been as thick and strong as a man's before the bull was five years old.

When the great days came more and more often and the good days began to run one into the next, Eryx had realized that something was changing. He was stronger now. He could feel that with every beat of his massive heart. With every step he took and every breath he drew and every movement of every muscle in his body.

The injections were not working. Not as they had before anyway. The carefully formulated mix of drugs designed to keep the minotaur, centaurs, and satyrs docile enough to be controlled yet strong enough for heavy labor had ceased to be effective on Eryx. Maybe he had grown, and his handlers had failed to compensate with a higher dosage. Or maybe his body had become so accustomed to the chemical cocktail that it no longer affected him as it once had.

The only thing Eryx was sure of was that no one had no-

ticed the clarity of his focus or the increase in his strength, and he had no intention of letting them. As long as his steps were slow and deliberate and his attention seemed labored, no one would look beyond what they expected to see from the carnival's prized beast of burden.

They wouldn't see what was right beneath their noses until it was far, far too late…

DELILAH

The ground beneath my wagon was strewn with fresh hay, and for the first time since I'd been hauled from the back of the Metzger's van in chains, I couldn't smell manure.

"Where are we?" The tent my cage sat in was about fifteen feet across and square. It was dimly lit by several floor lamps with filmy red shades. A folding screen stood near the back wall of the tent beside two round collapsible tables, each holding a neatly folded red-and-purple bundle of cloth. Tablecloths, I assumed. But I couldn't help thinking they'd make great pillows.

If my exhausted estimation could be trusted, I hadn't slept in twenty-eight hours. I'd had nothing to eat but soggy bread in at least fifteen.

"Please tell me this isn't where the succubi…do their thing," I said with a glance at the red lamps.

Gallagher dragged the third and final table toward the two against the rear wall. "This is the fortune-tellers' tent. The oracles work here—two of them anyway—but they won't need to set up for several hours, so we have a little time." Yet the tense line of his jaw told me that wouldn't be long enough for whatever he had planned.

"I have nothing but time. Literally. I have nothing else." I sat on my knees on the aluminum floor of my cart to keep my thin dress from riding up, and the diamond plate pattern bit into my skin.

Gallagher set the table down with a thump, and when he turned, his expression was as featureless as a stone wall and about as yielding. He pulled a cord attached to one canvas panel and the first of the two open flaps fell closed, cutting off most of the sunlight within the tent. When he reached for the second cord, my pulse tripped.

"Don't close that!"

He pulled the cord, and as the last flap fell, the outside world disappeared, leaving me alone with a man more than twice my size, whose job description included the phrase "break Delilah."

He seemed to be looking at me, but I could hardly see him in the dim lamplight. "We have work to do."

"I won't perform."

"All you have to do is sit there and look...beastly."

I scooted forward until nothing but wire mesh and my own resolve stood between us. "Even if I knew how to look beastly— and I don't—I wouldn't play along, and no punishment you can dish out would be worse than putting me on display like an animal." I sucked in a deep breath and pressed my palms against the floor of my cage to keep them from trembling. "Nothing."

Gallagher crossed huge arms over his broad chest, and even though I was seated in my cage, I still had to look up at him. "You're wrong about that."

The truly horrible thing was that I believed him. I'd never been hit or gone hungry. I'd never been electrocuted, robbed, or even really threatened. The worst things that had ever happened to me in my life had happened in the past eighteen hours, and I wasn't naive enough to believe I'd seen the worst the menagerie had to offer reluctant captives.

"But I am a caretaker," Gallagher continued, and I wondered how many of my thoughts he'd been able to read on my face. "My job does not typically include causing pain."

"So, what is your job, exactly?"

"In the menagerie we all have many duties. But in general,

I oversee the handlers and make sure the livestock is clean and healthy enough for work—both manual labor and exhibition. *You* are a special assignment. We need to uncover your species and draw it out for the public to see."

"That doesn't sound very pleasant."

Gallagher shrugged. "I don't think I'll have to hurt you."

His pragmatic address of my biggest fear surprised me. He wasn't making a threat; he was making a prediction. But I couldn't take it seriously. Everything that had happened to me since I'd first entered the hybrid tent had hurt in one way or another.

"And why is that?"

"Because I believe you truly don't know how to become the beast we all saw yesterday, and hurting you won't change that." His delivery was so sensible. He'd ruled out abuse because the time and energy spent causing me pain wouldn't be worth expending if it wasn't justified by the desired result.

I couldn't decide whether that made him more or less preferable to Ruyle, who was clearly willing to hurt me just for sport. Or pleasure.

"So, if torture's off the table, what's the plan?"

Gallagher scruffed his red baseball cap back and forth over his dark close-cropped hair. "If we can figure out what you are, we'll know how to trigger your transformation." He glanced at the watch on his wrist. "We really need to get started."

"Repeating the word *we* isn't going to make me feel like I'm part of some team effort, and neither will playing good cop to Ruyle's bad cop. I'm not going to develop Stockholm syndrome or fall for reverse psychology." I scooted to the back of my cage and sat with my knees tucked up to my chest, my dress pulled down as much as possible to keep me covered. "I'm not going to help you turn me into an exhibit."

Gallagher pulled a chair from beneath one of the tables at the back of the tent and sank into it in front of my cage. The

metal groaned beneath his bulk. "If you don't cooperate for me, the old man will assign you to someone else—probably Ruyle or Clyde—and your new handler will likely take his title a lot more literally than I do."

I shrugged, as if that prospect didn't completely terrify me. All I had left was free will. If I let them take that, I would truly have nothing.

"And if that doesn't work, the old man *will* sell you."

"To Vandekamp. I heard." I spread my arms, taking in the entire carnival full of atrocities. "How much worse could his menagerie possibly be?"

Some new bit of understanding settled behind his gray eyes. "Vandekamp doesn't run a menagerie. He keeps a private collection, and everything in it is for rent." Gallagher leaned closer to the cage, and something in his voice—something bleak and raw—kept me from looking away. "The man deals in exotic fetishes, Delilah. Vandekamp will break you, or he will let someone else pay for the privilege," he said, and every piercing word deepened the gash in my soul. "If you don't know how to access your inner monster, you'll have no hope of defending yourself."

I took deep, slow breaths to calm my roiling stomach. "Are you trying to scare me?"

Gallagher stood and threaded his fingers through the wire mesh between us. His grim stare captured mine. "I'm trying to convince you to unlock your arsenal. Why would you damn yourself to the role of victim when you could be scary enough that even if you *do* spend the rest of your life in a cage, no one would *ever* fuck with you?" His grip rattled the steel mesh and his gaze intensified. "I can see the destructive potential in you, Delilah. You're dangerous, and you could unleash that to your own benefit. Let me help you learn how."

You're dangerous. His words echoed in my head, and they made sense. They felt good.

Too good.

I hadn't yet found his weakness, but he'd found mine.

"Smart," I whispered, without breaking his gaze. "Trying to manipulate me into cooperating so I can protect myself." As if that were working for any of the other "dangerous" exhibits.

Gallagher let go of the cage. "You're going to believe whatever you want."

"Yeah. I am." Finally, he seemed to understand the inalienable certainty that had kept me running on no sleep, under threat of starvation, abuse, and exploitation. "That's one liberty you and this circus of inequity can't take from me." The anger slowly smoldering in my chest flared into true flames. "I can believe whatever I want, and unless you muzzle me, I can say whatever I want, and even if you cut out my tongue, I'll write whatever I want on the floor of my cage, in my own blood." I rose onto my knees and gripped the side of my cage. I was high on the truth, and on my own embattled nerve.

"If you cut off my hands, I'll write with my feet, and if you cut off my feet, I'll write with my nose, and if you cut that off, you may as well cut my whole head off, because no matter how you slice and dice me, you can't control what I think, or what I feel. You can keep me locked up for the rest of my life, however brief that may be, but you can never, ever own me. So why don't you march out there and tell Ruyle, and tell Metzger, and tell the guy who tacks up the posters, and the woman who sews the costumes, and the men who drive the big trucks that the only thing I have to say to any of you tyrannical bastards is *fuck you* and the circus train you rode in on. Now get the hell out of my face. I'm not going to help you."

I sat with my back against the end of my cage, spine straight, and tucked my feet beneath me. My heart hammered so hard it was all I could hear. I'd practically dared him to throw his worst at me, and I was sure I would regret that as soon as the real pain started. But pain and regret couldn't negate the truth, and I'd needed him to hear it as badly as I'd needed to say it.

Gallagher stared at me for a second, and I couldn't read his expression. He took a single step back and his eyes narrowed. "You're your own worst enemy, Delilah. When you decide to put all that passion into self-preservation, you let me know. But you better decide soon, or you'll lose the chance."

Then he turned and pushed his way through the tent flap, leaving me all alone with my thundering rage.

"Maggie, I need you to pull the medical records of every child born in the month of March 1980 and start making copies. The FBI is sending someone over for them this afternoon. If they're requesting records from every hospital in the country, there's bound to be a run on ink drums. Better stock up now."

—Memo from the Health President and CEO of Mercy General, Oklahoma City, dated September 4, 1986

DELILAH

"What is that?" I asked, eyeing several wet smudges of color smeared on a thin plastic board.

"Special effects makeup." A short woman in jeans and a red Metzger's shirt angled her palette so I could see the paint she was blending with a short pointed palette knife. She had spiky purple-and-blond hair, and nails with tiny saber-toothed cat skulls painted on them.

Surely she was as much a work of art as whatever she'd been painting.

One of the rougher handlers, Clyde, shoved me into a dentist-style reclining chair upholstered with as much duct tape as vinyl. My teeth clacked together when I landed and the upholstery creaked beneath me.

"Alyrose used to work in Hollywood." He pinned me down with one thick hand on my sternum while a skinny teenager with a healed-crooked nose cuffed my wrists to the arms of the chair.

Clyde's thumb strayed south of professional contact, and when I tried to object, he pressed harder, leaning with his weight on my chest until I couldn't breathe. I thrashed, rattling the cuffs. My flailing foot hit the kid trying to cuff my ankles to the chair.

Clyde chuckled. "An hour in here, and no one will know what an uncooperative little freak you are." The last cuff clicked closed around my ankle and he stepped back.

I pulled in a desperate breath. When the world rushed back into focus, I found him watching as I recovered from suffering he'd dealt out as casually as he might slap at a buzzing fly.

He was waiting for my reaction.

I shouldn't have taken the bait, but after no sleep and virtually no food, my restraint—fragile from the start—had been compromised. "Can she disguise what a sadistic asshole you are?"

He pulled his fist back, but he didn't look angry; he looked gleeful.

I squeezed my eyes shut, straining against my restraints. Bracing for the blow.

"Clyde!" Alyrose screeched, and I opened my eyes to find her holding him back with both hands, black paint smeared across his forearm. "I don't have the time or the skill to disguise a broken cheekbone. Get out of here. And take Abraxas with you."

Abraxas—the boy with the crooked nose—shuffled backward to stand near the door.

"She's a troublemaker, Aly," Clyde insisted through clenched teeth, glaring at me.

"So am I." She pointed her palette knife at the exit. "Get out."

Clyde pushed the door open. "I'll be right outside." He shoved Abraxas down the narrow porch steps, then followed him and slammed the door at his back.

"Why am I here?" I tried not to struggle against the cuffs, but just knowing I couldn't get up made me desperate to try.

"You're here so I can bring out your inner monster with the aid of a little cosmetic magic." Alyrose squirted dark paste from a thin tube onto her palette. "It's not a long-term solution, but since only a few people have actually seen your transformation, makeup should work for tonight."

"And if I refuse?"

Her smile looked genuine. "Gallagher says you're too smart for that."

Interesting.

While Alyrose blended colors and mixed translucent pastes and gels, I craned my neck to see as much as I could of her narrow, cluttered camper. Garment racks lined two walls, stuffed with clothes in every imaginable color and texture. High on one wall, a shelf was lined with foam mannequin heads, each wearing a different wig in a rainbow of colors, lengths, and styles.

The mallet lump on the side of my skull throbbed when I rolled my head to the side, noticing a small cluttered folding table. Amid piles of ribbons, buttons, straight pins, hot glue sticks, cloth flowers, and lace sat an open laptop, where Alyrose had obviously been designing a new poster for the carnival.

A surgical stand stood next to my chair, its shallow stainless-steel tray full of makeup sponges and brushes laid out as precisely as any surgeon's tools.

"You really worked in Hollywood?"

She closed a bottle of what looked like black paint. "For a little while. I only worked on one movie, though. *Nightmares from Hell.* Did you see it?"

I shook my head, and my hair snagged on a duct tape patch on the side of the headrest.

Alyrose shrugged and set her palette on a small table near my feet. "It went straight to DVD."

"And now you do makeup for the menagerie?"

"Oh, hon, I do *many* things for Metzger's. Money is tight and time is short, so we're all multitaskers. I design and maintain costumes, create posters, help groom the female exhibits where needed, and maintain a running inventory of all the supplies necessary for all of that."

"Do many of the others fake their transformations?"

She laughed. "No, I mostly cover bruises, brighten pale skin, and lighten dark circles. Sometimes I exaggerate trademark features, to make the exhibits look more exotic, but you're the first chance I've had to work real magic in years. Which was Gallagher's idea, of course."

Eagerness emanated from her voice, and as relieved as I was to have temporarily escaped the demand to "transform," I wasn't thrilled to have become Alyrose's new pet project.

She sat on a chair in front of her laptop. A few mouse strokes later, the poster she'd been working on disappeared, and a startling image replaced it. The face on-screen looked familiar, but bizarre.

My breath froze in my throat when I finally recognized the monster as myself.

My irises were *gone*. My eyes were a milky white, shot through with gray veins branching like tree limbs. More veins branched over the skin around my eyes, so dark they were almost black against cheeks so pale my skin might never have seen the light of day. My hair seemed to float around my head in fine tendrils, but I knew that if she'd had video instead of a still shot, those tendrils would be writhing. I'd heard about it. I'd felt it. But until that moment, I hadn't seen it.

It didn't seem possible. Even staring right at the evidence, I couldn't make myself believe what I was seeing.

"Where did you get that?" My voice was a ghost, so thin it seemed to have no substance.

"YouTube. Hasn't gotten many hits yet, so we should be able to fudge the details a little. I have solid white contacts, but I can't draw veins on them." She spun on her stool to face me, her gaze distant as she thought. "I'd love a few more reference images. Have they figured out what you are yet?"

"No." And I changed my mind nearly every minute about whether or not I wanted to know.

I couldn't turn away from the screen. I looked horrific. Monstrous. "Someone posted this online?" The magnitude of my living nightmare had just exploded.

"Yes, luckily for us." Alyrose rolled her chair toward me, opening an opaque plastic bottle. "We have a strict 'no photography' policy, but it only applies to the exhibits, and you weren't ours yet, so..." She shrugged and squirted pale liquid

onto a makeup sponge. "We'll start with your skin tone. Gallagher promised they'll have you dimly lit, and no one will be closer than three feet from you, so I think I can pull this off, if you cooperate. What do you say?"

I nodded, not because I had no choice, though that was basically true, but because she'd *asked*. Maybe treating me like a person was just her brand of manipulation, but as long as she was playing nice, I would do the same.

The alternative, I knew, would involve Clyde.

For the next hour, while she painted me to look like the monster I could hardly believe I was, I lay in Alyrose's repurposed dental chair under bright lights, trying not to feel grateful for the air-conditioning, and the quiet, and the relative solitude, because those were not things they had any right to deny me in the first place.

When the costume mistress was done with my face, she cleaned her equipment in a bathroom I couldn't see from the chair. I stared through an open doorway at an unmade bed and a portable television sitting on a chair. Alyrose's camper was both home and studio. And transportation. Everything she owned fit into those three rooms.

Twenty-four hours earlier, I might have pitied her, but now her meager assets represented wealth and luxury I could never again attain.

As low as personal possessions ranked on the list of things I'd lost, I couldn't help missing my clothes, and my shoes, and my bed.

I no longer owned anything but thoughts and memories, and with each minute that passed, I volleyed between outrage and grief over my loss.

Alyrose came back, wiping her wet hands on a clean white cloth, and made several more swipes on her computer track pad. The image of my face on her screen was replaced with an image of me from the waist up, facing away from the camera,

my hands raised, as if I were reaching for something. Jack, the handler with the cattle prod, stood between me and Genni's cage, mostly blocked from view by my body and hands.

She pressed a button on her keyboard, and the picture got bigger. Two clicks later, the screen showed only my pixelated right arm and the left side of Jack's face, blessedly blurred beyond recognition. "I can't get much detail from this, but it's the best shot I could find of your hands and arms. On the bright side, no one else will have a more accurate image to compare to the final product."

Alyrose turned from her computer and picked up a narrow, shallow box from the table, then rolled closer to me in her chair. She opened the hinged top of the box and tilted it so I could see several long, thin, sharply pointed pieces of black plastic, textured like finely grained wood. "These are your new fingernails."

"What are they?"

She set the box down and lifted one of the pieces into the light. "They're resin special-effects claws from a haunted house I worked on several years ago. They may be a little big, but we can trim them to fit, and in dim lighting, they should do the trick. But once we get them on, you're not going to be able to use your hands."

I shrugged, which was awkward with my wrists secured to the arms of the chair. "It's not like they let us play cards."

Holding one of the claws and a tube of theatrical glue, Alyrose frowned down at my fingers. "If I uncuff you one wrist at a time, are you going to be a problem?"

I shook my head. I *would* get a chance to escape—the universe owed me that—but one uncuffed hand wasn't going to do it.

Alyrose asked Clyde for the key to my cuffs, but he refused to hand them over on the grounds that I was dangerous and deceitful. She shut him up with the assertion that if I knew how to become a monster, her services wouldn't be required in the first place.

Clyde uncuffed my left hand, but refused to leave the trailer while only three of my four limbs were restrained.

She scowled up at him from her stool. "Why don't you see if Ruyle has approved her wardrobe? I can't get her dressed without her costume."

"I'm not leaving you alone with her."

Alyrose's thin paintbrush clattered onto the surgical tray. "I dress the oracles and sirens all the time with no one but Abraxas here to help, and nothing's ever gone wrong."

"They're trained, and sedated, and predictable, because they know their place. This bitch is dangerous and delusional, and the old man won't let us drug her until we know what she is. You should have seen her last night, trying to bargain with Gallagher, like this is some damn hotel and we're the staff sent to wait on her! She wasted half her breakfast this morning because she thinks she's too good for organ meat, and—"

"I didn't waste it, I tried to donate it. *You* threw it on the ground!"

Clyde flushed. "One more word and I will muzzle you!"

"A muzzle would ruin the makeup," I pointed out, thrilled by the opportunity to strip away his choices.

Suddenly Clyde's broad form loomed over me, backlit by the lights shining down at my chair. His face came closer, stale coffee breath wafting over me, and I was suddenly, absurdly aware that I hadn't brushed my own teeth in almost twenty-four hours. "What part of 'sold to the menagerie' do you not understand?"

His rage fed my reckless euphoria. He couldn't stand having his authority challenged, and that made him easy to manipulate.

I was in chains, but *he* was losing control.

"The legality. The iniquity. The reality." I shrugged again. "I don't understand any of it, really."

"Well, let me help you out with that. You don't decide how food gets distributed." His fists slammed into the arms of the chair, and I flinched as the entire structure shuddered beneath

me. "You eat what you're given or you go hungry. You do what you're told, or you go hungry." He grabbed my arms and lifted me until the cuffs cut into my wrists, and that's when I realized I'd poked the bear a little too hard.

I had the power to piss him off, but not the power to calm him down.

Terror squeezed my eyes shut.

"If that isn't enough to keep you in line, you better get used to this chair, because Alyrose will be covering up your bruises *every damn day*."

"Clyde," Alyrose scolded, while I stared at the back of my own eyelids, trying to stop shaking. I was certain with every passing second that he was about to punch a hole right through my face.

Instead, he drove his fist into my stomach so hard that for a moment, I was aware of nothing but pain.

My body tried to curl around the agony spreading through my midsection, but the cuffs prevented that. Tears filled my eyes, then ran over, and I was left gasping for air I couldn't use.

"Now look at her eye makeup!" Alyrose cried, but I hardly heard her.

I couldn't make sense of this violent new existence, where terms like *justice* had no meaning, *bondage* was a state of existence, and *hell* was the forecast for the rest of my life. One word began to play over and over in my head. It was the most powerful word I'd ever known, yet the most worthless syllable ever to be uttered by someone wearing more chains than actual clothing.

No. No. No. No. No...

I sucked in a breath, then lost it on the tail of a sob that racked my entire body. The physical reality of defiance had come as a shock. It turns out that expecting pain can't really prepare you for it.

"Clyde. That's enough." Alyrose's voice was soft, but firm. "Get the hell out of my camper and go track down her costume."

I couldn't see him with my eyes squeezed shut, but I could

measure his fury by the strength of each puff of breath that hit my face. For several tense seconds, he loomed over me, and I was afraid he'd take another shot.

But finally he stood. My chair rocked with the release of the armrests, but I kept my eyes closed as the camper door squealed open. His footsteps became heavier and more solid against the wooden steps outside.

"Get in there and keep an eye on that cryptid," Clyde said, and when the door slammed shut behind him, I opened my eyes to find Abraxas staring at me, wide-eyed, as if he were afraid to look away even long enough to blink.

I exhaled, and my heart finally stopped trying to beat a hole through my sternum. My entire midsection felt hot and swollen.

"Well, you certainly haven't made a friend out of Clyde." Alyrose picked up her paintbrush and returned to the dark veins she'd been tracing on the back of my left hand.

"Does he have *any* friends?" My voice sounded weak. It still hurt to breathe.

She shrugged. "He's kind of an ass, but he's good at what he does."

What he does?

"Is he the source of the bruises you cover up?"

Alyrose's tiny paintbrush stilled midstroke. "Some, yes." She sat up and rolled her chair toward my head until she could look straight down into my eyes. "Delilah, it's okay to pick your battles. Clyde doesn't forgive or forget easily, and provoking him will only get you hurt."

"So you think I should shut up and do as I'm told?" No surprise there.

"I think that the sooner you accept reality, the easier your life will become."

And that was the problem. As nice as Alyrose was, she was still human, and she still worked for Metzger's, and the bottom line for her and for everyone else employed by the menagerie

was that I wasn't just inhuman, I was *less* than human, therefore unfit for concepts like liberty and justice. The reaping wasn't going to be forgotten anytime soon, and people weren't just angry about it, they were still afraid.

Fear is a powerful, often irrational emotion, and mass fear on the scale of what followed the reaping has the power to shake any society to its core. As long as the world remembered, they would live in fear of all cryptids—regardless of whether or not any individual among us was truly dangerous.

Of course, not everyone supported stripping cryptids of all rights. But the dissenters were few among a dangerous and violent many, and most found it easy enough to simply ignore the problem—the way someone opposed to animal cruelty could still eat meat, I'd been guilty of that very thing myself. I'd abandoned the idea of becoming a crypto-vet because I didn't want to participate in the cruelty. But then I'd just come home and ignored the problem.

Looking at Alyrose and Abraxas, I realized that even some of the menagerie staff seemed to be doing the same thing. They weren't all hurting the captives, but neither were they trying to change anything.

Submission was the only solution they could conceive of to fix my problem. But with the imprint of Clyde's fist still throbbing in my stomach, I was much less interested in fixing a problem than in becoming one.

ROMMILY

The oracle curled her toes, and dirt squished between them. She liked standing up. She liked walking and staring up at the sun, turning her face into the breeze, even if the breeze was hot and dry.

Rommily lifted her arms, letting the wind blow through her hair and caress her fingers and make a whooshing noise in her ears. The crowd around her stilled as patrons watched the girl in the bright skirt, a matching handkerchief tied over the top of her head, her golden-brown gaze fixed on the sky. Adults stared and children pointed at her chains, their only clue—absent the white eyes that accompanied a prophesy—that the oracle dressed as a fortune-teller was a captive of the menagerie rather than a flamboyantly dressed patron.

Rommily could hardly feel the chains. She could hardly see the crowd or smell the popcorn. She didn't hear her handler when he told her to step back, but Kevin was used to her unfocused eyes and wandering steps, so he took her by the shoulders and guided her back into her usual spot against the front of the tent.

Even lost in the labyrinth of her own mind, as she'd been since that night in the rain, she understood that Kevin wasn't truly focused on her. She'd had a bad morning. Rommily had vague memories of screaming, and hands, and a sharp prick in her arm. But she was generally very little trouble for Kevin, and

when neither Ruyle nor Gallagher was watching, his attention tended to wander toward the siren tent across the midway.

The canvas at Rommily's back rustled in the wind, but the stakes had been driven deep and the material was too heavy to truly ripple or flap.

Several feet away, the talker was well into his ballyhoo, the rise and fall of his words designed to pull people into the tent, where they would sit across a small round table from a pretty oracle whose chains were hidden by long skirts and colorful tablecloths. Mirela and Lala would look into the customers' eyes and hold their hands, then deliver some small glimpse into the future.

Your next child will be a girl.

Your boss will recommend you for a promotion.

Your wife will find her lost wedding ring.

The oracles saw much more than they were allowed to say, because revealing that the new baby will have spina bifida, the boss's recommendation will be overruled, and the ring will be found in the neighbor's bed would have a discouraging effect on the cash flow.

Rommily used to sit in one of those chairs and sell incomplete information to people she would never meet again. But the things she saw now could not be sold, even if there'd been no fracture between her visions and her ability to express them.

A small boy stopped in front of her and reached for the chain stretched between her feet. His father pulled him away, then met Rommily's suddenly white-eyed gaze.

Her eyes narrowed. "Blood poisoning," she whispered. "Bacteremia."

The man picked up his child and hurried away from the fortune-tellers' tent.

"Hush, Rommily," her handler said into her ear, tugging on the cuff of one black leather glove. "You'll drive away the cus-

tomers." He knew better than to look into her eyes or touch her bare skin.

Rommily heard Kevin, but the sounds falling from his lips meant no more to her than the shuffle of shoes on sawdust, the crackle of a paper hot-dog wrapper, or the excited screams from the Zipper.

She took a step forward, and the chain connecting her ankles left a trail in the dirt. A woman with orange-streaked hair glanced up from her fried pie and met Rommily's eerily blank gaze.

"Pneumonia," the oracle whispered, and Kevin took her by the arm.

A boy with a pimple on his chin tried to snatch a bite of his girlfriend's ice cream cone, and when she pulled it out of reach, the back of her right hand bumped Rommily's bare arm.

"Cancer," the oracle said.

The girl frowned at her. "What?"

"Brain. Left hemisphere. Inoperable. There's nothing we can do. I'm so sorry."

Startled, the girl dropped her ice cream and ran into the crowd, leaving her boyfriend to chase her, but by then, more people were looking at Rommily.

"Fire," she said to a woman wearing jeans a size too small, then Rommily's focus skipped from face to face in the gathering crowd. "Collision. Heart failure. Suicide." She didn't know what all the words meant, but she heard them clearly, as they would one day—decades later, in many cases—be spoken to grieving friends and family members. "Aneurism. Natural causes. Overdose. Cirrhosis. Cardio—"

"That's enough!" Kevin pulled Rommily back against the tent and stepped in front of her to draw her attention from the crowd. For one fleeting instant, he accidentally looked into her strange, blank eyes.

"Multiple gunshot wounds to the torso," she whispered, and her eyes filled with tears.

"I know." His gaze fell to her chin and he dropped her arm. "You've told me."

"Running, and screaming, and blood."

"Rommily..."

"This is the man all tattered and torn, that kissed the maiden all forlorn." She put one finger beneath his chin and pushed up, trying to make him look at her, but Kevin swatted her hand away.

"Ruyle won't be happy if I have to put you back in your cage, and I don't think you will be either."

The oracle's mouth snapped closed, and a tear rolled down her cheek. The talker lured a few bystanders into the fortune-tellers' tent, promising 100 percent accuracy, and the crowd began to flow again.

Rommily was quiet for a while, and Kevin's attention began to roam. People wandered in and out of the tent, buzzing excitedly over Mirela's and Lala's predictions, and the sun continued to sink slowly toward the horizon.

When the wind died down and the sun slid behind the siren's tent, casting Rommily in shadow, she began to fidget with the folds on her skirt and shuffle her bare feet. Something was coming. She could feel it before she saw it, and when the bull rounded a curve in the midway, pulling a cart draped with stained canvas, led by the handler in a red baseball cap, Rommily began to wring her hands.

As the cart passed, its rear wheel bumped over a rut in the path and a seam in the canvas fell open. Half of a pale, black-veined face appeared in the gap, and a single cloudy white eye met the oracle's similar gaze.

A sudden onslaught of images sucked the air from Rommily's lungs and the warmth from her limbs, sending her stumbling into the front of the tent.

"Secret Mary," the oracle said, but the words were too weak to be heard. "Secret Mary!" she shouted, and people turned to stare. Kevin reached for Rommily with one gloved hand, but she pulled away from him, still focused on the canvas-covered cart. "Princess Sara. Jane, and Pip, and Oliver."

The bull stopped pulling, and the cart sat still on the midway while Kevin tried to rein in his charge, and still that white eye stared through the gap in the canvas.

As her handler tugged her into the tent, Rommily's shrill cry echoed into the crowd, and beyond.

"Fate's bastards, every one, and you least among them!"

DELILAH

"The makeup and claws are bad enough." Gluing the claws on had ruined my recent manicure, erasing the only remaining evidence that I'd ever been anything other than an animal in a cage. Only the threat of being placed under Clyde's supervision kept me from ripping the prosthetics from the ends of my fingers and scrubbing my face clean on the hem of my dress.

I'd told myself that cooperation wasn't submission; it was survival. But there was a limit to what I would endure in silence. "I won't wear that, and you can't make me."

"Wrong on both counts." Gallagher closed the tent flap, and that time I was actually relieved to be free of the curious, invasive gazes from carnival staff passing behind the tent in the makeshift alley that served as a supply path during business hours. He hung the black dress on the outside of my cage. But "dress" was a label the costume didn't deserve. It was more like scraps of black satin held together with sequins and a prayer.

"Really?" I propped my hands on my hips, careful of the fake claws, and challenged him with one arched brow. "I guess you could knock me out or sedate me and change my clothes for me, but don't you think the customers would be disappointed to find your shiny new exhibit lying unconscious on the floor of her cage?"

Gallagher's grim scowl was inspiration enough for me to continue.

"Or you could try to wrestle me into that thing the hard way, but Alyrose won't have time to repair any damage done to her masterpiece." I held my painted arms out for emphasis, and the glare from the light mounted on the center pole flashed on the tips of my fake claws. "You really should have made me change before she spent all that time and effort on makeup."

"I would have, if Ruyle had signed off on the costume in time." Gallagher stepped closer to the cage, but the bill of his cap left his face deeply shadowed. "You have to put the costume on, Delilah."

But we both knew the only card he had left to play was the violence card, and for no reason I could understand, he still hadn't laid it on the table.

Maybe his humanity ran more than skin-deep.

"Why are you here, Gallagher?"

"Because this is my job, and I *can't* let you get me fired."

But there was something he wasn't saying. His frame was too tense, his jaw too tight.

Gallagher squared his broad shoulders and cleared his throat. "You are out of options. You have to wear the costume. We all have to do things we hate. That's the nature of life."

"This isn't life, it's captivity. What do you hate doing?"

"I hate seeing you caged."

"Right." I sat on my heels. "You're the one keeping me caged."

"That doesn't mean I like it." He tipped his cap back and I could see his eyes, but I couldn't make sense of the visceral conflict I saw in them.

Conflict of what? Ideologies? Or something more personal? Loyalties?

"I hope you *do* find freedom someday, and I hope you tear some heads off in the process," he continued, holding my gaze so that I could see the raw candor in his, along with the risk he

took with every word he spoke. "But I won't be the one who lets that happen. I *can't* be the one."

His voice had gone tight and deep, as if the words bruised his throat, and there was something new in his eyes when he said them.

"Because you can't lose this job."

"That's right." His hand settled onto the black satin still hanging from the side of my cage. "Which is why you have to put on this costume."

"I'm not even sure *how* to do that." I studied the scraps of black cloth hanging against the side of my cage, searching for some structure I understood. A skirt. A bodice. A waistline. I saw none of that. "If the audience isn't supposed to see bruises, this thing's going to be a problem."

"Bruises?" Gallagher's brows furrowed, and I realized I should have opened my argument with that.

"Just one, really." I closed my eyes so I wouldn't have to see him look as I lifted the hem of my dress to reveal the dark purple blotch on my stomach.

"Son of a bitch," he growled.

I dropped my hem and opened my eyes to find him scruffing his cap over his hair.

"Clyde?"

I nodded. "Does this mean my exhibit is canceled?" Had I gained a reprieve *and* gotten Clyde in trouble?

But Gallagher shook his head. "We can't cancel your debut. I'll have to find you something more modest to wear."

Modest sounded promising.

He scowled at the skimpy black costume. "I could borrow something, but the oracles wear too much, the sirens too little. Alyrose will know what to do." His scowl deepened as he glanced at his watch. "Sit tight."

"As opposed to prancing down the midway?" I said as he

pulled the tent flap back, but he let the canvas fall closed without so much as a smile.

He'd only been gone a few minutes when the tent flap rose again.

"That was fa—" My words tumbled into a tense silence when my gaze fell not on Gallagher, but on Clyde, who was carrying what appeared to be a yard sign, turned away from me.

He laid the sign on a table already piled with boxes and supplies as the canvas fell closed behind him. "Why aren't you dressed?"

"Because my costume won't cover the bruise you left on my stomach." I expected knowledge that his boss was angry to take some of the wind from his sails, but when he only stalked closer to my cage, my confidence wavered. I backed toward the far side of the cart. "Gallagher went to Alyrose for an alternative, but he'll be back any minute. Any second," I amended with a closer look at his face.

Spite rode his features like violence rides a bullet.

"Well, no matter what you'll be wearing, you'll have to come out of that thing first." Clyde eyed the gray dress I still wore. "Why don't we surprise him and take care of that?" He shrugged, faking amiability while my pulse rushed so fast I felt dizzy. "One less thing on his to-do list."

"No," I said, but Clyde was already headed for the table by the closed tent entrance.

He reached for something behind a box on the table and lifted a long black stick with a forked tip and a red handle. An electric stock prod. Perhaps the very instrument of torture that had landed me in captivity in the first place.

A jolt of fear lit my lungs on fire until I realized the real problem was that I'd stopped breathing.

Clyde carried the prod toward me like a sword. "I'm going to open your cage, and you're going to get out slowly and handcuff yourself to the side. Then I'm going to cuff your other hand, and

if you so much as twitch, I will shove this stock prod somewhere where the welt won't show." He flicked the costume with one finger. "No matter what Gallagher brings back, it won't cover much, so my choices are pretty limited."

Air slid in and out of my lungs so fast it couldn't have been much use to the respiratory process.

"Calm down. You'll be fine if you cooperate. Ready?" Clyde pulled a key chain from a clip on his belt. He opened the lock on my cage, then slid the panel back with a metallic clatter. Cattle prod held ready, he tossed a set of handcuffs through the opening at me. "Put that around your right wrist."

"It'll mess up the makeup," I said with as much confidence as I could manage.

"Not if you're careful."

I studied him for a second, looking for any sign that he might hesitate to electrocute me, and when I found none, I clenched my jaw and clicked the metal loop around my right wrist, careful not to damage the prosthetic claws. Clyde was right. The theatrical makeup wouldn't rub off without some serious pressure, and if either of us had to put pressure on my bound arms, I'd have bigger problems than damaged makeup.

"Now crawl out of there and fasten the other cuff through the wire mesh."

Hay crunched beneath my feet, poking at my bare soles. My left hand shook as I secured my right to the front of the cage, but it shook even harder when Clyde slapped half of a second set of cuffs around my left wrist. I resisted instinctively when he tried to pull my arm back, but when he threatened my thigh with the cattle prod, I gave in, biting my lip to hold back the protest poised behind it.

This was payback. The bastard wanted to see my fear, and I would have swallowed my own tongue to hide it from him.

Still wielding the prod, he cuffed my ankles to opposite wheels of the cart, which was only possible because the leg

irons were separated by a fifteen-inch length of chain, designed to let prisoners walk.

And just like that, I was bound, spread eagle, to the front of my cage.

Clyde laid the cattle prod on the ground and went back to the table, where he picked up a large pair of scissors.

"Wait. You don't have to do that. Just uncuff me and I'll put the costume on. I swear." I was well beyond caring if it messed up the fake claws or showed off a bruise. Gallagher's threat had been accurate—life with Clyde as my handler would *truly* be hell.

"Shut up and hold still." He knelt in front of me and began slicing up the left side of my thin linen dress.

Fear thickened my tongue. "Won't Alyrose be mad about the damage?"

"Nah." The blade was cold against my hip as it sliced through first the dress, then the side of my underwear. "We got a couple hundred of these, and shit happens, ya know?"

I felt sick thinking of how often "shit" probably happened in the menagerie.

"I bet you had a real nice childhood, didn't you? Good schools? Birthday parties. Vacations. Right?"

My nausea swelled with the realization that Clyde's barbaric lesson actually had a point. And that it was starting to sink in.

I wasn't immune to the realities of life in captivity. The fact that I could read and add and navigate a map didn't make me the exception; it made me an object lesson. A target for all the handlers who'd grown up with fewer advantages than I'd had and who now had the opportunity and determination to prove themselves my betters.

Material fell away from my skin and I closed my eyes. Clyde's scissors cut through the side of my bra. He stood and looked down into my eyes.

"Did you go swimming and skating with your human friends? Let human boys touch you? You let all those boys think they

had something good and clean, didn't you? Something sweet and soft?" He severed both the shoulder of my dress and the strap of my bra in the same cut.

The soft snip made me flinch, but I clenched my jaw, determined not to give him the reaction he was after.

"I bet you never told them you were a dirty animal. A monster wearing a girl's face. What would they have said if they'd known? How do you think they feel now that everyone knows what you are?"

My resolve faltered when he stepped back to look at me, half-covered in flayed linen. In that moment, I understood that the menagerie was filled with two sorts of people. Those who felt that the inhumane treatment of cryptids was unfair, but needed the work. And those who were attracted to jobs like Clyde's because the position of authority came with a socially acceptable outlet for the true evil that burned within them.

I blinked away tears. Wars were not won from crying.

"Well, we all know where you belong now, no matter what you look like. As soon as you figure that out, your life's gonna get a whole lot easier."

Clyde's barbarically illustrated point came through loud and clear. The only way to avoid being forcibly put in my place was to step into it voluntarily. To give up any claim to humanity and admit that I belonged to Rudolph Metzger, because he'd bought me, and he could do whatever he wanted with me, and no one would stop him because the law wasn't concerned with the well-being of subhuman species. Not even those who'd acquired the prefix less than twenty-four hours before.

The choice wasn't really a choice at all. Fighting them every step of the way could get me killed. But if I submitted, I would die a little every day until they were able to drive my walking corpse like they drove the centaurs and the satyrs. Maybe they'd drug me, once they figured out what I was, but maybe they wouldn't have to.

How much trouble could I possibly be once I'd given up the possibility of ever being free?

Two more snips severed the material over my opposite shoulder, then the other side of my underwear, and scraps of ruined fabric pooled on the straw beneath me.

That linen dress had felt insubstantial when I'd worn it, but hindsight assigned it the strength of armor. I would have done anything to have it back.

Clyde stared. He looked simultaneously ravenous and satisfied. I wanted to cover myself, but the cuffs held me in place, exposed and vulnerable, wearing nothing but the shredded remains of my dignity.

I closed my eyes. The world seemed to be spinning too quickly, and I prayed that it would sling me loose. Dislodge me from this living hell.

Clyde stepped so close I could feel his breath on my face. He brushed hair from my shoulder, and my eyes flew open. "Don't touch me."

He only laughed and my skin crawled while his gaze wandered. "Do you want to know what you're worth?" He slid his fingers into the hair at the base of my skull and pulled my head back, so that I had to look up at him. "Can you guess what the old man paid for you?" The coarse cotton of his uniform shirt grazed my skin.

I held as still as I could. It took most of my concentration to keep my eyes dry, my mouth closed, and my psyche intact.

"Fifteen thousand dollars. Ten for the state of Oklahoma, five made out to the honorable sheriff himself—though that part's off the books. I bet that's less than your car cost, isn't it? Less than a year at your fancy college. If you turn out to be too much trouble, he'll sell you for half that and take the rest out of Gallagher's salary, but none of that reflects what you're really worth. Do you know what you're worth, beast?"

When I didn't answer, Clyde pulled back on my hair until

I couldn't close my mouth. Until my throat was stretched so tight I could hardly breathe. "You are worth *nothing*. No matter what the old man paid for you. No matter how much money you bring in for the menagerie. You will never be worth what it costs to feed and clothe you, no matter how little you eat and wear. Do you under—"

Suddenly he flew backward and his hand was ripped from my hair. I sucked in a startled breath, then lost it entirely when Gallagher spun Clyde around and slammed him into the side of the cage, inches from my left hand.

The boss of livestock pressed his forearm into the smaller man's windpipe, pinning him to the bars. "If you ever hurt her again, I will rip your limbs off and feed each distinct part of your corpse to a different exhibit."

I gaped at him, my heart pounding.

"Back off." Clyde's voice was weak and scratchy from the pressure on his throat. "I was just having a little fun with the uppity bitch."

"She is mine."

"I'm not," I insisted, though every self-preservation instinct I had was telling me to shut up and let them fight it out. "I'm not anyone's."

"Mine," Gallagher repeated, pressing even harder with his forearm. "The old man assigned her to me. I'm the boss of livestock. It's my paycheck on the line, and you will *not* fuck with my paycheck. Got it?"

"Fine," Clyde croaked. "I was just trying to help, but whatever."

Gallagher let him go but refused to back away, so the smaller handler had to sidestep him, rubbing his throat.

"Go see that the centaurs are fed and watered, and make sure Abraxas picks out their hooves before the show."

Clyde stomped toward the closed tent flap, his gait stiff, his

fists clenched. "Ruyle sent over the temporary sign. He'll need a name for her by next week."

"Noted." Gallagher picked up the stock prod, and I couldn't tell whether he intended to confiscate it or find a very special place to store it, so Clyde couldn't forget it next time. "Go."

Clyde left—quickly—and as soon as he was gone, Gallagher turned to me, still holding the stock prod. Anger had dilated his pupils and clenched his jaw, and with one look at him, a fresh bolt of fear shot up the length of my spine.

He dropped the prod on the table and pulled a ring of keys from a clip on his belt, the anger melting from his bearing. "I'm not going to hurt you, Delilah."

Relief washed over me, and it was harder than ever to resist feeling grateful for common decency disguised as gallantry. Gallagher wasn't going above and beyond. He wasn't risking his job for me. He was hardly even doing the decent thing—that would have required setting me free.

But that was very difficult to keep in mind, after what he'd just stopped. Which was why I had to reinforce the idea.

"I'm not yours," I said, still miserably aware that I was completely naked.

He thumbed through the keys. "You're my responsibility."

"That's not the same thing, Gallagher. There's a principle at stake."

His brows rose as he crossed the hay-strewn ground toward me, and his attention never wandered south of my eyes. "I thought your *survival* was at stake. You want me to call Clyde back so I can clarify?"

"Don't be an asshole."

Gallagher stopped several feet away, scowling. "You've grown bold, for a woman chained naked to a cage."

I tried to shrug. "You said you wouldn't hurt me."

"And my word is my honor."

The words echoed in my head. Something about the way he said it—the formal cadence—surprised me.

He unlocked my left wrist, and I dragged my focus back on task. *Escape*. Nothing else was more important. "So, all the keys work on any set of cuffs?"

"I'm going to pretend you didn't ask that." Gallagher stared at my right hand while he unlocked it, and in spite of his proximity and of the fact that he'd seen me naked the night before, he took no liberties.

He plucked my butchered dress from the ground and handed it to me.

I covered myself as best I could, trying to ignore the bits of straw caught in the linen, poking me in sensitive places.

"Are you hurt?" Gallagher knelt at my feet, and I stared down at the top of his red cap.

"Just my pride."

"A flesh wound, then." Metal clicked, and the cuff fell away from my left ankle. "No mortal blow was ever struck through someone's pride."

"Says the man standing fully clothed and untethered."

"Valid point." Gallagher left my right ankle chained to the cart while he retrieved a wad of black cloth from the table. "Put this on."

"I can't, not with the claws." I wiggled the fingers of my left hand while my right carefully clutched ruined linen to my chest. "What is it?"

"It's the best I could do." He slid a sheer, snug black tank top over my head, then over one arm at a time with more professional detachment than I'd seen from the doctor during my last physical.

Gallagher dropped into a squat in front of me and held the matching underwear near my left ankle. "Step through here." I slid my foot through the leg hole of the black bikini bottoms, then had to wait while he unlocked my other foot.

For about fifteen seconds, I was completely unrestrained, and the urge to somehow recognize the occasion was overwhelming. But I wasn't stupid enough to make a bid for freedom in broad daylight, only half-dressed, with a very large handler only inches away. Instead, I stepped through the second opening, and as he perfunctorily slid the material into place, looking to the side to give me as much privacy as possible, I swore to myself that I'd find another, better opportunity to run.

Soon.

"Thanks," I whispered, and saying that one word cost me a good deal of pride. I didn't want to be grateful for a kindness I shouldn't have been dependent upon him for in the first place. Surely that was how Stockholm syndrome began. But I *was* grateful. And it wouldn't hurt to have the goodwill of the man who was the biggest obstacle to my escape.

"Don't thank me, Delilah." He reached past me to slide the side of the cage open. "I'm not doing you a favor, I'm doing my job, and that won't always be pleasant for you." Gallagher lifted me into the wagon and handed me the costume Alyrose had made, without its hanger. "Get dressed. You go live in half an hour."

Live. I couldn't think about that without trembling, so I pushed the inevitable to the back of my mind and tackled the costume, though my concentration was hindered by the fact that I hadn't slept in almost thirty-two hours and had eaten nothing but a soggy slice of bread all day.

If not for the bathroom break in Alyrose's trailer, I would have had even more to worry about.

While I carefully puzzled my way into a configuration of satin and sequins that looked more like a harness than a costume, even over the tank top and bikini bottom, Gallagher moved around the tent, mounting and adjusting lights so that they didn't shine directly on my cage. He didn't offer to help me, in spite of my trouble with the claws. In fact, he hardly even glanced at me.

"Okay, this is as good as it's going to get," I said at last, and Gallagher looked up from the sign he was hammering into the ground in front of my cage.

Something raw and uncensored flashed behind his eyes, but it was gone before I could make sense of it. "Good. I'm almost done here, and I think they're ready for you out back." He gave the sign post one last blow, then set the hammer on the table next to the cattle prod.

"Out back? Is that secret code for something horrible?"

Gallagher crossed to the rear of the tent and knelt to unhook one of the canvas panels from its anchor. "In the menagerie, we don't hide 'horrible' behind code words. We put sequins on 'horrible,' drape ribbons around it, shine lights on it, and charge admission."

He pulled the tent flap back and the growl of heavy machinery crescendoed. Gallagher nodded to someone outside, then familiar, slow footsteps thudded toward us from behind the tent, a dull counterpoint to the incessant calliope music, the rumble of truck engines, and the ceaseless shouting of instructions from carnival employees.

"So, I'm that something horrible?" I sank onto my knees in my cage, already regretting the question. It didn't matter what he thought of me, since he could not be manipulated to benefit my escape.

Gallagher looked like he would answer, but then a shadow fell over the opening in the back of the tent. The minotaur ducked slowly beneath the canvas and his brown-eyed gaze met mine. For just a second, the drug-haze seemed to lift from his eyes as recognition filled them. But then his gaze fogged over again and his focus dropped to the ground in front of my cage.

"Over here, Eryx," Gallagher called. He harnessed the minotaur to the cage, then my cart began to roll toward the opening in the back of the tent.

Outside, daylight made me squint and the heat was like a quilt

draped over me, suffocating me. Tree limbs rocked and bowed in the distance, well behind the fairgrounds, but tents and food trucks blocked the breeze from most of the carnival.

Behind the tent, I found a small truck pulling an open trailer stacked with the disassembled casing of a menagerie wagon—a frame designed to fit over my naked cage. Even I had to admit that the casing was beautiful. The side panels looked like huge hand-carved picture frames. They were red, trimmed with ornate gold edges and corners, and embellishments that curled over the arched facades. The end panels were solid red, with "Metzger's Menagerie" painted in scrolling gold lettering.

Gallagher waved to several men waiting for orders, and two of the thick sweaty roustabouts lifted an ornate frame into place over one side of my cart, their arms bulging with effort. Two more rushed in with electric drills plugged into a generator on the back of the truck and began bolting the frame into place.

When all the facades were attached and my wagon sat low on its wheelbase from the additional weight, a man brought out a set of four matching wooden hubcaps, which were bolted to the front of the functional rubber tires to disguise them.

Just minutes after they'd started, the crew was done, and though I couldn't see any of it from the inside, I knew my cage had been transformed into a vintage-looking circus wagon, like the ones I'd seen the night before, as a carnival patron.

I exhaled, stunned and devastated by that thought. How could that possibly have been less than a day ago?

"Okay, Eryx, take her back in." Gallagher made a gesture toward the darker and slightly cooler interior of my tent, and as the minotaur pulled me into it, I noticed that though the roustabouts had all left, one red-clad handler had stayed behind to retrieve the bull.

When my embellished cage was in position and Eryx was gone, Gallagher closed and refastened the tent flap.

"So, these are my sequins?" I asked. He stood to look at me

and I propped my hands on the glittery hips of my costume. "This new cage is my ribbons and lights, right? Because I'm that something horrible, that Metzger's charges admission to see?"

Gallagher crossed the tent and gripped the steel mesh separating us. "You are only *one* of the horrible things at Metzger's."

I started to argue, even though I could no longer reasonably claim to be normal, but he shook his head. "Most people have something horrible hidden inside. A beast. A secret. A sin. What makes you and the other exhibits different is that your inner monster can't be explained by the laws of physics and biology as we know them. What people don't understand, they fear. What they fear, they lock up, so they can come see whatever scares them behind steel bars or glass walls and call themselves brave. But that only tells you who *they* are, not who you are."

"You're one of them." The accusation in my voice surprised me. I wasn't telling either of us anything new.

"Yeah. I am."

"But you're not afraid of me." I looked right into his eyes, and his gaze stayed glued to mine. "Why don't I scare you, Gallagher?"

His voice was so low it could almost rumble in my bones. "If what scared other people scared me, I wouldn't be very good at my job." He turned and walked out of the tent, leaving me to puzzle through his meaning alone.

GALLAGHER

Gallagher stood just inside the tent, watching the crowd file by behind the red velvet rope. The space was dimly lit and the shadows near the tent wall hid him almost completely. Gallagher had many unusual skills, but his talent for going unnoticed was among those he valued most when the press of the crowd began to drain his patience and sharpen his temper.

Delilah's tent was square, with a red-and-white-striped canvas. It was eight and a half meters across and could easily have held two or three wagon cages plus the crowd, but for her debut, she had the tent all to herself. If they expected her to play ball just one day after being sold to the menagerie, with no training and no time to adjust to her new place in the world, they would have to give her some space. And carefully controlled lighting.

When Ruyle and the boss canvas man had tried to overrule him on the tent issue, Gallagher had stared them down with stony silence. Then he'd backed them down with blatant physical intimidation, and when push came to brutish shove, neither had been willing to openly deny the boss of livestock what he wanted.

Few ever were.

Rudolph Metzger and Delilah Marlow were two of the exceptions. Metzger was old as dirt, and he signed the paychecks, but Delilah…

Gallagher's gaze found the dimly lit cage, where she sat staring at the hay-strewn ground, the very picture of civil disobedience.

Delilah could not be controlled.

Ruyle and the rest of the staff believed she'd been damaged beyond any usefulness as an exhibit by the circumstance of her youth.

What they couldn't understand—what Gallagher himself was only just starting to realize—was that her tireless defiance stemmed as much from nature as from nurture. She could be caged, but she could not be restrained. She could be bought, but she could not be owned.

Despite Metzger's ironclad demand, she could not be broken.

Gallagher studied her from the shadows. She sat with her legs folded beneath her, theatrically made-up hands resting on her knees, where the only direct light shining into her cage glinted off the points of her fake claws. She would not transmute. She would not perform. She would not even look at the viewers who'd paid for the chance to gawk at her.

Delilah negotiated when she was cornered. She cursed at Clyde when he bullied her. She wore wit like armor. Even having known her for only twenty-four hours, he suspected she was one of the strongest people he'd ever met.

Which told Gallagher that he'd made a mistake.

The old man could have her beaten, stripped, starved, isolated, drugged, or whipped, or he could simply turn a blind eye while the least noble among his men came at her in the night, and eventually they might actually crack her mental armor, along with her bones. But that wouldn't be breaking Delilah. That would be psychologically obliterating her and, as Rommily had proved, a mentally shattered menagerie exhibit was no good to anyone.

If Chris Ruyle weren't as dim as a box of busted lightbulbs, he'd see that they were already close to losing little Geneviève, thanks to Jack and his damn cattle prod.

Gallagher's only regret over what had happened to Jack was that he hadn't played a role in the bastard's downfall. That was all Delilah, and he'd loved watching her work.

He craved another glimpse of her potential, not because exposing her beast would save his job, but because he needed to understand her.

Delilah wasn't mindless violence like the adlet, or uncontrollable temper like the ogres. She was destruction given form and purpose. Hers was an elegant savagery—he'd seen that the night before. She hadn't ripped open Jack's flesh or pulled apart his bones, as any of the other beasts would have. Somehow, she'd inspired him to inflict damage upon *himself*.

Her violence was art.

Delilah's incarceration hadn't gone as he'd hoped. He'd thought she would be safe in the menagerie—surely anyone foolish enough to anger a woman who could scramble the human brain like an egg deserved whatever he got. And secretly, he'd hoped to see that very thing.

No one was more surprised than Gallagher to realize that she'd thought she was human. That she had no idea how to call on her beast. And that no matter how strong she was mentally, without access to her cryptid abilities, she was as physically vulnerable in the menagerie as any of the cubs, foals, and hatchlings in the petting zoo.

Despite her strength, she needed him.

Something primal twisted in his chest with that thought. Something alarming and intoxicating. Something fierce and suffocating, and Gallagher wasn't sure whether he should fight its clutch or submit to this strange, powerful grip on his soul.

I am needed.

Gallagher had never been needed. After a lifetime of searching for a purpose—a drive as ingrained in him as the need to breathe—he'd given up hope of ever finding one. His grim

cravings had never served anyone other than himself, but they could, with Delilah. They could *for* Delilah.

Yet many obstacles stood in the way of that possibility.

"What is she, Mommy?" a child's voice said near Gallagher's knee, and he looked down to find a small boy in khaki overalls holding his mother's hand while they both stared across the tent at Delilah in her display wagon.

"Some kind of monster." The mother pointed at the placard Gallagher had hammered into the ground in front of the cage. "That sign says they haven't figured out what kind yet, but that she's very dangerous."

"Is she gonna do something?"

"We've been standing here for ten minutes, and she hasn't moved a muscle," a man said from farther up the line. "I'm mermaid-bound. Who's with me?" His daughters squealed in delight, and Gallagher scowled as half of the crowd followed the young father out of the tent.

As intriguing as it was, Delilah's strength would be her ruin. If he couldn't bring out her beast and convince her to show it off, Metzger would sell her and she would be forever beyond his protection. Beyond his reach.

A young man stepped into the tent and slid into a dark alcove on the other side of the entrance instead of joining the line. His obvious desire to hide caught Gallagher's attention, and the familiarity of the man's features spiked the handler's temper. It took him several seconds to place the face half-hidden by the brim of a black cattleman-style cowboy hat, but then the circumstances fell into place.

The sheriff's station.

Tonight, Deputy Atherton wore civilian clothes.

Gallagher stepped out of the shadows, and three long steps later, he stood in front of the man in the cattleman hat, blocking his view and shielding him from Delilah's line of sight, should

she actually open her eyes. "Out," Gallagher growled, and the deputy frowned up at him.

"Excuse me?"

Gallagher hauled him from the tent by one arm, heedless of the smaller man's spiritless protests, then pulled him behind a bank of blue portable toilets. "Leave now, or I will pop your skull like a balloon."

Atherton took off his hat and stared up at Gallagher. Sudden recognition lit his gaze. "I remember you. You bought her."

"My boss bought her. Yours sold her. We failed her in equal parts."

Atherton looked surprised by the admission. He scuffed one boot in the dirt. "Could I talk to her? Just for a minute? I want to tell her I'm sorry."

An inarticulate threat rumbled from the handler's throat. "If you're still here in two minutes, you'll never speak again."

Atherton put his hat back on, and with it, he seemed to find mettle. "She's not a monster. She doesn't belong here."

Gallagher seized handfuls of the deputy's shirt and pulled him close. Atherton grunted. Stitches popped beneath his armpits.

"You think she doesn't belong here because she looks human?" the handler growled. "Or because you like her? You think deciding that she's the exception to everything you know about cryptids makes you noble, but it only exposes your ignorance. *No one* belongs here. But at least here she's accepted by her own kind."

"Maybe not." Still in the handler's grip, Atherton clumsily pulled a folded piece of paper from his back pocket and held it out.

Gallagher let him go, then snatched the paper and opened it. It only took him a few seconds to read the printout, but then he read it again. "This can't be right." He read it a third time.

Atherton shrugged. "Sheriff thinks there was a mix-up, so they're gonna run the sample again, but I thought you guys

would wanna see this. I don't know what it would mean for her, if this is accurate, considerin' money's already changed hands…"

"This can't be right," Gallagher repeated, as doubt battered against what had seemed certain moments before. "I *saw* her."

Atherton nodded. "You and more'n a dozen other people."

"Leave," the handler growled.

The deputy blinked, obviously surprised to realize he was still being expelled from the menagerie. "Can I just talk to her for a minute?"

Gallagher advanced on him, wearing the threat of violence as casually as other men wore clothes. "You can walk out on your own, or I can tell the ambulance where to pick you up."

"I'm going." Atherton backed toward the portable toilets, headed for the midway. "Just…take care of her, okay?"

"She will come to no harm on my watch." The handler gave the deputy an unguarded moment of eye contact. "My word is my honor."

When Atherton had gone, Gallagher read the printed report one more time, and his focus lingered on the information in an official-looking box at the bottom, after several paragraphs of explanation.

Subject: Delilah Elizabeth Marlow
Classification: *Homo sapiens sapiens.*

Blood tests on the initial group of one thousand surviving children from last month's massacre have confirmed that in fact, *not one* of them is human. Authorities aren't prepared to say exactly what species these things are, but it is becoming increasingly clear that women who gave birth in March of 1980 in the U.S. went home from the hospital cradling something *other* than their own natural children.

—From the front-page article of the September 20 edition of the
Detroit Daily Journal

DELILAH

"Claudio, are you awake?" I practically had to shout to be heard over the road noise, lying curled up on my right side with my nose inches from the side of my cage. My blanket was too thin to provide any real padding and I'd woken up the day before with bruises on my hips from the floor of my wagon.

"*Oui. Que tu vas bien?*"

"Yeah, I'm fine." But I hadn't really been fine in eight days, twelve hours, and a handful of minutes, if the weak light oozing into the travel trailer through the vent at the top could be trusted. Hunger and exhaustion were chief among my complaints, but the lack of bathroom facilities was a growing concern. "How much longer do you think we'll be stuck in here? I really have to pee."

Claudio scooted closer to the side of his cage. "According to roustabout chatter, this is a nine-hour drive. We must be getting close."

Nine hours in the travel trailer, plus at least three before that, spent sipping from my bowl of murky water while I'd waited to be loaded with the other exhibits. So, twelve hours and counting, with no bathroom break. I could only imagine that the bestiary trailer reeked to high hell, since I was set to bust my personal record.

And possibly rupture my bladder.

But my biggest fear was that drinking dirty water and eating

questionable meat would lead to some kind of bacterial infection. Unlike most of the other captives, I hadn't built up immunities in childhood.

"Papa," a soft voice called from Claudio's right, and I looked up to find Geneviève's golden eyes shining in the shadows. *"Dites-moi une histoire."*

"You need to go to sleep, *chère*," he replied, so softly I could hardly hear him over the road noise. But she would have heard him just fine. Shifters have great hearing.

"She wants a story?" Listening to the werewolves over the past week had brought back a lot of the French I'd learned in school.

"Oui," he said. "But she needs to sleep."

"Maybe a story would help her sleep. I know lots of stories."

Genni sat up, and I heard a high-pitched whine, which I interpreted as the lupine version of *"Pleeeeease,* Papa!"

Finally, Claudio nodded, and the pup settled in. "Have you heard about Hansel and Gretel?" I asked, practically shouting over the highway noise.

She shook her head, and Claudio chuckled. "She can hear you better than you hear her. You don't have to shout."

I nodded, then launched into the story about a girl who saved her brother from being eaten alive by a cannibalistic witch, and only halfway through did I realize Genni might miss the "girl power" message entirely, disguised as it was in action and gore. But when I finished, she curled up in the far corner of her cage and made a contented sound, deep in her throat.

Minutes later, she was asleep.

"Did you hear where we're going?" I asked, as Claudio's golden eyes shone at me in the gloom. Most of the handlers had stopped talking around me, since Ruyle had told them to quit arming me with information.

"Tomorrow's our first night in Texas." Claudio's blanket rustled. "Where is Texas?"

His question surprised me. "Have you ever seen a map of the U.S.?"

"I once saw one painted on the side of a ticket booth."

"At the bottom of the map, in the center." Claudio was smart, but he'd never been to school. He'd been born in a carnival near Avignon and sold to Metzger's as a teenager, and though he spoke fluent French and English, he could read neither language. "Texas is about the same size as France, but it's a lot dryer, and there's lots of open space. There are places in the western half where you can drive for hours without passing a single town." Which might explain our nine-hour ordeal.

Claudio nodded, taking it all in. "And where did we acquire you?"

"Oklahoma. That's just north of Texas. A century ago, it was full of buffalo, and horses, and cattle, and until the repeal of the Sanctuary Act, back in the eighties, we had skin walkers. A couple of the more prominent flocks of thunderbirds used to migrate through every fall."

I closed my eyes, trying to picture wide-open skies and magnificent giant birds, rather than the inside of a wide-load trailer, but the scents of hay and livestock were pervasive.

"Metzger's has a thunderbird," Claudio said. "Nashashuk. His mate died a few months ago, and *le vieil homme* is angry because Nashashuk is refusing food. Rommily says he'll die of an overdose of tranquilizer, though, so I suppose starving himself isn't going to work out."

"Rommily. What's her story?" I could see her across the narrow aisle between rows of cages, curled up between her oracle sisters in their long faded skirts. Mirela and Lala were friendly enough. Lala had even offered to trade her mostly unmoldy slice of bread for my nearly cooked hunk of cow liver, an exchange I'd jumped on, even though my exhausted body cried out for protein.

But Rommily...

In the week I'd been incarcerated, I hadn't heard her complete a single coherent sentence.

Claudio sat up on his blanket and blinked at me from across the aisle. "Did she say something to you?"

"Just names."

"What names? People you know?"

I shook my head. "I don't think so." *Secret Mary. Princess Sara.* "She just said several names and called them fate's bastards. It doesn't make any sense."

"*Elle est folle.* Everyone has a limit. An end to what can be endured." Claudio glanced at the end of his cage, beyond which his daughter lay sleeping in a pen of her own, beyond his help when the handlers mistreated her.

"Rommily hit her limit a few months ago," he continued. "Clyde took her to the restroom near the end of the night, and she wasn't back by the time they closed the front gate. They had the whole staff looking for her, then she just came wandering down the midway in the rain, her clothes torn and bloodstained. Most of what she sees now is death, and everything she says comes out broken. The best she can do is...hint. Drop clues."

"Clyde." His name tasted rotten on my tongue, and I couldn't spit it out fast enough. "That bastard!"

Fire flared deep in my stomach and my scalp began to prickle, as if my hair wanted to stand upright, and with a shock, I recognized the symptoms. *Finally,* my inner monster wanted to come out and play.

"Clyde swears he turned around for a second, and she was gone. He says he has no idea what happened to her."

"*He* happened to her," I insisted. Clyde had shattered Rommily, physically and mentally, and maybe that's what he'd had in mind when he'd chained me to the front of my cage. Maybe that's what would have happened, if Gallagher hadn't come in.

Could I be broken that easily?

The tingling in my scalp faded and the flames in my stomach

began to sputter, leaving me hollow and cold inside, and more than a little disappointed. I had no intention of performing in front of an audience, but if I had on-demand access to my beast, I could make sure Clyde got what he deserved. Just like Jack had.

"Clyde did it, and he'll pay for it," I whispered, lying down to stare at the ceiling of my cage. By the time sleep finally came, I was no longer sure whether I was promising Rommily or myself.

"Take off your clothes and slide them through the tray slot."

I didn't recognize the handler shouting orders at me, but I did recognize the hose he held, and I knew exactly what it was for. He'd already blasted it at the adlet, at Zyanya—the most feral of the cat shifters—and at poor little Geneviève, right there in their cages, lined up across from mine on a patch of grass behind the Denton County fairgrounds.

"I'm on hygiene plan A," I insisted, pulling myself to my bare feet with my fingers curled through the wire mesh. "I'm supposed to shower with the sirens, succubi, and oracles." I'd had enough trouble adjusting to group showers with sexual predators. Being hosed down in front of the entire carnival—that was too much to endure. "Ask Alyrose. She'll tell you."

"Today, you're on *my* list." Yet the handler made no effort to actually show me the list clipped to his clipboard. "So either you take your clothes off, or I accomplish your laundry and your shower in one convenient step."

Across the patch of grass, Genni sat shivering in one corner of her cage, even though the late-morning temperature had to be pushing ninety-five. She wasn't cold. She was nearly naked, soaked, and traumatized.

In the cage next to her, the drenched cheetah shifter prowled back and forth in feline form, hissing and spitting at anyone who came near. I understood why both the cat and the pup had been denied a proper shower, and the adlet was a no-brainer.

He hadn't left his cage once in the week I'd been with the menagerie. But I was no obvious threat.

"Just go ask her. Or Gallagher. I'm supposed to shower with group A, then head to Alyrose's trailer for makeup."

"You're not going on tonight, which means no shower and no makeup for you. Now take off the dress. You smell."

What? Gallagher hadn't said anything about a change in my schedule, and he would never have okayed a public hose-down.

My temper overtook both fear and logic. My fingers clenched around the mesh. "No."

The handler set his clipboard on the ground and twisted the nozzle on his hose. Water slammed into my chest and punched the air from my lungs, driving me to the far side of my cage.

The blast trailed lower, stealing my breath and pounding the entire width of my body with a thousand needles. I clung to the side of the cage, determined not to curl up and hide. Not to show further weakness. I sucked air in and spit it back out in staccato bursts as the bruising jet pelted my stomach and my legs, then worked its way back up, over my breasts and shoulders. But when the water hit my neck—a thousand tiny fists pummeling my throat—I lost control. I threw my hands up to protect my face and let loose the scream clawing at the inside of my skull.

When the spray stopped, I wiped my face as I lowered my hands, thankful the hose water would disguise my tears.

"Turn around," the handler ordered.

My teeth chattered as I crossed my arms over my thin, soaked dress and refused as civilly as I could manage. "Go fuck yourself."

He shrugged and leaned to the left to nod at someone behind me. Before I could turn to look, a second blast hit the back of my head, throwing me face-first into the wire mesh on the opposite side. Metal bruised my face and I tried to push myself back, but the pressure was too strong. I could only cling to the side of my cage, soaked and gasping, trying not to drown.

Then the first handler turned his hose back on and reality splintered into sharp missiles pelting every inch of me, from every direction. My eyes burned from the chlorine, my throat was raw from screaming, and my skin felt like I'd been rolling in shattered glass.

When the spray finally stopped, I collapsed to the floor of my cage, soaked and gasping, bruised all over from the pressure of the blasts, and just as vulnerable to wandering gazes as if I'd taken off my linen dress, as ordered.

I crawled into one corner of my cage and tucked my knees up to my chest, struggling to control the hitching, but I couldn't stop shaking. I couldn't stop crying. And when I finally calmed down enough to push soaked hair from my face, my right hand came away bloody. My collision with the side of my cage had gashed open my head, just above my hairline.

With a groan, I swiped at my dripping nose and looked up. Peeking through swollen eyelids, I found Clyde watching me, still holding the hose that had blasted me from behind.

By the time the sun hit the apex of its arch, my dress had dried, except where my back was pressed against the end panel of my cage. Hose water had been replaced by a thin sheen of sweat all over my body and my hair was a frizzy mass tangled around my face. My jaw ached from being clenched, and every time I looked up from the floor of my cage, I found someone staring at me as the staff worked to get everything ready for our first stop in Texas.

I'd been watching the parade of tent poles, massive sheets of canvas, and centaurs hauling cages for about an hour when the clanks and rattles of the food cart made my mouth water. I didn't *want* to want the scraps and entrails I'd come to expect from the food cart, but if every meal I'd been served in my week with Metzger's were to be scraped onto a plate, that pile would hardly equal two or three of my pre-captivity meals.

Hunger had become a perpetual state of being. Every time I passed a mirror, my cheekbones appeared sharper and my eyes a little bigger. My face seemed to be shrinking to the shape of my bones, and my knees looked knobbier than ever before.

My heart hurt when I saw Clyde in a stained apron, pushing the food cart between the two rows of cage wagons. Gallagher had never served a meal—the boss of livestock had more important things to do—so I hadn't really expected to see him, but I would have taken anyone other than Clyde.

Anyone.

"Hey, Drea, you all dried out yet?" Clyde stopped the cart in front of my cage, leering at me with one brow arched.

"That's not my name."

"It is now." He pulled a tray from the stack and filled one compartment with a ladle full of what appeared to be dark-meat chicken, swimming in broth so fragrant that saliva gathered in the corners of my mouth. I think I even saw a couple of noodles. "You can thank Gallagher for letting you keep your initial. Who knew he was such a softie?"

"You're all bastards." I tucked my feet beneath me and made myself let go of the wire mesh. "Someday someone's going to balance the scales, and I sure hope I'll be there to see it."

"Is that a prediction? You think you're an oracle now, *Drea*?" He pulled the heel from an otherwise empty bag of bread and dropped it right on top of my chicken soup.

"That's not my name." I couldn't drag my focus from the tray. My stomach cramped and my fingers clenched around handfuls of my dress. I couldn't think about anything but food.

"It's written on your placard. It's on the duty roster in the silver wagon. It's on the top line of the registration packet, all ready to send in and get you officially registered as a live exhibit, belonging to one Mr. Rudolph Metzger. We're still waiting for the blood test to tell us *what* you are, but the question of *who* you are has been answered."

Clyde flipped the latch on the tray slot, and the steel panel fell open. He slid my tray about a third of the way into the cage and I lunged for it, but he jerked it out of reach. "Say your name for me, and this is all yours. Chicken thighs in broth. The very last slice of whole wheat bread. And this fancy spring water. I brought it just for you, still cold from the fridge in my trailer." He pulled a bottle of water from the cargo pocket over his left thigh, and a drop of condensation rolled down the plastic to splat on the grass. "All you have to do is say your name."

My stomach growled. My throat ached and my tongue felt thick and unbearably dry. My fingers curled, as if they already held the tray. But to get fresh food and clean water, I'd have to give up my name—the only connection I still had to my mother.

I said a mental farewell to my lunch, then looked up to meet his expectant gaze. "I am Delilah Marlow."

"Oh, that's too bad, because there's no Delilah on the lunch list." Clyde's eyes narrowed and he shook his head in exaggerated disappointment. "This is for *Drea*." He dumped my lunch onto the ground, then set the empty tray back on the stack.

I blinked away tears and clenched my teeth against the sob building in my throat.

Clyde cracked the water bottle open and took a long swig from it, then screwed the lid back on and dropped the bottle into his pocket.

As he pushed the food cart past my cage, he planted one big black boot in my ruined lunch.

GENEVIÈVE

The pup huddled in one corner of her cage, knees tucked up to her chest, head buried in thin arms folded around her legs. Dirty toes peeked from beneath a curtain of long tangled hair that shone like gold when it was clean, but more often matched the grime the shower hose had managed to cake instead of rinse out.

"What'd the old man say?"

Genni peeked through her hair at the man with the mustache, but squeezed her eyes shut again the second his gaze met hers. Her arms tightened around her legs and her toes curled on the floor of her cage. She made herself as small as she could.

"He told me to make the deal," the tall man said. Genni knew he was the boss and that his name was Ruyle, though she couldn't read the letters sewn on his shirt. But her father secretly called him *l'imbécile grand*, and she thought that suited the tall man much better than his name. "He wants her gone before he gets back next week."

"But their offer's an insult. A werewolf bitch in perfect health is worth twice what they're quoting, and this one's never even been bred."

Geneviève cowered even tighter into her corner.

"Decision's not yours, Clyde," the tall man said.

"We're hardly getting paid as it is, and he just bought that arrogant free-range bitch when everyone knows the menagerie's in trouble," the shorter man grumbled.

Genni peeked above her arm to see his lip twitch, which made his mustache appear to crawl like a caterpillar.

"The equipment is outdated, the harnesses and muzzles are frayed, and if the government passes that new mandate, we'll have to upgrade to medical restraint cages. None of that will get any better if he accepts half what the pup's worth. I'm not taking another pay cut, Ruyle."

"With any luck, neither of us will have to," *l'imbécile grand* snapped. "The old man's looking at whatever we get for Genni as a down payment on a new bitch we can put in with Claudio. This time next year we'll have a cute little werewolf pup to sell, and hopefully another to keep in inventory. You know puppies bring in crowds."

"This one used to," the mustached man agreed.

Genni peeked through her hair again and saw *l'imbécile* shrug. "Yeah, but she's more trouble than she's worth now. We sell her to All American, and she becomes their problem. Let *them* try to breed the feral bitch."

Geneviève whimpered, and the sound of her own fear startled her so badly that she sank her teeth into her forearm until blood filled her mouth. The torn skin hurt, but that was nothing new. Ever since they'd put her in a cage of her own, pain had become a way of life. It was punishment, incentive, and bribe. It was the introduction to and the conclusion of every day. Pain told her to speak. Pain told her to shut up. Pain told her to move, and to be still. Pain was administered more reliably than either food or water, and there was no sure way to avoid it.

"Shit, she's bleeding." *L'imbécile* reached for the keys clipped to his belt, and Geneviève scooted as far from the door as she could, leaving a trail of blood across the floor of her cage.

"Shouldn't be." The man with the mustache frowned. "Werewolf bitches don't go into estrus 'til late November in the northern hemisphere. She's not even fertile right now."

"Someone's been doing his homework." Ruyle sounded impressed. "But that's not it. She bit herself again."

"Damn it!" the mustached man swore. "The electrical burns are bad enough. How are we supposed to tell All American she's in perfect health if she's covered in bite marks?"

"She's been like this since we sold her dam." *L'imbécile* slid the side panel open with a heavy metallic crash, and Geneviève flinched, but had nowhere left to flee.

"The problem isn't that we sold her dam," the mustached man insisted. "The problem is that we let dam and pup spend so long in the same cage. They should have been separated as soon as the pup was weaned. They *would* have been, if I were in charge of the livestock. I was next in line, after Venable."

Geneviève remembered Walter Venable. He'd been an old man with a shaky voice, firm hands, and even firmer opinions. When he'd retired the year before, she'd been sure that Clyde—the man with the mustache—would take his place, but then old man Metzger had hired Gallagher from outside the menagerie.

"You'll be in charge of livestock when the old man *puts* you in charge of livestock." *L'imbécile* reached into the cage for Genni's ankle, but she hissed and swiped at him with short, sharp claws growing from human hands. "Until then, you answer to Gallagher. But he answers to me." When Geneviève tried to tear his hand open again, *l'imbécile* turned back to the man with the mustache. "Give me the hypo."

Genni began to tremble when the man with the mustache slapped a syringe into his boss's palm. She clawed at him and tried to crawl away to avoid the needle, but only managed to tear open the boss's forearm, which made him curse at her in graceless, guttural English syllables.

On his third try, slippery from spilled blood, he grabbed the pup's left ankle and pulled as hard as he could. She slid across the cage toward him, thrashing and clawing at the blood-slick metal floor for purchase, but that was a struggle she had never won.

L'imbécile stabbed Genni in the thigh with the needle, then pressed the plunger, shooting fire into her leg. Geneviève screeched and the cage around her began to ripple and wave like a mirage. Her arms fell into the growing pool of blood. Her head rolled to one side and her eyelids grew insurmountably heavy as *l'imbécile* pulled her closer, widening the thick trail of blood on the floor.

"Muzzle." His voice seemed to distort the word like a funhouse mirror, stretching it thin in places and thickening it in others, but Geneviève knew that was the drugs at work.

The man with the mustache handed him a thick leather chin harness with straps on the sides and small holes in the part that would cover Genni's mouth. *L'imbécile* climbed into the cage to straddle her, staining both the knees of his pants and her grimy bikini bottom with his blood. He fitted the leather piece over her chin and mouth, then the man with the mustache lifted her head so the muzzle could be buckled at the back of her skull.

Genni moaned in protest, fighting the leaden darkness trying to suffocate her.

"Do everything you can while she's out." *L'imbécile* climbed down from the cage and pulled a white cloth from his pocket to press against his torn forearm. "Hose her down again, change her clothes, file her teeth and claws. Spray out this cage, and find out if Alyrose has anything to help heal those burn marks. Maybe a little of the phoenix tears. Then call All American back and renegotiate. You have less than a week to convince them she's domesticated and breedable, and worth more than they're offering."

"*I* have less than a week?" The man with the mustache turned from Geneviève to frown at his boss.

"If you can pull that off and Gallagher can't control that mutinous new monster of his, I'll see that you get his job."

"What about the old man? He likes Gallagher."

"He'll see the light if his boss of livestock costs him fifteen

grand the same month you make a few thousand by selling Genni."

The mustached man's grin smeared across reality as the pup's vision began to lose focus. "Thanks, Ruyle. You won't regret this."

The last thing Geneviève saw before encroaching darkness washed away all sight and sound was the nozzle of a fat, heavy hose aimed right at her.

DELILAH

Hours later, I lay with my newly mildewing blanket draped over me, listening to the centaurs snort and shuffle in their sleep in their custom-height horse trailers. Several cages down from Zyanya, the adlet growled, accompanied by a metallic screeching I could only assume was the raking of his claws against the aluminum floor of his pen. He was an active dreamer.

From even farther down, the berserker snored, a troll grunted in his sleep, and one of the pretty little *djinn* teenagers sang softly to the other in a language I couldn't even identify.

She finished her lullaby around the time Zyanya's brother, Payat, stopped mewling in his sleep, and suddenly the most prominent sounds were crickets chirruping from the empty field behind the fairground and muffled country music coming from one of the trailers in the gravel lot, where all the staff campers were parked.

I closed my eyes, hoping for sleep, even though my dress had never truly dried in the damp heat, but minutes later, footsteps crunched on gravel and my eyes flew open, every muscle in my body suddenly tense and on alert.

My heart pounded against my sternum as those steps drew closer, then stopped several feet away. I rolled over silently and stared into the moonlit aisle between the rows of wagons.

A handler stood in front of Zyanya's cage with his back to me.

He was tall, and typically thick, but I knew from the lack of a cap at the top of his shadow silhouette that it wasn't Gallagher.

"Zy," the handler whispered, softly rattling the side of her cage, and I recognized his voice. It was Wallace, who'd driven the van that had brought me to Metzger's.

"What do you have?" she asked, and he lifted a paper-wrapped bundle. Her head appeared near the mesh wall of her cage, cat eyes flashing from a dark human face, and she sniffed the air. "Pork sausage?"

"Quarter pound, from one of the grease joints," he whispered. "I noticed dinner was a little sparse tonight."

"Dinner's sparse every night." But then she only stared at him through the wire mesh separating them. He shrugged and started to turn toward the other female cat shifter—Mahsa, a melanistic Persian leopard—and Zyanya finally nodded.

When Wallace fumbled for his cage key, I rolled over to face the other direction, newly nauseated by the price Zyanya was paying, yet unavoidably jealous of what she'd bought. Similar scenes had played out several times during my week with the menagerie, and though I wanted to believe myself unsusceptible to such a bribe, the cramping from my empty stomach made me wonder what I might be willing to do after a few more days without food.

Zyanya's cage door squealed as it slid open, and the last thing I heard before I stuck my fingers in my ears and hummed a soft tune to myself was the low-pitched feline growl coming from her brother Payat's cage.

After Wallace had gone and Zyanya had quietly devoured her snack and licked her fingers clean, I realized I'd been hearing a familiar rhythmic thudding for at least a minute before the sound actually sank in. By the time I rolled over, Eryx was only feet from my cage, and though the handler guiding him was drenched in shadows, I recognized the baseball cap in his silhouette.

I sat up, my blanket clutched to my chest.

Gallagher didn't say a word to me. He just moved Eryx into position at the end of my wagon and strapped him up to haul.

The minotaur snorted softly while he was being buckled into the harness, and I got the distinct impression that he was greeting me.

"Shh, Eryx," Gallagher said, blocked from my sight by the end panel of my cage, and I heard him pat the minotaur, probably on the shoulder as I'd seen him do many times in the past few days. "Let's go. Quietly."

"Gallagher?"

When he leaned around the corner of my cage, his focus found my bloody forehead, then skimmed the smelly blanket I still clutched to my chest, and his brows furrowed. He put one finger over his lips, silently ordering me to be quiet, then disappeared around the end of the wagon again.

I leaned against the rear wall of my cart as it rolled across the grass and through a back gate into the fairgrounds. Gallagher led Eryx into the first tent we came to, where, during operating hours, the berserker awed audiences by transforming first into a bear, then into a massive wolf by donning and shedding the necessary pelts.

Gallagher unhooked Eryx from the cart, then led him out onto the midway. Metal clanked as he secured the minotaur's chains to…something, then my handler appeared in the tent again and lowered the open sidewall, leaving us alone in the dark.

"What is this?" I whispered, my heart thumping in my ears. What if I'd misread Gallagher completely? Was he about to show me a quarter pound of pork sausage and offer me a deal?

Something thudded in the dark, and he swore.

"Your phone probably has a flashlight app," I said, when another thud told me he was wandering around lost and blind.

"I don't have a phone." A second later, light flared from the

pole at the center of the small tent, illuminating the blue-and-white-striped dome and sidewalls. Against one wall was a long table draped in a white cloth, on which were arranged samples of the berserker's bear and wolf hides to be felt by spectators waiting in line, along with a collection of photographs of past performances and several framed "fast-fact" cards about the Nordic shifter species.

Gallagher twisted a nob on the center pole, and the light dimmed. He turned to me with his arms crossed over his chest, dark brows bunched low over gray eyes, which seemed to be... assessing.

"Why don't you have a cell phone?" I said, still shielding myself with the stinky blanket.

"I don't need one."

"Because you have no friends and family? Or because they don't want to talk to you? Did you abandon them, too?"

His assessment landed on my face and stayed there. "You look pale."

"I'll have to take your word for that, unless you want to haul my cage past the mirror maze." Hearing the hostility in my voice felt like discovering a beam of steel at the center of my spinal column, and I clung to that hidden strength, the only thing holding me upright at that moment.

"What have you eaten today?"

"Humble pie, my own words, and a little crow." I tugged the blanket higher, afraid that my dress might still be wet enough to see through. "All three taste like shit."

"You're angry," he observed, his focus glued to my eyes, as if he'd just pulled that arcane secret from the mystic depths of my soul.

"And tired, and hungry, and bruised. Does any of that matter?"

"It doesn't affect my job, no." Gallagher shrugged and tilted his head, and in the harsh light from above, his cap looked oddly

faded, as if it'd spent too much time in the sun. "But I don't enjoy seeing you suffer, Delilah."

"Well, then, I know how to make us both happy."

"I can't let you go."

"No, you *won't* let me go." I wanted to stand and pace, but the ceiling of my cage was too low, and because I'd hardly been out of it in two days, my legs were cramped from the lack of exercise. "You can keep lying to yourself about who and what you are, but don't expect me to believe it. You and your fellow handlers, the managers and acrobats and roustabouts and everyone else subsisting on the suffering of others—you're the real monsters."

Gallagher held my gaze.

"You're not going to argue?"

He shrugged broad red-clad shoulders. "Only a fool disputes the truth."

I blinked in surprise. "If you don't like seeing people suffer, then why—"

"I said I don't enjoy seeing *you* suffer."

I exhaled slowly, trying to interpret not just what he'd said, but what he hadn't said. My focus followed him as he crossed the sawdust-strewn ground and knelt to pull a backpack from beneath the table. "Why didn't I go on tonight?"

Gallagher pushed pictures and plaques out of the way and set his bag on the table. "Because Alyrose is running out of expensive supplies, and the time spent making you up to look like what you already are could be better spent on something else." He dug into the bag, then headed toward me with a bottle of water and a handful of protein bars. "The old man gets back in a few days, and if he doesn't see the real you, we're both screwed, Delilah."

"I'm screwed either way." I waved one hand at the cage surrounding me.

He shoved everything he held through the tray slot. The

bottle of water only bounced off the floor of my cage once before I snatched it.

I needed both hands to crack the lid, and when Gallagher's focus found the blanket, slipping beneath pressure from my upper arms, I hesitated with the water halfway to my mouth. "Take it back." I closed the bottle and pressed it against the mesh side of the cage, even though my dry tongue and throbbing head begged me to reconsider. "I don't trade favors for food."

"Favors?" He scowled as understanding surfaced. "I told you not to insult me with such insinuations. I'm not going to molest you. I just realized I don't have anything clean and dry for you to wear. I didn't know you'd be…mildewed."

I stared at him, trying to determine the truth, and finally his expression cracked, and exhaustion leaked out.

"Delilah, drink the water. Eat the food. There's no price. There will never be a price. My word is my honor."

I gave him one more second to reconsider. Then I ripped into the first protein bar with my teeth and ate half of it in one bite. "Why are you doing this?" I asked around a mouthful of peanuts and oats.

"The food is free. Answers aren't." He headed for the loose canvas panel, and I probably would have pressed for more information if I weren't busy stuffing protein bars into my mouth. "I'll be back with some clean clothes and a fresh blanket."

"Thanks," I said, but Gallagher ducked beneath the untethered sidewall without acknowledging me.

I ate all four protein bars in a span of minutes, stopping only to chug from the bottle of water, and when I finished, my jaw ached from chewing so hard and fast. I drained the last drops from the bottle, then turned to gather my trash into a neat pile—and froze when I found the minotaur staring at me.

He stood in front of the sidewall Gallagher had left loose, an enormous chain trailing from his thick bovine ankle beneath the tent wall to whatever our handler had left him tethered to.

Either my crunching had covered the sound of his entry or his chain was too heavy to rattle.

"Eryx?" My heartbeat thumped in my throat and echoed in both ears. The minotaur was nearly a foot taller than the top of my cage, and at least half as wide. For the first time since being conscripted into the menagerie, I was glad to be locked in a pen, even if the bull was drugged out of his mind.

There's never a good time to find out a minotaur has a bone to pick with you.

Eryx blinked, and his gaze held mine. He showed no inclination to ram my cart, or paw the ground, or even snort aggressively.

Fascinated, I scooted closer to the side of my cage, covering myself as best I could with the mildewy blanket. Ruyle had said the minotaur had the intellect of a cow, but his eyes looked human to me, and in my experience, rather than being the windows to the soul, they were the windows to one's thoughts. Which originated in the brain.

"Eryx, do you understand me?"

The minotaur's broad, thick forehead furrowed over his human eyes, and at first he only studied me. Then he nodded slowly, his enormous, curved horns dipping low with the movement, and I wondered if he'd ever nodded before. The gesture looked awkward and unpracticed.

"What are you doing in here?"

He tilted his head to the right, and though that gesture also looked awkward, his meaning was clear.

"Okay. Yes or no questions only. Um, did Gallagher send you in?"

Eryx shook his head.

"Does he know you're here?" I asked, and when he shook his head again, slowly, I wondered how much those massive horns weighed. If the thickness of his neck was any indication, they were quite a burden. "Do you need something?"

He seemed to think about that for a second, then shook his head again.

"Is there something you want to tell me?" I asked, and when he nodded, my pulse raced so fast I got light-headed. It took me a moment to realize that I wasn't about to pass out from exhaustion, hunger, or head trauma. I was exhilarated, like I hadn't been since long before Gallagher threw me into a cage like an animal. I had a mystery. A project. Maybe...a secret.

After a week trapped as much in my own head as in my cage, I finally had something to think about, other than my vague but persistent plans to escape.

"Eryx, does Gallagher know you understand...everything?"

He shook his head, and another little thrill of excitement shot through me. I felt like I suddenly had a secret ally.

"Does anyone know?" I asked, and when he didn't seem to know how to answer, I realized that my question was too broad. "Anyone on the staff?"

Another head shake, and I couldn't stop grinning. "Any of the exhibits?"

Eryx shook his head again, and frowned.

"Okay, what could that mean? Um...someone outside of Metzger's?" I said, and that time when the minotaur nodded, his eyes seemed to be shining. "Family?" He shook his head, so I tried again. "Friend?" But he only shook his head again. "Um...someone you knew before you came here?" He nodded, so I kept going. "A former...um...owner?"

That time when he nodded, I felt like my blood was on *fire*, and it wasn't just that I'd figured out something that Gallagher and Metzger didn't know. It wasn't just that I was now party to what was starting to feel like a triumphant conspiracy. It was the fact that Eryx's secret existed in the first place.

He had something private. Something all his own. Something they hadn't been able to take from him, in spite of the chains, and the drugs, and the forced labor and exploitation. Eryx had

won, even if his victory was small, and his success was due not to his size or strength, but to his wit and his patience. The "dim-witted" beast had outsmarted his human captors, and if he could do it, I could, too. I would just have to be smart about it. Like Eryx.

"So, what did you want to tell me? Am I going to have to guess?"

Eryx shook his head, and that time I could swear he was trying to smile. Carefully, he lowered himself to one knee in the sawdust. I could tell the position wasn't comfortable for him, either because his lower legs were bovine, or because his head, arms, and torso were so massive that it was difficult for him to find balance off his feet. The minotaur slowly turned away from me and reached for the ground with one hand, resting his opposite elbow on his knee for stability. When he began to draw in the sawdust with one thick index finger, I realized I was holding my breath.

I scooted to one end of my cage and craned my neck, trying to see what he was drawing, and after several seconds, I realized he wasn't drawing at all.

"Holy shit, you can write! Which probably means you can read, too." Surely there were other exhibits who could read and write—though the siren Lenore was the only one I'd met so far who wasn't raised in a carnival—but it had never occurred to me that the minotaur might be one of them.

Suddenly I felt like a bigoted asshole.

Eryx nodded without pausing, and when he shuffled to the right to start on the second word, he revealed the first. He'd written *RED* in uneven capital letters.

"Red. Okay." I had to bite my tongue to keep from yelling at him to write faster, damn it! He clearly hadn't had much practice, but I was about to crawl out of my own skin in anticipation and Gallagher could be back at any moment.

Finally Eryx twisted on his knee to look at me, and the sec-

ond word was revealed. *CAP* stood next to *RED*, written in those same shaky capital letters.

"Red cap." I frowned while he watched me expectantly. "Red cap. Whose cap, Eryx? Are you talking about Gallagher's hat?"

He shook his head, but then nodded, and I translated his frustrated contradiction into "no, but yes," a sentiment I'd often expressed with no more clarity, in spite of my fully functional human mouth.

"So, Gallagher's hat, but not his hat." And suddenly I got it. "You're talking about Gallagher himself, aren't you?"

Red cap was a descriptor. Maybe he didn't know how to spell *Gallagher*. Or maybe that would have taken too long.

Eryx nodded, and warmth spread throughout my chest. I was proud of us both, and not miserable for the first time since I'd woken up at the sheriff's station eight days before.

"Okay, so what about Gallagher? You want me to tell him something for you? Why can't you just spell for him?" But the minotaur was already shaking his head. "You don't want me to tell him anything?" Eryx nodded, and I assumed that meant I was correct. "So...you want to tell me something about him?"

That time I was rewarded with a grand, exaggerated head nod, and I realized the minotaur was just as frustrated with my slow comprehension of his words as I was with his pace in writing them.

But before I could guess again, the untethered sidewall rustled and Gallagher called from outside the tent. "Eryx? Where did you—"

The minotaur swiped one huge hand over the words he'd written half a second before Gallagher pushed back the blue striped canvas flap and stepped into the tent with an armload of material.

"Eryx, what the hell are you doing in here?" Gallagher dropped the linen-and-wool bundle on the table, knocking over

several of the berserker's pictures, then scowled at the minotaur, whose horns reached the handler's shoulders, even kneeling.

Eryx blinked up at him, and I realized that for whatever reason, the minotaur was playing dumb. And he was *good* at it.

"Well, get up!" Gallagher snapped. "Don't tell me you're stuck like that. It'd take a crane to lift you."

Eryx pushed himself to his feet slowly and with exaggerated effort, then let Gallagher lead him back outside. When the handler returned, he looked thoroughly perplexed. "What happened?" He plucked a clean dress from the pile on the table and shook it out on his way across the tent.

"I don't know," I lied. But my mental gears were grinding and smoking, trying to figure out what Eryx wanted to tell me about Gallagher, the man who held my safety and well-being in his big, rough hands.

"What was he doing in here?"

I shrugged, still clutching the dirty blanket. "He doesn't talk, remember?"

"A quality I'm starting to appreciate." Gallagher slid a fresh pair of underwear and a cotton bra through the tray slot in my cage. "Why was he on the ground?"

"He fell." I looked right into his eyes, but they narrowed with obvious suspicion.

"You're lying."

"Does that mean I don't get clothes?"

Gallagher huffed and let the dress hang from one finger. "This partnership is starting to feel a little one-sided. I give, and you take. Does that seem fair to you?"

My temper flared and my cheeks burned. "You said there would never be a price."

"I'm not asking you to pay. I'm telling you to learn how to transmute, so I can put you back in the show." He opened the tray slot again and pushed the clean dress inside. "That's not negotiable for either of us, Delilah."

"Don't you mean *Drea?*" I grabbed the dress, clutching the blanket to my chest with my free hand. "You can't change my name."

"I let you keep your initial."

"How magnanimous of you. Turn around," I snapped, and his growl was deep enough to impress a werewolf, but he turned.

I changed into the fresh underwear as quickly as I could. "I'm keeping my name." I pulled the clean dress over my head before he could get mad and decide to take the clothing back. "Is this really the best you could do?" I held out the hem of the new dress to show him that it was too small—more suited to one of the *djinn* girls than to a grown woman.

"You have a strange way of expressing gratitude."

"I'm better with logic, so let me put this 'gratitude' in perspective for you. I appreciate the fact that you've kept me alive, Gallagher, but I am entitled to life. I shouldn't need you to keep me from starving to death, and that's really all you're doing. You're flatlining on the morality EKG, expecting me to praise you as if you'd spiked an actual ethical pulse."

I threaded my fingers through the wire mesh and stood on my knees again, putting myself as close to eye level with him as I could. "I will get out of here. I can either go with you or through you."

His focus volleyed between my eyes, as if he were searching for something. "You're fearless." The pronouncement had the feel of an official ruling.

"Well, one of us should be."

He blinked, betraying a flash of anger. "You think I'm a coward?"

No. He'd taken plenty of risks for me. But at the end of the day, I was still locked in a cage. "I don't know what else to call a man who knows what's right, but refuses to act on it."

Gallagher was like a puzzle put together all wrong. The pieces shouldn't have fit, yet there he stood, made of equal parts com-

promise and rigidity. Compassion and mercenary determination to protect his paycheck.

"Don't mistake patience for cowardice, Delilah," he mumbled, and something grim and foreboding passed behind his eyes.

Anticipation raced through my veins like fire blazing along a trail of accelerant. Patience? I gripped the metal mesh tighter. "What does that mean? You're waiting for something? For what?" And what would he do when he got it?

I stared into his eyes, but the truth—if it was there—was buried too deep for me to see. "What are you doing, Gallagher? Are you planning something?" Or was he stringing me along with hope, to make me cooperate?

"You help me keep my job, and I'll tell you what you want to know."

"Promise? Because I hear your word is your—"

He scowled. "I swear on my life. And my word *is* my honor."

When I found no hint of doubt or hesitation in him, I exhaled. "Fine." I pushed the tray slot open and shoved both the mildewy blanket and my damp clothes onto the ground. "What do you want me to do?"

"Learn to transmute." He began to pace in front of my cage while he spoke. "I've been thinking about the one time it happened, and anger seems to have been the catalyst. But you're angry all the time, and that hasn't helped, so today I did what I could to re-create that kind of intense anger. However..." He shrugged, and the gesture looked all wrong on him. He had too powerful a build for such a casual motion.

"What does that mean? What did you do?"

Gallagher picked up the blanket, shaking sawdust from it. "I got out of the way." He crossed the tent and traded the dirty blanket for the clean one lying on the table.

"Out of the...? You...?" I sat back on my heels as the depth of his betrayal became clear. "You took the day off just to put me at Clyde's mercy. So he would piss me off." My throat felt tight.

"No." Gallagher spoke with such force that his denial could have driven a tent stake into the ground. "I had business in town today, and since I had to be gone, I took the opportunity to let him do what I couldn't." He slid the clean blanket through the tray slot, but I didn't even glance at it.

What he couldn't do. Starve me. Strip me. Humiliate me.

"Why couldn't you—" I hadn't realized how betrayed I felt until my voice cracked in the middle of the question. Even if he was only doing his job—keeping me healthy enough to perform—I'd come to expect decency, if not actual kindness, from Gallagher. "Why couldn't you do it yourself?"

"My reasoning doesn't matter." His stone-gray eyes betrayed nothing.

"He threw out my food and drenched me with a hose in front of God and half of the menagerie. He gashed open my head, then left me to pass out in my cage!"

The iron clench of his jaw was the only hint that my suffering bothered him. "I know."

"You know?" Rage exploded inside me. I shook the wire mesh as hard as I could, but it barely rattled. Of course he knew. He'd expected most of that, which was the reason he'd left me with Clyde in the first place.

His expression was carefully blank as he studied mine. "How do you feel? Any change in vision? Does your hair feel...weightless?"

I jerked back from the side of the cage. He was still trying to turn me into a monster by making me mad. "Stop! It's not going to work!"

His forehead furrowed and he grabbed the metal mesh, his grip just outside of my own, and for the first time since he'd pinned Clyde to my cage, I saw something real—something raw and wild—flash in his eyes. "We're running out of time, Delilah." The urgency in his voice stole my breath. "If you can't perform by next week, they will take you aw—"

Gallagher's mouth snapped shut so quickly I wasn't sure what I'd almost heard. "They'll sell you," he finished. "And I won't be able to protect you."

"Protect me? Is that what you think you're doing?"

His gray eyes widened almost imperceptibly. "That's *all* I've done since you got here. I'm making enemies. I'm disobeying orders. I'm breaking laws, Delilah. All to keep the old man from selling you to a collector who'll ring every dime he can out of you, then let some sick bastard pay for the privilege of finally ending your miserable life."

"Why do you care?"

Gallagher blinked, and whatever I'd seen in his eyes was gone, suddenly concealed by the stone facade he wore as easily as other men wore sunglasses. He let go of the cage and stepped back. "That isn't relevant."

"It is." If I knew I could trust him—that he wasn't just manipulating me into performing to save his job—I might be willing to compromise. "Tell me the truth."

"I've never lied to you."

"Then don't start now. Talk, Gallagher."

He exhaled slowly, then met my gaze from across the tent. "I was wrong when I said you were just like all the other beasts in cages. You're not. You came to the carnival passing for human, and you could have left the same way. The only reason you're not at home in your own bed, wearing your own clothes right now, is that you exposed yourself to help Geneviève."

"I didn't know what I was doing." I shook my head. "I didn't know what it would cost me. I can't take credit—"

"You'd have done it even if you'd known," he insisted, though I kept shaking my head. "That's who you are. I've seen that in a dozen other, smaller ways since you got here. That draws people to you, Delilah. It makes assholes like Clyde want to conquer you, and it makes people like Claudio want to be your friend. It makes me want to keep you safe, even if that costs me things

you can't possibly understand." And he clearly wasn't going to explain those things. "But the only way for either of us to protect you is to make sure you are valuable to the menagerie. You have to do what Metzger wants."

I was starting to concur, but not for reasons he'd like. I'd probably have significantly fewer chances to escape from a private collection than I would from the menagerie, where I was routinely removed from my cage and my handlers were often distracted by other duties.

"Gallagher, I don't know how. It's only happened that once, when Jack was hurting Genni."

"I'm still trying to figure that out." Gallagher stared down at me, frustration written in every line on his face. "Why is your transformation linked to the torture of a werewolf pup you'd never even met a few days ago?"

I had no answer. What did Genni have to do with—

"Maybe it isn't." I sat straighter as a fresh memory fell into place. "I felt it coming on in the travel trailer yesterday, but no one was being hurt." Though we were all suffering.

Gallagher came closer, and his shadow stretched across the ground. "What were you thinking about?"

"Rommily. Claudio was telling me about what happened to her, and I got so furious I couldn't think about anything else, and..." My words trailed off when I realized Gallagher was staring at me in astonishment. "What?"

"I can't believe I didn't see it." He stepped back and pressed both hands to the sides of his faded red ball cap. "The first time I saw you, I felt all this rage in you, but I misunderstood..."

I shook my head. He wasn't making any sense. "I wasn't angry until I saw Jack take a cattle prod to Geneviève." And I wasn't sure how he could have "felt" my anger, either way.

"The fury was always there," he insisted, and eyes that had previously looked as gray and unyielding as stone suddenly shone like polished steel. "You have an endless font of it, Delilah. You

are made of rage and power, all tied up in this deceptively delicate form." His focus never wandered south of my face, but I
felt his attention like a tangible force. "Your beast was just waiting for the right moment, for something to call it out of you."

"You're saying my inner monster is rage?" That didn't make
any sense, but I could hardly think it through because he was
still looking at me as if I were the only candle burning in a dark
room—the first glimpse of light strong enough to lead the way.

As if I were something he *needed*.

"Yes, rage, but rage with a purpose. It's been there all along."
Gallagher clutched the decorative frame of my cage and stared
down into my eyes with an intensity I'd never seen from him.
Or from anyone else. "This whole time I've been looking for
your species, but it's not that simple. Nothing with you is ever
simple. But my point is that you could be any species. You could
be a siren, or an oracle, or—"

His sentence ended so abruptly I thought he might have bit-
ten his tongue off with it.

Gallagher turned, and in three huge steps he'd crossed the tent
and snatched his bag from the table. He rummaged through the
front pocket, then came back clutching a folded sheet of paper
in one huge fist, his gray eyes bright with fervor. He unfolded
the page and held it up a foot from my face on the other side
of the steel mesh.

The first thing I noticed was how deep and worn the creases
were, as if he'd folded and unfolded the paper many times.
Then I saw the date at the top. "This is a week old." My voice
sounded strange. Hollow.

"Nine days," he corrected, and I realized I'd lost track of time.
But by then I'd found the box at the bottom, where the result
of my blood test was printed.

I blinked. Then I blinked again, but the words didn't change.

"This says I'm…human." But that couldn't be right. No
human could do what I'd done to Jack.

"That's why they're running your blood work again." Gallagher stared down at me. "They don't believe it either."

Confusion warred with shock inside me. I couldn't think straight. "How long have you had this?"

"Since your second night in the menagerie."

"Why didn't you tell me?" I demanded.

"Because I thought it was a mistake, and believing you were human would not have helped you bring out your beast. But the test is right. You're not a cryptid, Delilah, not that it matters anymore—"

"You think that doesn't *matter*?"

"—because what you are transcends species. You're an ideal. An abstraction." He gripped the steel wire with his free hand. "You are the incarnation of justice."

"Wait. *What?* I'm human, but I'm also rage…and justice?" He clearly had no idea how little sense he was making.

Gallagher nodded, his gray eyes shining with feverish excitement. "You're a *furiae*, Delilah."

"Furiae?" I frowned, thinking back to a class I'd had in college. Not a crypto-veterinary class—a literature elective. "As in, the Erinyes?"

"Yes." He grabbed a folding chair from beneath the table and set it in front of my wagon. "Those who avenge unrighted wrongs. That's you." He looked so satisfied. Almost euphoric. As if what he'd figured out somehow meant as much to him as it should to me.

"But the Erinyes aren't real. They're just the personification of a concept." Many, many cryptids were once assumed to be folklore and myths, but the Erinyes… "They're just symbols, Gallagher. Stories intended to reassure people that justice would be meted out in the afterlife if it was overlooked in this one."

"Oh, the Erinyes are real." He sat in the low chair, and for the first time since we'd met, he had to look up at me. "They're very rare, though, because they're not born. They're made."

"Made?" I wasn't sure how much to believe. I wasn't sure how much I *wanted* to believe. How could I be human, yet still have no rights? How likely were the authorities to believe a blood test, when at least fifteen people had seen me turn into a monster? "How are the Erinyes made?"

"Through sacrifice." Gallagher cleared his throat and leaned forward in his chair, capturing my gaze as if nothing in the world could mean more than whatever he was about to say. "People think they are masters of the universe because they've conquered the skies, and the seas, and the heavens. Because they can kill with the press of a button and speak to anyone else on the planet, anytime they like. But there are things older and wiser than humanity. Things more powerful and significant. Love, and loss, and birth. Pain, and bliss. Vengeance. They're more than just words, Delilah." The shine in his eyes was captivating. Practically hypnotic. "They're inalienable truths, in the most powerful sense of the word, and they're the only things that mankind can never truly touch, much less own.

"Every now and then, the universe decides to prove that by endowing a living being with the essence of one of those truths. You have been chosen to represent vengeance. To remind the world that mankind is not its own final authority. That burden is equal parts honor and curse, and it is nothing that humanity at large will ever accept. Or willingly allow to exist."

I could only stare at him, stunned by an outpouring of information I couldn't properly process. Most of it was churning in my head, slowly being ground into digestible chunks.

"What sacrifice put me here?" My voice echoed with shock.

"I don't know. Sometimes martyrs are brought back as *furiae*."

"But I'm not dead." Not that I knew of anyway. But then, the list of things I didn't know had never felt quite so comprehensive before.

"It's not always self-sacrifice. Each case is unique. We may never figure out how you became a *furiae*, but I have no doubt

it's true. That's why you couldn't transmute when Clyde abused you." He finally refolded the paper and slid it into his pocket. "You can't avenge yourself—your calling is purely selfless."

My thoughts were racing. I didn't want to believe it, but I couldn't come up with anything to contradict his theory. "But I've seen plenty of unjust things, and none of them ever turned me into a monster. Why now? Why Genni?"

Gallagher was quiet, and I could tell he was searching through his knowledge of the mythology for an answer that made sense. "According to the lore, each of the Erinyes was responsible for avenging a certain kind of offense. Maybe your specialty is avenging abused cryptids."

Clarity rushed over me. I'd always been fascinated by cryptids and bothered by the way they were treated. That was why I'd majored in crypto-biology in the first place. I'd thought my degree would help me make a difference. If I'd gone on to crypto-veterinary school, surely I would have seen the abuse firsthand a lot sooner. My inner beast might have shown herself years ago.

"So, you're telling me that I can avenge any captive in the menagerie, but not myself?"

Gallagher nodded. "You may also be able to avenge humans, even if they're not your specific calling, but you can't take vengeance on your own behalf."

"So, I'm totally helpless."

"No." He stood and looked straight into my eyes. "You have intelligence and courage. And you have me."

Yet he didn't seem to see the conflict of interest. "You're a jailer."

"That sums me up no more thoroughly than the word *prisoner* describes you." He came closer to the side of my cage, piercing me with the intensity of his steel focus. "I'm working on something, Delilah. I can get you out of here, so that you can better serve the demands of your calling. But I'm going to need trust,

patience, and cooperation from you, or it won't work. Can you do that?"

"Can you tell me what you're up to?" I said, and he shook his head, while mine spun with the possibilities. "Of course you can't. Do I have any other choice?"

"Not a good one. But my word is my honor, Delilah. Will you work with me?"

I exhaled and sat on my ankles in my cage. "Okay."

Gallagher nodded, and though he looked pleased, he did not smile. I wasn't sure he even knew how.

"The latest reports indicate that these 'surrogate' children brought home unbeknownst to their unwitting families somehow 'glamoured' parents into slaughtering all human siblings in a single bloody night. What kind of creatures are we talking about here, Ginger? Are they *fae*? What kind of *fae*, exactly?"

—Transcript from a September 24, 1986 interview with Ginger Cumberland, Head of Research at Yale's Crypto-biology Department, on *Wake Up America*

ERYX

The minotaur watched the carnival awaken from within his custom-made heavy-duty steel crate, but the carnival did not watch him back. The handlers and roustabouts never seemed to notice him until they needed him for heavy labor, and that was okay with Eryx.

The only advantage of having no speech was that most people assumed he also had no language and little comprehension beyond basic repetitive instructions.

Eryx was just fine with that assumption.

Before breakfast, Gallagher injected the usual dose of the usual drugs into his arm through the steel mesh and between the strong, thick steel bars. The bars on the minotaur's cage were twice as thick as those on the other cages because Eryx could have kicked out one of the regular bars in his sleep. In fact, he'd done that very thing during a bad dream the year he was fourteen and still in the possession of another carnival. The staff had risen to find him sleeping with one massive hoofed leg dangling from the side of his busted-open cage. The dislodged bar lay on the ground, and the wire mesh panel was twisted and torn around the bovine leg protruding through it.

Still, he'd never tried to run or to hurt anyone, and those who worked with him on a daily basis were so accustomed to his benign presence and tractable disposition that even though he was four times heavier and nine times stronger than the average circus roustabout, few ever worried for their safety around the giant beast.

They worried even less about information spilled near him, and Eryx soaked it up like a sponge, patiently waiting for the opportunity and ability to use what he knew. And the information didn't just come from the staff. Many of his fellow captives—even those who recognized intelligence in his eyes—assumed him incapable of betraying the secrets they let slip in his presence.

Eryx knew about the siren's stealthy lover, and the ringmaster's closet fetish. He knew about the old man's hypocrisy and he knew where Gallagher went when he slipped away from the menagerie some nights and came back...rejuvenated.

The bull knew where Rommily had disappeared to on that rainy night months before. He knew who'd been with her, and what had happened to her, and he knew that she would never be the same again.

And as Gallagher marched him down the row of wagons, past cage after cage and captive after captive, Eryx saw Rommily, sitting between her sisters, and he understood—not for the first time—that they were the same in many ways, the fragile oracle and the mighty minotaur.

Both knew important things, yet could not speak them.

Rommily looked up as he passed, and when her wide-eyed, fevered gaze found his, the minotaur stopped walking, heedless of the ring tugging at his septum and the impatient sounds of the handler in the red cap.

"Steel trap," she murmured, but his ears were so attuned to her voice that he would have heard even the softest sound to fall from her tongue. "One track. Speak mine. Boggle yours. Think alike."

The bull snorted softly, and her wheat-colored eyes narrowed, studying him as the handler turned to assess the problem. "Eryx. Let's go."

"Labyrinth, deconstructed!" Rommily shouted, as Gallagher urged the minotaur forward. "Eccentric rings! Fools will tumble. Blood will flow. And the bull shall stand tallest of them all..."

DELILAH

Geneviève's cage, which had been ominously missing from the lineup last night, was in place next to her father's when I woke up. I couldn't have slept for more than a couple of hours, with my thoughts flying around like debris in a storm, but she looked like she'd been awake all night.

"Genni!" I called, when I noticed her curled up in one corner of her pen, and to my relief, she looked up at the sound of my voice. "We missed you last night. Are you okay?"

She blinked, but made no response, and I noticed the fresh bandage on her forearm.

"What happened to your arm, honey?"

"What's wrong with her arm?" Claudio sat up and looked to me for a reply because he couldn't see into his daughter's cage. "I don't smell fresh blood."

"Genni, hold your arm out please," I said, and after a moment's hesitation, she complied. "The bandage is clean," I told Claudio, but I didn't mention how thin her arm was or how prominent her elbow looked because of that. "If there was blood, it's dry and covered. Genni, what happened? Did someone hurt you?"

Just asking made my chest ache. In my former life, if she'd said yes, I would have called child protective services. But because Genni was raised in the menagerie, her answer was largely ir-

relevant. If someone had hurt her, it wouldn't be the first time, and there was nothing I could do about it.

Or maybe there was.

If Gallagher was right, I might be the only one who *could* do something about it. But I wasn't quite ready to dive into the deep end of the vengeance pool.

I wasn't actually sure how to kick-start my inner *furiae*, and Gallagher and I had agreed that the rest of the staff should not know what we'd figured out. If they discovered that my life's purpose was at odds with their tendency to abuse the captives, I might very well be hurt—or at least isolated—beyond the ability to help anyone else. Yet what was the point of having a "calling," as Gallagher referred to it, if I couldn't perform the inherent duties?

Still, when Genni shook her head, relief rolled over me, taking some of the pressure off my response.

"Did you do that to yourself?" I asked, and she nodded, then mimed biting her own arm. "She bit herself," I told her father, and Claudio nodded in acknowledgment, his face a mask of worry. "Did they sew you up? Did they put cream on your arm before the bandage?"

Genni shrugged.

"She doesn't know," I said. "My guess is that she was unconscious."

"But she's okay now?"

"Seems to be," I said, well aware that "okay" was a relative term among menagerie captives.

Geneviève curled up on the metal floor of her pen and pulled her blanket up to her shoulders, then tucked both hands beneath her cheek like a pillow. *"Dites-moi une histoire, s'il vous plaît."*

"She wants to hear another story," her father translated, but I'd already figured that out. "She used her manners." He seemed pleased by that, and the rare glimpse at a normal parenting moment under such barbaric circumstances made my eyes water.

"Okay, let me think." She'd liked Hansel and Gretel, and I wanted to give her a story about a girl who triumphed over extraordinary adversity. Something relevant to her life. "Genni, do you know about the Black Bull-man of Norroway?" I asked, and when she shook her head, I sat cross-legged facing her and pulled my blanket into my lap, settling in for the story about a noble minotaur and his troubled young bride.

Halfway through, I looked up from where Genni lay watching me and discovered that Claudio, Zyanya, Payat, and Mahsa were all listening as well, and based on the silence from farther down the line, my audience had grown even bigger than I could see.

Breakfast was a small scoop of watery oatmeal—without utensils—and a boiled pig's foot, served by Abraxas. He didn't smile or chat with the captives, but he was a definite improvement over Clyde because everything he scooped onto the trays actually made it into someone's stomach.

I ate every bite of my meal, silently cursing myself for every scrap of food I'd ever wasted in my life before captivity.

I was leaning against the end panel of my cage, marveling at how much better I felt having eaten twice in a span of twelve hours, when Zyanya called my name from her ornate black-and-silver-framed crate across the aisle. "Hey," she said when I looked up. "Where did you go last night?"

"Excuse me?"

"I woke up in the middle of the night, and your cage was gone, but this morning you have clean clothes and a fresh blanket. Where'd you go?"

"Gallagher took her," a female voice called from farther down my own line of cages, and I recognized Lenore's melodic siren voice. I knew most of my fellow captives by voice better than by sight.

"He didn't *take* me," I insisted, afraid someone would think I'd made a late-night concession for food. Which was when I

realized my secret—*any* secret, actually—would be really hard to keep in the menagerie. "He just…"

"He made you work?" Claudio guessed, and I could have kissed him.

"Yes, actually. He says I can't go back on display until we figure out what I am." What he'd really said was that I couldn't go back on display until I figured out how to transmute without having to see someone else hurt. I'd come close on the travel trailer, but close wasn't good enough to charge admission for.

"Any clue yet?" Lenore asked from the wagon she shared with Finola.

Immediately the buzz of caged conversation swelled.

"I think she's a gorgon," the berserker called from three cages down. He was well out of my line of sight, but I'd grown to recognize the odd rattle in his voice. "Her hair looked like Medusa. I saw it that first night."

"I saw it, too, and there were no snakes," Zyanya insisted, seated with her knees sticking up near her shoulders, every bit the cat, even in human form. "No snakes, no gorgon. Plus, no one turned into stone."

"That stone part's bullshit," Finola, the other siren, called. I recognized her by the telltale melodic quality of her voice, even when she wasn't singing. "Gorgons don't actually petrify people—they exude some kind of hormone that paralyzes them. Besides, she can't be a gorgon. They're extinct."

After that, the discussion devolved into an argument over whether gorgons were actually extinct or just very, very endangered, and I let it proceed without me, grateful that everyone seemed to have forgotten about my illicit nighttime activities.

When the daily parade of captives toward the fairgrounds began, I watched with renewed interest, waiting for a glimpse of Eryx. Hoping he would look at me on his way past, or somehow acknowledge the new secret we shared, so I could stop worrying that I'd imagined him writing in the sawdust.

I wanted to know what he'd been trying to tell me. Did he know what Gallagher was up to?

Halfway through the cavalcade of weary exhibits in gilded cages, the white centaur and the buck pulled the oracle sisters by my crate and the moment my gaze met Rommily's, her eyes widened and glazed over with a white film.

"David! Dorothy! Heidi!" she shouted at me. "Siblings in serendipity, they welcome you!"

"Are those the names she said to you last time?" Claudio asked, and I could only shake my head, watching the oracles pass.

"Who are they?" Mahsa called from behind me.

"I have no idea."

"What were the other names?" the berserker asked, and in the aisle between rows, I could see his shadow silhouette turn toward mine.

"Um... Jane, and Pip, and Oliver. And a princess named Sara. And Secret Mary."

"*Sara, la princesse.*" Geneviève sat up and pushed her blanket off. "*Mon histoire préférée!*"

"What?" I turned to Genni, goose bumps rising on my arms. "Geneviève, what did you say?"

"She's talking about the girl in her favorite story," Claudio explained, pushing shaggy silver hair back from his face. "Mirela used to tell it to her, after Genni's mother... After they sold Melisande."

"*A Little Princess.*" I'd read it over and over as a kid.

"*Oui!*" Genni looked so hopeful I hated to disappoint her by not telling the story, but my brain was racing too quickly to stop.

"Holy shit! They're all characters."

"What?" Zyanya blinked big orangish eyes at me.

"Rommily's names. They're all characters from books. Sara, from *A Little Princess.* Mary, from *The Secret Garden.* Pip, from *Great Expectations.* Oliver, from *Oliver Twist.* David, from *David Copperfield.* Dorothy, from *The Wonderful Wizard of Oz.* Heidi,

from—well, from *Heidi*. I don't know who Jane is, but there must be a thousand characters named Jane."

Genni watched me, still waiting for her story, but her father looked puzzled. "Are they dead?"

"They're fictional. They were never alive in the first place." I shrugged. "You said Mirela told Genni about *A Little Princess*? Can she read? Weren't the oracles born here?" I had yet to meet anyone who'd learned to read after being born into captivity. Except maybe Eryx.

"No, they were bought as small children, after their parents were exposed and sold elsewhere," the werewolf papa said. "That was a couple of years after the old man brought me in from France."

"Were they old enough to read?"

"Mirela knows her letters," Mahsa said, smoothing long black hair over one dark shoulder, and I realized that everyone within hearing distance had gone quiet, listening. Most sat pressed against the aisle sides of their cages, trying to see as many fellow prisoners as possible. "She went to school for a couple of years before they were exposed. Sometimes she reads signs for us, so we know where we are. And I saw her teach letters to her sisters, in the dirt. When we were in the petting zoo."

The petting zoo.

An old memory flashed through my mind, and I connected the dots. I'd seen Mirela, Rommily, and Lala in the petting zoo when I was a kid. Mirela had been about my age, and I couldn't understand what three normal-looking girls were doing in the pen next to two small werewolves. They must have been new to the menagerie when I'd seen them.

The ache in my chest rivaled the rage in my soul. Small children ripped from their parents and sold into exhibition. That ache bruised even deeper when I realized I probably wasn't hearing about an isolated incident.

"She didn't read about Princess Sara, though," Claudio said. "She saw it on television. On a movie disk."

"A DVD." That made more sense. And if the oracle sisters had seen *A Little Princess* as a movie, they might have seen all the others the same way, long before they could have read the books.

"So why is she shouting the names of storybook characters at you?" Payat asked.

I could only shrug, my mind still racing. "Maybe she wants to tell me a story. Or maybe she wants me to tell one," I said, thinking of Eryx and our guessing game the night before.

Claudio shook his head once, firmly. "She doesn't ask for things anymore, and if her sisters didn't feed her, she would hardly eat. She has visions all the time, but she only shouts like that when she's seen something she really wants to tell someone."

What could Rommily possibly have seen involving a bunch of characters from books more than a century old, and what did any of that have to do with me?

Were any of them captives or prisoners?

Oliver Twist was stuck in a prison-like orphanage. Sara was forced to work for the owner of a girls' school, after her father died and left her penni—

"Orphans." The connection between the characters hit me like a punch to the gut. "They're all orphans. Sara, Mary, Pip, David, Oliver, Heidi, and Dorothy. And presumably Jane. Their parents are all…"

…*dead.*

Fate's bastards. "And I least among them…" My goose bumps receded beneath growing horror. "She's telling me I'm an orphan. Or that I'm going to be."

Movement to my right caught my eye and when the world zoomed back into focus, I saw Gallagher leading Eryx as he pulled a cage holding one of the squat, gnarl-limbed trolls.

"Gallagher!" I shouted, with no real forethought. He gave me a dark scowl, then kept walking without acknowledging me.

Normally, I would have let it go at that. Instead, I gripped the wire mesh and pulled myself onto my knees.

"Delilah, *don't!*" Zyanya whispered fiercely. "You're asking for trouble."

And I knew that. But my mother was the only person left in the world who'd cared about me both before and after captivity, and I didn't even know if she was alive. Getting ahold of her was worth whatever I'd have to endure for my insolence later.

So I steeled my nerve and raised my voice. "Gallagher! I need to talk to you."

His scowl became an angry glower and he handed Eryx's lead rope to Abraxas, who was passing in the opposite direction, with a barked order to wait for him. Gallagher stormed toward me, every step a bolt of thunder, anger firing in his gaze like lightning.

"Delilah, don't make it worse," Claudio whispered. But I was already committed.

"What the *hell* are you doing?" Gallagher growled, and the look in his gray eyes froze the blood in my veins. He looked like he might have ripped my head from my neck, if not for the steel barrier.

My mother was worth the risk.

"I need a favor, and I'm willing to pay." Though I wasn't sure how. "I'll… You can put me in the show tonight. I'll figure out how to transmute. I *swear* I'll make it happen." And if I couldn't, he would already have granted my favor.

"Gallagher?" Chris Ruyle headed toward us from the silver wagon, wearing his authority like a badge, and my heartbeat echoed in my ears. "Is there a problem?"

"Nothing I can't handle." Gallagher held my gaze with fury dancing in his own. "Don't forget where you're sitting." His voice rolled over me with a chilling hostility that made me wonder if I'd imagined everything that happened the night be-

fore. "You do as you're told, or you pay the price, just like all the other monsters in metal boxes."

He turned to stomp off, and desperation warred with my common sense. "Gallagher, *please!*" I called after him, gripping the wire so tightly it cut into my fingers. "I wouldn't ask if it wasn't important!"

He stiffened. Two steps later, he grabbed Abraxas by the front of his red tee. "No lunch for Drea today. No dinner either. Got it?"

Abraxas nodded, clearly terrified, and Gallagher let him go. "If you hear one more word out of her before I get back, hose her down."

His words were a shock almost as violent as the hose itself.

Gallagher snatched Eryx's lead rope and pulled the bull toward the rear entrance to the fairgrounds. As he was marched off, the minotaur turned to look at me, and I could swear I saw sympathy in his sad, human eyes.

Lunch came and went, and I was not served. Crews came to haul off the second troll, the lamia, the puca, the pair of *djinn*, and the berserker, but Gallagher did not return.

I didn't speak, even when Claudio and Zyanya both tried to draw me out of silence. Even when Geneviève asked politely in French for another story, I complied with Gallagher's gag order not for my own safety, but for my mother's. My last remaining parent, who was in serious trouble, if I'd interpreted Rommily's riddle correctly.

Or maybe she was already dead.

I would never know for sure without Gallagher's help.

After lunch, crew members leading pairs of drugged centaurs came to haul off the adlet and the cat shifters, leaving me alone with Geneviève and Claudio, who was trying to talk his daughter into performing her first live shift to keep her from being abused for refusal.

Early in the afternoon, two more hauling crews came for the werewolves, and my unadorned crate stood alone for the second day in a row. My growing hunger couldn't hold a candle to my need for a restroom, though I'd had nothing to drink since the small bowl of water that had come with my breakfast.

And through it all, I could think of nothing but my mother, hoping with every breath in my body that I'd misinterpreted the oracle's fractured prophecy.

Finally, as carnival performers headed toward the midway in black satin and red sequins glittering in the hot afternoon sun, Eryx and Gallagher appeared at the fairgrounds' back gate, headed my way. I could tell from my handler's gait that he wasn't as mad as he'd been earlier, but he didn't look happy either.

"Gallagher," I said as he fastened the minotaur's harness to my cage.

He leaned around the end panel. "Just shut up and sit still, and you might not end this day any worse off than you began it."

Out of options, I bit my tongue as Eryx pulled my cage through the gate, then into the alley behind a series of tents, avoiding the midway because the carnival was already open for business. Hours of operation were longer on the weekend, but I couldn't be sure whether it was Saturday or Sunday, and when I realized the day of the week no longer held any significance to me, I wanted to cry.

Eryx hauled me into my own small tent, and without a word, our handler unharnessed him and led him back outside, presumably to the hybrid tent, where the mighty minotaur should already have been on display.

Gallagher returned alone, still scowling from beneath the brim of his faded red cap. He hooked the bottom of the red-and-white tent sidewall into place, then stood to face me, thick arms crossed over an even thicker chest. "What the *hell* were you thinking?"

"That I need your help."

Gallagher's anger felt almost as ominous as Rommily's prophecy, but as tenuous as our partnership seemed, he was my only ally in the carnival. "That is *not* the way to get it," he growled as he unlocked my cage.

My legs ached in anticipation of truly stretching. Of walking. Of being out of that damn cage.

"If you ever pull something like that again, I'll have no choice but to let Ruyle punish you hard, fast, and in full view, just to keep my job." He pulled a pair of cuffs from a hook on the side of my cage, and I held my hands out so he could restrain me.

I didn't realize until the metal closed over my wrists that the restraint routine was so ingrained that I hadn't even given it conscious thought.

"There's *always* a choice," I insisted as he helped me to the ground. "Especially for those who aren't locked in metal boxes."

He led me out of the tent and through the back alley toward a row of blue portable toilets. "I *can't* lose this job, Delilah." The tension in his voice was an alarm, warning me that there was more to what he was saying than the sum of the words themselves. "Not yet."

"Why not? If you're going to break me out of here anyway, why can't we just go now?" Gallagher opened the toilet stall, but instead of stepping inside, I studied his gaze for some hint of what he was hiding. "We could leave tonight," I whispered. We could pile into his truck, or trailer, or whatever he drove, and I could call my mom from the road to check on her. Of course, I'd have to find a phone, since he didn't have a cell, and mine had been confiscated along with everything I'd owned.

"It's not that simple. Your escape is not my only concern, and this undertaking can't be rushed," he whispered. "I *cannot* lose this job before the time is right."

Tension twisted in my stomach. I suddenly felt as if I were standing in a pitch-black room, inches from some heinous danger I could sense, yet couldn't see. What would happen if I

stepped forward? "What are you up to?" Why was he keeping me in the dark?

"You don't get to ask that question." Gallagher nudged me toward the toilet, and I stepped inside. "What you get to do is turn yourself inside out, so we can all see the real you." His voice was muffled through the door. "You said you'd learn to transmute for tonight."

I stepped out of the stall, rubbing sanitizer from the dispenser onto my hands. "I said I was ready to make a deal. You help me, I'll help you."

"I'm *already* helping you. You have to do your part." Gallagher led me back to my tent and lifted me into my cage.

"Fine," I said as he locked me in. "But my condition stands. First I need you to call my mom and make sure she's still alive."

"Why would you think she's dead?"

"Because Rommily's spent the past two days trying to tell me that I'm an orphan. Or that I will be."

"No one knows what Rommily means most of the time, Delilah. That's why she doesn't work in the tent anymore."

But according to Claudio, banning Rommily from the oracle tent had more to do with the fact that since the day Clyde hurt her, her prophecies related almost exclusively to death, which wasn't marketable on the midway, because it scared the customers.

Her prophecy scared me, too.

"She called me an orphan, which either means that my mom is dead—or will be—or that she was talking about my biological parents. Whoever and wherever they may be. I'm not going to do another thing to help either of us until you find me a phone and let me talk to her."

A fierce, low growl rolled up from Gallagher's throat. "One phone call with your mother? One very *short* phone call, then you'll cooperate with me until the day you regain your freedom?"

"You have my word."

"Fine." He clipped the key ring back onto his belt. "I'll be right back, and you better be ready to work." Then Gallagher unhooked one of the sidewalls and disappeared into the carnival.

Time dragged while he was gone, and I had no way to accurately count the minutes. The clomp of hooves had replaced the ticking of the clock since I'd been imprisoned by the menagerie, and the sun's position in the sky had become a cosmic hour hand, tracing time as it circled the world around me. But neither of those was accurate enough to tell me how long I lay awake at night, how soon breakfast would come, or how long Gallagher had left me alone, locked in a cage.

Finally, he ducked into the tent again and pulled a cell phone from his pocket. He slid it through the tray slot in the side of my cage.

I took the phone, and an ache swelled deep inside me, equal parts bitter loss and rose-tinted nostalgia. The juxtaposition of the *before* and *after* halves of my life could not have felt more bizarre if I'd worn shackles and chains to work at the bank.

"Whose is this?" I dragged my finger across the screen to wake the phone up and exhaled in relief when I wasn't asked for a password, a concept so removed from my new existence that for a second, I couldn't remember its purpose.

Authorization. Permission to use.

"Alyrose's. She's taking tickets for the hybrid tent tonight."

I dialed my mother's cell number, and the phone rang over and over in my ear. Finally, her voice mail picked up.

"Hello, this is Charity Marlow. I can't come to the phone right now, so leave me a message. Unless you're a reporter, in which case you can go fuck yourself. Have a great day!"

The beep speared my brain, and I couldn't help smiling, in spite of the circumstance.

Gallagher frowned. "What's funny?"

"I just realized how much of my personality can be credited

to nurture, rather than nature." How had I never noticed before how much like my mother I was? "Hey, Mom, it's me," I said, when I realized that my voice message was already recording. "I'm fine, but I need you to call me back if you get this within the next few minutes. After that, don't call, because I won't have access to this phone." I squeezed my eyes shut, and two tears rolled down my face as every moment of homesickness, memory, and isolation I'd suffered in captivity suddenly coalesced into a single devastating pang of loss. "I love you."

I hung up, and a minute later I was still staring at the phone when it buzzed in my hand.

Fresh tears gathered in my eyes when I saw my mother's number on the screen, and in my haste, I said hello before I'd actually accepted the call. "Mom?" I said again, with the phone pressed to my head.

She sobbed into my ear. "Lilah!"

She was alive.

Hearing her say my name felt amazing, yet it also hurt, deep inside.

"Yeah, it's me. I'm okay, but I don't have long. Are you okay?"

"No, honey, I'm not," she said over the rumble of road noise. "Last week a heartless, corrupt backwoods sheriff sold my daughter to a traveling menagerie. But the Cryptid Conservation Society gave me the name of a civil rights attorney from—"

"Mom." My throat felt thick, and the word almost got stuck in it. "Are you *physically* all right? Are you sick? Or hurt? Has anyone threatened you?"

She hesitated a second, as if the question surprised her. "The reporters are persistent, and there've been a few threats. But nothing serious. And I feel fine. Why?"

"No reason." I tried to make my pulse slow, but I couldn't overlook the obvious—just because she wasn't sick or in danger now didn't mean she wouldn't be tomorrow. Or the next day. "I miss you."

"I miss you too, honey. You're in Texas now, right?"

I frowned, and a glance at Gallagher told me he'd heard her. "How did you know that, Mom?"

"Metzger's has a website, hon, and I'm not *completely* technologically incompetent."

"Okay." Gallagher held out his hand for the phone, as if I could just reach through the wire mesh and drop it onto his palm. "We don't have much time, Delilah."

"Who's that?" my mother asked.

"No one. I have to go." Tears blurred my vision, and I scrubbed my eyes with my free hand. Saying goodbye over the phone was just as hard as saying it in person had been.

"Can I call you back at this number?"

"No. I won't have access to a phone again." I sniffled and swiped at my nose with the back of my hand. "I just really needed to hear your voice."

"Me, too, hon, and I think I can do even better than that. The drive's not that long, and—"

"Don't," I said, and the word sounded like a sob. "Do *not* come here, Mom. I don't want you to see me like this."

"Delilah, there is no way I'm just going to leave you there to rot. I don't care if they declare you cryptid, or an alien, or the Antichrist, you're still my daughter, and they can't keep me away." Her engine noise softened and I heard a soft, familiar thump as she shifted into Park. "Anyway, I need pictures documenting your living conditions for the attorney—"

My chest ached fiercely. "Mom, do *not* hire an attorney." If she fought, Pennington and Metzger would throw her in jail.

She hesitated, and I could hear her breathing over the line. "Honey, it's starting to look like I'm going to have to hire her just to make them show me your blood test results. Unless you've already seen them?"

Gallagher tapped on the corner of my cage and I looked up to see warning in his stern expression.

"No." I felt bad about lying to my mother, but not bad enough to tell her the truth. After what I'd done to Jack, they wouldn't set me free no matter what my test results said, and she'd only be putting herself in danger if she kept digging. "Mom, I have to go, but I'm fine. Really. Don't come here, and don't hire the lawyer. That'll only make things worse."

My mother huffed. "I don't see how they could possibly be any—"

"Mom. Promise me!" My grip on the phone was so tight the plastic creaked.

After another moment's hesitation, she exhaled slowly. "Fine." I didn't believe her, but she would only have to keep her reluctant promise long enough for Gallagher to break me out. Which he'd said would be soon. "I love you, honey."

"I love you, too." I made myself hang up without thinking about it, so I couldn't lose my nerve. Then I pressed another series of buttons on Alyrose's phone.

"What are you doing?" Gallagher demanded, reaching for his keys.

"I'm just erasing my call from the log." I slid the phone back through the slot, and he took it. "Now, dial the weather line, or something generic like that. If you give the phone back and it doesn't show a call, Alyrose will get curious and ask you what you wanted."

"There's a weather line?" He stared at the phone as if he'd never held one.

"Yeah. It's archaic, thanks to the internet, but I think a lot of old people still use it." Like my mother. I gave him the number, and he dialed, then hung up a few seconds later.

"It's going to rain tomorrow." Gallagher slid the phone back into his pocket and when he left to return it, I huddled in the corner of my cage and let myself truly cry for the first time since waking up in the sheriff's station, in my own hometown.

Federal government rounds up more than 300,000 six-year-old "surrogate" children to be studied in secret labs

—Headline from the *Federal Inquirer*, September 30, 1986 edition

NALAH

The *ifrit* tucked a strand of wavy red hair behind her ear. She turned toward the sun, and the strand fell in front of her face again, subtle streaks of orange and yellow lit like a living flame. Nalah let the warmth soak into her skin, and when she closed her eyes, she could almost pretend she was back at home, a child of five lying on the grass behind the barn, waiting for her brother to finish feeding the cows.

The scent of manure fit. The warmth fit. The clanks and groans of wagons being hauled…that fit, too. The only thing left to ruin the illusion, as long as she kept her eyes closed, was—

"I can't stand this anymore."

Nalah opened her eyes and found Adira staring through the side of their cage, her pale fingers threaded through the wire mesh.

"It's too hot. Too dry. I'm going to shrivel up and blow away. Tell me we're almost home."

"We're almost home, Princess." The *ifrit*'s fingers found their way into Adira's long silver hair with no conscious thought, combing and gently untangling to provide comfort. "But the final mile is always the longest."

Adria twisted to frown at her companion, tugging her own hair in the process. "How can one mile be longer than any other?"

"I only meant that the most difficult part of the journey is yet to come."

The princess huffed. "What could be harder than sweltering for a year, locked in a cage, surrounded by beasts?"

"Overcoming distractions." Nalah gazed out at the alley behind their open tent, where she saw Gallagher leading an exhibit on foot. It was the new one—the girl with no notable features, aside from a crass tongue. Adira called her a "mongrel of non-specific origin," but as was often the case, the merid could not see beyond the surface to the heart of the problem.

Nalah understood that no matter what the new girl's species turned out to be and no matter how diluted her bloodline, Gallagher did not think of her as a mongrel. She could see that in the gentle way he held her arm, as if he did not want to add to her bruises. In the subtle way his lips moved when he spoke to her, as if he did not want to be overheard.

But the most telling evidence that Gallagher did not think of the new girl as just another beast was the fact that he spoke to her at all.

In the year he'd been at Metzger's, Nalah had never seen Gallagher converse with an exhibit other than Adira and herself. He gave instructions, of course. Sometimes he gave soft words of encouragement to the mute minotaur, along with a companionable pat on the shoulder. But he didn't speak with the other exhibits, beyond the necessary exchange of information. Nalah couldn't think of a reason the new girl might need so much private instruction, unless she were feebleminded.

But Delilah was not feeble in any sense of the word.

The only reasonable cause for Gallagher's interest in her was, well, interest.

Pain flared deep in the *ifrit*'s chest, and she gasped with the sensation.

Nalah had felt quite a lot of pain in her fifteen years. She had been sick from want of home, when she was first given to Adira

at the age of five. She'd been sick from drink not three months before they were imprisoned, the night Adira had told Nalah to sneak a bottle from the liquor stores, to wash away the fears accompanying the announcement of her betrothal to the *ifrit* crown prince. Nalah had been whipped by the menagerie's lot supervisor when she accepted blame for Adira's theft of a bottle of water, and she'd been consumed with the cramps of a consistently empty belly. She'd had hair pulled from her head, food taken from her hands, and flesh torn by the rough loss of innocence, but never in her life had anything hurt like the pain now stabbing at her chest like a spear of ice lodged deep in her heart.

She didn't realize she'd gasped again until Adira sat up with a frown. "Are you aware that the noises you're making are quite audible? Are you so very distressed that you must disturb my rest?"

"Apologies, Princess." Nalah took Adira's left hand and massaged it with both of hers.

Adira closed her eyes and squared her shoulders, as if to settle in for meditation. "And what was the cause for such a lapse?"

"Fear that Gallagher's attention has strayed from the task." Nalah's fingers never faltered, but her heart was not on the task. When Adira noticed, she opened her eyes and looked to where Gallagher and the new girl were passing by in the opposite direction. "She has already delayed your return and now seems poised to derail it entirely," the *ifrit* said softly.

"That is unacceptable." Adira pulled her hand free and turned to face the problem directly. Her pale blue eyes darkened like the ocean depths, and Nalah recognized the cruel edge in her voice. "How can we refocus his efforts?"

"By relieving him of the distraction."

"Fine. Kill her."

Nalah swallowed her initial, visceral excitement over the thought in favor of temperate council, but the words she could not say burned in her gut like lit coals. "I will roast her at the

earliest opportunity, if that is your will, Princess. But Gallagher may gravely object to the loss, and he is precious to your cause."

Yet Adira seemed unconvinced that losing the mongrel to an agonizing, fiery death could sour the handler's loyalty to her.

"Also, in the aftermath of the roast, I will be executed, and you will have no companion," Nalah added. "No one to serve at your side." The *ifrit* had no doubt that if they'd been in the merid's homeland, among flowing rivers, glistening lakes, and an entire population eager to serve, the princess would not have hesitated to sacrifice her lifelong companion—her best friend in the world—for even the slightest comfort. But such a loss could not be endured under the current cruel circumstances.

"What recourse have we, then?" Adira asked with a resigned sigh.

"A wildfire consumes both the crops and the weeds together, Princess. What we need is a controlled burn…"

DELILAH

"Dreeeaa…"

My eyes flew open and I struggled to bring the ceiling of my cage into focus in the gloom. I'd fallen asleep after Gallagher left to return Alyrose's phone, but the light in my tent had been on. He must have turned it out to let me sleep, when he'd returned.

"Someone wants to see you," Clyde's voice taunted, and something clanged against the side of my cage.

I sat up, my heart pounding in alarm.

Bright lights came on in the empty tent with a low-pitched buzz and I sat up, rubbing my eyes to shield them from the sudden painful gleam. While I blinked, wiping defensive tears from my face, I heard a new sound—a soft, wordless mewling I recognized instantly.

"Genni?" I spun around on my knees, blinking against the glare, still sluggish from sleep and half-blind.

The mewling grew louder. I rubbed my eyes again, then fell backward, startled, when Geneviève's face was smashed into the side of my cage. Wire mesh dug into her cheek, her brow bone, and half of her nose. Her eyes were damp and wide with fear, her mouth covered with duct tape.

"Let her go!"

Clyde pulled her back, brandishing a cattle prod in his free hand. "Gallagher may let you order him around, but that's not how I run things."

"Where is Gallagher?" I demanded, when my brain finally caught up with the rest of me.

"There was a sudden crisis in the mermaid tank. Some asshole clogged the filter with a handful of hay—can't imagine who would do such a thing. Since Gallagher's fixing things in the hybrid tent, I thought I'd fix things in here."

"What is this? What are you doing?" I scooted to the end of my wagon, trying to follow as he hauled the poor werewolf cub out of sight.

Genni whined.

"Sit still, or I'll kick your teeth in." Clyde reappeared on the left side of my tent and hooked the corner of one canvas panel to another, so that it was held open like living room drapes.

He ducked out of sight for a second, then rose, hauling Genni up by her hair while her squeals crescendoed behind the makeshift gag. "We'll be right out there." He gestured with the cattle prod toward the space behind a large game booth, and I frowned, trying to figure out what he was up to.

Genni's cage stood open behind the game booth, visible to me, but not to the crowd I could hear talking and laughing on the midway.

"What are you doing? What do you *want*?" I demanded. "Take her back to her dad. She has nothing to do with...whatever this is."

"Oh, but she does, thanks to you." Clyde stretched toward a portable stereo on the table and pressed a button with one knuckle of the hand holding the prod. Music blared, dark and melodically haunting, and loud enough to make my ears ring. Clyde set his prod on the edge of the table and held his free hand out toward me, fingers spread.

One, he mouthed, lowering his index finger. *Two*. When he got to five, he folded his thumb around his fist, then twisted to grab the cattle prod. Less than a second after he'd hauled Genni

out of the tent and into the shadow of the game booth, two side-wall panels began to fold up at the front of my tent.

My pulse racing, I turned to find Abraxas standing at the entrance, wearing a red sequined vest. Sneakers peeked from beneath the hem of his baggy black pants. He held a battery-powered megaphone. Before I could ask what he was doing or demand that he go get Gallagher, he lifted the megaphone and began shouting into it.

"Step right up, ladies and gentlemen! Step right up! Metzger's Menagerie is proud to announce a brand-new exhibit, opening right here, right now, for the first time ever. How special is this creature? So special that we don't know what she is yet!"

People began to wander into my tent, attracted by the music and the fledgling "talker" and I noticed that a red-velvet rope had been set up several feet in front of my cage. When I looked through the side exit of the tent, I realized the rope wasn't meant to protect the audience from me, but to keep spectators too far back to see what was behind door number two: Clyde, holding the little-girl-werewolf by a handful of her hair while he brandished the cattle prod in his other hand.

"We know her name is Drea, and that she's not the innocent, harmless creature she appears," Abraxas continued, while I struggled to slow my breathing and keep the world in focus. "But her species has yet to be identified, so step right up and take a look! Maybe one of *you* has the knowledge to unlock the mystery! If you can correctly identify the species of our mystery monster, you will win a set of four deluxe tickets to tomorrow night's show, which includes a private behind-the-scenes tour for you and three friends."

"She doesn't look like anything special," one man shouted over the music, twisting to glance at Abraxas. "She looks human."

"Is she a surrogate?" a woman called out from the back. "Is this safe? I read that they can influence your thoughts just from looking at you."

The nervous buzz of the crowd swelled and they moved as one toward the midway.

"Wait!" Abraxas held both arms out as if to block their path, his eyes wide with panic. He was losing his audience.

I resisted the urge to deny that I was a surrogate, because their fear was working in my favor.

"She's not a surrogate!" Abraxas called out. "We don't know what she is, but we know that for sure, and if you'll hang out for a minute—" He stopped when he realized he'd broken character, and the kid looked so flustered I almost felt sorry for him.

But then Abraxas stood straighter and relaunched what was obviously a prepared spiel. "Don't let her appearance fool you, ladies and gentlemen! Behind that innocent face lies a monster capable of scrambling a man's gray matter with her bare hands. And you lucky folks will be the *first* to witness her live transformation."

I gaped at Abraxas, but he only grinned and extended a broad-armed gesture my way, as if we were coconspirators in Clyde's outrageous ambush.

I gripped the wire mesh, and my gaze flitted from face to rapt face within the growing audience. They stared. They pointed. They whispered in their friends' ears while they waited, and all I could think about was that I was wearing a short, grimy linen dress, with unwashed hair and dirty feet.

Yet that was just the latest in the string of mortifications that my existence had become.

If I couldn't figure out how to transform in order to save my own life, what made Clyde think I could do it for their entertainment? Or that I *would*, even if I could?

Rage built in my belly. He was conspiring against Gallagher and trying to humiliate me, and I didn't need creepy eyes or sharp claws to give him what he deserved.

"You're all being scammed!" I shouted, riding high on the sudden vengeful impulse.

The chatter stopped, though the music kept playing. Abraxas stared at me, the megaphone hanging limp in his hand.

"No, seriously." I stared straight at the man who'd said I looked like nothing special. "I'm human. Less than two weeks ago, I was a bank teller. I had a boyfriend, and an apartment, and a mother. They took me right off the street and threw me into this cage, and if they can do that to me, they can do it to any of your daughters. They don't even need proof that she's not human. They just need an accusation, and once they have that, they'll haul your daughter off and sell her to a carnival, or a lab, or a private collection, where they'll torture her to try to get her to show you what kind of monster she is, and when that doesn't work—because she's *not* a monster—they'll let her starve to death and inventory her corpse as a dead cryptid of unspecified origin."

Wives looked at their husbands. Parents clutched their children close. No one seemed to know what to say or do.

"Don't believe me? Look in that backpack over there." I pointed to the table near the entrance, where Gallagher's bag still sat. "Folded in the front pocket, you'll find the results of the test they ran on me. You!" I pinned a woman near the back of the crowd with my gaze. "Go look."

She hesitated for a second, while Abraxas stared, obviously at a loss. Then she picked up the bag and unzipped the front pocket. She pulled the paper out and unfolded it. "It says she's human," the woman said, and the audience gasped.

Abraxas's eyes widened.

Several of the teenagers had their phone cameras aimed at me, in spite of the menagerie's rules, so I picked one and looked right at it. "Any minute now, they'll come out with a whip or a cattle prod, to try to shut me up, and when I collapse on the floor of this cage, still *completely human*, you'll know that what I'm telling you is true. And that if it can happen to me, it can happen to anyone."

I turned, ready to dare Clyde to come after me with his electrical prod, but he only glared at me through eyes narrowed into furious slits, his jaw bulging from being clenched.

Then he shoved the forked tip of the cattle prod at the inside of Geneviève's right thigh.

Genni convulsed and made a horrible sound from behind her duct tape, but no one in the tent could hear her over the music. Her legs folded, and she fell to the ground, but a thick clump of her hair remained in Clyde's hand.

I clutched the wire mesh so tightly it cut into my hands, but I couldn't make my fingers unfold. *Let her go!* I shouted, and only afterward realized the shout was trapped in my head, reverberating against the inside of my skull because my jaw would not unclench and release the words.

Clyde leaned over Genni and looked right at me. He brandished the cattle prod, then shoved it at her stomach.

Genni convulsed again. Her hands twitched and her head slammed into the grass over and over, and this time she seemed to be choking behind her gag.

No!

My skin began to itch, and my scalp started to tingle. My fingertips burned, and I let go of the wire mesh, under the impression for just a moment that it was actually shocking me.

The audience stared at me, stunned, and whatever they were seeing—whatever my body was doing—had completely undermined everything I'd just said and everything printed on the report that woman at the back still held. It's much easier to believe what we see than what we are told.

The tingling in my scalp became a full-fledged burning, and on the edges of my vision, I saw strands of dark hair twisting around my face. Lights flashed as people took more forbidden pictures and video footage. Then the room slid into crisp, hyper-clear focus. Colors looked brighter. Edges looked sharper. I could

see a tiny mole on the earlobe of the woman at the back of the tent, who still clutched my blood test results while she stared.

My fingers ached like knuckles in need of a crack, and when I held my hands up, I saw that my nails had tapered into curved, thin black points, more like needles than claws. I felt a steady pull to my left, as if the gravitational force had been reoriented to draw me toward Evan Clyde. I could practically *feel* his skin break beneath my hands, even with a steel cage and twenty feet of space standing between us.

The drive to make that act a reality was all-consuming.

Broiling with fury, I turned to find Clyde standing over Genni while she sobbed, fighting to breathe through her running nose. The cattle prod hung at his side. He was laughing. The bastard was *laughing*, because I'd given him exactly what he wanted.

He'd staged the entire thing to trigger my transmutation. In front of a live audience. Without Gallagher's knowledge or permission.

He'd hurt Genni for no reason at all.

"What did I—" Abraxas's voice cracked when his gaze met mine. Then he blinked and cleared his throat. "What did I tell you, ladies and gentlemen? She's something else, isn't she?" He turned toward the midway and stumbled through his pitch, drawing more and more people into my tent, where cameras flashed and phones recorded my misery, in clear violation of the menagerie's policy. A couple of small children started to cry, but their parents only picked them up and continued to stare at me with kids clutched to their chests.

Clyde set his electrical prod on the ground behind the game booth, then picked Genni up and tossed her into her open cage. He slammed the door shut and locked it while she shook and sobbed behind her gag, blinking at me from twenty-five feet away. Then he stored his weapon on the step rail of her crate and sauntered into the tent as if he owned it.

As if he owned *me*.

"Ladies and gentlemen, I'm going to have to ask you to put away your cameras." He waited while the audience complied reluctantly. "What you just heard Drea say before she graced us with her true face is a prime example of why monsters that look human are the most dangerous of their kind. Cryptids like this are capable of masterful feats of deception. They are silver-tongued beasts who will lie right to your face to protect the illusion of their humanity, which is exactly how this particular cryptid spent *twenty-five years* passing for human.

"Now, folks, I don't want you to worry about your safety—Drea is securely locked in a steel cage—but again let me say that we *do not know* what she is. The experts are flummoxed, but it's possible one of *you* can identify her species. On the table next to the entrance, you'll notice an empty jar and a stack of note-cards, which my assistant will be happy to pass out."

While Abraxas helped audience members fill out entry forms, I glared at Clyde, riding the current of fury coursing through my body, silently cursing the cage standing between me and a mind-scrambling end for the handler.

Justice for Geneviève.

The closer he came to my cage, the harder every cell in my body cried out for his suffering. I was drawn to him like metal to a human bastard of a magnet, but every time I reached for him, my claws slid through the wire mesh then stopped when my palms met metal.

I knew I couldn't get to him, but my body refused to accept that. The *furiae* within me suddenly felt like its own separate entity—inside of me, a part of me, but acting of its own accord.

People came and went with their kids and their astonished oohs and aahs. Abraxas continued to call spectators in from the midway. Clyde answered questions about where Metzger's had acquired me, and what I ate, and what havoc I might wreak if I ever escaped bondage. But as time passed after Genni's suf-

fering, my inner beast slowly retreated beneath my skin, biding her time. She still wanted to crack Clyde's skull like an eggshell, but she seemed to finally understand that her chance had not yet come.

My twisty, stand-up hair had already begun to fall limp when Gallagher stormed into the tent and grabbed Abraxas by the front of his shirt. A beat of hope and relief pulsed through me when he hauled the boy off his feet and ripped the megaphone away. I couldn't hear what he said over the crowd and the music, but the shapes drawn by his lips were familiar enough.

"What the hell is going on?"

Abraxas pointed to Clyde, stuttering some explanation I couldn't make out.

Clyde watched the interchange in smug satisfaction, his arms crossed over his Metzger's polo, and the *furiae* inside me stretched beneath my skin, resurrecting my urge to reach for him.

Gallagher dropped the boy and barked an order I couldn't hear. Then he marched through the crowd, jostling people out of his way, and slammed one huge fist down on the small portable stereo. I jerked, startled. Slivers of plastic and electronics rained onto the table and the sawdust-covered ground.

The music died, and the crowd turned to stare at him. The sudden silence echoed in my ears and for a second I was sure I'd gone deaf. Then Gallagher faced the audience, his bearing stiff and his fists clenched. "This exhibit is now closed," he growled. "Don't forget to purchase a Metzger's T-shirt or commemorative minotaur mug on your way out."

For a moment, everyone stared in confusion. Then Abraxas lifted his megaphone and began directing the audience back onto the midway.

By the time Gallagher hauled the boy-crier into the empty tent and dropped the open sidewall, my hair hung lank and tangled over my shoulders and my vision had returned to normal. My fingernails were still pointed, but those points were reced-

ing right in front of my eyes. Yet I could still feel the *furiae* just beneath my skin, like the seething undercurrent beneath the calm surface of a lake.

I'd never felt anything so persistent. So bloodthirsty. She was a part of me—she *was* me—but this new appetite for violence was so foreign that I couldn't help thinking of her as a distinct division of me. A hungry splinter faction of Delilah that could only be controlled if it were fed regularly. Suddenly, the result of my blood test made more sense. Becoming a *furiae* hadn't cost me my humanity; it had made me capable of holding others of my species accountable for their cruelty.

"You're *fired*!" Gallagher roared at Clyde from across the tent, and I shivered as the words rolled over and through me, soothing my inner beast like a cat being stroked. The *furiae* liked seeing Clyde reproached. "Get the *hell* out of my menagerie!"

"You can't fire me." Clyde pulled a trash can from beneath the folding table and brushed the remains of his stereo into it with a jarring clatter.

"I'm your boss!" Gallagher shouted.

The sidewall rose behind him, and Ruyle stepped into the tent. "And I'm yours. Clyde stays."

Gallagher turned on the lot superintendent, and my pulse rushed in anticipation of the confrontation. "He sabotaged the mermaid tank, then usurped my act and launched an unauthorized showcase of an ungroomed exhibit! He's damn lucky I'm *only* firing him." But the tight clench of his fists told me he was actually hoping for a more extreme solution.

As was I.

"Clyde transformed a useless cryptid from a drain on carnival resources into a profitable exhibit and engaged the audience in the search for her species. They're talking about it up and down the midway. Videos are already surfacing online." Ruyle unlocked his cell phone with a swipe of the screen. "Two thousand hits in twenty-four minutes. Most asking where we'll stop next.

That's the first time YouTube has ever worked in our favor." He held his cell up for Gallagher, and I couldn't clearly see the image paused on it, but I knew it was me.

Yet for the first time since discovering that I had an inner beast, I wasn't horrified or humiliated at the knowledge that she'd been gawked at. She'd *wanted* to be seen. But she'd wanted to be seen punishing Clyde for what he'd done, not as a monster sitting helpless in a cage.

"She's *my* project," Gallagher growled, and for once, I felt no need to object to the possessive nature of his claim. What he really meant but couldn't say was that I was his ally.

"Which is why you owe Clyde a debt—looks like you're going to get to keep your little pet." Ruyle turned to Abraxas, who still clutched the megaphone to his thin chest. "Take the jar to my office. There's a twenty waiting for you, as promised."

Ruyle glanced at me with a smug half smile, then he nodded at Clyde and ducked beneath the untethered side panel and out of the tent.

When Gallagher noticed Abraxas lingering, he turned to the boy with ice in his gray-eyed glare.

"I'm sorry." Abraxas started to hand him the megaphone, then set it on the ground between them instead. "I thought you knew. Clyde said this would be my chance to show Ruyle I could talk on the midway."

"Go," Gallagher growled. Abraxas blinked at him, then grabbed the jar full of paper slips and took off through the loose sidewall panel at a run.

"You, too," Gallagher said to Clyde, but the smaller handler only leaned with one hip against the folding table, smug and gloating.

"Don't you want to know how I got your pet freak to perform?"

"He tortured Geneviève." I turned to Clyde, and a resurgence of rage made my fingers tingle, but I swallowed the instinct,

loathe to give him a second show. "He cuffed her, gagged her, and shocked her with the cattle prod for *no reason at all*." My voice had taken on a husky quality, just as it had that night in the hybrid tent.

"Oh, I had a reason." Clyde tapped on the end panel of my cage, and fire surged through me. He turned back to Gallagher. "At first I thought Drea was a lost cause, on account of her raising, but then I realized that could be used against her. This one thinks like a human bitch." He hooked one thumb in my direction. "Which means you can make her do anything you want, if you push the right button."

"Take Geneviève back to the row," Gallagher ordered through clenched teeth.

"She's scheduled for a live shift in the center ring tonight."

"Take her back," Gallagher growled. "Give her some water and let her rest. Claudio can go on in her place."

"You're too soft on them." Clyde pushed back the sidewall panel, but hesitated before he ducked beneath it. "They're going to run all over you."

"If I didn't repair the damage mental runts like you and Jack do to the inventory, the old man wouldn't have a thing to put on display. Now go do your damn job."

Clyde ducked beneath the loose canvas flap and disappeared, still grinning.

Gallagher slid his fingers through the wire mesh between us, just outside of my own grip on the metal, and when he only breathed deeply for several long seconds, I realized he was trying to rein in his temper.

Finally, he turned and secured the loose sidewalls to stakes in the ground, effectively locking all the doors. Then he opened my cage and motioned me forward until I sat in the threshold, my legs dangling from the edge of the wagon. "Are you okay?" He pulled a bottle of water from one of the pockets of his cargo-style jeans and handed it to me.

"You should be worried about Genni, not me." I cracked open the bottle and drank a third of it in several large gulps.

"I'll check on her when I'm done here." Gallagher scruffed his faded red cap over his short hair. "So, Clyde figured out how to bring out your beast, but not what it is?"

I wedged the open bottle between my thighs to keep from knocking it over, and the cold condensation was a shock to my overheated skin. "I think he just re-created the circumstance that triggered my first transmutation and hoped for the best." Gallagher and I could have done the same thing—if we'd been willing to hurt someone innocent.

Clyde wouldn't hesitate to do it again.

My hand tightened around the water bottle. I closed my eyes, trying to absorb the conclusions and ramifications spinning in my head, but only one thing became clear. "We can't wait. We have to go now."

"I told you. That's not an option."

I opened my eyes again to find him watching me from inches away. "They're going to have to hurt someone every time I go on display, and the only way they're going to make any money under that business model is if they use acts that aren't profitable on their own. Which is only Genni and Rommily, right?"

Gallagher nodded, his teeth clenched tightly.

"That is *not* okay with me!" The words grated against my throat on their way out, as the *furiae* asserted her influence on my vocal chords.

"Agreed, but we can't leave yet. I made a promise, and I can't go back on my word, Delilah. Not even to set you free."

"You made a promise to someone else?"

Gallagher nodded.

"To one of the other captives?" An odd beat of jealousy flashed through me at the thought.

"I can't... Look, I'd rather get you out of here tonight. Right now. But my word is my honor."

I knew I'd lost before he even finished the familiar phrase. Anger ground my teeth together, and I tried to scoot back into my cage, to put distance between us.

He caught me with one hand around my ankle. "Delilah. I'm *going* to set you free." Gallagher tugged me forward until my legs dangled from the cage again, and we were inches apart. "You have my word. But now I need yours. I want you to promise me you're going to be patient and wait. No more stunts like you pulled yesterday."

"I'm not promising you anything. You said it yourself—I'm supposed to be avenging unrighted wrongs. Instead, I'm the reason Genni was tortured tonight, and that's going to happen over and over unless we do something about it. Clyde was right. As long as I'm in this cage, I'm worth less than the food it takes to keep me alive."

Anger flashed across Gallagher's face. "That is *not* true," he growled. "You are judge, jury, and executioner—the physical embodiment of retribution." Fervor burned in his eyes, kindling a blistering response deep inside me, where the *furiae* was stirred by his words. "You serve no one and nothing except the concept of justice itself, and no ignorant brute of a handler could possibly understand your worth."

For a second, I couldn't breathe. The conviction in his voice was stunning. It was absolute. No one had ever in my life believed in me as much as Gallagher did in that moment. I could see that in his eyes as clearly as I could hear it in his voice.

"What you do is important to the world. Who you are is important to me. You are worth fighting for, and *I will fight for you*. But you have to be willing to compromise until the time is right."

I stared at him, trying to understand. Where had his conviction come from? Every other human I'd met since being sold to the menagerie had treated me like an animal, but Gallagher seemed to be polishing a pedestal for me.

I didn't deserve his conviction. Regardless of whatever calling I served, all I'd done so far was get people hurt. I couldn't let that happen again.

"I can't compromise someone else's safety just so Metzger's can get a show out of me," I insisted.

"Then figure out how to give them what they want some other way. On your own terms."

As if I hadn't thought of that. "How?"

Gallagher closed his eyes and scruffed his hat over his hair again as he thought out loud. "Injustice triggers your transmutation, but do you have to actually *see* that injustice, live?" His eyes opened, and his gaze met mine. "Could you possibly just think about an instance in the past? Meditate about it?"

"I think that's what was happening that time in the travel trailer, and I've tried that a couple of times since, but I was never able to make it work. But tonight when I saw Clyde hurting Genni, my inner beast was just *there*. She was drawn to him, in a way she couldn't be when I was locked up in the travel trailer, because he wasn't there."

"Because *he* wasn't there…" Gallagher's eyes brightened, and after a second, I caught on.

"Clyde wasn't close enough to be punished in the travel trailer, so my beast never fully manifested. I don't need to see the abuse—I just need to see the abuser!"

Gallagher nodded. "That's what it sounds like anyway."

I frowned as a new realization dawned. "But I see Clyde all the time without sprouting claws."

"So maybe part of it is that meditation," he suggested. "Maybe if you visualize giving him what he deserves?"

"We need a trial run." Warmth blossomed in my gut and my fingers began to itch. My beast was still there, just beneath the surface of my skin. She was still eager. And she was pissed off that she hadn't gotten the man she'd shown up for.

Gallagher shrugged. "I could send Clyde in here on an errand."

I shook my head. "I want a *real* trial run." My voice took on that fuller quality, as if the words were somehow heavier than they should have been. "Give him a reason to unlock my cage, and I'll take care of the rest." I was suddenly viscerally certain that I could do it. That now that she'd been unlocked, the *furiae* wouldn't let me truly rest until she'd drawn blood.

"Delilah, I can't let you kill Clyde."

I could feel my beast crawling around inside me, restless, stretching to fill the shape of my limbs. "I don't know that he'll die. What I do know is that I'm supposed to hurt him. He deserves it."

Gallagher frowned and took a step back, and I realized he'd heard the beast in my voice. He stared into my eyes, then stepped closer again. "Delilah?"

"I can feel her." I reached out for him, and he took my hands. "She wants him, Gallagher, and I *have* to give him to her."

"But—"

"She won't rest until she draws blood." I hardly recognized the sound of my own voice, or the odd echo it carried.

Gallagher's eyes widened, but instead of backing away, he leaned closer to me, as if he were drawn to my beast. His pupils dilated until his irises almost disappeared, and his hands tightened around mine. "Okay."

"Okay?"

He nodded. "But I can't give you Clyde." His voice was deep and even gruffer than usual, similar to how Brandon had sounded when he was aroused. Only Gallagher's interest didn't look or feel like anything as simple as physical titillation. The fire in his eyes was part empathy and part fascination—a vicarious anticipation of what he'd just agreed to let me do. "Will your beast take anyone else, for now?"

"Wallace." I didn't even have to think about it. His name was

just there, along with the memory of him standing in front of Zyanya's cage, extorting sexual favors from a half-starved captive in exchange for food.

Gallagher let go of my hands and reached for the door to my cage. Each movement was fast and sharp, as if he couldn't wait to fulfill my request. "I'll send him to take you to the bathroom."

"No, it can't happen here," I said. "The staff has to see me transmute while no one's being hurt." To protect Genni and Rommily from future pointless abuse.

Gallagher nodded again, breathing faster now. He swallowed, and I realized he was trying to rein in his excitement. "Give me five minutes," he said as he slid my cage door closed and locked it. He wanted to see what I could do. He could hardly wait.

That made two of us.

Leaders of the cryptid community deny any knowledge of or involvement in the mass slaughter of innocent children now known nationally as "the reaping," but most government officials remain skeptical.

—Opening line from a front-page article in the
Chicago Post, October 4, 1986

GALLAGHER

The boss of livestock hardly saw the crowd that split before him, instinctively making way for the large man marching down the center of the paved midway, clearly on an urgent mission. He hardly heard the organ music or smelled the fried food either, because he was lost in his own thoughts. In the memory of Delilah's eyes, before color had returned to them and the veins had faded. Of her voice when the *furiae* had seized it, adding a dark and thrilling depth to the normally mellow notes.

That voice had called out to him, not with the actual words spoken, but with the power of the tone itself. Listening to Delilah speak had triggered wordless flashes behind his eyes—images he kept buried not because they bothered him, but because they *excited* him.

Blood. Unseeing eyes. Torn flesh. Broken bone.

Not thinking those thoughts was an exercise in willpower—a way to control his craving for violence—but the more time he spent with Delilah, the harder it became to maintain that willpower. She made him want to give in to a basic nature neither of them could ever truly escape.

But that would not be wise.

Not yet.

Gallagher never lied, not even to himself, so denying that he had an interest in Delilah wasn't possible. In truth, he thought about her all the time, but he couldn't say precisely when this

captivating new fascination had developed. It was a strange feeling: part burning curiosity about what she could do, part utter fixation on why she'd been charged with that task. But it was her purpose—the clear-cut objective of her existence—that occupied most of his idle thoughts.

The universe had a plan for Delilah. She'd been given an exquisite and devastating ability and had been burdened with its use because she was everything Gallagher was not.

He marched past the sirens' tent, then the oracles' tent, and he was halfway to the red-trimmed succubi tent before he realized he'd taken off in the wrong direction. Wallace was at work in the hybrid tent. Gallagher's head was not in the game. Because Delilah was in his head.

Growling to himself, the boss of livestock executed an abrupt about-face, without noticing the strange look that Rommily's handler gave him from outside the oracles' tent. Gallagher was thinking about Mike Wallace, a man he'd been working alongside for a year. A man he'd eaten with, traveled with, and shared the occasional drink with.

A man he was about to deliver into the claw-fingered hands of Lady Justice herself.

Gallagher wondered if Wallace would die. That thought did not bother him.

He wondered if Wallace would bleed and scream. That thought excited him, dumping adrenaline into his veins with every beat of his heart. He itched to see Delilah standing over a limp body. Blood dripping from her fingers. Hair floating around her face. Power emanating from her every pore.

He ached to be the one who put her in that position, yet he could not quite swallow his envy of her.

The world would never embrace his cravings as it would embrace Delilah's, once those in need of justice understood what she was. She would be their champion; he would be their nightmare, as fate had decreed on the day of his birth.

Unless she gave him purpose.

Gallagher stopped in midstride and several passersby had to dart around him to avoid a collision. He could ask her. The words were there—written long before he was born, memorized before he'd even learned to spell them—but the precedent was not. Tradition did not support the most radical impulse Gallagher had ever had. Delilah was not a proper candidate for the position, and even if she were, he had not yet earned the right to request her consideration.

There were preliminary advances. Prescribed offerings. A conventional exchange of sentiment. But there was no time for most of that, and she would understand little of it anyway.

Gallagher's plan would not work.

Yet he could think of nothing else. She needed him, and he needed purpose.

Resolved, the boss of livestock marched on with his head high and his spine straight, headed for the hybrid tent with fresh intent. The sacrifice of Mike Wallace would serve three different but vital functions. The handler's suffering would feed the *furiae's* appetite for justice and it would free both Genni and Rommily from the pain of triggering Delilah's transmutation.

But most important, Mike Wallace would serve as Gallagher's official tribute of blood to Delilah—the first sacrament of formal devotion.

PART THREE

ÉMANCIPÉ

DELILAH

While I waited in my cage in the quiet, empty tent, I could feel the *furiae* moving inside me. It was a strange sensation, and every time I decided it was psychosomatic—after all, she and I were one and the same—she would stretch again, as if she were trying to break free of my body, and I would reconsider.

I'd never felt her like that before. Not even the day she'd attacked Jack in the hybrid tent. In the nearly two weeks I'd been at Metzger's, I'd tried countless times to call her forth with no luck, but now that she'd been awakened, she would *not* go back to sleep. At least, not until she got what she wanted.

It reminded me of how my mother had described her pregnancy to me once. She'd said that when I'd finally kicked hard enough to make my presence known, she realized I'd been kicking for days, but she'd had no understanding of the sensation.

Of course, as it turns out, she wasn't feeling me at all. She was feeling Elizabeth.

I'd been jittery and uneasy for the past few days, except when I'd been too weak from hunger to move. I'd attributed that psychological unease to being cooped up in a cage, but in looking back, I could see that much of my discomfort was the *furiae* pacing inside me, eager to avenge injustice hidden beneath the striped canvas and behind the bright lights.

In a sudden surreal moment of epiphany, I realized I was incubating not a child, but a cause. I had become the mother of

retribution, and my vengeful offspring would kick until she got her way.

She wouldn't have to wait long.

Gallagher never came back. Wallace ducked into my tent holding the minotaur's guide rope, grumbling that the assignment was beneath him as he led Eryx into my tent. The minotaur met my gaze, and I wondered how much he knew about our trial run. I wondered how much he knew about *everything.* The handlers' tongues wagged freely around him because they thought he was mindless.

No one ever seemed to truly notice him, except for me. And Gallagher.

Eryx blinked at me deliberately as Wallace harnessed him to the end of my cage, and I wondered what he was trying to tell me.

"They ever figure out what you are?" Wallace slapped Eryx on the shoulder, and the massive minotaur hauled my cage slowly toward the rear of the tent.

"They figured out I'm dangerous," I said, and Eryx snorted.

Wallace lifted a flap at the back of the tent. "You've been misinformed. What you are is caged."

"Only a fool believes his eyes above all other senses." I could tell from his dismissive glance that he had no idea I was quoting Gallagher.

Wagon row was still nearly empty when Eryx hauled my cage into place. Most of the hybrids were still performing in the big top, but Genni was there in her cage, as were several of the humanoid captives, who had no role in the final show. Several roustabouts were carrying supplies toward the rear entrance to the fairgrounds, and the man who ran the pie car was headed toward the silver wagon.

My audience was small, but it would have to do.

Wallace left Eryx harnessed to my wagon while he ordered me to put my hands through the tray slot, so they could be cuffed.

Then he unlocked my cage door. He wasn't supposed to leave the minotaur unattended while he took me to the portable toilet, but like most of the other handlers, Wallace assumed he had nothing to fear from the docile, drugged beast, as long as he was tied to something.

The *furiae* twisted frantically inside me as Wallace slid the door open. Anticipation tingled in my fingers.

"Make it quick," the handler snapped, waving me forward, and he seemed to have no idea that by cuffing my hands in front instead of at my back, he'd underestimated me just like he'd underestimated the minotaur.

My vision sharpened dramatically as I shuffled on my knees toward the open side panel. My fingertips burned, and I heard several soft cracking sounds as the nails lengthened and hardened into needle-points.

"What the hell?" Wallace's eyes widened as my hair began to rise off my shoulders under its own power. He tried to slam the door shut as I reached for him, and he might have crushed my hands if Eryx hadn't lurched forward at that very moment, pulling the cage side panel right out of Wallace's grip.

I swayed with the sudden motion, then the *furiae* threw herself over the threshold. My knees crashed into Wallace's stomach. He hit the ground on his back, screaming.

The *furiae* grabbed his head. My sharp, narrow nails slid through the flesh at his temples.

The handler's screaming soon stopped, but by then, several others had risen to fill the shocked silence. Wallace's eyes rolled up until only the bottoms of his irises were visible. He began to shake as if I were electrifying him.

Footsteps pounded toward us as he writhed in pain beneath me.

When I stared down at Wallace, I saw him not convulsing on the ground, but standing in front of Zyanya in the middle of the night. I heard him unlock her cage and unzip his pants.

How do you like it?

"Help him!" someone shouted. Shadowed silhouettes fell over me, but I didn't look up.

Frenzied cheering echoed from the cages behind me.

"Someone get a mallet! And a muzzle!" Ruyle shouted. He'd emerged from the silver wagon, but was scared to get too close to me.

"I got it," Gallagher called, and I finally looked up. He held a tranquilizer gun, aimed right at me. He fired, and pain bit into my thigh.

Stunned, I fell back on my heels and my fingers were ripped from Wallace's temples. I collapsed against a wagon wheel as the world swam around me.

Blood dripped from the sides of Wallace's head as he struggled to sit up, but his eyes regained no focus.

Gallagher marched toward me, rifle aimed at the ground, and though his gray-eyed glare betrayed no involvement in my little trial run, I could tell from his easy gait that he was as pleased with the result as I was.

The last thing I saw before the world went dark was Mike Wallace's bloody right hand, clawing at his own gory groin through the unzipped crotch of his jeans.

He'd torn his briefs—and what lay beneath the material—to shreds.

It was late when I woke up in my cage on wagon row, which I only knew because the carnival was dark and quiet. The silver wagon's windows were unlit, as were most of the personal trailers in the dirt parking lot.

As far as I could tell from my limited perspective, all the other cages had been hauled back into the usual configuration of two parallel lines, and I thought everyone was asleep until Claudio sat up across the aisle from me.

"Delilah." His long thin fingers gripped the side of his cage.

Dim light from the edge of the parking lot shone on nails that were thick, curved, and yellow, even in human form. "*Mon Dieu*, what have you done?"

I frowned at Claudio, well aware that he could see me much better than I could see him in the dark. "I don't..." I knew who I was and where I was but everything else was kind of foggy.

"Gallagher said you tried to escape. He had to tranquilize you."

And all at once, the whole thing came back with a rush of adrenaline, remembered pain, and primal satisfaction. I could practically feel the *furiae* purring inside me like a smug cat.

"Wait, Gallagher said I tried to escape?" But Gallagher never lied. His word was his honor.

Claudio shrugged. "He said you got out of your cage." And that much was true. Claudio—and everyone else—had probably assumed the rest. "You're lucky they didn't put a bullet in your head."

"No, *they're* lucky she didn't rip them all wide-open," Zyanya said from her the cage. All I could see of her was the light reflecting from her feline eyes in the dark. "Whatever she did to Wallace left a bucket of blood soaking into the dirt." Her silhouette moved among the darker shadows, and her next words were half whisper, half throaty growl. "Smells like dinner."

"I didn't do that." I'd hardly even seen it, before Gallagher's tranquilizer knocked me out. "All I did was touch him." I'd touched skin, then pushed through that into skull, then into the fragile, malleable tissue of his brain.

"Then what the hell happened to the bastard?"

"He tried to rip off his own man parts," Lenore whispered from farther down the row. Even at a volume almost too low to hear, her melodic voice made me want things I couldn't possibly articulate. Dark things. Primal, violent things. "He might have actually succeeded."

"Why would he...?" Mahsa began, but the leopard shifter didn't seem to know how to finish her sentence.

"Because Delilah touched him," Lenore whispered, and her cage wagon creaked as she moved around in it. "Whatever she did made him want to hurt himself."

The groan of metal and whispered murmurs from farther up wagon row told me that others were waking up. Listening.

"But why like that?" Payat asked, from Zyanya's other side. "Why not make him dig his own eyes out, or bite off his tongue?"

"I didn't know." I couldn't explain what I'd been thinking when the *furiae* took over. I wasn't even sure I understood it. "I just wanted justice. I wanted him to understand what he'd done wrong and to punish himself in some manner that fit the offense."

"That was *his* choice?" the berserker called. "Why wouldn't he just climb into a cage?"

"She's talking about a different offense," Payat said, and I could tell from the angle of his glowing eyes that he was staring at the end panel of his cage in his sister's direction.

"You..." Zyanya crawled forward until I could see her in the light thrown from the lamp in the parking lot. She sat in a deep squat, with her knees up near her ears. "You did that for me?"

"And for everyone else he's coerced with threats or promises to give something he had no right to deprive you of in the first place."

"That's a crime?" Zyanya sounded stunned.

Lenore huffed, and even that rough exhalation of air seemed to carry oddly expressive notes. "No," she said. "Not here. Not against us."

"I deal in morality, not in law," I whispered, oddly pleased by the opportunity to twist Sheriff Pennington's words into a more satisfying truth. "Wallace can't misuse a body part he doesn't have."

"Yeah, well, I can't digest meat I don't eat," Zyanya snapped, but I could hear the truth in the raw, vulnerable quality of her voice, as if she were on the edge of relieved tears. She was pleased not just by the fact that someone had acted on her behalf, but by the knowledge that she'd been found worthy of the action.

The fact that she'd had reason to doubt that broke my heart.

"They won't underestimate you again," Claudio warned.

I was fine with that, because they would also never again torture someone innocent to make me perform.

My gaze landed on Genni, who lay in her wagon, unmoving, and I couldn't distinguish most of her from the shadows.

"Is she okay?" I whispered.

"I don't know." Claudio was pressed against the side of his cage, trying to get as physically close to his daughter as possible. "I've been calling her name, but there's been no response."

"I can't see her very well either," Finola said from the crate on my right, which she shared with Lenore. "But her wagon was already here when we got back, and I don't think she's moved since then."

"What happened to her?" Claudio's voice was thick and growly with worry, as if his vocal chords were more canine than usual. "Did anyone see?"

"Clyde electrocuted her." I tried to strip all emotion from my voice, half-afraid that now that I'd unleashed the *furiae*, she would be on a hair trigger.

The father pressed his face into the side of his cage until the mesh made a grid on his face, pale in the moonlight. "Why?"

"To trigger my transmutation." The last word got lost in a sob I couldn't choke back. "I'm so sorry, Claudio. I couldn't make him stop."

"You can't blame yourself for what they do," Lenore insisted.

"Well, you *can*," Zyanya purred from the cage on the papa wolf's other side. "But that won't fix anything."

Claudio spoke into the corner of his cage closest to his daughter. "Geneviève? Genni, *chère, dis quelque chose.*"

The werewolf pup rolled toward the side of her cage, but her eyes did not open.

"She's okay. I think." I'd almost said *she's alive*, but I didn't want her father to know I'd had any doubts. "Genni, wake up, honey." The duct tape was gone, and I couldn't see or smell any vomit.

"Geneviève!" Claudio snapped, his voice sharp and commanding, with more than a hint of fabled werewolf aggression. *"Réveille-toi!"*

"Papa?" she whispered, and Claudio exhaled deeply.

"Are you okay, *chère*?"

"J'ai mal à la tête."

Her head. "She hit her head on the ground." A lot. "Are you nauseated?" I asked.

"Comment?"

"Do you feel like you're going to vomit?" I clarified. "Throw up?"

"Non."

"Does anything look...strange? Are you seeing okay?"

"Oui." She pushed herself upright, and her knee brushed something that crinkled like cellophane. When I squinted into the dark, I made out one of Gallagher's ubiquitous protein bars. He must have slipped them to her at some point after I'd been recaged.

"There's a snack bar next to your left knee. I think you'll feel better a lot faster if you have something in your stomach."

Genni reached down for the bar, then tore into the wrapper with her teeth. For a couple of minutes, we all listened to her chew. Farther down my row, one of the *djinn* was singing to the other, and both trolls had started to snore again.

"So..." Zyanya said, when Genni didn't vomit or pass out, and everyone had relaxed a little. "What are you?" Her golden

eyes shone at me in the dark. "Why would they have to torture Genni to bring out your beast?"

"It doesn't have to be Genni." I crossed my feet beneath me on the aluminum floor, which was already warm from my skin. "Clyde electrocuted her because that's what was happening when I transmuted the first time. He still doesn't know what I am."

"But you do." Zyanya's cat eyes practically glowed at me from the shadowy depth of her cage, and I realized she was shrewder than I'd given her credit for. "How long have you known?"

"Known what?" the berserker asked from a couple of wagons down.

"What is she?" one of the succubi called, though I couldn't tell if I was hearing Trista or Zarah—the sisters sounded just alike.

"Born of blood and wrath!" The shout came from a cart several down and across the aisle from mine, and I recognized Rommily's voice. "The crone is set upon her path!"

Zyanya pressed against the steel mesh to see as far down the aisle as she could. "What the hell does that mean?"

"She's a *furiae*," Mirela said, and I could tell from how surprised she sounded that even Rommily's sisters were rarely able to interpret her riddles.

"As in…an Erinyes?" Lenore's voice was high-pitched with excitement. Or maybe with disbelief. "My grandmother's people called them the Eumenides—the kindly ones—to avoid insulting them."

I scooted closer to the Lenore end of my cage, so I could hear her better. "Did she say what they look like?"

"The old stories describe them with snakes for hair, bodies as black as coal, wings like a bat, and bloodshot eyes."

I was two for four, assuming twisting, gravity-defiant locks could be seen as the logical interpretation of "snakes for hair."

"But the truth is that no two Erinyes look alike, because 'Erinyes' isn't a species," Lenore added. "It's a… It's like a calling. A pull from some higher purpose. An Erinyes can be a were-

wolf, or a dryad, or an elf, or any other species capable of feeling the sting of injustice."

"Yeah, that fits with what Gallagher told me," I said, and when the *djinni*'s lullaby ended abruptly, I realized my audience had grown. "As it turns out, I actually am human. How's that for irony?"

"Delilah, this is wonderful!" Lenore's voice sounded like sunshine. Like hope, joy, faith, and anticipation, and when she spoke, I started to feel all those things, too. Which was why her handlers wore earplugs during her performances—the modern-day Odysseus really could've sailed his ship into the rocks under a siren's influence.

"They will have to let you go!" Claudio said, his accent thicker than usual with emotion.

"Oh, no, they won't." I'd been thinking about that a lot. "I'm not sure my test results will matter, considering that there's footage out there showing my transmutation. I'm still a monster in their eyes. And even if by some miracle I actually got a court to verify my test results and get me out of here, they'd just charge me for what I did to Jack and to Wallace, which would either get me locked up and isolated for the rest of my life or executed."

"But Gallagher knows?" Claudio said.

I started to answer, then thought better of it. Gallagher couldn't afford to be seen as less than loyal to the menagerie, and he'd already given Genni a protein bar, probably in full view.

"He thinks there was a mistake at the lab. They're rerunning the test. But that won't help me."

"Mysterious ways..." Rommily murmured, so softly I could hardly hear her.

"What does that mean?" I asked the world at large, and to my surprise, Lenore had an answer.

"The Lord works in mysterious ways." The siren's crate squealed. "My grandmother said it all the time. Rommily means that you're meant to be here. Don't you see? You were sent to

us, Delilah. My grandmother said the Eumenides would only be called forth when and where they are needed."

And that was exactly what had happened. Gallagher was right. My purpose was to avenge the wrongs committed against cryptids, and I'd been called forth when and where I was first needed.

"You're where you're supposed to be." Lenore's voice felt like a call to action, and my heart pounded harder. My inner *furiae* was eager to accept that call. "No place on earth needs you more than we do. You can *avenge* us." Her pitch dropped into a range most women weren't capable of, and a shiver rolled through me, accompanied by the phantom taste of blood on my tongue. "You can kill them all, and…set us free."

Lenore could have launched ships and formed armies with nothing more than her voice—her pull was much stronger than I'd realized. Claudio had told me once that the only reason she and Finola didn't try to talk their way out of their cages in broad daylight was because Finola's older sister had been shot on sight for doing that very thing.

Fear is often more effective than chains at keeping people in captivity.

"You chameleons are all alike," Zyanya growled, breaking the siren's spell. "You pass for human for most of your lives, then when you get captured, you think you can just overthrow the system and take your life back, but that's not how it works. Even if Delilah could kill them all and set us free, how long do you think we'd stay free? Where would we go? There's no place for cryptids in this country, except as entertainment and playthings. And even if we make it to the Mexican border alive, it's not like they're welcoming everyone across the river with open arms." Moonlight reflected from her cat eyes and shone on the tips of her elongated canines. "You dream all you want, songbird, but leave the rest of us out of it. Hope is much more dangerous than any damn cattle prod."

With that, the cheetah shifter slunk to the other side of her cage and curled up in the shadows.

"Don't listen to her," Lenore insisted. "You're here for a reason, Delilah. You can do what the rest of us can't."

And for the first time since I'd been locked up, I realized that my escape from Metzger's would feel more like abandonment to those I left behind.

I wasn't sure either part of me could live with that.

CHARITY

"You in town for the circus?" The convenience store clerk rang up Charity Marlow's coffee, breath mints, and two energy drink cans with a handheld scanner, then swiveled the display to show her the total.

"No." Charity dug a twenty from her wallet and laid it on the counter. "Just passing through." And anyway, the menagerie would be pulling up stakes first thing in the morning, according to the schedule posted online.

"Too bad." The clerk counted out her change. "I saw it last night. Hell of a show. The Courtyard Inn on the highway is booked solid for the first time I can remember."

"Is that the only hotel in town?"

"It's really more of a motel, but yeah, that's all we got since the Bluebell shut down a few years ago. You need a place to stay?"

"No," Charity lied, as the cashier packed all of her purchases except the coffee in a small brown paper bag. "Thanks." She slid her change into her pocket and took the bag, then headed out into the brightly lit parking lot with her new cell phone in her hand.

Alone in her car, she locked the doors and set her coffee in the cup holder, then touched a series of icons on her phone screen. Shelley Wells had shown her what to buy and helped her set up her email account on a device that had only one button, yet

about a million functions. She still only understood three of them—telephone, email, and internet.

The texting program seemed promising, but Charity had no one to text. Most of her friends had quietly backed away from her after Delilah was arrested. Shelley had made it clear that her involvement ended with setting up the cell phone and, as hurt as she was, Charity couldn't blame her. Any good mother would be willing to take risks for her daughter, but she couldn't justify dragging someone else into danger.

The progress icon cycled for a minute or so, while Charity stared at the tiny email inbox, mentally crossing her fingers. She'd been waiting for a reply from Paige Wilmington, the civil rights attorney, for three days, and as far as she was concerned, any attorney whose services required old women to mortgage their homes should be on call twenty-four hours a day.

Wilmington's work was usually pro bono, at least on the front end; if she won her clients' cases, she took a percentage of the settlement. She'd successfully sued police departments, school systems, and even the Veteran's Administration, multiple times. But because she'd never won a case brought on behalf of a cryptid, she couldn't afford to work for free.

In the end, Charity had decided she'd rather have her daughter back than keep her home. No one who knew her was surprised. But at some point along the way, Ms. Wilmington had decided that she stood a much better chance of keeping Charity out of jail than of freeing Delilah.

Finally, the email program loaded, and a single new message appeared. Charity's hand tightened around her phone as she read, squinting at the small print.

Mrs. Marlow,
I'm sorry to say that we've been denied access to Delilah's blood test results based on your own admission that you are not her biological mother. This is a setback, for sure, but it's

not a roadblock. I'm appealing the decision, and while we're likely to get the same ruling from the circuit court, the appeal will put us on the judicial radar on a national scale, and that kind of attention can really only help our cause.

Either way, we're still going to need those pictures. Let me know when you have them.

Sincerely,

Paige Wilmington

Charity pressed the only actual button on her phone and dropped it onto the passenger-side floorboard in disgust.

That was the problem with civil rights lawyers. They were always more concerned with the big picture—with throwing light onto the problem—than with fighting for any single oppressed individual.

Delilah couldn't spare that kind of time, and Charity's budget could not support a two-year fight toward a—likely unfavorable—Supreme Court ruling.

Still, nearly two weeks of research and planning had revealed only two other alternatives. She could try to buy Delilah from Metzger's, but that would be financially unfeasible, even before she applied for the necessary permits and bought the required equipment and facilities.

Or she could help Delilah escape. The obstacles in that case were both financial and logistical. How would she break Delilah out of the menagerie? Even if they managed to escape, where could they go? The last cryptid to escape from official custody was shot to death in the street like a dog, and the relative who'd helped him escape was sentenced to life in prison.

Charity started her engine and backed out of the parking lot, then drove east for a mile and a half to an empty lot she'd scouted on the way into town. She'd slept in her car before, and she could do it again, especially fueled by the knowledge that Delilah now slumbered under much harsher conditions.

Charity dreamed about the woman in the mirror and the baby in her arms, then woke up with tears on her cheeks. Failure as a mother had already torn Elizabeth from her.

She was *not* going to lose Delilah, as well.

DELILAH

The squeal of metal woke me, and I had to blink several times to bring the man-shaped shadow standing in front of Genni's wagon into focus. The lock clicked, then he slid the side of her cage open slowly, to dampen the noise. The *furiae* stirred inside me. Geneviève was only thirteen!

I sat up, ready to wake the whole world with my outrage, but then I recognized Gallagher's distinctive, broad outline as he helped the werewolf cub from her wagon.

She stood mute and docile while he closed and locked her cage, then opened Claudio's. Genni curled up next to her father, and Gallagher slid two bottles of water and a few more of his ubiquitous snack bars into the cage before he closed it.

"You lied to me," I whispered, as he quietly unlocked my wagon.

His brows rose in silent question.

"You told me you weren't a nice guy."

He shook his head as he slid open the side panel of my cage. "I have never lied to you, Delilah."

He cuffed my hands and helped me out of my cage, and a few steps later, I spoke too softly for anyone else to hear. "Where are we going? Is tonight the night?" I still had no idea what his plan for breaking me out entailed, and I felt almost as imprisoned by that ignorance as by my chains.

"Gallagher!"

The strained whisper came from my left as Gallagher led me toward a fairgrounds service entrance, and we both turned to see the teenage *djinn* seated side by side on their knees, in their shared cage.

Gallagher groaned, but veered toward their wagon, positioned first in the double row. "What?" he growled, pulling me to a stop at his side.

The one on the left—the paler one with the silver hair—turned to her cage mate expectantly.

"I need feminine supplies." The redhead's voice was soft, and she stared at the floor of her cage while she spoke, her face flushed even beyond what was normal for an *ifrit*.

Gallagher groaned again, and I scowled at him. The poor thing was already humiliated by the circumstance, and he wasn't making that any easier.

"Just go get her something!"

His eyes flashed at me in silent censure, but he knelt to chain one of my ankles to the axle beneath their cage, then took off toward the supply trailer at a jog.

"You are called Delilah, are you not?" The silver-haired *djinni* was young and coldly beautiful. Her wide blue eyes literally twinkled in the light from the parking lot, and her hair shimmered like water flowing through a starlit river.

"Yes. And you're…Nalah?"

She flinched, as if I'd insulted her. "I am Adira, a merid, highborn among glittering fountains and glistening seas. Nalah is my *ifrit* companion." She tossed a careless gesture at the girl next to her.

Nalah was one of the most stunningly beautiful girls I'd ever seen. Her smooth skin was golden bronze and nearly glowing, her long hair so many shades of crimson it seemed actually to be on fire, even in the dim light from the parking lot. Next to her, the merid looked pale and cold.

"Nalah hails from a land of roaring flames and broiling des-

erts, but I would never hold her unfortunate origin against her. She serves me very well." Adira gave her companion a lofty smile, and I had to bite my tongue to hold back the criticism ready to leap from it.

"Okay…" It was hard for me not to frown. "Good for her."

Adira nodded, accepting my congratulations with haughty ease. "Delilah, why are you out of your cage in the middle of the night?"

I scrambled for a logical explanation, since I couldn't tell her that my handler and I needed to discuss his plan to set me free. "Gallagher wants me learn how to call my inner *furiae* on demand. Without having a…target to aim for."

That was close enough to the truth that I didn't feel bad about lying to my fellow captives.

"You seem strangely eager to cooperate," Adira said, and the criticism in her voice made me bristle.

"If I'm not useful, Metzger will sell me to a collector." I shrugged. "We do whatever it takes to survive, right?"

Nalah nodded solemnly, the oranges and yellows of her irises leaping like flames, practically glowing from the shadowed interior of their wagon.

"Of course," Adira agreed. "But we'd heard that *you* were above such concessions." Her tone was full of reprimand and I wondered whether she was using the royal "we" or was including Nalah in her backhanded compliment. "We're especially surprised to see that you've submitted to Gallagher, out of all the handlers, considering his role in your captivity."

I bit back the urge to defend him. "He had no role. Metzger put him in charge of me."

Adira and Nalah exchanged a private, ominous look, then the merid turned back to me. "Did he mention why?"

Unease crawled beneath my skin at the suggestive arch of her brow. "No."

Adira turned to her young companion, wringing her hands in

sudden, overblown uncertainty, and I couldn't tell whether she was a drama queen by nature or intentionally putting on a show. "Maybe we shouldn't tell her. I can't see how it would help."

"Would you want to know, if your positions were reversed?" Nalah's voice was soft and steady. Comforting, but somber, just like both her bearing and her expression. My attention was repeatedly drawn to her, in spite of her cage mate's histrionics.

"I would." Adira nodded. "Manipulation is their strongest weapon, and I'd want to know if it were being wielded against me." She seemed completely ignorant of her own hypocrisy.

"Then you must afford her the same rights you would claim for yourself," Nalah advised. "She deserves no less."

"Your counsel is wise without fail." Adira turned back to me with exaggerated solemnity. "Gallagher was put in charge of you because he is the reason you're here."

"What?" I backed away from their wagon as far as the ankle chain would allow. That couldn't be true. They were playing some kind of cruel prank. "No." I shook my head firmly. "Metzger bought me. I was there."

"The old man wrote the check, but Gallagher advised the purchase," Adira insisted. "Gallagher told him what you'd done and where they'd taken you after...your display in the hybrids tent." She paused for dramatic effect, and my heart thudded painfully. "You're here, locked up, a possession of those who were once your equals, because of Gallagher."

"No. You're wrong." I reveled in the numbness of denial, a psychological narcotic, because they couldn't be right. They *couldn't*. "I don't know what kind of stupid adolescent game you two are playing, but I've sat through enough community theater to know an amateur performance when I see one."

"She doesn't believe us." Adira shook her head in exaggerated pity.

"I'm sure she means no slight against your honor, Princess," the companion murmured. "Delilah has obviously grown fond

of Gallagher, and hearing the truth about him must be difficult." Nalah laid her free hand over her heart. "Truly, she has
my sympathy."

"Mine as well." Adira studied my expression, but I could find
only ice in her blue-eyed gaze. "If you don't believe us, ask Gallagher. I'm sure he will tell you the truth." The merid watched
me closely as she struck the final blow. "His word is his honor."

I flinched, and she noticed. She'd been waiting for it.

Gallagher had told them the same thing he'd told me—that
his word was his honor. Were they the other captives he'd made
a promise to? If so, what had he promised them?

I sank to the ground on my knees and ran both hands through
my tangled hair. I wanted to believe the *djinn* were lying—
their delivery hadn't exactly reeked of sincerity—because from
the very beginning, Gallagher had treated me better than any
of the other handlers had, and it wasn't just the extra food and
water. He spoke to me like a person. He spared my dignity. He
argued with me.

People do not bicker with cats and dogs. They give pets orders and expect to be obeyed.

I didn't want to believe that the only Metzger's employee
who thought of me as a person was actually the reason for my
imprisonment.

Cryptids have been warned by the federal government to stay in their homes as the investigation continues into the origins and instigation of "the reaping," amid growing pressure from the public.

—Public service announcement, issued October 10, 1986

DELILAH

"Get up."

Startled, I looked up to see Gallagher walking toward me carrying a plastic grocery store bag. He opened the *djinn*'s cage and handed the bag to Nalah, then locked the cage again and freed my ankle. The whole time, I watched him, trying to see if I'd missed something. Maybe it was naive of me to believe him just because he'd told me I could, but I'd never caught him in a lie to anyone. Not to my fellow captives or to his own coworkers.

He'd said I was meant to be free, yet the *djinn* girls claimed he was the reason I'd been bought by Metzger's in the first place.

I had no reason to trust Adira and Nalah over Gallagher, yet in spite of their manipulative delivery, everything they'd said made sense. Gallagher was in the hybrid tent when I was exposed. He came with Metzger to buy me from the sheriff. The old man had put him in charge of me, as if he'd had some reason to hold Gallagher accountable if I failed to perform.

I probably never should have trusted him in the first place, but because I had, the sting of his betrayal was sharp and deep.

"Let's get moving." Gallagher reached for my arm, but instead of hauling me to my feet, he simply helped me up, and again my resolve faltered. I couldn't decide from one heartbeat to the next whether I was being unfair to him by suspecting him or unfair to myself by wanting him to be innocent.

He frowned with one look at whatever conflict showed on my face. "What's wrong?"

"I'm a captive in a traveling zoo," I snapped, caught between a pressing need to demand the truth and a fear that doing so would end any chance I had of escaping with him. "A better question would be 'What's right?'"

Gallagher's frown deepened, but instead of replying, he led me through the service entrance to the deserted fairgrounds, which sported a blacktop midway and kiosks built like little storybook cottages. I felt like a hostage in a warped fairy tale as we passed a cobbler's shop, a small castle tower, and what appeared to be the cabin from Goldilocks's infamous home invasion.

With every step, my leg shackles scraped the blacktop, reminding me that my status as a prisoner might be Gallagher's fault.

I assumed we were going to my usual tent until he guided me through another service entrance. Just outside the carnival proper, a camper sat about fifty feet from a flatbed pickup truck with the Metzger's logo painted on one door and an empty livestock cage lashed to the bed.

"We took the long way, so no one would see us, but everyone else is parked just around that corner—" he pointed at a curve in the exterior fairgrounds fence "—so we still have to be quiet."

"Why are we here? Is that yours?" I gestured toward the camper.

Gallagher nodded. "I thought you might like a break from tents and cages and folding furniture. Not that I have much better to offer." He led me to the camper and unlocked the door. "There's a light switch on your left, but don't flip it until I get the door closed."

He helped me up the steps in my chains, then followed me inside, and for a moment, he seemed to take up the entire tight space.

Fear skittered up my spine until it hit the lump in my throat.

I couldn't even breathe without brushing his arm or chest, and I was suddenly, terrifyingly certain that I'd just made the biggest mistake of my life. Not that I'd had any choice.

I stumbled forward to put much-needed space between us and collided with what felt like a hollow wall.

The door latched behind me with a solid click. A second later, the light came on, and I found myself staring at a small wood-paneled refrigerator.

"Have a seat." Gallagher scooted past me and pulled two bottles of water from the fridge. "Anywhere's fine," he said, when my focus skipped from the booth-style table against one wall to a small sofa, then to an unmade bed at the back of the trailer.

I sat on the closest of the padded booth benches.

Gallagher set both bottles of water on the table, then he knelt in front of me and removed my handcuffs. They hit the chipped top of the table with a clank.

He sank onto the sagging built-in couch, his elbow resting on the tiny kitchen counter. "Water?" He gestured at the bottles, but I shook my head. "What's wrong, Delilah?"

"Are you the reason I'm here?" The words fell out before I could rethink my approach. "Did you tell Metzger to buy me?"

For one single, unprecedented instant, Gallagher's thoughts were unguarded, and I saw the truth. He leaned forward on the couch, his bearing instantly tense. "Okay, first of all, Rudolph Metzger doesn't do anything he doesn't want to do—"

I stood, and he rose to slide between me and the door, and suddenly oxygen seemed to be in short supply.

"Delilah, wait. Please listen." He reached for me, and when I backed away, I hit my hip on the edge of his tiny kitchen cabinet.

"Is it true?" I snatched the handcuffs from the table top, which was only an arm's length away in the tight space. "Is this because of you?"

He exhaled heavily, but held my gaze. "Yes."

"You soul-rotting *bastard*!" I threw the cuffs at his face and

tried to push past him for the door, all promises to bide my time—to wait for his mysterious plan to unfold—forgotten. "You lied to me!"

Why did that knowledge hurt, when I should have expected it? Why did I feel so betrayed, when I should have known better than to trust anyone who dressed me in linen scraps accessorized with steel cuffs?

Gallagher refused to budge, and I realized he was actually broader than the door—he probably had to turn sideways to get into his own home. "I have *never* lied to you." His gray eyes flashed in anger, as if he were mortally wounded by the insult. "You never asked if buying you was my idea. If you had, I would have told you the truth."

"You lied through omission," I insisted, glaring up at him, and bewildered lines creased his forehead. "You intentionally withheld information I had a right to."

His confusion cleared like clouds blown away to expose the sky. "That's not a lie, that's a *deception*," he said as if the distinction somehow relieved him of guilt. "Deceit is a much more complicated, nuanced concept. I've never lied to you, or to anyone else. Ever." He looked like he wanted to say more, but no more came.

A river of lava pumped through my veins. "Are you seriously trying to absolve yourself using semantics?"

"Please sit and let me explain."

"I don't have any choice, do I?" Yet he'd already said "please" twice since closing the door behind us. "You give the orders and I follow them. That's how the relationship between captor and captive works, right?"

"I'm not your captor," he growled. "And you sure as *hell* aren't my captive."

"I'm wearing several pounds of metal that would suggest otherwise." I lifted one foot, and the chain connecting it to my opposite ankle clanked against the floor. "You were never going to

set me free, were you? So what was your plan? Get Metzger to buy me like a piece of meat, then swoop in and string me along with snacks and water and promises you never make good on?" I frowned up at him, still trying to puzzle it through. "What was the point?"

He hadn't asked me for anything, other than patience and co-operation with my "act," and the only deception I could pin-point was his admission about buying me.

"You don't understand." Gallagher reached for me, but I backed up until my spine hit the narrow bathroom door. "I don't want to hurt you—I want to protect you."

"Is that what you said to those pretty little *djinn* girls? Did you buy them, then promise to let them go, too?" Despite the lack of evidence, in the absence of a more logical theory, the obvious—and vile—conclusion seemed most likely. "They're *children*, Gallagher!"

"Adira told you...?" Gallagher lifted the faded cap from his head and raked his fingers through his hair. "Damn it!" His fist slammed into the table with an iron thud and it broke into two pieces, then fell apart.

I jumped, startled, and bumped the bathroom door again.

The table *fell apart*, like a stack of children's blocks. I stared at it, stunned, and my vague need to escape his trailer became a command to flee, from every muscle in my body.

Gallagher stepped in front of the broken furniture, as if out of sight really might mean out of mind. "It was old and poorly constructed. Delilah, Adira's..." He rubbed his forehead and started again, but I hardly heard him. I was still staring at the table he'd destroyed as easily as I might rip a sheet of paper. "In her homeland she was royalty—given everything she ever wanted, no matter what it cost anyone else—and she refuses to acknowledge that her circumstances have changed." Gallagher tilted my face so that my gaze met his.

I flinched away from his touch, but had no more room to retreat.

"She manipulates people into doing what she wants," he said. "She's a troublemaker."

"But is she a liar?" I didn't care about her motives. "Or was she telling the truth?"

"She doesn't even know the truth. She told you something she heard out of context, because she got scared. I've never touched either of those girls beyond my duties as a handler, and I had nothing to do with Metzger buying them," he growled, huge fists clenched in response to accusations that clearly offended him. "They were here before I took this job." He stood straighter, and the top of his cap brushed the ceiling. "I swear on the solemn honor of my name."

I frowned, caught off guard by archaic phrasing he didn't seem to have noticed, and suddenly I remembered how my mother's Southern accent had always thickened when she was angry or upset.

"Moreover, I will tolerate no further unwarranted denigration of my character, from you or from anyone else."

"Denigration of your...?" Fire flushed my cheeks and scalded my ears. "*You're* the bastard who put me here, and you never had *any* intention of setting me free."

He reached for me again, and when I sidestepped his touch, I almost fell onto his bed. "I talked Metzger into buying you to save your life."

I rolled my eyes. "Because I'm so safe here, half-starved, surrounded by child-abusing rapist handlers." I half expected him to deny the circumstances I'd described, but I should have known better. I had yet to catch him in a lie.

"You're safer here than you'd be anywhere else." When he took a step back, I realized he was trying to set me at ease. As if it had just then occurred to him that closing in on me would have the opposite effect.

"Why on earth would I be safer here?"

"Because *I'm* here!" His spine straightened with the claim, and his next words carried the first hint of vulnerability he'd shown. "Because if you'll let me, I'll make sure no one can hurt you."

With a sudden bolt of surprise, I realized I was finally seeing a crack in the steely facade he'd worn from the moment I'd first met him. The longing that showed through that crack was somewhere between the lust for a beautiful woman and the craving of a juicy steak.

Gallagher was looking at me like Shelley might look at a pair of designer shoes she could never afford. Like my mother had looked at the only new car she'd ever had, convinced she didn't deserve it, but resolved to take care of it.

He was looking at me the way I looked at freedom, with iron-clad determination to take it for myself and make the most of it.

"Clyde hurt me," I whispered, stunned and disoriented by the strange, restrained desire I could hear in his voice and see in his eyes, yet couldn't make sense of. It felt cleaner than lust and more formal than physical attraction. Almost like...chivalry.

Real chivalry—not simple manners, but archaic courtly valor.

Suddenly I remembered Gallagher helping me dress with his gaze averted, after Clyde had cut my clothes off. The clean clothes and blanket he'd brought me, after my confrontation with the hose. The food and water he gave me. How *fundamentally* insulted he'd looked when I'd asked what his favors would cost me.

Whatever he was showing me felt...urgent. Significant, in some way I couldn't truly understand.

"You said if Clyde touched me, you'd rip him apart. Then you let him hose me down." I'd considered that a failed threat, rather than a broken promise, but Gallagher flinched, and I was fascinated by his reaction.

"I apologize. I didn't know how else to bring out your beast and keep you from being sold into a situation I couldn't protect

you from. I chose to let him hurt you a little now to keep some-one else from hurting you worse later. But I swear on the solemn honor of my name that I will keep my word. Evan Clyde will pay for what he did to you. He will pay in pain, and in terror, and in pints and pints of glistening blood."

Chills rolled through me not just at his words, but at the hushed, reverent quality of his voice when he said them. At the eager look in his eyes. He felt and sounded nothing like the steely-eyed boss of livestock I'd come to know. This Gallagher felt larger and more powerful in some captivating way that had nothing to do with his physical size. It was as if he'd just put on a costume.

Or had finally taken one off.

"If you'll let me, I will rip apart anyone who lays a hostile hand on you. I swear on my life, and my word is my honor, Delilah." This time when he reached for my hands, I let him take them, because I believed him. His voice sounded like truth. His every utterance felt like fact.

My head swam and my pulse roared in my ears.

He squeezed my hands, the pads of his fingers rough against my palms. "I can protect you. I *want* to protect you. I want to fight for you."

Warmth gathered low in my stomach. "What does that mean?" Why did the intensity of his voice hint at more than his words seemed to say?

Gallagher knelt and unlocked the cuff around my right ankle. He looked up at me from his knees, still holding my dirty foot. "My people believe that from birth, each of us owes the world a service, in exchange for the seeds we sow and the air we breathe."

His people? What people? How could I have spent so much time with him, yet know so little about him, beyond his role in the menagerie?

Why would a man who kept sentient beings in cages be so concerned with truth and honor?

"That service must be selfless and it must cost us something, because that which costs nothing is worth nothing." He gently lowered my right foot and lifted my left. "I have nothing to offer the world except physical strength, the simplest, most humble of all gifts. But *you* have something truly extraordinary to give, and it has cost you everything."

My chest felt so tight that breathing had become a blissful agony.

He unlocked the other cuff, and the shackles fell away, but his hands did not. His fingers felt warm and strong, yet made no demands and took no liberties. "You are bold, and fearless, and even the darkest parts of you serve at the discretion of your compassion and empathy. You *exist* to seek justice, and it has become increasingly clear to me since I met you that the most worthy service I will ever be able to offer the world is the facilitation of your work."

"Facilitation? You want to help me be a *furiae*? How? By getting me out of here?" Was that why he wanted to help me escape—so he could feel like he deserved every breath he took?

That sounded pretty odd, but who was I to criticize someone else's culture, especially if it led him to set me free?

"By freeing you, and by protecting you, so you can live out your purpose with no fear for your personal safety."

"Wait, like a bodyguard?" That was hands-down the strangest proposition I'd ever received, and on the surface, it seemed to make little sense. Yet somehow it *felt* reasonable. Gallagher looked and sounded sincere, and I had no trouble picturing him in that role. "You're serious?"

"Of course." He looked up at me from his knees. "I've spent my entire life searching for an opportunity to serve. You are that opportunity, Delilah." He cleared his throat. "Will you consider me as your champion?"

"My champion?" That sounded like a hell of a lot more than a bodyguard. And I was suddenly very aware that he was still holding my bare, filthy foot.

"Yes. Your defender and guardian."

My heart thumped so loudly I was sure he could hear it. Those words obviously meant something very specific to him. Something primal, which the *furiae* stirring contentedly inside me seemed to understand, but I couldn't quite wrap my mind around.

"What does that entail, exactly?" Hadn't he already sworn to rip hands off for me?

Gallagher released my foot, then stood straight and tall—all six and a half feet of him. His speech took on the cadence of a formal vow, and I could only stare up at him, riveted. "As your champion, I will serve at your side. I will protect you with every bone in my body and every beat of my heart. I will rip apart anyone who comes between us, and I will litter the ground with the corpses of our enemies. I will be your sword and your shield, in all matters. If you will have me."

"My sword and shield." My throat felt inexplicably tight, and his camper suddenly looked unsteady, as if it might start spinning at any second. "Do you understand how strange that sounds?"

"To you? Yes. But for my people, it's an honored tradition. It's a way of life."

"And just who are these people?" I knew of several religions and a couple of cults which required less formal vows.

Gallagher's expression softened, and he looked pleased by my interest. "You have my word that when I have the chance, I will tell you everything you want to know about my people and our traditions. But right now, we're pressed for time, and I need your decision."

He looked nervous for the first time since I'd met him, as if I had the power to break him with a single word, when he'd

spent the past year working with beasts strong enough to pull his head from his shoulders. Literally.

"I'm not sure I understand what I'm getting into," I admitted, my thoughts racing. "Would I be obligated to *do* anything?"

His brows rose. He looked almost impressed that I'd thought to ask. "Only to seal our alliance when the probationary period concludes, if you choose to continue the partnership."

"Seal...how?" I was assuming he had something more *mature* in mind than cutting our palms and shaking hands. Was that why he'd brought me to his home?

I glanced at his bed, but I should have known better.

Gallagher looked painfully offended.

"Delilah, this is the most honorable relationship my people recognize. More so even than marriage, because conjugal pairings are typically built upon a foundation of lust, which is notoriously capricious. I know you don't understand, but assuming that I'm asking for anything improper from you is a grave insult to my honor."

"Oh. I'm—I'm sorry." I looked down at my bare feet, my face flaming. But I wasn't sure what other conclusion I was supposed to draw. I'd never met a man who valued honor over sex. That wasn't human nature—honor didn't propagate species.

"No need to apologize. Our relationship would be sealed with your acceptance of four offerings and the recitation of a sacred vow."

"Presents and a promise?"

"No. Offerings and a vow," he insisted, and finally I understood that for him, words were as important as actions. His words were specific. They seemed to carry power.

"Gallagher, your people... They aren't human, are they?"

For a moment, he only stared at me, his features so perfectly blank they had to be hiding something big. Something important. Then I understood the problem. His word was his honor, so he couldn't lie. But telling the truth would be dangerous.

"It's okay," I said. "I won't tell anyone. You have my word."

Gallagher exhaled slowly. "No. They aren't human."

Exhilaration surged through me with each beat of my heart. He was hiding in plain sight, in a position of authority, and had been for at least a year. No wonder he didn't abuse the captives. No wonder he'd talked Metzger into buying me. He really did think he could protect me. Maybe he could.

"What are—"

Gallagher shook his head. "I can't tell you anything else right now, but I will hold you to your word. And you still haven't answered my question. Will you consider me as your champion, Delilah? I swear on my honor—on my life—that *no one* will get to you without going through me."

An alliance with a strong and by all appearances honorable ally, who had the keys to my cage and a personal interest in keeping my secrets. An alliance with a trial period. That was exactly what a woman with a big mouth, no self-defense skills, and no civil rights needed.

"Okay," I said, and adrenaline rushed through me, amplifying my heartbeat until I could hear it in my ears, the rhythm of my very existence. I'd been certain the universe owed me a break, and what it had given me was Gallagher. I'd have been a fool to turn his offer down.

"Are you sure?" His gaze searched mine, looking for doubt.

I shrugged. "If we're allies, you'll *definitely* get me out of captivity? Soon?"

"I swear on my honor."

"Then, yes, I'm sure."

"You have to say the words," he insisted, taking my hands as he looked down into my eyes, and he was almost smiling.

Almost.

"There are words?" Of course there were words. Words, evidently, meant everything to his people. Whoever they were. "What are these words?"

He grew solemn again, as if someone had flipped a switch. His eyes even looked darker, and a beat of doubt pulsed along with my heart. "You have to say you'll take me as your sword and shield."

I sucked in a deep breath and swallowed my doubt. I would get no better opportunity to escape, and he'd already taken many risks for me. "Gallagher, I will take you as my sword and shield." *Probationally.*

Without releasing my hands, he gave me a formal nod— almost a bow. "And so you shall have me."

"Great." I gently pulled my hands from his grip and took a step back, just then realizing that I was both unbound and un-caged for the first time since being sold as livestock. "So, now what? How are we going to get me out of here? Where are we going to go? Can we leave tonight?"

"We're going to Mexico, and no, we can't leave tonight." Gallagher leaned back against the kitchen countertop, and I re-alized he towered over his own refrigerator. "And we're taking Adira and Nalah."

I started to ask why, when Genni and Rommily were clearly faring much worse in captivity, but then I understood. "You made them a promise, too." I frowned. "Wait, are you cham-pioning them, too?"

That hint of a smile was back, as if he wanted to laugh, but wasn't allowed. "No. A champion can only have one benefac-tor. And I didn't promise the girls. I promised Adira's father. He hired me to return his daughter."

"What?" I sank onto the couch, trying to puzzle through that unexpected revelation.

"I applied for the job at Metzger's so I could stay close enough to break her out when the menagerie swings near the southern border. That's the only way to avoid going on the run during a nationwide manhunt. Adira and Nalah can't pass for human." He

shrugged. "We'll never make it if border patrol—not to mention the rest of the country—knows to look for us."

"How did you get this job without lying?"

Gallagher's gray eyes shone. "Fortunately, in the entire year I've been here, waiting for the southern loop of the menagerie circuit, no one's ever actually asked me if I'm here to free the *djinn* from captivity."

"A year." I had trouble wrapping my mind around that. "Her dad must be offering one hell of a payout."

"He can afford it." Gallagher sat on the edge of one of the padded benches and propped one elbow on the broken table. "Her father is Bruhier, sultan of the merids."

"Wait, she really is royalty?" He'd told me, and *she'd* told me, but I hadn't really believed it. "How did she wind up in the menagerie?"

"She ran away a week before her wedding, and because she's not the brightest merid in the pond, she fled north, into the U.S. She'd been here less than a week before she and Nalah were captured, and old man Metzger swooped in with his checkbook."

"She was a runaway bride more than a year ago?" Adira looked very young, even having lived in such rough conditions. "How old is she?"

"She's sixteen now." Gallagher shrugged. "Each culture has its own customs. That's no different for cryptids than for humans. Adira's marriage to the crown prince of the *ifrits* is supposed to unite the two *djinn* kingdoms, or something like that. My job is just to take her home. What happens after that has nothing to do with me."

"But she doesn't want to get married." Anger stirred in the pit of my stomach at the thought of a teenager forced into marriage.

"And I'm not going to make her. I told her what her father was offering, and she decided she'd rather take her chances at home than sit in a cage here."

I couldn't blame her for that. "Do the other handlers know who she is? Does Metzger?"

"Everyone's heard her talk, but I don't think many believe her. Which is probably for the best. She's worth quite a lot to her father."

"Which is why you took the job?" That didn't sound much like the man who'd volunteered to be my champion. "For the money?"

"There is no money. I wanted to go south of the border, and the sultan has provided passage."

"You have passage into Mexico?" Even having grown up human, I knew what that was worth. Few cryptids even made it to the border thanks to the U.S. Border Patrol, and of those who did, fewer than half were accepted into Mexico. Worried about a flood of refugees, the sultans south of the border only took in those who could pay, or who could otherwise benefit the kingdom.

"Sultan Bruhier sent a pass for each of the girls, and one for me."

Passage for three. "No wonder the girls are scared. They're afraid I'll take one of the spots."

"Yes, but it won't come to that. My trip into town the other day was so I could contact Adira's father, to ask for a fourth pass."

"What did he say?"

"He's considering it. I'm supposed to call again from the next town."

"Can't you just borrow another cell phone?"

Gallagher shook his head and shifted on the couch. "I can't risk anyone finding a call to Mexico on their bill, or someone walking in while I'm on the phone. But I'll get another pass, Delilah. I'm not going to leave you here. My word is my honor, remember?"

How could I forget?

Gallagher stood and scruffed his sun-bleached baseball cap back and forth over his short hair, a habit I'd noticed my first day in the menagerie.

"You need a new hat." I stood and reached up to thump the bill, and he tensed. "This one's all faded."

"I'll wash it soon, and it'll look as good as new," he insisted, but I had my doubts.

Gallagher picked up the cuffs and leg shackles, and a familiar, devastating dread glued my bare feet to the cheap linoleum.

"I can't put those back on." I couldn't climb back into that horrible cage. Not with liberty so close. Not with Gallagher's promise to free me still echoing in my head.

"It's not for long. We drop stakes near Laredo in a couple of days, then this'll all be over."

"Swear?" I said, as he reached for the doorknob.

Gallagher hesitated, his brows tugged low by the weight of what I was asking for. "I can't foresee all the possible complications, but I swear I'll do my best to set all four of us free there."

"Thank you," I said, when I realized that was the best I was going to get.

Gallagher gave me an almost formal nod, then gestured for me to precede him outside. He turned off the light, then followed me onto the steps, clanking like a captive thanks to the metal he carried. He was about to recuff me when a growl cut through the night, too loud to have come from wagon row.

"What the hell?" I whispered.

"Pipe down, Papa, or I'll light you up until your insides boil," Clyde said, and I gasped at how close his voice was. He had to be right behind the camper.

"Stay here," Gallagher whispered, carefully lowering the cuffs and shackles to the ground, so they wouldn't clank again. He rounded the end of the RV, and after a moment's hesitation, I followed, barefoot.

I'd recognized that growl, and I'd sure as *hell* recognized the soft canine whine accompanying it.

Geneviève was in trouble.

Congress officially repeals the Sanctuary Act, stripping cryptids of protection under the U.S. Constitution. Millions lose their jobs and homes in the immediate aftermath.

—From a December 12, 1986 article in the *Tulsa Herald*

DELILAH

From the shadow of Gallagher's camper, I could see the figures gathered near the flatbed truck, but they hadn't noticed me yet.

Eryx was harnessed to Claudio's wagon, which he'd obviously hauled from wagon row toward the truck with an animal crate strapped onto the bed. The truck's headlights threw two cones of bright light over the grass, which made the ambient darkness look even darker.

"Come here, you little bitch, or we'll have to do this the hard way." Clyde had opened the side panel of the werewolf's cage and was brandishing a cattle prod at the father and daughter inside, both in canine form.

Gallagher stepped into the beam of the headlights, and Eryx's brown eyes widened. "What the hell are you doing?"

"My job." Clyde didn't turn, nor did he seem surprised by Gallagher's presence; he'd obviously recognized the camper. "Ruyle signed the papers on the little bitch this afternoon, and I'm supposed to have her in Wichita by noon."

That's when I realized Clyde had parked the menagerie's flatbed truck next to the camper *hoping* to attract Gallagher's attention. Because he wanted to gloat.

My hands curled into fists. He couldn't sell Genni. She was just a kid—the only child her father had left!

Clyde brandished the prod at Claudio, who scuttled back, growling while he shielded his daughter with his own body.

"Unfortunately, separating the whelp from her sire is a real pain in the ass. Any idea why this cage is at double capacity?"

Gallagher ignored the question. "Ruyle didn't say anything to me about selling Geneviève."

"That's because you are no longer in the loop. Once the old man gets back and signs off on it, you'll be answering to me. If you wanna get a head start on that, come help me get her onto the truck."

"She's not going anywhere until Ruyle verifies that you're not just poaching menagerie assets. Close the door and back away from the cage," Gallagher ordered.

"I don't answer to you anymore." Clyde turned back to the werewolves. "Papa, send the pup out here before you both get hurt."

Claudio growled louder, baring sharp teeth, still firmly installed between his daughter and the handler.

"Have it your way." Clyde thrust the electrical prod at Claudio. The wolf lunged. He began to convulse from the voltage just as his muzzle clamped down on Clyde's bare right forearm, and for one long, stunning moment, mutual foes shared a splendid dance of agony.

A high-pitched squeal leaked from Clyde's lips, but it contained none of the volume or power I'd expected in response to a brutal werewolf bite. All at once I realized the electrical voltage was flowing into him through the werewolf, completing a circuit that prevented Claudio from letting go of Clyde's arm and Clyde from letting go of the cattle prod.

Genni's whine crescendoed into a yowl of terror. Eryx twisted in his harness, trying to get a look at the problem.

Gallagher lurched forward to interrupt the cycle, but I darted out of the shadows to pull him back. "Use something that doesn't conduct. Like…wood. Or plastic." We glanced around and found nothing on the ground, so I raced to the flatbed truck and pulled a shovel from the large tool bin behind the cab. Gripping it by

the wooden handle, I swung the shovel at the cattle prod, knocking it out of Clyde's grip.

The prod thumped onto the grass four feet away.

Claudio let go of the handler and backed shakily into the corner of his cage, where Genni began to lick his face and nuzzle him. Clyde collapsed onto the grass in a bright beam from the truck's headlights, clutching his mauled forearm, jaw clenched to deny the pain an outlet. For one long, tense moment, no one moved. No one spoke.

Then Eryx stamped one hoof, his human eyes wordlessly demanding an update—he hadn't seen much from his position at the front of the cart.

"It's okay." I crossed my fingers, hoping I was right. I had no idea how much voltage had gone through Claudio, but I couldn't reasonably hope it had fried the handler without mentally damning the werewolf to the same fate.

Clyde looked up at the sound of my voice, still clutching his arm, and at first his stare was blank. Then he frowned, and I froze like a deer in oncoming headlights when I realized he was coming out of his stupor. And that he recognized me.

"What's..." Clyde cleared his throat and pushed himself to his feet, still holding his ruined arm, while blood ran between his fingers. He slammed the cage door shut without ever taking his focus from me, but he was speaking to Gallagher. "What the *fuck* is she doing out here, and where the *hell* are her restraints?"

"You're hurt," Gallagher observed, with an almost clinical detachment. Clyde was also shiny with sweat and pale, even in the glare from the headlights. He'd lost a lot of blood.

"You need to go to the hospital." I glanced at the Metzger's truck, then at Gallagher, and the rage I found etched into his face sent chills deep into my bones. His fists were clenched. His teeth were grinding. His eyes had darkened until I couldn't be sure they held any color at all.

Clyde glanced from Gallagher to me, then back, and the ob-

vious misunderstanding surfaced in his eyes, already glassy with blood loss. "You have five seconds to deal with your little whore, before I wake up the whole damn menagerie."

The snarl that rumbled from Gallagher was like no sound I'd ever heard. It wasn't human. It wasn't feline, or canine, or ursine, or anything like the grunts and grumbles of a troll, or giant, or even the berserker. It was a sound of raw power and pure rage.

Gallagher seemed to be standing on the edge of some crucial precipice. The monster within me understood the storm of violence roiling off him like clouds in advance of a downpour, but the rest of me couldn't make sense of what I was seeing. What I was feeling. What the very charge in the air told me was about to happen.

"Gallagher?" I kept my voice low and steady out of instinct, the way one might address a gunman with his finger on the trigger, or a dog with its teeth already buried in flesh.

He turned to me, and Clyde dived for the cattle prod. Gallagher lunged at him so fast I could hardly track the movement. His massive right shoulder slammed into Clyde's solar plexus, driving the air from his body an instant before they both hit the ground.

Gallagher clamped one broad hand over Clyde's mouth, then reached for the cattle prod. I thought he'd rip it from Clyde's grasp. Instead he ripped Clyde's arm from his body, with no more effort than it might take to tear a breadstick in two.

I blinked, shocked beyond all words. All thoughts. Then blood began to soak through Clyde's empty left sleeve, and my legs folded beneath me. Horrified, I held back screams with both hands over my mouth while Clyde howled into Gallagher's palm.

Eryx snorted and pawed at the ground with one hoof. Claudio and Genni stood on all fours in their cage, panting while they watched, evidently unbothered by the savage spill of blood.

My sight lost focus and I started to shake while Gallagher pulled Clyde apart. Piece by piece. One-handed. An arm landed

several feet in front of me, followed by a blood-filled left boot. A bare leg hit the side of Claudio's cage and he and Genni both scuttled back, then edged forward again to watch the show.

When it was over, Clyde lay in blurry, red-streaked pieces on the grass between the werewolf cage and Gallagher's camper. Empty, blood-soaked scraps of clothing littered the ground. More blood gathered in out-of-focus pools on the grass and dripped from the wire mesh side of the crate.

I couldn't breathe. I couldn't think.

I couldn't believe what I'd seen, even with evidence of it lying all around me in gruesome bits and pieces.

"What…what…what…?" My chin quivered, and I couldn't get beyond that one word. I swallowed and started over, staring up at him from my knees in the blood-splattered grass. "What the *fuck*, Gallagher?"

He turned to me slowly, moonlight shining on an arc of blood splattered across his face. "I said I would rip him limb from limb for touching you. My word is my honor."

My teeth began to chatter, in spite of the heat. I had no idea what to say.

Gallagher knelt among the dismembered remains of his foe and took his faded baseball cap off. I watched, stunned, while he set his cap upside down in a pool of blood and stared at it. At first, I thought he was praying.

Then a drop of blood rolled up and over the edge of Clyde's empty black boot, and I gasped. Once I'd noticed that one small motion, I could see all the others.

I could see the pattern.

Blood flowed all around me—from everywhere it had landed during the massacre, as well as from the severed body parts— but it flowed *toward* Gallagher's hat. It rolled, and streamed, and gathered in defiance of gravity, over blades of grass and twigs and trash blown from the carnival midway. Blood trickled through the wire mesh side of Claudio's cage and fell in fine beads from

Gallagher's face and clothing. It all collected in the pool beneath his hat, but that pool didn't widen. It didn't deepen. In fact, it seemed to be shrinking.

As I watched, the blood from the puddle soaked into Gallagher's hat, pulled up through the fibers like a spill into a paper towel, and I couldn't look away.

"What's happening?" I whispered, and when he didn't answer—didn't even look away from his bloody hat—I tried again. "Gallagher, what the hell is happening?"

He didn't answer, but Eryx snorted, so I tore my gaze from the deliberate flow of blood and looked at the minotaur. And that's when I finally realized that whatever was happening, he'd known about it all along.

Red cap. He'd written it in the sawdust, but I hadn't understood what he'd been trying to tell me.

I still didn't.

"Is this what you were saying?"

Eryx nodded. Geneviève whined and I looked up to find her father sitting next to her in human form, casually nude as shifters often seemed to be by necessity, one arm wrapped protectively around her canine shoulders. "Did you know about this?" I whispered, and he shook his head. "Do you know what's happening?"

Claudio shook his head again, and Eryx snorted in obvious frustration. Claudio could speak, but had no answers, and Eryx clearly understood, yet couldn't speak.

Finally, when the last drop of blood had soaked into Gallagher's gruesome baseball cap, leaving the gory crime scene eerily absent of mess, he picked up his hat, which now glistened with thick, dark blood.

"No!" I cried, when I realized what he was about to do, but he set the hat on his head anyway.

I braced myself for the sight of blood running down his face, into his eyes, and over his chin. But that didn't happen.

The blood stayed in his hat, and after a few seconds, the hat stopped glistening. It looked...dry. It looked normal—as clean and bright red as it must have been the day he'd bought it.

Assuming such a hat *could* be bought.

"Delilah." Gallagher stepped over Clyde's torso and veered around his right leg, then sank to his knees in the grass next to me. "Delilah," he said again, and when I didn't look at him— when I could only stare at my hands, clenched around handfuls of my dirty linen skirt, he lifted my chin until I met his gaze.

His eyes looked normal. Gray and...worried. "Delilah, are you okay?"

"What is this? What happened?" I brushed his hand away and tried not to be swayed by the fact that the rare glimpse of true concern in his expression was for me. "What are you?"

"I am a redcap." He answered without hesitation, and seemed almost relieved by the opportunity.

"A redcap." I thought back through everything I'd learned about cryptids in college, but couldn't place the species.

"We're also known as *fear dearg*." He took my hands, and they finally stopped shaking. "It means 'red man' in—"

"In Celtic," I finished for him. And suddenly I understood. "You're *fae*."

"*Fae*, yes, but of the solitary variety. I serve no king or queen." There was something oddly fragile in the admission, and for once, his eyes hid nothing. His pain was mine to observe. "I have no home."

"How are you here? There are no *fae* here, Gallagher."

"None that you know of." He squeezed my hand, then brushed hair back from my forehead. "The *fae* are better equipped than any other cryptid species to blend in with humanity."

Which was why I'd learned as much about them in mythology class as in any of my biology courses.

"Glamour," I said, and he nodded. "What do you really look like?"

He seemed surprised by the question. "This is my actual appearance."

"But *fear dearg* is small—like, three feet tall—and his teeth are sharp and pointy, and his fingers—"

Gallagher scowled. "Yes, and *furiae* are hideous old hags who fly on bat wings and have snakes for hair. How often have you known folklore to be completely accurate, Delilah?"

"Okay. Fair point." But shock still dulled my thoughts and slowed my tongue. "I guess the blood part's real, though? You have to kill to survive?"

"Yes." His gaze was open. Brutally honest. "If the blood ever completely dries from my cap I will die," he explained, one side of his face brightly lit by the headlights. "We are warriors by nature—*fear dearg* crave slaughter. In the past, we've been mercenaries, assassins, and hunters. Some worked for pay, but most would work for the thrill of the kill. However, a few centuries ago, a group of *fear dearg* who did not relish the death of innocents broke away to form their own tribe. The *honora militem.* Members of the *militem* swore to take as victims only those who deserve a painful end. They took an oath promising to repay the earth for the resources they used by dedicating their lives to selfless service. Most became champions."

The strange tradition. The formal words. The strong drive to facilitate my calling. "You're *militem.*"

"I am what's left of *militem.*" He shifted on his knees in the grass, as if the admission made him uncomfortable. "When I was a boy, there was a civil war, such as has never been fought among humans. I and a few others are all that remain, scattered across the globe."

"Your word is your honor…" I mumbled, and another piece of the puzzle slid into place. "*Fae* cannot tell an outright lie." But according to conventional wisdom, they were masters of deception.

No wonder he'd stressed the distinction.

"Which is why we take the oath—it prevents us from killing the innocent, even in desperate times, when our caps begin to dry. Without the oath, most *fear dearg* would give in to the irresistible lure of violence. Even now, having just bathed my cap, my hands itch to rip flesh and break bone."

I could see the stress that resisting the biological urge put him through. No wonder he was always tense. Living in such close proximity to fragile flesh and pumping blood must have been torture similar to that of a celibate man walking through a nudist colony.

"Your cap looks dry now." I stared at his hat, remembering how faded it had been minutes earlier, yet how bright on the day we'd met.

"I use glamour to disguise my traditional red cap as a human baseball cap and the drying of blood as the fading of color, but I have no choice about the truth behind the illusion. Clyde had to die. I had to dip my hat in blood. And you had to know the truth. Though this is not how I would have chosen to show you."

The truth. "You're a monster. Like me." I wanted to condemn what he'd done. I wouldn't sentence my worst enemy to the mutilation Clyde had suffered. But what right did I have to denounce Gallagher's nature, when mine wasn't so very different?

"No." He took me by both arms and stared right into my eyes. "Your calling is sacred. You are the physical incarnation of justice. The force that balances the scales. You are everything antithetical to my nature. *I* am a monster. And now I must clean up a monster's mess."

Gallagher stood and pulled me up with him, and I realized the wolves and the minotaur were still watching us. And that the sun would soon be up. And that the ground was still littered with body parts.

"Stay here. Don't touch anything," Gallagher said, and before I could nod, he disappeared around the corner of his camper. A

second later, the front door squealed open, and I heard his footsteps as he walked through the small space.

"Are you okay?" I asked Claudio. I wanted to get closer, to see for myself, but I couldn't make myself step over Clyde. Any part of him.

The werewolf nodded. "A redcap. How could we not have known?"

"Eryx knew," I said, and the minotaur snorted in acknowledgment.

"This won't stop them," Claudio said, and I realized he'd moved past the recent slaughter to his own tragedy. "They'll still sell Geneviève. The deal's already been struck."

"No." I wrapped my arms around myself, shivering in spite of the warm night. "Gallagher won't let it happen." He might be at Metzger's for Adira, but that hadn't stopped him from treating Eryx with respect and helping me. He would help Genni, too. She was an innocent.

Claudio shook his head. "There's nothing he can do without exposing himself."

Genni whined, her muzzle resting on his leg.

"He's right," Gallagher said, and I whirled to find him headed our way, carrying a large black trash bag.

"You can't just let them give Genni to another carnival," I insisted, crossing my arms over my thin linen dress. "What's the point of being strong enough to rip a man limb from limb if you can't stop bad people from selling children?"

"I can't stop them, and if I try, I'll either lose my job or expose my species." He bent to pick up Clyde's arm, then dropped it into the open bag. "There'll be nothing I can do to help *anyone* if that happens."

"Fine. I'll get her out of here." I held my hand out, palm up. "Give me your keys."

"No." He bent for another body part, and his trash bag began to bulge with morbid shapes.

"I'm not just going to let them take her, Gallagher. She's only a kid!" I said, and Genni whined in what I assumed was agreement. "You're supposed to be facilitating my life's work!"

"Which I'm doing, by keeping you from getting yourself killed." Gallagher stood and met my gaze. "Beyond that, I have another promise to keep, which I can't do if I have to expose myself by killing anyone who touches you when they hunt you and Genni down."

"What?"

He exhaled slowly, obviously grasping for patience. "As you might recall, I swore to rip apart anyone who lays a hostile hand on you."

Alarm coursed through me with the stunning realization. "You meant that literally." As evidenced by the body parts still scattered all over the grass.

"Of course." Gallagher shoved a severed hand into his bag. "My word is my—"

"Honor." I gripped handfuls of my own hair, too frustrated to think straight, then combed through the tangled strands with my fingers. "I know."

"Then you understand that if you let them sell Genni, she will live, as will all the police and idiot civilian hunters who won't have to go through me to get to you."

"He's right," Claudio said. "Sell her, but sell me with her. We'll go without a fuss, and I promise that if you keep us together, neither of us will ever tell a soul that you're not human. Ever."

Gallagher dropped the last arm into his bag and stepped closer to Claudio's cage. "I swear that I will try, but I can't promise it'll work." Claudio nodded, and Gallagher held his gruesome goody bag out to me. "Will you hold this open?"

"No way in hell." I stepped back, arms folded firmly over my chest.

Gallagher rolled his eyes, then handed the bag to Eryx, who

held the opening wide while the handler picked up Clyde's torso and dropped it inside with a leaden thunk. Gallagher took the bag back and pulled the red drawstrings tight, then glanced around the scene of the crime in satisfaction.

My gaze was drawn to his gruesome bundle. "An hour ago, I would have sworn that a man's body wouldn't fit in a standard trash bag, and that even if it did, it'd be too heavy to lift."

"Pieces always fit better than the whole," he said. "And a corpse weighs less after you drain the blood."

"Spoken like a true psychopath." And I was starting to suspect that Gallagher could have lifted several corpses at once, even still full of their lifeblood.

"This is what I am." He threw the bag over his shoulder like Santa with a really morbid surprise, then stepped closer. "I am a monster, born and bred to kill. This is what that looks like. I cannot change my nature. I can only use my oath to reshape it, like tight clothes will reshape the physical form." He reached for my hand, and I let him have it. "Or I can unleash it, and let the bodies fall where they may. Delilah, I've sworn to unleash the violence that swims in my veins for *you*."

"You killed Clyde because you had to."

"I had to kill someone, but it didn't have to be him. I killed him because he saw you unrestrained. Because he hurt you. I killed him because he humiliated you and made you bleed. I killed him because you were not safe here while he still breathed."

"I know." And killing a coworker couldn't have been the ideal scenario—there would be questions, and possibly an investigation. "Thank you."

"There is no need to thank me. My honor is sullied when you suffer, and it shines when you are well." He stepped closer and lowered his voice, but I was pretty sure the werewolves could still hear him. "Unfortunately, we have to endure your captivity for a little while longer."

My gaze followed his to where my chains still lay on the grass. Reluctantly, I let him recuff my wrists, and when he knelt to do my ankles, the black bag recaptured my attention. "What about the body? I mean, the pieces."

Gallagher gave me a small, morbid smile. "Fortunately, we travel in the company of several different species of flesh eaters, each of whom will be glad for the treat."

"The adlet?"

"And the trolls. And the ogres. And the wendigo, the aswang, and the cyclops. And the lamia, if we had the corpse of a child, though I try never to have the corpse of a child. But the lion head of the chimera will be good for a hand or foot, as will the griffin."

"Sounds like you've done this before."

"Many times. But never with the body of a coworker."

The sky was beginning to lighten when Gallagher led us all back to wagon row, my arm in his left hand, Eryx's lead rope in his right, Claudio and Geneviève trailing behind in their wheeled cage. "How can you stand this?" I whispered as we walked. "You're one of us. How can you stand to keep the rest of us in chains and cages?"

"If I could free them all, I would. But that's well beyond one man's ability. Even mine," he added, before I could cite his supernatural strength as an asset. "I can't stop a bullet with bare flesh, and I can't stop the slaughter that would result when everyone I set free is hunted down. The best I can do is get you, Adira, and Nalah over the border, and hope that the others eventually find their way south." He spoke softly because neither the wolves nor Eryx knew Gallagher's true reason for being at Metzger's, and I'd promised not to tell.

Most of the others were asleep when he locked me into my cage, then did the same for Genni and Eryx, and by the time

he came back through with his black bag full of horrors, Geneviève was already deep asleep in her cage.

Though he hadn't gotten much sleep either, and I'd had none at all, neither Claudio nor I were able to close our eyes for more than a long blink, and I couldn't help wondering if I'd ever sleep again without dreaming of flying body parts and blood-soaked hats.

DELILAH

While Abraxas was serving breakfast to Payat two cages down from mine, one of the handlers came running toward wagon row and skidded to a breathless stop a few feet from the food cart. My heart thudded in my ears while I waited to hear that body parts had been found in one of the cages or that Gallagher had been arrested. But the handler only asked Abraxas if he'd seen Clyde.

I glanced at Claudio. He said nothing, so I followed his lead.

"Not since last night." Abraxas dropped a ladleful of oatmeal on Payat's tray, then cursed when he remembered that cat shifters were supposed to receive 70 percent protein.

"He was supposed to be halfway to Wichita by now with the werewolf bitch," the handler said. "But no one's seen him since he got up at four this morning to load her onto the flatbed truck."

Abraxas slid Payat's tray into Lenore's cage, then leaned back and glanced down the row in my direction. "Genni's right there."

"I *know* she's there. Gallagher found her cage sitting by the side entrance to the fairgrounds, not fifteen feet from the flatbed, with Eryx still harnessed to the cart. He put her back in line and locked up the minotaur, and says he didn't know anything about the sale until he reported the incident to Ruyle this morning."

"I didn't know about the sale either." Abraxas scooped sev-

eral chunks of organ meat onto another tray for Payat. "Are we sure it's legit? Did anyone call Clyde?"

"Been calling him all morning, but he's not answering. Ruyle's so pissed off his face is purple."

Abraxas shrugged and slid Zyanya's tray through the slot in her cage. "Clyde'll probably show up with a hangover in a couple of hours."

The other handler looked doubtful, but he only nodded, then tapped the side of the food cart. "Hurry up with this. We're shorthanded with Clyde missing, and that'll get worse when Gallagher heads to town for supplies."

When Abraxas had served everyone and pushed the food cart back to wherever it belonged, Zyanya looked up from her empty tray and arched one brow at me. "So, what really happened last night?"

"How should I know?" I avoided looking at her, hoping there wasn't some weird cheetah shifter trait that let her hear my racing pulse.

"You left with Gallagher in the middle of the night, and you were with him when he brought the wolves back this morning." She made a show of sniffing the air in my direction. "Though you're not carrying enough of his scent to have done much rolling around."

"It wasn't like that." Yet I could feel my cheeks flush.

"What about the predawn snacks Gallagher handed out to all the fastest, most thorough eaters?" Payat asked, holding his tray aloft, ready to be licked clean. "They smelled an awful lot like a certain missing asswipe handler."

I shrugged. He didn't need me to confirm what his nose and eyes had already told him. "Are you going to report him?"

Zyanya laughed out loud, exposing the sharp cat canines jutting from an otherwise human mouthful of teeth, and several softer chuckles echoed from farther down the row. "For feeding one monster to several others? No, and neither will anyone

else. Though I don't understand why he did it." She turned toward Claudio, though he was blocked from her sight by the end panels of both of their cages. "Why would he cover for you, Papa wolf?"

I blinked, surprised by the conclusion she'd drawn, until I realized she could probably smell some trace of Clyde on Claudio, from the big pre-mortem bite the werewolf had taken out of the handler.

"To cover his own rule breach," Claudio said, looking right at me. "For letting Genni into my cage and for taking Delilah out for the night. We agreed to call it even."

Zyana snorted. "I'd say you came out ahead on that one, Papa."

No one argued.

"What did Ruyle say about Claudio?" The question tumbled from my tongue the minute Gallagher finished anchoring the canvas flap.

He crossed the tent toward me, digging his keys from his pocket, and his steps looked a little lighter, his eyes a little brighter, probably thanks to the newly bright hue of his bloodhat.

"Ruyle won't let him go with Genni. The old man plans to breed him with a new purchase." He unlocked the side panel of my cage and slid it back, and I sat on the edge, with my legs dangling over. "I'm sorry. I tried."

"I know."

Gallagher lifted me out of the cage and set my bare feet in dry sawdust.

My gaze found the handcuffs hanging from a hook on the end of my cage. "Should I put those on? What if someone comes in looking for Clyde?"

"Ruyle had the entire menagerie searched before 10:00 a.m. All they know for sure is that Clyde's not here. The gate opens

in a couple of hours, and everyone else is too busy covering for him to bother us before then. So, no restraints for the moment." He leaned to his left and smacked the handcuffs, which made them swing like a pendulum. "Two days from now, if you like, we will throw these on the fire and watch as flames consume them."

"Does steel burn?"

"Only at very high temperatures. Fortunately, an *ifrit's* fire can burn anything."

I stepped back for a better look at his expression. "Wait, you mean Nalah can just melt through her cage anytime she wants?"

Gallagher shrugged. "She's young, so if she can't yet, she'll be able to soon. But not without frying Adira in the process, which is why they're in the same cage. Nalah is the only captive *ifrit* in the country kept unsedated—none of the others have a reason not to burn through both cage and handlers." He set up two folding chairs in front of my cage. "We should all be thankful that she's even-tempered and fanatically loyal to that spoiled little merid."

"Wow." I sank onto one of the chairs. "Speaking of double occupancy, most of my fellow inmates think Claudio killed Clyde. He's not correcting them."

Gallagher's eyebrows rose. "Why do they think that?"

"Zyanya smelled Clyde on him. And she saw me come back with you, so now everyone seems to think we're doing something...illicit."

Gallagher frowned. "This isn't some unseemly fling to fuel gossip. We're upholding an esteemed traditional imperative."

"Yes, but we're doing that *illicitly*," I pointed out. "People are going to talk."

"Well, they're wrong. And to demonstrate the honorable nature of this merger, I have something for you." Gallagher sank onto both knees in front of my chair and pulled what appeared to be a narrow leather envelope from his backpack on the ground.

His steady eye contact told me that whatever was inside was important to him, and I wondered if I was being given some kind of test.

He reached into the leather wrapping and pulled out a short, thin blade with a simple leather-wrapped handle. "I took this from the corpse of my first kill—a soldier fighting against the *militem* during our civil war."

"I thought you were just a kid during the war." I stared at the knife. It was humbly appointed, but the edge of the blade looked as thin as a sheet of paper. I knew nothing about weapons, yet even I recognized the extraordinary skill that went into its production.

"I was eleven. This is my oldest possession, and it represents the day I accepted my calling as a warrior. I would be honored if you would accept it, as a symbol of my devotion to our partnership."

"Gallagher, I can't take your knife." It was clearly his most precious possession, and beyond that, I had nowhere to hide it.

His brows dipped low in dismay, bordering on bafflement. "There is no more appropriate offering from a champion to the one he serves. This knife holds great value to me, and giving it to you means that I hold you in equal worth. If you refuse the blade, you'll be refusing my services. My honor will never recover from the blow."

"Wait, if I don't take your knife, you can't be my champion?" Meaning he couldn't free me from captivity?

"Yes. This is the last of the four offerings. You readily accepted the others, and you seemed satisfied with the probationary period of our arrangement. This is the last step required to seal our union."

"Wait, are you saying the trial period is over? It's only been twelve hours!" By my best guess, in the absence of a watch.

Gallagher nodded. "The probationary period is defined by action, not by the passage of time."

"What?" I felt like a child floating in the ocean, fighting an undertow she could neither see nor understand. "What action?"

Gallagher spoke as if the answer should have been obvious, and maybe it would have been to a redcap. "My first kill on your behalf."

Clyde. But… "Are you saying the probationary period lasted less than an hour?"

"Twenty-three minutes, by my count." His gray eyes shone. "A feat that would have been celebrated, if I still had friends or relatives with which to share the news."

"I don't have any either, anymore." None except my mother, who would only be put in danger by contact with me.

"If you accept the knife, you'll have *me,*" he said, and I could see the truth of that burning in his hungry gaze. "For the rest of your life, or until mine is taken as the price for failure."

I stared at him, stunned. "For the rest of my life? That's a hell of a commitment." And not what I'd signed up for.

"A redcap may only take the role of champion once—it's a lifelong devotion. It's your choice, whether or not to accept me, but you need to decide. You've already accepted the first three offerings and we have concluded the probationary period."

What had I accepted from him, other than kindness and a modicum of respect? He seemed to sense my confusion.

"The champion must offer and have accepted gifts of food, shelter, blood, and weapon—the pillars of life for a warrior."

Food. Well, yes, I'd taken his food.

Shelter. I hadn't… But, yes, I had. Clyde had said my private tent was Gallagher's doing.

"Okay, I took food and shelter from you, but I didn't know what I was doing. You said there'd never be a price."

"There is no price." Gallagher shrugged. "I would have given them to you regardless. But the point is that you accepted them from me, which indicates that you found me worthy of the offering."

"Okay, but what about blood? I haven't taken your blood."

"It's the blood of an enemy, delivered into your hand." Gallagher's eyes flashed with what could only have been bloodlust with the memory. "Michael Wallace." Whom he had, in fact, sent right to my cage.

Shit. "So… I accept your knife and get a champion for life, or I reject it and lose—" Any hope of getting out of Metzger's. "—you?"

He gave me a single, solemn nod. Despite the multitude of doubts rolling around in my head, I saw no other choice. Without him, even if I escaped, I would never get to the border. And even if I did make it, I would have no way to cross.

"There is no more sacred union among my people, Delilah. I will serve at your side with every beat of my heart and every breath in my body. If you will have me."

His words—and the righteous hunger fueling them—gave me chills.

I nodded. "Fine. I'll accept your knife, and with it, your service." I lifted the knife from his palm, and the next word caught in my throat. "Forever."

"I swear you will never regret those words." Gallagher stood with the ease of a much smaller man. "Redcaps are the greatest warriors in the world." His gray-eyed gaze shone with the first glimpse of true pride I'd ever seen in him. "Once, there were entire armies of us, each pledged to defend the crown we swore loyalty to. We stormed kingdoms and left battlegrounds littered with the bloodless corpses of our enemies. We don't exist in such large numbers anymore, and I have no crown to serve. Instead, I lay all that I have and all that I am at your feet. Use me well, and ours will be a union spoken of for centuries to come."

His words were obviously part of some ancient ceremony, but as I listened, I realized they were also true. If I gave the *furiae* full reign and he ripped people apart to protect me, we would be spoken about, and not just in oral traditions passed down by

a fearsome but unknown species of *fae*. We would make history on television and online, and in any newspapers still being printed. We would gain twenty-first century notoriety the likes of which he probably couldn't even imagine.

Humanity would *have* to see us. They would have to see what they'd done.

"May I hold that for you, until you are free to wear it?" Gallagher asked, and I realized he was staring at his knife.

My knife.

"Oh. Yes, please." I gave it back to him, and he slid it reverently into its humble sheath.

"How much time do we have left?" I gripped the seat of the metal chair on either side of my thighs, and he glanced at his watch. "A couple of hours until the gates open. Another hour after that before your show. Genni will be gone by then." He met my gaze with regret. "Tonight Ruyle's going to use Claudio to force you to perform."

"But they don't need to torture anyone! That was the whole point of the Mike Wallace incident."

"They know you can transmute on your own," Gallagher explained. "But they don't know that you *will*. They're holding Claudio in reserve, just in case."

My fist curled around a handful of gray linen. "We can't let him torture Claudio."

Gallagher slid the knife back into his backpack. "Even if we could stop him, Ruyle would just replace Claudio with one of the kids from the petting zoo. That was actually discussed this morning, Delilah."

Anger flared like a bonfire in the pit of my stomach, and bitter irony was fuel for the flames. Lenore had been so sure I could save them, but Geneviève had been hurt because of me, and her father could soon suffer the same fate. They'd both be better off once I was gone, I told myself. But that was a lie, and I damn well knew it.

My escape wouldn't stop handlers from abusing their authority or management from stripping new acquisitions of their very
identities. My absence wouldn't give the captives better food or
more substantial clothing, nor would it free them from chains
or cages.

After I left, the menagerie would still load captives in sweltering cargo trucks, where they would be forced to soil themselves. Handlers would still starve, strip, whip, and hose down
the captives. They would still put children on display in their
underwear. They would still extort sexual favors in exchange for
food. And one night, another missing captive might be found
wandering down the midway, dripping blood.

My escape would only benefit me.

And without Gallagher there to prevent the worst of the
abuse…

I stood, and the metal chair squeaked with the motion. "Gallagher, we can't go."

"What?" He looked up from his bag, his forehead furrowed.

"You can send Adira and Nalah over the border but we can't
just leave the rest of them here to suffer. I'm supposed to *avenge*
them, not abandon them."

"Delilah, there's nothing else we can do for them. Ruyle already wants me fired, and when Metzger finds out I didn't break
you—that I wasn't even the one who got you to transmute—
he'll be ready to send me packing. We can't stay."

He turned to pick up his bag, but I seized his hand and with
it, his attention. "Gallagher, I can't walk away from this place
while they're all still locked up! They're just like us. You said
you'd be my sword and shield in all things. I thought your word
was your honor."

"And both are beyond reproach." He set his bag on the ground
and glared down at me. "If we stay here, they'll eventually kill
you, even if they have to go through me, and I will have failed.
I'm leaving, and I'm taking you with me."

"No! I'm staying, and so are you. You're a warrior, right?" I stared up at him, reckless exhilaration firing through me with each beat of my heart.

"You know I am." He was still scowling, but something stirred behind his eyes in response to my excitement. What moved me would move him, evidently. For the rest of our lives.

"Then why wouldn't you want to fight? War is all or nothing, right? You take everything, or you lose everything?"

He nodded, and curiosity showed through his stern facade like the bulge of muscles through his sleeves. "When it's done right, war is a *glorious* commitment to a cause. The fallen die as heroes. The survivors change the world. There is no more noble commitment."

"That's excellent, because I have an idea." A crazy, dangerous, impractical, and quite possibly ill-conceived idea that would either bring freedom to every sentient, sane captive at Metzger's or get every last one of us killed. "We're not going to leave the menagerie. We're going to *take* it."

"Take the menagerie? As in mutiny?" His narrowed eyes said he couldn't tell whether or not I was joking.

"Yes. A hostile takeover. A mini-emancipation. Blood will be shed, and wrongs will be righted. This is *our fight*, Gallagher. This is what we were meant to do."

"Delilah…" Each syllable of my name was weighted with his skepticism. "Even if we could take control of Metzger's—and what glorious bloodshed that would be—what are we going to do with a caravan full of cryptids?"

"Any chance the sultan would let us drive the whole menagerie over the border?" I was mostly kidding—I hadn't thought that far ahead—but Gallagher frowned as he leaned back against my wagon, clearly considering the possibility.

"Not literally. But if the captives were all willing to swear fealty, and there was good press to be gained…" He shrugged. "Maybe, if I pitch the idea with just the right spin."

Anticipation tingled in my every nerve ending. "Can you go back into town and give that your best shot?"

He nodded. "But I need to know exactly what you're planning here, Delilah."

"We're a couple of days from the border, right?" I said, and he nodded again. "You can pass for human, obviously, and I *am* human." Not that my species had mattered, in the end. "Lenore passed for, like, twenty years, and there are others who could pass for employees with sunglasses, or hats, or work gloves, just long enough to get us to the border." I stood, grateful for the freedom to pace as I thought. "And if we could get Alyrose on board, with her skills and supplies..."

Gallagher took my arm before I could pace very far. "Speaking of Alyrose, what are you planning to do with all the human employees? I can only kill the ones who directly threaten you."

"And those will be yours to tear apart. But with any luck, the rest will simply walk away," I said, and when his frown deepened, I patted his massive left biceps. "How much do you know about *encantados*?"

Gallagher's frown lingered for a second, then his eyes widened, and I knew he'd caught on. "We have two. Renata and Raul. As a species, they're very smart, very curious, and very mischievous. In captivity, they're kept heavily sedated, which only works because they transmute into dolphins instinctively every time they hit the water."

"How long would it take for the sedation to wear off?"

He shrugged. "I administer a specially formulated dose every twelve hours."

"There's no vet?" No wonder I'd never been examined by one.

He shrugged. "Cryptid vets bill as much per hour as a lawyer, and even if we could afford one full-time, they don't typically favor the camper-and-pie-car lifestyle. The old man brings one

in every three months to perform the required quarterly exams and reassess all the dosages."

For the first time since graduation, I could actually see a potential use for my crypto-biology degree. "So, if you were to skip a dose, both *encantados* would be fully functional in less than twenty-four hours?"

"Functional, and a hazard to every human in the room. There's a good reason the name of their species means *enchant* or *bewitch*." Gallagher's eyes widened as understanding dawned in them. He studied me with what looked suspiciously like respect, not for the beast that could make men spill their own blood, but for the idea that might let us take the menagerie without shedding a single innocent drop. "You may be the most brilliant woman I've ever met."

"I *may* be? Come back when you're sure." I climbed into my cage, for once eager to be locked up so he could put in motion the first stage of my plan.

"I'm sure," Gallagher said as he slid the door closed between us. He placed one hand against the mesh, and I laid mine against it, fascinated by the combination of warm flesh and cold steel. "It is my profound honor to serve at your side."

GALLAGHER

The name of the town closest to this latest county fairgrounds escaped Gallagher. He'd seen too many in the past year to count, but what he did remember about this particular town was that it lacked pay telephones entirely. The day before, he'd been forced to purchase a six-pack of some beer he'd never heard of for the privilege of using the convenience store's line for a call to Mexico.

If he hadn't mastered the art of the phone card nine months before, he might have had to wait and pray that the next town had a telephone booth.

The bell over the convenience store door chimed, and an unnaturally cold blast hit Gallagher as he stepped inside. The air smelled stale—like artificial coolant and dust—and as he headed for a row of cold glass cases at the back, he was struck with the sudden certainty that the owner was preserving himself through refrigeration just as surely as he was preserving his beer and soft drinks.

At the register, Gallagher set a small carton of cheap beer on the counter, along with a twenty-dollar bill, and the man behind the register handed him the wireless phone handset without being asked. He remembered Gallagher from the day before.

Few people ever forgot the man in the red cap.

Gallagher dialed from memory as he walked to the other side of the store, and someone answered on the second ring. "Gal-

lagher for Sultan Bruhier," the menagerie handler said, without waiting for a greeting from the other end.

An unfamiliar voice replied, "One moment," and a second later Bruhier was on the line.

"You've called for a decision about your friend's passage?" The sultan rarely wasted time with pleasantries, and Gallagher respected that about him.

"Actually, I have a revised proposal for you. I will deliver your daughter and her companion as promised, and if you grant Delilah passage under the same terms you've granted me—admission with no obligation of fealty—we promise to bring with us up to three dozen others prepared to swear allegiance in exchange for citizenship."

For a long moment, the sultan was silent. "You're asking for additional passage for thirty-six?" His lyrical accent stressed odd sounds and syllables.

"I'm offering up to thirty-six new citizens to add strength to your kingdom and honor to your name. The whole world will know that the generous merid sultan has taken mercy upon a host of abused refugees. Your people will further adore you. There is nothing but benefit for you in this arrangement."

"Yet not enough," the sultan insisted. "I will accept your terms with one condition. You must also bring me a human named Christopher Ruyle. My eyes and ears in the U.S. tell me he is responsible for the purchase of Adira and her companion."

Gallagher could not verify the truth of that statement, but Ruyle was far from innocent. "Agreed. Look for us in two days, at the crossing near Laredo."

"If I may ask," Bruhier said, before Gallagher could hang up, "who is this woman, that you would go through so much trouble for her?"

"She is…" Gallagher considered his reply carefully. "Worthy. I have offered myself as her sword and shield, and she has accepted."

"You're her champion?" the sultan said, surprise thick in each word, and Gallagher gave an affirmative grunt. "Does she mean that much to you?"

"She means that much to the *world*." Gallagher pressed the button that would end the call, then he returned the telephone to the clerk. As he walked out into the heat of the day without the beer he'd paid for, Gallagher reveled in a private moment of triumph.

He'd been waiting for this day his entire life.

Millions flee the country as the federal government begins assigning cryptids to walled-in reservations, to protect the human community from the threat of further attack.

—January 2, 1987 headline in the *Toledo Tribune*

DELILAH

They came for Geneviève in the middle of the afternoon. Two of them—handlers I recognized but couldn't name—with Ruyle driving the transport flatbed. Genni began to whine the minute she saw him. She'd been in wolf form all day.

Claudio growled when Ruyle got out of the truck and took a tranquilizer rifle from the gun rack mounted behind the seats. "Settle down, Papa," the lot supervisor said. "You know how this works."

Claudio's growl only deepened, and when a feline yowl joined in, I looked up to see that Zyanya and Payat were both in cheetah form, pacing back and forth in their cages, while on the other side of Payat, Mahsa sat on her haunches, growling, her black tail swishing angrily behind her.

"Fuss all you want," Ruyle said. "This is happening."

When the handlers approached Genni's cage, she huddled in one corner, her silver tail curled protectively around the rest of her body. One of the handlers unlocked the side panel and slid it open just far enough for Ruyle to stick the barrel of his rifle inside.

Genni whined and trembled. Claudio paced and growled. Zyanya, Payat, and Mahsa made deep, angry bleating sounds. The trolls and ogres grunted. From farther down wagon row, metal clanked and clanged as the other captives rattled cage doors in protest.

The communal outrage made my heart ache.

Ruyle fired his rifle. Genni yelped, and her whole body twitched. She blinked twice. Then her head sank onto her front paws and her eyelids fell.

The supervisor lowered his gun and the other handler slid the cage door all the way open. He reached inside, hesitantly, and when Genni didn't move, he grabbed her left rear paw and pulled her to the opening. The handlers carried her to the cage strapped onto the flatbed of the transport truck, and Ruyle followed, still aiming the rifle, just in case.

When the cage slammed shut behind his daughter, Claudio howled. The sound was an outpouring of anger and grief, and it pierced me like a spear straight through my soul.

One of the handlers slid into the driver's seat and started the engine, and the cacophony from wagon row rose into an ear-splitting din of growls, howls, grunts, screams, and clanking steel. When the truck drove off and Genni was gone, I sat with my knees pulled up to my chest, and I only realized I was crying when tears fell onto my arm.

Claudio howled for his lost daughter until he lost his voice, as well.

"Claudio," I whispered, as the thud of Eryx's hooves faded into the distance, along with the squeal of the loose wheel beneath Payat's cage. There was no one left on wagon row now except Lenore and Finola, in the crate to my right, and Zyanya and Claudio across from us. "Can you hear me?" I asked softly, but the werewolf didn't even look up from the corner of his cage.

"He can hear you," Zyanya said, and I realized I would have to take her word for it.

"You're going to get Genni back," I said, and the cheetah shifter clucked her tongue to scold me.

"Don't give him false hope. How can he get her back when he can't even get out of that cage?"

"I'm going to get him out," I whispered, and Zyanya snorted. "I have a plan, and it's going to work," I insisted. "This time tomorrow, we will all be free."

Zyanya made another rude sound from deep in her throat and Claudio didn't even open his eyes, but from my right, Lenore cleared her throat. "Do you mean it?"

"Yes. Be ready," I told her. "We'll need your help."

Hours later, I realized none of them had asked me who else "we" included.

"We've only got an hour before you're due in Alyrose's trailer for costuming," Gallagher said, lifting the sidewall as he stepped into my tent.

"Did you talk to the merid...king? Or whatever?" I asked, the instant the canvas fell closed behind him.

"He's a sultan. His name is Bruhier." Gallagher pulled a bottle of water and a cylindrical silver package from his backpack, then dropped the bag on the table beside the tent entrance. "And, yes, I called him from town. He's agreed to everything we asked for—"

Relief washed tension from my limbs, and I had to fight the urge to squeal with excitement.

"—on the condition that we deliver Chris Ruyle to him." Gallagher opened the tray slot and slid the bottle of water through, along with what turned out to be a hot dog fresh from the midway.

"Thanks," I said, my mouth already watering from the scents of beef and mustard. "Why does the sultan want Ruyle?"

"So he can take the pound of flesh he feels he's owed. Though no doubt it'll be much more than an actual pound. Ruyle is the one who bought Adira and Nalah for the menagerie," Gallagher explained.

I swallowed my first blissful bite, then gulped from the bottle of water. "So you're just going to hand him over to be tortured?"

"Yes." Gallagher didn't even blink. "That's the price for your freedom and for that of every other sentient cryptid at Metzger's."

Ruyle was an asshole and a generally reprehensible human being, but death by torture at the hands of a *djinn* sultan? At least Clyde's death had been quick. If brutal and messy. "There has to be another way."

"He's not innocent, Delilah."

"I know, but torture? Are you sure he deserves it?" I was supposed to be avenging injustice, not perpetuating it.

Gallagher frowned. "He sanctioned what Clyde did to Genni to bring out your beast. He's the one who'll be torturing Claudio tonight. And he's the one who suggested bringing in one of Zyanya's cubs from the petting zoo, if hurting Claudio doesn't work."

"Zyanya has kids?" How had I not known? In the two weeks I'd been with the menagerie, she hadn't been taken to see them once, and they certainly hadn't been brought to her.

"Three-year-old twins. A boy and a girl. And Ruyle would see them electrocuted just to make you perform."

My dinner went tasteless on my tongue and in spite of my empty stomach, I had to force myself to swallow. Fire burned in my gut at the thought of Ruyle anywhere near Zyanya's babies. He was a monster. The *furiae* stirring inside me agreed.

"Give him to the sultan."

Gallagher laid one hand on the beautifully carved frame of my wagon. "I was thinking we could hand him over in your cage."

"Poetic justice. I like it." I took another bite of my hot dog, then spoke around it. "Why didn't you just use Clyde's cell to call the sultan? It's not like he'll be around to check the call list."

"The *fae* can't use cell phones. Or computers. Or most other electronic devices. They crash about a minute after I start pushing buttons, which is one of the reasons my camper is thirty

years old. That, and it was cheap." He curled his fingers through the mesh side of my cage.

"Wow. No electronics?"

He nodded. "After millennia of hiding from humanity— often in plain sight—the avoidance of electronic technology will no doubt be what someday exposes us. On an individual basis, at least."

I chewed my last bite of hot dog while I thought about that, and I decided that most of the *fae* were safe for the moment— no state in the union had enough manpower to go door to door checking for cell phones and digital cable.

"Where do we stand with the *encantados*?" I asked as I slid the hot dog wrapper to Gallagher through the tray slot.

"Both received an injection of pure saline at noon today. By midnight, any human who gets within earshot of them will completely lose touch with reality."

"Does that include me?"

Gallagher frowned. "I guess we'll find out. I'll bring ear-plugs, just in case."

"Thanks. What time do the gates close tonight?"

"Eleven," he said.

My pulse spiked at just the thought of what we were about to attempt. "So we should start introducing the staff to Raul and Renata around…what, 2:00 a.m.?"

He nodded. "That should work. With any luck, by the time the sun rises, you'll be a free woman."

That night, they gave me a real talker and a bigger tent, which was open across the front so the crowd could spill out onto the midway. Alyrose had dressed me all in black and applied sparkly, scrolling black makeup, which, she'd assured me, would only enhance my "natural look," once I'd "become the monster."

I caught a glimpse of myself in the mirror, when Freddie— chest hair still poking from the unbuttoned top of his Metzger's

polo—pulled me out of the dental chair to haul me out of Aly-rose's trailer. The makeup artist had left my hair down in a wild tumble of dark waves so they would be free to twist on their own later. She'd emphasized my newly hollow cheekbones and enlarged my eyes with several shades of powder and lots of blending. The sequined costume hid my visible ribs, yet emphasized my narrow waist. Alyrose had given me the kind of dangerous, ethereal beauty both sirens and succubi were born with, and I hardly recognized myself.

Yet the beast within me stirred, content with what she saw and eager to add to the effect.

A sheet of canvas was draped over my cage when they opened my tent, so I could be revealed with a splash at the appropriate time. I could hear chatter from the audience. I could smell their popcorn and corn dogs, their beer and their sweat. I could feel their excitement.

It was hard not to hate every single one of them.

"We don't know what she is yet," the talker called from outside my tent. "But we know what she can do, and you do not want to miss one of the most dramatic transformations in the cryptid kingdom!"

That was a flat-out lie. The phoenix bursting into flames, then rising from his own ashes—that was dramatic. The shifters taking on two completely different forms—three, in the berserker's case—that was dramatic. My bloodshot eyes, long nails, and crazy hair didn't really compare.

However, I took a certain amount of petty satisfaction from the fact that Gallagher and most of my fellow captives knew what I was, while the rest of the staff did not.

When the sheet of canvas slid off my cage, the audience and I stared at each other, but they seemed…disappointed. Even with the dramatic black makeup and sparkly costume, I looked human.

"She may seem normal now, but you've seen the posters,"

the talker said, draping the canvas he'd removed from my cage over a folding chair. "Our mystery monster is a sight to behold."

They'd made posters?

I turned to my left and saw Chris Ruyle standing next to Claudio's cage, just outside my tent, concealed from both the audience and the midway by a large framed canvas panel, probably printed with an ad for one of the acts. Claudio lay on the ground in wolf form, muzzled so that he could not howl. He wore a nylon harness—a sturdier version of the kind guide dogs wear—which was chained to a tent stake.

Ruyle stood just out of Claudio's reach, holding an electrical prod, but Claudio didn't even seem to know he was there. At first I thought the wolf had been sedated, but when he blinked, I saw that his eyes looked clear.

He wasn't medicated. He was in mourning.

My heart broke for him, but my blood…my blood *boiled* for him.

I let that anger flow through me unchecked, and the *furiae* took over from there. My fingers and scalp began to tingle. My vision sharpened until I could see individual hairs on Claudio's pelt, and when the audience *oooohed*, I knew that my eyes had changed. Static electricity propelled my hair away from my head, and my throat throbbed with a dull ache even as my fingertips began to burn.

I stared out at the spectators through my cage and found all gazes on me. Mothers held their infants. Fathers clutched older kids' hands. Teens and single adults were filming with their cell phones, and no one told them to stop.

"Drea, why don't you turn a circle and give us a good look?" the talker said, his chest all puffed out, as if he'd had something to do with making me perform.

"Fuck you," I said, nice and clear, in spite of my fuller voice, so everyone could hear.

A couple of teens near the back of the crowd laughed, but the mothers scowled and covered their children's ears.

"Sorry about that, ladies and gentlemen," the talker called with an amiable chuckle. "Most of our exhibits were born and raised in the carnival, and they hear a lot of rough language."

"Most of our handlers are full of shit," I added, drawing more laughter from the back of the crowd. "I learned to cuss the same place all of your kids did. In middle school."

I'm pretty sure my online debut went viral.

Because I drew a pretty big crowd, Ruyle kept me on display until shortly before the main gate closed, and for the first time since I'd been sold into the menagerie, I was one of the last to make it back to wagon row.

My pulse raced for the entire two hours it took the staff to get everything sealed up and put away for the night, and I couldn't have fallen asleep if my life had depended on it.

By 1:00 a.m., by my best guess, the independent contractors had packed up their rides and booths and moved on toward their next stop, and most of the circus performers, handlers, and roustabouts had retired to their trailers and campers.

Over the next half hour or so, I watched the Metzger's employees' lights go out one by one. After that, there was nothing left to do but measure the passing seconds in the snores and grunts of trolls and ogres.

When Gallagher finally stepped silently out of the shadows, I was so startled I nearly screamed.

"You ready?" he whispered, pulling his key ring from the loop on his belt.

"I've never been more ready for anything in my entire life."

He unlocked the cage and helped me down, and when I stepped onto the grass unfettered, my heart pounded so hard I was afraid it would wake every shifter on wagon row.

"Let's go," he whispered, and I followed him through the

unlocked rear gate and across the darkened menagerie into the empty hybrid tent, where a single pole-mounted light remained lit. Gallagher knelt to pick up a bag stowed just inside the entrance. "I had to guess at your size. Alyrose's clothes looked like they'd be the best fit."

I reached into the bag and pulled out a red Metzger's polo and a pair of jeans. At the bottom of the bag was a pair of black hightop sneakers.

"In the dark, if we put your hair up, I don't think anyone will recognize you."

He was right, but that had less to do with the dark than with the fact that no one on staff would ever expect to find me uncaged, unchained, and dressed like a normal human being.

Alyrose's shirt and jeans were loose, but by some miracle, her shoes fit me perfectly. When I was dressed, Gallagher led me across the hybrid tent toward the special canvas room adjoining it, where several of the rarer cryptid hybrids—including the minotaur—were displayed during operating hours.

My friends and I hadn't made it that far during our tour the day I'd been exposed.

"Let me know immediately if you start to feel strange at all," Gallagher said, and when I nodded, he pushed open the tent flap and gestured for me to precede him inside.

Eryx had already been returned to wagon row, but the other two acts spent all of their time, except during transit, in that canvas room, and once I saw them, I understood why.

The largest of the two mermaids couldn't have been longer than four and a half feet, and maybe weighed eighty pounds, at most. Yet despite their small stature, if I'd come across them in the wild, they would've been more than enough to keep me out of the water.

Isla and Havana had webbed hands, scales climbing the sides of their necks, and bulbous eyes on either side of pointy, fish-like faces. The mermaids had human mouths and noses, along

with a set of gills just below their ears. Though they were clearly able to breathe both in and out of water, only a few inches of air stood between the surface of the water and the tank's covering, and there was too little space inside the tank for them to do more than slowly circle each other, their long seaweed-like hair floating around their faces.

"Delilah," Gallagher called, and when I reluctantly tore my gaze from the poor mermaids, I found him waiting for me next to the other, even larger tank. A young man and woman, each about the size of a human twelve-year-old, sat on Plexiglas benches built into the aquarium, near the open top, their bare human feet dangling in the water. "This is Raul." Gallagher gestured to the man. "And this is his sister, Renata."

"Nice to meet you," I said, trying not to notice the fact that they were completely nude, and fully mature, despite their size.

Raul grinned. *"Encantado,"* he replied, and when Renata laughed, I realized he'd made a pun out of the greeting.

Their age was difficult to determine because their pale skin was flawlessly smooth and completely hairless. And like the dolphins they would become the minute they were submerged in water, each had a small blowhole—vestigial, in human form, if I remembered correctly—at the top of his/her smooth, bald head.

"Gallagher says you're to thank for clearing our minds," Renata said, and after hearing her voice, I decided she was a little older than my original guess. "To what do we owe the pleasure, of both lucidity and your company?"

I shrugged. "We're staging a coup, and we need your help."

Raul's bright blue eyes widened and he turned to Gallagher. "Is she serious?"

Gallagher nodded. "But first, we need to know whether or not you can enchant her."

"We can't," Renata said, and when I shot a suspicious glance her way, she shrugged. "I've been trying to make you cluck like a chicken since you walked into the room."

"What are you?" Raul asked.

"Human."

He frowned and pulled himself up on the edge of their tank, his arms dangling on the outside while his feet kicked gently in the water. "What else?"

"She's a *furiae*," Gallagher said. "We don't—"

"And what are you?" Renata demanded, leaning forward on her Plexiglass bench for a better look at him. She'd just discovered that Gallagher—whom she'd been too sedated to try to enchant before—wasn't human either.

"He's a redcap." I propped both hands on my hips and stared up at them. "Look, if you're on board, we need to get—"

"On board?" Raul repeated, and I wondered if they were ever going to let me complete a sentence. "You're asking us?"

"If we were ordering you, this wouldn't be much of an emancipation," I pointed out. "No chains. No cuffs. No sedatives. We want you to voluntar—"

Renata's hairless brows rose. "If this is truly our choice, what's to stop us from just walking out of here right now?"

"The fact that on your own, you'll almost certainly be caught, and probably shot on sight." Because few humans would be willing to get very close to them. "However, if you help us, we can guarantee you full citizenship in a sultanate south of the border. The deal's already in place. But we need you to help us take the menagerie."

Renata turned to her brother, and for a moment, the *encantados* only stared at each other. Then she shrugged, and he returned the gesture, and as one, they turned back to us. "How can we help?" Raul asked.

It took serious effort to conceal my excitement. "By doing what you do best…"

We got Raul situated in the small canvas room with two folding metal chairs, which—he insisted—were all he needed. He

didn't even want any clothes. I set up two more chairs for Renata in the main hybrid tent, just outside the red circus ring, where the wagons would have been on display during business hours.

When everything was ready, Gallagher headed into the employee lot to get the first staff member, while I went back to wagon row to recruit some help.

"Eryx," I whispered, standing next to the first cage in line—a reinforced steel crate mounted on a custom heavy-duty wagon base. The minotaur's cage didn't have a fancy frame because during exhibition hours, he stood for hours on end chained to a tent stake in the ground.

"Eryx," I whispered again, and the bull snorted, startled out of whatever dreams made his thick human fingers twitch. His eyes opened and slowly focused, and when I was sure he recognized me, I smiled and put one hand on the corner of his cage. "How would you like a permanent change of address?"

I held up Gallagher's key ring, and the minotaur's eyes widened. "Shhh…" I said while I unlocked his crate, and he peered out into the dark, on the lookout for trouble. "We're letting the staff know that they're no longer needed, and we could use your help."

I led him—unchained, possibly for the first time in his life—to the back of wagon row. Several of the other captives twitched or rolled over in their sleep, but they were accustomed to sleeping when and where they could, and if any of them woke up, I couldn't tell.

At the end of the row, I asked Eryx if he would be willing to help, and in response, he harnessed himself to my empty wagon, eagerness shining in his brown human eyes.

On the way to the hybrid tent, I caught movement in the shadows to one side of the deserted midway and froze, one hand on Eryx's arm to bring him to a silent halt. A second later, Gallagher stepped out of the shadows, flanked by two large handlers in jogging shorts and tees they'd obviously slept in. I couldn't

hear what he was telling them, but as per the plan, it sounded urgent.

When they disappeared into the hybrid tent, I waited several seconds, then tapped Eryx's shoulder. "I think we're good."

We followed them inside just in time to see Gallagher lead the second handler into the small canvas room. The first sleep-groggy handler stood in the middle of the main tent, hands clasped at his back, as if he were waiting for an important meeting to start.

"Come on in, David," Renata said, and the man in shorts jumped, startled, as if he hadn't seen her sitting right in front of him. "Have a seat." She waved one hand at the folding metal chair facing hers, and I watched, amused, while David sat, his spine straight, picking nervously at his fingernails.

"Is something wrong, Mr. Metzger?" he asked, staring right at the *encantado*.

"Unfortunately, I have to let you go today," Renata said, and the handler frowned, his mouth already open to object. "It's nothing you did. This is a budgetary issue. We're making cutbacks in every department."

"But I've been with the menagerie for three years!" David cried, and I wondered what he was seeing. Did he think he was in the silver wagon, staring across one of the metal desks at old man Metzger?

"And I'm sure you'll find work with another outfit in no time. I think you'll find that if you head out immediately, you'll miss the morning rush hour. Please leave your uniforms and any menagerie property with Gallagher. Best of luck to you, son." Renata gave him a dismissive nod, then pretended to shuffle papers on a desk that didn't exist.

Stunned but compliant, David stood and walked out of the tent without even a glance at me or at Eryx, who still stood harnessed to the wagon. When the tent flap fell closed, Renata stood and stretched with her thin pale arms over her bald head,

beaming a smile that seemed to take up the width of her entire face. "Damn, that felt good! How was I?"

"You were incredible." Far better than I'd had any reason to expect from a cryptid who'd spent most of the past few years in a medicated stupor. "He thinks he was let go?"

"He *was* let go. By the old man himself, in his office. The images were already in his memory. I just had to dig them out and project them for him," she explained, and suddenly I understood why Renata and her brother spoke more like my former, human friends than like most of the other captives—even sedated, they were inundated by thoughts and images from the minds of every human they saw. "Right now, David wants nothing more than to drive his camper back to Alabama and park it in his ex-wife's driveway until she agrees to take him back."

"That's brilliant, Renata!" I couldn't believe how well the plan had worked.

"I hear this whole thing was your idea," she said, as I helped Eryx out of his harness.

I shrugged. "We couldn't do it without you. Or you," I added, turning to Eryx, who blinked at me in acknowledgment. "Okay, two employees down, many still to go. It's going to be a long night." Yet it was already the best night of my entire life.

"Hey, what's going on?" a voice called from behind me, and I spun to see Abraxas standing in the entrance, holding the loose canvas flap back. His eyes widened when he recognized me, in spite of my Metzger's uniform, and before I could stop him, he turned and took off down the midway, headed straight for the employee lot.

"Damn it! Gallagher!" I yelled over my shoulder. Then I raced into the dark after a terrified kid armed with knowledge that could derail our plans before we'd even gotten them off the ground.

ABRAXAS

His heart pounding like thunder in his chest, Abraxas Lasko raced up the aluminum camper steps and hammered on the door with his fist. When he got no response after two seconds, he glanced into the dark around him, on alert for any movement from the shadows, then banged on the door again.

"What?" Chris Ruyle yelled from inside. "It's two-thirty in the morning!"

"Mr. Ruyle?" Abraxas called in as loud a whisper as he could manage. "You gotta come now. Something's wrong!"

Footsteps echoed from within the camper, and the boy heard a scraping sound as Ruyle flipped the latch. He swung the door open, and Abraxas barged inside, then slammed the thin door at his back. "What's—"

"Some of the beasts got loose." His chest heaving with each breath, the boy peeked through the dusty curtains over the grimy sink. "They were in the hybrid tent, no chains or nothin', just walking around and talking to each other!"

"Fuck!" Ruyle pulled on a pair of boots without socks, then clipped his key ring to his belt. "Let's go get Gallagher. Stupid brute doesn't have a phone."

"I tried him first." Abraxas turned and peeked through a window on the other side of the small room, completely missing Ruyle's irritated glance at the admission. "He's not in his

camper. I can't find Freddie either, and Clyde's still gone. We gotta do something! Do you have a tranq rifle?"

Ruyle shook his head and unlocked the door. "They're in a crate—at the back of the hybrid tent."

"We might be able to get to them," Abraxas whispered, following the lot supervisor quietly down the steps and onto the gravel lot. "The beasts chased me when I ran out, so they may not be in the tent anymore."

"How many were there?" Ruyle stepped carefully, to keep his boots from crunching on loose rocks, and the boy tried to follow his example. "What kinds?"

"Three, that I saw. That new female we picked up a couple of weeks ago—"

"I *hate* that bitch," the supervisor mumbled.

"—and one of the dolphin shifters. And the minotaur."

Ruyle cursed beneath his breath. "It'll take several darts to bring the bull down. Come on."

"Should we wake someone else up?"

"They'd only be in the way," the supervisor said as they stepped out of the lot and onto grass, and he seemed to breathe easier now that every footstep didn't call attention to them. "The only men as qualified as me to bring down the minotaur are Clyde and Gallagher. It'll probably take half a dozen of us to move him once he's out."

"This ever happened before?" Abraxas asked, adrenaline firing through his veins, and Ruyle snorted.

"A centaur broke his lead rope once and made it a couple hundred yards before I dropped him with a hunting rifle. But we never had one break out of his cage, much less three at once. They had to've had some help. Someone's head's gonna roll."

"Any guess who?" Abraxas asked, and Ruyle eyed the boy in the moonlight as they passed through the menagerie's rear entrance.

"How old are you, kid? Eighteen?"

The boy followed his supervisor between two tents and past a bank of portable toilets. "Nineteen in a couple'a weeks, sir."

"And how long you been with us now?" Ruyle whispered, rolling his feet on the paved midway to mute his footsteps.

"Three months." Something moved in the gloom to his left, and Abraxas jumped, but when he stared into the darkness, he found only shadows.

"Welcome to the trenches, kid. You ever shot a tranq rifle?"

"I shot my dad's Winchester .38," the boy whispered, as they approached the hybrid tent.

"I guess that's close enough." Ruyle put one finger to his lips and aimed an exaggerated wide-eyed look at Abraxas, who nodded. Then the handler pushed open the loose canvas panel and stepped into the tent.

Abraxas followed him in, then immediately stepped to the right of the entrance, his pulse swooshing in his ears.

"What the— Mr. Metzger?" Ruyle frowned and glanced around the tent, but Abraxas could tell he wasn't seeing the red ring in the middle, or the striped canvas sidewalls, or Delilah Marlow's circus wagon. Nor was he seeing Renata, the smooth-skinned dolphin shifter, who calmly told him to have a seat and remove his key ring from his belt.

"Did you have any trouble?" Delilah whispered from the shadows to his right, and Abraxas shook his head, grinning, and crossed his arms over his thin chest.

"Worked like a charm," he said, as the lot supervisor sat in a folding chair near the middle of the tent, as if he could neither see nor hear them. "This was really your idea?" That's what Gallagher had told him, when he'd chased the boy down and offered him a choice.

Delilah nodded.

"How many is this?"

"Ruyle's the fifth, but he's a special case," she said. "We still

have a long way to go, and it'll get trickier once the first few start leaving."

The minotaur snorted, towering over them both from her other side, and Abraxas laughed softly. "Eryx thinks you've got it in the bag. I agree." He reached in front of Delilah to extend his fist toward the minotaur, who only stared at it, brows drawn low. "You have to make a fist and bump mine," Abraxas whispered. "For solidarity."

"Like this." Delilah returned the fist bump in demonstration.

When Eryx gave it a try, he knocked the boy back by several steps.

Abraxas chuckled softly and rubbed his knuckles. "I just fist-bumped a minotaur."

Eryx snorted, and Delilah grinned. "Well, I hope you're both right, and the rest of them go this smoothly."

"So, everyone will think they were fired?" the boy asked, watching as Ruyle approached the empty circus wagon under the mistaken impression that the opening was an air conditioner vent in need of repair.

"The ones I don't hate will think they quit, and Ruyle here is headed somewhere special, but yeah, that's the general idea," Delilah said. "No bodies. No questions from the authorities or from worried relatives."

"Hey!" Abraxas called as Ruyle gripped the side of the cage, preparing to climb into it. The supervisor's eyes widened in surprise; he'd obviously forgotten all about the boy. "If I say something to him, will he remember later?"

"Not if you don't want him to," Renata said.

"I want him to." Abraxas crossed the sawdust-strewn ground toward the handler, and Ruyle's expression grew more confused with every step the boy took. "Remember that Winchester .38 I told you about?"

The supervisor nodded hesitantly, his eyes half-focused.

"I fired it at the hunter chasing my cousin Thea into the

woods, to keep him from selling her at auction. She was half-dryad on her dad's side. Thea got away, and I've been trying to find her and bring her home ever since." Abraxas pulled himself up to his full—if slight—height and punched the handler in the face. Ruyle stumbled backward and hit his spine on the cage.

Renata calmly told the former supervisor to climb into the vent and begin his repairs and when Ruyle had obeyed, Abraxas slammed the door shut and locked it. "The bastard who tried to take my cousin died facedown in the dirt. Ask me, you're getting off easy."

DELILAH

It took us three hours to convince all the handlers and performers that they had been fired or had quit jobs they were no longer satisfied with, and it would have taken a lot longer than that without Abraxas's help. Once Raul and Renata really got into the swing of it, they were able to convince about half of their victims to leave their campers in the possession of the menagerie and hitch a ride home with a friend, which left us with more vehicles than we had people qualified to drive them.

By the time we started firing the miscellaneous staff, at about four-thirty in the morning, Raul, Renata, Eryx, Abraxas, Gallagher, and I were running on nothing but adrenaline and the thrill of tentative success. About a third of the trucks and campers had left the campgrounds, carrying two-thirds of the employees we'd already dealt with, and all of wagon row was awake and wide-eyed, buzzing with rumors of the staff exodus.

When Gallagher had escorted the petting zoo "nannies" to the hybrid tent to convince them both that they'd quit, Eryx hauled the children one cage at a time toward wagon row, where I used Gallagher's keys to reunite parents with children.

Zyanya cried when she saw her twins. "You did it!" she whispered, clutching the side of her cage while I unlocked it. "I can't believe you did it." Yet fear echoed in her voice and was evident in her grip on the metal wire. As excited as she was, she expected our coup to fail and dreaded the price we would pay.

"It's not over yet," I admitted. "But as soon as we're rid of the staff, we'll let you all out. In the meantime, I thought you'd like some company while you wait."

I lifted both squirmy toddlers into their mother's cage, and when she scooped up her excited, mewling, human-form kittens, my vision blurred beneath tears of my own. Even Eryx sniffled. I gave them two packs of hot dogs and three bottles of water from Clyde's refrigerator, then left them to their reunion.

While Zyanya coddled and examined her kittens, checking every inch of their tiny bodies for marks or injuries, speaking to them in hushed, tender tones, I opened the next wagon. Claudio looked up when I set some scavenged clothes and a pair of shoes on the pressed aluminum cage floor, along with a backpack full of food and water, and a pair of dark sunglasses. "Go get your daughter," I said.

Claudio ran his hand over the blue tee, and his eyes watered.

"You can throw them in the backpack, if you want to go after her in wolf form. It has a strap here that'll fasten around your stomach." I demonstrated clicking the fasteners together. "You should be able to run with it on—"

"It's not that," he said. "I've never worn such a shirt. Or such a color. I've never carried...possessions."

I smiled. "Welcome to emancipation. New clothes for everyone."

"Enjoy it, for however long it lasts," Zyanya said, and when I leaned back to scowl at her, she shrugged, a quiet child cradled in each arm, their pudgy little hands clutching possessively at their mother's dress, as if they were afraid to let her go. "You know it's true. They'll catch him. Or they'll kill him. They'll probably kill all of us when we're caught, to make an example." She nudged one of the packets of hot dogs, which she couldn't open with her hands full of toddler. "Your heart's in the right place, but you've just served our last meal."

"That's not true," I insisted as Claudio began to pull on the

new clothes with a shifter's typical immodesty. "You all have passage over the border and guaranteed citizenship in the merid sultanate. We'll reach the border tomorrow. No more cages. No chains. No late-night visits in exchange for food. You and your kids are going to be free, Zyanya. For good."

Her laugh was harsh and bitter, and I instinctively recoiled from the sound. "You don't get it, do you? These aren't my only children, Delilah," she said, and it took a moment before a brutal understanding crashed over me. "Two more were sold off years ago, separately. I can't leave them here to suffer any more than Claudio can leave Genni. Half of wagon row will refuse to cross the border for the same reason."

"But what about *these* children?" I demanded, gesturing to the curly-headed toddlers. Surely she wouldn't condemn them to captivity just because the older ones were locked up.

"If they truly have passage, I'll send them over the border with Payat."

Her brother grunted in consent from the cage on her other side.

I could only stare at her, frustrated almost beyond words by how much I'd failed to consider. How little I'd seen of the larger picture. Still, there was only so much even a *furiae* could do, and she might not get another chance at freedom. "Zyanya, if you stay here, they'll catch you eventually."

"I know. Claudio knows it, too." She carefully laid her mewling twins side by side on her blanket, then crawled closer to the side of her cage and lowered her voice. "But how could either of us live in peace while our children are suffering?" Her orangish gaze pinned me from a foot away, as light from the parking lot shone on her dark skin, and despite the differences in their ages and appearances, something in Zyanya's expression reminded me of my mom.

My mother would move heaven and earth if she thought it would help me, and Zyanya would do the same for her children.

"Okay. Maybe we can wait another day or two," I said as a new idea began to form. "Do you know where your other kids are? Maybe we could buy them back in Metzger's name before we cross." I turned back to Claudio, who was trying to figure out how to tie his new boots. "We could do the same for Genni. Gallagher knows who bought her."

"What about my daughter?" one of the succubi demanded from farther down the row.

"And my son," the berserker added.

"Our parents," Lala called from the oracles' cage.

"And my mother and my little sister," Lenore said. "We were separated when we were exposed. I can't leave the country without them."

Calls rang out from the full length of wagon row, and the demands were overwhelming. My heart thumped too hard and my throat felt tight. I hadn't understood the breadth of the problem. The scale of their suffering.

I'd never felt like such a fool in my life.

"Did you really think it would be that easy?" Zyanya demanded softly, with one look at my stricken face. "Did you honestly think you could spend two weeks in our shoes, then swoop in and solve all our problems?"

"I…" Is that what I'd thought? Had I truly been that naive?

"I get that you want to fix this, Delilah," Zyanya said, as she pulled open one of the hot dog packets. "It's in your nature. But this isn't the kind of thing that can be fixed by making a couple of men claw their own privates off." She took a bite from the first stick of beef. "You're in way over your head, *furiae*."

"We can't go," I said, before the bathroom door could even swing shut behind Gallagher. I'd dragged him into the nearest building I could find, and only realized it was a men's room when I noticed the urinals.

"We can't go where?" But his deeply furrowed forehead told me he knew exactly what I was talking about.

"Gallagher, they won't cross the border with us. They all have family members who were sold off, and I can't leave knowing they're all going to be recaptured or killed just for trying to save their kids. Or their parents. Or their siblings."

"So, what, we get captured along with them?" he demanded. "How will that help?"

"We won't get captured. We've taken the menagerie, and no one knows! Don't you get it? Metzger's can travel all over the country, and as long as it looks like we're keeping cryptids in cages, no one will know any different. We could buy back their relatives as we go, then just drive the whole caravan back to Mexico. We might even be able to pick up a few strays, like you guys picked me up. We'd be *saving lives*, Gallagher. That's making a difference."

"Delilah, that's a beautiful thought, but—"

"Don't patronize me!" I snapped, anger sizzling beneath my skin.

His gaze hardened. "I'm not patronizing you. I'm telling you it won't work. Metzger's is broke. Maybe we could get Genni back. We haven't been paid for her yet. But then we'd only be able to buy one or two more—assuming we can find them—before the funds are exhausted. And that's if we don't spend anything on food or fuel, which is well beyond the bounds of practicality."

I crossed my arms over my chest and stared up at him in the fluorescent glow from overhead. "Isn't the menagerie a business? Won't people pay to come see us?"

"Yes, but—"

"Wouldn't that be the most satisfying irony ever?" I demanded. "Using the money we take from human audiences to buy freedom for cryptids?"

He nodded. "There is a certain poetic ring to it, but are you sure they'd want to perform?"

"I think that's a question worth asking." I shrugged. "We'd only have to use the cages for performances, and we could change the show. Cut out anything demeaning or cruel. We could be showing off, instead of being exploited. We could show people how much beauty there really is in the cryptid world!"

Gallagher's resistance was starting to weaken. "Okay, I'm not saying it's not possible, for a little while anyway," he said. "But, Delilah, you said it yourself—the menagerie is a business. There are fees, and inspections, and bookkeeping, and advertisement. The administrative aspects never end, and we've just fired everyone who knows about that stuff."

"We haven't fired everyone yet. We know Abraxas will stay—he's looking for his cousin. And there's Alyrose."

"She won't—"

"She might," I insisted, leaning against one of the grimy gray toilet stalls.

"She'd be risking jail time if we're caught."

"We're risking a hell of a lot more than that. I'm going to ask her."

"Delilah." Gallagher put a hand on each of my shoulders. "If this is what you want to do, I'm with you. I always will be. But I want you to think about this for a minute. You're less than a day away from absolute freedom. No running. No hiding. No chains. Are you willing to give that up for a chance—a very *slim* chance—that we can find a handful of cryptids spread out all over the country?"

"Am I willing to risk my own freedom for the chance to give that same thing to several dozen others?" I stared up at him. "Gallagher, that's the *only* thing I'm willing to risk my freedom for."

I sneaked Renata through the thickest shadows to Alyrose's trailer, where Abraxas had promised to meet me with Kevin—the last of the handlers—in tow. The costume mistress answered

her door in a blue satin robe, her normally spiky purple hair hanging limp around her ears. Her sleep-puffy eyes widened when she recognized me. "What the—"

Then she noticed the *encantado* standing behind me, still nude, because every piece of clothing we'd offered her had irritated her smooth, sensitive skin.

Alyrose made an inarticulate sound and tried to slam the door in my face. I stuck my foot in the jam, and when she backed farther into her trailer, I led Renata inside.

"We're not here to hurt you," I said, but Aly couldn't tear her gaze from the *encantado*. Renata looked around the trailer with wide eyes, taking in the furniture, and costumes, and makeup, and I wondered if that was the first time she'd ever physically existed in the kind of setting she'd been re-creating for her victims for the past couple of hours.

Alyrose shifted nervously, reclaiming my attention. "We're taking the menagerie, and I'm offering you a choice few of the other staff members are getting. Because I think you're a decent person."

"You're *taking* the menagerie?" Her eyes swam in fear; she still thought we'd come to kill her.

"Yes. Total mutiny. In fact, we're almost done. Do you know what Renata is?" I asked, and when her gaze strayed to the *encantado* again, as Renata ran her fingers over a feather boa hanging from a full clothing rack, I stepped between them to regain her focus. "Aly. Do you understand what she and her brother can do?"

The costume mistress nodded, and her focus shifted back and forth between us. "They can alter memory and perception."

"Exactly. Renata and Raul are helping us send the staff away peacefully. There hasn't been a single injury so far. If you want, we can do that for you. You wouldn't remember any of this. You'd just believe you decided to move on from the carnival

lifestyle. Or…you can stay. We'd love to have you, and we could really use your help."

"With what?" Finally, she looked more curious than scared.

"We're going to run the menagerie ourselves. *For* ourselves. The only way we can stay free in the U.S. is to maintain the illusion of the traveling menagerie, as if nothing's changed. And we could use a good costume mistress. But you need to understand up front that it won't be like it was before. Sentient, nonviolent cryptids will only be in cages for performances."

"The adlet?" Fear lined Aly's forehead.

"We can't set him free. He's a predator through and through. But he'll have decent facilities and food. We'll do what we can for him, and for anyone who's truly a threat to others, within those limitations. You'll be safe here with us if you stay, but if we get caught, you'll get caught with us." I wanted to be upfront about that, too. "So…what do you say?"

Her eyes were painfully wide, and her fingers were curling and uncurling at her sides, as if she didn't know what to do with them. "Do I have to decide now?"

"Five minutes ago would have been good. If you choose to stay and later decide you don't like it, you can leave then, under the same terms."

Alyrose looked from me to Renata, as if to confirm what I'd promised. Or maybe to make sure this whole conversation wasn't really just an enchantment.

"If I were enchanting you, you wouldn't see me," Renata said, as she thumbed through a book of fabric samples, but her reassurance sounded more like a threat.

Alyrose took a deep breath, and finally she nodded. "Okay. I'm in."

On our way out of Alyrose's trailer, I stopped and turned back to her. "Hey, do you have anything Renata could wear while she's out of the water? Everything we've given her irritates her skin."

When Aly pulled off her own satin robe and gave it to the *encantato*, I knew that I'd been right to trust my gut. Regardless of her species, Alyrose was one of us.

We passed wagon row on the way back to the hybrid tent, and halfway down, I put one hand on Renata's satin-clad shoulder to stop her. Something was wrong. Turning, I studied the wagons. Everyone was awake, and many of them were still slowly nibbling the snacks I'd brought, obviously worried that my plan would fail and it might be a long time before they were fed again.

I could understand that fear.

But one of the cages looked...

I let go of Renata and marched toward the siren cage—where Finola sat alone. "Where's Lenore?" I demanded, panic painting my voice in shrill tones.

"Kevin came for her, but—"

I took off running with Renata on my heels, and behind me Finola was still shouting, "Delilah, wait...!"

KEVIN

Kevin was already awake when Gallagher knocked on the door of the camper next door. He was already dressed, and had brushed his teeth and combed his hair nearly an hour before. Holding one boot, he peeked between the dusty metal blinds, as paranoid men were apt to do, and saw Gallagher lead Hallie and Farah—the human contortionists—toward the fairground. At two in the morning.

And they weren't the first to go.

Kevin's hands shook as he pulled his last boot on, listening carefully for more footsteps. More knocks on hollow metal doors.

Over the past half hour, he'd seen the boss of livestock come for two other staff members. Then Abraxas, that kid they'd picked up near Saint Louis a few months before, had pounded on Ruyle's door across the way, spouting some story about a breakout. Kevin might have fallen for it, too, if anyone had sounded the alarm. And if he hadn't already seen several other handlers lured quietly from their beds in the middle of the night.

Two of them had come back, climbed into their campers, and driven right off the lot. The others had yet to return.

Something very strange was going on. Maybe it was nothing. Maybe there was a perfectly good explanation. But a man with secrets like Kevin's couldn't afford to take that chance.

Kevin sneaked out of his camper the moment Gallagher and

the acrobats disappeared around the corner, his keys jingling in his pocket, his left boot untied. He stuck to the shadows on his way toward wagon row, and ducked behind a portable toilet when he saw a dark-headed female employee jogging toward the fairgrounds as if her feet were on fire.

One glance at wagon row had confirmed that something was wrong. The cheetah shifter was cradling her cubs—in her cage! Several others were eating what looked like raw hot dogs, probably stolen from one of the vendor's carts. And they all had bottles of water.

If this was a breakout, why were none of the exhibits loose? Who was feeding them? Why were the employees abandoning the menagerie one by one in the middle of the night?

Lenore sat up straight when she saw him, her eyes wide with obvious relief. "Kevin!" she whispered around a bit of... Was that a candy bar clutched in her right hand? No, a power bar. Who had given her a power bar?

"Come on. Something's wrong, and this is our chance." He unlocked her cage with practiced ease, then hauled her onto the ground with one arm around her waist.

"Wait, I have to tell—"

"Shh..." Kevin slid the cage door shut and locked it with a regretful glance at Finola, who stared at him in bewilderment. He felt bad about leaving her there, but he really had no other choice.

Kevin's grip on Lenore's hand tightened as he pulled her across the gravel lot toward his trailer. She stumbled and cried out for him to wait, but he kept running, hauling her along as fast as he could, his heart pounding against his sternum. Whatever was going on would soon attract the cops, and they'd have to be long gone by the time that happened.

"Kevin, wait!" Lenore's voice flowed over him like water over a riverbed, eroding his willpower. Washing away his immediate haste, but leaving his deeper-rooted anxiety intact. It was a

soft insertion of her will over his, and it was his irritation that stopped him, as much as it was the pull from her voice:

"You swore you'd never do that," he snapped, skidding to a halt on the gravel beneath his boots.

"It's an emergency," she said, by way of an apology. "It's a coup, Kevin. A mutiny. The cryptids are taking over the menagerie."

"So I see. We need to be at least sixty miles away before anyone else figures that out," he insisted, tightening his grip on her hand when she tried to pull free. "This is our chance to get away." He'd been waiting for an opportunity for years, biding his time in a red polo that bound him to the carnival as surely as her chains bound her. But he'd been expecting a simple distraction, like a tent fire, or an escaped centaur. He'd never dreamed of an opportunity like this.

"No," Lenore said. "This is our chance to *stay*."

"But when the cops get here—"

"The cops won't get here. No one's going to report this, Kevin. The employees don't even know this is happening. They all think they've been fired, or that they quit. It's really kind of funny. And pretty smart."

"They think…?" Well, that would explain why they were all leaving, instead of sounding an alarm. "How?"

Lenore smiled, and her entire face lit up. "The *encantados*. Delilah woke them up."

"Delilah?"

"Yes. I told you, she was sent to us. She did this for us, and we *owe* her."

"We don't owe anyone anything. Not after what you've been through."

Kevin had ached to touch her since the moment he'd first seen her, so long ago, and no matter how many times his greedy hands fulfilled that wish, he couldn't get enough of her.

He would *never* have enough of her. But this was his chance

to try. "Come on. We're leaving, and we're going to put this all behind us."

"No." Lenore's voice held no pull, but neither did it hold any doubt. She tugged her hand from his grip and stood firm. "You leave if you want. Maybe you should. If I come with you, we'll always be on the run."

"Lenore…" he said, but she shook her head.

"This wasn't fair to you." She spread her arms to indicate the entire menagerie. "But running won't be either. Maybe you should go find someone whose most frequent accessory isn't steel bracelets. Someone you can share a real life with."

Anger flared deep in his chest. He pulled her close, and when she flinched, a pang of guilt rang through him, but he didn't release her. He couldn't. "Don't ever say that again," Kevin growled through clenched teeth. "I will never let you go, Lenore. You're mine, and I don't care what some scrap of paper in an old man's filing cabinet says. I have a document that predates his."

"Let her go."

Kevin heard the words a split second before he was pulled off his feet. Lenore gasped, jerked forward by his desperate grip on her arm until his fingers loosened and she slid free.

Gallagher lifted the smaller handler until his boots barely dragged on the ground. Light from the parking lot shone on his bright red cap. His thick left hand curled into a fist, already drawn back for a blow that would surely shatter Kevin's cheek.

"Wait!" Kevin's focus slid from Gallagher's face—half-shadowed from the light by the bill of his hat—to where the new exhibit stood behind him, unshackled and dressed in a Metzger's polo. "This isn't what you think."

"I think you're a predatory asshole who's about to get a free makeover," Gallagher growled.

"No!" Lenore stepped forward, pulling at Gallagher's arm. "Leave him alone. Please." Her wide violet eyes and furrowed

forehead pled just as hard as her words, threaded through with a calming undertone. "You don't understand." She sucked in a deep breath, then let it out slowly. "He's my husband."

DELILAH

"If I could have everyone's attention, I think we're ready to get started." I cleared my throat and stepped up onto the center platform of the white three-tiered podium in the middle of the red ring. The circus wagons—holding all of the sentient cryptids, except for the adlet—were arranged around the outside of the ring in two rows, staggered so everyone could see. "And while we talk, Abraxas and Gallagher are coming around with more water."

I nodded, and the kid began distributing bottles from the cooler full of ice Gallagher hauled behind him, as if it weighed nothing.

"When do we get out of these cages?" the berserker shouted, and both trolls echoed the sentiment in their slightly less articulate...style. "If this is a coup, why are we still locked up?"

"Why are *they* here?" Mirela, the oldest of the oracles asked, glaring at Alyrose and Kevin.

"Why are they already unlocked?" Adira demanded, eyeing Eryx, Claudio, and Lenore.

"You're all going to be let out in a few minutes," I assured them. "I just want a chance to explain what's happening before any of you decide to wander off."

"You're going to let us go?" one of the succubi—Zarah? Or maybe Trista?—said, disbelief thick in her husky voice.

"Of course, if that's what you want. But I'd like to invite you to stay and—"

"Why the hell should we stay?" one of the giants demanded in his booming voice, and that triggered another outbreak of questions. Which was when I remembered that crowd control was more of a problem in a democracy than in any other version of society.

"Be quiet and let her speak." The voice was soft, yet it cut through the cacophony like an oar through water, and when I glanced to my right, I saw Lenore smiling at me, clutching her husband's hand.

"Thank you," I said, then I turned back to the wagons. "In case any of you haven't figured it out yet, we've taken over the menagerie. Renata and Raul have helped us get rid of all the staff members except for Alyrose, Kevin, and Abraxas without spilling a single drop of blood." Which I was proud of on a personal level—even though Gallagher was disappointed—because if we were caught, at least the headlines couldn't read Savage Cryptids Slaughter Staff and Seize Circus. Not truthfully anyway.

Our actions would speak louder than our words ever could. People would know that we'd spared our human captors, though they had rarely spared us.

"Alyrose, Kevin, and Abraxas have agreed to stay and help us because they're sympathetic to our cause. For those who don't know, Kevin is Lenore's husband. He took a job at Metzger's years ago, to stay near her."

"What about Gallagher?" someone shouted, but I couldn't identify the speaker.

"He's a redcap," Adira said with a petulant pout, obviously irritated that she hadn't been let in on our coup before the fact. Nalah was curled up in the opposite corner of their cage, her yellow-orange eyes burning brighter than ever.

"Yes," I said. "Gallagher's been working here on behalf of Adira's father, in order to return her to her homeland. Which

brings me to my next point. Adira's father, Sultan Bruhier, has offered each of you full citizenship in the merid sultanate. Those of you who wish to accept can cross the border with Adira and Nalah tomorrow.

"However, those of us standing before you plan to keep the menagerie open and run it as a masquerade of sorts. We plan to use whatever money we earn to reunite whoever stays with us with their lost relatives. Those who choose to stay will still look like prisoners to the outside world, but in reality, we'll all be living free behind the facade of captivity. We will continue to put on exhibitions and charge admission, but the money will go toward feeding us and freeing your children, parents, and siblings from whatever institutions they were sold into."

A cautiously optimistic buzz rose from the cages, as my fellow former captives discussed my plan and questioned its chances of success. The conversation encouraged me. I'd been worried most of them would be too scared of reprisal to seize freedom when it was offered, but that didn't seem to be the case.

"Will we still be in the ring?" Mahsa shouted, to be heard over the other voices.

"Yes, but the acts will be all ours. We'll redesign the show. You can wear whatever you want and perform whatever tricks you like, so long as they'll impress a human audience and bring in cash without hurting anyone. You can show them whatever you want them to see of your culture and your abilities."

"What about cages and chains?" Finola called, with her seductive siren voice.

"And sedatives?" That came from the back, maybe from one of the centaurs.

"No sedatives," I said. "And we'll only use chains and cages during exhibitions and inspections, to maintain the illusion that Metzger's is still a real menagerie. You'll all have a healthy diet and better facilities. And real clothes. And proper hygiene. You'll have everything Metzger's can possibly give you. Including au-

tonomy. You'll decide what you want to eat, and when. You'll choose your clothes. You will raise your own children."

Stunned reactions buzzed from the wagons, and I recognized both eager acceptance and disbelief. Fear, skepticism, and astonishment. Some of them were instantly won over, and even those who seemed convinced we were doomed to fail sounded inclined to at least give it a chance.

"Of course, all this comes with a risk," I continued, from the top tier of the podium. "If we get caught, we'll all be back where we were before, if not worse. That means more captivity and abuse for the cryptids, and jail time for human accessories. I need you all to understand that before you decide. Nothing is gained without risk." I took Ruyle's key ring from Gallagher when he held it up for me. "Now we're going to come around and unlock everyone, and Alyrose has brought over a selection of clothing for you to look through—"

On the left edge of my vision, one of the tent panels rose, letting in the first rays of sunlight, and I turned toward the movement just as my mother stepped hesitantly into the hybrid tent.

I froze in midsentence, momentarily convinced that I was hallucinating. That Renata had been lying about her inability to enchant me, and now she was either trying to give me the gift of a reunion or throw me entirely off my game.

Then Gallagher made an aggressive move toward my mother, and I lurched after him and grabbed his arm. "Wait! That's my mom."

Gallagher stopped and made a confused sound deep in his throat, but I couldn't tear my gaze away from my mother. "Delilah?" she said, and tears blurred my vision. My mother was alive, and she was fifty feet away, and I wasn't an orphan after all.

I hopped down from the podium and raced across the sawdust-strewn ground toward her. The tent flap fell closed at her back, and her arms opened. I slammed into her so hard I almost

knocked us both over, then she was crying, and I was laughing, and we were both talking at once.

"What's happening, Lilah?" she asked, as I buried my face in her hair and breathed in the scent of her shampoo. With that scent came random memories from my childhood, relevant to that moment only because she'd smelled the same in each of them, and because the scent of artificial strawberry would forever be linked to the safest, most stable moments of my life.

"We're taking over the menagerie," I said, still caught between laughing and crying, and when my mother pulled away to look at me, I realized that the rest of the tent had gone still and quiet, watching our reunion.

"You're taking the menagerie?" my mother said, and I almost laughed at her expression. "And here I thought you'd need to be rescued."

"She does," Ruyle said, and when I turned toward his cage, intending to tell him exactly where to shove his unwanted commentary, I found him standing in deep shadows three feet away, one hand at his ear.

He was aiming a rifle at my head.

DELILAH

"I want you to climb back in your cage," Ruyle said. "Right now."

A glance to the right revealed that my cage stood wide-open against the rear sidewall.

How the hell had he gotten out, when I still held his keys?

Gallagher growled from my right, and I realized he'd followed me across the tent. I could tell from his stiff bearing and from the anger emanating from him like heat from a fire that he was mentally ripping the former lot supervisor limb from limb.

"Put the gun down," Lenore said, and the compulsion in her voice rolled over me on its way to Ruyle. I knelt beneath the power in her words, intending to put down the key ring just in case it might be mistaken for a gun, until Gallagher caught my arm and pulled me back up, breaking the siren's spell. Which probably wouldn't have been possible, if it'd actually been aimed at me.

When Ruyle didn't respond, I squinted and noticed the orange tip of an earplug sticking out of his left ear. To his right, a crate of supplies—including guns, tranquilizer rifles, handcuffs, and earplugs—stood open. I still couldn't understand how he'd gotten free, but with his mind clear once the *encantados'* enchantment had faded, he'd obviously raided the stock in the shadows while I'd talked and everyone else was distracted by the prospect of freedom.

I scanned the tent, looking for Raul or Renata, but they'd returned to their tanks to rest and rehydrate after hours of work on our behalf. They could not help us.

"Gallagher, cuff your cryptid slut, then cuff yourself. Kevin, cuff your wife, then slap some duct tape over her mouth." When no one moved to comply, Ruyle cocked his rifle—still aimed at my head. "Do it! Or I'll blow Drea's face wide-open!"

Gallagher growled again, putting to rest any doubt that he wasn't human.

Heart slamming against my chest with every beat, I slowly slid my hands into the air, and Gallagher did the same, demonstrating that he didn't have any cuffs and would have to find some. Kevin acted out the same concept, charades-style, since the former supervisor couldn't hear us.

"Lift up the top of the podium." Ruyle gestured to the platform I'd stood on. "We keep extras in there."

Kevin knelt to do as instructed, his jaw tightly clenched.

"Where's the bull?" Ruyle demanded, as Kevin tossed a set of cuffs to Gallagher, and that's when I realized Eryx had disappeared at some point during my speech.

Kevin stood with another set of cuffs, while everyone else stared, most too terrified to move.

Gallagher was wound so tight I was afraid he'd explode and take half the tent with him. His glare was fixed on Ruyle with the savage hatred of a thousand *fear dearg*, and for a second, I could almost imagine him on the battlefield, surrounded by his red-capped brothers in arms, ready to paint the earth red with the blood of their enemies. "I'm going to tear you—"

"Don't say it!" I hissed, as he slowly pulled my arms behind my back, stalling for time. "We need him alive."

Suddenly another side panel was lifted from the outside, and bright morning light poured into the tent, momentarily blinding us all. "Hey, where the hell is every—" Carter, the handler who'd driven off with Genni in her cage, stepped into the tent

and froze, as blinded by the darkness as we were by the light of day.

Startled, Ruyle turned toward the new arrival, and his aim tracked away from me. Gallagher tackled his former boss, and the rifle went off as they fell, gunfire echoing within the walls of the tent.

Someone screamed—a bloodcurdling, primal screech of agony—and as I turned to see who'd been shot, I spotted Eryx in a dark corner of the tent, suddenly exposed by the intrusion of light. The bull snorted and pawed the ground, and my pulse tripped too fast. I saw no sluggishness in his eyes. No drugged glaze.

What I *did* see was a very familiar destructive rage.

"No—!" I shouted.

Gallagher stood and pulled the lot supervisor to his feet, ripping the rifle from him at the same time.

The minotaur charged, and the ground trembled with every thundering step.

Gallagher turned to look just as Eryx drove his curved right horn through the supervisor's stomach, tearing him from the redcap's grip.

Ruyle made a gruesome, wet choking sound, which I could hardly hear over the screaming, and my stomach pitched.

Eryx stood up straight, snorting in triumph, with Ruyle still impaled on his gore-smeared horn. The lot supervisor howled. He struggled and kicked, eight feet in the air, but the huge bull-man didn't even sway beneath the weight. Blood poured down Eryx's head, between his eyes, then dripped off his bovine nose as Ruyle's struggles quickened his own gory demise.

"Eryx, put him down!" I shouted, horrified not just by the violence, but by the loss. We *needed* Ruyle alive.

The minotaur blinked at me, and what I saw in his eyes bruised me all the way to my soul. The source of his rage was pain. Deep, profound pain and loss.

He shook his head slowly, declining my request while Aly-rose and Lenore and several of the cryptids still locked in cages wailed, horrified by what we were witnessing. Eryx seized the feet flailing weakly in front of his face and pulled with such force that his horn ripped Ruyle's torso in two, from belly button to left shoulder.

Blood poured over the mighty minotaur. Ruyle's arms stopped flailing.

I gasped, and my hands flew up to cover my mouth, along with my horror.

Eryx gave a mighty bovine bellow, then hurled Ruyle's dripping, half-bisected corpse far over my head, where it smacked the opposite side of the tent and slid down the sidewall, leaving a thick, gory smear in its wake.

All the air leaked from my lungs. No Ruyle, no passage. The sultan would not let our people in. All of our hope and effort and ideas had been for nothing.

Zyanya was right. I was hopelessly naive. I'd just sentenced us all to death.

Terrified into motion, Carter dropped the tent flap, temporarily blinding us all again, and dived toward the open crate of weapons. On my right, Kevin overcame his shock in time to reach into the open podium and pull out a pistol, just as Carter aimed a gun in my direction with one shaky hand.

"No!" My mother stepped in front of me as Carter pulled the trigger. Kevin fired four times, in rapid succession.

My mother fell into my arms as the handler stumbled backward into the tent wall, blood pouring from his chest. He slid to the ground as a dark pool quickly formed around him.

I sank onto the sawdust with my mother on my lap. Tears blurred the red mess her chest had become, and my screams joined the other voice still shrieking over another casualty I hadn't yet discovered.

My mother blinked up at me, pain tugging her features into a

mask of suffering. "Mom…" I pressed both hands over the hole in her chest, but blood poured between my fingers. Her wound was too big. There was nothing I could do.

"I always loved you best," she whispered, and I leaned closer to listen, as my tears fell onto her hair. "Maybe that was wrong, but it's the truth. I always loved you most…" Her body stiffened beneath my hands, then her eyes fluttered closed. She took two more short, halting breaths. Then she went still.

I threw my head back and screamed.

"Delilah." Gallagher tried to pull me up, but I fought him, determined to stay with my mother. "Delilah!" He took me by both arms and hauled me to my feet, heedless of my blows, as if he didn't feel them. "Your mother died an honorable death, and the earth welcomes her nourishing blood. Don't take that from her by letting her death be in vain."

I choked back another sob and scrubbed tears from my eyes, finally pulling his face into focus.

"Warriors die, Delilah, and your mother was a soldier. I know that without ever having met her. Make her proud. Keep fighting. There are still people depending on you."

I nodded shakily, and he let me go. "I'm okay," I said. Later that might not be true, once my loss had a chance to sink in, but for the moment, he was right. I had to stand straight and keep going, or I might never get up again.

The sidewall behind Eryx swished. I couldn't see the source of the movement, with the minotaur blocking it, but Gallagher let out a mighty roar, then lunged for the loose panel. I hardly processed his absence. All I could see was blood. All I could think about was how badly I'd failed everyone I'd tried to help.

A hand settled onto my arm, and I looked up to find Eryx staring down at me, blood still dripping from his horn and rolling down his face and chest.

"Did you let Ruyle out of the cage?" I demanded, tears standing in my eyes as another chunk of hope died a fiery death, deep

within my soul. The minotaur nodded, and I found no remorse in his eyes. "Why?"

Eryx pointed at the ground, where I found letters written in the sawdust, in the minotaur's labored but legible print. One word.

Rommily.

When I looked up to ask for more, I found him pointing at Ruyle's ruined corpse, still propped against a far sidewall of the tent.

"It was Ruyle? Ruyle broke Rommily?" I said, and Eryx nodded slowly. Firmly. "Are you sure?" I asked, and again he nodded. "I understand. He had to pay." But now, unless Gallagher could renegotiate with the sultan, we would all pay for the sins of one horrible man.

I turned to look at Rommily and found her standing on her knees in her cage, between her sisters, all three gripping the metal mesh.

Rommily met my gaze boldly. "And the bull shall stand tallest of them all."

Chills rose all over my skin. I had no idea what she was talking about, but it seemed to mean something to Eryx. He walked toward the oracles' cage with slow, deliberate steps, then slid his thick fingers through the mesh. With bulging arms and a mighty bellow, he ripped the sliding panel right off the cage and dropped it on the ground at his feet. Then he reached out for Rommily.

She placed her small hand in his huge grip and let him help her out of her cage, unfettered. Then she wrapped her thin arms around him as far as they would go and laid her cheek on his massive human chest, heedless of the fresh blood.

When I finally looked away from their private, bittersweet moment, I saw that Alyrose, Kevin, Abraxas, and Lenore had started unlocking crates. People were climbing out of their cages, many for the first time, unfettered. But they were not celebrating. They weren't even talking. They stared, almost as one, at a

cage near the center of the circle, where the screaming that had begun right before my mother was shot had become a high-pitched keening.

I pushed my way through the crowd, dread eating at me from the inside, but before I'd gotten close enough to see, the crowd began pushing against me, backing up as one unit. I slid between the berserker and one of the giants and gasped at what I saw.

Nalah sat on the floor of her cage, holding Adira's limp body. Blood covered the merid from the bullet hole in her neck all the way to her waist. But Nalah was clean. She was also completely nude, and I didn't understand why until I felt the heat radiating from the cage. Her internal temperature had risen so steeply it had burned both the blood and clothing from her flesh.

"You!" Her gaze met mine, and the yellows and oranges in her irises burned brighter. Her normally golden skin had taken on a darker hue, glowing from within like a lit coal. "*You* did this." Nalah stood and laid Adira on the floor, where the merid's skin sizzled against aluminum that glowed red with heat. "You took *everything*. You had no right. Now she is gone." Nalah extended one hand toward her companion's corpse. "And he is pledged." She threw her other arm out toward the wall of the tent, and I realized she was talking about Gallagher. "And you will pay for your theft with the fire of a *thousand* suns."

My pulse leaped into my throat as a wave of heat washed over me, and the *djinn* cage began to melt right in front of us. Adira's corpse burst into flames, but Nalah didn't seem to notice. She gripped the metal mesh, and it melted beneath her fingers, just as the floor began to bow beneath her feet.

Heart pounding, face flushed from the heat, I took a step back as she pushed her way through the melting metal screen and stepped onto the ground. "I will sear the flesh from your bones and make a stew from your organs." Sawdust burst into a thousand tiny sparks beneath her feet. "I will dance in your ashes. I will—"

A soft thwack echoed from behind me. A tranquilizer appeared in the *ifrit*'s bare thigh, and she crumpled to the ground. A drift of sawdust burst into flames beneath her hair, then died as the fuel was consumed.

Gallagher pulled me back from Nalah's still form and clutched me close. "She doesn't know what she's saying. She's lost everything." He aimed the tranquilizer rifle at the ground.

"She has us," I said, as—deep inside me—the *furiae* seemed frustrated by the injustice of the young *ifrit*'s loss, and by the fact that there was no vengeance to be had on her behalf. The princess's killer was already dead. "But we'll have to keep her sedated until she can accept Adira's death."

Gallagher nodded. "That may take a while. I hope your masquerade idea works, because we may need it long-term. Bruhier will *never* let us in now. We'll be lucky if he doesn't take out a contract on us both."

"No Mexico?" Lenore said, and I looked up to find the siren and her husband standing over Carter's corpse. The pistol still dangled from Kevin's hand.

"I'm so sorry," I said, but Kevin didn't seem to hear. He was staring at his former coworker's body.

"You didn't have any choice," Lenore told him. "You saved Delilah's life."

Eryx and Rommily stepped closer, and the oracle's eyes were huge as she stared down at the corpse. "Multiple gunshot wounds to the torso," she said.

Kevin's eyes went wide, and he stared from the oracle to the body at their feet. His empty hand went to his own chest, as if to verify that he was still whole, and Rommily's smile looked satisfied, as if she'd finally broken through a barrier she'd been chipping away at for years.

"Hey, Gallagher, what do you want me to do with him?" Abraxas called. I turned to ask what he was talking about, and

my jaw nearly fell open. Rudolph Metzger lay unconscious at his feet.

Gallagher had lunged at the moving tent flap to find the old man, about to make an entrance and discover the coup.

"The hood of his truck is still hot—he must have just gotten back. I want to see if the sultan will accept him as a peace offering." Gallagher bent to pick the old man up like a baby, then slid him into the cage Ruyle had vacated. "Would you like the honor?" He stepped back and leveled a grand gesture at my open wagon.

Nodding, I grabbed the cage door, ready to slam it shut.

"Wait!" Mirela ran toward us and skidded to a barefoot halt, with Lala not two steps behind her. "Don't forget this!" She tossed the old man's top hat into the cage, and it landed square on his little potbelly.

"And this!" Lala slid his formal black walking stick in next to him.

I slammed the cage shut, severing Rudolph Metzger from his liberty, once and for all.

RUDOLPH

The old man woke up on his side, in the dark, and no matter how many times he blinked, his surroundings would not come into focus. There was not enough light to see by.

His head ached fiercely, and a gentle probe with his fingers revealed a tall, tender bump on the back of his head, but for his life, Rudolph could not recall how he'd gotten it.

The world jostled and bounced beneath him, jarring him terribly, and when he tried to stand, his knees and hips screamed with arthritic pain. The room jumped beneath him again, and he smacked his elbow on something hard.

Rudolph sucked in a deep, calming breath through his nose, trying to get a handle on impending panic, and that's when he noticed the smell. Stale hay, and...manure.

And urine.

Fear began to gather at the back of his mind. Rudolph felt around on the floor, and his fingers bumped over a raised pattern. His heart began to thump. His throat constricted. He reached a little farther, and the tips of his fingers brushed something hard and thin. He slid his hand up, and his fingers pushed through a grid of some kind. A hard, metal...grille. Like a chain-link fence. Or the side of an animal crate.

No!

The room jostled him again, and that time Rudolph recognized the motion and racket for what they were. Road noise.

The harsh bounce of low-quality shocks. The squeals and groans of one of his custom-built wide-load cryptid transport trucks.

"No!" Rudolph shouted aloud that time, but there was no response. "Gallagher, let me out of here, you son of a bitch!"

His voice was reflected back to him from the steel sides of the cavernous cargo trailer. He was alone. But as the trailer sped toward the Mexican border, Rudolph Metzger understood that the blessing of solitude would not last much longer.

And if he was very, very lucky, neither would he.

DELILAH

"Here they come," Zyanya whispered as she approached the ticket booth, staring over my shoulder at the first few cars as they pulled into the gravel parking lot. She tugged at the elastic hem of her sequined leotard, where it met her thick black tights. "Why is there no music? They'll never believe this is a real menagerie if there's no calliope music, Delilah."

"We're having technical issues. Abraxas is on it," I assured her.

"Great." Zyanya rolled her eyes, which looked very dark, but human, thanks to Alyrose's contact lenses. "Put the kid in charge of all the technical equipment. How could that possibly go wrong?"

"He's the only one who's ever seen it run," I reminded her, powering up the ancient credit card machine in my booth. "And anyway, kids always know how to work new technology before adults do. It's like their birthright." I neglected to tell her that the broadcast system was at least a decade older than Abraxas and hopelessly outdated, just like everything else at Metzger's.

Zyanya nodded, but her left hand strayed into her apron pocket to fidget with her emergency sunglasses. I'd given them to her in case she lost a contact lens, and she kept touching them to reassure herself that they were still there.

"Are you ready?"

She nodded again, her lips moving silently as she went over the prices in her mind. Zyanya had never gone to school, and

after a week of lessons, she still couldn't spell her own name, but she'd picked up simple change-making very quickly, earning herself a place in the cash-only booth. She was the first disguised cryptid our customers would see—a test case of sorts—and I could practically hear the anxiety in her voice.

A door slammed shut in the parking lot, and she jumped. "Maybe you should have put Lenore here. Or Finola."

"You're gonna be fine," I said as she stepped into her booth. Besides, I needed them taking tickets at the bestiary and the hybrid tent, which were unsupervised positions. "Just don't open your mouth very wide." So the customers wouldn't see her sharp canines.

"Are humans so easy to fool?"

I shrugged. "People see what they expect to see, and you look the part." She was *stunning* in the glittery costume and makeup Alyrose had fixed up for her, and as long as she kept her gestures grand and her smile small, she'd be just fine. We'd already fooled the independent contractors who'd provided the game booths, pie carts, and rides. In comparison, customers should be easy.

"Delilah!" Lala skidded to a halt next to my booth, kicking up a cloud of dust around her sparkly black slippers. She would spend the evening as a talker for Mirela in the fortune teller's tent. "The berserker's cage clasp broke, and he won't let us chain it shut. He seems to truly think we won't let him back out again."

"Okay." That was understandable. Most of the former captives viewed their freedom as a tenuous state, and for some, the illusion of captivity was still too realistic to be endured. "Turn his cage around, so that the door's on the back side, and leave it closed, but unlatched. If that doesn't satisfy him, remove his cage from the lineup and let him work as a handler tonight. Alyrose left extra red shirts in the supply trunk. If the customers notice him missing, tell them the vet pulled him from the exhibit because he's sick."

Worry melted from Lala's expression when it became clear that I wasn't going to kill the messenger. Time was the only thing that could heal the flinch response they'd all acquired from years of abuse, and that fact broke my heart on an hourly basis. "Okay. I'm on it!" She smiled and turned to run back the way she'd come. Lala ran everywhere she went, now that there was no cage to restrict her.

"Lala!" I called, with a glance at the parking lot, where the first families were already heading toward us. "Hurry. The hybrid tent will have customers in less than five minutes."

She nodded and raced back the way she'd come. I laughed as I watched her go.

"Family of four," Zyanya mumbled, as the first group approached. "That's four tickets, at one hundred four dollars each. If they pay with four hundreds and a twenty, I'll give them back four one-dollar bills..."

"Relax." I smiled at her from across the space between our booths. "You've got this." And most people would pay with a credit card anyway.

"I hope you're right."

Before I could insist that I was, static buzzed from the speaker over our heads, followed by a loud burst of calliope music, adding the sound track necessary to complete our illusion. Zyanya visibly relaxed. She ran one hand over the top of her head, toward the bun pinned at the back of her skull, and gave me a small smile. "I'm ready."

"All right. Let's do it!" I whispered as the first family approached. The father wore a skeptical frown, but the mother looked excited. The kids—a boy and a girl—had wide eyes and timid smiles.

I reached into my pocket for a wad of flash cotton and a flint wheel, mentally crossing my fingers as I prepared the only magic trick I knew. When the kids were about five feet away, I lit the

cotton and presented my handful of flames with a flourish. In my open palms sat four shiny red tickets.

The children's eyes brightened and their jaws dropped open.

I smiled and waved them through the gate. "Welcome to the menagerie, where beauty and grace shine from every cage and peek from every shadow. You've never seen anything like the exotic wonders within, so keep your eyes open, ladies and gentlemen, because in our world of spectacle and illusion, what you see isn't always what you get."

★ ★ ★ ★ ★

ACKNOWLEDGMENTS

Thanks first and foremost go to Mary-Theresa Hussey, whose initial confidence in this project got the ball rolling. Your influence and excitement continue to mean the world to me.

Thanks also to Michelle Meade, my new editor, whose enthusiasm and guidance have been nothing short of brilliant. Your vision for this project is stunning, and I only hope I've risen to meet the challenge. Thanks for ideas and rapid-fire brainstorming phone calls, and for bringing everything together.

Gratitude, as always, goes to my agent, Merrilee Heifetz, who's never dropped a ball in her life. She even picks up mine, when my juggling falters.

Thank you to my critique partner, Rinda Elliott, for being the world's best sounding board, and for all the crazy text messages she answers, at all hours.

Thank you to the amazing art and production teams at MIRA Books. I am honored to say I work with the best!

And finally, a big thank-you to Holly, Sarah, and Kelley, for talking me through the initial mental roadblock I erected in spite of my own efforts. You ladies are amazing, and I am in your debt!

This one is for my husband and children,
who suffered with me through three years, several rewrites,
a shifted release date and the loss of my longtime editor while I wrote *Menagerie*.
It's been a long road, but I think it's been worth it, and I can't thank you all enough.

ISBN-13: 978-0-7783-1605-3

Menagerie

For questions and comments about the quality of this book, please contact us at CustomerService@Harlequin.com.

www.MIRABooks.com

Printed in U.S.A.

First printing: October 2015
10 9 8 7 6 5 4 3 2 1

NEW YORK TIMES BESTSELLING AUTHOR
RACHEL VINCENT

MENAGERIE

MIRA

TABLE OF CONTENTS

PREFACE

THE LAST HALF OF THE 20th century is ushering in a period of unprecedented change. Never in such a short time span have individuals and nations experienced such a radical restructuring of the social, political, and economic structures of life. Western societies, once bastions of economic stability, are finding themselves under economic siege. The Third World countries are staggering under a load of debt, while Central America, Africa, and the Middle East find themselves in a political mine field. Plots to gain military advantage, discussions concerning the future of the arms race, and the awareness of the potential for global catastrophe keep the average citizen on an emotional roller coaster. Furthermore, this restructuring is being directed by technological innovation and fueled by a human quest for power, money, and sexual advantage. Like it or not, the human race is being catapulted into a new age.

This restructuring of life is not merely an American phenomenon; it is global. No one is immune from those forces responsible for such change. They are constantly at work creating new and socially acceptable forms of economic and political enslavement by redefining the nature of human existence in terms of consumption. Although the world experiences tremendous disharmony, at the same time nations are becoming increasingly tied together by common economic concerns that demand unified problem-solving stragegies and global cooperation.

Individuals are increasingly defining their hopes, dreams, and life aspirations in terms of economic success. Unfortunately the church has not only accommodated itself to such interpretations of life; many church leaders—especially televangelists—are incorporating these interpretations into their message. Christianity is gradually being shuffled off to the fringes of life. In part this is because the church is allowing those structures for proclaiming the gospel to become obsolete. It is responding to life's concerns in an inadequate fashion. Moreover, the church has permitted the biblical message to be devalued and to become archaic in the face of modern society. Regrettably, some in the church are taking an active but unreflective role in trying to relate to an ever-changing world. The results have been disastrous; they have unwittingly allowed the forces of this "power complex" to define the mission of the church through the very structures that are used to propagate the gospel. "Power complex" is an expression used by Lewis Mumford in his two-volume work, *The Pentagon of Power*, to describe "a new constellation of forces, interests, and motives" that shape and condition life in ways impossible prior to mechanization (2:166). From Mumford's perspective the world is interconnected by a web of forces that operate independently of the welfare of humankind. For Mumford, the power complex thrives on enlarging its own power and sphere of influence.

This book joins the concept of the power complex to the Pauline portrayal of the principalities and powers. It then applies that understanding to the practical issues of church structure and congregational life. This is not to say that such a perspective is the necessary starting point for understanding the place of the church in society; rather, the concern is for the practical implications: I hope to develop a frame of reference for examining questions related to how the church should structure its life in a changing world if it is going to fulfill its mission. On the one hand, the very structures that enable the church to exist as a social entity are at the same time part of the power complex. Consequently, it is driven by forces alien to the gospel. On the other hand, as the community of the Spirit, the church is to point beyond itself to the kingdom of God, which it both embodies and awaits. Thus, a tension exists; or one might say there is a spiritual conflict. While the church must use meetings, buildings, finances, programs, and policies to structure itself, these can become enslaving. Spiritual "merchandizing and consumerism" can replace discipleship. Christianity thus becomes another commodity to be marketed, packaged, and sold in the marketplace of the world's values. Christian community becomes supplanted and restructured by the power complex—principalities and powers that are competing for the future of the human race. Such a predicament is according to the values of the world and not according to Christ.

The good news is that Christ has disarmed the powers. The church can indeed live out the true meaning of the gospel, but not without conflict. This book examines the spiritual conflict of the Christian church in terms of the modern power complex and explores practical issues related to developing and maintaining meaningful structures for congregational life.

Finally I am in debt to the following individuals who deserve special thanks for their assistance and feedback in preparing this manuscript: Patrick Alexander, Clifford Christians, Susan Johnson, U. Milo Kaufmann, William Menzies, and Cathy Walker.

PART 1: The Power Complex

THE POWER COMPLEX

"THE MOST IMPORTANT FACT about our current historical situation is hard to accept: that our modern world is in its last day and that we are—ready or not, like it or not—entering a turbulent period of transition to a very different world of postmodernity."[1] Frederick Ferré is right. As we enter the closing decades of the 20th century, we are in the midst of a global revolution that will forever alter the course of human life and history. The world as we know it is passing from the scene like a dinosaur.

This revolution is not simply technological in nature; it is also spiritual insofar as it shapes the essence of what it means to be human. More fundamentally, the failure to recognize the spiritual dimension of what is commonly recognized as "secular" is a tragic mistake. Never in the history of humanity have so many spiritual forces been actively competing to shape life. This is true not only with respect to individuals, but even more so regarding the corporate realities of modern life. Spiritual forces are active within the institutional power complex which has developed into a global network of forces. Furthermore, no living being is immune from the effects generated by this behemoth which thrives on turbulence and change.

Fueled by technological advances, change permeates nearly every aspect of life. To survive, both individuals and institutions must adapt to a changing environment. Engulfed by feelings of insecurity and loss, many feel as if the ground beneath them is shifting. And it is. The past 100 years have produced steady changes in society at a rapidly increasing rate. The introduction of electrical appliances into the home revolutionized the entire Western household in the short span of two decades

(1912–1932).[2] The automobile, radio, and television radically transformed the nature of daily life in the course of one generation.
Such changes, however, are minuscule when viewed in light of
the technological innovations introduced since the Second World
War. The microchip has accelerated both the intensity and comprehensive character of change. The explosion of knowledge and
the management and dissemination of information are restructuring the political, economic, and social fabric of human existence.
One result is a shift in and erosion of the life-values to which
people cling for direction and meaning. An uncertain future
adds to the turbulent character of the present.

Historically, value changes in society have occurred so slowly
that in the life span of a single individual, few major transitions
could be observed at all. Today this is no longer true. Life-values
change more than once in a single generation. The 20th century
was ushered in with a vision for peace and utopia. World War I
abruptly destroyed that vision. Each decade that followed represented further upheaval and change. Change now permeates
existence.

Connected to the frequency of change is the sheer diversity
and quantity of forces altering the way we live. Prior to the
16th century, modifications in society occurred through a limited
number of channels including trade, military force, and oral
communication. Rural population, immobility, lack of central-
ized power, and slow communication contributed to long-term stability. Today the forces bringing about change have grown exponentially: governments, businesses, schools, industries, television,
radio, newspapers, books, musicians, terrorists, scientists,
doctors—the list is endless. Not only has the social, psychological, spiritual, and physical nature of humanity undergone
permanent modification, but also the ecological balance of the
earth has been affected.

Asphalt roads and jet streams dissect our world; structures of
steel and concrete eat up farm land; mechanical equipment
erodes our soil; impurities collect in the atmosphere; waste
and debris litter the landscape; and, noise fills the air. Life
is immersed in traffic, speed, motion, lights, signs, and sounds
—sounds of cars, buses, planes, motorcycles, trains, trucks,
furnaces, clocks, machines, gadgets, tapes, crowds, and the

almost inescapable presence of radio and television. Sound and motion engulf life. Yet for many it results only in motion sickness. Activity replaces meaning and purpose.

An abstract notion of progress linked to a techno-materialistic attitude justifies the radical change in human existence. The primary needs of food, shelter, companionship, and love, which condition human existence, are interwoven with manufactured needs and are turned into psychologically conditioned human wants. Furthermore, the spiritual significance of human need has become a merchandizable aspect of life itself.

A power complex composed of an entangled network of forces now conditions human existence. No one escapes the influence "it" transmits through every available medium—every institution, whether political, industrial, commercial, economic, medical, educational, or religious. Every source of communication and power, whether personal or impersonal, is an integral part of the life-shaping system we have created, but which now largely functions beyond both our control and welfare. The spiritual significance of this power complex, however, has evaded the modern world, and to a large extent even the church. The only term strong enough to characterize the nature of these powers is death.

As an institutional reality, the church is very much a part of the modern power complex. The question must be asked, *How should the church structure its existence, not only to adapt to the changing environment, but also to survive and expose the power complex that undermines the message of the gospel and the Christian conduct of life?*

From a biblical perspective, Christians are engaged in a spiritual conflict, not against flesh and blood, but against principalities and powers. Yet how are such powers to be viewed and understood in modern life? What is the nature and extent of the conflict that the church faces? Furthermore, what are the implications for the life of the church in terms of its organization, conduct, and commitments?

These questions are the focus of this book. The way in which local congregations respond to these questions will determine the future of the church. In more than one respect, the human race stands at a crossroads. One nuclear accident, a single terrorist bombing, and the voices of leaders in Moscow and Washington bring us to the realization that we may be many nations and peoples, but we are one world with all human beings sharing a destiny tied together by common hopes and fears. On the one hand, we face the fear of nuclear annihilation, war, and global chaos. Yet on the other hand, as individuals, our concerns, fears, hopes, and dreams are not that different from those who have gone before us: the excitement and joy of love; sleepless nights and tired days caused by little children awake in the night; the pain, turbulence, and relief of launching our children into the world; the struggles of selecting a career and paying bills; elderly parents with chronic health problems; job changes; car problems; family vacations; retirement; Super Bowls and barbecues; funerals and hospitals; check-out lines and traffic jams; weddings and divorces—these are the day-to-day realities that occupy us.

In the midst of this, where is God? In a society that knows no limits to the power of marketing, is Jesus to be merchandized as a product and set on the shelf between the Alka-Seltzer and Tylenol? Is he to be promoted on TV along with McDonald's and Budweiser? Can God's grace be transformed and packaged technologically? Can spirituality be constructed as a do-it-yourself kit using tapes, books, computers, radio, and television? Can we become the architects of our own spirituality? Can spirituality have different dimensions to it such as "yuppie," "punk," "country," "classical," "new age," or "avant-garde"?

We are faced with serious questions and no easy answers. While many of the issues confronting the church are not new, the global circumstances and technological realities surrounding us are. These are the issues faced here. How is the church to order its life for the future? Our starting point is to examine the theological significance of the principalities and the powers. Only then can we deal with fundamental organizational concerns.

— 1 —

THE PRINCIPALITIES AND THE POWERS

EVERY PERSON DIES—Democrat, Republican, white, black, male, female, rich, poor, fat, thin—it makes no difference; death conquers everyone. Death, the ultimate enemy, is the payment for sin (Rom. 6:23). Sin must not be understood only as an act, but also as a "sphere" of existence. In that sphere, which all human beings enter at birth, death is the ruling power. Sin and death completely condition and control human existence (Rom. 5:12; Eph. 2:1-2).

The result of sin's entrance into the world is not just lying, stealing, cheating, and killing. Far more tragic consequences exist. Rather, our very perception and understanding of human existence becomes twisted and distorted. In our attempt to secure purpose and meaning, which sin strips away, we end up destroying not only ourselves, but others along the way.

The Apostle Paul describes this sphere of existence as "the present evil age" (Gal. 1:4) or "the domain of darkness" (Col. 1:13). "The prince of the power of the air" controls this age, and those in it "walk according to this world" (Eph. 2:2). Over against this stands the "new creation" (2 Cor. 5:17), the "kingdom of the Son" (Col. 1:13), or the "age to come" (Eph. 1:21). In these Christ reigns "above all rule and authority and power and dominion" (Eph. 1:21). The two ages stand in conflict with one another. One is a kingdom of sin and death; demonic powers govern it. The other is a kingdom of life and righteousness; in it Christ is Lord.

The present evil age will not last forever. Eventually, death and all evil powers will be destroyed (1 Cor. 15:24). For now, though, an interim period exists in which the two ages coexist

(see Figure 1-1). This results in a spiritual conflict in the life of
every Christian (Eph. 6:12). The powers are still attempting to
gain control of life. This creates a dynamic tension in the
formation of values, in decision making, and in the conduct of
daily life.

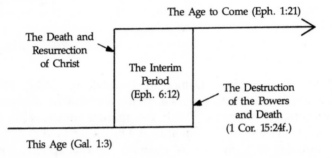

FIGURE 1-1

William Stringfellow notes that regardless of how it appears
to us, every value, goal, policy, action, routine, and enterprise
embodies the reality of death. Death is not just biological extinction. Rather, as Stringfellow puts it, "The moral reality of death
involves death comprehended sociologically and anthropologically,
psychologically and psychically, economically and politically, soci-
etally and institutionally."[1]

The Principalities and the Powers

The reign of death (Rom. 5:14, 17) is a manifestation of the
rule and control of sin (Rom. 5:12). Simply put, death is the
ultimate end, not only of humanity, but of all creation. The
creation exists in the "death-sphere" of sin. For this reason the
creation groans awaiting the day of redemption (Rom. 8:19f).
Nothing escapes death's contamination. The only alternative is to
be transferred into the new creation (Gal. 6:15).

Once we grasp this biblical picture of sin and death, we see
that death operates not only in living organisms, but also in structures, institutions, and systems. Death conditions all phases and
aspects of life and creation, both personal and impersonal,
organic and inorganic. The principalities and powers govern life.

The terms "principalities" and "powers" were common religious terms during the time of Paul, but they have little meaning to the average person today. The tendency is to think of them as counterparts to the demonic forces found in the Gospels. However, that is misleading. Our first task is to discover what Paul meant when he used these terms, and second, to apply that understanding to our own historical setting. Two main sources can help us better understand what Paul meant when he used words like principalities and powers: Jewish apocalypticism[2] and Hellenistic astrology.[3]

The Background of the Powers

The various terms associated with the powers began to appear in Jewish apocalyptic literature before Christ. This literature expressed hope that God would intervene in the world and overthrow the forces of evil. A sense of urgency and expectation existed that God was about to vindicate his people. An end-time battle was expected between the forces of light and the powers of darkness. This battle was not simply political or historical; rather, it was a spiritual conflict with the "powers in high places." These "powers" were thought of as angelic in nature. In part, the nature and development of this thinking stems from the OT.

Foreign gods and idols continually confronted the people of Israel. The covenant oath found in Joshua, chapter 24, challenges the people to choose between the Lord, the God of Israel, or the foreign gods. In choosing to do the will of the one true God, the foreign gods had to be put away, but this command was not easily enforced.

The prophets attempted to eradicate pagan worship, but often had little success. Many Israelites took pagan religions seriously.[4] Foreign gods were viewed as subordinate to and accountable to Yahweh.[5] These powers, particularly those understood as angelic in nature, became known as "gods," "sons of gods," or "messengers."[6] They were viewed as members of the heavenly council who met around the throne of Yahweh.[7]

> Who is like thee, O LORD, among the gods?
> Who is like thee, majestic in holiness,
> terrible in glorious deeds, doing wonders? (Ex. 15:11)

> Ascribe to the LORD, O heavenly beings,
> ascribe to the LORD, glory and strength. (Ps. 29:1)

G. B. Caird suggested that the title "lord of hosts" can be understood in the light of this development. The term "host" refers to these angelic powers. Similarly, the "host of heaven," usually seen as denoting the sun, moon, and the stars, refers to the heavenly court.[8] Thus according to Caird, "When Israel came into contact with the astral deities of the east, she was ready to accommodate them, not as gods in their own right, but as angelic viceroys with delegated power."[9] Each nation was viewed as having its own ruler, except Israel, who was ruled by Yahweh:

> And beware lest you lift up your eyes to heaven, and when you see the sun and the moon and the stars, all the host of heaven, you be drawn away and worship them and serve them, things which the LORD your God has allotted to all the people under the whole heaven. But the LORD has taken you, and brought you forth out of the iron furnace, out of Egypt, to be a people of his own possession, as at this day. (Dt. 4:19, 20)

The author of Jubilees states this view in clear terms around 150 BC:

> . . . there are many nations and many peoples, and all are his, over all hath he placed spirits in authority to lead them astray from him. But over Israel he did not appoint any angel or spirit, for he alone is their ruler. (Jubilees 15:31–32)

This view of subordination helps us to understand Israel's view of foreign religion. First, the reality of pagan religion was recognized. Pagan nations had angelic rulers that had to be reckoned with. And because these angelic rulers were subordinate to Yahweh, these nations were also under divine influence. Therefore, Israel saw opposition from foreign nations coming not just from the hands of pagans, but potentially from the Lord. And finally, Israel saw itself as having an exclusive, direct relationship with Yahweh.

After the Davidic rule, Israel went into a state of apostasy. The people lived under the influence of one ruler after another, and their own national aspirations became frustrated. Even though Israel's neighbors were immoral and superstitious, they prospered. Ultimately, however, they would have to pay for their sins. The angelic rulers or powers allotted to each nation would be held responsible for the sins of the people, and the powers, along with the people, would pay for such sin:

> God has taken his place in the divine council;
> in the midst of the gods he holds judgment: ...
> I say, "You are gods,
> sons of the Most High, all of you;
> nevertheless, you shall die like men,
> and fall like any prince."
> Arise, O God, judge the earth;
> for to thee belong all the nations! (Ps. 82:1, 6–8)

The Hebrew writers were sure the pagan empires, along with their angelic rulers, were doomed to final defeat:

> For the LORD is enraged against all the nations,
> and furious against all their host,
> he has doomed them,
> has given them over for slaughter. (Isa. 34:2)

During the intertestamental period a shift began to take place in the thought of the Jewish people regarding the heavenly host, the sons of God. In the Septuagint (LXX) the terms "powers," "authorities," "principalities," and "rulers" are applied to angelic beings. Caird identified the following scriptures which illustrate this: [10]

> Praise him, all his angels,
> Praise him, all his host! [LXX=all his powers] (Ps. 148:2)

> Bless the LORD, all his hosts [LXX=all his powers],
> his ministers that do his will! (Ps. 103:21)

In Daniel, the princes of Persia, Greece, and Israel, who were understood as angels, become the rulers of the age in the LXX (Dan. 10:13, 21; 12:1). [11] In the Psalms we find "YHWH of hosts" translated "Lord of the powers." The Hebrew text of Ps. 96:5 denounces the heathen gods as "idols," but the LXX uses the word "demons."

In the Pseudepigrapha we encounter other references to the powers and the evil spirits. The evil spirits are subject to Satan and serve him (Jub. 10:8, 11). In addition to Satan, other personified leaders of evil are identified, including Belial, Satanail, Semjaza, Asazel, and Mastema. Nature is a prime medium for the powers, who are portrayed as exerting their influence through disasters, plagues, and disease. The powers work through the "elements."

Babylonian astrological practices existed alongside of Judaism during the OT era. Astrology was also prevalent in the Hellenistic world during the time of Paul. According to J. Y. Lee, ". . . astrological belief had one of the most significant impacts upon the life and thought of the Hellenistic world at the time of Paul's ministry."[12] The power of the stars and planets was believed to control human destiny.

Astrological belief found its way into Jewish apocalyptic thought. D. S. Russell observes that considerable interest was "shown in the movements of the heavenly bodies and their influence on the affairs of men."[13] The stars and the planets became identified with the "elemental powers." Those powers were viewed as capable of controlling life and of exerting their influence upon nations. Within that milieu Paul portrayed the powers as enemies of the gospel.

In summary, the powers gained prominence in Jewish thought several centuries before Christ. Originally they were identified with God's heavenly host of angels, but later they took on a demonic character and were viewed as hostile to both people and God. The hope and expectation was that God would overthrow the powers in a final, end-time, cosmic battle.

The Pauline Terminology

H. Schlier comments, "The realm of principalities and demons is of interest to the New Testament only because they must be resisted and the world protected from them."[14] Paul, the only NT writer to refer to the powers, did not present a systematic, theological statement concerning their nature, creation, or purpose. Instead, he used a wide variety of terms to describe the powers and apparently made no effort to distinguish one term from another. These terms include rule, authority, power, thrones, lordship, world rulers of this darkness, the spiritual host of evil in the heavenlies, the authority of darkness, every name that is named, and the elements of the world.[15] In addition to the powers is Satan or the devil.

The Role of Satan

The Hebrew word *satan* is a purely Semitic word meaning "to oppose" or "to be an adversary."[16] Satan generally refers to the personified ruler of evil, but it does have other common uses as illustrated in the following OT passages.

> the angel of the LORD took his stand in the way as his adversary (*satan*). (Num. 22:22)

> Send the man back, that he may return to the place to which you have assigned him; he shall not go down with us to battle, lest in the battle he become an adversary (*satan*) to us. (1 Sam. 29:4)

> But David said, "What have I to do with you, you sons of Zeruiah, that you should this day be as an adversary (*satan*) to me?" (2 Sam. 19:22)

> But now the LORD my God has given me rest on every side; there is neither adversary (*satan*) nor misfortune. (1 Kgs. 5:4)

> And the LORD raised up an adversary (*satan*) against Solomon. (1 Kgs. 11:14)

From these passages, the character of Satan, the personification of evil, becomes more clear. Von Rad suggests that Satan should be understood not simply as an enemy, but in a more specific sense as an enemy with respect to the law.[17] The adversary (*satan*) raised up against Solomon (1 Kgs. 11:14) is not merely an enemy in the general sense of the term, but an adversary in the specific legal sense. This *satan* is raised up because Solomon sinned; God's judgment must be carried out. The role of *satan* is that of a prosecutor in the heavenly court. Furthermore, these *satans* or adversaries can be sent to carry out the purposes of God.

Satan appears only three times in the OT as a superhuman personality (Zec. 3:1; Job 1 and 2; 1 Chr. 21:1). In both Job and Zechariah, Satan appears with the definite article (*the* Satan). In these two instances, "Satan" is probably not a proper name, but the title of an office (the Adversary).[18] In the book of Job,

Satan, along with the "sons of God," appears in the heavenly court where his demonic nature becomes manifest. Even though the office of "Satan" is divinely appointed, he becomes not only the adversary of Job, but also of God. His attack on Job, which is permitted by God, is actually an attack on God. No indication is given as to how this demonic nature surfaces, but in Satan's zeal to fulfill his role, he becomes hostile to both man and God.

For Paul, Satan is the personified leader of the powers. He is called the devil (Eph. 6:11), Belial (2 Cor. 6:15), the evil one (2 Thes. 3:3), the tempter (1 Thes. 3:5), the serpent (2 Cor. 11:3), the god of this world (2 Cor. 4:4), and the prince of the power of the air (Eph. 2:2). What is of interest, however, is that Satan is rarely mentioned in passages focusing on the meaning and significance of Christ's coming, death, and resurrection; instead, in those texts we encounter the cosmic powers.

The Powers

According to Paul, the powers exist in high places (Eph. 3:10). Both Berkhof and Schlier understand Paul to mean the atmosphere around us when he speaks of the air (high places). In that sense, the powers are in the very air we breathe. Concerning this, Schlier comments, "If men expose themselves to this atmosphere they become its carriers, and thereby contribute to its extension." Contamination is inescapable.

A key attribute of the powers is that they penetrate daily life, yet go unrecognized. They strategically position themselves to direct and control even the mundane affairs of life. By doing so they become gods. Paul wrote:

> For we are not contending against flesh and blood, but against the principalities, against the powers, against the world rulers of this present darkness, against the spiritual hosts of wickedness in the heavenly places. (Eph. 6:12)

Even though the powers are now in conflict with humanity and hostile to God, that was not always the case. God created the powers for our benefit. Concerning this, Paul wrote:

> For in him all things were created, in heaven and on earth, visible and invisible, whether thrones or dominions or principalities or authorities—all things were created through him and for him. (Col. 1:16)

By definition, one who has authority has the power to command and to enforce laws. God established the powers to maintain order in the cosmos. Without order life becomes reduced to chaos. The "powers," created to serve as God's ministering agents over his creation, were to provide the structure for life to develop in a meaningful and orderly way. These powers, however, became hostile to God. Rather than maintaining order, they took on the status of gods and began to regulate human existence and destiny. As a result, they became demonic, and men and women became enslaved to a world order over which they had no control. No direct explanation is given in the Scriptures as to how this happened, but, from a Pauline perspective, this development is tied to "the elementary principles of the world."

The Elementary Principles

The phrase "elementary principles" comes from the Greek word *stoicheia* and is used four times by Paul (Gal. 4:3, 9; Col. 2:8, 20). Scholars translate *stoicheia* a variety of ways including "elementary principles" (NAS), "basic principles" (NIV), "rudiments" (KJV), and "elemental spirits" (RSV, NEB).

Paul indicates that the *stoicheia* victimize humanity. They have the power to ensnare individuals through deceit:

> See to it that no one makes a prey of you by philosophy and empty deceit, according to human tradition, according to the *stoicheia* of the universe, and not according to Christ. (Col. 2:8)

A close relationship exists between human tradition and the *stoicheia*. Not only do both lead to empty deceit, they are contrary to Christ. Furthermore, their power lies in the ability to regulate life. This is illustrated in the passage below:

> If with Christ you died to the *stoicheia* of the universe, why do you live as if you still belonged to the world? Why do you submit to regulations, "Do not handle, Do not taste, Do not touch" (referring to things which all perish as they are used), according to human precepts and doctrines? (Col. 2:20–22)

The *stoicheia* impact human existence through precepts and doctrines. Human traditions, therefore, take on spiritual reality when they regulate life—they become powers. In addition, those powers become demonic when they take on ultimate meaning.

This entire process is illustrated below as we examine the development of the *stoicheia*.

The original meaning of *stoicheia* relates to the "elements of a series or list of things."[19] For example, each letter of the alphabet can be described as an "element." Electric typewriters use typing "elements." Greek philosophers used the term *stoicheia* to describe the basic elements or building blocks out of which they believed everything else was formed. Earth, fire, water, and air were understood in the Greek world to be the four basic "elements" out of which everything was formed. We still use the word "elements" to refer to the forces of nature—man against the elements.

In later developments, *stoicheia* became identified with animated spirits. Eduard Lohse notes:

> In the Testament of Solomon, the "elements" are described as beings who appear to be persons. Solomon sees seven spirits coming and asks them who they are. He receives the answer: "We are the elements, the cosmic rulers of darkness." A group of thirty-six spirits likewise introduces itself with the words: "We are the thirty-six elements, the world rulers of the darkness of this age."[20]

The *stoicheia* or the "elements" came to be seen as cosmic powers who were able to exert influence over the lives of men and women. They were to be worshipped. Lohse explains this development as follows:

> In Hellenistic times this reverence was explained by the assertion that man is formed out of the same elements from which the entire cosmos had been fashioned. Thus it is necessary not only to possess knowledge about the elements, the movement of the stars, and the powers of the cosmos, man must also become part of the cosmic order insofar as he offers the powers and principalities the requisite reverence and submits to the laws and prescriptions they impose upon his life.[21]

The *stoicheia* made demands upon life. Paul identified these demands with "human traditions, doctrines and precepts." Their power surfaced in the form of decrees which regulated life, enslaved people, and became the building blocks for a social order alienated from God.

The Christian, however, is not to be controlled by the *stoicheia*, which exert their influence through regulatory power.

Paul indicated that Christ disarmed the powers at the cross (Col. 2:15). This disarmament occurred through the removal of regulations (Col. 2:14). The believer is no longer to be enslaved to judgments concerning food, drink, festivals, new moons, or even the Sabbath (Col. 2:16). These are all decrees which have been taken out of the way by the cross. At the cross, the believer died with Christ, not only to sin, but also to the *stoicheia* (Col. 2:16). Therefore, they are not to regulate life. Only Christ has the right to make ultimate demands on one's life.

The Galatians had problems with such regulations. Concerning their situation, Paul wrote:

> Formerly, when you did not know God, you were in bondage to beings that by nature are no gods; but now that you have come to know God, or rather to be known by God, how can you turn back again to the weak and beggarly elemental spirits (*stoicheia*), whose slaves you want to be once more? You observe days, and months, and seasons, and years! I am afraid I have labored over you in vain. (Gal. 4:8-11)

In both Galatians and Colossians, Paul indicated that the *stoicheia* are hostile to God. Their enslaving influence is exerted through regulations. These regulations claim to draw individuals closer to God, though in reality they do the opposite.

Christians are warned that they too can be deceived and become victims of the powers. The lack of spiritual discernment and the inability to recognize the powers at work, even in the most mundane areas of life, are perhaps the greatest handicap facing many Christians and congregations today. Without such recognition, individuals become easy prey for the "god of this world."

Summary

As we examine the biblical picture of the principalities and powers, five points stand out:

(1) The powers, created for and through Jesus Christ (Col. 1:16), were to benefit all creation. While their exact purpose is not explicitly stated, it appears the "powers" were to underpin the creation by maintaining order and reducing chaos. At times these powers were viewed as angels associated with both nations and

cosmic forces. Their influence was exerted through decrees and human traditions.

(2) In an undisclosed way, the powers became hostile to God and were disarmed at the cross (Col. 2:15). The powers lost their rightful place in God's order when they took on the status of gods. Rather than aiding people they enslaved them, demanding rigid obedience to decrees and traditions which were justified apart from God. The law itself became a tool of enslavement. However, when Jesus died he disarmed the powers through the removal of enslaving decrees and regulations. In Christ, the believer dies to the *stoicheia*. Christ's victory is to be proclaimed to the powers through the church (Eph. 3:10). These powers are now subordinated to the authority of Christ (Eph. 1:21f). Furthermore, they are unable to separate the Christian from the love of God (Rom. 8:38).

(3) The Christian, however, is still in conflict with the powers (Eph. 6:12). The powers rule this age, which will continue until Christ delivers the kingdom to the Father (1 Cor. 15:24). Although the age to come began with Christ's resurrection, there is an interim period where the two ages (this age and the age to come) coexist. The conflict between the domain of darkness, conditioned by sin and death, and the kingdom of the Son, characterized by life and righteousness, reflects the current struggle.

(4) The powers will be destroyed when the kingdom is delivered to the Father (1 Cor. 15:24). Until then, the "prince of the power of the air," who determines the course of this world (Eph. 2:1–3), directs the powers.

(5) Even though Christians are set free from the control of the powers, they can rearm them and become enslaved all over again by submitting to their decrees and traditions (Gal. 4:8–11; Col. 2:20–23). Christians face danger if they are unable to recognize the tactics and presence of this spiritual host, which infiltrates everyday life and shapes attitudes, values, and behavior according to the ways of the world. Therefore, Christians are to develop a new mind which is to result in a new way of life (Rom. 12:1–2).

Life is impossible without the powers. Societies cannot exist without order. From a biblical perspective, however, that order separates men and women from God and brings individuals under the tutelage and bondage of decrees and traditions that lead to death. While the powers were created to sustain life and history, they now destroy life as God intended it. Furthermore, the powers are able to sabotage Christian existence and the life of local congregations. We must now discuss the influence and existence of the powers in modern life. What form do the powers take and in what sense do the powers regulate life today? What are the resulting implications for the church?

— 2 —

THE POWERS IN MODERN LIFE

POWERS CAN BE PERSONAL or impersonal. God is a personal power. Angels are personal powers. Personal powers exist independently of one's belief in them. Impersonal spiritual powers, however, have no reality apart from individuals assigning it to them. Yet once created, these powers exert influence back on their "creators." For example, an idol is an impersonal power. Although an individual creates it and the idol has no reality in itself, nevertheless, as it takes on the status of a god, it captivates its own creator. The result is empty deception (Col. 2:8).

Impersonal spiritual powers exist in all societies. These powers are present in the symbols, motivations, and structures of social groups. Thus we can speak of the "spirit of capitalism" or the "spirit of competition." While these "spirits" have no existence apart from human beings, once in existence they have the potential to condition and shape life. Their influence is primarily exerted through institutions.

Impersonal powers shape us not only as citizens and consumers, but also as devoutly religious people. The very structures we embrace and utilize to maintain life and serve God are powers that shape and influence our own existence and commitments.

No institution, structure, or system—whether it is religious, educational, political, social, recreational, medical, economic, moral, commercial, industrial or whatever—is able to escape the influence of the demonic. Sin and death condition all aspects of life. Furthermore, once the impersonal spiritual powers that surround our daily life make a bid for ultimate control, they acquire spiritual significance, and individuals are subordinated to their authority. In a biblical sense they become *stoicheia* as they regulate and control life. Concerning this, Jacques Ellul writes:

> Thus a social factor like religion, political power, technology, or propaganda will still be the work of man in its earliest forms, so that at its commencement it can still be modified by man. Man is the master and arbiter of its destiny. But as this factor solidifies in its means and methods, as it extends its sphere of application, as it invests itself with spiritual meaning, man progressively loses his possibilities of intervention and modification. A reversal takes place. Man no longer organizes the object. The object has its own life and it develops like a true organism according to its own necessity for him. [1]

Never before in the history of mankind have such diverse global forces existed to condition, control, and literally destroy human life. These forces, characterized in particular by political, military, and economic power, operate independently of the welfare, needs, and desires of humanity. Survival and expansion drive them. Powers hostile to life and God control the "rulers of this age."

The Rise of the Modern Power Complex

To understand the rise and development of the modern power complex, we must direct our attention back several centuries. The complexity of modern life, which contributes to the pervasive influence of the powers, originated in the 16th century with the emergence of a new world picture. The machine, perhaps more so than anything else, symbolizes the changes that were to take place in the following centuries.

From the 15th century on, exploration, discovery, trade, and invention opened up a new world unknown to previous generations. The natural environment began to give way to mechanization. As individuals became consumed with subduing and controlling nature, life became increasingly technical. In the process many benefits were reaped. But, not only did humanity become a benefactor, it also became a victim of its own efforts.

While science and technology brought about significant improvements in the quality of life, undesirable consequences also occurred. Every aspect of life was affected. Unfortunately, the negative consequences of technological development cannot be discarded while the positive aspects are kept. The two are tied together. Furthermore, at this stage the social, political, and economic forces that are linked to technological development are too complex and diversified for any individual, group, or nation to isolate for adjustment.

Simply put, the destiny of the world is uncertain, and rather than being a victim of nature's floods, hurricanes, tornadoes, earthquakes, droughts, and disease with which it has always been able to cope, humanity is now the victim of the work of its own hands, a far more ignominious fate. Men and women are impotent in the face of global phenomena directly resulting from "progress."

The church must be concerned about the spiritual conditioning of individuals in this environment. When viewed in light of the biblical perspective of the principalities and powers and the *stoicheia*, the hostility of the current world forces to the spiritual well-being of humanity becomes glaringly apparent.

The powers should not be dismissed as an outdated, mythological way of understanding life. Rather, the "powers of this world" are gods and rulers seated in high places who vie for total and absolute control of life. Their reality is hidden in systems, structures, and institutions, the very fabric of daily life.

The powers consume men and women by directing their quest for a better life, happiness, meaning, prosperity, power, or even spiritual fulfillment. The spiritual reality of the powers goes unrecognized. Human beings give the powers their passionate support and promote them without realizing what they are doing or that they are paying with their lives. The powers of death go unrecognized for the lack of a credible witness to expose them.

To understand the nature of the conflict we must understand the opponent. In the words of Jacques Ellul:

> Man's enemy is no longer another class of men, nor is it a relatively simple system set up in the interests of a special class. It is a collection of mechanisms of undesirable complexity—technics, propaganda, state, administration, planning, ideology, urbanization, social technology. Man is set in these complexes which no one can control, but whose functioning strictly governs the state, the future, the sphere of liberty, conformity, and adaptation. Man is less and less the master of his own life.[2]

These complex forces governing us must be viewed in light of the biblical teaching concerning the principalities and powers.

Our struggle is not against flesh and blood (Eph. 6:12). Nor is it against society or mankind; rather, it is against those structures which regulate life according to the elements, according to human traditions, and not according to Christ.

Our aim is to trace out, in part, the philosophical, social, and technical developments that have led to the current complexities, fabrications, and control of human life by a host of impersonal spiritual forces. To do this four points will be examined: (1) the formation of a mechanical-objective world view; (2) the mechanization of life; (3) the disjunctive development of society; and (4) the perceptual fragmentation and institutional shaping of reality.

The Mechanical World View

Lewis Mumford, in his two-volume work, *The Myth of the Machine*, documents the influence of the machine and mechanization on human development. Mumford portrays the "new world picture" as coming into final articulation with the development of the glass lens. Related to the glass lens was the invention of the telescope and microscope, which led to the reevaluation of religious truths that had been held as self-evident for centuries.

Mumford notes that the Copernican revolution removed man from the center of the universe and the lens reduced him further in size when compared to the solar system and galaxy. Certain religious beliefs, which beforehand were purely speculative, were brought into the arena of observation within space and time. Individuals became aware of an orderly solar system with regular planetary motion around the sun. Such regularity became the model for a new social order. The refinement of the clock aided in the formation of regularity within human interaction. Before long, regularity led to predictability and predictability to control.

The old order, based on Christian revelation and centered on God, gave way to the new order based on matter, motion, and human reasoning. Objectivity became of utmost importance. The subjective dimension of life, based on feelings, taste, and emotion, was rendered unimportant—at least in understanding the nature of the world and universe which not only surrounds us, but in which we as human beings live. Mumford points out that what went unrecognized was that humanity, in its own subjectivity, was removed from its own world and environment.

From the 15th century on, the world became increasingly viewed as a mechanical system to be understood and controlled rationally. The hereafter, which had been at the heart of medieval life, no longer counted. The here and now guided life.

Discovery, trade, and invention provided the backdrop for a new world based on a mechanized, orderly understanding of life. It provided the foundation not only for the development of physics, but also for the development of a new social order. People soon forgot that any other way of life ever existed. It took only a short time for human life to be reduced to and evaluated in terms of abstract concepts such as speed, time, money, and power. As Mumford notes, "speed shortened time; time was money; money was power. Farther and farther, faster and faster became identified with human progress."[3]

The development of the new world view can be credited in large measure to Copernicus, Kepler, Galileo, Descartes, Leibnitz, and Newton. Focusing on Galileo's distinction between the primary and secondary qualities of things, Mumford points to Galileo as the single greatest contributor to this new world view. For Galileo, the primary qualities of matter referred to size, shape, number, and rate of motion. These qualities are objective and can be verified by methods of weighing, timing, and measuring. Most importantly, these qualities can be quantified.

Galileo believed that only mathematics afforded complete certainty. The secondary qualities of a thing, such as color, sound, odor, texture, and the like, are all subjective qualities. The perception of these qualities may differ from one person to the next and are nonquantifiable. Therefore, to Galileo, secondary qualities of matter were far less important than primary qualities. In separating these qualities, Galileo intended to separate objectivity from subjectivity.

For Galileo, the real world was the objective world made up of matter and motion which could be reduced to quantitative, mathematical expressions. The subjective world became suspect and relative. The human being as a living soul became reduced to a product of mass and motion. Thus objective science was born at the expense of the real world of experience. One portion of human and physical reality replaced the totality of life. The ultimate goal was to free oneself from subjective presuppositions that could distort the true objective nature of reality. Furthermore, it was believed that this was an achievable goal.

The orderly, measurable, objective, mechanized world of the scientist soon found its way into philosophy and finally society itself. Descartes, for example, viewed the individual as a "machine made by the hands of God." The body was viewed as a mechanical system in union with the soul. The ultimate goal was the mechanization of the social order, regulated and controlled by a political absolute.

Thomas Hobbes, a contemporary of both Galileo and Descartes, introduced this objective-mechanistic thinking into the realm of politics. Hobbes, who met with Galileo in 1636, came away with "the main outline of his philosophical system, in which the method of geometry and the concepts of the new science of motion were to be applied to man in society."[4] Later, in the 1640s, Hobbes began work on his trilogy where man, body, and citizen were portrayed as part of a mechanized social system.

Hobbes, like Descartes, advocated political absolutism. A benevolent, political dictator who maintained social order would be the best form of government. This power was to arise out of the consent of the governed. Anarchy was to be kept in check. Hobbes contended that when working properly, society could function with the order and predictability of a machine. The basis for such logic was the presumption that men and women were no more than animated machines that could operate like cogs in a mechanical social framework. The goal was to regulate human life resulting in an ordered, peaceful society.

This emphasis on order, control, and regulation contributed to both the compartmentalization and quantification of life. Compartmentalization was reinforced by viewing behavior in terms of social roles. Initially, the meaning of "role" was a part played by an actor in a play. Later it came to mean expected social behaviors or a specific function or position in society.

In the course of one day, a person engages in many different roles. For example, a man might take on the roles of father, neighbor, laborer, consumer, citizen, and so on. The power complex defines and shapes those roles. Human behavior is broken down for analysis so that it can be socially determined and controlled.

As behavior became dissected and prescribed, daily existence became increasingly quantified. From a macroperspective, individuals became part of a statistical order. The categories of race, sex, age, education, income, employment, religion, and so on provided the framework for the analysis and interpretation of social and individual needs. Social problems became defined statistically. As a result, policy makers now turn to technicians for information and answers. The future offers little hope of deviating from this path.

The Mechanization of Life

This mechanized world-view lent itself to the quantification of daily behavior. Speed, regularity, and order became further linked with power and productivity. As Giedion noted decades ago, the gradual changes and sometimes very simple objects that were introduced into society accumulated into forces that shook the very roots of human life. While we cannot thoroughly document this transformation here, nevertheless, it is beneficial to gain some appreciation for the changes that altered our existence.

The invention and development of machines played a major role in the transformation of society. The use of machines can be traced back thousands of years. For the most part, human ingenuity and technical development were a direct response to the necessities of human survival or to the spiritual world. The fundamental human need for food and shelter provided incentives for the development of new techniques. In addition to material factors, spiritual and magical interests also led to invention and creativity.

While machines existed in society for long periods of time, their existence did not greatly alter life-values. Mechanization did not significantly penetrate society until the elimination of the complicated handicrafts between the 14th and 19th centuries. The 11th century saw a resurgence of technical development which was stimulated by both trade and war. By the 15th century, trade contact with the Near and Far East, and the discovery of America, made available immense new sources of raw materials and technological innovations. Up until that time the craft guilds were the primary industrial providers.

The guild, besides providing goods and services for local geographical areas, also provided the basic educational and welfare needs for its members. According to Mumford, as long as the guilds contributed to the local community, mechanization was not possible. The guild membership regulated business and strived to maintain a balanced economy. By the 14th and 15th centuries, however, larger industries began to invade the domain of the smaller trade shops. Quantity began to replace quality. The guilds, monitors of the worker's skill and the quality of his work, became associations of hired workers. Their chief concern became obtaining fair wages and decent working conditions. By the end of the 16th century the guilds were abolished and wealthy merchants increasingly controlled production. According to Siegfried Giedion, "This was the predestined hour for mechanization."

Prior to that time, the emphasis was not on the tool or the machine, but on the craftsman; not on the quantity or speed of production, but on the quality of the product. The technology of the Middle Ages is reflected in the Romanesque and Gothic cathedrals. Concerning these structures, Mumford comments:

> Not merely muscular strength, mechanical skill, and physical courage went into the fabrication of these buildings: emotions, feelings, fantasies, remembered legends—in fact the community's total response to life—took form in these supreme technological achievements. [5]

These buildings reflected the life-values of the workers and the community. The community was made up of various craft guilds, each of which, to some degree, embodied the basic values from which medieval life was sustained and directed—the ultimate value and reality being the human soul and its eternal welfare. But as the social orientation changed and mechanization took command, quantification of life emerged as the new guideline for determining purpose and meaning. The bottom line of the account ledger took on ultimate meaning. Life became increasingly evaluated in terms of profit and power.

Mumford indicates that with the breakdown of the craft guilds production began to be separated into component operations resulting in the division of labor. The work tempo became faster and less flexible. As industrialization began to occur, large capital investments became necessary for ships, machinery, and wages. This contributed to the formation of stock companies with absentee ownership. The result was inevitable—the exploitation of anonymous workers whose worth was evaluated in terms of profits.

The army, the mine, and the factory all paved the way for mechanization to be applied to human beings. Human activity and ability were translated into units of energy or money (human capital and resources). Regimentation, order, and efficiency became the guidelines for human development within the military or industrial settings. Through this progression society became transformed into what Mumford describes as a new power complex composed of a "constellation of forces, interests and motives, . . . capable of planetary and even interplanetary extension."[6]

The power complex, directed by its own internal logic, has developed so that it is indifferent to human need or welfare. The only standard it remains accountable to is its own continued existence and expansion. The power complex is self-justifying. Reasonable and rational forces control and dominate life—or at least we would be led to believe so.

The existence of a global force was impossible prior to the mechanization of life. During the Middle Ages limited and diverse contributions from a variety of workers, farmers, and craftsmen who were dependent on one another to meet shared needs sustained life. Mumford credits spiritual values, aesthetic design, and qualitative excellence for holding in check the quantification of life. That is not to say that life was romantic, meaningful, or easy; rather, a very different set of forces were at work shaping life than exist today.

Mechanization fragmented the medieval community; this led to a capitalistic mentality with a renewed emphasis on private ownership and material accumulation. The welfare of the community was no longer necessary for the welfare of the individual. Mumford sums it up by saying, "The idea of a powerful and expensive life supplanted the ideal of a holy or humane one."

This did not all occur in one generation or even in one century. Steady developments along these lines took place from the 16th century to the present. The expansion of the railroads, urban growth, and the demise of the complicated handicrafts paved the way for mechanization. Giedion has observed that the introduction of electric fans, irons, toasters, wringers, vacuum cleaners, ranges, and refrigerators revolutionized the American household between 1912 and 1932.[7] The mass production of automobiles went hand in hand with the mass production of food and the mechanization of nutrition. The tin can paved the way for ready-made foods and chain-franchised restaurants.

Mass production and mass distribution contributed to the homogenization of society. Many products penetrate every segment of our culture, and in several instances, the world. Fast food restaurants and time-saving cooking techniques have altered our interaction patterns with both family members and friends. Life has been shaped to exist in the "fast lane." Yet, rather than streamlining our time and energies, we often find ourselves facing additional decisions and commitments. Meaningless activity pulls life apart. We must constantly choose between a maze of options on how to use our time, energy, and resources. Many of these decisions, like deciding which pair of shoes to buy, have little value, but can become a major endeavor.

When viewed from the vantage point of one day, life can become a string of activity slots. People glide in and out of roles at work, at home, with friends, while shopping, and also at church. At the end of any given day, it may be difficult to integrate all of that activity (motion) into a meaningful whole. Rather, life becomes fragmented into units of doing, going, watching, but rarely being. Living itself can become little more than a technique.

Life in the 20th century is a complex, unfolding, technological drama, altered often and repeatedly. This is not to say that technological developments are bad. Technology makes the world a better place to live. Furthermore, God gives us the capacity to create and to shape the world. Our concern is not with that ability or goal. Instead, we must try and understand our present condition in light of the Scriptures. Once we recognize the fallen state of humanity, and the pervasive influence of the "powers" over human destiny, we are faced with a world that offers an illusion of peace, hope, and security, but which leads to death and destruction. This structural-philosophical framework serves as a medium for the *stoicheia* of the world and has a direct impact on the life of the church. Part of that impact is discussed below.

The Techno-Economic Realm & the Disjunctive Nature of Society

A third factor contributing to the influence of the powers in today's world is the disjunctive nature of society. Sociologist

Daniel Bell describes society as a composite of different realms, each responding to its own set of norms and values. Most sociologists divide society into three such realms—the *techno-economic*, the *polity*, and the *culture*. Each realm has its own agenda and needs which can, and do, conflict with the other realms. Political institutions dramatically influence economic concerns and vice versa. Tremendous tensions develop between competing sectors of society creating an impact on both families and individuals. According to Bell, various social realms generate conflicting goals which create contradictions in the way we live.

The techno-economic realm of society is concerned with the production and distribution of goods and services. Rationality, economizing, and efficiency characterize this sector of society. Value is measured in terms of utility, which is in turn translated into monetary terms.

Regarding the social structure of the techno-economic realm, Bell writes:

> it is a structure of roles, not persons, and is laid out in the organizational charts that specify the relationships of hierarchy and function. Authority inheres in the position, not in the individual, and social exchange is a relation between roles. A person becomes an object or a "thing" not because the enterprise is inhumane, but because the performance of a task is subordinated to the organization's ends. [8]

The modern techno-economic realm is a result of capitalistic development since the 16th century. Prior to that time, the primary social unit, whether it was viewed in terms of the community, the family, the tribe or the guild, was a group. Within Western society, during the period of mechanization, the emphasis shifted to the individual. The self-made, self-sufficient individual became the new role model for society. As long as society was viewed from a corporate perspective, rather than an atomistic one, production was geared toward the needs of the larger group. Such needs were initially defined in terms of human survival. Once society became reoriented towards the individual, a new life perspective developed. Needs became replaced with wants, which became defined psychologically rather than biologically. Individual consumption became limited only by financial resources, the accumulation of which became the chief aim in life.

Bell notes that in the formative years, Puritan restraint and the Protestant work ethic held capitalism in check. But in the long run the materialistic spirit won out. Bell claims:

> The greatest single engine in the destruction of the Protestant ethic was the invention of the installment plan, or instant credit. Previously, one had to save in order to buy. But with credit cards one could indulge in instant gratification. The system was transformed by mass production and mass consumption, by the creation of new wants and new means of gratifying those wants.[9]

The temptation of instant gratification dates back to Jesus' encounter with Satan in the wilderness. The credit card now replaces the creative word of God.

Ignited by the possibilities created by mass production, the techno-economic revolution fostered a new consumer mentality based on individual ownership. Consumption gave birth to a new lifestyle. According to Bell, the consumption mentality, with its emphasis on spending and material possessions, undermined the traditional value system's emphasis on thrift, frugality, self-control, and impulse renunciation. By the early 20th century, technological developments had paved the way for the spirit of materialism through mass production, mass distribution, and mass advertising. Major tensions developed between the techno-economic realm—with its emphasis on cost, benefits, efficiency, and role behavior—and the cultural realm which wished to explore the meaning of human existence.

The techno-economic order classifies individuals according to roles. Function replaces personality, and in turn, roles can become more important than people. Human interaction unfolds as an exchange between predefined role behavior. We become clients to lawyers, patients to doctors, students to teachers, customers to salespeople and so on. Interaction is brittle and routine and results in little meeting of minds or souls.

Roles, however, cannot define human behavior. Not only is this true in practice, but our culture places emphasis on personhood—that individuals have personal worth and value and that we are "somebody" and not simply "something." The dominating influence of the techno-economic order, however, contributes to a depersonalization of society. To a large extent, people are seen and responded to, not as individuals with personal needs and characteristics, but as functional representatives of a particular role. Thus, one's feelings of self-worth and value can become dependent, for example, on a job title.

For centuries, the family and the church transmitted the traditional values of society. The value of the individual and his or her identity were preserved. In the new techno-economic order, however, values—including the value of individuals—are readily altered through movies, books, radio, television, magazines, and newspapers. Spending and enjoyment dominate the materialistic spirit of our age and tie personal value to a particular lifestyle principally controlled by the power complex. Identity is tied to cars, clothes, and homes. Travel, adventure, and fashion are all part of what Bell calls "a world of make-believe in which one lives for expectations, for what will come rather than what is."

Yet in this fast-moving, high-paced, consumption-dominated sphere the most fundamental question of human existence—Who am I?—remains unanswered. The techno-economic order erodes the cultural value base and results in not only an ongoing identity crisis for many people, but also the inability to answer such basic questions as, Why am I here? Where am I going? and What should I do? These questions fade into the background in a society based on a credit card mentality where the answers and fulfillment of life's struggles and needs will be taken care of with the next purchase, a nicer home, or a better job. The next purchase, however, is never enough and humanity's conditioned appetite for consumption reduces existence to a perpetual pursuit of pleasure. In this context, God is viewed through the lens of leisure, recreation, ownership, and comfort. Faith and morality become redefined to accommodate the materialistic spirit of this evil age.

In this environment, forces bombard those attempting to shape their minds and in turn their consumption habits, political behavior, wants, and in the end their very understanding of life is assaulted, including their perception of God. As a result, the principalities and powers reign supreme, dominating and shaping human life to such an extent that no one escapes their influence. The diversity, intensity, complexity, and continual multiplication of the social, political, and economic forces at work attempting to shape us cannot be adequately recognized or coped with apart from Christ.

The church is not immune to the influence of this power complex. Technique, mechanization, impersonal role behavior, and the rationality and logic of our age can subordinate life in Christ. However, such life is not according to Christ, but human tradition, according to the *stoicheia* (the basic building blocks) of the world.

The church is to enable Christians to grow and mature into strong believers equipped to deal with the problems and pressures of life. This endeavor is not an individual one, but is based on mutually edifying relationships within the body of Christ. For this to occur there must be unity in both spirit and mission as well as an organizational structure that supports that mission—a topic which we must explore later.

The Fragmentation of Reality

The final aspect we will discuss that contributes to the strength of the powers in modern society is the fragmentation of reality. Most people unconsciously divide reality up into multiple spheres. For example, science, religion, politics, or other influences combine to shape our understanding of reality. One of these dimensions of life may be more influential than another. As discussed above, that results in tensions as value conflicts may develop from one realm to another.

Among these spheres, one presents itself to us as the ultimate reality. Whatever this sphere, it shapes and integrates our life-values and understanding of the world and our place within it. During the Middle Ages, Christian theology provided the basis for understanding creation and existence. During the 16th and 17th centuries, science and political ideologies paved the way for new interpretations and theories concerning life and the universe. Today, a significant portion of the world's population views and interprets reality through the lens of communism. Every person frames and structures reality on the basis of some world view. That world view then acts back on the individual affecting how meaning and history are interpreted.

In addition to holding some ultimate perception of reality, we are faced with finding meaning in the daily mundane affairs of human existence. This is partially accomplished through the development of a "natural attitude," i.e., the routine attitude of everyday experience. For example, we take for granted the way we walk down the sidewalk. That is, we are not conscious of the actual process of walking unless walking presents itself to us as a problem. If the sidewalk is icy or I have broken my foot then I become more conscious of what walking actually involves. I can no longer take the process for granted, but must actually concentrate on walking. When that process occurs, I have suspended my "natural attitude" and have replaced it with a "reflexive attitude" that focuses on the problem at hand. Generally, daily life is taken for granted. The natural attitude is suspended, however, when a problem occurs or something happens which is not understood. For that moment we are faced with uncertainties that require reflection and clarification.

The fact that my "natural attitude" corresponds to the "natural attitude" of others allows for meaningful and stable relationships within society. For example, there is a common agreement that a green light means go and a red light means stop. This agreement extends to the interpretation of most daily experiences. This means that we share a common view of reality, because at certain points "my meanings" and "your meanings" converge.

Nevertheless, as Berger and Luckmann point out, we are capable of suspending this natural attitude. When problems or unusual circumstances develop, we begin to ask questions in an attempt to give meaning to the reality at hand. Reality is no longer taken for granted. The "reflexive attitude" replaces the "natural attitude."

Two major factors influence our understanding of daily experience. The first is language. The ability to communicate directly affects our ability to interpret and understand the world around us. The fact that I speak English rather than Japanese shapes my understanding of the world. Second, available knowledge influences my perception of everyday reality. Within any given society, there is a stock of available knowledge. For that society to continue over time and to maintain order, a certain amount of that knowledge must be available to and acknowledged by the entire population. Those shared understandings allow for meaningful interaction and the development of mutual commitments.

In a sense, then, reality becomes defined on the basis of our socio-cultural setting. This socio-cultural setting stands as an objective reality apart from us, even though it is a product of our own making. As children we enter the world of our parents which confronts us as a given reality. We have had nothing to do with its formation, and in the early stages of life we will learn of this world as it is transmitted to us by our parents, "significant others," and later by various social institutions. As we grow we discover that certain attitudes, values, and behavior are to correspond to different life situations. We will develop a natural attitude that allows us to function socially in a meaningful and acceptable way in our environment.

Related to this is the habitualization of human activity that occurs within institutional settings. [10] Over time, certain patterns of behavior emerge within social structures that become normative. Social and institutional norms regulate human conduct. At the institutional level, these patterns of behavior take on a reality of their own and confront the individual as "an external and coercive fact." [11] The institution, having a history that precedes that of the individual, stands as a part of the given reality and persists despite the attitude of the individual concerning it. For example, although I may not like certain governmental rules and regulations, I cannot wish them away. They are part of the given reality of my world.

While institutions are a product of human activity, they are capable of outliving their founders and of developing their own reality. Once this happens, "the product acts back on the producer." [12] Furthermore, as Berger and Luckmann observe, "The more conduct is institutionalized, the more predictable and the more controlled it becomes." [13]

The final outcome is that an individual's natural attitude is shaped by a multitude of institutional realities. Whatever is learned as objective truth is internalized as subjective reality and has the power to shape the individual. That is, once I am told that the world is a certain way and I accept that as being true, then I internalize that knowledge and use it to interpret the world around me. Regardless of whether that knowledge is true, once it becomes internalized it becomes the basis for my understanding of life and reality.

Throughout most of history, a person's primary understanding of the world came from family, religious beliefs, the local community, and the power complex. Today this is no longer a simple process, but is conditioned and complicated by the multiplicity of power structures that determine human existence. This presents a problem in trying to discuss "reality." We must ask, Of whose reality are we speaking—the reality of the news media, the military general, the punk rocker, the starving peasant, the nuclear physicist—who? Is life a reflection of some "objective reality" that can be processed and coded? Or is it more complex, more subjective, more elusive? Since the individual is faced with multiple, often competing, realities, how do we conceptually organize life and the world to maintain some sense of meaning and direction?

These multiple spheres of reality become synthesized into some overall view of life. Each sphere becomes a subuniverse within a larger universe of meaning. For example, a person's religious views may govern his or her perception of politics. Every person develops some overall framework to interpret life whether it is mythological, scientific, political, theological, or otherwise.

For the Christian, divine revelation provides the underpinning for the understanding of reality and life within the world. In particular, God reveals himself through his Word, Jesus Christ, as mediated by the Holy Spirit and testified to in the Scriptures. The Bible is part of God's special revelation and stands as the ultimate and infallible authority concerning God's dealing with humanity. Yet within the modern world, and since the 16th century, this revelation has become eclipsed and has little impact on institutional life. Even when God is recognized there are no guarantees that such recognition will have any significant impact on the development and structure of the related institutional realities.

The institutional life of the church is an aggregate of multiple realities, shaped and conditioned by an endless variety of factors having their origin, not in divine revelation, but in the techno-socio-cultural development of modern life. Furthermore, that cannot be changed—it can only be recognized. Such recognition is to lead to ongoing self-examination. The church is not immune from the shaping influence of the powers. However, without this recognition, the church can become enslaved to and victimized by its own religiosity.

One problem the church faces is proclaiming the gospel in a world whose outlook on life is conditioned by institutional realities that undermine divine revelation and leave the individual to the fate of complex social forces. Furthermore, Christians are redefining and redirecting their own version of the Christian message—shaped by social, economic, and political forces that are hostile to God—to justify self-serving interests. A new gospel is created to accommodate a new lifestyle.

For the church to unveil the illusionary promises and death-infested content of the powers, it must witness to the grace of God and the wholeness of life in Christ. This witness cannot exist apart from the Christian community that is to embody and manifest the objective nature of divine revelation to the world. This truth is to point both to the reality of God and of his saving grace in Jesus Christ.

For this community to endure, its members must develop and maintain a shared understanding of the Christian life and mission. Ongoing support must be present based on mutual edification and support. Furthermore, there must be a shared basis of knowledge which provides the foundation for living and the framework for decision making. It is not enough to say that this basis is the Bible. While this is true, the truth of the Bible must be communicated and understood in a corporate sense and then practiced and lived out on a daily basis. For this to occur, social structures must exist which support it. Unfortunately, what does exist in too many instances are individuals, all viewing the world through different lenses, who gather together for meetings. These meetings represent the intersection of shared religious beliefs, which produces a common purpose for meeting, but not a common life. The result is a loosely associated group of people rather than the biblical concept of community.

These shared religious beliefs may consist of selected moral teachings, isolated facts and myths, and a mixture of personal ideas and notions which become embedded in a culturally determined framework for understanding and interpreting life. In this context, systematic Christian thinking and reflection that attempt to understand human existence and social realities in a broad and biblically based theological framework are abandoned for superficial and personal religious meanings. When this occurs there is no corporate basis for life in the world, and personal interpretation replaces divine revelation. However, personal interpretation is ultimately sabotaged by the technical, economic, political, and social spheres of life which not only impact our understanding of truth and reality, but which also shape values, attitudes, and behavior. The powers, not men and women, rule and reign. No one escapes their influence. For the Christian, obedience to the Spirit of God is to overcome that influence in the context of a supportive community of believers in Jesus Christ.

The Christian community is to expose the powers; however, that involves creating and maintaining social structures that reinforce Christianity. Christians are called to a life of servanthood, embracing the values of the kingdom of God and manifesting love, peace, and joy. Through the church the life and judgment of God are to be prophetically revealed.

Summary

In summary of our discussion concerning the powers and modern life the following points should be noted:

(1) Spiritual powers are both personal and impersonal. Structures, systems, ways of thinking, and institutions all become channels or mediums through which the powers exert their influence and control.

(2) The complexities of modern life can be discussed in a variety of ways. We have examined mechanization, the polarization of the objective and subjective dimensions of life, the fragmented and contradictory nature of man's social development, and finally, how modern society structures reality.

(3) Galileo, Descartes, Hobbes, and others provided the philosophical framework needed for the "objectifying" of life. Especially important in this development was Galileo's distinction between the primary and secondary qualities.

(4) From the 15th century on, trade, invention, and exploration contributed to mechanization. The abolishment of the craft guilds, industrial growth, and the formation of stock companies reinforced the quantification of life. The mines, the factories, and the military were the first places where mechanization was widely applied to human beings.

(5) While society became knit together through mass production, mobility, and instant communication, the daily life of the individual became fragmented into a variety of impersonal roles and relationships. Techno-economic development characterized by

consumption and instant gratification eroded cultural traditions. Psychologically conditioned human wants replaced biologically determined human needs. Self-image and self-worth became progressively tied to a materialistic lifestyle. Life became role-dominated, slot-oriented, and mass-marketed.

(6) Reality itself became divided into subuniverses of meaning. In this context social, political, and economic realities shape the individual's natural attitude. Divine revelation, which should undergird the Christian's understanding of life and the world, is under attack from every direction. Without the support of a healthy Christian environment, the individual is left to the fate of complicated social realities. Little difference can now be seen between the natural attitude of the Christian and the non-Christian.

(7) The modern milieu supports the life of the powers and contributes to their dispersion throughout human existence. Freedom in Christ can exist only where the powers are recognized and exposed. Nothing in Scripture indicates that the Christian is immune from the influence of the powers. Rather, we are engaged in spiritual conflict with them.

3

THE QUEST FOR MEANING

WE HAVE SEEN THE STRONGHOLD of the powers in this world and can more clearly understand the intensity and the nature of the conflict in which Christians are involved. The fragmentation of society, the family, and ultimately the individual, generates an uncertainty in both self-identity and future direction. The result is that society is engaged in a search for meaning. This is true because humanity is not sure of its ultimate destiny. The social barometer points to change, but no one knows the direction.

During the next 25 years humanity is going to face the question of survival in a new and dramatic way. The world is already saturated with military, religious, political, and economic tensions. No solutions are in sight. Violence is an inevitable response of those whose dignity, self-worth, and rights have been stripped away through political and economic means. Even though the evening news regularly carries a new installment of the drama, the next chapter remains uncertain.

The overall atmosphere of modern life contributes to a lack of ultimate meaning and shared values. Since the future is uncertain, many people live for the moment. This results in a focusing on the immediate, which enslaves them to passing whims. Moreover, life is reduced to a consumer market—chartable, predictable, and enticeable. Men and women can be programmed to pursue objects and things that offer an illusion of hope, prosperity, power, and security, but which in the end are empty. Existence can be transformed into a "thing," used, manipulated, and discarded.

The mounting crises facing us will continue to make the quest for meaning even more difficult. Americans think of mean-

ing in terms of consumption. Cars, homes, travel, and possessions are part of the pursuit of happiness. Americans are not
only accustomed to, but demanding of a lifestyle that absorbs as
much energy as possible. The goal is comfort, but such a goal is
not without cost. For many, the end will be bitter disappointment. An unpredictable economy shatters the dreams of millions
to possess and accumulate. However, that is only part of the
drama.

Domestic problems plague many families. While financial
pressures contribute to family tensions, a combination of negative
forces have led to the unraveling of many families and individual
lives. Traditional values that provided a foundation for personal
and family stability have eroded, leaving many with no meaningful frame of reference for decision making.

Increasingly, children are exposed to the adult world at earlier
ages, but without the means to understand the significance of the
encounter. They find themselves engaging in adult roles, but without the emotional maturity necessary for healthy development.
For example, children are engaging in sexual relationships at
earlier ages. The result is tragic and devastating. Too frequently,
children are being treated as little adults in a society where
grown men and women have trouble coping with the pressures
of life.

Human beings can easily view one another as a means rather
than as an end. For many, a meaningful end no longer exists.
Only things exist, and existence itself is reduced to the pursuit
and preservation of things. Such values are especially widespread
in television and advertising—media that not only reflect, but
promote superficiality.

Local congregations contribute to the problem of misplaced
values when they preach a religious version of the "American
Dream." The tragedy is that this occurs without Christians being
aware of it. A number of factors contribute to this concern, including competition, social independence, church structure, and
citizenship.

Competition

Social competition contributes to an ongoing search for personal meaning and worth. Early in life we are taught to measure

our self-worth in relationship to others. In an environment that values beauty, youth, power, skill, wealth, fame, and creativity, the conditions are set to reinforce within many people feelings of inferiority and low self-esteem. The consequences are painful.

A competitive spirit permeates every aspect of our society. It is found not only in sports, but also in education, business, politics, marriage, family life, and also within religion. Not all competition is bad, yet many forms have a negative impact on the formation of self-worth. Competition focuses attention on human characteristics and accomplishments. Rather than viewing life as a gift, people view life as a contest. Some win, some lose. Winning becomes deceptively associated with beauty, money, status, power, comfort, sex, and consumption. The mass media create and promote symbols of success. Then from an early age, the competition begins to be "successful." In the process, the meaning of life becomes obscured.

The rules of competition in the modern world are stacked against the poor, the uneducated, the elderly, and the destitute. If we view the world through a lens of competition, then we must realize that God aligns himself firmly with the disadvantaged and helpless.

The church is engaged in this struggle. Its purpose, however, is not to compete with the world, but to unmask the destructive forces of death and to bring life. The church is not to imitate the world or to be a part of the world. Christians are not to rely on competition to secure meaning. The kingdom of God turns our perceptions of life upside down. To compete means to lose.

The spirit of competition enters into our lives in manifold ways. It appears in the way we relate to others. We may find ourselves trying to manipulate others through our emotions, intellect, or physical appearance. We may be competing with an image of success that has saturated our society; that of a superstar—powerful, wealthy, and sexy.

There are more subtle ways that the spirit of competition enters our lives. One is for the use of our time. We may find ourselves inundated with an overwhelming number of community, business, or social activities competing for one of our most valuable resources. Over against these are church events. How do we decide to use the free time that we have? In the business world, efficiency and productivity are two key concepts that govern the use of time. In the church it is ministry. But unfortunately, ministry is frequently equated with involvement in activities, rather than with a way of life.

We must avoid allowing activities to program our lives; rather, our use of time must be governed by clearly defined biblical values. Activities become enslaving when they regulate existence and determine when, where, how, and by whom things will be done. This problem can develop in local churches. Activities that are scheduled to help Christians grow and to reach the lost demand the attention of every dedicated believer. But when these events turn into a flood of unending activity, they undermine their very purpose. People end up filling activity slots. No real ministry occurs, only motion. Even though the motivating factors for involvement may be ministry and serving God, they become confused with activity slots rather than with a way of life. Such ministry should reflect abundant life in Christ, but can lead to feelings of weariness when we are involved and guilt when we are not. The goal is to bring us closer to God. The end result, however, may simply be to keep family members busy every night of the week.

Time is a precious commodity. Jesus spent time alone with his Father in the wilderness. We can learn from his example. There, while alone with God, the glitter and tinsel of personal ambition and popular acclaim should fade away. The holy presence of God is to replace the swirling motion that surrounds existence. In that moment we come face to face with eternity. We stand naked before God. Our true character and spirit are revealed. Only then can we truly discover who we are and who he is. The ultimate importance lies not in what we do, or how we compare with others, but in understanding who it is that we call Lord.

Competition is closely tied to money. Human existence and meaning in life have become merchandizable. This leads to competition in the packaging and marketing of enticing products. Lifestyles are advertised like tools in a hardware store. Money is the life-force of the power complex, and the world competes for our money Just as meaning can become lost in a sea of activities, so too, it can become twisted and distorted through greed and avarice.

Jesus Christ lays claim to the whole person, including our finances. Money is a tool. The church must use money to fulfill its mission as the people of God. We are accountable to God to be good stewards of all that he has given to our care. Our commitment to Christ and his lordship must determine how we use all resources. Otherwise, we will find ourselves falling victim to the powers of this world, which compete with God for our finances. One of the most effective tools used by the powers to deceive us is the godless use of money.

A third area of competition is sexual. God created men and women as sexual beings. Sexual drives are a normal part of every human being. However, the power complex exploits natural sexual drives by promoting lust and distorting sexual intimacy. Sexual competition exists at all levels of society. It is used to sell products, to nourish fantasies, and to exploit the weak. Sexual awareness is closely tied to one's self-image and self-esteem. Advertisers recognize the vulnerability of people in these areas and take advantage of sexuality to achieve a profit.

In summary, competition affects our lives in a variety of ways that can lead to a sense of meaninglessness and actual bondage to the power complex. Christians are not immune from these forces. Once we recognize who this Lord is who calls us to himself, we realize that there is no competition. He demands all. He is all in all.

Social Independence

A second factor contributing to meaninglessness and having a dramatic impact on personal growth and congregational life is social independence. Rather than the church existing as a community of believers who are building one another up in love, it can turn into a group of individuals who simply attend a common meeting. Certain beliefs may be held in common, but faith in God becomes a personal and private affair. This leads us to examine a personal versus a public faith.

Americans highly value personal freedom and liberty. No one wants to exist under a totalitarian regime where he or she is told what to do and what to believe. We esteem both personal privacy and the freedom to act according to our conscience. In a collective sense, the church values and enjoys these rights too. We don't want the government telling us how to run the church. We do not hold our beliefs accountable to public officials in Washington, D.C.

Our personal beliefs are not open to public debate. However, in what context, if any, should personal religious beliefs be subject to outside accountability?

At this point we come to a critical crossroads. While our beliefs are personal—that is, no one can believe for another—these beliefs take on meaning only in a public context. To state this more strongly, Christian faith takes on meaning only when it is proclaimed publicly. A private faith is always selective in what it views as important. A public faith must stand prepared to give an account of itself. To be relevant, it must address the broader issues that affect both its immediate social context and even more broadly, the world.

Here we must come to grips with the biblical account of creation. God created everything. Everything he created was good; it was perfect. Furthermore, men and women were created in God's own image. In a way beyond our comprehension, individuals reflect the divine character. Our discussion of a public and private faith must take into account God as Creator. There is no such thing as divine selectivity when it comes to dealing with issues that relate to the welfare of the world. The Scriptures reveal a God who is concerned about all creation.

Death, the ultimate enemy of the human race, has infested and contaminated all creation. God's plan of salvation is not limited to individuals, but includes the entire created order. The vision is of a new heaven and a new earth. Just as Christians cannot isolate themselves from the pressing agenda of life, passively waiting for the eschaton, the same is true of the corporate church. To segregate the gospel from life's issues violates God's intervention in human affairs. The prophets understood this. Their proclamation of God's word was a public testimony, not only to Israel, but to the nations of the earth. God is the God of heaven and earth. Joel proclaimed, "And the LORD roars from Zion, and utters his voice from Jerusalem, and the heavens and the earth shake" (Joel 3:16). Micah exclaimed, "Hear, you peoples, all of you; hearken, O earth, and all that is in it" (Mic. 1:2). The prophets maintained a cosmic vision of God: "The LORD is coming forth out of his place, and will come down and tread upon the high places of the earth. And the mountains will melt under him and the valleys will be cleft, like wax before the fire" (Mic. 1:3).

This public aspect was present in the life of Jesus. Not only was his life public, so was his death. The same holds true for the ministry of the early church. Its faith was proclaimed publicly and brought about public response. A private faith attempts to protect itself from public scrutiny. It loves darkness rather than light. A public faith often brings reproach not only from those outside the faith, but also from those within. When Amos' message began to cause those in positions of leadership embarrassment, they attempted to silence him. Amaziah, the priest of Bethel said to Amos: "never again prophesy at Bethel, for it is the king's sanctuary, and it is a temple of the kingdom" (Amos 7:13).

Amos' response was hardly what Amaziah expected or appreciated:

"I am no prophet, nor a prophet's son; but I am a herdsman, and a dresser of sycamore trees, and the LORD took me from following the flock, and the Lord said to me, 'Go, prophesy to my people Israel.'

"Now therefore hear the word of the LORD.
You say, 'Do not prophesy against Israel,
and do not preach against the house of Isaac.'
Therefore thus says the LORD:
'Your wife shall be a harlot in the city,
and your sons and your daughters shall fall by the sword,
and your land shall be parceled out by line;
you yourself shall die in an unclean land,
and Israel shall surely go into exile away from its land.' "
(Amos 7:14–17)

A public expression of faith brought slander and hardship to the prophets. They were ridiculed, viewed as traitors, and on occasion were killed. Jesus was crucified; the apostles and other early Christians were martyred because of the public proclamation of faith. The confession, "Jesus is Lord," takes on meaning only when it is proclaimed publicly.

Authentic faith follows in the same tradition of the prophets and apostles, although this means more than giving a public testimony of faith in Christ. It must be revealed through a way of life. Furthermore, this must be done institutionally as well as individually.

The prophets forcefully proclaimed God's message of justice for the poor and judgment on the corrupt. Without respect for political power, wealth, or religious stature, the prophets declared, "Thus saith the Lord." Jesus spoke with even greater authority than the prophets. He entered into the condition of humanity as the Word made flesh.

The church cannot exist and fulfill the purposes of God without a public faith. God's grace brings about individual transformation, which is then to be expressed corporately. God's love and judgment are to be manifest. No part of life is to be left untouched. Public faith is likely to receive rebuff, criticism, and persecution, not only from the outside but from within the church as well. However, this is the cost of obedience and honesty. The church will never fulfill its mission by protecting itself. Authentic faith must be manifest through a public expression. This is true for both individuals and corporate structures. The church plays a vital role in the public expression of faith.

Structure

Structure is a third factor contributing to problems of meaning in the church today. No congregation can exist without structure. Structure involves more, though, than policies, meeting times, and leadership. More fundamentally, social structures arise out of patterns of behavior grounded in the attitudes, perceptions, beliefs, motivations, habits and expectations of human beings. A social structure is no more harmonious than the individuals who comprise it. Furthermore, numerous historical and cultural influences condition the institutional nature of the structure. To appreciate the nature of any given social structure, we must identify the forces which shape its components. Some forces reinforce Christian life; others do not.

No social structure, including a church, can escape the influence of the power complex. A church cannot exist as a closed system, insulated from the rest of the world. While the goal is for local congregations to provide the framework for establishing Christian community, this is not an easy task. The challenge is twofold. First, individual Christians must be aided in developing a biblical perspective on life that will help them in establishing a frame of reference for decision making and involvement in the world. Second, a structure must be maintained that provides a supportive framework for the overall mission of the church including worship, instruction, fellowship, and evangelism. The difficulty is in counterbalancing and overcoming the impact of the power complex on individual lives. Furthermore, caution must be taken that the structures do not enslave their creators.

Congregational structure must arise out of the biblical mission of the church. Yet the particular structures adopted largely determine the mission of the congregation. A structure has the potential to take on spiritual authority. It can make claims and demands on the individual or group. Even though the original intent is to reduce chaos and maintain order to complete the mission, a reversal can take place which brings about enslavement.

Paul warns Christians to avoid enslavement to rules and regulations that become spiritual ends in themselves and remove our freedom in Christ (Gal. 4:8–11; Col. 2:20–23). Regulations become self-justifying. On the surface they appear to contribute to godliness, but they are of no value. This point is of particular importance concerning social structures. As new dimensions are added to the structure, they can produce positive effects for the congregation. But, as the structure increases in complexity, it progressively gains more control in shaping the mission of the church. Furthermore, as the system develops it becomes accountable only to its own internal logic. These characteristics point to a reversal whereby the structure itself becomes invested with spiritual authority adversely affecting the lives of its members.

One major concern of the system becomes self-preservation. The structure will develop and solidify in such a way as to prevent change or loss of existence. What began as a force for good turns into a power that maintains the *status quo* for better or worse.

Without a supportive community of believers and role models, the Christian faces an uphill struggle. The pervasive influence of the "elemental" thinking of this world which shapes our understanding and interpretation of reality is difficult to escape. Not only does it have a stagnating influence on individual Christians, but, more dramatically, it also adversely affects the corporate life and organization of entire congregations. For example, once abundant life is redefined to match the thinking of this world (i.e., success, prosperity, status, power, prestige, and so on), then the demonic structures take over, and even as Christians we will promote them and support them as long as they, and not the Bible, provide us with an understanding of what Christian life actually means. In light of this, our analysis of structure becomes critical. Is one's church structure reinforcing the attitudes and motivations of humanity apart from God? Has it turned into an impersonal spiritual force that rigidly controls the lives of those who are involved? Has the structure reached a point of *status quo*, where preservation of the past takes precedent over adapting to the future? Does it serve us or do we serve it?

Structure is a necessary part of our lives together as human beings. Without structure we would be enslaved to chaos. As Christians, however, we must monitor the structures we create and change them when necessary to nurture the fullest and most visible expression of life in Christ. Otherwise, the structure itself, based on its own momentum, will take on a leading role in determining the mission of the church.

To maintain healthy congregational life, the following four dimensions must give life to the structure:

1. A community of believers, empowered by the Spirit, who are actively engaged in mutual support and love.

2. Active obedience in the hearing and doing of the word of God.

3. The full exchange of the manifold grace of God.

4. The ability to change the structure to allow for the most meaningful expression of each of the above points.

The pragmatic issues related to developing and strengthening supportive congregational structures will be more fully addressed later. Our attention now turns to a fourth factor related to the quest for meaning—citizenship.

Citizenship: Aliens and Strangers

As Christians our citizenship is in heaven. The author of Hebrews expresses it this way: "For here we have no lasting city, but we seek the city which is to come" (13:14). In Christ we are called not only to a new life, but also to a new homeland. Abraham, who by faith left his home not knowing where he was to go, symbolizes the Christian pilgrimage. He became a sojourner, looking for a city which has foundations, whose builder and maker is God.

Important implications follow from this for Christians today. We too are called to be nomads, without roots in this world. We are not to seek a city without foundations; such cities cannot endure. This is characteristic of life apart from God. Jesus spoke about it in reference to the house built upon sand (Mt. 7:26). The house was demolished as a result of the rain, floods, and wind. The foundation was not secure.

We are warned throughout the Scriptures that attempts to build life apart from God will result in death. Yet we are always ready to begin construction of Babel, a gateway to heaven without God. We dream of building an alabaster city, gleaming with promises and hope of a better life. Yet no such city exists.

The city is symbolic of our pursuit of community, relationships, progress, and domination. Human activity revolves around the city. In all aspects, both good and bad, the city reflects the nature of the human race. Here in the earthly city, the Christian can never feel at home. Our dreams, hope, and faith must be directed to another city where our life is hid with Christ in the heavenlies.

The Christian can find no permanent roots in the earthly city because it is a place of death. The focus is not on biological death; rather, it is death in the most ultimate sense of the term—separation from God. Within cities, the influence of the principalities and powers becomes exponentially multiplied. The city itself is a principality. The control, subjection, and determination of human life becomes interwoven into the city itself. The power complex conditions every aspect of life.

Our summons to a new city does not mean that we are to drop out of the mainstream of human existence. We are not to leave the city. Nor can we escape the influence of the city; instead, our lives in Christ point to a new existence and possibility for the human race. Rather than reflecting destruction, exploitation, manipulation, greed, power, lust, and death, our lives together as Christians should point to a new social order which is only possible through the power of the Spirit. Where the Spirit is, there is life.

As Christians, our decisions, behavior, and attitudes are to reflect an awareness of and commitment to our heavenly destination. Even though that future life is hidden from view, we know that when Christ appears, we too shall appear with him in glory

(Col. 3:3; 1 Jn. 3:2). We shall be transformed into his image and likeness. This hope of glory enables us to live in this world as strangers and aliens, freeing us to live a life of risk.

The church's presence in the world is to point to the God of love. The church is to expose the world's false illusion of life. A stark contrast should exist between the city of God and the city of man. In the midst of human suffering a community must exist that points to the new Jerusalem, the city of God:

> You see this city? Here God lives among men. He will make his home among them; they shall be his people, and he will be their God; his name is God-with-them. He will wipe away all tears from their eyes; there will be no more death, and no more mourning or sadness. The world of the past has gone. (Rev. 21:3-4, JB)

In this community of believers, regardless of how small it may be or how imperfect it is, the grace of God brings life. Meaning is lost in the church when it forgets it is not of this world. When we stop living as aliens and strangers we allow the cares of life to overtake us. Meaning for the Christian is related to risk taking. When we count all things as loss, Jesus Christ becomes more fully known. In turn, the grace of God sustains us even more.

Jesus summed it up when he said, "Seek first his kingdom and his righteousness and all these things shall be yours as well" (Mt. 6:33). We must learn to live as aliens and strangers, to be in search for the city to come. To embrace the Christian faith means to locate ourselves in the midst of the earthly city to expose the forces of death. We must join ourselves to other Christians, who in active obedience are following Jesus Christ. Through that fellowship the city of God is to become visible.

Lack of meaning in the church arises when the city of God is confused with the city of this world; when we forget we have a home not made with human hands; when resurrection power is forfeited for fear of suffering; when the glory of God is exchanged for power, prestige, or wealth; when we fail to see that worship of ourselves replaces the adoration of Jesus Christ. The questions the church must face are, Is life truly gained through loss of life, and if so, is the church willing to live out its own message? Where is our citizenship—heaven or earth?

Summary

For most people the future is uncertain. Lack of shared values and goals coupled with the immense domestic and foreign concerns creates uncertainty as to where we as a nation and a world are heading. In this atmosphere of uncertainty meaning becomes vague and distorted. It becomes difficult to discern why we are here, where we are going, and what is the purpose of life itself. In this environment the powers are able to captivate our thinking.

Of grave concern is the lack of spiritual insight in the church concerning this struggle (Eph. 6:12). The same spiritual powers at work in the world are also at work in the church. This has been dealt with as we have examined competition, social independence, structure, and citizenship. As Christians we are not to be conformed to this world, but transformed by the renewing of our minds (Rom. 12:2). Only then can we discern the will of God and live it out in such a way that the disfiguring of life in the world becomes visible for what it really is.

The church must remain sensitive to the leading and guidance of the Holy Spirit who may call us to symbolic activity which is unexplainable and inaccessible by purely rational thinking. If the principalities and powers are to be exposed, the church must live a life of risk. In the weakness of the church, the power of God will be found. When this occurs the powers will be exposed and meaning will be discovered afresh.

— 4 —

DECISION MAKING AND THE WILL OF GOD

A PRELIMINARY STEP IN EXPOSING the powers and in testifying of God's grace is recognition—recognition of sin and death, and recognition of Jesus Christ. In the initial chapters, a biblical, theological, and social perspective was developed concerning the principalities and the powers. The argument was presented that a complex of powers, both personal and impersonal in nature, shape life as we know it. To a large extent these powers operate outside of humanity's interests and welfare. In addition, the spiritual dimension of this complex has for the most part remained hidden.

Churches are not immune from the influence of these powers. The structure of a congregation is a regulatory power itself which either helps or hinders the church in fulfilling its mission. The church should be an agency of both grace and justice, proclaiming God's word and sharing his love. This requires obedience, insight, knowledge, and action based on a clear understanding of and commitment to God's will.

The mission and structure of the church must reflect this understanding and commitment, which provides the foundation for worship, evangelism, discipleship, and community. One essential foundation stone for building and maintaining an effective congregational structure is knowing the will of God. God's will should provide the basis for action and decisions. This chapter will explore the nature of God's will and its implications for decision making and action.

A Personal Blueprint?

The will of God is a mystery to many Christians. Although one is committed to Jesus Christ, he or she may still feel that

God's will is vague. "God has a wonderful plan for your life," or so we've been told. But just how are we to know what it is? Important questions concerning God's will surface throughout life. Who does God plan for me to marry? Should I finish college? Does God want me to change jobs? These are not uncommon questions.

God's will is often viewed as a personalized blueprint, different for each individual. Yet this blueprint is not easy to read. Exactly how does a person come to know and fulfill God's will? Does a personal plan for the life of every Christian exist?

There is no question that God calls individuals and sets them apart for ministry. Paul, Noah, Abraham, Moses, David, and many others are examples of how God chooses and uses individuals for particular purposes. Concerning Jeremiah, the Lord said:

> Before I formed you in the womb I knew you, and before you were born I consecrated you; I appointed you a prophet to the nations. (Jer. 1:5)

Although God called Jeremiah to be a prophet before he was born, does that also mean that he had a personal plan for Jeremiah for every moment of every day of his life? We must distinguish between God's call or will for an individual and the personal responsibility for decision making that all human beings share. For example, it was God's will that Paul be an apostle, but was it God's will for Paul to make tents? Or is Paul's tentmaking simply a response to the necessity for food and shelter? How comprehensive is God's will in determining specific decisions?

As we examine the Scriptures we discover that the will of God is not viewed as something vague. One will search in vain, however, for a personalized blueprint. What we find is a God who manifests a personal concern for his creation. The emphasis is not on a "plan" but on a "relationship." The Scriptures reveal a God who desires to have an intimate relationship with us. This is not a mechanized relationship which prints out a schedule and program for our lives. Such an intimate relationship is possible only through Jesus Christ; moreover, it is based on grace and is characterized by holiness and freedom. Through Christ, the individual believer is freed from sin. Jesus said,

Truly, truly, I say to you, everyone who commits sin is a slave to sin. The slave does not continue in the house for ever; the son continues for ever. So if the Son makes you free, you will be free indeed. (Jn. 8:34–36)

Yet paradoxically, this new freedom results in a new form of slavery—a slavery to righteousness. This new slavery is to result in "right relationships" with God, with ourselves, and with our neighbor.

These relationships manifest God's will and since they are dynamic and not static, God's will must be continually experienced. Each moment calls for a decision for or against God. The very thought that God programs these decisions destroys the possibility of both freedom and holiness. Our freedom to choose allows for the possibility of holiness. In these choices, God's will is to become manifest in our lives.

The Basis for Decision Making

It should not be deduced that God will direct all of our actions and decisions if we can only tune into his wavelength. Understanding God's guidance involves personal struggle. This is true, not because God's will is nebulous, but because it is revealed through a personal relationship with Jesus Christ. This relationship does not demand obedience to a list of commandments, but rather it asks for personal transformation. This transformation results in ongoing reflection concerning existence and one's relationship with God and neighbor. This struggle itself leads to personal growth and maturity in Christ. It reflects a desire "to know him" (Phil. 3:10). Without an encounter with the Christ, there can be no special revelation of God.

Our encounter with Christ must be translated into a way of life requiring specific decisions and commitments. The necessities of life confront Christians, just like they do all people. Consequently, to meet these needs work consumes much of life. All human beings are faced with the question of survival. Future uncertainty results in the ongoing search for meaning and fulfillment. Life appears as a question mark. There is to be a significant difference in attitude between the Christian and the non-Christian in responding to work and the future.

On the one hand, the power complex creates an environment

whereby individuals are geared to think about and evaluate life based on self-serving interests; consequently, a materialistic spirit dominates our age. Jesus, on the other hand, focused attention on the kingdom of God and righteousness. Christians are not to connect personal meaning with materialism. Life cannot be defined or sustained in that way. Rather, life is a gift from God. Furthermore, meaning can only be grasped from an eschatological perspective. Rather than focusing upon the "now," we must understand and view "now" through the lens of the future coming kingdom of God. "Now" all things are to be counted as loss (Phil. 3:8). Jesus illustrated this concern, using Noah as an example:

> As were the days of Noah, so will be the coming of the Son of man. For as in those days before the flood they were eating and drinking, marrying and giving in marriage, until the day when Noah entered the ark, and they did not know until the flood came and swept them all away, so will be the coming of the Son of man. (Mt. 24:37–39)

Apart from God, men and women are unable to discern issues of ultimate spiritual importance. As in the days of Noah, out of the hope of securing personal meaning, we focus on temporal concerns. At the same time, the presence and mandate of God goes unnoticed, even though he is preparing for judgment. The seriousness of the moment goes unrecognized. Existence becomes lost through self-serving interests.

The New Testament Perspective

There is no such thing as a comprehensive statement within the NT concerning the will of God. Yet the will of God is not viewed as inaccessible. The NT concern is not so much in *discerning* God's will as it is with *doing* God's will. The following passages address this issue.

Matthew 7:21–23

> Not every one who says to me, "Lord, Lord," shall enter the kingdom of heaven, but he who does the will of my Father who is in heaven. On that day many will say to me, "Lord, Lord, did we not prophesy in your name, and cast out demons in your name, and do many mighty works in your name?" And then will I declare to them, "I never knew you; depart from me, you evildoers."

Here Jesus emphasizes the decisiveness of doing the will of God. Most importantly, it is not to be confused with religious activity. Jesus does not treat God's will as something vague. Doing or not doing the will of God determines one's existence. The emphasis is on a way of life. Furthermore, this way of life is embodied in Christ himself, as the Gospel of John shows us:

John 6:38–40

> For I have come down from heaven, not to do my own will, but the will of him who sent me; and this is the will of him who sent me, that I should lose nothing of all that he has given me, but raise it up at the last day. For this is the will of my Father, that every one who sees the Son and believes in him should have eternal life; and I will raise him up at the last day.

Jesus clearly describes the will of God. God's will is that everyone who sees the Son and believes in him should have eternal life. Any discussion concerning the will of God must begin and end with Jesus Christ. The will of God focuses on one paramount issue—life. Apart from Christ there is no life. In Christ, there is eternal life.

As we seek the will of God we must always return to one fundamental point: God's will can never be severed from the life and mission of Jesus Christ. To discover the will of God we must personally encounter the living Christ. Such an encounter does not produce a blueprint for living to be mechanically followed. But it does enlighten us to a way of life which is embodied in the Christ and empowered by the Spirit. Furthermore, it is a life of faith (Gal. 2:20).

As humans we desire to control our destiny and to have a handle on the future. We believe that if we know what is coming we can equip ourselves to meet the challenge. If possible, we want assurances and guarantees concerning the future. An uncertain future translates into anxiety. Therefore, technological man uses every means available to determine, shape, and enlighten the coming days and years. We learn to anticipate, to cope with reality with the hope that by doing so we are preparing for a better future. Some assume that if we know God's will, then we should clearly understand everything about our life as it unfolds before us. This understanding is to provide a handle on the future, which allows us to be better equipped to secure personal meaning. Jesus exposed this approach to life as leading to death.

Meaning is in no way related to our ability to determine the future or to protect our existence. Actually, the opposite is true. The Christian who places trust in God and is therefore able to risk all is the one who finds life. Concern for the future fades into the background precisely because the future is known. Our future life is hidden in Christ (Col. 3:4), and our security rests in the cross. One's decision for Christ eternally settles the future. Any attempt to eliminate personal risk or cost fails to understand the provision that God has made for us in his Son. Those who would know the will of the Father must come to know and trust his Son.

Ephesians 1:9

For he has made known to us in all wisdom and insight the mystery of his will, according to his purpose which he set forth in Christ.

Colossians 1:9–10

And so, from the day we heard of it, we have not ceased to pray for you, asking that you may be filled with the knowledge of his will in all spiritual wisdom and understanding, to lead a life worthy of the Lord, fully pleasing to him, bearing fruit in every good work and increasing in the knowledge of God.

The will of God is not hidden to the believer, but has been fully disclosed in the person of Jesus Christ. It can be understood with all wisdom and insight. Paul indicates, however, that while this revelation has taken place (Eph. 1:9) the believer may still not have received it in the fullest sense (Col. 1:9–10).

The knowledge of God's will is to be used to lead a life worthy of the Lord. Such knowledge must be translated into and manifested by good works. Kingdom values and commitments characterize this new life, which is based on a growing understanding of God's will and demonstrated by a lifestyle that bears fruit in every good deed. Knowledge and action yoked together manifest God's will through good deeds.

As Paul indicated in the above Ephesian passage, the purpose of God is set forth in Christ. Knowledge of God's will emerges out of our relationship with Jesus Christ and our understanding of his life and teaching. Therefore, to develop meaningful insights concerning the will of God, one must come to know his Son Jesus. Jesus Christ is revealed through the work of the Spirit. The

Holy Spirit gives life to the proclamation of God's word making Christ real to those who hear.

The Bible provides the authoritative account of the life and mission of Jesus Christ. However, to comprehend fully the will of God, the Spirit must transform factual knowledge about Christ into faith. God's will is then to become manifest in both the individual life of the believer and in the corporate witness of the church—the community of the Spirit. Such revelation is always redemptive in nature. It may not answer specific questions, but it will always provide the framework for responsible decision making.

Romans 12:2

Do not be conformed to this world but be transformed by the renewal of your mind, that you may prove what is the will of God, what is good and acceptable and perfect.

Our perception of reality influences our understanding of God's will. Paul placed significant importance on the renewed mind of the Christian. Those apart from Christ demonstrate a distorted and confused view of reality. The powers of this world condition their thinking. Forces such as power, lust, and greed govern decisions. Paul indicates that all human beings are conditioned this way. Those in Christ, however, are to manifest a new understanding of life both in thought and deed. However, this new understanding must be nurtured and developed. It requires the renewal of the mind. Through this renewing process God's will becomes clarified.

A Christian can forfeit the spiritual discernment now made available through Christ and maintain a warped view of existence. The powers are still at work attempting to shape thinking and thereby severely hinder the healing grace of God in one's life. The will of God becomes vague for this person because a clear picture of Jesus Christ is not possible. Christ is not being formed within; the new life is not developing in a healthy way. Furthermore, the individual must take responsibility for this. Paul commented on this in his letter to the Ephesians:

Now this I affirm and testify in the Lord, that you must no longer live as the Gentiles do, in the futility of their minds; they are darkened in their understanding, alienated from the life of God because

of the ignorance that is in them, due to their hardness of heart.
. . . Put off your old nature which belongs to your former manner
of life and is corrupt through deceitful lusts, and be renewed in the
spirit of your minds, and put on the new nature, created after the
likeness of God in true righteousness and holiness. (Eph. 4:17–18,
22–24)

Paul urges transformation, not simply conversion. The will of
God becomes clarified through the process of transformation.
This involves both study of the Scriptures and participation in
the life of the church. Daily decisions and commitments are in-
creasingly to reflect growing Christian maturity as defined in the
NT. Local congregations are to provide the context for spiritual
growth and development leading to an increased appreciation of
God's will.

Central to this metamorphosis is the renewal of the mind. By
developing the mind of Christ, we no longer allow temporal concerns to govern our thoughts; things in heaven, not things on
earth, shape our existence. There is to be a new eschatological dimension to our thinking. Because our citizenship is now with
Christ in the heavenlies, we no longer need to secure meaning or
direction for our lives from the earth. That is why personal temporal concerns are no longer to dominate our existence. The
eschatological perspective does not make temporal concerns unimportant though. The opposite is true. All aspects related to life
and God's creation are to be seen from a redemptive perspective.
Life is to be embraced fully and enjoyed.

Many people are unable to get an accurate picture of Jesus
Christ from the church. Those factors that should distinguish a
Christian way of life from life in general are difficult to find. No
precise conception of the Christian life is visible; rather, what is
present are conceptions of religion or morality that are substituted
for Christian discipleship.

In some congregations, morality has replaced transformation.
In others, the gospel has been exchanged for a political ideology.
Yet in others, the gospel has simply been adapted to a cultural lifestyle. The church no longer plays a central role in the lives of
most people, including, unfortunately, even some of those who attend. Politics, advertisements, Wall Street, television, and other
forces are more influential. For many, going to church is simply
one more activity on the week's schedule.

The cross of Christ has not lost its power to transform human life. For transformation to occur, however, the same message must be proclaimed that energized the early church: Christ crucified and risen from the dead. This message loses its power when it is refashioned for self-serving interests. The will of God becomes distorted when the church is concerned basically with convenience, comfort, and accommodation. Without transformation, the church lacks distinctiveness. When no clear definition of Jesus Christ is present, God's will is no longer discernible. Humanity is left on its own.

1 Thessalonians 4:3

For this is the will of God, your sanctification.

Holiness, not morality, is at the heart of Christian life. Greek philosophy and Roman law both emphasized codes of morality. The law was at the heart of Judaism. Pagan religions emphasize forms of morality. While morality is important, it is not at the center of Christian holiness. Jesus summoned his followers, not to a code of morality, but to a radical new life requiring total transformation and active obedience to himself. While the process of sanctification is not spelled out in the NT, nevertheless, holiness is central to what it means to be a follower of Jesus Christ. However, nowhere is holiness simply equated with morality.

From a Christian perspective, the act and process of sanctification are revolutionary in nature. While sanctification involves moral imperatives, it does so in a way that makes it unique. What is embraced is not a law, a code, or a set of principles, but Jesus Christ. Christian holiness comes into existence through Jesus Christ. Those who belong to Christ are "set apart," and what makes them distinctive is life in the Spirit. The trademark of this life is love for God and neighbor. Good works, which are pleasing to God, characterize the Spirit-filled life.

The Process of Sanctification

Sanctification involves different aspects that are held together in a dynamic tension. This tension results from the Christian's life in the two overlapping ages—this age and the age to come. Our citizenship is with Christ in the heavenlies, but sin and death govern the context of our daily lives. As a result, Christian life has both a present and a future context to it. The present must take into account the need to press on toward perfection through personal commitment and obedience to Christ. The future reflects that same perfection as a *fait accompli*. Christ has already established our holiness. From a biblical perspective, the process of sanctification reflects the tensions that arise out of both a present and future orientation concerning spiritual development. The following five theses illuminate this process.

Sanctification and the Already/Not Yet

Sanctification is both an accomplished fact and an ongoing process. Sanctification or holiness (they both translate the Greek *hagiasmos*) is not something to be achieved. Only God "sets apart" the believer in Christ. As part of the salvation process, sanctification is a work of grace. Holiness is a gift from God.

Jesus' death and resurrection are the basis for sanctification. Nothing can be added to that basis. Those who accept Christ as Lord are made complete in him. Yet the perfect nature of the Christian's life remains hidden in Christ:

> For you have died, and your life is hid with Christ in God. When Christ who is our life appears, then you also will appear with him in glory. (Col. 3:3–4)

From an eschatological perspective, God views every Christian as holy in Christ. However, the manifest nature of that holiness is revealed only at the appearance of Christ (1 Jn. 3:2–3).

Every believer is instructed to pursue a life of perfection requiring personal commitment and perseverance. Christians are to be holy (1 Pet. 1:16). The holy life of the Christian depends on a life of discipline and active obedience to kingdom values and principles set forth in the Scriptures. Just as we once yielded our lives to sin, life is now to be dedicated to righteousness for sanctification (Rom. 6:19).

Sanctification and Expectations

Certain qualities of life are expected from those who are set apart. Holiness demands purity. Those who follow Jesus Christ are to manifest a godly way of life. The most important aspect is love for God and neighbor. Jesus mentioned other qualities including meekness, showing mercy, peacemaking, generosity, humility, servanthood, reverence, sexual purity, and faith. These and other qualities mentioned in the NT (e.g., Col. 3:12–4:6) are not a product of human virtue and endeavor, but of the Holy Spirit. Yet, the individual is not a passive participant in their expression.

Human and Divine Cooperation

Sanctification is a result of both divine activity and human effort. Sanctification has its basis in the death of Christ. While holiness is a gift from God and not a result of works, the individual must still embrace that gift and allow it to become a living reality in his or her life. As Paul stated, salvation must be "worked out":

> Therefore, my beloved, as you have always obeyed, so now, not only as in my presence but much more in my absence, work out your own salvation with fear and trembling; for God is at work in you, both to will and to work for his good pleasure. (Phil. 2:12–14)

Spiritual development is an ongoing process requiring human effort (Rom. 6:19). Divine sanctification is revealed through personal consecration. Such consecration, however, is not the result of human power, although it involves an act of the will. Instead, the strength comes from God who has given us everything we need for life and godliness (2 Pet. 1:3).

The Work of the Spirit

Sanctification is a work of the Spirit in the life of the individual; it results in obedience to God. We are "set apart" in Christ for a purpose. That purpose is obedience to God which is to result in good works (Eph. 2:10).

The Spirit of God makes the new life in Christ possible. While this new life requires personal commitment and dedication to Christ, it is not based on human effort. Jesus said, "The Spirit gives life; the flesh counts for nothing" (Jn. 6:63). Clearly, throughout Jesus' teaching he emphasized new life as a result of the Spirit. Not only does the Spirit give life, he leads the believer into all truth (Jn. 16:13); he testifies of Christ (Jn. 15:26); he is a counselor (Jn. 14:16); and he gives the believer power (Acts 1:8). The Spirit sanctifies (sets apart) Christians for a life of holiness and obedience. This is illustrated in the opening verses of First Peter:

> Peter, an apostle of Jesus Christ, to the exiles of the Dispersion in Pontus, Galatia, Cappadocia, Asia, and Bithynia, chosen and destined by God the Father and sanctified by the Spirit for obedience to Jesus Christ and for sprinkling with his blood: May grace and peace be multiplied to you. (1 Pet. 1:1–2)

Jesus expected his disciples to be obedient. He said, "If you love me, you will do what I command" (Jn. 14:15). To proclaim Jesus as Lord requires submission to his lordship. The lordship of Christ becomes a reality in the Christian's life through the Spirit of God. The Holy Spirit frees the Christian from the power of sin and empowers the believer to lead a holy life. Paul emphasizes this in the letter to the Romans:

> For the law of the Spirit of life in Christ Jesus has set me free from the law of sin and death. (Rom. 8:2)

> those who are in the flesh cannot please God. But you are not in the flesh, you are in the Spirit, if the Spirit of God really dwells in you. (Rom. 8:8–9)

> for if you live according to the flesh you will die, but if by the Spirit you put to death the deeds of the body you will live. (Rom. 8:13)

One prominent theme surfaces: the Spirit gives life. Those led by the Spirit of God belong to God (Rom. 8:14). Sin conditions and controls everyone else; its end result is death. The sanctifying work of the Spirit gives life and is to result in obedience to Christ. However, this is not obedience to a list of rules, but to a person. A relationship exists with God who loves us and will not allow anything to separate us from his love (Rom. 8:38–39). The Spirit makes us God's own children (Rom. 8:16).

A New Perspective

Sanctification requires a new understanding of life. As an ongoing process, sanctification requires that the believer arrive at a new understanding of life and purpose. This new perspective comes from a personal encounter with the living Christ and results in personal transformation.

Reading or reflecting about Jesus does not transform existence. Transformation occurs when Jesus is personally encountered and there is a surrender of one's self to the lordship of Christ. After such an encounter, the world is viewed differently. The kingdom of God unexpectedly breaks into the individual's life. The old passes away, the new comes. Every aspect of life must be given over to God.

This transformation from the domain of darkness into the kingdom of the Son (Col. 1:13) is reflected in daily conduct. The way one thinks shapes this new life (Eph. 4:22–24). The mind itself must be transformed. Paul speaks of this transformation in sacrificial terms (Rom. 12:1-2). True sacrificial worship arises from a proper perspective of God's will and is to be reflected in the pattern of one's life. Every thought is to be taken captive and made obedient to Christ (2 Cor 10:5).

Freedom and Sanctification

Sanctification or holiness empowers us to take on the true character of Christ. Jesus Christ our life is also our sanctification (1 Cor. 1:30). He sets us apart to be used by God. Just as the vessels in the temple were consecrated and set apart for special use, so too, the Christian is a holy vessel, cleansed by the blood of Christ and sanctified by the Spirit. As such, the believer is set free not only from sin, but also from the entire order of life which exists apart from God. Therefore, those who are sanctified in Christ are completely free. Yet this freedom is maintained only through full consecration and dedication to the service of God.

Self-centeredness destroys the possibility of both freedom and holiness. One cannot be set apart for use by God and at the same time view existence and the world in a way that promotes self-interest. The clutches of self-deception snare those who follow that path. What appears on the surface as a means to secure life turns into a perpetual search for meaning. Only the word of God can strip away illusions that seek to control life. In turn, those who encounter Jesus Christ and who live a life of holiness experience freedom and responsibility. The discernment of God's will becomes central to living a holy life. However, the "concept" of God's will can be used to lead a life of deception and slavery. More than once it has been said, "God has told me to do this or that" and when all is done it becomes clear that reference to God is being used to justify one's actions. Insecurity, guilt, or some other personal need may foster that behavior, or it may embody a more blatant form of manipulation. In any respect, it leads to self-deception and bondage. Simply because it is claimed that God is at the source of one's decisions or actions does not make it so.

Self-justification, claiming God as the cause of our actions, can lead to irresponsibility and harm. God does lead us, he does speak to us, he does reveal his will to us, but always in a way that leads to greater maturity and growth in Christ. Actions and decisions that are motivated by self-interest rather than service of Christ are part of the old self which must be put off. Righteousness and faithfulness to Christ must characterize the new life. Revelation is the means for encountering the will of God; sanctification is the basis for clarifying God's will. Without holiness, no one will see the Lord (Heb. 12:14).

Summary

In summary these points stand out concerning our discussion of decision making and the will of God.

(1) The New Testament emphasis is not so much on discovering God's will as it is on doing God's will.

(2) The will of God is not vague or nebulous. Jesus explicitly identifies it with his mission of salvation (Jn. 6:40).

(3) Paul indicates that God's will is now made available to be known with all wisdom and insight (Eph. 1:8–9; Col. 1:9).

(4) We come to know and understand the will of God as we come to know and understand Jesus Christ. The Holy Spirit, through both the Scriptures and the church, reveals Jesus Christ to us.

(5) The Scriptures are the only infallible witness to Jesus Christ.

(6) The church reveals Jesus Christ as it surrenders itself to God; as each individual member finds his or her proper place in the body of Christ; as the body builds itself up in love through the mutual care and support of every member; and, as the church reveals the holiness of God by engaging in acts of righteousness.

(7) God's will is to be reflected in a holy life. Holiness can never be encapsulated in a creed or code. It can be found only in Jesus Christ, who is himself our holiness. Therefore, the will of God can never be reduced to a blueprint because it violates the person of Christ.

(8) Holiness embodies Christian freedom and in turn the transgression of all value systems apart from the word of God. This freedom is realized in the Christian life through service to Christ.

(9) The will of God does not give us a handle on the future. Rather it defines the future in terms of our hidden life in Christ. Therefore, temporal concerns are not to govern Christian decision making. Instead, decision making is to arise from an eschatological perspective. Faith in Christ is to guide life commitments. Decisions are to be made in the context of the church, and then as individuals, we must live out personal decisions in a socially responsible way. In doing so, we must be accountable to the Holy Spirit, the Scriptures, God's people, and his creation.

Nothing in Scripture indicates that such decision making is automatic or obvious. Rather it involves personal struggle and ongoing reflection and review. Some will claim this is too vague; that God directly leads and guides us. God does lead and guide us; however, we come to recognize God's leading and guidance through his Son Jesus Christ. He alone matters. We do not need audible voices, visions, or miracles to know the will of God. If he chooses to use these means to reveal himself, they must still be interpreted in light of Jesus Christ.

Jesus Christ does not reveal the answer to every question or the solution to every problem. He does reveal to us how to live out our decisions before God and man in faith, risk, and love.

God, after He spoke long ago to the fathers in the prophets in many portions and in many ways, in these last days has spoken to us in His Son, whom He appointed heir of all things, through whom He made the world. (Heb. 1:1-2 NAS)

PART 2: Structural Dynamics

STRUCTURAL DYNAMICS

CHRISTIANS ARE TO BE A PEOPLE of distinction, a holy nation. This understanding is to provide insight into the decisions that we make and guidance for the way we live. God's will is that we are to be holy. This applies not only to individuals, but also to the church as a corporate body of believers. In turn, this has implications for congregational structure and the practice of ministry.

The Nature of Ministry

The structure of the church should be directly tied to a philosophy of ministry. Furthermore, such a philosophy should emerge out of a dynamic interaction between biblical exegesis, faith, and one's circumstances. Ministry should be based on an intentional plan and design that grows out of biblical insight, social sensitivity, and theological awareness.

Congregational leaders must work at building a conceptual approach to ministry. The alternative is a haphazard one based primarily on reaction and intuition. Those who follow this latter course are likely to experience confusion, frustration, misunderstandings, and a high rate of turnover among leaders. A lack of clear direction and the absence of shared understanding among congregational leaders erode the partnership essential for fruitful ministry. Therefore, a need exists for common goals and commitments among leaders concerning the future ministry of the church. There must be a plan of action.

Plans do not surface out of a vacuum; rather, they are based on perceptions, assumptions, and some base of knowledge. Our starting point in developing a conceptual approach for ministry will be to explore eight theses. These theses, stated below, provide the foundation for the remaining chapters on building effective structures for congregational life.

The Foundations of Ministry

(1) *Ministry arises out of some understanding of reality.* Obviously, not all people view reality in the same way. Our culture, language, history, traditions, values, and circumstances influence our understanding of reality. A person born and raised in Japan views the world quite differently than someone from Harlem or the Middle East.

(2) *Ministry occurs in specific cultural and historical settings.* Factors related to space and time impact the structure and nature of Christian ministry. Ministry structures are culturally grounded. That is, all approaches to ministry grow out of some cultural background. What works in one culture may not work in another.

Various settings generate relative demands on ministry. For example, political, economic, social, geographical, and technological factors all have a significant impact on Christian ministry. It makes a difference whether ministry is oriented to an inner city environment or to a cluster of islands in the South Pacific. Factors such as high unemployment, hunger, or the availability of electricity affect both ministry strategies and needs.

(3) *The Scriptures provide normative guidelines for ministry.* All biblically grounded ministry should share common features. For example, *diakonia* (service) and *koinonia* (partnership) should characterize all Christian ministry. Ministry should be conducted in a spirit of humility and love. Baptism, communion, worship, evangelism, and discipleship should be present in some form in every church.

(4) *Ministry is a mixture of normative and relative components.* First, there must be an integration of biblical concepts and practices into specific cultural and historical settings. An important task is to develop a corporate understanding of and commitment to the biblical mission of the church. Second, that mission must be put into effect to meet the needs created by any particular setting. Relative demands that change from one setting to another create the need for variations in the approach to ministry.

(5) *Ministry is a spiritual activity dependent on the Holy Spirit.* In the life of the individual Christian, the Spirit of God empowers and sustains Christian service. The result is the manifestation of God's grace through the gifts of the Spirit that bring salvation, healing, strength, and hope into the lives of God's people. Without the Spirit, ministry is hollow and ineffective. Spiritual discipline is at the heart of effective ministry.

(6) *Ministry depends on individual commitment.* God uses individuals. The ministry of each individual is central and indispensable to the growth and maturity of the church.

(7) *Ministry is a corporate enterprise.* While ministry is based on individual contributions, it is a collective responsibility. To use a biblical analogy, one person plants, another waters, and yet another reaps. The combined effort of each member enables the church to fulfill its mission in the world.

(8) *Ministry is to glorify God.* The model of all Christian ministry is Jesus Christ. Christian ministry is not to be based on self-serving interests; rather, ministry should fulfill God's will. The ultimate goal is to glorify God through service both to God and neighbor in a spirit of humility and grace.

These eight theses provide a conceptual starting point for examining and evaluating congregational structure. No one approach to ministry is valid for all peoples and all times. Yet, normative features should be present in all Christian churches. Each situation must be examined in light of prevailing environmental circumstances, and plans for congregational mission must be developed and implemented that will effectively communicate the gospel, sustain congregational life, and expose the powers of this age.

— 5 —

THE SOCIAL STRUCTURE OF THE EARLY CHURCH

STRUCTURES PLAY A SIGNIFICANT role in shaping the life and mission of the church or any social organization. Structures provide not only stability, but also the framework necessary to carry out the organizational mission. An effective structure will enable the organization to achieve its goals; but, ineffective structures can just as easily sabotage efforts.

Social structures do not exist apart from people, but arise out of the life and interaction of people who are tied together through common commitments. This chapter will examine the social structure of the early church. First, the meaning of *ekklēsia* (church) will be explored and, second, various components which gave life to the social structure of the NT church will be reviewed. This will provide a preliminary basis for discussing the issue of church structure in a changing technological world.

The Meaning of *Ekklēsia*

Scholars generally agree that the word *ekklēsia* is used in two distinct ways in the NT. It primarily refers to a local assembly; to a lesser degree, but equally important, it refers to the corporate people of God. For our purposes several important questions surface. They include: What were the dominant characteristics of local churches? What kind of relationships existed between local congregations? How should we understand the relationship between the church as a local assembly and the church as the people of God?

Local Assemblies

Paul referred frequently to local assemblies such as the church at Corinth (1 Cor. 1:2), at Cenchrea (Rom. 16:1), or Thessalonica (1 Thes. 1:1). Some churches met in homes (Rom. 16:5, 23; Col. 4:15; Phm. 2). Paul also spoke of the churches of Christ (Rom. 16:16), the churches of the Gentiles (Rom. 16:4), all the churches (1 Cor. 7:17), the churches of Asia (1 Cor. 16:19), and the churches of Galatia (Gal. 1:2).

In the above passages, Paul refers to actual gatherings of believers and not to the church as an organizational reality. The churches in Asia or Galatia do not belong to a formal church organization. Each assembly of believers exists as the church. The gathering together of believers defines the church as is illustrated in 1 Cor. 11:18: "when you assemble as a church."

Was there only one church in each city? While Paul uses the plural in reference to the churches in a region (Asia), or in a group (Gentiles), he uses the singular in addressing the church at Corinth (1 Cor. 1:2; 2 Cor. 2:1) and Thessalonica (1 Thes. 1:1; 2 Thes. 1:1). We should not assume from this that only one church existed in each city; we can only be sure that the epistle was directed to an assembly of believers in those cities. Factors such as the number of believers, meeting space, location, and meeting times would influence how many assemblies existed in a community. Each gathering, however, was understood as a church. Home meetings illustrate this. According to Banks, most homes would have accommodated an assembly of only about 35 people.[1] Undoubtedly, many homes would have been needed to accommodate the Christians living in Corinth or Rome. Many churches must have existed in those cities.

If many gatherings existed in a single city, then that city had many churches. When and if those churches gathered together for a common meeting, they did not meet as many churches, but as a single church. It appears there was a common meeting, at least on occasion, at Corinth. Therefore, when Paul wrote to the church at Corinth, he addressed the entire assembled group of Christians. However, Paul did not write to the church at Rome, but "to all God's beloved in Rome, who are called to be saints" (1:7). Perhaps he did so because the church in Rome was too large or unable to meet together as one single assembly.

Houses were common meeting places for the church. While some houses had large rooms where a large group could meet, such as on the Day of Pentecost, most homes were more modest in size and could accommodate only a small group. Several such churches existed in Rome (Romans 16). One thing is clear in the NT: the term *ekklēsia* is never used to refer to the meeting place. Such usage did not occur until much later.

No clear indication exists in the NT as to how frequently the church met or how the meeting was conducted. During the formative period of the church, believers attended the temple as well as met in homes on a daily basis. Paul instructed the Corinthians to set aside a contribution on the first day of every week (1 Cor. 16:2). This does not necessarily mean, however, that they met together to receive a collection. Christians did meet together in homes for prayer meetings, teaching, and preaching, but little is known of the frequency or times of these meetings.

Little is also known about how the meeting was conducted. The church met regularly together for common meals and to celebrate the Lord's Supper. Paul taught that if edification were to occur, then order was necessary; however, his guidelines were flexible. Paul instructed the Corinthians, "When you come together, each one has a hymn, a lesson, a revelation, a tongue, or an interpretation. Let all things be done for edification" (1 Cor. 14:26). No indication exists that worship services were well organized; in Corinth just the opposite was the case.

The Relationship Between Local Assemblies

Little evidence can be found of formal organizational relationships between different churches. The church at Jerusalem did have some pastoral oversight and relationship with the church at Antioch. On one occasion the the Jerusalem leaders sent Barnabas to Antioch, and after the Jerusalem Council, they sent representatives to Antioch with a report (Acts 11:22; 15:27f). Apparently the Jerusalem congregation did not control the prophets and teachers of the Antioch church, which included Paul and Barnabas. Paul saw his own apostolic authority as coming directly from God.

Paul did encourage congregations to demonstrate love for other churches. The collection of a relief offering from the Gentile churches for the Jerusalem church reflects that commitment; but, Paul's personal appeal and commitment are the main forces behind that outreach, not formal ties between the churches. A similar commitment also appears in the agreement between Paul and the Jerusalem leaders to remember the poor (Gal. 2:9–10).

Paul did instruct churches about their relative state and mission, but again, we cannot be sure that any strong organizational bonds existed between congregations. The linkage that did exist appears to be more at the relational level between specific individuals and leaders than anything else.

The Universal Church

While much of the focus in the NT, and especially in Paul's epistles, is upon local churches, there is also teaching concerning the universal nature of the church. The primary sources for this are found in Ephesians and Colossians, where Paul presents the church as a heavenly community in which all believers participate. Seated with Christ in the heavenly places (Eph. 2:6), the believers from all generations join in a heavenly assembly.[2]

The universal nature of the church also has a theological basis in Paul's concept of the the believer's being "in Christ." Since all Christians are "in Christ," they are all united in one body. The universal church is more than the sum total of all existing congregations. It can be best understood as the spiritual gathering together of all believers "in Christ," a gathering which transcends both space and time.

The Organizational Development of the Church

We have seen that *ekklēsia* primarily denotes an assembly of believers. To survive, all social groups must organize. The church is no exception.

The Social Setting

To understand the structure and life of the early church, it is necessary to understand the times in which it came into being. The letters of Paul are the earliest documents of the Christian church and reveal the dynamic development of congregations throughout Asia Minor. The missionary enterprise and the establishment of churches took place within the religious and social milieu of the 1st-century Roman Empire. Changing social trends and the growth of voluntary associations characterized this period.[3] For centuries the city-state and the family played a central role in the development of community life.[4] However, the expansion of the Roman Empire and the disintegration of power at local levels contributed to the demise of the polis (city) in terms of building and sustaining relationships.

The search for identity and the need for meaningful relationships contributed to the growth and success of associations or partnerships. Sampley notes that many different associations emerged during the 1st century, including funeral associations, trade guilds, associations of farmers, herders, youth, women, and religious associations.[5] According to Banks, the principle underlying these associations was *koinōnia* which was characterized by a voluntary sharing or partnership.[6] Sampley goes a step further arguing that the *koinōnia* of the early church can best be understood based on the Roman legal model of a consensual *societas*, a common legal contract entered into by partners during that period. This contract was a legal apparatus "where each of the partners contributed something to the association with a view towards a shared goal."[7] As such, *societas* could be based solely on a verbal, but legally binding, agreement between the parties.

Sampley maintains that the Jerusalem conference where Paul and Barnabas were given "the right hand of fellowship" by James, Cephas, and John is an example of such a partnership at work in the early church (Gal. 2:9). Furthermore, he suggests that Paul's relationship with the church at Philippi can better be understood in light of the Roman legal contract of consensual partnership. Together, Paul and the Philippians established a formal partnership to proclaim the gospel. He further contends that the concept of *societas* "provided a social framework in which Christians could understand and creatively fulfill their mutual obligations within the community."[8] Thus, the social framework of voluntary associations and the legal understanding of partnerships provided an environment conducive for the growth of the church. *Koinōnia* became central to the life of the church.

In contemporary terms, *koinōnia* is often equated with fellowship. In the early church, however, it would have been viewed more in the framework of a serious partnership in which both parties were committed to common goals. In the early church the basis for *koinōnia* was the common life in Christ. Christian *koinōnia* was to result in a shared partnership committed to evangelism and edification.

Banks observes that most voluntary associations averaged around 30–35 members, but could be as large as 100 or as small as 10. Therefore, the appearance of Christian house churches and other private meetings characterized by *koinōnia* would not have been out of place within the Greco-Roman world of the 1st century. From a sociological perspective such meetings would have been a reflection of the growing social trend toward voluntary associations.

The prevailing social attitudes and structures of the 1st century affected churches in the same way that contemporary structures affect us. At times, those structures were adopted to further the development and expansion of the church. Yet the prevailing values and attitudes that characterized the social milieu were contrary to Christ and had to be "put off" so that the new life could be "put on" (Eph. 4:22–24). While the structures of the early church were not totally foreign to the Greco-Roman world, the message and the Christian way of life was.

The Jewish Background

The early church was a distinct group within Judaism. While the early church was affected by the Greco-Roman world in which it emerged, it must be emphasized that in its formative period, it existed as a distinct group within Judaism. Not only were all the leaders of the early church Jewish, they also resided in Jerusalem and worshipped at the temple (Acts 3:1ff).

It took years before Christianity became distinct and separate from Judaism. Many Jewish Christians desired to make certain Jewish religious rites and practices normative for Christians as well. This created division and tension between Jewish and Gentile believers. Some of these differences were never settled and fragmentation resulted. The council at Jerusalem was called to address some of these concerns. While some issues were resolved, not all Jewish Christians were pleased with the final outcomes. There never was a total healing in the church between Jewish and Gentile Christians.

The early church has been compared to the Qumran community. From an organizational standpoint, this group, commonly known as the Essenes, differed from the early church in one dramatic way: whereas the Essenes withdrew from society, Christians were fervently evangelistic and penetrated society with the message of Jesus Christ. Unlike other Jewish sects, Christians proclaimed that Jesus was the Messiah, not only for Jews, but also for Gentiles. Eventually Gentile Christians dominated the leadership of the church. Nevertheless, its origin, development, and beliefs cannot be understood apart from its Jewish heritage.

Apostolic Leadership

The early church was loosely organized and revolved around the leadership of the apostles in Jerusalem. Most of Jesus' disciples came from Galilee, but they relocated in Jerusalem after the resurrection. After the Day of Pentecost, the disciples assumed the primary leadership roles in the church at Jerusalem. Their duties included teaching, preaching, and praying. We are not told what other responsibilities they had, although they did receive money to be used in caring for the poor (Acts 4:34).

The book of Acts suggests that although the apostles were recognized as having special authority in the church, not much emphasis was placed on formal organization. The organization that did exist surfaced in response to ministry needs. The primary guiding force of the earliest community was the leading and guidance of the Holy Spirit. That is not to say that organization was unimportant or did not exist; but, what did exist was loosely structured and tended to adapt to changing needs.

Servants

As the ministry of the Jerusalem church grew in both scope and complexity, servants in addition to the apostles were formally recognized. The addition of new leaders in the church was directly related to problem solving associated with caring for the poor. While initially the Jerusalem church was made up entirely of Jews, they could be divided into distinct groups. The primary lines of division came between the Palestinian Jews who spoke Aramaic and the Hellenistic Jews who spoke Greek. Some tension existed between these two groups because the Palestinian Jews viewed the Hellenists as second-class citizens.

Many Greek-speaking Jews lived in Jerusalem and had their own separate synagogues. Apparently, the Palestinian Christians were active in the Aramaic-speaking synagogues while the Greek-speaking Jewish Christians maintained contact with the Hellenistic synagogues. As a result of evangelistic efforts, Jews from both groups became Christians. The tension that existed between these two groups before they became Christians continued even after they believed in Christ. The tension ultimately surfaced in a dispute concerning relief arrangements for the widows.

It was not uncommon for Hellenistic Jews, who were born and raised in the Greco-Roman world outside of Palestine, to return to Jerusalem during later adulthood. According to Haenchen, "the widows of such men had no relatives at hand to look after them and tended to become dependent on public charity."[9] The church became one such source of charity.

The Hellenists raised a charge against the Palestinian Christians because their widows were being overlooked in the daily distribution of food (Acts 6:1). No indication is given as to who was responsible for the distribution or how it was carried out. The discussion does not focus upon who was at fault, but rather upon how the apostles remedied the injustice. In part, the problem was due to the growth of the church (Acts 6:1). Even though the Jewish community had a relief system for the poor, the Christians developed their own arrangements to meet these needs. This was done both informally as believers shared their possessions with one another (Acts 4:32) and more formally as designated funds were given to the apostles for the needy (Acts 4:34, 35). It is not clear, though, that the apostles were directly involved in the actual distribution of resources to those in need.

The problem was solved in the following manner. The Twelve gathered the entire community of believers together. Two things are noteworthy here. First, this is the only place in Acts where the Twelve are directly mentioned. They are clearly viewed as the leaders of the church. Second, the entire community was involved in the resolution of the problem. Although this should not be construed as democracy, it does point to the importance of the shared life and mission of the church in decision making and problem solving.

The community of believers was to choose seven men who would assume responsibility for the daily distribution of food.

Not only were these men to be full of the Spirit, they were also to have wisdom. In this context wisdom would include the prudence to handle the community's money and see that the charitable funds were properly administered.

This proposal pleased the community and seven men were selected. We are not told how the selection process occurred or how long it took. Once chosen, the men were presented to the apostles who prayed and laid hands on them. According to Bruce, the laying on of hands "formally associated the seven with the twelve, as their deputies to discharge a special duty."[10] But, it was more than just a ceremony. The laying on of hands was associated with the transmission of blessing and power.[11]

What is the significance of this event for the organizational development of the church and the related issue of church structure? Traditionally, the focus has been on the establishment of the office of deacon. To gain some insight into this issue we first focus our attention on the biblical concept of *diakonia* (service) and the related word group *diakonos* (servant, deacon), and *diakonein* (to serve).

In secular Greek *diakonein* (to serve) primarily meant to wait at the table or attend to someone's bodily needs. In the broad sense it was used to describe service rendered to another person. The person performing *diakonia* (service) was a *diakonos* (servant).[12] Normally such service was viewed as menial.

The NT concept of *diakonia* (service) plays a central role both in the life of Jesus (Mt. 10:45; Lk. 22:27; Rom. 15:8) and leaders in the early church (Acts 1:17, 25; 20:24; 21:19; Rom. 11:13; 1 Cor. 12:5). Leaders were to be humble servants (1 Cor. 3:5). The biblical focus for church leaders is not on preeminence but on service. As Cranfield observes, such service was to be rendered to God (2 Cor. 6:4; 1 Thes. 3:2), to Christ (1 Tim. 4:6; Jn. 12:26), to the new covenant (2 Cor. 3:6), to the gospel (Eph. 3:7; Col. 1:23), and to one another (Mk. 9:35; 1 Pet. 4:10). Special service is to be given to those in need (Mt. 25:31–46; Rom. 15:25–27; Heb. 6:10; Acts 6:2; 2 Cor. 8:14f).[13]

On three occasions *diakonos* refers to a position within the church (Phil. 1:1; 1 Tim. 3:8, 12). In each instance, the office of bishop is also mentioned. At no time, however, are the duties or responsibilities of a deacon described. According to Cranfield, the main thrust in the NT is not on the office of deacon, but on the calling to *diakonia* (service) shared in common by all Christians regardless of status or position. Jesus Christ sets the example of humility (Phil. 2:5f) that believers are to follow. He was a servant to the sick, poor, afflicted, victimized, and outcast. To those in need he showed compassion.

The serving of self-interests or the seeking of power, prestige, and status are contrary to authentic *diakonia*. *Diakonia* must arise out of a pure heart where the concern is for the other and not for one's self. Finally, Cranfield points out that *diakonia* is both a responsibility of the individual (Gal. 6:2) and of the congregation (Acts 6:1; 1 Cor. 16:1–4).

From this perspective, where *diakonia* is understood as a normative expression of faith in Christ, we must examine the appointment of the seven men in Acts 6. The Seven are not called deacons, although the cognate noun *diakonia* (service) and verb *diakoneō* (to serve) are found in the passage. The emphasis, however, is not on the establishment of a formal office (deacon), but on the proper care and service for those who are in need.

Today's "care-taking" role of deacon may include the oversight of finances, the supervision of building and grounds, or other responsibilities necessary for the day-to-day operation of the church. Obviously these are important tasks requiring special care and attention. The biblical emphasis on *diakonia* (service), however, focuses less on these areas and more on the needs of people. More specifically, the major concern is care for the poor, infirm, and wretched. The ministry of the Seven went far beyond that of being "benevolence officers." At least two of them are preachers and evangelists, and it is likely that the Hellenistic segment of the church regarded all seven as leaders.

To conclude that clearly defined organizational procedures were being established when these seven men were chosen would be wrong. Frequently the apostles are portrayed as overseers or pastors while the Seven are viewed as deacons or caretakers of the church's financial responsibilities. That image is foreign to the text. While the Seven did take over specific responsibilities related to the distribution of food, that in no way eclipses the charismatic nature of their ministry reflected in teaching, preaching, and the doing of "great wonders and signs" (Acts 6:8). At least Stephen and Philip were active in the development and expansion of the church much in the same way as the apostles. They receive more attention in Acts than do any of the original apostles except for Peter and John.

As indicated, nowhere does Paul clarify the duties of a deacon, though he does differentiate deacons from elders. The only noteworthy difference in the list of qualifications for elders and deacons, is that elders must be able to teach (1 Tim. 3:1–7). Otherwise, the qualifications are almost identical. All that can be said is that the title *diakonos* (servant, deacon) indicates a responsibility to serve, however that service might be defined. Apparently, the major thrust in the early church was service to the poor.

It is not clear that deacons were present in all churches, although Paul and Barnabas appointed elders in every church (Acts 14:23). Nor can we be sure how deacons were elected to their place of ministry, whether they were appointed by apostles or elders or whether they were chosen by the community. Furthermore, if we are to use the men in Acts 6 as a model for the ministry of a deacon, then we must recognize that their service in the church went far beyond the traditional technical and narrow definition given to the role. It becomes difficult to distinguish the ministry of Stephen or Philip from that of a preacher or evangelist.

Elders

In addition to apostles, elders quickly emerged within the leadership structure of the local church. By the time the council of Jerusalem was held (Acts 15), elders had come to play a significant role in the leadership of the early church. No indication is given of their exact duties or as to how they surfaced in importance, but by that time they were directly involved in examining doctrinal issues and making decisions that affected the entire church (Acts 15:2, 7). However, the context for decision making was not behind closed doors, but in open session including the entire congregation (Acts 15:12, 22).

Luke first introduces the elders in Acts 11:30. In Acts 15, whenever the apostles are mentioned the elders are mentioned as well; this indicates that they held a position of significant importance within the church (Acts 15:2, 4, 6, 22, 23). The letter summarizing the outcome of the council that was sent to the church at Antioch is from both the apostles *and* elders (Acts 15:23).

Haenchen maintained that Acts 15 marks the turning point of apostolic rule within the church.[14] No further mention is made of the apostles with respect to the Jerusalem church, which later was led by James, the brother of Jesus, and the elders (Acts 21:18). The apostles may have left Jerusalem to engage in missionary activity, although there is no specific evidence for that. James, however, did become the leading figure in the Jerusalem church after the departure of Peter.

Paul and Barnabas appointed elders in each church they founded (Acts 14:23). These appointments may have been based on the model of the Jerusalem church (Acts 11:30), which had adopted the terminology from Judaism. Paul and other biblical writers did not feel confined to the term elder and used other designations interchangeably. Elders were called bishops or overseers (Acts 20:17, 28; Phil. 1:1; Titus 1:5–7; 1 Pet. 5:1, 2); those who are over you (1 Thes. 5:12); leaders (Heb. 13:7); and shepherds (Acts 20:28; 1 Pet. 5:2). Elders were to be able to teach (1 Tim. 3:2) and were called on to pray for the sick (Jas. 5:14). They were also involved in major church decisions (Acts 15).

All indications are that elders were to follow in the legacy of the apostles and to watch over the church, protect it from error, and to promote the ministry of God's word and prayer. Furthermore, those who effectively carried out these responsibilities were to be accorded double honor (1 Tim. 5:17) which included financial remuneration.

One question that remains is whether or not monarchical bishops existed in local congregations distinct and separate from the elders. At Philippi (Phil. 1:1) and Ephesus (Acts 20:17, 28) we are presented with a group of bishops and no distinction is made between bishop and elder. Later, however, the title "bishop" is used in the singular (1 Tim. 3:2; Titus 1:7), even though elders (Titus 1:5; 1 Tim. 5:17) and deacons (1 Tim. 3:8) appear in the plural. Nowhere, however, do these three titles of bishop, elder, and deacon appear together, which might suggest a hierarchy of three distinct offices. In the Titus passage (1:5–9), the initial reference is made to elders who are to be appointed in every town. A list of qualifications is then presented, but the term bishop now occurs replacing that of elder.

Is the bishop to be understood as an elder who has special authority and responsibilities above and beyond the other elders, or is the term bishop a synonym for elder? The latter appears to be the case. The singular use of bishop denotes that the qualifications are to be understood generically and are applicable to all individuals who are elders or bishops. Even if one concludes that there is a distinction between elder and bishop in the Pastoral Epistles, and that the office of bishop must be understood in a monarchical sense, that arrangement is not uniform or normative in the early church (Acts 20:17, 28; Phil 1:1). However, by the early part of the 2nd century Ignatius of Antioch strongly defended the monarchical episcopate.

By the end of the 1st century, the organization of local churches had developed along several lines. The two-tiered system of presbyters and deacons (with the term bishop being used interchangeably with presbyter) was one approach and is reflected in the second epistle of Clement of Rome to the Corinthians. The same pattern is found in the Didache. However, Ignatius defended a three-tiered system with emphasis upon a monarchical bishop supported by both presbyters and deacons.

Henry Chadwick claimed that four factors contributed to the development of the monoepiscopate, where one of the presbyter-bishops rose to a position of superiority and acquired the title "bishop."[15]

1. The right of the senior member of the presbyterial college to ordain ministerial candidates.

2. The presiding member of the presbytery normally conducted correspondence between churches giving him special recognition and status.

3. The senior member served as a representative to solemn gatherings of other congregations and would take part in the laying on of hands and prayer.

4. The presiding member served as a focus for unity in the light of heretical challenges.

For a time the bishop was viewed as a first among equals in relationship to the other presbyters (elders). Eventually, however, the bishop assumed a higher role following in the tradition of the apostles while the presbyters took on a lower role.[16] The three-tiered system of one bishop in one city with presbyters and deacons was firmly established during the 2nd century. Later, by the 4th century, church organization and development became increasingly tied to the Roman political system with the emperor making imperial nominations for the bishop of important cities.[17]

Prophets and Evangelists

The ministry of prophets and evangelists played a central role in the life of the early church. Later their importance diminished. In addition to apostles, elders, and deacons, prophets and evangelists also played a prominent role in the life of the early church. Nonetheless, there is little descriptive information about prophets or evangelists in the NT. What is known can be summarized as follows:

(1) There was a group of prophets in the Jerusalem church (Acts 11:27f). Christians in other congregations accepted their status as prophets and in the Acts 11 account these Jerusalem prophets go to Antioch where one of them, Agabus, foretold by the Spirit that there would be a great famine over all the world. Based upon that prophecy, the disciples at Antioch determined to send relief aid to the Christians in Judea. On another occasion, Judas and Silas, leading men among the brethren at Jerusalem and prophets, were also sent to give a message to the church at Antioch (Acts 15:22, 32). Judas and Silas are also portrayed as preachers and teachers.

(2) A group of prophets and teachers was also present in the church at Antioch (Acts 13:1). Barnabas and Saul are identified along with three other men as "prophets and teachers." Nothing indicates that some of the five were prophets and the rest teachers. Lucius of Cyrene, one of the five, possibly helped to establish the Antioch congregation (Acts 11:20). These five men are clearly portrayed as leaders in the church.

(3) Paul wrote to the Corinthians that God appointed first apostles, second prophets, third teachers, and then the other charismatic ministries (1 Cor. 12:28). The placement of prophets behind apostles indicates their importance.

Only two or three prophets were permitted to speak at an assembly. Furthermore, what they said was to be evaluated carefully (1 Cor. 14:29f). While prophetic utterances were viewed as a revelation from God, nevertheless, all things were to be done in order with the prophet controlling when and how he spoke (1 Cor. 14:13–33). There seems to be no limit on how many prophets might exist in one congregation. It is possible, though not likely, that any Christian could prophesy.

(4) Paul wrote that the church was built on the foundation of the apostles and prophets with Jesus Christ being the chief cornerstone (Eph. 2:20). The time-honored interpretation of this passage is to view the apostles as Jesus' disciples along with Paul, and the prophets as the OT prophets; however, these is good reason to understand "prophets" to mean the itinerant charismatic figures in the early church.[18] Paul identified such prophets as having a special place in the church (1 Cor. 12:28–29). Furthermore, apostles and prophets are mentioned together in Eph. 3:5 and 4:11, where together they are identified as central to God's plan in establishing and nurturing his church.

From this viewpoint, prophets played a major role in the early church and were central to its life. Although there is no indication that they were involved administratively in the organizational structure of the church, nevertheless they were viewed as leaders, served as apostolic representatives, and frequently acted as teachers and preachers. With the decline of the charismatic nature of the church, the role of the prophet disappeared, while the formal establishment of a two- or three-tiered system of leadership grew in importance. The bishop became the central authority figure.

(5) Philip, one of the seven men chosen to serve the widows, is the only identified evangelist in the NT, although Timothy is instructed to do the work of an evangelist. Philip's daughters all prophesied (Acts 21:8, 9). No further information is given concerning the daughters, although Eusebius notes that they were buried with their father at Hierapolis in Asia.[19]

Philip is credited with initiating the revival in Samaria along with the performance of miraculous signs, especially healings (Acts 8:5–8). He is also portrayed as evangelizing the Ethiopian eunuch (Acts 8:26–39) and proclaiming the gospel to many towns (Acts 8:40). He may have founded churches at Lydda, Joppa, and Caesarea.[20] Paul mentioned evangelists as God's gift for the building up of the church (Eph. 4:11).

In summary, Luke and Paul portrayed prophets and evangelists as having an active and important role in the early church. Prophets were more prominent than evangelists. They are not presented as office holders, but are described as Spirit-filled men and women who spoke according to special revelation. Their prophetic utterances were to be tested and confirmed by the church.

Some prophets were also teachers. The Apostle Paul was also a prophet and a teacher (Acts 13:1). While bands of prophets were associated with particular churches such as at Jerusalem or Antioch, other prophets developed an itinerant ministry traveling from one city to another. According to the Didache, these wandering prophets had to be carefully tested to distinguish valid ministries from freeloaders and shysters. The comment is made, "But whosoever shall say in spirit, 'Give me money, or other things,' ye shall not listen to him."[21]

As for evangelists, the focus is on the proclamation of the gospel to the unsaved and is illustrated by the ministry of Philip. Philip and others like him were viewed as having a special calling to that work. In certain respects, the ministry of an evangelist was similar in nature to the missionary activity of Paul, but without his apostolic authority. Thus, when Philip preached in Samaria, his work came under the supervision of the Jerusalem apostles. Both prophets and evangelists were active in the development of the early church.

Other Ministries of Grace

Church organization was closely tied to the expression of spiritual gifts. The emphasis in the early church was not so much on elected positions or recognized offices, but on the ministry and expression of the Holy Spirit in the lives of individual believers. The central event in the establishment of the church was the giving of the Holy Spirit on the Day of Pentecost. Without the Spirit there is no church. The basis of life in congregations must be clearly distinguished from creeds, liturgies, structure, or offices. The church receives its life, not from its organizational structure, but exclusively from the Holy Spirit. Furthermore, the work of the Spirit in sustaining and nurturing God's people is accomplished through the charismatic nature of the body of Christ.

From a biblical perspective, congregational structure is not so much based on organizational designs as it is a reflection of the charismatic ministry of individual believers who collectively shape the local church. The metaphor "body of Christ," more than any other image, captures the charismatic nature of the church.

The body metaphor points to several truths concerning the church. First, the church can be viewed as an organism of active members.[22] Each believer is a member of the body of Christ (1 Cor. 12:27). Each member of the body has his or her own special function, which, when done properly, contributes to the welfare of the whole (Eph. 4:16). Therefore, no part is greater than another, since all are indispensable (1 Cor. 12:22). Second, the body is one, although it is made up of many members (1 Cor. 12:12, 13). The body metaphor symbolizes the unity of the church. Unity, though, does not mean uniformity, since the body is made up of many different members with different functions. Yet it is the same Spirit that empowers and inspires all. Third, Christ is the head of the body (Eph. 4:15–16). As head, Jesus Christ is to be preeminent in all things (Col. 1:18). As Guthrie notes, the headship of Christ points toward the universal unity of the church.[23] Fourth, the metaphor implies that the body must mature and develop. This is specifically stated in Eph. 4:15–16. The body grows when each individual member functions properly. Love is central to proper growth.

Based on the image of the church as the body of Christ, an understanding of spiritual gifts and the importance of each individual member's contribution to the welfare of the whole body becomes central to comprehending the early church's structure and development. This becomes clear as we examine the relationship between God's grace and spiritual gifts.

God's grace (*charis*) comes to humanity as a gift (*charisma*). The historical manifestation of that gift and its source is the Son of God, Jesus Christ (Jn. 3:16; Eph. 4:7). That grace is sufficient for every human need (2 Cor. 12:9). Activated by the Holy Spirit, the grace of God transforms, empowers, and sustains individual believers. The outcome is that Christians are not only forgiven, they also become gifted. The spiritual manifestations of *charis* (grace) in the life of the individual and the church are called *charismata* (gifts). For example, Paul comments in his letter to the Romans, "Having gifts (*charismata*) that differ according to the grace (*charis*) given to us, let us use them" (12:6; see also 1 Cor. 12:31). These gifts are present for the edification of the body of Christ.

Such grace and gifts are not limited only to the most prominent or visible members of the church. Since all Christians are gifted by the grace of God, the total contribution of each individual member of the body of Christ is necessary for the proper growth and maturity of the church (Eph. 4:16). Every member has an essential part to play (1 Cor. 12:14ff). Specific lists of gifts are mentioned in Romans 12 and 1 Corinthians 12. These lists are not intended to be comprehensive, for God's grace is manifested in diverse ways.

Several important implications follow from this portrayal of the church as a charismatic community. Since salvation is by grace, the interaction and service rendered by believers to one another is essential for the welfare of the corporate body and individual Christians. God's grace enters the church through several different channels. First and foremost, God's grace flows sovereignly and directly into the life of the individual Christian through the ministry of the Holy Spirit. This relationship with God through Christ is both eternal and direct. The believer has continual access to the grace of God through his Son Jesus.

Second, Christians are to encounter God's grace in the lives of one another. As servants, individual believers are to be channels of God's saving grace through Christ. This means that congregations can be healthy only if individual members are willing to allow God's grace to flow through and into their lives. There must be a willingness both to give and receive. Those individuals who cut themselves off from other believers are actually cutting off the flow of God's grace into their lives. The result is spiritual poverty.

The early church was a charismatic community. While certain gifts, such as apostle and elder, played a strategic role in the organizational life of the church, the overall emphasis was on the contribution of all members. In part, whatever organization there was emerged out of the spiritual life of the community as individuals expressed God's grace through specific forms of service and commitment. The flow and content of meetings, the daily interaction of believers, and the decision-making process could not be separated from the leading, guidance, and expression of the Spirit of God in the life of the church. This was not a formal or static process, but one which was alive, creative, dynamic, and often spontaneous as individuals responded to the Spirit of God.

Summary

No fixed pattern of church organization existed in the early church. Based on the preceding examination, the formal organizational development of the early church must be viewed more in light of relative sociological influences than of normatively prescribed patterns intended for all people in all times.

Church life cannot be reduced to a blueprint, plan, or formula. Nor can it be passed on from one generation to another. It must be continually rediscovered. Born out of a personal encounter with the living Christ, Christian life is a relationship built on trust and characterized by love. Life itself becomes restructured around a new center of value and power. The true key to the dynamism of the early church, or for any assembly of believers, is found not in an organizational structure, but in that structure of life which is empowered by the Spirit, grounded in faith, and expressed in love.

6

STRUCTURAL DYNAMICS: COMMUNITY

THE PRECEDING CHAPTER EXAMINED the social structure of the early church. Rather than discovering a set pattern, we found a flexible community guided by the Spirit of God, yet also shaped by the social, political, and economic realities of contemporary life. The emphasis was less on structure and more on the charismatic nature of the body of Christ. The life of the church was primarily understood as a spiritual reality. Submission to Christ as Lord and Savior was to shape that reality. While that submission is to have a direct impact on congregational structure, the reverse is also true.

Church structure has an immediate and dramatic impact on the life and mission of a church. Therefore the mission of the church cannot be separated from the structures which it utilizes in attempting to fulfill that mission.

Two conflicting realities surface as we continue our analysis of church structure. The church exists at one and the same time within two separate dimensions. First, the church exists as a sociological reality subject to the same forces and laws which govern and shape the development and life of all social groups. [1] From this viewpoint the church can be studied like any cultural, political, economic, philosophical, technological, or scientific development of any historical period and setting. For example, the electronic church is a product of the 20th century.

As a sociological reality the church reflects the political intrigue, bureaucratic development, social stratification, class conflicts, and boredom that occur in all social institutions. In that sense, the principalities and powers are no less a part of church history than they are of any other institutional history. The institutional church cannot escape the influence of sin and death on its organizational development any more than can any other social reality. However, what should set the church apart from other institutions is the recognition of this very fact.

As a sociological reality, the institutional church is very much a part of the modern power complex. When the church fails to recognize this involvement, or attempts to deny it, it becomes vulnerable to the conditioning and enslaving control of the elements of this world.

Only by recognizing its involvement with the power complex can God's people expose the principalities of modern life. This exposure does not take place primarily through contrasting institutional structures or organizational development, but through the reality of the church—the people of God—as the eschatological community of the Spirit. This leads to the second dimension of the church's existence.

While the sociological nature of the church cannot be denied, neither can it accurately inform us of the authentic nature, life, or mission of the church. The Spirit empowers, gifts, sustains, and sets apart the church. As such it is distinct and separate from the modern power complex and stands in deep contrast to earthly traditions and the thinking of this age. As an eschatological community, the church represents the lordship of Christ and the life of the Spirit. The church exists as a tangible reality of that which is to come illuminating not only the future, but also the current ambiguities of life.

Christian life cannot be embodied in or derived through liturgies, creeds, rituals, doctrinal statements, or institutional structures. It cannot be found in a specific form of government or transmitted through a set of policies or procedures. Nor can it be derived through rational planning or human understanding.

The new life exists only through faith in the crucified Lord and comes to men and women as a gift brought by the Spirit of God. The church as a sociological reality, with a history reflecting the impact of sin and death, is at the same time the community of the Spirit, holy in the sight of God. This paradox must be maintained as we continue our examination of the life and structure of the church.

Structure and the Lordship of Christ

In the early church the lordship of Jesus Christ was understood and accepted. To proclaim Jesus as Lord could result in death. As Ellul reminds us in *The New Demons*, early Christianity sought to bring the lordship of Christ to bear on every aspect of life. This meant that the existing social structures could not remain exempt from the lordship of Christ. Ellul writes:

> Consequently, if the God of Jesus Christ was indeed the God of all creation, his presence must be perceptible not only in the individual conscience but in the social structures as well—all social structures without exception.[2]

As a result of the unwavering commitment of Christians to the lordship of Christ, Christendom arose. Eventually, the life and practice of the church impacted the political and social structures of the Roman Empire. At the same time, however, the church itself was changed. Over time, everyone in society was viewed as a Christian regardless of whether a living faith in the risen Lord existed or not. The efficacy of the grace of God was independent of the "believer's" faith. Christianity was transformed from a living faith into a religious and social ideology. The Christian creeds, rituals, and dogmas became both politicized and habitualized within society and provided the foundation for the institutionalization of the Christian faith. Form and function replaced the charismatic life of the church.

Our feelings of this transition may generate a sense of loss, but as Ellul notes this development arose out of the belief that the lordship of Christ must be manifest in history.[3] He comments:

> If we want each Christian to live out his faith in a concrete way in his personal life, how can we not want all Christians to do so in a collective way? And if Christianity is political, can we help but want a political order that is inspired by faith?[4]

This Christian order declined with advances in science, trade, and invention. The dominating influence of the church, that had existed for centuries, evaporated nearly overnight. Today, the church has moved from the center of social life to the fringes.

Partnership and Service

For centuries, the social environment helped to maintain the life and structure of the church. Such a supportive environment no longer exists. Turbulence and change now characterize the environment. The challenge for Christian leaders is to develop new wineskins. Structural alternatives must be sought that will support and nurture the life and mission of the church. Such structures must reinforce the charismatic life of the church. They must also promote both partnership and service.

Koinōnia or partnership was central to the life and structure of the early church. The biblical concept of *koinōnia* extends far beyond the limited notion of fellowship emphasized in many churches today.

Church fellowship activities conjure up images of picnics, dinners, softball games, and informal socializing before and after church services. While these experiences are important, they do not embody the central thrust of biblical *koinōnia*, although they reflect aspects which play a vital role in its maintenance in a congregation. *Koinōnia* is directly tied to the life of the congregation as a community of believers who have entered into a collective partnership with Christ and with one another. One central element in this partnership is *diakonia* or service. Two principal terms denote this relationship—*doulos* (slave) and *diakonos* (servant).[5]

T. F. Torrance observes that the concept of slave refers to status rather than function. He wrote, "The *doulos* lives under the total claim of God and is completely subordinate to Jesus Christ, to whom he belongs body and soul."[6] *Diakonos* refers to function. The *diakonos* does what has been commanded. According to Torrance, "Christian service or *diakonia* is not something that is accidental to the Christian, but essential to him, for it is rooted in his basic structure of existence as a slave of Jesus Christ."[7]

Christ is the example for all Christian service, and through him we understand the true meaning of *diakonia*. Such service is not compatible with self-serving interests or the acquisition of power or status. Unfortunately, it is not uncommon for structures that were created to help in the process of serving, to become instruments of power that distort Christian life. Those involved in such structures can be blind to their own spiritual impoverishment. Like the Laodicean church, they believe they are rich and prosperous, when in reality they are wretched, poor, blind, and naked (Rev. 3:17).

The vitality of both partnership and service is directly linked to the degree that the congregation exists as a community of believers. The lack of a supportive environment makes this task difficult. While the life of the church is primarily a spiritual matter, nevertheless, its spiritual manifestation is linked to its institutional life. From an organizational viewpoint, an important question is how the congregation can strengthen its basis for community life. To answer this question, we must examine the nature of community in our technological world.

The Nature of Community

The word community is used in so many different ways that it can refer to a small group or the entire human race.[8] Ordinarily though, community is tied to a location such as one's hometown. It refers to the social organization among individuals in a particular locale.[9] Used in this way it conjures up images of a pleasant, personal, uncomplicated way of life vastly different from the urban, institutionalized experience of today. Community expresses the desire for shared life with others, a sense of communion, of close family ties, and a common destiny with those whom we share a common bond.

Community and the Urban Environment

Community is often set over against urban impersonality. Community denotes a positive image of the warm, friendly village life which arises out of shared values and perspectives. It revolves around close family ties and shared religious beliefs. In contrast, urban life is portrayed as cold and business-like. Sterility, rationality, and logic characterize relationships.[10] The implication is that community can be found in the confines of the warm, friendly village, but not in the cold, calculating city. The problem is that these expressions distort reality because they are both one-dimensional and oversimplified.

There is no doubt that the modern urban environment has altered traditional forms of community. Meaningful, abiding relationships which provide mutual support become more difficult to establish and maintain. When people live together, know one another, and share the same problems, they are more likely to develop common perspectives and work together toward shared goals. Historically this is seen in the establishment of villages. Individuals did not come together as a loose aggregate or because of a series of accidents; rather, they banded together in cohesive groups. This led to the development of specific roles and responsibilities and contributed to feelings of mutual interdependence and security.

As villages evolved into cities, this interdependence took on new, more complex social, political, and economic forms. Eventually the individual became involved in different groups, associations, clubs, or organizations, each of which influenced personal goals, values, and perspectives concerning life. The authority of the church began to diminish as people became more cosmopolitan.

During the Middle Ages the church provided the basic reference point for social interaction. However, with the relativizing of values within the context of rapid urban growth and the expansion of various forms of social, political, and economic involvement, the church found itself only one of many voices seeking the individual's allegiance.

Group involvement became less determined by geography and increasingly determined by personal interest. Both necessity and the individual's search for happiness and personal satisfaction shaped group involvement. In the process, commitment and loyalty to any particular group or "community" weakened as individuals made commitments to several different groups. Social mobility and transient lifestyles also contributed to short-term relationships which undermined community life.

The modern world pulls men and women out of their secluded environment into the complexities of contemporary life. An individual's occupation, leisure time, friendships, spending habits, and religious involvement are no longer firmly attached to a stable pattern of life. The question exists whether or not any form of meaningful community can exist within a turbulent social environment. What will bind that community together? How will shared commitments be developed and maintained?

What type of personal interaction will exist? The answer to these questions affects the nature of a congregation's life and mission.

Community and Location

Community cannot exist in a vacuum, but does it have to have a specific geographical location? Historically, communities have been tied to particular settings, but this is no longer always the case. People who live in one town may work, go to church, do their shopping, or visit friends in other locations. In essence, a community revolving around a specific place has been abandoned for new social forms. Jacqueline Scherer notes that these new forms bind us socially while allowing us to be physically free. [11]

Social mobility directly and significantly impacts the maintenance of geographical communities. It allows people to expand their choices concerning where to place loyalties. Scherer comments:

> As a result, modern communities are not the stable enduring collectivities of the past, rooted to a fixed place, and fixed in both composition and direction. Mobility also makes it possible for modern man to belong to several different types of associations at the same time and, possibly, to more than one community. [12]

"Interest" communities have replaced geographical communities. Thus we can speak of the cosmopolites or the socialites, the museum and concert-goers, the sports fanatics and the like. The mass media allow for psychological mobility. [13] Television, radio, newspapers, magazines, and books enter our homes and prepare us for a new world. According to Scherer, "communality" is the term which refers to social nearness regardless of physical distance.

Television, which promotes a form of technological community, exemplifies communality. In the church, the use of television has nurtured the growth of mega-religious systems. These technological communities are held together by shared religious beliefs and revolve around a charismatic leader. These programs evoke authentic emotional response, but technological relationships replace human ones. The result is "technological grace." No geographical community exists—only a mailing list which is used for fund raising.

The formation of such communities raises serious questions concerning church structure and the edification of Christians. Technological grace reinforces spiritual architecture whereby the individual becomes the designer, contractor, and builder of spirituality in the privacy of his or her own home. No accountability exists. Spirituality becomes reduced to symbols and images that appeal to the broadest audience. Christianity is merchandized. These images then convey to the broader public a characterization of Christianity far-removed from the biblical teaching concerning discipleship.

The church cannot avoid the impact of technology on the formation and maintenance of community. Technological grace is here to stay. Although it raises serious questions, it also has positive dimensions to it. The focus must be on how such technology can be harnessed to reinforce the Christian mission. Those who fight the intrusion of technology in the church will lose.

Community and Congregational Life

For many people the church is less of a community and more of an association. It takes its place alongside of social clubs, political parties, places of work, and now television programs. It is not always easy to know who belongs to the community and who does not, who is committed and who is not. Expectations for membership can be hazy or nonexistent. Little or no accountability may exist.

Personal values, attitudes, and behaviors are shaped in an environment where the difference between the church and the world is not always clear. One thing is clear, however: the world does not support a Christian way of life. For the church to grow, it must exist as more than a loose association of individuals who happen to attend a common worship service. As a true spiritual community, the local church must provide the framework to build caring relationships based on shared commitments arising out of a common partnership with Jesus Christ. For this to occur, a network of relationships must be developed that reinforces a Christian way of life. These relationships must be more than technological. In essence, we must find our participation in and understanding of the world originating out of a Christian environment. The church cannot be thought of as a building, a mailing list, or just another group. Instead, it must be seen as the community of which we are a part and the context for our growth and development as Christians; moreover, it must serve as the source of strength for our involvement in the world.

At one time or another, all social groups, including the church, are faced with tensions between the individual and the collective group. While the basis for group survival is shared beliefs, practices, and commitments, at times the individual may feel pressured by the group to conform. This may result in feelings that personal creativity is being sacrificed or that group membership can be maintained only at the expense of the loss of personal identity. To maintain a positive relationship between the individual and the group, common commitments must exist.

The church must work at maintaining a healthy balance between individual freedom and corporate life. On the one hand, the individual stands accountable to God and will be judged according to what he or she has done in this life. On the other hand, God has chosen the church to fulfill his purposes on earth. The individual is to become an effective member of the body of Christ. Spiritual growth occurs only in the context of *koinōnia* (partnership) and *diakonia* (service). This involves not only personal relationships and shared commitments, but also corporate responsibility.

The context for decision making should reflect both partnership and service. Mutual trust, support, and commitment must be at the heart of the process. When this occurs, the community life of the church is strengthened and the basis for ongoing effective ministry is maintained. The question we must now face is, what practical steps can and should be taken to build effective structures for congregational life and ministry which support community?

7

STRUCTURAL DYNAMICS: THE BASIS FOR COMMUNITY AND PARTNERSHIP

CHURCHES MUST CREATE STRUCTURES that will nurture Christian life. While that sounds obvious, it is not an easy task to accomplish. Effective congregational structures should encourage both partnership and community within the congregation. Furthermore, each setting is different. What works well for one church may not be effective somewhere else. There are normative dimensions to effective church structures, however, that should be present regardless of time or place.

If a structure is to support the life of the church, special attention must be given to the areas of relationships, shared values, congregational mission, clarified expectations, mutual support, and accountability. Collectively, the successful development of each of these areas, as guided by the Holy Spirit, provides the basis for community and partnership in the congregation.

Building Relationships

The church cannot effectively fulfill its mission unless its members develop *meaningful relationships* with one another. The establishment of these relationships requires personal interaction and sharing. This can only occur as individuals spend time together. For churches to develop a strong infrastructure, relationships among members must go beyond casual acquaintances and reflect strong friendships and binding commitments.

In the early church Christians experienced ongoing relationships and often daily contact with one another. They worshiped together, ate together, prayed together, and were involved in mission together. They shared a common life which arose out of their being together. They knew one another and were aware of one another's needs. In part, the social environment supported these kinds of relationships. Today that is no longer true. The environment makes those kinds of relationships more difficult to establish and maintain. What still is true, however, is that meaningful relationships require significant investments of time and energy. Furthermore, in-depth relationships are not possible with a large group. Rather, each individual needs to have his or her own "social space" in the congregation, where his or her presence is felt and absence is noticed. In essence, each individual should be tied into the larger infrastructure through participation in a small group, however that group is defined. It may be the choir, the Sunday School staff, a home Bible study group, or involvement in a ministry.

Simple involvement in activities cannot guarantee the development of these types of relationships. Programmed involvement in one another's lives can lead to detached relationships. Meaningful relationships must grow out of friendship, out of play, eating together, sharing dreams, common worship experiences, Bible studies, and working together side by side. As Christians this must go even deeper and arise out of a shared sense of mission and service to Christ. While it may not be possible for each individual to have in-depth relationships with everyone else in the church, nevertheless, there should be a collective sense of mission, partnership, and commitment that extends throughout the entire congregation. The small relational groups that make up the infrastructure should be tied together through a shared sense of calling to the kingdom of God.

How large can a congregation become without doing damage to the meaningful development of relationships? Actually, size is not the main issue. The key concern is with the quality of the relational infrastructure of the congregation. Some large congregations do a better job of integrating new members or converts into the life of the church than do some smaller ones. Size and structure must be considered in relationship to a congregation's ability to maintain a sense of community. The cement that holds people together is related to each of the factors discussed below.

Shared Values and a Sense of Mission

If a congregation is to reflect the life of Christ, a corporate identity as the people of God must exist. *Shared values,* which give rise to a *sense of mission,* must sustain congregational life. Out of these shared values the actual structure of the congregation begins to take shape. Once in existence, social structures dramatically influence values. Therefore, congregational structures must be periodically reviewed and modified to reinforce the life and mission of the church in relationship to changing congregational needs and circumstances.

The existence of shared values within the church is related to the development of the mind of Christ among the individual members. The biblical emphasis is on unity and likemindedness. Likemindedness promotes the clear sense of direction necessary for effective ministry.

As Christians, our values should be tied to our new life in Christ. The two primary channels for the development of these values are the Scriptures and the church as mediated by the Spirit of God. The life of the church should stand in harmony with the Scriptures. The Scriptures provide guidelines for the development of congregational life, but they do not provide a blueprint for church structure.

Education and planning are vital to the development of shared values and a sense of congregational mission. If these latter qualities are to contribute to community and partnership, leaders must work at establishing a shared basis of knowledge and commitment in the congregation. Each member of the church must have a minimal knowledge and understanding of what it means to be a Christian, and more particularly, what it means to be a confessing member of that congregation. Such learning cannot take place on the basis of formal training alone. While sermons, Christian education classes, and other organized activities are critical for this to occur, this understanding must also develop through a process of socialization that ties the individual into the congregational infrastructure.

Since people have different levels of maturity and have different abilities and needs, a multifaceted educational process must be developed. For example, while new Christians need a basic understanding of the Christian life, they must also be incorporated into the life of the church. Several different learning processes must be occurring simultaneously. As the new Christian matures in the faith, substantive changes requiring additional training and support should occur in his or her life. This developmental process is critical for the maintenance of shared values and like-mindedness within the congregation. It provides the basis for a shared body of knowledge and helps to create the foundation for unity of vision and purpose. Each of the following areas should be included in the developmental process:

New Christian	**Maturing Christian**
1. Beginning knowledge of the Bible	1. Ongoing mastery of biblical knowledge
2. Beginning devotional life	2. Ongoing devotional life
3. New Christian friendships	3. Committed Christian friendships
4. Initial spiritual discernment	4. Growing spiritual discernment
5. Attendance at church activities	5. Contributing member of the congregation
6. Introduction to congregational life and goals	6. Clear understanding of and commitment to congregational life and goals
7. New way of life	7. Ongoing integration of Christian truth into daily life

This process does not automatically occur, but requires both personal commitment and a supportive, relational infrastructure and organizational framework. Both leadership and planning are essential components of this process.

A person cannot develop a clear understanding of and commitment to congregational goals if no such goals exist. A congregation with a clear sense of direction and purpose is more likely to experience growth and maintain unity than one that speaks of its future in broad generalizations. It is one thing to say, "Our church is committed to evangelism," and quite another thing to have an evangelistic strategy that the congregation understands and embraces. If congregations desire unity, growth, and maturity then they must develop shared values and a clear sense of mission. These two qualities, along with supportive relationships, are vital for congregational maturity. In themselves, however, they are not enough to sustain congregational life. Clarified expectations, mutual support, and accountability must also be present.

Clarifying Expectations

The gospel makes demands on those who are called Christians. Jesus said, "Why do you call me 'Lord, Lord,' and do not what I tell you?" (Lk. 6:46). As Christians, we must submit to the demands of Scripture and embrace a way of life that reflects kingdom values and goals. Submission to God and to other Christians is central to Christian faith. We must be careful, though, not to confuse a submissive lifestyle with ritualistic obedience to religious forms and regulations. The very practices and structures that are designed to support life with God can enslave us. For example, the Pharisees replaced the Lawgiver with the law. We must be careful not to do the same with our own faith practices.

On the other hand, to be part of a community we must give allegiance and support to structures and practices that place demands on us. Wherever communities exist there will always be some friction between group structure and goals and personal desires and choices. To fulfill our collective mission as God's people, we must be willing to make personal sacrifices on behalf of a higher calling and purpose. A process of self-examination must take place in the life of each individual Christian concerning personal commitments. This process is essential for church leaders.

Over half a century ago, Reinhold Niebuhr argued that "a sharp distinction must be drawn between the moral and social behavior of individuals and social groups...."[1] Individuals, he claimed, are endowed with a degree of sympathy and are able to consider the interests of others, and at times will even put the interests of others before their own. Yet within social groups other factors, which do not always reflect the way an individual member of the group might respond to a particular situation, affect decisions. Niebuhr wrote,

> In every human group there is less reason to guide and to check impulse, less capacity for self-transcendence, less ability to comprehend the needs of others and therefore more unrestrained egotism than the individuals, who compose the group, reveal in their personal relationships. [2]

Church leaders have the responsibility, through teaching and example, to clarify expectations for the individual member's involvement in the congregation, daily lifestyle, and role in the mission of the church. A congregation's membership statement should state its expectations. Furthermore, those expectations must be viewed in a covenantal fashion and become binding upon those who agree to their terms. Otherwise, what is the purpose of membership? Those congregations lacking formal membership must still outline what it means to be a covenantal member of that particular community. Each local church must develop its own structural framework to maintain and encourage community and partnership. Otherwise, effective ministry is not likely to occur. *Clarified expectations* concerning ministry involvement are essential. Such expectations must be developed, however, in direct correlation to two factors: *mutual support* and *accountability*.

Giving Support and Being Accountable

The body of Christ is not simply to build itself up, but it is to build itself up in love. Love is the key element in defining the life of the church. It can be expressed in many different ways, but in the end it always edifies and strengthens the entire body of believers. Love points to the truth revealed in Jesus Christ and expresses God's care, concern, and provision for his creation. The body of Christ is to reflect the love of God through its life and ministry.

The church is not to be a sterile, legal monitor of good and evil, but as a community of believers it should reflect God's true intention for human life. The expectations discussed in the preceding section should not be viewed as "decrees" or as a legal code, but rather as something which helps to define what Christian partnership means. As Christians work together, their collective effort is to result in *mutual edification and support*. Acts of mutual love and concern are to characterize the mission of the church.

Christianity is not an individualized struggle for perfection. The early Christians had a sense of *accountability* that goes along with the common life. Discipline played an important role in the life of the church. Today it has little impact in the church, because our culture places a high value on individual privacy and choice. The cultural credo is "Keep your nose out of my business." Western individualism and Christian community approach life from two different perspectives.

That is not to say that Christianity devalues the importance of individual rights and freedom; on the contrary. But Christianity views the individual in relationship to Jesus Christ, to the church, and to God's entire creation. As Christians, our lives and values are to be grounded in the life and mission of the church. Those who are a part of that mission are required to be accountable to God and to neighbor.

For several reasons, discipline and accountability in the church are nearly impossible in the existing social environment. First, many congregations do not provide a healthy or supportive environment for meaningful discipline. There may not be a true sense of partnership or of binding commitments. Individuals may not know one another very well and feel threatened to share openly personal needs or problems. Second, there are few means of accountability unless some form of covenantal relationships exist. Third, if a person feels uncomfortable in one congregation because of personal sin or conflict, he or she can go down the street to a different church. And finally, when and if some form of discipline is initiated, it frequently is more destructive than redemptive, precisely because the basis for redemptive discipline does not exist in the congregation to begin with. Accountability is only one dimension of partnership and community. Without the other qualities of congregational life that we have discussed, genuine accountability is not likely to exist.

If we take Christian growth seriously, we must be accountable. But this is to occur in an atmosphere of mutual love and care. We become accountable to one another as we grow in mutual trust and love. True accountability arises out of meaningful relationships where we sense the freedom to share personal concerns without fear of rejection. Christian accountability is related to relationships which are growing in love and humility.

The six qualities discussed above—meaningful relationships, shared values, a sense of mission, clarified expectations, mutual support, and accountability—are essential for the development and maintenance of Christian community and partnership. The dynamic interrelationship of these factors that leads to the basis of community and partnership is illustrated in Figure 7-1.

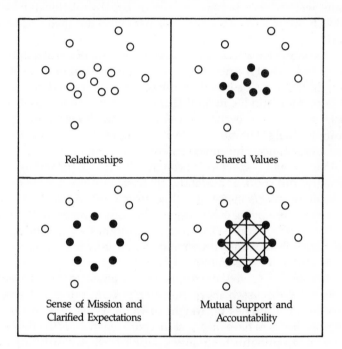

FIGURE 7-1

The issue is how these factors can be developed in our current social environment. One contributing element is a congregational covenant.

Structure and Covenant

Meaningful structures must arise out of the life and mission of a people. A covenant can help in developing such structures.

The formation of a covenant can give definition to congregational values and commitments. It can also aid in clarifying expectations and in providing a basis for accountability.

Covenants are a very normal part of life. We make a covenant with the bank when we take out a loan, or with a landlord when we sign a rental agreement. As citizens, we have made a covenant with our government to obey the law. Marriage ceremonies are covenantal acts as are any formal binding partnerships. Covenants were a very important part of Israel's relationship with Yahweh. Jesus formed the new covenant with the shedding of his blood.

A congregational covenant is an agreement of partnership between individual members concerning the life and mission of the church. It should be based on the congregation's understanding of its mission and life in light of the Scriptures and its particular social setting. The covenant should define the basis and nature of an individual's commitment to the congregation and clarify expectations concerning involvement. It can serve as a basis for evaluation with respect to the congregation's understanding of its ministry. But most importantly, the covenant must arise out of the congregation's sense of calling from God. As such, a covenant must be a living expression of the commitments and calling of that congregation. When and if it becomes a legalistic agreement, rather than an expression of community and partnership, it has outlived its usefulness.

In some congregations membership is similar to the covenantal relationship discussed above; however, in many others it is simply a social act. It carries no weight or value. What is necessary, if membership is to have meaning in a congregation, is the development of meaningful boundary conditions that clearly identify commitment and partnership.

Congregational Boundaries

Every organization has boundaries. Boundaries serve two purposes. First, they give definition to a system, and second, they regulate access between the system and its environment. For example, a football field's boundaries define the playing field. Only players or officials can cross the boundaries and enter the playing field during the game. In addition, the rules of the game also serve as boundary conditions. Those rules define what is a valid game. They also regulate how the game is to be played. If a player does not stay within the boundaries of the rules, his team will be penalized.

Boundaries can either be physical or conceptual. For example, the football field has physical boundaries. There is no question whether a person is inside or outside of those boundaries. The game of football also has conceptual boundaries composed of the rules of the game. Those boundaries regulate the playing of the game and define whether what is being played is actually football.

In addition to *physical* and *conceptual* boundaries, organizations also have *sentient* boundaries. Those boundaries reflect the feelings, perceptions, and attitudes of individuals toward the organization. If a person has a favorable view of the organization, then the sentient boundary is low or open for that individual. However, if the individual has negative feelings about the organization, then the boundary conditions are high and the person is unlikely to cross them. For example, some people love football and others hate it. For the first individual the boundaries are low, but for the second person they are high. All social organizations have sentient boundaries. The boundaries exist in the feelings and perceptions of individuals. These feelings attract some and repel others.

Churches have similar boundaries. On the one hand, the church facilities have defined geographic boundaries. On the other hand, the church proclaims "rules of life" which serve as "boundaries" for conduct. Those boundaries may be very restrictive or very open and undefined. Furthermore, they can be regulated to achieve different results. The location and time of the church service serves as a boundary condition. For example, if a congregation changed its service time from 10:00 A.M. to 6:00 A.M. it would be making the boundary more closed. Since fewer people are willing to get up early, the change in time would affect their involvement.

Different boundaries are needed for different aspects of congregational life. Evangelistic outreaches must have open boundaries. A non-Christian is more likely to attend a picnic or visit someone's home for dinner than to attend a church service. Discipleship groups, on the other hand, must have fairly closed boundaries. If the goal is to develop commitment and discipline, then the boundary conditions must be designed to aid that process. For example, regular attendance may be required at an evening Bible study to be a member of the discipleship group. Ongoing absence may result in being dismissed from the group. That requirement helps to close the boundary and more clearly define group membership.

A covenant helps to define congregational boundaries. For instance, congregations may have vast differences in the nature of their membership boundaries. An open boundary would define membership in terms of being present for the Sunday morning worship service. A closed boundary would make very specific requirements of personal commitment and responsibility. As the required level of commitment increases, the boundary becomes more closed.

Boundary conditions affect the life and structure of every congregation. The following three figures illustrate the nature and impact of different kinds of congregational boundaries on the life and mission of the church.

CHURCH A

FIGURE 7-2

The following factors characterize Church A. First, many of its members do not attend the Sunday morning worship service. The membership boundary is very open. Membership may mean making an annual contribution or signing a membership card. However defined, membership requires a low level of commitment.

The life of the church revolves around attendance at the Sunday morning worship service, and other events play only a small role. In all likelihood, this congregation's structure does little to develop any strong sense of community.

CHURCH B

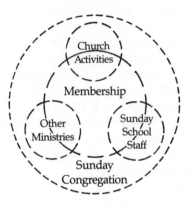

FIGURE 7-3

Members of Church B are much more involved in the life of the church. Membership requires a higher level of commitment than Church A. More possibilities exist for involvement in small groups and for building relationships. A greater degree of shared values, a sense of mission, mutual support, and accountability are more likely to exist in Church B than in Church A.

CHURCH C

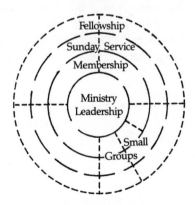

FIGURE 7-4

Church C uses several boundary conditions. First, it has a fairly closed membership boundary that requires a high level of commitment and participation. All leaders are required to be members. The congregation has different types of small groups requiring different levels of commitment. As one moves toward the center of Church C, one is more likely to experience community than would be the case in the other two churches. At the same time, more demands are placed on the individual.

In examining the above churches it becomes clear that different boundary conditions affect levels of participation as well as the nature of the participation. If a congregational structure is to aid in the development of community, the leaders must build a shared basis of knowledge and commitment and create the proper structures and means to achieve the church's mission. A covenant can aid in that process.

Summary

To fulfill its mission effectively, the church must exist as a community of believers with a clearly defined sense of mission and partnership. Not all structures are equally valuable in maintaining the community life of the church. Good structures will help the congregation to develop supportive relationships, shared values, a sense of mission, clarified expectations, mutual support, and accountability. These factors, when empowered by God's Spirit, provide the basis for community and partnership. Various types of boundary conditions are required to develop and maintain these areas of congregational life. One element that can aid in the development of these areas is a congregational covenant. Other structural factors include leadership, facilities, education, and meetings. These topics are the focus of the following chapters.

8

CHRISTIAN LEADERSHIP

L EADERSHIP IS ESSENTIAL FOR the survival of any organization. It is an integral part of all social structures. Furthermore, the nature and quality of leadership are not determined solely by those who are called leaders, but rather by the relationships that those leaders develop with other members of the organization and of society. Therefore, leadership can only be understood or studied as a relational quality between two or more persons. That is not to say, however, that individuals do not have personal leadership qualities. Yet the true expression of those qualities becomes visible only as a social reality.

The Nature of Leadership

Different social environments require different leadership styles and skills. The leadership style of a Marine drill sergeant would differ from that of a college dean. Yet while there may be fundamental differences in the *style* of leadership, other basic leadership skills should be the same. One task that we face is to determine if there are unique or specific qualities that characterize Christian leadership. First, we must explore some general aspects of leadership.

There cannot be leaders without followers. There are many reasons that one person may follow another. They may have no option. Force or coercion may characterize the relationship. Another may follow for lack of knowledge, skill, or ability. Others may follow out of self-serving interests in an attempt to gain money, power, or status. Yet another may follow out of respect or love. In any case, there can be no leader without a follower.

Leadership involves both power and authority. Two essentials of power are motives and resources. James MacGregor Burns notes that powerholders have both the motives and resources to create change in the behavior of another person.[1] Both motivation and resources are required to maintain power. A person may have the motivation to achieve a specific goal, but if the required resources are not available, the person is powerless. On the other hand, one may have the resources, but if there is no motivation, then nothing will happen and no expression of power will occur. For power to exist, there must be both resources and the motivation to use them to achieve a particular result.

In examining church leadership, we must identify both the motivations and resources that contribute to legitimate power. Such power is necessary for effective leadership. Leaders without power cannot prevent chaos or provide direction to others. Power can be abused, but when properly channeled, motivated by godly desires, and carried out in an appropriate way, it contributes to both social stability and human welfare.

Jesus the Leader

Jesus' own life manifested power. He spoke with power and authority. He had power to forgive sins, heal the sick, raise the dead, and command the forces of nature. All authority in heaven and on earth has been given to him. Christ's followers also have power—power to become the children of God, and to be witnesses of Christ (Jn. 1:12; Acts 1:8). Power that comes from God edifies rather than destroys. It liberates rather than enslaves. Furthermore, the expression of Christian power has at its source only one motivation—love.

All motivation that originates from a source other than the love of God and neighbor will become misguided and result in misfortune. Love of money, status, power, prestige, success, or self can replace one's love for God. When these forces become the fuel for our motivation we quickly become entrapped by the demonic and develop a distorted perspective, not only of life, but also of God.

The Lord God is replaced by our own views, which reinforces the misguided and tragic motivations whose false promises of satisfaction and security lead only to death and destruction. Yet while this is taking place, our own sense of spirituality and well-being may be falsely promoted. Not only do we betray the true intentions of our Savior, but we applaud ourselves in the process. We seek encouragement concerning the importance and value of our commitments and work, and these assume ultimate meaning. We would lead ourselves to believe that the final outcome of God's kingdom rests with our own sense of success or failure.

Regardless of how well intended, any life motivation that does not have as its source the love of God will eventually become self-destructive. Furthermore, no leader can insulate himself or herself from the institutional structures in which he or she lives and acts. Since sin and death govern the structures of modern life, it follows that all leaders, including Christians, can never assume that they are operating from pure motives. We are engaged in a life and death struggle with forces that would gain the upper hand by leading us to believe that we are depending upon God, when in reality we are relying on our own sense of self-righteousness and spirituality. Such people are blind—blind to their own sin (Jn. 9:40); blind to their own poverty (Rev. 3:17); and blind to their own self-serving ways (Lk. 11:42-44).

While Jesus calls us to perfection, there can be no movement toward godliness unless we abide in him. Those who abide in Christ must depend on his strength and power rather than their own wisdom or efforts. Those who would grow in love and character must engage not only in self-examination, but in the searching of the heart that comes directly from the Spirit of God (Ps.139:23). Such examination can be painful as the darkness of our inner life and motives becomes revealed in the pure light of a holy God. Yet those who are motivated out of love earnestly desire the cleansing power of the Holy Spirit.

Leadership and Power

The power that comes from God is not to be used for personal gain, political advantage, or social recognition. Such power is not revealed in the customary fashion through pomp and circumstance; rather, it is most clearly evident in humble service. Love of God is reflected in spiritual humility. Self-interest sows the destructive seeds of pride, but humility produces the fruit of peace and joy. The abiding satisfaction of serving God and doing his will replaces personal ambition. Without love there can be no true humility; without humility there can be no inner peace. Those motivated by self-serving interests are bound to a life of striving. Pride and ambition become linked to the insatiable quest for personal fulfillment. That quest is at the heart of all power and authority outside of Christ. Such power is devastating, not only because it can lead to the destruction of human life through maniacal quests for domination, but more subtly because it can lead to the blind self-justification of death itself.

Our world views death as a justifiable means to promote peace, security, and even personal fulfillment. This is true not only with the deployment of nuclear weapons, but also through the maintenance of economic, political, and legal systems that survive at the expense of human dignity and welfare. From a biblical perspective death is not just the biological extinction of human life, but the result of sin. The infestation of death becomes rooted and grounded in the very structures of life itself. The result is the perpetuation of systems and structures that maintain order without respect for God or man. The road to both corporate and individual survival becomes deceptively paved with the stepping stones of self-interest. Yet while this path leads to spiritual poverty, it becomes portrayed as the true road to spiritual and personal freedom. Yet the power complex shapes it every step of the way.

Christian leaders are to manifest power, but such power is to lead others to the cross of Christ, not to the pinnacle of the temple. Spiritual power does not intimidate, but liberates individuals from sin, death, and fear. Love of God and neighbor are the motivating forces. Humility of spirit is manifested. Healing, peace, forgiveness, and joy are promoted. It reflects the glory of God and points to the reality of a new age. It is the power of love. Such love binds us to God with such force that no power of darkness can break the bond. The power that raised Christ from the dead will sustain us until Christ returns. It is the power of the cross of Christ. To those who are perishing it is foolishness, but to us who are being saved, it is the power of God (1 Cor. 1:18).

The essential essence of Christian leadership is therefore spiritual. However, by spiritual we do not mean a disposition, an attitude, or an emotional state. Rather, it has to do with the very structure of one's life—a structure based on faith in Christ.[2]

Leadership and Love

Christian leaders should be time-tested disciples manifesting a mature and stable commitment to Christ. Life is not to be grounded in the transient values and shifting tides of the social order, but in the eternal Word of God. Commitment to Christ involves the totality of one's existence. Jesus said, "you shall love the Lord your God with all your heart, and with all your soul, and with all your mind, and with all your strength" (Mk. 12:30). The motivation of love must therefore extend into every aspect of life. Love with the heart is not enough—one must also love with the mind. Furthermore, we are to direct all of our personal energy into the service of Christ.

While love of God is the sole motivation of Christian leadership, the next issue is how that motivation becomes transformed into tangible, practical service. That involves the use of resources. Without resources we are left with spiritual energy, but no way to harness it.

There is an infinite number of resources available for serving Christ. Christ instructed us to give ourselves completely to God, with all of our heart, soul, mind, and strength. These four aspects of commitment are central to Christian leadership and to the development of legitimate power. They undergird the power to serve.

To love God with all of one's heart requires an emotional investment. Commitment to God is not based on calculation; it requires passion: "As the deer pants for streams of water, so my soul pants for you, O God" (Ps. 42:1). Jeremiah experienced it as a burning fire in his heart (Jer. 20:9). Such desire is not simply a sentimental attachment, but it reveals the complete surrender of one's self to the calling of God.

This commitment of the heart is expressed by an act of the will—the love of God with one's soul. The manifestation of such love is demonstrated in obedience to Christ and is to summon forth all of one's strength. Love of God with one's heart, soul, and strength result in power—power to live a life worthy of the calling of Christ. In addition, however, the mind is a resource for the manifestation of love. As such it is to aid in the creation and support of effective structures for congregational life.

Leadership and Knowledge

One of the greatest resources for service God gives to us is the mind transformed by the Holy Spirit. Our ability to think, reason, and create separates us from the rest of the earthly creation. The human mind can lead us away from God or enable us to serve him more faithfully. In either capacity, it is the most potent of all human operations. The function of the mind is not an inherently spiritual operation. As part of the created human nature, thinking allows both the interpretation and creation of knowledge. That knowledge becomes among the most important resources at humanity's disposal. Love and knowledge become two of the foundations of power.

Intrinsically knowledge is neither good nor bad; instead, the ethical concern is how that knowledge becomes integrated into the structure of one's life and how it is translated into behavior. Knowledge, or the lack thereof, will affect every aspect of a person's life. At the same time, however, life decisions and actions are not based on knowledge alone. Personal perceptions, feelings, motivations, and emotions all affect behavior. Therefore, life cannot be approached solely on the basis of rationality.

As we examine Christian leadership, we must therefore recognize that the mind plays a central role in shaping the structure of life, which in turn determines the nature of our existence. Christian transformation occurs through the renewal of the mind (Rom. 12:2). The renewal of the mind affects both the cognitive and affective domains. There is to be a change not only in how one sees the world, but also in how one feels about life. This is to result in a change in how one acts.

The Holy Spirit should guide the expression of feelings or thoughts into words or actions. Anger, wrath, malice, slander, and foul talk must be transformed into compassion, kindness, lowliness, meekness, and patience (Col. 3:5–17). However, that transformation will not automatically occur in anyone. Spiritual discipline and personal commitment are required.

For one to grow as a leader, more than one's emotional life must come under the direction of the Holy Spirit. Responsibilities must be recognized if duties are to be carried out effectively. No matter how great one's motivation or how disciplined one's personal life, without the proper knowledge to do one's work, the individual is left powerless.

Some leaders in the church pit knowledge that comes from hard work and study over against spiritual discernment. These argue that the former is not important; the latter is all that matters. That is not a biblical view. Knowledge is important at every level of life. Knowledge of the gospel is essential for salvation (Rom. 10:14–17). To grow in the faith, Christians need knowledge of the Bible and the ability to apply that knowledge to the issues of daily life. Without proper knowledge, people perish (Hos. 4:6).

A problem begins once we separate knowledge into categories of "sacred" and "secular." For the Christian, life cannot be subdivided into spiritual and nonspiritual components. Faith in God must be linked to every aspect of life. Once these divisions begin, so-called secular knowledge becomes suspect; however, this is a false dichotomy. Knowledge is a tool or a resource. The division of life into "sacred" and "secular" categories has often hindered the church in the proper utilization of knowledge. This is true in the area of church leadership.

Leadership is both an art and a science. As an art it is closely tied to the personal intuition, feelings, instincts, and sensitivity of individual leaders. Such qualities are not so much taught as they are inherent to the individual. Furthermore, they play a major role in shaping how we relate to both life circumstances and other people. As a science, leadership is based on theories and techniques. While no social science claims the same precision or verifiability as the natural sciences, nevertheless, certain generalizations can be developed with respect to leadership practices, which, if employed, are more likely to lead to desired outcomes than if one acts solely on the basis of intuition. This is not an either/or process, though. Effective leadership embodies both intuition and theory.

Summary

From a Christian perspective, leadership theories must be screened through a biblical framework that focuses on the fundamental values of faith in Christ. Christian leadership is a charismatic reality depending primarily on the guidance of the Holy

Spirit. It must be recognized, though, that from an organizational perspective, many of the findings that apply to leadership in general, also apply to church leadership. This is true because, as was noted earlier, the church is not only a spiritual reality, but also a social institution subject to the same forces that govern the life of other social realities. Therefore, knowledge related to leadership practices in social organizations is important to church leaders. Rather than being avoided, such knowledge should be studied, analyzed, and applied when helpful in fulfilling the mission of the church.

Leadership skills do influence how effective church leaders can be. Some tend to confuse the leading of the Spirit with intuition or feelings; however, spiritual leadership goes beyond feelings and is based on love and the effective use of resources. That requires planning as well as prayer. Church leaders must actively work at growing in their knowledge of the Bible and other disciplines relevant to their leadership responsibilities. They must be able to understand the meaning and implications of biblical Christianity in relationship to their own personal, historical, and cultural setting. Finally, leaders must be capable of building, sustaining, and nurturing relationships with other people in a way that strengthens the church and promotes the gospel.

9

STRUCTURAL DYNAMICS: BUILDINGS AND MEETINGS

I N HIS DEFENSE BEFORE the Jewish council, Stephen said, "Yet
the Most High does not dwell in houses made with hands"
(Acts 7:48). Nevertheless, that truth has not slowed down the
construction of "the house of God." Church buildings have
played a prominent role in the life of congregations since the 3rd
century. Furthermore, their use reflects both the life and mission
of local congregations.

A Historical Perspective

J. G. Davies has conducted extensive research on the development and use of church buildings. The following summarization
reflects some of his findings.

(1) *The church did not own buildings until the third century.*
Around AD 200, Minucius Felix made the following comment:
"We have no temples or altars." According to Davies, this statement accurately describes the state of the church at that time. [1]
He identifies three reasons why the early church did not own or
construct its own buildings. [2] First, the funds were not available
to engage in any large-scale building programs. Second, congregations were normally small and did not need large facilities.
Third, as potential victims of persecution, it would have been
unwise for Christians to draw attention to themselves through
public building programs.

Perhaps more important than any practical reasons for not
owning church property was the theological perspective of the
early church. Unlike Judaism, the early church did not associate

the worship of God with a particular place or location. The focus
was not on a temple or building, but on the spiritual reality of
the people of God. Believers did not *go* to church; rather, the
church *assembled* together. The emphasis was not on the place, but
on the gathering together. For this reason the biblical writers
never used the word church (*ekklēsia*) to describe a building. It
was used only to refer to the assembly of believers, either in a
local or universal sense. Davies indicates that many early Christian
writers emphasized this point. For example, Hippolytus noted,
"It is not a place that is called church, nor a house made of
stones and earth. . . . What then is the church? It is the holy
assembly of those who live in righteousness."[3] According to
Clement of Alexandria, "it is not the place but the assembly of
the elect that I call church."[4]

This view of the church reflects the NT emphasis on the
community of believers. A temple not made by human hands replaces the physical temple. The assembly of believers becomes the
temple of the Holy Spirit (1 Cor. 3:16). Buildings played no prominent role in the worship of God in the early church.

(2) The early church met primarily in houses. House churches
were common during the first three centuries. They are regularly
referred to in the NT (1 Cor. 16:19; Col. 4:15; Phlm. 2). Davies
notes that the dining room, which was usually located on the top
floor of the house (Acts 20:7, 8), was most frequently used for
meetings. Not only was it generally the largest room, but it also
lent itself to the common meal which was a central element in the
act of worship.

Normally these houses were owned by a congregational member who lived there and invited the church to use the home for
its gatherings. According to Davies, some changes in this arrangement took place during the 3rd century. As congregations grew
in size, wealth, and influence, they began to acquire, either
through gift or purchase, their own houses. Such places of assembly could be called "the house of God," a phrase used by
Tertullian.[5]

Davies illustrates this development by describing a house
located at Dura Europos on the Euphrates which was built shortly
after AD 200. A Christian congregation acquired the house in
AD 231 and modified it to serve as a meeting place. In addition
to knocking out walls to make a meeting room to accommodate

50 people, a baptistery was added to the right of the entry-way. The exterior, however, was not altered and maintained a domestic appearance.[6] Later in that century more elaborate buildings began to be constructed for church use.

(3) *As the church began to own its own buildings, it became viewed as sacred-space much in the same way as other religious temples or shrines.* With the ascendancy of Constantine, church buildings began to play a more prominent role in the life of local congregations. Eusebius indicates that bishops began to acquire money, property, and materials to build churches.[7]

As church buildings became viewed as sacred, the nature and use of the buildings began to change. The common meal, which was a central element of the worship service in homes, was reduced to a celebration of the bread and wine. The buildings lent themselves to a greater degree of formality and a clearer distinction between priest and laity. This viewpoint persisted throughout the Middle Ages until the Reformation, when Luther, Calvin, and Anabaptist leaders began to redefine the nature of church buildings. The Protestant leaders tended to strip away the emphasis from "holy buildings" and focused it more on "holy people." The Protestant churches moved away from the Gothic structures, which were believed to be too closely identified with Catholicism, to more modest rectangular auditoriums, often with galleries. However, according to Davies, even though these buildings may not have been viewed theologically as "holy places," in practice they were treated as such. Later this led to the development of church halls, which were used for social purposes while the sanctuary was reserved as sacred-space for worship and preaching.

The Reformation had no impact on the Roman Catholic Church's view of church buildings as sacred-space. The view that had been held throughout the Middle Ages—that church buildings were to be patterned after Solomon's Temple—continued. The Anglican Church also adopted this viewpoint.

While many of the Reformers reacted against the elaborate quality and design of Catholic churches and advocated a greater degree of simplicity, the designs of the architects of baroque cathedrals reflected their view of the holiness and majesty of God. Influential architects, such as Leon Battista Alberti (1404-72), translated their theological perspectives into magnificent architectural realities. According to Davies, the belief that God is the king of kings, required that church buildings display all the glory that was due him. As a result, baroque architecture "was inspired by the desire to offer to God all the riches of the world."[8] Davies comments, "The mine and slave owners, who financed these buildings, were concerned to honour God by decorating his palaces with the greatest possible sumptuousness and at the same time to thank him for the treasures he had bestowed upon them."[9] This also resulted in a more pompous and elaborate liturgy.

Church Buildings: Contemporary Issues

Since the Reformation the debate over the use, design, and function of church buildings continues to rage, and for a variety of reasons. One of the central issues today is cost. The primary issue with respect to cost is whether or not a congregation can justify spending large amounts of money on land, buildings, maintenance, and utilities when much of the human race is coping with inadequate housing, malnutrition, and poor health care. The question of how a church spends its money is not simply a financial issue, but is very much a moral one. We must begin by asking what does Scripture tell us about the use of money for buildings and the mission of the church.

In the OT great sums of wealth were expended in the construction of the temple. The temple not only symbolized the majesty of God, but was the place of direct access to his presence. But for Christians, the temple ceased to function in either capacity. First, the majesty of God was no longer attached to any building. Instead, the glory of God was reflected in earthen vessels (2 Cor. 4:6, 7). Second, all Christians have direct access to God through Jesus Christ by the gift of his Spirit. Therefore a particular place or location was unimportant. This was true for Jesus as well as for the early church.

The early church placed no emphasis on the purchase of property or the construction of buildings. While facilities of some kind were required for meetings, the focus was not on the meeting place, but on the charismatic life of the assembly. More attention was given to caring for the poor and helping those in need. This commitment surfaced directly from the life of Christ. Jesus identified with the poor, the sick, the destitute, and the outcast. Jesus' followers embraced these same commitments.

The biblical emphasis is on God's concern for human life. Direct warnings are given to those who would seek to accumulate material possessions, not because the possessions are bad, but because the love of possessions destroys the foundation for life. The Christian perspective is "for we brought nothing into the world, and we cannot take anything out of the world, but if we have food and clothing, with these we shall be content" (1 Tim. 6:7–8). While the early church did not own a building, it did develop a relief system to care for the poor. It must be concluded that the ownership of property must be evaluated in light of a higher value—that is, human need and welfare.

The problem in relating that to church buildings today is that economic decisions and their implications are not always clear-cut. The economic realities of our age are complex, difficult to understand, and impossible to forecast. They are inexorably linked to the political, social, and technological structures of modern life. The life situation and circumstances of the poor and needy cannot be separated from these power-structures. Furthermore, as a social institution, the church is a member of the power-structure.

Church structures can and do contribute to the plight of the world's outcasts. Furthermore, power and authority in the church are tied to the way in which Christians use money. There is little to indicate that Christians or churches use money differently than other individuals or groups.

It can be argued that churches have spent too much money on buildings at the expense of human need. Yet the real issue is not a general one but a specific one of personal accountability to God and neighbor concerning the use of money. Every situation has a unique set of circumstances which impacts how money is spent, what facilities are needed, and how facilities are used. It is easy to condemn church building programs in light of global human needs. The real problem, however, is not with building programs, but with the equitable distribution of goods and resources. Some congregations have invested sizeable sums of money into facilities, but in return the use of those facilities has enabled the same congregation to multiply that investment many times over. The focus should not be that buildings are costly and therefore bad, but that the church's use of money should be based on biblical values that recognize the need to promote God's love and justice in the world.

To build or to help the poor are not mutually exclusive options. Those who would reduce this to a simple dichotomy fail to recognize the potential complexities and paradoxes. First, churches must use money to help the poor and to proclaim biblical commitments and values. The jar of costly perfume must be broken—even wasted. Such decisions are not rational. Second, churches must also be good stewards and use funds wisely. That requires reflection and hard work. These two commitments can create tensions in deciding how to use money.

A congregation's use of money and facilities must reflect a sensitivity to the social setting and environment of the church. Whether property is owned or not, or what kind of facilities are used, have a significant impact on the congregation's ability to fulfill its mission. On the one hand, facilities can discriminate and create barriers to the gospel. On the other hand, they can promote interaction, learning, and personal and corporate growth. The question is not simply whether or not to own property, but how that property is used.

The Use of Buildings

The focal point of most church buildings is the sanctuary. It is used for worship, preaching, and for other events including funerals, weddings, baptisms, educational classes, congregational meetings, musical presentations, and plays. However, many sanctuaries are used only a few hours each week. This circumstance causes some to question whether the church can justify spending large sums of money on such idle facilities.

There are two primary reasons why sanctuaries have sparse use. One reason is that most sanctuaries have fixed pews that greatly restrict the use of the building. A second reason derives from the view that the sanctuary is sacred-space and must be protected from any secular or social use. Therefore, only events of a sacred or spiritual nature can be conducted in the sanctuary. Pews were not introduced into church buildings until the 13th century. Prior to then no seating was provided except for the aged or handicapped. By the 16th century many churches were equipped with wooden seats. [10]

The high cost of construction affects the design and use of some church buildings. Some sanctuaries are now being designed as a multipurpose room. Moveable seats are used instead of pews. Thus the sanctuary doubles as a worship center and a fellowship hall. Often the intent is to view such a building as stage one in a multiphased-plan of development which is to lead to the construction of a traditional sacred-space sanctuary. It is unlikely that the use of sanctuaries will undergo any dramatic changes in the future. However, such limited use must be called into question.

The selection of portable chairs instead of fixed pews can greatly enhance the use of the sanctuary. Such chairs allow for various seating arrangements that are more conducive for sharing and interaction. Fixed pews reinforce one-way communication from the pulpit to the congregation. Little if any personal interaction occurs. It hinders the charismatic life of the church.

From a NT perspective nothing supports the view that buildings are sacred. Therefore it may be argued that facilities should be designed and selected to support the congregational mission in the most functional, yet least expensive way. However, it must be remembered that expensive is a relative term and what is expensive in the short-term may prove to be cost-effective in the long-run.

The cost for artistic design and aesthetic beauty are not easy to evaluate. While the Reformers were correct in their critique of the extravagance in the church, we must be careful not to undervalue the importance of symbolism. On the one hand, the majesty of God demands the best that we have to offer him. On the other hand, God identifies with the poor, and our use of funds and way of life must also reflect that commitment. The key is to maintain a balance and to recognize that there is room for both symbols in the life of the church.

One final point needs to be made concerning facilities and congregational size. A congregation may arrive at a point of equilibrium where the existing facilities maintain the activities of the church, but do not allow for growth. Frequently, larger facilities are the only alternative considered. While larger facilities may be justified, other options may prove to be more productive in the actual fulfillment of the church's mission.

The life and vitality of any church must be distinguished from the facilities it chooses to use. During the past 30 years, the Chinese church has experienced sustained growth even though its buildings were confiscated. Yet in the United States it is not un-common to hear the argument that inadequate facilities limit church growth. On occasion that might be true, but the true vitality of the church cannot be tied to a building.

While buildings may be an asset, they can also be a liability. They may drain a congregation's financial resources, limit its size, and define the type of meetings that it plans. More impor-tant than being a building, a church's design must contribute to the realization of the mission of the church and the development of its members' life. The ultimate key is not a program or a place, but the community of the Spirit united in faith, hope, and love.

Specific Types of Meetings and Activities

To develop a well-balanced framework for Christian growth, different types of events must be planned. The setting will vary from one event to another. In general, meetings or activities can be classified in the following categories of worship, education, fel-lowship, service, and evangelism.

(1) Worship. Corporate worship is central to Christian life. It provides the context for mutual edification, inspiration, celebra-tion, awe, and reflection. Ralph Martin defines worship as "the dramatic celebration of God in his supreme worth in such a man-ner that his 'worthiness' becomes the norm and inspiration of human living."[11] Martin notes that the practice of worship is a "veritable kaleidoscope of patterns and forms" throughout Chris-tendom.[12] Forms of worship vary from informal charismatic house meetings to highly structured liturgical productions.

Not all forms of or approaches to worship are equally desir-able. While there is not a set biblical pattern for worship, certain themes do emerge that should play a prominent role in how wor-ship is conducted. Praise, teaching, prayer, public confession, cele-bration of the Lord's Supper, Bible reading, baptism, and giving —both of one's self and one's resources—are important dimen-sions of worshiping of God. The Holy Spirit is central to Chris-tian worship. We are baptized into one body by the Spirit (1 Cor. 12:13). The giving of gifts for the common good is a work of the Spirit (1 Cor. 12:7). The Spirit inspires worship, helps us to pray, and leads us into all truth. The Spirit of God gives life.

(2) Education. Education is essential for the growth of every Christian. Historically Sunday School is a late addition to congregational structure, but the didactic or instructional dimension of Christian life has always been of major importance. As a teacher, Jesus used the educational techniques of his day to teach his followers about the kingdom of God. Education is necessary to help believers develop a world-view consistent with biblical revelation. The message of the Bible must be communicated to every follower of Christ to provide a biblical basis for decision making and action within the world. Christians must understand the implications of their faith for the complex and changing issues of modern life.

Approaches to Christian education must take into account the developmental issues facing individual believers within all age groups. Adults, for example, should not be viewed as a homogeneous group facing the same life questions and concerns. To be effective, adult education must utilize theories and techniques designed for adults. Learning must be viewed as a lifelong endeavor.

As church leaders plan congregational meetings, educational factors should play a significant role. However, this means more than simply scheduling a class, time, and teacher. If learning is to occur, it will require careful planning, preparation, and the utilization of instructional formats that reinforce the educational objectives. Education must mean more than simply conducting lectures. The process of planning these events will be more fully discussed in the next chapter.

(3) Fellowship. Fellowship allows people to establish, nurture, and sustain relationships. While most fellowship occurs at an informal level and on the basis of personal friendships, planned leisure activities significantly aid in developing the "social fabric" of the congregation. The building of the informal relationships provides the foundation for the support structures and greater in-depth sharing necessary for the maintenance of both personal growth and congregational life. Therefore, strategically designed fellowship activities are a critical aspect of the congregation's planned events.

(4) Service and Evangelism. As the body of Christ, the church matures as each believer is able to employ the gifts entrusted to him or her by the Spirit of God. While much of this ministry may be individually motivated and directed, it can be stimulated and reinforced through careful planning. Not every Christian is

able to share his or her gifts in the context of a worship service or other traditional church meetings. We must recognize that the use of ministry gifts extends beyond the context of traditional church meetings to the realities of everyday life.

We cannot avoid involvement in people's lives if we are truly to express the love of Christ. Whether it is organizing a work day to paint the house of an elderly person, collecting and distributing food to the needy, or working through community agencies, the church must include such items on its agenda.

Organized activities are also important to Christian evangelism. While each Christian is to share his or her own faith in a public way, a corporate framework must also be developed to aid the congregation in its biblical responsibility for world evangelization. Events such as mission conferences, visitation programs, and evangelistic Bible studies should be included in the design of a comprehensive strategy of evangelism.

Evangelistic efforts should be the result of careful planning that takes into account the needs of potential converts, strategies to proclaim the gospel, and support structures to enable Christians to become more effective in the sharing of their faith in Christ.

Planning Meetings and Activities

Designing the type of meetings and events that have been discussed above can be effectively accomplished only by developing a perspective that takes into account overall congregational life and mission. The key is to develop a supportive environment that reinforces Christian growth. The goal is to help Christians to develop a way of life, not simply to be involved in numerous activities. Actually, a person can attend church quite regularly on Sunday morning without getting to know other people. When that person is absent it can easily go unnoticed. Therefore, it becomes imperative that congregations develop the support structures that undergird community and partnership. One essential factor is to organize both informal and formal activities for meeting needs related to worship, education, fellowship, service, and evangelism.

Some congregations have three services a week—Sunday morning, Sunday evening, and a midweek service. Frequently these meetings follow a similar design. The pastor speaks to the people who sit and listen. Not only does such a format discourage interaction and the building of relationships, it is one of the worst possible approaches to learning. In order to strengthen congregational life, church meetings must be redesigned to encourage the formation of partnership and community.

One meeting, such as a large group gathering on Sunday morning, cannot meet every need. In designing meetings attention must be given to such factors as participants' needs, setting, arrangements, format, leadership skills, content, and size. Many different settings and formats should be used. For example, during a twelve-month period the following resources and settings should be considered in responding to congregational needs and mission:

1. Worship Services	15. Discipling
2. Home Hospitality	16. Ministry Trips
3. Personal Devotions	17. Recreational Activities
4. Fellowship Meetings	18. Hospital Visitation
5. Small Groups	19. Meals
6. Classes	20. Plays, Drama
7. Conferences	21. Musical Presentations
8. Committees	22. Church Newsletter
9. Work Groups	23. Cassette Tapes
10. Choir	24. Books
11. Ministry Groups	25. Video Tapes
12. Retreats	26. Radio
13. Seminars	27. Television
14. Counseling	28. Computer Programs

Few congregations avail themselves of the variety of settings and tools at their disposal. Since adult needs and interests vary, a planning approach that uses multiple settings and topics will be more effective than one that does not.

One question is how many meetings a congregation should sponsor in the course of a week or month. This will vary from one church to another depending on congregational size, needs, and resources. Since people have different needs, more than one type of support program will be required. For example, a young person who enters a live-in drug rehabilitation program may require a very structured and supportive environment. In the course of a week he may attend five chapel services, three church services, a Sunday school class and several Bible studies. On the other hand, a mature believer who works full-time in a Christian ministry will need less structured support. Single adults may desire more planned activities than married couples with young children at home. The key is to recognize that people face different problems and personal needs. What is important is not how many meetings a person attends, but the quality of available support that leads to Christian maturity. Church leaders must work at building and maintaining such support systems.

Summary

Church buildings and planned events play a major role in defining the life of a congregation. The challenge the church faces today is to construct church facilities that combine wise stewardship, meaningful symbolism, and productive use. To do this, congregations must reflect on the use of their funds in relationship to all levels and dimensions of human need. Careful attention must be given to not only congregational needs, but social and global needs as well. Furthermore, the type, setting, and frequency of activities must be integrated into an intentional design of ministry that embodies biblical values and responds to the spiritual needs and developmental issues and tasks of congregational members. This requires a balance between formally planned worship, education, fellowship, service, and evangelism and the reinforcement of spontaneous and informal involvement of congregational members in one another's lives.

— 10 —

PLANNING AS A SPIRITUAL DISCIPLINE

N O CHURCH CAN EXIST without structure. Greeley is emphatic in that "a community without structure is a non-existent community, because all human groups, even the most simple, quickly evolve established patterns of behavior."[1] However, no two churches develop identical structures. As Dudley observes, many factors contribute to the individuality of a congregation including its policy, location, history, leadership, environment, culture, theological orientation, and membership.[2]

Structures evolve in many different ways. Once in existence, though, they are not easy to change. Therefore it becomes imperative that we build structures supportive of ministry goals. Strategies must also be developed to change ineffective structures. Such strategies are easier to outline on paper than they are to implement successfully in practice.

Structural Foundations

Supportive structures do not automatically appear. They must be thoughtfully built on a solid foundation consisting of biblical insight, theological awareness, social responsibility, practical understanding, and ethical commitment. Failure to plan adequately will result in structures that are less likely to provide adequate support toward the fulfillment of mission goals. On the other hand, structures that emerge out of a clear sense of mission and partnership within the congregation will enable the local church to be more effective in its ministry.

Reasons for Planning

There are two basic reasons for planning. Simply stated they are: (1) To know where you are going; and (2) to figure out how to get there. A well-known Christian leader was asked, "If you only had four years left to live, what would you do?" His response was, "I would spend the first year planning what I would do in the remaining three."

Too often, church leaders take a reactionary approach to planning. Significantly, the history of the early church is called the *Acts of the Apostles* and not the *Reactions of the Apostles*. Congregations must develop proactive strategies for their future. We must become initiators of change rather than simply responders to change. That requires planning.

One of the primary reasons that clergy leave the ministry is the feeling that they are operating by the "seat of their pants." Many ministers are not adequately trained in the practical areas of organizational development and administrative leadership that are essential parts of congregational life. A lack of competency in these areas will limit congregational effectiveness and inhibit church growth. Unfortunately, many institutions that train ministers place inadequate emphasis on these practical areas, even though they are vital for pastoral ministry and congregational life. To be effective, pastors must demonstrate a broad range of competencies beginning with the biblical and theological disciplines, but extending into practical areas related to organizational, administrative, and social skills.

Some individuals tend to view planning as contrary to or in some way hindering the leading of the Holy Spirit. The assumption is that spontaneous actions are more spiritual and therefore superior to carefully designed "human" plans, which allow little opportunity for flexibility. Such plans are thought to place God in a box, leaving little room for the Spirit's work.

Planning can create barriers to spontaneous change. In part, that is one of the contributions of planning! Not all spontaneous change is good or desirable. Nor should it be assumed that actions that are spontaneous are more spiritual than those which arise out of careful planning and reflection. The gift of administration is no less spiritual than the gifts of healing or speaking in tongues (1 Cor. 12:28).

Congregational meetings are to be conducted with a sense of order and reverence. This does not mean that there should be no spontaneity or charismatic expression, for the church should be a charismatic body. Nevertheless, it should be remembered that only a fine line separates spontaneity from confusion. Without planning, the latter is likely to occur and we know that confusion is not biblical (1 Cor. 14:33).

Rather than viewing planning as a barrier to the Holy Spirit, it should be understood as opening up new possibilities for the Spirit to lead us. Proper planning is not a cold, sterile process, but one that emerges out of spiritual discipline. The formulation of strategies and goals should emerge as much as from prayer and Bible study as from organizational insights. It should not be viewed as an either/or process, but as one that encompasses a broad range of *both* spiritual *and* organizational disciplines. The fact that the church exists as a social reality demands the latter. The reality of the church as the community of the Spirit requires the former. Effective planning is a spiritual enterprise that demands careful preparation, creative expression, and personal commitment. Those gifted in the church as administrators will have skills in these areas. Regardless of our place in the church, we will be better equipped to follow the Spirit's leading if we are prepared!

The Benefits of Planning

There are numerous benefits to planning. Some of these include the following:

(1) When approached as a spiritual discipline, planning opens up new possibilities, direction, and insights from the Holy Spirit. Planning that is energized by the Holy Spirit results in both personal and corporate edification. The individual benefits by seeking God, exploring the Scriptures, personal reflection, and through developing a holistic approach to planning that provides perspective and balance. The church benefits when leaders have a clear vision for the future that arises out of personal commitment to the lordship of Christ, an openness to the leading of the Holy Spirit, and a systematic approach to planning that maintains a comprehensive overview of congregational life and mission in light of biblical, social, and organizational insights. Once leaders are able to translate a vision for congregational life into an effective strategy for

mission and action, every member of the church should find the resulting structure and framework more able to empower individual believers in their work for Christ. The result should be the overall edification of the body of Christ (Eph. 4:11f).

(2) Planning provides the context to consider alternative courses of action which may lead to very different end results. Not all ministry outcomes are equally desirable, and some outcomes are not desirable at all. Planning allows leaders to consider these outcomes in advance, and to reflect on the meaning of these consequences for the life of the church. If no planning is done, the future becomes mortgaged to random activities and *ad hoc* commitments. We find ourselves always responding to environmental conditions over which we have little control.

(3) Planning helps us to consider the future in light of the present and the past. The question, "How do you get to Chicago?" cannot be answered until one knows the point of departure. We are not simply going somewhere, we are coming from somewhere. To make meaningful plans for the future we must begin by realistically assessing where we are and where we have been.

Social structures do not change overnight. Institutions arise out of routine behavior; patterns develop over time and become the distinctives of its structure. These patterns represent an institutional "momentum" that is not easily redirected. Those responsible for planning must identify the force of that momentum. In part, this is done by monitoring the history, traditions, and values of the congregation. Any plan which greatly deviates from these factors is likely to cause upheaval. On the other hand, those who acknowledge and understand the congregation's history will be in a better position to advocate change. Therefore, whoever plans must make an effort to reflect critically on and review the overall life and history of the local church.

First, a congregation must review its life and mission in relationship to the biblical message. The question should be asked whether or not a proper balance exists in the church between such biblical emphases as evangelism, worship, and caring for the poor. Are certain areas being promoted at the expense of others? Is a restructuring of priorities and commitments necessary to achieve a balance with biblical themes and emphases? Before these questions can be answered, a biblical perspective on the mission of the church must be developed.

Second, a congregation must develop a self-understanding of its own life. Important questions such as the following must be answered: What are the perceptions and feelings of members about the structure and mission of the church? What are the primary forces shaping those perceptions? What needs exist within the congregation, and which of those needs are most important?

Third, a congregation must examine its standing in the local community as well as review environmental factors that will impact its future. This may include an examination of economic projections, employment data, building forecasts and so on. Other questions must focus on how the church is perceived in the community. What kind of reputation does the congregation have? How do different community groups perceive the church? How do those perceptions correspond to the self-perception of the congregation itself?

Fourth, the church must review its mission in light of the church worldwide. How does the congregation relate to the larger church world? Has the congregation isolated itself from important issues and concerns that need attention from all Christians? Is the church participating in a meaningful way with the entire body of Christ? Does the church promote well-being in its relationships with other congregations?

Fifth, the local church must explore its life and mission in relationship to the pressing world agenda. An understanding must be present that the church is part of a global community with common concerns related to energy, food, the environment, the poor, economic issues, and the paramount issue of nuclear destruction. Christians cannot avoid the concerns of mankind without violating their reason for being—to bring light and life into a world of death and darkness. For this reason local congregations must develop a global perspective in reviewing their own ministry commitments.

Sixth, congregational finances must be carefully studied. How is the money being used? Is its use compatible with the congregation's mission and the biblical material? What is the financial base of the congregation? Will that base change in the near future? Does the congregation have a budget? Does the congregation responsibly oversee all of its resources?

Future planning takes on meaning only when it is conducted with a sense of appreciation for and understanding of the past and present. Each of the above areas plays an important role in coming to such an understanding.

(4) Planning can help build shared goals and mutual commitments among leaders and congregational members. When planning is conducted as a shared process, involving both leaders and those who will carry out the plans, the likelihood of success increases. The opportunity to interact, dream, and finally to arrive at a consensus produces a powerful bonding element between those involved in the planning process. However, for this to occur the process must be open allowing for full discussion and expression. All who have participated in the planning process must own the end result.

(5) Planning provides a basis for action. Planning is of little value unless specific ideas and strategies are translated into concrete actions. While the plans cannot guarantee specific outcomes, they do clarify what should and can be done to move toward a future that is desirable and to avoid one that is not.

(6) Planning increases congregational effectiveness. A congregation is effective only to the extent that it achieves its desired outcomes based on the biblical mandate in light of prevailing circumstances. An ineffective congregation is one that, for whatever reason, is not adequately fulfilling its biblical mission. Based on the above discussion, our ability to plan and implement carefully designed strategies should lead to a greater degree of effectiveness in fulfilling our mission. However, one point must be kept in focus. The life of the church can never be sustained or brought to life on the basis of planning. The Spirit of God is the only essential basis for meaningful and effective congregational life. That basis distinguishes the church from all other social realities.

All successful enduring organizations plan. However, any congregation that places planning at the center of its existence will quickly become sterile. Only when planning becomes a spiritual discipline, empowered, sustained, and directed by the Spirit of God, does it takes on vitality within the church. Spirit-directed planning, however, provides the necessary framework for decision making that aids the congregation in fulfilling its mission. Congregations with such a plan can expect to be effective as individual members band together with singleness of mind and heart to fulfill the calling of God through specific actions and commitments.

Approaches to Planning

The matrix in Figure 10-1 illustrates one way the planning process can be examined. The four dimensions in the matrix related to planning are tactical, strategic, intuitive, and intentional.

Two types of planning are tactical and strategic. Tactical planning is responsive in nature. More limited in its scope, it tends to be both short-term and reactionary. For example, if a fire damaged the church facilities a tactical response would be required. Temporary plans would be developed to respond to many different needs including where the congregation would meet.

Strategic planning is visionary in nature. Rather than only responding to circumstances, strategic plans are designed to shape future circumstances in a way the planners view as desirable and, to the extent possible, to avoid undesirable circumstances. Often, tactical planning and strategic planning overlap.

Two approaches to the planning process are intuitive and intentional. An intuitive approach to planning is based on personal insights, feelings, instincts, beliefs, and emotions. It is a "gut-level" reaction. On the other hand, an intentional approach to planning is based on the systematic collecting, analyzing, interpreting, and application of relevant data. The intuitive approach is the art of planning; the intentional approach is the science of planning. Both play an important role in the planning process.

The matrix in Figure 10-1 is based on the intersection of the *two types* of planning (tactical and strategic) with the *two approaches* to the planning process (intuitive and intentional). The result is the four quadrants discussed below.

Types of Planning

		Tactical	Strategic
	Intuitive	1	2
Approaches to Planning			
	Intentional	3	4

FIGURE 10-1

Tactical-Intuitive (quadrant 1). Tactical-intuitive planning is short-term and reactionary. Based on personal feelings and insights, coping patterns characterize this approach to the planning process. In a personal emergency, such responses are instinctive. However, organizations which exist within dynamic environments and rely heavily on tactical-intuitive approaches to planning will experience ongoing turbulence and instability. One result will be psychological displacement among employees and low morale resulting from never knowing what the destiny of the organization is from one day to the next. While skilled leaders, drawing on years of experience and insight, are able to make good tactical-intuitive decisions, if that process becomes the norm for the organization, problems are inevitable. Environmental circumstances control the destiny of that organization.

Tactical-Intentional (quadrant 3). Tactical-intentional planning anticipates different scenarios in advance, and based on the best data available, it develops a range of limited responses to the probable outcomes. Such planning recognizes that unintended outcomes are possible and develops contingency plans. Rather than being guided by intuition alone, a tactical-intentional approach reacts according to a predefined set of options based on research and analysis.

Strategic-Intuitive (quadrant 2). A strategic-intuitive approach to planning often characterizes organizations headed by a strong, charismatic leader. Such leaders often use instinct to guide and direct the organization. The risks associated with this approach increase in direct proportion to the complexity of the organization and the degree of turbulence in the environment. Hunches can only carry people or institutions so far. However, intuition may be the deciding factor when the decision makers are faced with a range of options that are based on research, but which are inconclusive.

Strategic-Intentional (quadrant 4). Organizations which invest heavily in research and development value the strategic-intentional approach to planning. The goal of this method is to make long-term informed decisions that optimize the mission of the organization based on the best relevant information available. While this approach is the most expensive and time consuming, it is also the most effective. First, it requires the organization to define clearly its mission and to identify those environmental factors which affect its future. Second, time must be taken to assess these factors and their impact on the organization's mission. Third, plans must be developed that take into account environmental forces, organizational resources, and the mission of the organization. The goal is to optimize the likelihood of the organization achieving its mission in the most effective and efficient way.

In today's rapidly changing environment, the strategic-intentional approach is essential—not just for secular organizations, but also for the church. For example, if the church is to develop effective ministries devoted to strengthening family life, it must first understand the kind of forces that are affecting family life and which are likely to have long-term implications for the nature of family development. If a local congregation is planning to build a new facility, it must first have a clear understanding of its mission and the type of space that will be needed to meet the needs of that mission. Many economic, social, and environmental factors will need examination.

Effective planning cannot be done in a vacuum. Furthermore, a spiritual dimension must guide how the church engages in the planning process that is not taken into account by secular organizations. Prayer must play a central role in the church's planning process. Some Christian leaders attempt to polarize God's leading through prayer and spiritual discernment from the hard work of collecting, assessing, interpreting, and applying information to the decision-making process. However, both processes are essential and are not contradictory. When yoked with the proper motivations and commitments, they form the basis for planning as a spiritual discipline.

The Process of Planning

Having examined the reasons for planning, the benefits of planning, and approaches to planning, we must now explore the process of planning. What follows is not intended to be a blueprint for all times and places, but rather an illustration of the kinds of issues the planning process should address. Seven planning steps will be examined below.

Step One: Clarifying the Mission

The planning process begins by developing a statement clarifying the mission of the congregation. This step involves defining the purpose of the congregation's existence. As such, the mission statement should express the biblical mandate for God's people in a particular setting. While this statement may change over time, the essence of the mission remains the same as it has since the Day of Pentecost. But the particular methods for carrying out the mission do change according to a particular setting. Congregations may express the mission of the church in different terms, emphasize unique priorities, and engage in various actions and commitments, but the essence of the church's mission transcends space and time.

The value of developing a mission statement is not just the result, but the process itself. It aids in promoting the spirit of partnership, shared goals, and common commitments among participants. Several important benefits to the congregation emerge from that process.

(1) The development of a mission statement helps congregational members and leaders to think biblically about the church. As a normative expression of the mission, the statement attempts to embody the biblical mandate given to the church. This forces those involved in drafting the statement to review and enter into dialogue with the Bible in an attempt to understand, identify, and communicate scriptural directives and themes concerning mission and commitments for congregational life.

(2) The mission statement helps congregational members and leaders to reflect on the message of the Bible as it relates to their world and life circumstances, both as individuals and as corporate members of society and the world. The mission statement should enlighten the congregation as to what it means to be God's people today, and how the expression of Christian faith touches the world.

(3) The development of a mission statement helps Christians to think about how their church functions and provides a positive framework for them to consider how they think it ought to function. It helps members to consider why certain things are done and why others are not. This may lead to new emphases, a change in priorities, or it may reinforce well-established patterns.

(4) Finally, the development of a mission statement helps to promote partnership concerning the church's goals and commitments. A congregation that has a clear sense of identity and direction, and in which both leaders and members are committed to the same agenda, has a stronger foundation for congregational life than one where those traits are not present.

The lack of a mission statement will not hinder a congregation which has a clear sense of purpose and shared commitment in fulfilling that purpose. The key is not the mission statement, but the sense of vision, direction, and commitment which is present in the congregation. When clarity and commitment are not present, one can expect to encounter a variety of concerns that emerge as a direct result of conflicting perceptions or interpretations of what the church should be doing and how it should be done.

Step Two: Writing the Mission Statement

The question now addressed is the practical one of how a congregation develops a mission statement.

(1) Who should be involved in writing the statement? The response to this question determines the entire process. The answer depends on the size, leadership, and general state of affairs in the congregation. From a democratic perspective, the inclination is to invite as many people as possible to be involved. While there are certain advantages to that, not all congregations should lean in that direction. For example, a congregation with a history of problems may need strong outside leadership and support from judicatory officials or district officials. There may be a need for strong, directive leadership from the outside to help that congregation plan. The same may be true of a new congregation of recent converts who have little understanding or appreciation of the Scriptures. Since the mission statement is to reflect a normative expression of the biblical mandate for the church, it would be unwise to leave its development largely in the hands of novices in the faith.

When mature leaders are present to guide and oversee the process, the development of a mission statement can become an educational experience for everyone. However, when that is done and as many people are involved as possible, the leaders of the church should develop the basic framework of the statement in advance to ensure a solid biblical basis for the document.

Several positive results can emerge when most of the congregation are involved in the process. Those investing personal time and energy are more likely to feel some sense of commitment and obligation to the end result precisely because they had some part to play in its formation. A sense of partnership can emerge out of the process which helps to bind people together to fulfill a shared vision for the future of the congregation.

Adults show commitment to a thing to the extent that they have made some personal investment in whatever that thing might be. That investment may be in the form of time, money, personal energy, or moral commitment, but if that investment is not there, neither will there be much of a commitment. Therefore, the best of all circumstances exists when the formulation of a mission statement evokes high levels of personal investment from as many congregational members as possible, but in such a way that it does not set people up for the bitter disappointment if the mission does not proceed as expected.

The process must begin with congregational leaders and then extend into the life of the congregation in such a way that there is a clear sense of partnership. If leaders simply hand over a statement to members without their input, it will have little impact on their lives or their involvement in the congregation, unless some personal investment can be developed *post facto*. It will appear as a sterile doctrinal statement with little vitality. However, if the statement becomes the focus of serious attention and reflection, both through the pulpit and other mediums of communication, then it can serve a supportive role in defining commitment and clarifying vision for the future of the church. At some point the corporate body must formally commit to or ratify the statement.

However the statement evolves, or whether it evolves at all, one thing is essential: the leadership must have a shared understanding of congregational mission if any hope for effective ministry is to occur. If a mission statement is to be developed, that process should include all key leaders in the congregation.

(2) What should be included in the statement? The statement should consist of several parts reflecting the major biblical emphases concerning congregational life. Some writers categorize the mission of the church in terms of worship, instruction, fellowship, and evangelism. Others list such categories as spiritual journeying, caring, and empowering.[3] Whatever categories are used, they should be biblically based and should encompass the total breadth of the church's mission. Furthermore, the overall statement should reflect the particular emphases of the congregation in light of its own local ministry commitments.

(3) How should the statement be written? The process will vary depending on how many people are involved, the number of leaders who are available, and the amount of time and the nature of the facilities for completing the process.

Qualified leaders should identify in advance the primary biblical themes, images, or categories to be focused on in the statement. One approach is then to break into small groups to discuss the material and to identify ideas that can be used in writing statements in each defined category. Each group should be given the opportunity to present its findings. Later, the leadership should formulate a statement based on the interaction and findings of the groups concerning each mission area. The statement should then be presented to the entire congregation to stimulate reflection and discussion concerning the future mission and commitments of the congregation.

(4) How often should a mission statement be written or reviewed? If a congregation does not have a mission statement a good time to develop one is at the beginning of a major planning endeavor. Once the statement is written, the leadership should review it on an annual basis. It should be revised only if the congregation comes to a new understanding of its mission and alters its commitments.

The mission statement should be used to help potential members understand the direction of the congregation and the commitments that are expected by those who formally identify with the church. At least once a year, the pastor should develop a series of sermons focusing on the mission of the church. Ideally, this should occur near the time the church leaders gather to plan for the coming year. The goal is to maintain a clear sense of vision among the leaders and members for the mission of the church.

Developing a mission statement is simply the beginning of the planning process. Once the leaders and members of the church accept the statement, the next task is to identify and prioritize congregational needs. The statement provides a basic framework for exploring the question, Where are we in light of where we want to be? This leads us to the process of needs assessment.

Step Three: Assessing and Prioritizing Needs

A need can be defined as a gap between what is and what is desired. Closing that gap may involve increasing knowledge,

improving skills, changing attitudes, altering behaviors, or transforming the total situation. According to Pennington, needs can
deal with desires, interests, or deficiencies. [4] An assessment of
these needs can help congregational leaders identify desires and
interests in the congregation and community that deserve special
attention. While providing information to improve existing programs, a needs assessment can also help plan more intelligently
for the future.

There are at least five dimensions to a comprehensive identification of ministry needs: (1) normative needs; (2) expressed needs;
(3) felt needs; (4) comparative needs; and, (5) environmental needs.

(1) Normative Needs. In the process of assessing needs, some
opinions and insights should be more highly regarded and valued
than others. For example, a pediatrician has a greater understanding of the health needs of children than an architect. But if you
want to build a home, then the insights of the architect become
important. In considering the life and mission of the church, we
must ask where we can gain normative insights concerning
congregational needs.

The starting point in developing a normative needs assessment is understanding the Bible. One task of congregational
leaders is to identify, interpret, and apply biblical material to
guide congregational development. To aid this process, qualified
experts should be consulted. These individuals might include
seminary professors, denominational officers, or experienced pastors and leaders who have devoted their life to Christian service.
Selected books and articles can also provide valuable insights. Of
the five areas being considered, the normative assessment carries
special weight in the final analysis of the findings.

(2) Expressed Needs. A critical part of the needs assessment is
to document the expressed needs of the target group. If the needs
assessment focuses on the entire congregation, then as many
members as possible must be included in the study.

Two types of information should be collected from church
members. The first is what individual members view as congregational needs. For example, some mothers may feel the need
for more toys in the nursery. Other members may be concerned
with what time the services begin or end. These needs focus
on the congregation as it currently exists in contrast to what
is desired.

The second type of information to be collected focuses on individual needs. It attempts to clarify the question, "What are the primary needs in your life?" Some members may need help raising their children. Others may be coping with health problems or have a personal desire to grow in their knowledge of the Bible. These needs vary from one individual to another. Leaders need to know what needs exist among members and if certain needs are more prominent than others. For example, the church may need a class for young mothers or a greater focus on the concerns of older adults. People may be struggling with life issues that current church programs are not addressing. An expressed needs assessment can clarify those concerns.

Expressed needs can be identified through soliciting informal feedback, conducting personal interviews, or by distributing and collecting questionnaires. The best approach is one that combines several of these methods. If questionnaires are used they should be filled out and collected at the same time, otherwise, few will be returned.

(3) Felt Needs. Felt needs are present among congregational members, but ones which they are unlikely to express. They may not be shared out of fear of personal embarrassment, reprisal, being misunderstood, or of not wanting to hurt someone else. For example, a teenager may feel the need to talk about masturbation, but is unlikely to express that need openly. People will not share concerns with others if they believe they may be misunderstood. There are many reasons that felt needs remain unexpressed, but a comprehensive needs assessment should attempt to identify these needs as well. One approach is to use an unsigned questionnaire which encourages people to express needs without fear of personal identification.

(4) Comparative Needs Assessment. This technique examines a comparable situation to identify issues, concerns, strategies, and program ideas that can provide insights into one's own setting. For example, the youth minister may examine youth programs in other congregations in order to generate ideas and provide a framework for better understanding his or her own ministry. This approach can be applied to any area of congregational life. The review of past programs in one's own church can also be used to generate ideas.

(5) Environmental Needs Assessment. Churches cannot operate as closed systems. Leaders need an understanding of community

affairs and issues that impact the church. They should be aware of census data and other demographic information, and should be in touch with other community leaders.

A comprehensive needs assessment should be conducted well in advance of any major planning effort. Several approaches can be used to collect data. They include interviews, questionnaires, reviewing past programs, comparative studies, collecting informal feedback, and conducting a literature review. An examination of current Christian literature is a good place to start to identify trends and needs in the church. By spending a few hours in a local library or Christian bookstore, important themes can be identified which provide a perspective on congregational needs. Interviews should be conducted with key congregational leaders and other individuals who have an understanding of the life and mission of the church. Questionnaires can be distributed to any target group in the church. One example of assessing needs is outlined below:

1. Identify the particular areas or groups to be studied.
2. Determine the amount of time and resources that are available to conduct the study.
3. Design a strategy to collect data in each of the following needs assessment areas: (a) normative needs (b) expressed needs; (c) felt needs; (d) comparative needs; and (e) environmental needs.
4. Implement the data collection procedures.
5. Process and interpret the data.
6. Prepare the findings for the purpose of planning.

It is impossible to respond to each identified need. Therefore, needs must be prioritized in each area or category that was studied.

Step Four: Establishing Goals

Once needs have been identified, the next step is to establish goals. The purpose of goal setting is to identify what is to be accomplished during a specific period of time. Goal statements should be formulated on the basis of the mission statement and the needs assessment. If goals are achieved, this should help to close the gap between existing circumstances and desired circumstances. If they are to be effective, everyone who has some responsibility for seeing that they are fulfilled must comprehend what is to be achieved and what his or her specific role or duties are in seeing that the stated result is attained. Otherwise, lack of direction resulting in confusion and wasted effort can sabotage the process.

Several types of goals should be developed. First, long-term goals should be distinguished from short-term goals. Long-term goals should be developed first. They should clarify the direction and commitment of the church for the next three to five years or longer. Long-term goals also provide the context to develop short-term goals. Short-term goals focus on the specific actions needed to attain long-term goals, and the response to immediate needs.

For example, if a long-term goal is to establish a Christian radio station within the next four years, related short-term goals may focus on gaining approval from the FCC, securing funding, and locating a facility within a specific time frame. Other short-term goals will need to be established as the process unfolds to achieve the goal of putting the radio station on the air within a four-year period.

Step Five: Identifying Mission Tasks

Once the goals are developed, the next step is to identify and organize specific tasks to accomplish each goal. Large projects must be broken down into smaller, manageable tasks. Plans help to identify how many workers will be needed. They also help to clarify what workers will do and when it is to be done. Well-conceived plans increase the likelihood that goals will be accomplished. Once the plans are developed, the work should begin.

Step Six: Implementing and Monitoring Action Plans

Timing is a major factor contributing to the success or failure of any project. If a proper foundation has been developed, the actual work will proceed with less time, effort, and waste than if plans are whipped into place at the last minute or in a reactionary way. Results are also more likely to be positive. Unfortunately, many leaders do not prepare far enough in advance and then find themselves scrambling at the last minute to pull things together. Strategies based on careful reflection and relevant data are far more effective.

Once the work begins, tasks must be monitored. How this is done will depend on the complexity of the project, the number of people involved, and the deadlines that must be met. Leaders must stay informed on the development of important tasks or projects. Whether this is done on a daily, weekly, or on some other basis will depend on the specific goal being achieved.

Step Seven: Evaluation Procedures

The most difficult step in the overall process is evaluation. The most common approach is to evaluate goals to see if they were achieved. However, program evaluation goes beyond examining the fulfillment of goals. For example, a congregation may fulfill the goal of establishing three new adult elective classes on Sunday morning, but that tells us nothing about the value of those classes, their impact on either the individuals involved or the congregation, or to what extent those classes contributed to helping the church fulfill its mission. All we know is that three classes were started. A need exists to determine the value of those classes. Should they be continued, stopped, or modified in some way? What impact did the classes make on the church and on the lives of those involved? Evaluation involves value judgments. What is of value to one person may not be to another. Thus, the basis for value decisions must be clarified.

Just as there are different dimensions to assessing needs, the same is true concerning evaluating programs. Programs must be evaluated from different perspectives. The starting point is with the Bible. We must critically reflect on what we are doing and what we have done on the basis of biblical insights and understanding.

Second, evaluation must go beyond examining the fulfillment of goals. Rather, evaluation findings should portray the broad impact of plans, strategies, actions, commitments, and programs on the church and its members. Also, if possible, some assessment should be made of the impact on the surrounding community. For example, a church may set goals to increase membership. Suppose that at the end of the stated period the goals were not achieved. Does that mean that the program was a failure? The answer depends on the breadth and perspective of the evaluation.

If we examine the program only on the basis of the stated goals, we must conclude that it failed. However, that does not tell us the true impact of the program on the life of the church, on its individual members, or on the surrounding community. While the church may not have grown to the desired level of membership, perhaps the program contributed to a renewed sense of partnership among existing leaders and members. The program may have increased interest among nonactive members, or resulted in the healing of family problems. It may have inspired a new sense of hope and commitment within the church. However, if we only examine the program on the basis of the stated goals, the other outcomes will not be properly assessed or understood. The full impact of the program will go unnoticed and unappreciated. Therefore, if judgments are to be made about specific programs or commitments, the broad impact must be examined. This is known as goal-free evaluation. Focusing only on goals may be deceptive.

Evaluation techniques are similar to those used in assessing needs. Techniques can be formal or informal and include conducting personal interviews, soliciting informal feedback, distributing and collecting questionnaires, or utilizing various testing procedures. The findings can be presented in the form of a verbal or written report, or as a case study. A combination of these approaches is best.

Evaluation strategies should be planned before the event or program even begins. The evaluation process begins at the start of the program and not at the end. Evaluation must be ongoing. Findings should be used to modify the program if necessary. Once the program is over, evaluation findings should lead to preliminary judgments concerning future events. The results may help to identify issues or needs that should be taken into account when considering the future of the church.

Other Planning Considerations

In the remainder of this chapter, two other important factors will be explored. The first is the role of consultants in the planning process. The second is an examination of the church planning calendar.

Church Consultants

Increasingly, consideration is being given to using consultants in various aspects of the church's ministry. Several questions surface concerning the role of consultants in the church. They include: (1) Why should an outside consultant be used? (2) When should a consultant be invited? (3) How is a consultant selected? and, (4) What should be expected from a consultant?

(1) Why should a consultant be considered? A qualified consultant can make a valuable contribution to the local church. This is true for several reasons. First, someone from outside the congregation can bring a fresh sense of objectivity that contributes to a better understanding of congregational life. Second, a properly selected consultant should bring tested expertise that may not be available within the congregation, but which is vital to the planning process. Third, someone from outside the congregation can raise valid issues that may not be raised otherwise, especially if these issues appear to be self-serving. For example, if the pastor is being underpaid, he or she may feel uncomfortable raising it as a concern. If the consultant recommends a salary increase, it may be received differently than if the pastor recommends it. Fourth, once the consultant leaves, his or her recommendations can be accepted or rejected on the basis of their merit and there is not a personality left to deal with. On the other hand, if someone from within the congregation is called upon to do an analysis and make recommendations, if those recommendations are rejected, it may also involve feelings of personal rejection as well. This can lead to further complications. Fifth, in problematic situations, the consultant may help to provide the balance of power needed to move the congregation forward in a positive direction. Sixth and finally, a skilled and knowledgeable consultant more than pays his or her own way. Generally, the costs involved are minimal in light of the potential benefits if the congregation is prepared to utilize the skills of the consultant which it invites.

(2) When should a consultant be invited? Consultants should be employed for specific reasons. Information or advice is of no value if there are no plans to use it. One time to use a consultant is approximately every four years at the beginning of a major planning effort. The consultant can conduct a needs assessment or be involved in ministry evaluation. Consultants can also address specific problems or issues that require specialized expertise. This might occur during a building program or when planning to start a Christian school. The areas in which a consultant can help are almost unlimited.

(3) How is a consultant selected? When selecting a consultant several sources should be considered. Denominational churches should inquire with denominational officials to see what services they can provide or if they can make personal recommendations. Other sources are seminaries and Christian colleges. Professional associations such as the National Association of Church Business Administration can also provide referrals. Ministerial associations and colleagues in the ministry are also potential sources of assistance.

(4) What should be expected from a consultant? There should be a clear understanding and written agreement of what the consultant's responsibilities will be between the church leaders and the consultant before he or she ever comes. Church leaders need to negotiate with the consultant what will be done, how it will be done, when it will be done, and how much it will cost before any agreement is made.

Churches should not expect consultants to solve their problems. Consultants should be expected to provide expertise in sharing insights, collecting and interpreting data, and to provide recommendations if requested. Consultants should be viewed as helpers that can aid the church, but not as the answer to every church need.

Finally, while a consultant may be used only in special circumstances, an outside resource person should be invited to speak to the church leadership on a more frequent basis such as once a year. Not only can this provide needed inspiration, but can serve as an opportunity for continuing education for leaders and can address areas of need in the church. Some people address needs only when a problem is present. The best approach, however, is preventative care.

A consultant can be of great assistance to the pastor. Even though the pastor may be as qualified as the resource person, or even more so, yet it is helpful to have an outside person's perspective. At times someone from outside the congregation can present topics in a way that helps congregational members or leaders better appreciate the issues or concerns. The special nature of having an outside speaker can heighten both the importance and meaning of the event. In problematic situations such a person can play a vital supportive role in helping to maintain order and clarify direction.

The Planning Calendar

This final section addresses the question, When is the best time to plan? The general tendency is to wait too long and then pull everything together at the last minute. This can and should be avoided. One step to see that this does not happen is to develop a yearly planning cycle.

One approach to developing a planning cycle is to break the year down into smaller planning periods. These periods should have natural beginning and ending points. The school calendar often affects the identification of these periods because of its great impact on family life. For church planning, the following five periods stand out:

1. January–Easter
2. Easter–May
3. June–August
4. September–November
5. December

Each period has its own unique characteristics. The period from September–November provides a natural point to begin new programs. Children are returning to school and families are settling down from vacations and weekend travel. December is a month to itself. The Christmas season dominates this period. January–Easter is a solid block of time to initiate new ideas, make adjustments, and build toward Easter, one of two periods, along with Christmas, that provides a seasonly supported approach to evangelism and church growth. Easter through May is a time of new life and expectation. The summer months are more transitory. Outdoor activities increase, vacations are taken, and people are gone more frequently on the weekends. All of these factors play an important role in developing plans.

Several different types of planning meetings should be scheduled. They include: (1) a yearly planning retreat; (2) monthly reviews; (3) weekly and/or daily updates; and (4) once every three or four years a major congregational review.

(1) Yearly Planning Retreat. Some time during the year should be set aside to develop plans for the next calendar year. One of

the best times to do this is during the summer months. Concurrently, a review should be made of the upcoming fall events.

May provides a good time to conduct evaluations or needs assessments. Many events are winding down in anticipation of the summer months and it provides an appropriate time to solicit feedback. That information can then be used in making decisions about upcoming events at the yearly planning retreat.

If possible, this meeting should be held out of town away from possible interruptions. The best setting is one that provides a positive environment for personal interaction and fellowship. The retreat may last several days, but definitely should be overnight if possible. The experience of staying together helps to build camaraderie among the leadership. Recreational activities add to the building of personal relationships necessary for effective planning.

The key church leaders should attend the retreat. Normally this will include the pastoral staff and the elders or church board. In larger churches with a multiple staff, a separate retreat for the pastors may be beneficial. Each congregation must determine its own needs.

During the retreat consideration should be given to assessing where the congregation is with respect to its mission and goals. Several approaches can be taken in discussing the life of the congregation. One is to review the various subsystems that make up the functional areas of congregational life. These may include such areas as the Sunday services, Christian education, youth programs, ministry teams, leadership, buildings and grounds, and so on. Another approach is to consider the dimensions of the church's ministry which cut across all areas of congregational life. This may include such dimensions as discipleship, evangelism, worship, fellowship, and other biblically defined areas of Christian life and commitment.

While the primary focus of the meeting is to plan for the coming year (January–December), time should also be spent in reviewing plans for upcoming fall activities and commitments. Each person should come prepared with specific plans and ideas related to his or her own areas of responsibility.

If a mission statement has never been developed, the retreat provides a good setting for formulating one. The real goal is to leave the meeting with a clear sense of direction for the next year. This time together should also be inspirational. Bible reading, prayer, personal reflection, and sharing should play a major role in the retreat. Another minister or resource person might be invited to speak to the group on topics of inspiration and challenge.

(2) *Monthly Reviews.* Most churches have leadership meetings of one kind or another on a monthly basis. If clear plans have been developed for the entire year, then this meeting can be used to monitor events as well as to consider pending business. Leaders must continually be looking several months ahead while at the same time they consider the realities of the moment.

(3) *Weekly Reviews.* The pastor should maintain weekly contact with leaders who are working on important projects. It may come through a formal meeting, a phone call, or a brief informal visit. Communication is vital for effective ministry. In some cases, daily updates may be necessary. The point is to maintain the contact necessary for achieving the desired results. Lack of communication creates the environment for conflict, misunderstanding, frustration, and disappointment.

(4) *Major Congregational Review.* Depending on the size and nature of the congregation, a major congregational review should be planned every three or four years. The purpose of the review is to conduct a major needs assessment and to gather information to help leaders and members reflect on the life and direction of the church. The information can be used to formulate long-range plans, improve existing programs, and plan new events. Leaders should consider using an outside consultant to aid them in conducting and planning the review.

Every congregation is unique. Therefore major planning approaches will differ from one congregation to the next. One approach is outlined below.

Steps in Conducting a Congregational Profile: One Example

1. Leaders determine that a major review is in order.

2. An experienced and trusted consultant is contacted to help develop a profile of the congregation. His or her duties and responsibilities are negotiated and agreed on. The church leaders send a written confirmation to the consultant.

3. The consultant receives background information from the leaders concerning the church before arriving.

4. The consultant arrives at the church on a Friday morning and spends the day meeting with the pastor and other leaders and discussing the life and mission of the church.

5. On Friday evening, the church leaders meet with the consultant for dinner. Afterwards they review and clarify the mission of the church.

6. On Saturday morning, the consultant leads the group and conducts a normative needs assessment based on the leadership's perceptions of congregational life.

7. On Saturday afternoon, the consultant conducts individual interviews with the leadership to identify dreams, strengths, and needs concerning the church. Again this represents a normative assessment by the leadership.

8. During the Sunday morning service on the next day, the pastor gives a sermon which focuses on the mission of the church. At the conclusion, each person is asked to fill out a questionnaire which the consultant has prepared in collaboration with the church's leaders prior to his coming. The questionnaire focuses on personal needs, congregational needs, and demographic information. The questionnaire is collected before the people are dismissed. The congregation has been notified well in advance that this event will take place and members understand that the church is engaged in a major review of its commitments and direction.

9. On Sunday afternoon, the results of the questionnaire are tabulated. The consultant continues to conduct personal interviews if they are needed

10. On Sunday evening the consultant gives a preliminary verbal report to the leaders. A written report is to follow within the next several days.

11. During that week, congregational members meet in small groups in homes or at the church to share their dreams about the future of the church. Each group is led by one of the leaders who met with the consultant over the past weekend.

12. The following Friday, the leaders depart for an overnight retreat. That evening and Saturday are spent in discussing and prioritizing ministry needs. Both long-range and short-range goals are developed concerning the church's mission. Strategies are discussed to fulfill individual goals.

13. Over the next several weeks, the pastoral staff, church

leaders, and other involved workers develop detailed strategies to fulfill the goals. If needed, goals are refined and specific action plans are created.

14. Within a month, the pastor presents the leadership a comprehensive plan of action which then receives final approval.

It might be argued that what looks fine on paper rarely works out in reality. However, that is not always true. Actually, those who plan are much more likely to achieve desired results than those who do not. The latter become victims of their circumstances. The former shape their circumstances.

In the final analysis we must remember that planning is a spiritual discipline. Its worth, value, and vitality must come from the Holy Spirit. Planning is an exercise in Bible study, prayer, reflection, sharing, building relationships, dreaming, deciding, and making commitments. When carried out with those factors in mind, along with hard work and careful preparation, plans can be transformed into realities.

— 11 —

EMERGING TRENDS

T HE STRUGGLE TO BUILD enduring social structures that enable man to live a peaceful and prosperous existence has been a challenge for every generation. Over time, however, the nature of that quest has changed. Technology has altered both the conduct of daily life and the relationship between individuals and institutions. The primary forces which now regulate human life are not easy to define or to change. They are made up of a complex network of structures that transcend national boundaries and affect the lives of both individuals and social systems. Adjustments or changes in one domain of life trigger responding changes throughout the entire world system.

The Challenge

Religious systems are very much a part of this network. The very structure the church uses to carry out its mission in the world is part of this global network of forces. The fundamental character of this "structure of powers" cannot be altered.

From a biblical perspective, man, as well as his systems, structures, and institutions, bears the marks of sin and death. Yet these power structures, even in their fallen state, are necessary for the preservation of life. Therefore, governments and power structures are ordained by God. That does not mean, however, that governments or other power structures are godly—they are simply necessary.

A religious person might assume that a religiously based structure is more desirable than a secular structure, but this position fails to recognize the fundamental character of power in this age. While not all power structures are equally desirable, their difference lies not in essence, but only in degree. The "powers" of this world are doomed to ultimate destruction (1 Cor. 15:24f). The mission of the church is not to reform the power structure; that is impossible. Rather, the church is to expose the power complex. This does not occur by creating alternative structures. Any structure that the church creates is as much a part of the power complex as is any other structure. That does not mean that we are not to work at creating structures which reflect, at least to the extent possible, the basic values which we esteem and for which we are willing to make personal sacrifices. It is simply to note that our citizenship is not of this world, and that we still await a city—a new social structure of life—that is not of this age. Until then, the social structures of life, including church structures, will never provide the basis or framework for enduring peace or stability. It is hoped they will reduce chaos, promote civil liberty, and provide some sense of justice and equality. Christians must never cease to express God's love in practical ways that impact the social structures in which we live. Yet we must also recognize that they can never be fundamentally transformed. The structures cannot give life, but they can take it away.

The hope of the church cannot be found in the political realities of world systems. Nor can the message of the church be clearly seen through such realities. They can only distort it. In the same capacity, the social structure of a congregation can twist the plain meaning of the gospel. While the structure is essential to maintain the corporate life of the church, it is useful only as long as it allows that life to be expressed in such a way that it is in harmony with God's rule and intention for human life. Unfortunately, no congregation is able to achieve that in a complete sense. Furthermore, there is no such thing as a perfect structure. All structures are constantly changing in terms of their effectiveness because the environment is constantly changing. The dynamic relationship between the institutional nature of the church and its environment requires ongoing adaptation mandating structural change if the church is to remain effective in its mission. Some of the trends that churches must consider and respond to in this adaptation require some elaboration.

Emerging Trends

(1) Church structures must adapt to changing forms of family life.
First it must be recognized that there are many different types of
families and that family patterns continue to change over time.
The traditional model, a two-parent family with two children, is
no longer adequate in considering the needs of families. In developing an intentional approach to family ministry the following
points must be taken into consideration.

Family life is developmental. The needs of families and of their
individual members change over time. Family life is made up of
many different stages commencing with marriage and followed
by, in most cases, parenthood, the preschool family, the elementary age family, families with adolescents, launching children into
the adult world, the empty nest, retirement, loss of spouse, and
death and dying. Furthermore, there are many variations of these
stages caused by divorce, widowhood, or never marrying. The
church must understand and respond to these changing issues
and needs.

Single-parent families have special needs. Single-parent families
make up a significant percentage of all American households, yet
the church largely ignores their unique needs. Of this group,
those who are divorced often feel locked outside the church. Not
only do they wrestle with concerns related to finances, sexuality,
raising children, and career, but they must also deal with potential feelings of guilt, anger, low self-esteem, and a host of other
emotions which are often complicated by feelings of being rejected by the church. The needs of widows and widowers are
also largely neglected, leaving them to cope on their own or to
seek support systems outside the church. Furthermore, the children in single-parent households have special needs as well. Yet
little if any attention has been given this group, although many
children in every congregation fall in this category.

Nontraditional approaches to family ministry are needed. Traditional programs are not sufficient to meet the changing needs of
families in today's world. If the church is to provide effective and
meaningful support, it must reexamine its mission in respect to
the changing needs of family life focusing on the needs of every

family member. Support systems must be developed that respond to the various tasks that families face. This will require a reexamination of the congregation's educational program, as well as the type and frequency of meetings which the church sponsors in attempting to provide help to congregational and community members. The traditional format consisting of one or two services on Sunday and a mid-week service must be reconsidered in light of environmental changes affecting family life.

(2) *The church must adapt its mission to changing population trends.* Demographically, the number of young people in our society increased significantly following World War II. Today, however, as an overall percentage of the total population, the number of young Americans under age 25 is on the decline while the number of middle-aged and senior citizens is on the rise. The population shift has had a dramatic impact on many school districts resulting in the closing or merging of numerous schools. At the same time an increased emphasis on adult education and lifelong learning has developed.

(3) *The church must be prepared for more, not less, government regulation.* We have entered an era where religious influence and the nature and extent of that influence have become a political issue. As religious organizations attempt to influence the political system, that system will also influence the practice of religion at both national and local levels. At the local level churches can expect to become more regulated through zoning laws, which will affect both the size and use of church buildings. Church schools and home schooling will also be further scrutinized with respect to standards. At the federal level, the Supreme Court will be increasingly involved in passing judgments concerning the separation of church and state. Consequently, congregations and religious groups will probably find their freedoms shrinking rather than expanding. As Christians become more active politically, churches can expect tighter controls related to tax-exempt status. Confrontations between church and state are likely to increase rather than decrease.

(4) *Technology will increasingly transform the nature and structure of church ministry.* During the decade of the '70s religion came of age with respect to the use of the electronic media. Moving out of the Sunday morning ghetto, several religious satellite networks were launched. Various church organizations began to promote

the use of teleconferencing. Sustained growth in these areas is continuing in the '80s and new attention is being directed toward the development of Christian videos and computer software for both congregations and individual believers. The church is entering a new era of technology that will alter the nature of support systems available for Christian growth and development. The nature and value of these changes are already becoming the focus of debate and discussion.

One significant issue is the relationship between technology and community life, the latter being viewed as threatened as individuals utilize technological support systems in the privacy of their own home at the expense of building and nurturing congregational relationships. In the near future, individuals will be increasingly able to subscribe to a wide array of Christian media designed to enrich personal growth and development. Traditional church programs will be forced to integrate technology into the structure of congregational life. While Sunday morning worship services will be the least affected, nearly every other area of congregational life will feel the impact during the next decade. Furthermore, these changes will occur regardless of church size or location. Basically, no one will be left unaffected.

(5) *Individual Christians will continue to develop loyalties and commitments tied to "mega-religious systems" that transcend the local church or church denomination.* While this has already occurred to a certain degree, it will increase in the future as a direct result of technology's impact upon the values and commitments of individual believers. The primary medium in defining these "mega-religious systems" will be television.

While these mega-religious systems have existed for a long time, their potential to come into existence and grow has never been greater. There have always been a few religious leaders with a large following that transcends the local church. Today, however, that number is rapidly increasing. In the future it is likely that within one congregation, individual believers will express a wide range of loyalties and commitments to various mega-religious systems that will be competing for limited resources to survive. While there is no indication that these systems have drained finances from local congregations, that does not mean that they have not affected the local church. However, it is not clear what the nature of that impact is or might be in the future.

For the most part these mega-religious systems provide a degree of religious gratification and personal support without making any personal demands except for financial support. Furthermore, since these requests are made through the impersonal medium of television, there is little social pressure to respond. They allow for a private religious experience with no accountability. There is no indication, though, that these systems will replace involvement in the church. They will, however, influence that involvement.

(6) Congregations will have to reexamine the nature and use of church buildings. In general, church buildings will be designed to become more multifunctional in use. The high cost of construction will be one cause. Most congregations cannot afford large facilities that remain unused for the greater part of the week. More sanctuaries will be designed to accommodate meetings other than just Sunday morning worship. The removal of fixed pews will help to accomplish this. A shifting emphasis on adult education and the integration of media and computer technology in the life of the church will also affect the nature and use of church buildings.

Summary

It cannot be determined whether the changes discussed above will have a positive or negative impact on the church. Neither is it clear how the church should respond to such changes if they do occur. However, one thing is certain—the church will change as a result of the turbulent nature of our environment. The question is not if, but how those changes will take place. The theses running throughout this book point to important implications related to the future and nature of the church. They are as follows:

(1) Social structures, including that of the church, are part of the power complex necessary to maintain life, but also capable of controlling and regulating existence.

(2) The church exists as both a social reality and an eschatological community. The former requires an institutional structure; the latter is a spiritual community which is to expose the demonic elements of life while it points beyond itself to the saving grace of God in Christ.

(3) While there are some biblical guidelines for the social structure of the church, it is to be determined largely by the prevalent needs within the community of believers and the nature of the society in which that community exists.

(4) The current nature of society is redefining the "delivery systems" through which and the settings in which individuals receive spiritual support and information. Such systems are becoming more geared towards self-directed learning and personal growth in the privacy of one's own home.

(5) Whether it wants it or not, or whether it is ready for it or not, the church will ultimately follow the same models and utilize the same technological systems as used by public institutions in providing a wide range of support services in the areas of education, family life, and personal growth. Those who resist these changes will ultimately find themselves utilizing these systems anyway. It is only a matter of time.

(6) It is necessary for dialogue to begin within the church, carefully reflecting upon the nature of these changes, their potential impact on congregational life, and the alternatives that local congregations have in responding to widespread and influential environmental trends.

(7) Congregations must explore ways through which they can guide the intrusion of technology into the life of the church and utilize it in positive ways, rather than finding themselves in the undesirable position of responding to changes over which they have no control and which potentially undercut important values and goals essential for effective and fruitful congregational life.

These are not easy issues to confront or discuss. Nor does the church face an easy task in building and maintaining social structures that, to the extent possible, reflect kingdom values and symbols in the midst of a turbulent society and world that is itself in the throes of a major historical transition creating unparalleled social change. Nevertheless, this is the death-defying mission of the church—to be a chosen race, a royal priesthood, a holy nation, God's own people, declaring the wonderful deeds of him who called us out of darkness into his marvelous light!

ENDNOTES

Introduction to Part 1: The Power Complex

1. Frederick Ferré, *Shaping the Future* (New York: Harper & Row, 1976) 1.
2. Siegfried Giedion, *Mechanization Takes Command* (New York: Oxford University Press, 1948) 42.

Chapter One

1. William Stringfellow, *An Ethic for Christians and Other Aliens in a Strange Land* (Waco: Word Books, 1973) 70.
2. See G. B. Caird, *Principalities and Powers* (Oxford: Clarendon Press, 1956).
3. See G. H. C. Macgregor, "Principalities and Powers: The Cosmic Background of St. Paul's Thought," *New Testament Studies* 1 (1954–55) 17–28.
4. Caird, 11.
5. Ibid., 6.
6. Caird, 2; D. S. Russell, *The Method and Message of Jewish Apocalyptic* (Philadelphia: Westminster Press, 1964) 236.
7. See Psalm 89:6, 7
8. 1 Kgs. 22:19f; Neh. 9:6; Dan. 8:9–11; Job 38:7; see Caird, 4.
9. Ibid., 4.
10. Ibid., 11.
11. Ibid., 12.
12. Jung Young Lee, "Interpreting the Demonic Powers in Pauline Thought," *Novum Testamentum* 12 (Jan. 1970) 59–60; also D. E. H. Whitely, *The Theology of St. Paul* (Philadelphia: Fortress Press, 1971) 23.
13. Russell, 19.
14. Heinrich Schlier, *Principalities and Powers in the New Testament* (New York: Herder and Herder, 1961) 14.
15. George E. Ladd, *A Theology of the New Testament* (Grand Rapids: Eerdmans, 1974) 402.
16. Edward Langton, *Satan* (London: Skeffington and Son, 1945) 10; Caird, 31.

17. Gerhard von Rad, *TDNT* 2:73.

18. Langton, 9.

19. Eduard Lohse, *Colossians and Philemon* (Philadelphia: Fortress Press, 1971) 96.

20. Ibid., 97.

21. Ibid., 98.

Chapter Two

1. Jacques Ellul, *The Ethics of Freedom* (Grand Rapids: Eerdmans, 1976) 40f.

2. Ellul, 27.

3. Lewis Mumford, *The Myth of the Machine* (New York: Harcourt, Brace, Jovanovich, 1964) 2:37.

4. R. S. Peters, "Hobbes, Thomas," *The Encyclopedia of Philosophy,* (New York: Macmillan, 1967) 4:31.

5. Mumford, 2:135.

6. Ibid., 2:166

7. Giedion, 42.

8. Daniel Bell, *The Cultural Contradictions of Capitalism* (New York: Basic Books, 1976) 11.

9. Ibid., 21.

10. Peter Berger and Thomas Luckmann, *The Social Construction of Reality* (Garden City: Anchor Books, 1967) 56.

11. Berger and Luckmann, 58.

12. Ibid., 61.

13. Ibid., 62.

Chapter Five

1. Robert Banks, *Paul's Idea of Community* (Surry Hills: Anzea Books, 1979) 49.

2. Ibid., 54.

3. J. Paul Sampley, *Pauline Partnership in Christ* (Philadelphia: Fortress Press, 1980) 6; Banks, 19.

4. Banks, 20.

5. Sampley, 6.

6. Banks, 21.

7. Sampley, 11.

8. Ibid., 115.

9. Ernst Haenchen, *The Acts of the Apostles* (Philadelphia: Westminster Press, 1971) 261.

10. F. F. Bruce, *The Book of the Acts* (Grand Rapids: Eerdmans, 1971) 130.

11. Haenchen, 264.

12. C. E. B. Cranfield, "Diakonia in the New Testament," in *Service In Christ,* ed. James I. McCord and T. H. L. Parker (Grand Rapids: Eerdmans, 1966) 37.

13. Cranfield, 37.
14. Haenchen, 462.
15. Henry Chadwick, *The Early Church* (Baltimore: Penguin Books, 1971) 49.
16. Ibid., 50.
17. Ibid.
18. Markus Barth, *Ephesians,* 2 vols. (Garden City: Doubleday, 1974) 2:314.
19. Eusebius, *The History of the Church* (Baltimore: Penguin Books, 1965) 141.
20. Haenchen, 313.
21. *Documents of the Christian Church,* ed. Henry Bettenson, 2nd ed. (New York: Oxford University Press, 1971) 65.
22. Leonhard Goppelt, *Theology of the New Testament,* 2 vols. (Grand Rapids: Eerdmans, 1982) 2:146.
23. Donald Guthrie, *New Testament Theology* (Downers Grove: Inter-Varsity Press, 1981) 745.

Chapter Six

1. Paul Tillich, *Systematic Theology,* 3 vols. (Chicago: University of Chicago Press, 1951–63) 3:165.
2. Jacques Ellul, *The New Demons* (New York: Seabury Press, 1975) 4.
3. Ibid., 15.
4. Ibid.
5. T. F. Torrance, "Service in Jesus Christ," in *Service in Christ,* ed. James I. McCord and T. H. L. Parker (Grand Rapids: Eerdmans, 1966) 1.
6. Ibid., 1.
7. Ibid., 2.
8. Rene König, *The Community* (London: Routledge & Kegan Paul, 1968) 43.
9. David W. Minar and Scott Greer, eds., *The Concept of Community* (Chicago: Aldine Publishing Company, 1969) ix.
10. *The Community* (New York: Time-Life Books, 1976) 24f.
11. Jacqueline Sherer, *Contemporary Community* (London: Tavistock Publications, 1972) 13.
12. Ibid., 15.
13. Ibid., 14.

Chapter Seven

1. Reinhold Niebuhr, *Moral Man and Immoral Society* (New York: Charles Scribner's Sons, 1960) xi.
2. Ibid.

Chapter Eight

1. James MacGregor Burns, *Leadership* (New York: Harper & Row, 1978) 12.

2. See James F. Cobble, Jr., *Faith and Crisis in the Stages of Life* (Peabody, MA: Hendrickson Publishers, 1985).

Chapter Nine

1. J. G. Davies, *The Secular Use of Church Buildings* (London: SCM Press, 1968) 1.

2. Ibid., 1f.

3. Ibid., 4.

4. Ibid.

5. Ibid., 6.

6. Ibid., 6f.

7. Ibid., 10.

8. Ibid., 127.

9. Ibid.

10. Ibid., 138.

11. Ralph Martin, *The Worship of God* (Grand Rapids: Eerdmans, 1982) 54.

12. Ibid., 82.

Chapter Ten

1. Andrew Greeley, *The Crucible of Change* (New York: Sheed and Ward, 1968) 52.

2. Carl Dudley, "The Practice of Ministry," in *Building Effective Ministry* (San Francisco: Harper & Row, 1983) 213.

3. Paul Dietterich and Russell Wilson, *A Process of Local Church Vitalization* (Naperville, Ill.: Center for Parish Development, 1976).

4. Floyd Pennington, ed., *New Directions for Continuing Education 7: Assessing Educational Needs of Adults* (San Francisco: Jossey-Bass, 1980).

BIBLIOGRAPHY

Allen, Donald R. *Barefoot in the Church*. Richmond: John Knox Press, 1966.

Banks, Robert. *Paul's Idea of Community*. Surry Hills: Anzea Books, 1979.

Barth, Markus, and Fletcher, Verne H. *Acquittal by Resurrection*. New York: Holt, Rinehart and Winston, 1964.

Barth, Markus. *Ephesians*, 2 vols. Garden City: Doubleday 1974.

Bell, Daniel. *The Cultural Contradictions of Capitalism*. New York: Basic Books, 1976.

Berdyaev, Nikolai. *Slavery and Freedom*. New York: Charles Scribner's Sons, 1944.

Berkhof, Hendrikus. *Christ and the Powers*. Scottdale: Herald Press, 1962.

Bernard, Jessis. *The Sociology of Community*. Glenview: Scott, Foreman, and Company, 1973.

Bloesch, Donald G. *Wellsprings of Renewal*. Grand Rapids: Eerdmans, 1974.

Bonhoeffer, Dietrich. *Life Together*. New York: Harper & Row, 1954.

Bruce, F. F. *Colossians*. Grand Rapids: Eerdmans, 1957.

_____. *The Book of the Acts*. Grand Rapids: Eerdmans, 1971.

Bultmann, Rudolf. *Theology of the New Testament*, 2 vols. Trans., K. Grobel. New York: Charles Scribner's Sons, 1951, 1955.

_____. *Jesus Christ and Mythology*. New York: Charles Scribner's Sons, 1958.

_____. *Kerygma and Myth*. Trans., Reginald Fuller. New York: Harper & Row, 1961.

Caird, G. B. *Principalities and Powers*. London: Oxford University Press, 1956.

Cerfaux, Lucien. *Christ in the Theology of St. Paul*. New York: Herder and Herder, 1959.

Chadwick, Henry. *The Early Church*. Baltimore: Penguin Books, 1971.

Charles, R. H. *The Apocrypha and the Pseudepigrapha of the Old Testament*. Oxford: Clarendon Press, 1969 edition.

Clark, Stephen. *Building Christian Communities*. Notre Dame: Ave Maria Press, 1972.

Cullmann, Oscar. *The State in the New Testament*. New York: Charles Scribner's Sons, 1956.

Davies, J. G. *The Secular Use of Church Buildings*. London: SCM Press, 1968.

de Jonge, M. *The Testament of the Twelve Patriarchs*. Assen: Van Gorcum and Co., 1953.

Drake, S. "Galileo, Galilei." *The Encyclopedia of Philosophy*, 3:262–67. New York: Macmillan and Free Press, 1967.

Dudley, Carl, ed. *Building Effective Ministry*. San Francisco: Harper & Row, 1983.

Dulles, Avery. *Models of the Church*. Garden City: Doubleday, 1974.

Dupont-Sommer. *The Essene Writings from Qumran*. Gloucester: Peter Smith, 1973.

Ellul, Jacques. *The Technological Society*. New York: Vintage Books, 1964.

———. *The Ethics of Freedom*. Grand Rapids: Eerdmans, 1976.

———. *The New Demons*. New York: Seabury Press, 1975.

———. *The Betrayal of the West*. New York: Seabury Press, 1978.

Ferré, Frederick. *Shaping the Future*. New York: Harper & Row, 1976.

Forbes, R. J. *The Conquest of Nature*. New York: Frederick A. Praeger, 1968.

Foster, George M. *Traditional Cultures and the Impact of Technological Change*. New York: Harper & Row, 1962.

Francis, Fred. "Humility and Angelic Worship in Col. 2:18." *Studia Theologica* 16 (2, 1962): 109–34.

Furnish, Victor Paul. *Theology and Ethics in Paul*. Nashville: Abingdon Press, 1968.

Gibbs, John G. *Creation and Redemption*. Leiden: E. J. Brill, 1971.

Giedion, Siegfried. *Mechanization Takes Command*. New York: Oxford University Press, 1948.

Girdlestone, R. B. *Synonyms of the Old Testament*. Grand Rapids: Eerdmans, 1973.

Goppelt, Leonhard. *Theology of the New Testament*. Grand Rapids: Eerdmans, 1982.

Greeley, Andrew. *The Crucible of Change*. New York: Sheed and Ward, 1968.

Guthrie, Donald. *New Testament Theology*. Downers Grove: Inter-Varsity Press, 1981.

Haenchen, Ernst. *The Acts of the Apostles*. Philadelphia: Westminster Press, 1971.

Hall, Cameron. *Human Values and Advancing Technology*. New York: Friendship Press, 1967.

Heidegger, Martin. *The Question Concerning Technology and Other Essays*. New York: Garland Publishing, 1977.

Hengel, Martin. *Property and Riches in the Early Church*. Philadelphia: Fortress Press, 1974.

Homans, George. *The Human Group*. New York: Harcourt, Brace & World, 1950.

König, Rene. *The Community*. London: Routledge & Kegan Paul, 1968.

Kuhns, William. *Environmental Man*. New York: Harper & Row, 1969.

Ladd, George E. *A Theology of the New Testament*. Grand Rapids: Eerdmans, 1974.

Langton, Edward. *Satan*. London: Skeffington and Son, 1945.

_____. *Good and Evil Spirits*. New York: Macmillan, 1942.

Lee, Jung Y. "Interpreting the Demonic Powers in Pauline Thought." *Novum Testamentum* 12 (1 1970): 54–69.

Leivestad, R. *Christ the Conqueror*. New York: Macmillan, 1954.

Ling, Trevor. *Significance of Satan*. London: SPCK, 1961.

Lohse, Eduard. *Colossians and Philemon*. Philadelphia: Fortress Press, 1971.

Macgregor, G. H. C. "Principalities and Powers: The Cosmic Background of St. Paul's Thought." *New Testament Studies* 1 (1954–55) 17–28.

Malherbe, Abraham. *Social Aspects of Early Christianity*. Philadelphia: Fortress Press, 1983.

McCord, James I. and Parker, T. H. L., eds. *Service in Christ*. Grand Rapids: Eerdmans, 1966.

Meeks, Wayne. *The First Urban Christians*. New Haven: Yale University Press, 1983.

Minar, David and Greer, Scott. *The Concept of Community*. Chicago: Aldine Publishing Co., 1969.

Morris, Leon. *The Cross in the New Testament*. Grand Rapids: Eerdmans, 1965.

Morrison, Clinton. *The Powers that Be*. Naperville: Alec R. Allenson, 1960.

Mumford, Lewis. *Technics and Civilization*. New York: Harcourt, Brace & World, 1934.

_____. *The Myth of the Machine*. New York: Harcourt, Brace, Jovanovich, 1964.

Niebuhr, Reinhold. *Moral Man and Immoral Society*. New York: Charles Scribner's Sons, 1960.

Peters, R. S. "Hobbes, Thomas." *The Encyclopedia of Philosophy* 4:30–46. New York: Macmillan and Free Press, 1967.

Poling, David. *The Last Years of the Church*. Garden City: Doubleday, 1969.

Reicke, Bo. "The Law and the World According to Paul." *Journal of Biblical Literature* 70 (1951) 259–76.

Rudin, Maximilian. *The Devil in Legend and Literature*. Chicago: Open Court Publishing Company, 1931.

Sampley, J. Paul. *Pauline Partnership in Christ*. Philadelphia: Fortress Press, 1980.

Scherer, Jacqueline. *Contemporary Community*. London: Tavistock Publications, 1972.

Schlier, Heinrich. *Principalities and Powers in the New Testament*. New York: Herder and Herder, 1961.

Snyder, Howard. *The Problem of Wineskins*. Downers Grove: Inter-Varsity Press, 1975.

_____. *The Community of the King*. Downers Grove: Inter-Varsity Press, 1977.

Spengler, Oswald. *Man and Technics*. New York: Alfred A. Knopf, 1932.

Stringfellow, William. *An Ethic for Christians and Other Aliens in a Strange Land*. Waco: Word Books, 1973.

Tillich, Paul. *Systematic Theology*, 3 vols. Chicago: University of Chicago Press, 1951–63.

Theissen, Gerd. *Sociology of Early Palestinian Christianity*. Philadelphia: Fortress Press, 1978.

Theological Dictionary of the New Testament. Ed. G. Kittel and G. Friedrich. 10 vols. Trans. G. Bromiley. Grand Rapids: Eerdmans, 1964–76.

Vahanian, Gabriel. *God and Utopia.* New York: Seabury Press, 1977.

Vaux, Kenneth. *Subduing the Cosmos.* Richmond: John Knox Press, 1970.

von Rad, Gerhard. *Old Testament Theology.* New York: Harper & Row, 1962.

Weiss, Harold. "The Law in the Epistle to the Colossians." *Catholic Biblical Quarterly* 34 (1972) 294–314.

Whitely, D. E. H. *The Theology of St. Paul.* Philadelphia: Fortress Press, 1964.

Yoder, John H. *The Politics of Jesus.* Grand Rapids: Eerdmans, 1972.

INDEX OF SCRIPTURES